Envoy of Jerusalem

Envoy of Jerusalem

Balian d'Ibelin and the Third Crusade

Helena P. Schrader

Envoy of Jerusalem: Balian d'Ibelin and the Third Crusade

Published by Wheatmark®
1760 East River Road, Suite 145
Tucson, Arizona 85718 USA
www.wheatmark.com

ISBN: 978-1-62787-397-0 (paperback)
ISBN: 978-1-62787-398-7 (ebook)
LCCN: 2016943614

Contents

Cast of Characters

(Names in **bold** are historical figures.
Names with * appear more than once.)

Royal House of Jerusalem

Maria Comnena, * Dowager Queen of Jerusalem, great-niece of the Greek Emperor **Manuel I, Queen of Jerusalem 1167-1174**

Sibylla, Queen of Jerusalem 1186-1190

Guy de Lusignan, her second husband, **King of Jerusalem 1186-1190**

Isabella of Jerusalem, Sibylla's paternal half-sister, daughter of **Maria Comnena** and King Amalric, **Queen of Jerusalem 1190-1204**

House of Ibelin

Balian, third son of Barisan, 1st Baron of Ibelin, Lord of Ibelin from 1177, known to the Arabs as Ibn Barzan (son of Barisan), Lord of Nablus by right of his wife from 1179

Maria Comnena, * Dowager Queen of Jerusalem, his wife

Helvis, John, Margaret, and **Philip,** their children

Eschiva, * Balian's niece (daughter of his brother Baldwin), wife of **Aimery de Lusignan***

Hugh, Burgundia, Helvis, and Aimery, their children (they had a total of six children historically, but only the names of the first three are known)

Henri, youngest son of the 1st Baron of Ibelin, younger brother of Balian

Eloise, his wife

Household of Balian d'Ibelin

Ernoul, Balian's squire, 1181-1194

Georgios, Balian's squire, 1187-1199

Father Michael, Balian's confessor and the children's tutor

Father Angelus, Maria's confessor and the children's tutor

Sir Roger Shoreham, formerly a sergeant, knighted at Jerusalem

Centurion, Balian's veteran destrier

Ras Dawit, Balian's young destrier

Hermes, Balian's palfrey

Knights of Ibelin and Nablus

Sir Bartholomew, feudal tenant of Ibelin

Sir Galvin, a household knight of Scottish origin

House of Lusignan

Guy,* fourth son of the Lord of Lusignan, **King of Jerusalem** by right of his wife, Sibylla

Aimery,* third son of the Lord of Lusignan, Constable of Jerusalem

Eschiva,* his wife, daughter of the Baron of Ramla, niece of Balian d'Ibelin

Geoffrey, second son of the Lord of Lusignan, crusader

Hugh "le Brun," eldest son of the Lord of Lusignan, nephew to Guy, Aimery, and Geoffrey

Crusaders

Richard I Plantagenet, "the Lionheart," King of England, known to the Saracens as "Malik Rik"

Berengaria of Navarre, his wife, Queen of England

Joanna Plantagenet, sister to Richard of England, Dowager Queen of Sicily

Conrad de Montferrat, brother of Queen Sibylla's* first husband William de Montferrat, second husband of Isabella* of Jerusalem

Philip II Capet, King of France

Hugh, Duke of Burgundy, leader of the French crusaders after Philip II's departure

Henri, Count of Champagne, third husband of Isabella of Jerusalem

Barons of the Crusader States

William of Tiberius, Prince of Galilee, stepson of Raymond of Tripoli

Ralph of Tiberius, his younger brother

Humphrey de Toron IV, first husband to Isabella of Jerusalem*
Reginald, Lord of Sidon
Pagan, Lord of Haifa
The lordships of Beirut, Botron, Gibelet, Jubail, Scandelion, Nazareth, Caymont, Caesarea, Bethsan, Arsur, Blanchgarde, Bethgibelin, and Hebron existed historically, so reference to lords of these baronies is accurate, although details of names and personalities are lacking.

Members of the Militant Orders and Church Leaders

Gerard de Ridefort, Grand Master of the Knights Templar, 1184-1189
Robert de Sablé, Grand Master of the Knights Templar, 1191-1193
Garnier de Nablus, Grand Master of the Knights Hospitaller
Heraclius, Archbishop of Caesarea and Patriarch of Jerusalem, 1180-1190
Randolf, Bishop of Bethlehem, later Patriarch of Jerusalem
Bishop of Lydda, captured at Hattin
Bishop of Beauvais, French prelate and crusader
Baldwin, Archbishop of Canterbury, English prelate
Sister Adela, a Hospitaller nun

Saracens

Salah ad-Din Yusuf, Sultan of Egypt and Damascus
Al-Adil, Salah ad-Din's brother
Farrukh-Shah, Salah ad-Din's nephew
Al-Afdal, the eldest of Salah ad-Din's seventeen sons
Imad ad-Din al Isfahani, Salah ad-Din's secretary and biographer
Khalid al-Hamar, a young, red-haired Mamluke

Other Characters of Note

Beatrice and Constance d'Auber, daughters of Sir Bartholomew
Bart, Amalric, and Joscelyn, Beatrice's sons
Anne, Constance's daughter
Godwin Olafsen, a Norse armorer
Haakon Magnussen, a Norse sea captain
Erik Andersen, his chief mate
Mariam, a Syrian pastry master
Alys, a tavern singer

The Ibelin Family
in the 12th Century

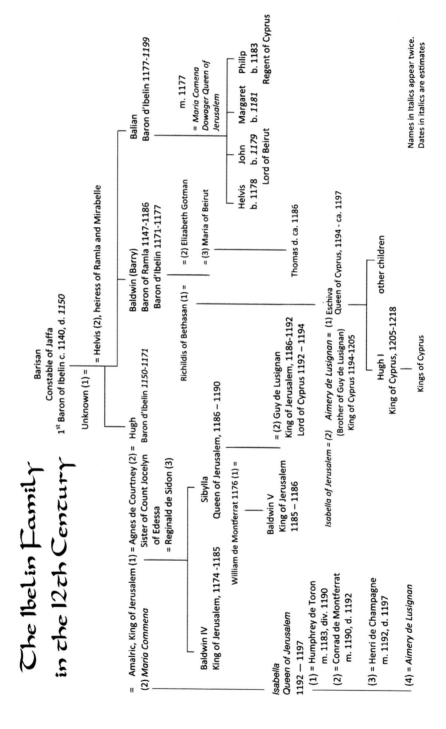

Barisan
Constable of Jaffa
1st Baron of Ibelin c. 1140, d. *1150*

= Helvis (2), heiress of Ramla and Mirabelle

Unknown (1) =

Balian
Baron d'Ibelin 1177-1199

m. 1177

= *Maria Comena*
Dowager Queen of
Jerusalem

Helvis   John   Margaret   Philip
b. 1178   *b. 1179*   *b. 1181*   *b. 1183*
                Lord of Beirut   Regent of Cyprus

Baldwin (Barry)
Baron of Ramla 1147-1186
Baron d'Ibelin 1171-1177

= (2) Elizabeth Gotman

= (3) Maria of Beirut

Richildis of Bethasan (1) =

Thomas d. ca. 1186

Hugh
Baron d'Ibelin *1150-1171*

Sibylla
Queen of Jerusalem, 1186 – 1190

William de Montferrat 1176 (1) =

= (2) Guy de Lusignan
King of Jerusalem, 1186-1192
Lord of Cyprus 1192 – 1194

Aimery de Lusignan = (1) Eschiva
(Brother of Guy de Lusignan)   Queen of Cyprus, 1194 - ca. 1197
King of Cyprus 1194-1205

Hugh I   other children
King of Cyprus, 1205-1218

Kings of Cyprus

= Amalric, King of Jerusalem (1) = Agnes de Courtney (2) =
(2) *Maria Commena*   Sister of Count Jocelyn
                                    of Edessa
                                    = Reginald de Sidon (3)

Baldwin IV
King of Jerusalem, 1174 -1185

Baldwin V
King of Jerusalem
1185 – 1186

Isabella
Queen of Jerusalem
1192 – 1197

(1) = Humphrey de Toron
m. 1183, div. 1190

(2) = Conrad de Montferrat
m. 1190, d. 1192

(3) = Henri de Champagne
m. 1192, d. 1197

(4) = *Aimery de Lusignan*

Isabella of Jerusalem = (2)

Names in italics appear twice.
Dates in italics are estimates

Kings/Queens of Jerusalem 1131 – 1212

Kings of Jerusalem

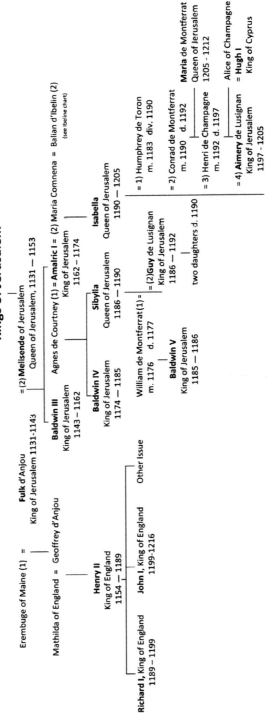

The Greek (Byzantine) Emperors in the 12th Century

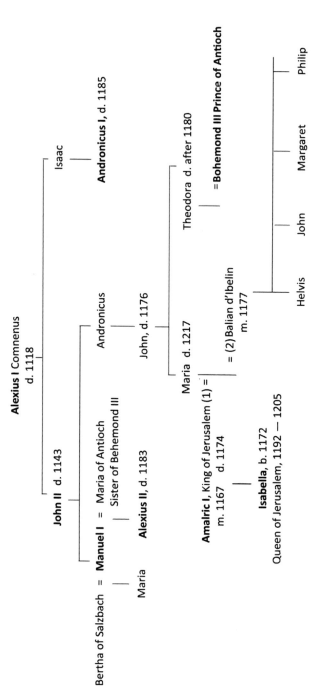

Names in bold are ruling monarchs

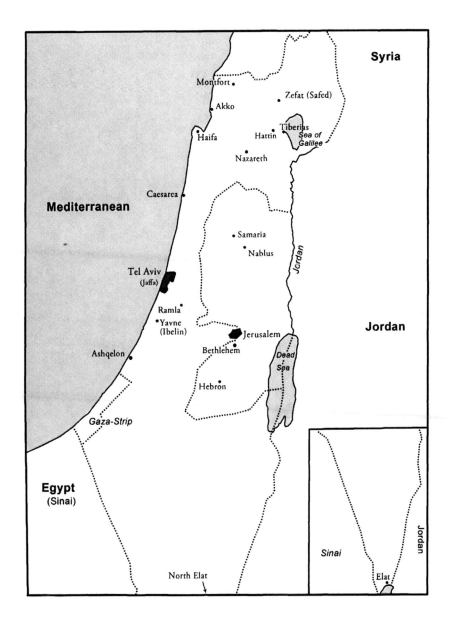

Map of the Holy Land Today (Modern Israel)

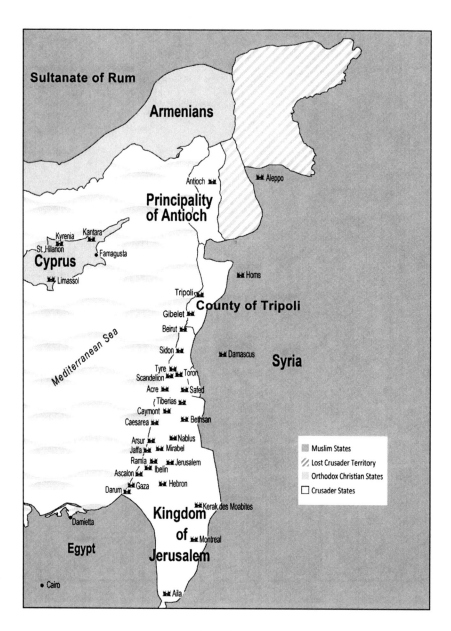

Kingdom of Jerusalem

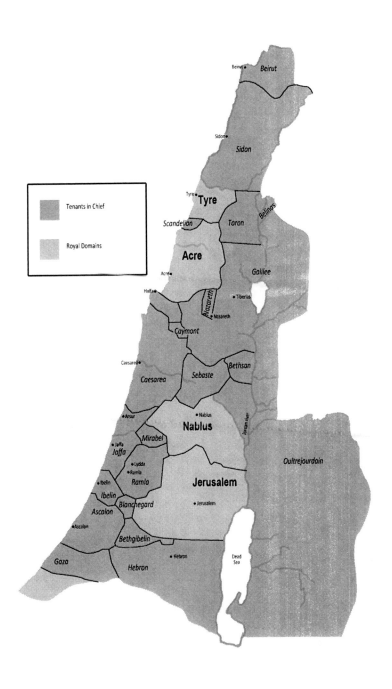

Baronies of Jerusalem

Introduction and
Acknowledgments

THIS IS THE THIRD BOOK IN a biographical novel of the historical figure Balian d'Ibelin based on the known facts about his life. The first volume was published under the title *Knight of Jerusalem* and covered the period 1171–1177. The second volume, *Defender of Jerusalem*, described the fateful years leading up to and including the disastrous Battle of Hattin and the fall of Jerusalem to Salah ad-Din in 1187. *Defender of Jerusalem* was a B.R.A.G. Medallion Honoree. It won the "Silver" (second place) for Religious/Spiritual Fiction in the Feathered Quill 2016 Book Awards, the 2015 Chaucer Award for Historical Fiction set in the Middle Ages, and (at the time of publication) is a finalist for the M.M. Bennetts Award for Historical Fiction.

The historical Balian was born in the mid-eleventh century in the Christian Kingdom of Jerusalem. He was the youngest son of the first Baron of Ibelin and as such did not inherit land or title. He entered the historical record in 1177, when he played a prominent role in the Frankish defeat of Salah ad-Din at the Battle of Montgisard alongside his older brother Baldwin, the Baron of Ramla, Mirabel and Ibelin. Shortly afterwards he married the Dowager Queen of Jerusalem, Maria Comnena, and his elder brother gave him the smallest of his three baronies, Ibelin. These events are described in volume one, *Knight of Jerusalem*. To avoid confusion with King Baldwin, Baldwin de Ibelin is referred to as Barisan or "Barry" throughout this trilogy.

Defender of Jerusalem describes in fictional form the events of the following decade. The deteriorating health of the "Leper King" makes it imperative for the

High Court of Jerusalem to find a suitable husband for Baldwin's sister Sibylla, the heir apparent to the throne. Her first husband has died of malaria leaving Sibylla pregnant, and the search for a new consort has begun when the book opens. Balian's elder brother, "Barry", harbors hopes of gaining Sibylla's affections and hand, but has the misfortunate to be taken captive by the Saracens in the Battle on the Litani. While he is engaged in raising his ransom in Constantinople, Sibylla is seduced by Guy de Lusignan. Agnes de Courtenay, mother of both Sibylla and the dying King Baldwin, manipulates her son into consenting to a marriage between the lovers.

Ramla is now an embittered enemy of Guy de Lusignan. The latter rapidly alienates the other barons of the kingdom with his arrogance and ignorance. Recognizing his mistake in letting his sister marry Lusignan, King Baldwin attempts to persuade Sibylla to divorce Guy. Her refusal to separate from Guy makes her increasingly unpopular with members of the High Court. Her mother becomes afraid that as a result the barons will bypass Sibylla at her son's death in favor of his half-sister Isabella, the daughter of King Amalric by his second wife and Agnes' hated rival, Maria Comnena. Fearing the loss of power that such a solution would entail, Agnes convinces her son to remove Isabella from Maria and Balian's care. Aged only eight, Isabella is sent to the border fortress of Kerak under the guardianship of the notoriously brutal Reynald de Châtillon. Denied the right to even visit her mother for the next three years, she is married to Châtillon's stepson, Humphrey de Toron, at the age of eleven.

In 1185, Baldwin IV succumbs to his disease and is succeeded by his eight-year-old nephew, Sibylla's son by her first marriage. The boy dies less than a year later. This is the moment Sibylla and Guy have been waiting for. They usurp the crown of Jerusalem without the consent of the High Court. An attempt by the High Court to crown Isabella and Humphrey as (legitimate) rivals to Sibylla and Guy collapses when Humphrey sneaks away to do homage to Guy.

Robbed of an alternative king, most of the barons of Jerusalem acknowledge Guy, but the proud Baron of Ramla and Mirabel prefers exile to submission. He turns his infant son and all his lands and titles over to his younger brother Balian and leaves the kingdom. The Count of Tripoli chooses open rebellion and signs a separate peace with Salah ad-Din. Only a new Frankish defeat enables Ibelin to act as peacemaker between Tripoli and Lusignan, effecting a reconciliation between them in which Tripoli does homage to Lusignan.

Less than a year after his usurpation, Guy proves the worst expectations of his detractors correct. He leads the entire Christian army to an avoidable but devastating defeat at the Battle of Hattin. The entire fighting force of the Kingdom of Jerusalem is destroyed, either killed or captured. Only Tripoli,

Sidon, and Ibelin manage to escape from the encirclement. The latter leads some three thousand survivors to the city of Tyre.

Denuded of fighting troops (because these mustered and were lost at Hattin), the rest of the kingdom falls, city by city and castle by castle, to the forces of Salah ad-Din. Within two months, only the coastal city of Tyre remains—and Jerusalem.

In Jerusalem are gathered some sixty thousand Christian refugees. Among the women and children are Balian's wife, Maria Comnena, and his children. He obtains from Salah ad-Din a "safe conduct" to cross Saracen-held territory and go to Jerusalem to remove his wife and children from the city before the impending siege. Ibelin swears to enter without weapons and remain only a single night.

On his arrival in Jerusalem, however, the inhabitants go wild with jubilation, thinking that they at last have an experienced commander capable of organizing the defense of the city. Ibelin realizes he cannot leave. He sends word to Salah ad-Din of what has happened. Salah ad-Din chivalrously sends his own bodyguard to escort Balian's family to safety, while Balian prepares to defend Jerusalem. The city is populated by fifty women and children for every fighting man. Ibelin knights eighty youths in a single ceremony, and organizes the women and priests to support the men he has.

Expecting an easy victory, Salah ad-Din sends in his troops without artillery support, but the waves of infantry are repulsed. Salah ad-Din then brings up his siege engines, but in a daring night raid Ibelin and his knights destroy several of these while the lepers of Jerusalem mount a diversion to facilitate the attack. Salah ad-Din is forced to withdraw, but redeploys his troops and brings up sappers to undermine the walls. Late in the afternoon of September 29, a large section of the northern wall is brought down. Although the Christians manage to defeat the first attempts by Salah ad-Din's troops to rush through the breach, by nightfall it is clear they will not be able to beat off many more attacks. Ibelin leads a last desperate sortie to kill Salah ad-Din, but is rapidly repulsed.

In the morning the Christians prepare to die or be enslaved, but then Ibelin remembers that Salah ad-Din had told him he did not want to risk damaging the Dome of the Rock in a siege. He takes a white flag and seeks to negotiate with Salah ad-Din. Even as they speak, Salah ad-Din's banners appear on the walls of Jerusalem; Salah ad-Din scoffs that one does not negotiate for a city one already holds. At that moment the Saracen banners are thrown down, and Ibelin "plays his trump," threatening to destroy all the holy places in the city and kill all the civilians before sallying forth with what men he has left to die a martyr's death while killing as many of Salah-ad Din's men as possible.

To save the sacred sites from destruction, Salah ad-Din agrees to allow the Christians in the city to ransom their lives and freedom. Ibelin and Salah ad-Din agree to ten gold pieces per man, five per woman, and two per child, but Ibelin recognizes that many of the people in Jerusalem are refugees who have already lost everything. He therefore negotiates the payment of a lump sum of thirty thousand gold pieces for ten thousand paupers. The Christians are given forty days to raise their ransoms.

This volume opens in Tyre on the day news reaches it that Jerusalem has capitulated.

I wish to thank my test readers for their careful and constructive criticism, and my editor, Christy Dickson, for her patient, meticulous, and professional editing. I am also indebted to Mikhail Greuli for his evocative cover.

Helena P. Schrader
Addis Ababa
2016

Chapter 1

Tyre, October 1187

THE HARBOR-SIDE TAVERN WAS FILLED TO overflowing with fighting men. Whether they had escaped the carnage at Hattin, been left to garrison cities that had since surrendered, or come from overseas in ignorance of the catastrophe that had obliterated the Kingdom of Jerusalem, they had all washed up here. It was the only place left for a man still determined to defend the Holy Land to go. Every other city in the entire Kingdom of Jerusalem had fallen in the three bitter months between July 4 and today, October 3, 1187.

Today they had been shaken by the clamorous shouts of "Allahu Akbar!" and the beating of Saracen drums. They had rushed to the walls prepared to fight off a new assault, only to discover these shouts marked not the start of an attack, but rather the end of one. Riders from the enemy camp, just out of range, pumped their swords triumphantly in the air as they shouted: "Jerusalem! Jerusalem is ours!" Those with an understanding of Arabic translated for the newcomers and the less linguistically skilled: Jerusalem had fallen to Salah ad-Din.

Most of the fighting men collected in Tyre recognized that the fall of Jerusalem had been inevitable—more so than the fall of Acre, Haifa, Sidon, Gibelet, Beirut, Caesarea, Jaffa, and Ascalon. The latter had been defensible coastal cities capable of reinforcement and supply by sea and manned by garrisons worthy of the name. Jerusalem, in contrast, had been denuded of her defenders when the feudal army marched to Hattin. That army had been composed of the flower of both secular and sacred chivalry, the knights, sergeants, and Turcopoles of the Kingdom, and the knights and sergeants of the militant orders. The garrison left behind had been made up of middle-aged merchants, Syrians, Greeks, and pilgrims.

Yet while the garrison was old, ineffective, and small, the population of the city had swollen with refugees. From along the Jordan valley and other inland settlements, Christian women, children, and elderly—all those who had not been at Hattin—had fled to the Holy City after the destruction of the Frankish army at Hattin. By some accounts as many as one hundred thousand Christians had taken refuge there; the more likely number was sixty thousand.

And now they were either dead or slaves.

The thought depressed the men in Tyre. While their military minds had known Jerusalem was indefensible, their Christian hearts had hoped for a miracle. For those native to Outremer, it had been a hope fed by desperation: Jerusalem was the last place their own loved ones might yet be free—if they weren't already in Tyre. Of all the defeats of the last three months, this was the worst.

In the dingy harbor-side tavern, despair hung in the smoky air. These men had survived to fight another day. They had taken heart when Conrad de Montferrat had sailed into Tyre harbor and spat defiance at the victorious Sultan. They had fought with him and for him, and they had believed that not all was lost after all.

But now Jerusalem was lost. The site of Christ's Passion. The home of the Holy Sepulcher. Lost. What was there left to fight for?

A youth with a lute in his left hand shoved his way between the tables toward the serving counter. He was thin and bony. His light-brown hair was overlong, as if he couldn't afford a barber, and his face was marred by acne. One shoulder hung distinctly lower than the other, and when he tried to hoist himself up to sit on the countertop, he gave a gasp and his face screwed up with pain. The innkeeper shook his head in annoyance and warned in a low growl as he helped him onto the counter, "This better be good, Ernoul."

Ernoul didn't answer directly. He sat on the countertop with his feet dangling and settled his lute under his right arm, grimacing slightly as he lifted his left to the neck of the instrument. Then his face cleared. He took a deep breath and played a few chords.

Some men were talking or dicing, but most had come here to drink themselves into oblivion. They were in no mood for entertainment. The young man on the counter elicited indifference at best and aroused hostility from many. One man called out resentfully: "Go back to your great hall, puppy! Your lord might like a love song, but we're in no mood for it!"

"How can he? His lord was in Jerusalem!" the man across from the speaker retorted bitterly.

On the counter, Ernoul cleared his throat and began to sing:

"Salah ad-Din, you have the grave,
And you have made our brothers slaves . . ."

Instantly the squire had their attention. Across the room a dozen desultory conversations stopped and men glared at the singer. Hostility hung in the air. They didn't need to have their noses rubbed in it by the likes of this puny, shabby squire!

Ernoul appeared not to notice. He sang in a low, soft, melodic tenor:

"But we survived, we are alive . . ."

The men in the tavern were transfixed. Not a man raised his mug to drink, not a foot clumped on the floor, not a word was spoken. They were staring at the squire as he continued more certainly in his firm and resonant voice.

"Salah ad-Din, you have the Tomb,
But it is dark, deserted gloom;
For Christ is risen! And by our side!"

Ernoul seemed to draw strength from their rapt attention; his voice grew stronger, louder as he continued.

"We are with Him; we have no fear
Of you, your army, or your emirs;
Christ on our side, we cannot die!"

The squire had struck a chord in the dingy tavern, and more than one scarred and bearded veteran found himself close to tears. Others crossed themselves or said the Lord's Prayer in an affirmation of the faith they had too often neglected.

Still Ernoul sang, the melody mutating slightly.

"Christ is with us, Salah ad-Din.
Christ is with us, we cannot die,
But we will fight you—until you do!"

"Hear! Hear!" someone shouted, but his comrades hushed him.

Ernoul raised his voice and though he reverted to the original melody, he picked up the pace and volume as he sang out:

"The day will come when we will win,
When we will take Jerusalem
For Him, not us, for Christendom!

"We are alive, Salah ad-Din,
We are alive and cannot die;
We will retake Jerusalem!"

With a flourish on the strings and a bow of his head, Ernoul indicated he was done.

For a stunned second no one in the tavern moved, and then they burst into thunderous applause. Some men stamped their feet; others clapped their hands or pounded on the tables with their pottery mugs. The acclamation was so powerful, enthusiastic, and unexpected that Ernoul's ears turned bright red, and he readily took the mug shoved at him by the relieved tavern-keeper. The cheers had turned into calls for "Again! Again! Sing it again!"

Ernoul put the mug aside, wiped his lips on the back of his linen sleeve, and straightened his crooked shoulders as best he could. The receptiveness of his audience had taken him by surprise; it flattered and elated him like a drug, blotting out his pain.

By the time he'd repeated his song two more times, the more musical of his listeners had already picked up the tune. By the fourth time, they were all singing with him. The song that had seemed so melancholy and mourning when sung by a lone squire had become a fighting song laden with defiance and determination.

The Church of the Holy Trinity was one of the oldest in Tyre, allegedly dating back to the reign of Emperor Constantine. As Mass ended and the clergy withdrew on slipper-shod feet, a lady kneeling in a side chapel dedicated to St. George crossed herself, rolled back on her heels, and stood. She was shrouded in a dark veil trimmed with a single band of gold embroidery that covered her head and body all the way to her knees. Standing, it was clear that she was both tall and slender. She took a coin from her purse, purchased a thin beeswax candle, lit it, and stood it upright in the box of sand. The light from a half-dozen candles already burned.

The lady turned and flung the lower right corner of her veil up over the opposite shoulder to partially cover her face, but even so she heard someone whisper in awe, "The Dowager Queen!"

On the steps of the church, two beggars closed in on her. One pushed his legless body on a wooden platform with little wheels that squeaked piteously. The other, more importunate, pressed in close, whining, "Alms, my lady! Alms! I lost my hand at Hattin." He held up a stump wrapped in dirty rags.

"You'll rot in hell for your lies, Peter of Paris!" a gruff voice barked out of the darkness, adding: "You lost your hand for cheating at dice ten years ago!" A burly man in chain mail under a voluminous cloak emerged from the shadows. The knight was no longer young. His mustache and hair were completely white, and his face was deeply lined by life, but the sword at his hip was not decorative, and he moved with the vigor of a man still capable of wielding it. The beggars melted away before him, and the Dowager Queen gratefully hooked her hand through his offered elbow.

"Thank you for waiting for me, Sir Bartholomew," she greeted him. "I'm afraid I was longer than intended."

The old knight growled back, "Plenty to pray for this night, my lady."

The Dowager Queen stopped in her tracks and looked up at him in sudden understanding. "Your daughters and their children! Do you think they were in Jerusalem?"

"I've had no word from them at all," Sir Bartholomew answered grimly. "None."

Queen Maria Zoë Comnena digested that fact as they resumed walking. Sir Bartholomew held a fief from her second husband, the Baron of Ibelin. He had no sons, just two grown daughters, the eldest of whom was already a young widow before Hattin, and the younger married to a man who had fallen at the battle. Although Sir Bartholomew had fought his way off the field of Hattin, he, like the rest of the surviving fighting men, found himself cooped up in Tyre while the rest of the Kingdom fell city by city and castle by castle to Salah ad-Din. Sir Bartholomew's daughters and their still-young children had been left behind on their peaceful manor just a few miles from Ibelin—land now held by the Saracens.

Sir Bartholomew broke in on her thoughts. "There's really no reason to think they made it to Jerusalem. More likely they went to Jaffa. It was closer." But Jaffa had fallen to the Saracens before Jerusalem, and if his daughters had not found their way to Tyre by now, then they were almost certainly dead— or captives. Slaves. Maria Zoë shuddered at the thought, and her hand closed around her companion's elbow in a gesture of helpless sympathy.

"My grief is only a single tear in the sea of misery, my lady," Sir Bartholomew summarized his situation astutely.

"That doesn't make it less intense," Maria Zoë countered. They continued in silence through the darkened streets.

The city was overcrowded, and even now, after Compline, many people lingered on the streets for lack of a better alternative. Most of the refugees were housed in warehouses by the port, and these lacked comfort, lighting, privacy, and sanitary facilities. Brawls were common, and it wasn't necessarily the worst individuals who sought escape in the open streets. Still, Sir Bartholomew's hand dropped instinctively to his hilt as they passed a trio of young men loitering at the entry to an alleyway. The young men watched the knight and lady with appraising eyes, weighing the obvious wealth of a woman in gold-trimmed silks against the risk of taking on an armed knight.

Fortunately, Sir Bartholomew and the Dowager Queen did not have far to go. They reached their lodgings after rounding the next corner. The narrow, three-story building crushed between similar structures belonged to a Genoese merchant family. The day after the news of Hattin reached Tyre, the merchant had packed his family, his valuables, and as many of his wares as possible into the fastest Genoese galley in Tyre harbor. He left behind his household staff—an aging Greek Orthodox couple and two Syrian grooms—most of his furnishings, and cellars well stocked with food and wine.

The presence of staff had discouraged plunder in the days to follow until, on July 14, Conrad de Montferrat had taken command of the defense of Tyre. Montferrat had both established order and expropriated all vacant property. When the Dowager Queen of Jerusalem arrived in the city weeks later, he had put this house at her disposal. There were those who saw this as a calculated insult. She was, after all, a member of the Greek imperial family as well as Dowager Queen of Jerusalem. Furthermore, she was accompanied by her daughter, the Princess Isabella of Jerusalem. It would have been more appropriate, they suggested, for her to be housed in the archiepiscopal palace, the largest and most representational residence in the ancient city. But Montferrat himself already occupied the palace, and he had no intention of moving out for a dowager and her daughter.

Maria Zoë had not protested. The merchant residence was beautifully appointed with tiled and mosaic floors, glass in all the windows, beds, tables, and other essential furnishings. Furthermore, it had a fully functioning kitchen and a garden with its own well. Most important, however, it offered her and her children a degree of privacy that they would not have enjoyed at the archiepiscopal palace.

When she accepted the residence, however, she had not realized that fourteen of her husband's knights were already in Tyre. Her husband had commanded the third largest contingent of troops at the Battle of Hattin, leading under his banner not only the knights of Ibelin and his personal household, but the knights of her dower barony of Nablus and his brother's baronies of Ramla and Mirabel. When he led the breakout late in the battle, some two hundred knights and over one hundred squires survived the charge with him. Many of them were strangers and had gone their own way. Others had relatives in Tripoli or Antioch and had continued to these territories. The rest, however, had remained in Tyre. When the news reached them that the Dowager Queen had come to Tyre, they flocked to offer their services to her.

Service, however, was a double-edged sword: it required patronage in exchange. That entailed bed and board at a minimum. Furthermore, the Queen had arrived with her own small household, which included not just her five children, but her sister-in-law with two more children, her husband's niece with three, the children's nanny, her waiting woman, a priest, and a groom. Together with her husband's knights and squires, this amounted to a household of over forty people. Consequently, the merchant house was packed to overflowing.

One of the squires was standing guard, and he hastened to open the door for his lady and Sir Bartholomew. "We were getting worried, my lady," he exclaimed in an anxious voice that reflected more the overall state of nervous tension ignited by the fall of Jerusalem than any rational worries about the safety of the Dowager Queen.

"Nothing to worry about, Stephan," Maria Zoë answered, removing her veils now that she was inside.

They were in a vaulted entryway, lit by a single oil lamp hanging from a hook at the peak of the arch. The vault was lined with empty shelves on which the merchant's wares had once been displayed. Now these shelves were laden with straw pallets on which the squires slept. A second vaulted chamber containing the kitchen intersected at right angles at the far end of the chamber, and a brick fireplace sat nestled in the corner of the juncture. Maria Zoë could hear voices and see shadows cast on the far wall by people gathered around the solid oak kitchen table, and she knew that the squires and household staff were gathered there. She did not disturb them, but rather turned to enter a small cobbled courtyard lined with stone troughs sprouting rosemary, thyme, and lavender, and mounted the stone stairs that curled around two sides of the courtyard to give her access to the hall located above the kitchen.

This was the largest room in the house, with glazed windows overlooking both the interior courtyard and the walled garden on the other side. It had a hooded fireplace at the far end and a gallery over the near end. The floor was paved with mosaics in an elegant floral pattern of blue, white, and purple. A small, more intimate solar or receiving room, opened off the hall at the far end near the fireplace, while a door under the gallery connected with an internal stairway leading to the upper floor.

The knights of her household lived and slept in the hall, so it was hardly surprising to find them gathered over several pitchers of wine as she entered. The heated discussion came to an abrupt end at her appearance, and the men respectfully rose to their feet to bow to her. Maria Zoë sensed, more from the scowl on Sir Bartholomew's face than from anything she'd actually overheard, that the discussion had been about what would happen to them now that her husband was presumed dead.

Maria Zoë turned to Sir Bartholomew and thanked him for escorting her, dismissing him at the same time. She took a hand-held glass lamp in one hand and her skirts in the other and mounted the interior wooden stairs to the floor above. On the landing she stopped to listen. There were four chambers on this floor. The largest had been turned into a nursery for her two youngest children, her sister-in-law's two little boys, and her niece's two babies along with the nurse. The smallest of the four rooms was where her confessor and her children's tutor, Fathers Angelus, and the three school-aged children slept. The remaining two rooms were for herself, her adult daughter Isabella, her sister-in-law Eloise, and her husband's niece Eschiva.

The nursery seemed thankfully still. Either the children had not grasped the significance of the fall of Jerusalem, their nurse had managed to quell their fears, or they had simply been given enough wine to make them sleep. From the schoolroom, on the other hand, Maria Zoë could hear the angry voice of her eldest son. John was now eight, and he was a bright, alert child. He had been very cognizant of what fate had awaited them in Jerusalem—and overjoyed when his father arrived like an archangel to spirit them away to safety. That his father had decided to remain behind in Jerusalem while the Ibelin women and children were sent to safety in Tyre, however, had outraged him. He'd been too frightened to want to remain, but he'd been furious with his father, too. He was querulous now, and she could sense the rage in his voice even without hearing his words. Why, why, why did his father have to die? Why had he thrown his life away when he could have been *here*, with us, safe in Tyre?

Maria Zoë knew she ought to go to him and comfort him, but how could she? How could she help when part of her felt the same childish rage? Better to leave him to the seasoned and stoical Father Angelus, whose calm voice rumbled in answer to the boy's high-pitched anger.

Maria Zoë turned and continued down the hall. The next room was silent, she noted with relief, because she had no desire to face her sister-in-law Eloise. At last she reached her own chamber and took a deep breath, knowing that her daughter Isabella would be waiting up for her on the other side of the door. Part of her would have preferred to be left alone, but what sort of daughter would go to bed when her mother had just learned she was a widow?

Maria Zoë pushed open the door to find not just Isabella but also Eschiva, her husband's niece, sitting beside the little table by the window overlooking the street. The young women had been raised together for several years as children, and their friendship had withstood separation and marriage. They were evidently in earnest conversation, but jumped up at the sound of the door opening.

Isabella ran to her mother. "Mama! We were getting worried! Are you all right?" Isabella was fifteen years old, and even her mother could see she had left childhood behind and was now very much a nubile beauty with a womanly figure as well as a lovely face. She seemed to fly across the room to take her mother in her arms, her expression of concern both sincere and melodramatic.

"I'm not on the brink of collapse, if that's what you mean," Maria Zoë answered her daughter, at once muting her emotions and patting her in thanks. With their arms locked, Maria Zoë and Isabella returned to the table as Eschiva slipped onto the wooden window seat to vacate her chair for the Dowager Queen.

In this company, Eschiva often felt like the dowdy sparrow or the poor cousin. Maria Zoë might be thirty-three years old, but she was still a strikingly handsome woman. She had, after all, been selected as a bride for King Amalric in part because she was an exceptionally pretty child, and it was largely from her that Isabella had her budding beauty. Eschiva, on the other hand, had never been deemed a great beauty, and she had not withstood the trials of life as apparently unscathed as Maria Zoë. Eschiva had grieved for the loss of two infants and had been abandoned by both her parents. At twenty-two she looked more like thirty, a fact underlined by her simple linen wimple and plain cotton gown. Here in the company of princesses and queens, she remained nothing but the wife of a landless younger son—that, or the wife of a man whose brother had squandered a kingdom on a single day, the wife of the constable of a kingdom that no longer existed.

A single candle burned in a silver candlestick on the little table, but there was a silver pitcher filled with wine, another with water, and three silver chalices as well—all goods the Dowager Queen had sagely packed onto the backs of protesting brood mares as she salvaged as much as possible of her movable fortune from Jerusalem. As Maria Zoë settled herself in an armed chair softened with cushions, Isabella reached for the pitcher. "Mixed or pure, Mama?"

"I think I need it pure, sweetheart," Maria Zoë admitted, leaning her head against the high back of the chair and closing her eyes for a moment. Then she half opened them and considered her companions. Eschiva might technically be only her niece by marriage, but she had come to live with Maria Zoë and Balian at Ibelin when her mother retired to a convent. She had remained in their household two years, and the bonds forged in those two years had never weakened. Eschiva looked to Maria Zoë more as an elder sister than as an uncle's wife, while Maria Zoë's protectiveness of Eschiva had been tempered by growing respect for her strength in adversity and her common sense. It was to Eschiva, therefore, that she directed her next remark: "So what have you decided we should do?"

Eschiva started slightly, surprised by the Dowager Queen's directness, but she was pleased by this mark of the older woman's respect for her common sense. "Well, the first thing we need to do is demand more information from Salah ad-Din. After all, we don't know for *sure* that Uncle Balian is dead. He might have surrendered and been taken captive, as were our husbands." Eschiva's husband, Aimery de Lusignan, and Isabella's husband, Humphrey de Toron, had both been taken captive at Hattin and were being held in the citadel at Aleppo.

Maria Zoë considered the two women before her. Both were nodding vigorously.

She shook her head and reminded them: "You know as well as I do that the burghers of Jerusalem said they would kill their own families and then sortie out to certain death before they would surrender Jerusalem."

"But the Patriarch condemned that as unchristian, and Uncle Balian opposed it as fanaticism," Isabella pointed out passionately.

"Men are always braver *before* a battle than after one," Eschiva added, with a cynicism Maria Zoë had not expected of her. "I don't mean Uncle Balian," Eschiva hastened to explain, mistaking Maria Zoë's expression of surprise. "No one can doubt his courage, but the rest of the men—they were merchants, tradesmen, and clerics. Remember, too, that no one crowed louder about fighting for Christ than my brother-in-law Guy, yet he surrendered, did he not?"

Maria Zoë only raised her eyebrows, too exhausted to give vent to her feelings about Guy de Lusignan. She reminded the younger women instead, "My lord husband broke his word to Salah ad-Din when he chose to remain in Jerusalem rather than just bring me and the children to safety. Salah ad-Din is ruthless to those he thinks have betrayed him."

"But the Sultan sent his own men to escort you to safety," Eschiva pointed out.

Maria Zoë dismissed her comment with a wave of her hand and retorted tartly, "He did that because he didn't want to provoke my cousin in Constantinople."

Eschiva and Isabella exchanged a glance. They *wanted* to believe the Sultan would be generous; so much depended on it.

As if sensing their distress, Maria Zoë softened her stance. "You are right to suggest appealing directly to Salah ad-Din, Eschiva. He still wants the goodwill of the Greek Emperor, and he will respond to an inquiry from me with courtesy—regardless of the news. If he has killed Lord Balian, then I can request his remains. If he holds him prisoner, I can ask what ransom he wants." She nodded and reached for the wine.

Isabella and Eschiva drank too as Maria Zoë sipped cautiously, evidently lost in thought as she stared at the candle. "There is one thing that puzzles me," Maria Zoë admitted softly. Her two companions looked at her expectantly. "In all their jubilation and triumph today, the Saracens failed to brag about the slaughter that had taken place. That's not like them, you know. They revel in telling us of their bloody deeds. It was from *them* that we learned of the execution of the captive Templars and Hospitallers. They were *proud* of hacking off the heads of bound and kneeling prisoners. And they promised to 'wash away' the slaughter of eighty-eight years ago in a new river of blood. Remember how our escort told us that 'If your horses walked in blood up to their fetlocks, ours will *swim* in blood'?"

Eschiva nodded and gripped her chalice, remembering how terrified she had been when one of the escort delivered this message with an expression of gleeful hatred. She had been sure it was a prelude to violence against them, and she had started praying frantically. Instead the red-headed *Mamluke* had been called to order by the escort commander, and they had been treated courteously thereafter. Isabella, however, jumped to her feet in agitation. "For all their silks and perfumes, they are more bloodthirsty than ravenous wolves! They are—"

"Hush, Isabella," her mother admonished, gesturing for her to sit down. "The point is: they did *not* brag about the rivers of blood and mountains of corpses they had created in Jerusalem. They did not even taunt us with the fact that my husband's 'faithlessness' had been repaid. It would have been more in character if they had described in detail the way they had tortured him to death."

Isabella and Eschiva were staring at the Maria Zoë" in horror, seeing for the first time the nightmares she had concealed from them. This was what she had been living with since their departure from Jerusalem: the fear that the man she loved would not meet a noble death in battle, but live to be tortured and humiliated. It was a fear she had not dared breathe to anyone, because she had not wanted to add to their already considerable uncertainty and grief. She had carried it alone.

Now she looked from her daughter to her niece and back again, and something like hope shimmered in her eyes. "I'm sure they would have gloated if they *could*, which means it didn't happen. Jerusalem has fallen, but there was no slaughter in the streets, and Lord Balian was not publicly tortured and butchered. So, we must find out what *did* happen."

Conrad de Montferrat was even now, at the age of forty-two, a stunningly handsome man. His good looks, superb manners, and gift for languages had enchanted the court at Constantinople when he had accompanied his younger brother Rainer to the latter's wedding with Emperor Manuel I's only daughter Maria. At the time he too had been bedazzled, not by any woman but by the Queen of Cities itself. The city on the Bosporus had enchanted him with its size, grandeur, and elegance. He had been mesmerized by the depth of culture and tradition cultivated by the Eastern Empire—not to mention its wealth. Conrad had, furthermore, left behind his mousy German wife, and in addition to admiring the splendor of court ceremony, the magnificence of the architecture, and the delectability of the cuisine, he had greatly enjoyed the sexual sophistication of certain Greek wives and widows. Conrad had been quite prepared to spend the rest of his life in Constantinople—and then his brother's new father-in-law had had the temerity to die of old age.

The new regent, the Emperor's second wife Maria of Antioch, had been understandably suspicious of her stepdaughter, and the atmosphere had chilled immediately. Courtiers are quick to smell which way the wind is blowing, and Conrad discovered that while no one dared scorn his brother Rainer, they had fewer scruples about closing their doors (and boudoirs) to the brother of the husband of the former Emperor's daughter. Constantinople rapidly lost some of its charm, and Conrad had departed—in the nick of time. Within a year of his departure, his brother and sister-in-law had been murdered by the usurper Andronicus, along with Maria of Antioch. Indeed, the entire community of Latin merchants—women, children, and priests included—had been slaughtered by the population in a bloodbath.

It was a lesson in Greek treachery that Conrad should have learned, but the memories of that golden city had been more powerful than the lessons taught by that slaughter. He had been seduced a second time. Thinking that things had changed for the better when Andronicus was torn to pieces by a raging mob and replaced by the lowly Isaac Angelus, Conrad had returned to Constantinople. The lure had been Emperor Isaac Angelus' sister Theodora. Since Conrad's German wife had conveniently died childless, there was no impediment to this marriage. Conrad had seized upon it gleefully, reveling even more in the title of "Caesar" that it bestowed upon him.

But the splendor of Constantinople was largely a façade. Beneath the glittering gold of the tiles and the shimmering purple silk lurked treachery and poison. Theodora had proven haughty, avaricious, vain, and viperous. Like the Greek ladies who had welcomed and then rejected him before, she was as sexually sophisticated as a Turkish whore—and as intellectually devious as a Roman cardinal. Like the others, she could caress with one hand and poison with the other. No sooner had Conrad successfully defeated the rebellion of Alexios Branas and returned to Constantinople in triumph, than his wife and her brother turned against him. With his spectacular success—riding bareheaded into the thick of the fighting and thrusting Alexios Branas from his horse in the midst of the battle—Conrad had made himself a threat to the less martial Isaac.

Conrad had only escaped the jealousy of his patron and the vengeance of Branas' supporters by fleeing aboard a Genoese galley. He had not known (or cared about) the destination of the vessel when it cast off, but on learning it, it had suited him well enough: it was bound for Acre in the Kingdom of Jerusalem. His father had held a fief in Jerusalem ever since his elder brother William had married Queen Sibylla. Conrad had blithely assumed that his father would be pleased to see him again, and likewise assumed that his undoubted talents would soon win him lands and titles, if not heiresses or dowagers.

At Acre, however, the bells that usually announced the imminent arrival of a ship failed to ring. The captain, a wary old sea dog, opted to drop anchor offshore until the silence could be explained. Shortly afterwards a pilot boat approached to inquire their business, and the captain asked for the latest news (as any seaman long at sea would do). The news shocked them to the quick. "Allahu Akbar!" the pilot sang out. "The glorious Sultan Salah ad-Din, may God shower blessings upon him, has obliterated the polytheists, curses upon their infidel souls, and controls Acre these four days past."

They'd weighed anchor and run out the oars to dash up the coast for Tyre. Here, although the city was still in Frankish hands, the population was in a state of mindless panic mixed with profound demoralization. It was flooded with refugees and the walking wounded from Hattin. The lord of Tyre, the Archbishop, had already taken ship to bring word to the West of the catastrophe of Hattin and appeal for a new crusade, leaving the city leaderless. Most of the richer merchants and churchmen were busy packing up their valuables and frantically bidding up the price of passage aboard the few ships still in the harbor. The poor, meanwhile, were trying to steal what was left behind by the rich, and the fighting men were bickering about whether to continue on to Tripoli, to which the Count of Tripoli had already fled, or to try to defend Scandelion or Toron. Of the two barons remaining, Sidon was rumored to favor a surrender to Salah ad-Din, while Ibelin could think of nothing but begging the Sultan for a safe-conduct so he could rescue his wife and children from the now isolated and indefensible Jerusalem.

Conrad had been disgusted by the lot of them and equally determined to put an end to the disintegration of the Kingdom. It was obvious to him that Christianity was about to lose its hold on the Holy Land unless someone made a stand—here in Tyre. The city of Tyre was the most defensible in the Kingdom. It had been built in biblical times on an island off the coast. Furthermore, except for the entrance to the harbor itself, the coast was littered with underwater rocks that prevented an assault by sea. Although the city was joined to the mainland by a causeway, over the centuries this narrow tongue had been made defensible by a moat and a series of three walls, each higher than the one before.

Conrad had taken one look at the defenses and determined that Tyre was the ideal place for making a stand. It was virtually impregnable to assault and almost equally well suited to withstanding a siege, since it could be resupplied by sea unless blockaded effectively. It sat less than 90 miles from Tripoli and 260 from Antioch. Even if, God forbid, Tripoli and Antioch fell, the rich Greek island of Cyprus, just 150 miles offshore, was completely secure.

Conrad's own enthusiasm for the defense of Tyre had been contagious—particularly among those too poor to escape by sea. Sidon had withdrawn to his castle of Belfort inland, and Ibelin had gone off on his fool's errand to Jerusalem, leaving Conrad to be made the ruler of Tyre by popular acclaim. No Caesar of old had ever been more tumultuously proclaimed, Conrad thought.

He had organized the defenders into an effective garrison. For him and under his leadership, they had dug ditches beyond the outer wall to the east and built up the sea walls and harbor mole as well. A chain had been fixed across the harbor entrance. An inventory of stores, weapons, armor, and vacant houses had been made, and the treasury of the absent Archbishop had been confiscated. Conrad de Montferrat was master of Tyre, and from here he intended to recapture the entire Kingdom of Jerusalem—whether for Christ or for himself was a moot point, since he tended to see them as one and the same thing.

The arrival of Queen Maria Zoë Comnena in early August with a bevy of women and children had surprised but not unduly unsettled Conrad. Such a highborn lady could only be met with the utmost courtesy. She was a niece of the late Greek Emperor Manuel I, after all, and so by marriage she was a kinswoman. She brought with her, furthermore, her daughter by King Amalric of Jerusalem, the Princess Isabella. Conrad was not indisposed to play the role of gallant protector to a dowager queen and a nubile princess, particularly not after their first encounter had revealed that both women were beautiful in their different ways: Queen Maria Zoë stately, elegant, and dark, Princess Isabella blooming and soft.

He had been less pleased to discover, however, that Queen Maria Zoë had rapidly attracted a small but potent entourage of fighting men. Conrad had dismissed Ibelin as an insignificant baron only concerned about his personal affairs, and had been surprised to discover that among the knights and—more surprising—sergeants of Outremer he enjoyed a reputation for courage and leadership that was unequaled by any of his peers. Conrad had been inwardly disgruntled to discover that the arrival of Queen Maria Zoë had caused a minor sensation in the city (*his* city) and that hundreds of men had converged on the modest house he had assigned to the Lady of Ibelin to pay her and her (absent) husband homage.

It was perhaps natural that her second husband's vassals and household knights felt honor-bound to his lady, while the knights of Nablus, her own barony, were naturally still pledged to her. It was less self-evident, and so distinctly disturbing, to realize that hundreds of sergeants and archers from across the lost Kingdom likewise looked to this obscure native baron for leadership— even when he wasn't here! The knights of the Dowager Queen and her second husband rapidly formed themselves into a close-knit and quasi-independent force who could count on the unofficial support of a wider cross-section of fighting men. They would take his orders, Conrad believed, but only as long as Queen Maria Zoë did not contradict him. At the moment, of course, there was no reason why she should, but he knew from experience how independent and self-confident Imperial Greek women were. It would be foolish, he knew, to imagine that their interests would always align perfectly.

The news that Queen Maria Zoë was requesting an interview was, therefore, cause for consternation. "What does she want?" he asked the clerk who had brought him the news.

"I imagine she wishes more information about what happened in Jerusalem," the priest answered unimaginatively. Conrad had inherited the staff of the archiepiscopal palace when he took up residence in it, and the staff was all clerical. That sometimes had its advantages. Priests were on the whole better educated, more discreet, and less inclined to theft, drunkenness, or disorder than secular servants. In this case, Conrad couldn't decide if the man was mocking him or simply stupid.

"How in the name of our Blessed Savior should I be able to give her more information about what happened in Jerusalem?" Conrad snapped back.

"Do you want me to send her away?" the priest asked next.

"Don't be ridiculous! She's the Dowager Queen of Jerusalem! See her to the solar."

Almost before he had finished speaking, Conrad jumped to his feet and made his way to his chamber. He hastily changed into one of his better silk surcoats, brushed traces of dirt from his suede boots, and combed his thick dark hair and mustache before hastening back to the solar. A few paces before the door, he slowed himself to a dignified pace and entered the solar with measured and weighty steps. (He had observed court etiquette well during his sojourns in Constantinople.)

He was startled to find two women awaiting him. The priest (he cursed him inwardly) had neglected to mention that the Dowager Queen was accompanied by her daughter, the Princess Isabella. Although he had seen Isabella before, notably on her arrival in Jerusalem, something about the way she looked today ignited his interest. She was dressed in burgundy trimmed with gold embroidery, and the insides of her wide outer sleeves were lined with shimmering sky-blue silk that matched the veils encasing her face and throat. She was *really* a very beautiful young woman, Conrad concluded, as he bowed gallantly over her hand. "Madame, what a pleasant surprise."

Turning to her mother, he repeated his deep bow, and compensated for the breach of protocol in greeting her daughter first with a flood of welcoming words in passable Greek that stressed how honored he was to receive his "beloved" and "most esteemed" kinswoman. He ended with a declaration of shared distress over the fate of her husband.

Maria Zoë had not missed either the fact that Conrad all but devoured Isabella with his eyes or the fact that her daughter had blushed. More than blushed, really: Isabella looked like an unfolding blossom. She commented on neither fact. "My lord, I am here to ask a favor of you," she announced instead.

Conrad bowed again and indicated that the Dowager Queen should take one of the large high-backed armed chairs at a table before a window that looked north along the coast. He assured her, "I would be delighted to be of service to you, Madame, provided it is within my power to do what you ask."

Maria Zoë settled herself in the chair, her abundant purple silk taffeta skirts spilling in gracious folds around her legs and her sleeves enveloping the arms of the chair. Hem, sleeves, waist, and neckline were all trimmed with gold needlework studded with rolled amethysts, Conrad noted. He smiled to himself because she had clearly dressed in some of her finest to see him. "Yesterday," Maria Zoë opened, "we were informed Jerusalem had fallen to Salah ad-Din. However, there were no specifics about the fate of my husband, who commanded the defense. I wish to send a messenger to the Sultan requesting that information."

Conrad nodded and answered, "Understandable, Madame. Very understandable." He found he had to make a conscious effort not to let his eyes shift to Isabella's lovely face. It was ridiculous in a man his age, with as many conquests as he'd had, to be infatuated with a mere girl, he told himself, but the desire to look at her again was almost irresistible.

A priest glided into the solar with a tray of refreshments that he began offloading onto the small round table. Maria Zoë pointedly watched him offload the silver pitcher, chalices, and bowls (all objects that belonged to the absent Archbishop of Tyre), thanked the priest, and waited for him to depart again before asking Conrad, "Does that mean you will allow me to send someone?"

"I'm not sure, Madame. Whom should I put at such risk? Anyone issuing forth from Tyre and requesting an audience with the Sultan Salah ad-Din is as likely to face immediate execution as to be escorted to the Sultan. I can hardly order a man to take such a risk for the sake of information about the fate of one man, can I?"

"I have several volunteers, Monsieur, if that is your only concern."

She made it sound as if she did not believe he was really worried about the fate of the messenger, while the reference to volunteers was a pointed reminder to Conrad that she had men willing to do her bidding. Yes, it would be wise not to underestimate this woman, Conrad concluded. "In that case, Madame, I can only wish them Godspeed." He opened his hands in a gesture of invitation, but his gaze slid back to Isabella and his smile was directed at her rather than her mother.

Isabella smiled back, and it lit up the whole room. "Thank you so much, Monsieur!" she exclaimed enthusiastically. "You can't know how much this means to my mother and me! Sir Bartholomew has promised to bring me back word of my lord husband as well," she explained with juvenile candor.

Maria Zoë, watching closely, saw Conrad flinch before assuring Isabella smoothly that he was more delighted than ever to assist her in any way he could, and that he was "enchanted" to see two wives so concerned for the fate of their husbands. Maria Zoë rose to her feet to the rustle of silk taffeta and held out her hand. Conrad and Isabella hastily got to their feet and Conrad bowed low over Maria Zoë's hand. He then turned and, with a smile only for her, bowed even lower over Isabella's hand. "Please, come to me with whatever requests you have. I will always try to accommodate."

Maria Zoë nodded and her lips smiled, but her eyes met Conrad's coldly as she noted cynically, "As you have today."

After they left the palace and were riding side by side back to their own residence, Isabella, who was still beaming, remarked to her mother, "Monsieur de Montferrat is very gallant, Mama, don't you think?"

"He is very polished, well traveled, and good-looking," Maria Zoë answered.

Isabella considered her mother, sensitive to her tone as well as her words. "That doesn't sound entirely approving, Mama."

"It's not. Conrad de Montferrat is exceedingly ambitious and far too sure of himself for his own good."

"I'm not sure what you mean by that," Isabella admitted.

"Hmm," Maria Zoë replied. She had no intention of telling her daughter that Conrad was a notorious seducer and settled for saying, "He calls himself 'Caesar' in his correspondence, although it is an empty title now that he has fled Constantinople, and he occupies the archiepiscopal palace as if he owned it."

"But the Archbishop is away and no one knows when he will return. Why shouldn't he live in the palace?"

"Lord Balian didn't move into the royal apartments in Jerusalem just because Sibylla abandoned the city," Maria Zoë reminded Isabella. "But no matter. Conrad de Montferrat has saved this city for Christ, and as long as we hold it, aid can come from the West. God willing!" She crossed herself and prayed that it would be so.

Chapter 2

Jerusalem, October 1187

THE SHEER SIZE OF THE ARMY spread out on the hills around Jerusalem made Sir Bartholomew's throat go dry. It was all too reminiscent of Hattin: the same bright-colored tents of the emirs surrounded by rows and rows of plain-colored smaller tents for the common soldiers; the same corrals for the horses; the same long lines of tethered camels. To the Frankish knight's well-trained eye, it was clear the Sultan had drawn all his forces together for the assault on Jerusalem. The army mustered here easily numbered forty thousand men, of which more than ten thousand were cavalry. What chance had Jerusalem stood against such a force?

Sir Bartholomew knew that the Templars and Hospitallers had mustered for Hattin with their entire mobile force. That meant that while they had left knights to garrison strategic castles like Safed and Krak des Chevaliers, they had taken the full complement of knights, Turcopoles, and sergeants from their headquarters at Jerusalem. Only the sick, the infirm, and the non-combatant lay brothers had been left behind to maintain their establishments. King Guy had likewise taken the entire royal household—knights, squires, and Turcopoles—along with the hundreds of sergeants from the royal domains and those who owed service to the Canons of the Holy Sepulcher. Not a single fighting man below the age of forty had remained behind in Jerusalem when the feudal army marched out to face Salah ad-Din's invasion.

The Dowager Queen had told Sir Bartholomew that her husband had knighted over eighty youths of good family and described how he'd organized the merchants, tradesmen, and clerics, particularly those from the non-Latin Christian communities. But the Lord of Ibelin still held a city where women and children outnumbered men capable of bearing arms by fifty to one. So Ibelin had organized the women, too.

Sir Bartholomew shook his head in wonder, for as he approached the city he could clearly see the evidence of a fierce and far from one-sided battle. Even from a distance he could make out the hulking and listing wrecks of burned-out siege engines. He next saw many dark stains on the white stone surface of the walls, marking where the defenders had poured burning pitch on their assailants. Nearer still, the dusty earth was littered with crossbow shafts and broken pieces of equipment. Various bloodstained rags, the remnants of clothes cut away, testified to the wounded who had bled out here. The rows of neat Saracen graves bore silent witness to the Sultan's losses. No, Jerusalem had not collapsed or surrendered easily. It had been overwhelmed.

Sir Bartholomew had traveled this far under a white flag, and a young Mamluke, Khalid al-Hamar, had been detailed to escort him to the Sultan. The youth was a redhead, probably from the cold regions north of the Black Sea, but it was unlikely he had any memory of the land of his birth. He was now the Sultan's man, ambitious and talkative. He provided Sir Bartholomew with a running commentary about the battle for Jerusalem, to which Sir Bartholomew listened only partially. The older man was more interested in the testimony of his own eyes than in the bragging of a stripling young enough to be his grandson. He noted that the moat had been almost completely filled to enable the Sultan's troops to get closer to the walls. More impressive still, a solid stone structure protected the entrance to the tunnel used by the sappers to dig under the walls. The sight of the collapsed section of the northern wall, easily forty yards long, took Sir Bartholomew's breath away. Khalid grinned and made a gloating remark that Sir Bartholomew's numbed brain could not take in. They must have been able to pour hundreds of men through that breach, the old soldier calculated, and followed them up with thousands more. They would have slaughtered everyone in the city in just a matter of hours!

Yet the absence of vultures wheeling overhead and the lack of swarming flies suggested that the city was not clogged with corpses. On the contrary, the air smelled of nothing more offensive than dust and Saracen latrines along the moat. Puzzled, he looked beyond the Saracen sentries guarding the breach in the wall and caught his breath in amazement. He could see the Temple of God rearing up against the cloudy sky, and it was still crowned by the cross of Christ. That didn't make sense in a city that was now controlled by the Muslims. The Temple of God was known to the Saracens as the Dome of the Rock. It had been built over a rock that, they claimed, bore Mohammed's footprint from his ascent into heaven.

Sir Bartholomew reached out and caught his escort's arm to get his attention. "The cross," he pointed; "why is it still there?"

"The forty days aren't up yet," the Mamluke answered puzzlingly, as if that explained everything.

Before Sir Bartholomew could ask any more questions, however, they reached the northeast corner of the city and turned to start descending into the Kidron Valley. The Tomb of the Virgin, the Grotto of the Agony at Gethsemane, and the Church of St. Saviour stood out like islands of light amidst the swarming mass of Saracen troops. Surprisingly, they did not appear to have been totally trashed, much less gutted by fire. Beyond the valley, the Mount of Olives was scarred by felled trees, however, and the sight stabbed at Sir Bartholomew's heart. Those trees had once given shade to the Savior. They had been cut down simply to make a large place for the Sultan's brilliant yellow tent and a pasture for his horses. Such was the price of defeat.

Khalid al-Hamar unnecessarily pointed out the Sultan's tent to Sir Bartholomew, and he nodded absently, still trying to figure out what was going on. All the gates of the city were manned by Mamlukes—but he had seen no one moving in or out. The reference to forty days suggested the surrender had been agreed upon but not yet implemented. The city had been given forty days. To do what?

They rode together through the denser rows of the Sultan's personal bodyguard camped within the olive grove. Between trees, tents, and campfires there was hardly room for the horses to find a footing, and they had to weave their way slowly. Finally they reached the space before the Sultan's tent and dismounted. While a boy took the reins of his horse, Khalid gestured for Sir Bartholomew to follow him inside.

Once inside, the Frank was told to wait, while Khalid continued deeper into the partitioned tent. Other Saracens of various ranks, imams and Sufis as well as fighting men, cast him curious glances as they came and went. Sir Bartholomew's patience wore thin. He had come a long way, and he wanted to know the fate of the citizens of Jerusalem. He couldn't bear the suspense much longer, he thought.

Khalid returned and announced that al-Adil, rather than the Sultan, would receive him. Sir Bartholomew nodded stiffly. The Sultan's brother was good enough for him. He followed the red-haired Mamluke into a room completely carpeted with painted canvas and on which a table and cushions had been arranged neatly. He was told to sit, and he sank down behind the table. His nerves were getting the better of him, however, and he couldn't keep his hands still. They galloped in place on the carved surface of the table. Egyptian manufacture, he noted, with ivory inlay.

"You requested an audience with the Sultan?" a deep, cultivated voice asked from behind.

Sir Bartholomew drew himself back up onto his feet with an unconscious grunt. (For an old man, it was a long way up from sitting cross-legged on the floor.) He bowed to a man wearing long-flowing, elaborately embroidered silk robes and a satin turban, and then reached inside his gambeson and removed the Dowager Queen's letter. "My lady, Maria Zoë Comnena, Dowager Queen of Jerusalem, Lady of Nablus and Ibelin, has charged me to bring this letter to the Sultan," he explained in passable Arabic. Sir Bartholomew had been born and raised in the Holy Land, and he had learned to speak Arabic from the Syrian Christian servants and the tenants.

Al-Adil held out a beringed hand, and Sir Bartholomew crossed the space between them to place the letter in it.

"May I open it?" asked al-Adil. "Or is it for the Sultan's eyes alone?"

"You may open it, but it is in Greek."

"Ah." Al-Adil turned and ordered Khalid to fetch him Benjamin, a Jewish scribe literate in Greek, then indicated Sir Bartholomew should sit down again. He ordered refreshments for both of them, but before the fruit juice and nuts arrived an elderly man in the robes and long curls of a Jew joined them. Al-Adil indicated he should sit with them and handed him the Dowager Queen's letter.

The Jewish secretary cautiously sliced through the Queen's seal with a little knife he carried in his belt. He then unfolded the letter and spread it out. He leaned over and read intently, nodding to himself as he went along. Only when he had read to the end did he sit upright again and look at al-Adil. "Do you want me to read it aloud?"

"For now, a summary would suffice," al-Adil replied.

"The Dowager Queen politely and deferentially requests news of her husband, the Lord of Ibelin, the return of his remains if he is dead, or his release if he is captive."

"Write a faithful translation of the letter for my brother," al-Adil ordered the secretary, "and bring it to me when you are done."

After the secretary had departed, al-Adil turned to Sir Bartholomew. "Rest assured your lord is in good health," he told the old knight. Sir Bartholomew's relief was so great that he crossed himself without thinking about where he was.

Al-Adil continued, "He agreed to surrender Jerusalem intact in exchange for us allowing the survivors to ransom themselves. We gave them forty days to raise their ransoms—after which those who have paid will be allowed to go free, while those who have not will be enslaved. Ibn Barzan is engaged in raising the necessary ransoms for himself, his household, and the many poor and destitute in the city. He has another thirty-two days before the ransoms are due."

"May I be allowed into the city to see him?" Sir Bartholomew asked anxiously. He had promised the Dowager Queen that, if her husband was alive, he would try to see him. He had imagined visiting a man held in a dungeon, possibly in chains. The thought that he might see Ibelin as a free man was both amazing and elating, but the news that the city's residents and refugees likewise stood a chance of rescue was downright intoxicating. Sir Bartholomew could hardly contain the hope that his daughters had found their way to Jerusalem. And if they had, they would surely have found safety with the Ibelin household. He could already picture himself embracing them and sweeping his grandchildren up into his arms again.

"Of course," al-Adil answered, opening his hands and smiling. "You may go at once," he suggested generously.

Sir Bartholomew could hardly stop himself from just jumping up and running out. He managed, however, to bow and thank al-Adil before rushing outside. Here he found his horse, remounted, and started as fast as he could to weave his way through the crowded orchard toward the Jehoshaphat Gate.

He had already reached the foot of the valley and was starting up the far slope when the gate ahead of him opened. A Frankish knight emerged from the gate, riding a large but graying palfrey. The man was exceptionally tall but slender, and he sat very upright in the saddle. He was not wearing his helmet, but he wore chain mail, and over this a surcoat particolored in gold and scarlet. Sir Bartholomew at once recognized the Lord of Ibelin and spurred forward.

Ibelin caught sight of Sir Bartholomew and likewise urged his horse to a faster gait. They reached one another in a swirl of dust, drew up, and dropped from their saddles before the horses came to a complete halt. The two men embraced heartily, indifferent to the large and curious Saracen audience around them.

After that first exuberant greeting, Sir Bartholomew drew back and exclaimed in excitement, "My lord! We thought you must be dead! We heard Jerusalem had fallen, and your lady—"

"She made it safely to Tyre? With the children?" Ibelin interrupted to ask, the fears that had haunted him still shadowing his eyes.

Sir Bartholomew's smile broadened even more. "Yes. She, the ladies Isabella and Eschiva, and all the children are safe and well. Your lady sent me with a letter to the Sultan requesting more information about *you*. Al-Adil told me you lived, and I was on my way to find you. I still can't believe it!"

Reassured that his family was safe and well, Ibelin could focus again on the immediate problems. "I negotiated a surrender that allows us to ransom ourselves," Ibelin reiterated what al-Adil had already said. Yet as he spoke Sir Bartholomew noted the weariness and worry that had carved out his cheeks and drawn his eyes deeper into their sockets. Ibelin did not look particularly pleased to still be alive, the older man noted with surprise—until Ibelin burst out hotly, "The ransom's more than many poor people here can pay! The Hospital has turned over all the money King Henry of England deposited with them, but it's not enough. The city's filled with refugees—women and children, people who've lost everything already!"

"My daughters?" Sir Bartholomew asked, unable to withstand the suspense a moment longer.

Ibelin started, looked at the old knight in horror, and then slowly shook his head. "They're not here, Bart. Didn't they get to Tyre?"

Sir Bartholomew swallowed to keep his constricted throat from closing entirely as he slowly shook his head. The short flare of hope was already extinguished.

"I'm sorry," Ibelin told him honestly, laying a hand on his arm. "I'm so sorry," he repeated. But in the next instant his agitation had overwhelmed his sympathy and he burst out, "But, God help me, if I can't find another thirty thousand dinars, *tens of thousands* of innocent women, children, and clerics are going into Saracen slavery!"

Sir Bartholomew understood Ibelin's distress, and recognized that the baron was focused on the total tragedy rather than one man's individual grief. He nodded to indicate he understood, but he also felt utterly helpless. If the girls and his grandchildren weren't here and they weren't in Tyre, then they were *already* in Saracen captivity—or dead.

Ibelin was still thinking and speaking of the wider tragedy. "I'm going to meet with the Sultan again in the hope we can renegotiate the ransom for the poor," he told his friend. "I have no other choice," he explained in a voice both tortured and furious, "because nothing I can say or do has convinced that *bastard* Heraclius to part with even a *portion* of his treasure for the sake of the poor! The *Patriarch of Jerusalem*"—Ibelin's voice was laden with contempt, disgust, and outright disbelief—"prefers to retain his gold and silver plate to buying the freedom of Christians!"

The muezzin's voice was fading out and the Sultan sat back on his heels, then pushed himself up off his prayer rug. He gestured to a slave boy to roll it up and put it back in its place. He reseated himself on thick cushions behind the ivory-inlaid table that he used as his writing desk, and again took up the translation of the letter from the Dowager Queen of Jerusalem.

Behind him he heard someone enter and glanced over his shoulder. His brother had entered, asking, "Am I interrupting?"

Salah ad-Din shook his head and indicated that his brother should join him, asking, "You have seen this letter?"

"I skimmed over the translation," al-Adil admitted. "What are you going to answer?"

"I will tell her the truth," the Sultan answered simply.

"Which is?" al-Adil pressed him, his eyes intent on his brother's face.

"That her husband will go free at the end of the forty days."

"You aren't going to accept his offer to stand surety for those who cannot pay?" al-Adil asked back, sounding both surprised and displeased. Ibelin had made this offer this afternoon: that if he could not find an additional thirty thousand dinars in Jerusalem, he would surrender his own person to the Sultan as a hostage until the sum could be raised in the West.

"No," Salah ad-Din answered firmly. "It is worthless. He cannot possibly raise another thirty thousand dinars. All that talk about the Pope in Rome paying is nonsense," he scoffed. "The Pope is no more likely to pay for the paupers in Jerusalem than the Caliph in Baghdad is!" "Furthermore," he continued, "the troops are already grumbling about being denied plunder and slaves. I am counting on some twenty thousand Christians being unable to pay so we can divide them among the troops. Since most of the Christians in the city are women, this will do much to appease their displeasure. One woman for every two men should be enough to restore their good humor for a few weeks."

Al-Adil shrugged agreement, but insisted, "Ibn Barzan is a dangerous opponent. Surely it is better to keep him in our hands than to let him go free, regardless of what happens to the Christian whores. If you let him go, he will certainly fight us again at the next opportunity."

Salah ad-Din raised his eyebrows and eyed his brother. "You sound like you are afraid of him."

"Hardly," al-Adil snapped back, annoyed at his brother's aspersion on his courage. "But why let him go free? At the very least we could insist that his wealthy wife pay a high price for him."

"She is not so wealthy anymore, now that we control all the lands her late husband Malik Amalric settled upon her."

"Her father's family is wealthy," al-Adil insisted.

Salah ad-Din admitted, "True enough—but while I did not want to risk the Greek Emperor's wrath by laying hands on his kinswoman, I'm not sure his sense of family loyalty would extend so far as to pay a large ransom for her Frankish husband. It is more likely we would simply end up with yet another high-ranking—but not particularly valuable—prisoner on our hands. Besides, I gave him my word."

Al-Adil pressed his lips together. His brother was quite capable of breaking his word when he thought it was expedient, but he also knew that his brother *liked* to think of himself as a man of honor. If he was going to get on his high horse and stress his sense of honor, then it would not be productive to argue with him. Al-Adil could not resist adding, however: "You will live to regret this, Yusuf. I warn you Ibn Barzan will do all he can to regain his lost lands. He will never accept our control of these places holy to his foolish faith. He will go all the way to the kingdom of the Norsemen to get help, if he has to."

Salah ad-Din shrugged. "Then he will die an unhappy man in a cold and distant place. We have won. Allah in his infinite generosity has heard our prayers and has granted us this great triumph. In less than four weeks, we will tear down the cross and raise the half-moon of Islam over the Dome of the Rock and the al-Aqsa mosque. We will drive out the polytheists, and I will establish madrassas in their churches. This is no time to be petty or vindictive. I let my emotions run away with me when I allowed the Sufis to execute the Hospitaller and Templar prisoners after Hattin. Yes, they were fanatics who would never make good slaves, and, yes, it was better to kill them—but we should have done it quickly and cleanly, as I killed Arnat al-Karak. Now that I hold the entire Kingdom, my blood has cooled, and I can afford to be generous."

"Tyre still holds out," al-Adil reminded him stubbornly.

Salah ad-Din made a gesture as if he were shooing away a fly. "It is only a matter of time until Tyre falls, and the more mouths they have to feed inside the walls, the faster they will submit. I will let Ibn Barzan escort a third of the refugees from Jerusalem to Tyre. That should fill the city to overflowing, foster sickness and shortages, and so soften the city for ready surrender. We'll follow on the heels of the Christians expelled from Jerusalem, and be ready to lay siege to Tyre as soon as the refugees are all inside. It will fall before the winter solstice," he predicted confidently.

"If that is so, you will have Ibn Barzan in your hands again."

"Yes, and his wife and sons," the Sultan agreed, reaching out to pick up the letter from Maria Zoë Comnena again. "I am quite curious about this woman."

Al-Afdal raised his eyebrows. His brother had four wives and countless concubines. He could not imagine what interest his brother had in a Greek woman, who he guessed was over thirty years old. He admitted, "it is said she was remarkably beautiful when she came to Jerusalem as a young bride, but that was twenty years ago. She is probably fat and sagging now."

Salah ad-Din shrugged. "Pretty flesh is plentiful and readily accessible. I am sure to find something to my taste among the women and girls who cannot pay their ransom, but this woman," he tapped his forefinger on the letter, "is intelligent, and that is a great rarity among her sex."

"What makes you think she possesses intellect?" al-Adil asked, surprised.

"The letter," his brother answered with a smile as he tapped it again. "She constructed it very cleverly: never sounding arrogant, yet never sliding into piteous pleading. When she wrote it, she did not know if her husband was alive or dead. She appealed to my sense of honor—duly citing the Koran—in requesting the return of his remains should he be dead, and she mustered her arguments for clemency, should he be alive, as masterfully as you muster my army." He flashed his brother a smile.

"Surely that was the work of a clever clerk, not a brainless woman," al-Adil countered, annoyed by his brother's credulity.

Salah ad-Din shook his head. "Our good Benjamin told me the letter was composed in the Greek of the imperial class but without the usual embellishments of a scribe. Furthermore, he swears, it was written by a woman's hand." The secretary Benjamin was a master at analyzing calligraphy, which was one reason he enjoyed favor despite being a Jew. "Benjamin believes she wrote it herself, rather than risking it to dictation. He claims that all the imperial women of Constantinople are very well educated."

"How can you educate a woman?" Al-Adil scoffed in exasperation. "They do not have the brains for it, so all teaching is wasted on them. The only thing a woman needs to know is how to please her master and how to honor Allah and his messenger, may Allah's blessings be upon him."

"Possibly, yet *this* woman at least appears to have absorbed a great deal of learning since she speaks three languages, I am told, and writes so eloquently. It makes me wonder if Allah in his infinite wisdom did not give some women a little bit of manliness. . . ."

Al-Adil was not convinced, but he cared too little about an old woman married to a Frank to bother arguing with his brother about her. He confined himself to remarking caustically, "If she has a brain in her head at all, she must be very different from her successor on the throne of Jerusalem!"

Salah ad-Din burst out laughing. "Indeed, they must be as different as day and night! Allah be praised that it is Sibylla who is now the *faranj* Queen, for Sibylla is without doubt the stupidest woman I have ever encountered in my entire life!"

Aleppo, October 1187

Sibylla, Queen of Jerusalem, snuggled closer to the naked body of her husband. She lay on her side under his shoulder, her knee across his hips and her face against his rib cage. With her right hand she played absently with the bronze-colored hairs on his chest. Guy was a wonderfully handsome and virile man, she thought to herself contentedly, still warm and languid from their love-making. She did not understand why other people refused to see his virtues. Some were just jealous, of course, like Barry, who had been furious because Guy replaced him in her bed. Others were bigots, like Tripoli and Sidon, who thought only men from Outremer could rule the Kingdom. And her poor brother Baldwin had hated Guy simply because he was all that Baldwin wasn't: strong, handsome, and vigorous.

But it made no sense the way the survivors of Hattin blamed Guy for their defeat. Could Guy help it that the Saracens outnumbered them, or that they poisoned the wells? Could Guy stop the wind from fanning the fires? Guy had fought bravely to the very end. He hadn't run away like Tripoli and Ibelin. He was no more to blame for the catastrophe than anyone else.

Guy's breathing was becoming deeper as he drifted off to sleep, and Sibylla squirmed to wake him up again. "Guy, I have something to tell you."

"Hmm?" he grunted, reluctant to return to consciousness and with it, awareness of his imprisonment and helplessness.

"You're such a good lover, Guy," Sibylla opened, knowing it would please him, "and we've been making love so often" (what else was there to do in captivity?) "that you have filled my womb with life."

"What?" His eyes flew open and his whole body tensed. "What did you say?"

"That I'm carrying your child again—at last." Despite Guy's unquestionable virility, Sibylla had not conceived until they had been married three years. She had then given birth to a daughter who had died before her second birthday.

"Are you sure?" Guy demanded, slipping out of Sibylla's embrace to look down at her from a sitting position. His expression was not exactly overjoyed.

"Of course I'm sure," Sibylla answered, annoyed by his lack of delight. She looked up at him with a frown hovering on her brow. Sibylla was big-breasted, round-bellied, and an eager and creative bedmate, but her face had never been her best feature, and it was turning round and flabby. "I had my last flux three weeks before I came to join you. I was worried that it would come right after we were reunited and you would be angry, but it never came. Now we've been together ten weeks and still it hasn't come. There are other signs, too," she added, thinking he might have noticed her swelling breasts on his own. "Aren't you pleased?"

"Pleased? How can I be pleased?" Guy demanded, unable to fathom her stupidity. "What if you're carrying a son at last?"

"But that's what I want and pray for," Sibylla told him blankly. "I thought you wanted a son, too."

"Of course I want a son!" Guy retorted furiously, flinging back the covers and swinging his feet over the edge of the bed to stand up, his back to her.

"I don't understand!" Sibylla wailed. "I'm with child and it may well be the son we've hoped and prayed for. Why are you angry with me?" She was near to tears.

"You stupid goose!" Guy snapped, reaching for his braies and stepping into them in obvious haste. As he drew the drawstring tight he reminded her, "Have you forgotten we're prisoners? What do you think Salah ad-Din will do when he learns you are with child?"

Sibylla gazed up at Guy with an open mouth that expressed her utter lack of imagination. "But what should he do?"

"Seize the child, for a start, and then either kill him or—more probably—raise him with his own sons, make him a Muslim, and *then* send him back to us and say: 'Behold your king!' Jesus God, woman! It's bad enough that you insisted on putting yourself in his hands, but now—" He threw up his own hands in helpless frustration and reached for his shirt.

Sibylla pointed out petulantly, "It takes two to make a child. If you didn't want me to become pregnant here in Aleppo, then you shouldn't have been trying so hard."

"I didn't think—never mind!" Guy pulled a shirt over his head and shouted in the direction of the door to the adjacent chamber, "Henri! Henri! Come help me dress!"

Sibylla rolled herself into the sheets to cover her nakedness and lay with her back to her husband, swallowing down tears of self-pity. She loved Guy more than anything in the world. All she wanted to do was please him. She'd abandoned Jerusalem to be with him in captivity, and what thanks did she get? Her subjects had hissed and jeered at her as she left Jerusalem, and her barons had received her here with stony hostility. Guy had been the only one to welcome her. That had been enough at the time, but now he was snarling, too. She just didn't understand.

When Guy was fully dressed, he crossed to the anteroom shared by Sir Henri, who was serving him as a squire since he had none, and Sibylla's maid, and passed through it to pound on the door that led out into the corridor. "I want to visit my brother!" he told the guards posted on the other side of the locked door. "I need to speak urgently with my brother!"

Although he was sure the guards spoke enough French to understand him, they pretended not to and answered in Arabic or Turkish or one of their other ugly-sounding tongues. "Tell them what I want!" Guy ordered Sir Henri.

Sir Henri smirked with an inward sense of superiority. He had been born in Ibelin, the youngest of the first Baron's four sons, and like most of the Latin settlers he had learned rudimentary Arabic as a child in order to speak to the native population. Although he had never mastered it as fully as his older brother Balian, he had over the years acquired a serviceable vocabulary, and had more than once passed himself off as a Bedouin—a ruse that did not require extensive or intellectual conversations. He viewed Lusignan's complete ignorance of the language as intellectual laziness and misplaced arrogance, but it also increased his own utility to the captive king, and so he welcomed it, too.

Guy de Lusignan was a man without friends at the moment. Never popular and widely viewed as a usurper even before the disaster at Hattin, he was now despised for leading the Christian army to an unnecessary defeat and losing the entire Kingdom as a result. Henri shared his peers' contempt for Guy's leadership, but he saw in their open rejection of Guy an opportunity as well. Henri was under no illusion about being in a position to pay his ransom; not only was his estate at Amman lost, but the baronies of his once wealthy and powerful older brothers—Nablus, Ramla, Mirabel, and Ibelin—were likewise all in Saracen hands. Thus he had little prospect of release and might spend the rest of his days in the darkness of the dungeon—unless he could find someone *else* to pay his ransom.

Guy de Lusignan, to be sure, had lost his kingdom and so his income, but he *was* an anointed king. Henri figured that there were rich and powerful kings in the West who would not want a fellow Christian monarch to remain in Saracen hands. By toadying up to Lusignan, Henri had already gained the privilege of sharing the King's comparatively comfortable suite of rooms, and he hoped that when the time came he would also gain release from captivity altogether—through Guy's good offices.

For now, Henri informed the guards that his lord wanted to visit the other prisoners, and received the answer that they would inquire if it was allowed.

"Damn them!" Guy raged, furious with his stupid wife. It was all her fault that they were now in this ridiculous predicament. "Damn them!"

While the King and Queen of Jerusalem were housed in a two-room suite on the upper floor of one of the many towers, the other prisoners were not so lucky.

When guards eventually came to escort Guy to the other prisoners, he was led on shallow, sloping stairs to the very bowels of the great fortress. The passages were wide and tall but poorly lit, and the air was stale and foul long before they reached the large, cavernous cellar in which the other "prisoners of rank" were held.

The arrival of King Guy with an escort caused a minor sensation—or at least a distraction. Several men roused themselves from their straw pallets, not out of respect but from curiosity.

"Come to join us?" Haifa asked sarcastically, looking up but not rising from his chess game with Caesarea.

The white-haired Marquis de Montferrat, father of the man who, unbeknownst to him, was now defending Tyre, hushed Haifa with a wave of his hand. He was no more enamored of Guy de Lusignan than the rest of them, but he did not think Christian lords should present a spectacle of internal bickering to their jailers.

"Where's my brother?" Guy asked in answer, looking around the seemingly vast underground hall, which was composed of a series of vaulted chambers supported by massive stone pillars.

"Down that way," Caesarea gestured vaguely, and Guy had no option but to continue deeper into the darkness. With each step he distanced himself more from the hanging lanterns, and the air seemed both colder and stiller. Suddenly something moved on his right and he shied to the left, instinctively feeling for his hilt. But he had no sword. None of them did.

His brother Aimery loomed up out of the darkness. "Come to see how the rest of us live?" he mocked.

"It's not my fault you aren't housed as well as I," Guy answered defensively.

"No, of course not—no more than it is your fault that we are prisoners, that the Kingdom of Jerusalem is lost, that thousands of Christian corpses lie rotting on the field of Hattin unshriven, that—"

"Stop it! We've been through all that a thousand times. You insist on blaming me, and I know I am not to blame! Gerard de Ridefort gave me bad advice—"

"You didn't have to take it!"

"What's done is done. I'm here about something else."

Aimery considered his brother with a sense of hopelessness. Guy might be able to wash himself clean of all guilt for the catastrophe that had befallen them, but Aimery could not. He was honest enough to know he, too, bore his share of guilt—if only for encouraging Guy to come to Outremer, and more especially for enabling him to become King against the wishes of the High Court.

Guy meanwhile was studying his elder brother, and he was not pleased by what he saw. Aimery was letting himself go, Guy noted with disapproval and a sense of superiority. He was haggard, growing a beard, and he smelled unwashed. But Guy still needed his advice. So Guy dropped his voice and took his brother by the elbow to move with him to the back of the vault with the words, "We need to talk."

Aimery did not resist; his will was lamed. He could not forget, as Guy apparently did, that their father had spent five years in a Saracen prison and died there. Aimery, furthermore, had been a prisoner of the Saracens once before. Shortly after first coming to Outremer, he had fallen into Saracen hands and been locked away in a worse place than this. At the time, he'd been unable to imagine how his brothers still in France would learn of his capture, much less how his eldest brother might be persuaded to pay his ransom. When he learned King Amalric had paid his ransom, he'd been overwhelmed with gratitude. He still prayed for the dead King's soul, but the memory of that previous rescue only increased his current state of depression. While his oldest brother was as far away as ever, the King of Jerusalem was right here beside him—and there was no Kingdom left from which to raise the ransom.

"Sibylla's pregnant," Guy whispered into the dank, stagnant air of the dungeon.

Aimery stared apparently blankly at his brother before remarking resentfully, "Congratulations." Guy's wife had surrendered herself voluntarily to the enemy so she could be with her husband, thereby giving Salah ad-Din control of the woman through whom Guy derived his claim to the throne. The way Aimery saw it, it had been political idiocy, but it had given Guy the pleasures of sex.

"Aimery! I thought at least *you'd* understand," Guy hissed. "What if it's a son? What if Salah ad-Din seizes the boy and raises him a Muslim?"

Aimery raised his eyebrows. The idea was far-fetched—or was it? "Well, then, send your wife away before the Sultan finds out about her condition. She came here voluntarily; she should be allowed to go again at will. She could feign illness or some such thing."

"Do you really think the Sultan might let her go?" Guy asked dubiously.

Aimery shrugged. He didn't really care. Even if Guy and Sibylla had a son, he had no kingdom to inherit anyway—or not a Christian one. He might just as well be Muslim, and then he might be made emir of Jerusalem one day. To his brother he said, "There's no harm in asking."

"Sibylla might not want to go," Guy admitted, thinking out loud. "She loves me so well, she can't bear being parted."

Aimery wanted to vomit. Guy was so proud of his wife's loyalty and devotion, when it was actually the cause of catastrophic misfortune. If she'd been willing to divorce Guy as she promised before her coronation, the Kingdom might have had a competent leader, one who would have led them to victory rather than defeat. To his brother he remarked, "Well, then, you'll have to remind her of her duty of obedience. She *did* vow at your wedding to obey you, remember."

"You're jealous of her love for me," Guy concluded condescendingly. "Eschiva could have come with Sibylla, but she chose to go to Tyre with the Dowager Queen and Isabella instead."

"Eschiva put the welfare of our children above our personal affection," Aimery replied with as much dignity as he could muster. If he hadn't been so despondent, his brother's gloating would have made him angry.

"Of course," Guy agreed in a placating tone. "Of course."

"Let us hope your wife will show the same concern for her offspring, now that she is pregnant at last," Aimery replied pointedly.

"Of course. I'll go talk to her. And the Sultan? How do I ask him about this?"

"Why don't you have young Toron write a letter for you? Unlike the rest of us, he can write, not just speak, Arabic."

"Yes, that's a good idea," Guy agreed, and without further ado he turned and hurried back toward the exit, determined to carry out his plans at once.

Aimery sank back onto his pallet. It was filled with old straw and lumpy. He lay down on his back and stared up at the stone blocks of the ceiling. He had no idea if it was day or night, but probably day or his brother wouldn't have been walking around, he reasoned. He was no longer sure exactly how many days he'd been here, although he scratched the wall beside his pallet each time they were fed on the assumption they were fed daily. There were now sixty-seven scratches on the wall. His last imprisonment had lasted exactly ninety-six days and he had nearly gone mad in that space of time. Reynald de Châtillon, on the other hand, had survived *fifteen years* in a dungeon.

Aimery shook himself. He had to *want* to survive—even if it were for fifteen years in this darkness. He had to find ways to survive. He had a son and two lovely daughters, and no matter what Guy said about her, Eschiva was a good and faithful wife. Furthermore, Eschiva was more intelligent than Sibylla, and she knew she could do more for him by staying free and raising his ransom than by sharing his captivity. Eschiva had made the right choice to stay with the Dowager Queen and Princess Isabella. They were the very best hope Aimery had of freedom. As long as Eschiva was in the company of these powerful women, she was in a position to petition his brothers in France. Even more promising, Isabella's first cousin was King Henry II of England. If anyone could ransom the men captured at Hattin, it was King Henry. He was immensely wealthy, and he had already pledged to come on pilgrimage before the disaster at Hattin. He would surely come now to regain the Holy Land, and he would want men around him who knew the country. Who better than the former Constable of the Kingdom?

Aimery knew he was grasping at straws, but he had to or he would go mad.

"Ah, so you are the famous Lord Humphrey de Toron!" the elderly Saracen exclaimed with a smile and a gracious gesture, indicating that the prisoner should sit opposite him on a waiting cushion on the floor. He was obviously not a fighting man and wore neither arms nor armor. Nor was he a wealthy merchant clothed in the bright colors and elaborate styles of the souks and bazaars. Instead, he was dressed in the simple, striped kaftan of a humble man— except that the cotton was crisply clean and exceptionally fine, and he had several gold rings on his fingers.

Humphrey bowed over his hands in thanks and sank warily down on the cushion, acutely conscious of how badly he smelled. He had not been given an opportunity to wash since his capture at Hattin. The dried blood had eventually just worn off, but the accumulated dirt and the stench of his own body only got worse. "I apologize," he said, bowing his head again, "for my sorry and unwashed state. It is not my habit to go about smelling worse than a stable and as dirty as a peasant."

The man opposite smiled in sympathy. "Be assured, I do not think you ill-mannered. Rather, I will do all in my power to see you are given the oppor-tunity to wash and obtain a change of clothes. Let me introduce myself: I am Imad ad-Din al-Isfahani. I had the great honor to serve the illustrious Sultan Nur ad-Din, may Allah show him mercy, as his secretary, and, undeserving as I am, the brave Salah ad-Din, may God's blessing upon him a thousand-fold, has, in his infinite wisdom, seen fit to allow me to continue in the same humble position, for which I thank Allah five times a day."

Humphrey bowed his head and crossed his hands on his chest as he assured the secretary, "I am deeply honored to find myself in such exalted company, and am even more ashamed of my unsavory condition."

Imad ad-Din dismissed his concerns with a wave of his hand and a smile. "That will all be put right. But first, please partake of a little refreshment." He indicated a beautifully displayed spread of delicacies, from goat's cheese in honey to figs encrusted with pistachios. There was minced meat wrapped in grape leaves, rice with parsley and pine nuts, and more. Even before Humphrey could protest, his host clapped his hands, and a boy scurried forward to offer Humphrey a bowl of water in which to wash his hands. A second boy handed Humphrey a linen cloth on which to dry them, and a third offered him a tray on which a broad silver goblet containing iced sherbet, smelling of lemon and decorated with a sprig of mint, was offered.

Humphrey gratefully washed his hands, but did not partake of the sherbet until he had bowed to his host and exclaimed, "I am overwhelmed by your generosity and hospitality, and wish to understand why I have been honored by such undeserved kindness and attention, Excellency."

"Ah." Imad ad-Din smiled, and his leathery face crinkled along the deep lines cut in it by decades in the sun. "It is because, my dear Humphrey—if I may call you that?" Humphrey bowed his head in agreement, "It is because I was the man who read your recent missive to his magnificence Sultan Salah ad-Din, may Allah grant him long life, and I was delighted by your sophisticated and elegant style. Such a refined command of Arabic is a rarity even among educated men of my own people. But to find a master of Arabic in a *faranj* was so astonishing that I said to myself at once, I must meet this unusual man! When my lord and master, my Allah grant him long life, asked me to return to Aleppo on other matters, I took the opportunity to inquire after you. You can imagine my astonishment when I learned you were neither a scholar nor a man of my own generation, but hardly more than a cub and a man of the sword."

Humphrey was deeply moved by the elderly scribe's praise, and he bowed his head again. "You flatter me, Excellency. I have studied your literature diligently and have endeavored to imitate it to the best of my humble abilities, but I am only a novice. I am flattered that my efforts—poor as they undoubtedly were—were not too rude or ill-formed for the Sultan's ear."

"Not at all, not at all—though, of course, there were slight errors that I automatically corrected when reading aloud. Nothing that you could not master with more opportunity to study. It would give me great pleasure to be an instrument for helping you develop your gift for the language of the Prophet, may Allah's blessings be upon him. I hope you will accept my offer?"

Humphrey stopped in the act taking a spoonful of the sherbet. "Your Excellency—I—I don't know what you mean. I am your prisoner, as you see."

"Young man," the elderly scholar opened with a smile, "your condition is no reflection on your personal virtue or your intelligence; it therefore need cause you no shame. You are a prisoner because it was your misfortune to be born and raised a worshiper of icons at a time when Allah in his righteousness has given the Faithful a great leader who, in accordance with His will, has triumphed over his enemies. Do not be downhearted on account of that. We can still be friends.

Come, tell me more about yourself." Imad ad-Din gestured for Humphrey to
eat and drink as he spoke.

"My grandfather," Humphrey began cautiously, "was Constable of the
Kingdom of Jerusalem. He once had the exceptional honor of meeting the
Caliph of Cairo to conclude a treaty with him."

Imad ad-Din nodded and exclaimed softly, "Ah, now I know where I had
heard your name. He too was a great scholar, I believe, no?"

"Yes," Humphrey agreed readily. "He was a master of many languages and a
scholar of both history and poetry. My father died when I was very young, and
I was raised for ten years by my grandfather. He had a large library with many
books of Arab poetry that he used to teach me the language."

"How lovely!" Imad ad-Din exclaimed with genuine enthusiasm. "What
could be a more perfect way to learn Arabic?—other than reading the Koran,
of course."

Humphrey shook his head, confused. He was only nineteen years old and he
was feeling disoriented. The trauma of Hattin, followed by the brutal execution
of the captured Templars and Hospitallers, sat deep. Spending more than three
months in the dank darkness of a dungeon had done little to heal the scars of
that horror. It did not help that Humphrey was younger than most of the other
captives, and routinely ignored because he did not enjoy the respect of his fellow
barons. They scorned him because he had given up his barony for a money fief
and because he wasn't a very competent fighting man, either. It was, he supposed,
a wonder that he had survived Hattin at all.

Imad ad-Din was more than three times his young guest's age, and it was
not difficult for him to see how fragile Humphrey's nerves were. The secretary
sympathized. This young man was no brutal barbarian, like most *faranj*. He was
sensitive and intelligent and educated. Imad ad-Din was finding it easy to like
him, which made it all the easier to do his master's bidding of befriending him
and milking him for information as well as ensuring that he, the husband of the
Princess Isabella, was turned into a friend of the Sultan—if not of Islam itself.

Imad ad-Din let the subject of the Koran slide for now and pressed
Humphrey to continue with his autobiography. "Your grandfather was a great
man, but he was from Toron. My master, however, told me he would free you
in exchange for the surrender of al-Karak. What is your connection to Arnat
al-Karak?" Imad ad-Din knew the answer already, of course, but he did not want
Humphrey to know how much he knew. He thought a display of too much
knowledge might make the young Frank suspicious of his motives.

"He was my mother's third husband. I was forced to live with him after my
grandfather's death. He was a horrible, brutal man! A dishonest and dishonorable

man! He deserved his fate!" Humphrey spoke with conviction that was all the greater for his emotions having been pent up for so long. He had hated Reynald de Châtillon almost from the moment they had met. His years under Châtillon's tutelage, serving as a squire, had been sheer hell. Châtillon had taunted, tormented, insulted, and physically abused Humphrey, all in the name of "making a man of him." His mother had stood by cheering her husband on, and everyone else had looked the other way—either from fear of their lord or because they were made of the same cruel cloth!

Humphrey had never before dared say what he felt or thought about Châtillon to anyone but Isabella. The thought of Isabella, however, brought tears to his eyes. He tried to cover his raw, exposed emotions by reaching for one of the figs.

The perceptive Imad ad-Din could see his young guest's distress. The Sultan was wise, he thought. This was a vulnerable youth, a youth whose ties to his fellow Infidels were weak and frayed already. It would be child's play to make him an instrument of their own design. For now he remarked only, "It pleases me to hear you are not an admirer of Arnat al-Karak. He was Islam's most hated enemy."

"Christendom's, too!" Humphrey declared passionately. "He attacked Christian Cyprus and he tortured the Patriarch of Antioch. He was a barbarian through and through, true to no faith!" Humphrey felt much better for having said that.

Imad ad-Din nodded, adding with calculated flattery, "You are wise beyond your years, young man."

Humphrey looked down in pleased embarrassment. At last he was with someone civilized enough to understand him!

Imad ad-Din often paced about his garden when he experienced "writer's block." He was currently engaged in composing an account of Salah ad-Din's greatest victory, his conquest of the Holy City of Jerusalem, which he wanted to present to the Sultan's sons. This was to be a masterpiece. More than a mere chronicle, it was to be a work of such literary eloquence that centuries from now, even those who knew the story well would read his work for the pleasure that the words gave. It was a work of prose, to be sure, but it was to have its own melody, and the use of cadence and alliteration would elevate it above the common clacking of ordinary scribes to a work of art.

Only at the moment, the words weren't coming.

Imad ad-Din paused to consider one of the hibiscus bushes. It appeared to have some kind of lice. Annoyed, he frowned and called sharply to his gardener. The slave, who was clipping grass beyond the fountain, hurried to throw himself at his master's feet. He was a old man, bent permanently from digging, weeding, and clipping in the garden.

"What is this?" Imad ad-Din demanded sharply, his elegant fingers grasping one of the blooms by the stalk and pointing the face toward his slave.

"Yes, Master," the slave agreed. "I have sent for beetles that will eat the lice, but they haven't come yet."

Imad ad-Din was not fool enough to believe every lie an old slave told him. "If there are still lice in the hibiscus a week from now, it will go ill with you," he warned, and dropped the subject.

Continuing his aimless stroll, he came upon a slave woman scrubbing the tiles of the paved walkway. She had a bucket of water, a scrub brush, and several rags to do the work. Her skirts were soiled and damp from kneeling on the wet tiles, and sweat had soaked the sides of her gown so often that the cloth under her arms was badly stained. Sweat also dripped from a face bright red from the exertion and the unaccustomed exposure to the Syrian sun. Imad ad-Din remembered being told she had been a "great lady" among the Christians, a woman used to commanding a large household.

As an admirer of the great Islamic theologian Imam Ghazali, especially his excellent work *The Revivication of Religious Science*, Imad ad-Din disapproved vehemently of women being allowed such power. As Ghazali had made clear in his brilliant analysis of the Koran, the most precious gift that Allah had given man was reason, and the purpose of that reason was to enable man to pursue knowledge and truth through study, especially study of the Koran. Women, lacking reason and being purely sexual by their nature, were a threat to man pursuing his destiny. Indeed, women's ability to distract men was a satanic power that could only be defeated throught the strict control and segregation of women. The best was to make them as invisible as possible—until after a day of intellectual or martial activity, a man paused to take pleasure with the woman of his choice, be she wife or concubine. A woman in a position of authority was, therefore, an abomination, something typical of primitive and polytheist societies that remained enslaved and degraded by their fascination with females.

Imad ad-Din noted with satisfaction that this new Christian slave shrank back at his approach, cowering on the side of the path to make way for him. Even better, she kept her head down and turned away from him, and he nodded with approval. It was good to see these Christian whores learning their proper place and adopting modest behavior.

He caught his breath, and increased his pace to all but run to his study. The words were coming! He settled himself with unusual haste before his writing table and took a clean sheet of papyrus. Dipping his quill in the ink, he began to write:

How many well-guarded women were profaned, how many queens were ruled, and nubile girls married, and noble women given away, and miserly women forced to yield themselves, and women who had been kept hidden stripped of their modesty, and serious women made ridiculous, and women kept in private now set in public, and free women occupied, and precious ones used for hard work, and pretty things put to the test, and virgins dishonored and proud women deflowered, and lovely women's red lips kissed, and dark women prostrated, and untamed ones tamed, and happy ones made to weep! How many noblemen took them as concubines, how many ardent men blazed for one of them, and celibates were satisfied by them, and thirsty men sated by them, and turbulent men able to give vent to their passion. How many lovely women were the exclusive property of one man, how many great ladies were sold at low prices, and close ones set at a distance, and lofty ones abased, and savage ones captured, and those accustomed to thrones dragged down![*]

Imad ad-Din sat back with a sigh of satisfaction, and thanked Allah for the inspiration. It was perfect! Not only did it describe so well what had happened to the Christian women condemned to slavery after their towns, cities, and castles fell to the forces of the Sultan, it described the justice of Allah in humiliating these arrogant and unnatural females. Christian women, until they were captured and taught better, did not know their proper place and went about with no sense of shame. These women, who once dared to look men in the eye and talk to men who were not their kinsfolk, deserved every humiliation they suffered at the hands of Believers. Imad ad-Din was certain that nothing offended Allah quite so much these brazen women, for while polytheist men were merely foolish to allow women so much power, the women themselves were satanic, seeking to end the civilizing influence of reason which Allah's messenger, may Allah's blessings be infinitely with him, had brought to all believers.

In the garden, Beatrice had collapsed and rolled herself into a ball of misery, sobbing helplessly. She begged God earnestly to take her to Him. She could not

---

[*] This is a verbatim quote from Imad ad-Din al-Isfahani's *al-Fath al-Qussi fi-l-Fath al-Qudsi*, paragraphs 47-69, translated from the Arabic by Francesco Gabrieli.

take any more. It was that simple: she could not take any more. Scrubbing tiles
on a garden path was not really so terrible, of course, but it was one humiliation
too many.

She had survived the rapes, refusing to remember how many men it had
actually been, clinging to the need to protect her children. But then they had
taken her children away—simply sold them to utter strangers and dragged
them, screaming and crying, from her arms. When she tried to follow, they had
surrounded her, pushed her to the ground, and then from three sides they had
kicked her with hatred as they spat and cursed her: "Polytheist filth! Pig-eating
whore! Barbarian bitch!" The slave trader had been forced to intervene to stop
them from "damaging his property" further.

After that she had been too bruised and numb to care what happened
to her. The trader had sold her off for a pittance, complaining bitterly about
how the market was flooded with "stinking, icon-worshiping filth," and how
an honest slaver couldn't make a decent living anymore. She had been taken
down a dark alley and shoved through a door into a room full of other women.
They had gaped and pointed, ridiculing what was left of the gown she'd been
wearing on the day of her enslavement. They had cackled and giggled and
held their noses to show her what they thought of her. Eventually a man had
come and scolded them, making them take her to a chamber where she could
wash herself. After that he had given her sandals and a rough cotton gown to
wear. Then they had taken a pair of scissors to her hair and had shorn her.
No scarves or veils were allowed her, because she was no longer a "decent"
woman—she had known too many men, none of whom were her husband.
She was just a slave.

Her face and neck were now burned from exposure to the sun, her knees
bruised not from praying but from cleaning floors, and her hands blistered and
cut from laundry and other work. But that might have been bearable if there
had been any human left in the whole world who knew her name or cared how
she felt.

The touch of a hand on her shoulder made her rear up in terror. They were
sure to beat her for not doing her work—or rape her again, if it was a man.

It was a man, but it was a old, bent, and wrinkled man, and he was making
calming gestures with his hand and soothing sounds. "Hush, hush," he said to
her gently. "Crying will not make it better."

"Nothing will make it better!" Beatrice lashed out in agony, before she
registered that he had spoken French. She gasped and held her breath. "You
speak French?" she asked the gardener, hardly daring to believe it. It seemed like
forever since she had heard her own tongue.

"Yes," he answered in French. "I was born long, long ago in the peaceful village of Moustiers-Ste.-Marie in gentle Provence."

Beatrice swallowed down her tears and gazed at the old gardener. "How did you come to be *here*?"

"Much the way you did, child," he answered gently. "I joined the Benedictines at the age of twelve and was ordained at seventeen. I came out to Outremer at the age of twenty-two in the company of six of my brothers. Only I had the misfortune to go to County of Edessa, and within two years Nur ad-Din had defeated our nobles and knights. When they overran our abbey, the abbot and many of my brothers were crucified for not converting to Islam."

"And you?" Beatrice asked, horrified. "You converted?"

The old man smiled wearily. "I pretended to, but God knows that when I pray I pray to Christ, and although I have learned the incantations and chants of our tormentors, in my heart I say the Mass morning and night."

Beatrice stared at him, not knowing what to think.

"You have it easier," he told her softly, "because they do not expect women to convert at all. They prefer women not to, in fact. As long as you are a Christian they can treat you like filth, but if you converted, some of the more enlightened imams would argue they ought to show you more respect."

"Father." Beatrice bestowed the title on her comforter because she desperately needed to believe he was still a priest and so a lifeline to her faith. "They have taken away my children." As she spoke, the pain overwhelmed her, and tears started flooding down her sunburned face. "All three of them! Even the baby, Joscelyn. He's only six! Six! What can they do with a six-year-old? Why couldn't they let us stay together—" she broke down entirely. The old monk took her into his arms and held her until the storm of misery had subsided a little.

Then, as she lay shaking but no longer wailing in his arms, he told her, "Perhaps he is the lucky one. If he is comely and well made, they will raise him a good Muslim, and maybe he will one day be a Mamluke—proud and fierce. How old are the other children?"

"Amalric is ten and Bart is eleven," she gasped out, trying to wipe some of the tears from her face with her dirty hands.

The priest/gardener nodded knowingly but said nothing. Anything could happen to boys that age. They might end up in some tradesman's shop, fed barely enough to survive, chased from one chore to the next, and subjected to beatings from dawn to dusk. Or they might land in the home of some rich man who would take particular pleasure in having blond boys (he assumed the boys were blond because Beatrice was very fair) serving them at dinner, washing their feet, and fanning away the flies and heat. Or if they were very unlucky, the boys might be castrated and sent to guard a rich man's harem or land in one of the sordid, sunless dens in the deepest bowels of the souks where men who preferred boys took their sinful pleasure.

"Will I ever see them again?" Beatrice asked the priest through tear-filled eyes.

The priest shook his head. "It is unlikely, child. I overheard the master saying that Jerusalem has fallen, and tens of thousands of new slaves will soon join us. Here, let me wash your face," he offered. Beatrice's hands were so grimy that she had only managed to smear dirt across her face with her own efforts. The priest/gardener dipped his hands in her bucket of water, rubbed them clean, and then gently smoothed them over her face. As he did so he spoke softly to her. "I will not make you false promises or awaken false hopes, child. In this life we are slaves, and we are condemned to suffer. I know I shall never escape—and who could ever rescue us, now that Jerusalem is lost? We must not imagine our lives will improve, but I have found over the decades that there are moments when Christ smiles at me—through an oleander bush," he pointed to one along the side of the garden, "or out of the eyes of a saucy pigeon." Again he gestured toward an audacious bird approaching them along the path with curious yet nervous jerks of its head.

"What is your name, Father? And where can I find you?"

"It would bring great joy to my old heart, child, to be called again by my name in Christ: Father Francis. And you?"

"Beatrice d'Auber. My father, Sir Bartholomew, held a knight's fee from the Baron of Ibelin. Bart—Bart would have inherited—"

Father Francis shook his head and stroked her shoulder. "Don't think about it, child. It will do you no good. That world is gone forever."

Chapter 3

Jerusalem-Tyre Road, November 12, 1187

THE COLUMN WAS ALMOST FIFTEEN THOUSAND strong: mostly women, children, and elderly, but with a stiffening of roughly three hundred youth and middle-aged men capable of bearing arms. They were predominantly Franks, but the column included nearly four thousand Armenians and about three thousand Syrian Christians as well. They had, until yesterday, made up about a fourth of the population of Jerusalem, and today represented one-third of those souls who had raised a ransom of ten dinars per man, five dinars per woman, and two dinars per child in order to escape slavery. Some fifteen thousand of their fellows had not been so lucky and were now on their way to the slave markets of Syria, while two other columns of ransomed Christians were wending their way towards Jaffa in the west and Ascalon in the south respectively.

The pace was slow. The terms of surrender stated that anyone who could pay his or her ransom could leave the city with all their movable goods and chattels, so the column was made up of wagons, carts, wheelbarrows, and pack animals as well as people. They lumbered along at the pace of the slowest, while the armed escort provided by the Baron of Ibelin and his remaining knights rode up and down along the sides of the column like sheep dogs, trying to keep people and beasts moving.

Godwin Olafsen had nothing but the clothes he was wearing and the crippled boy on his back. The boy was his son Sven, who had lost the use of his legs in an accident in Oslo ten years ago. Godwin had sold his shop and come with his wife to Jerusalem in search of a cure. On arrival they had followed the

Via Dolorosa on their knees in prayer, but Sven was still a cripple. They had no money to return to Oslo, so Godwin had taken work as a journeyman, although he was a master. Slowly he had established himself, but just months after he had finally become his own master again, the defeat of the Christian army at Hattin had destroyed his fortunes a second time.

"You can set the boy down here!" a woman's voice called out cheerfully. Godwin looked around bewildered to see who had spoken. Although Godwin was a strong man, he was lagging a bit and had fallen to the side of the column. As he looked toward the voice, he saw a fat woman in widow's weeds seated on the driver's seat of a large wagon pulled by two powerful horses. She was patting the empty seat beside her. "You can join me, too, if you like," she offered.

Godwin did not have to think twice. He jogged over to the wagon, and then turned his back to it so that Sven could sit on the side for a moment. The boy had strong arms, and with the help of the fat widow, he was quickly pulled up beside her on the driving seat. Godwin followed him lithely. "Thank you, good widow! You are the second miracle in a single day. I pray the good Lord will shower His mercies upon you as he has on me this day!"

"Well, well," the widow answered with a dubious smile. "I never thought to hear the day we were driven from Jerusalem called a day of miracles, but I'm happy to help. I'm Mariam, by the way. Most people know me as Mariam the Pastry Lady—though that sells my other sweets short. I'll bet your boy here could do with a spot of marzipan." As she spoke, she smiled at Sven and saw his eyes widen.

Godwin could hear his wife's voice scolding in his head, "The boy needs a solid meal, not sweets!" But his wife was not here, and he nodded to Mariam. "He would be very indebted to you if you could spare such a luxury."

"Well, then, take the reins for a moment, and I'll see what I can dig out of the back here." She handed the reins over to Godwin and twisted around to dig in the basket nestled just behind the driving seat. This was clearly her provisions for the day, and when she turned around again she had the whole basket on her ample lap. "I don't know why, but I have the feeling you could do with a bit more than marzipan—or at least your Dad could." She addressed herself to the still wide-eyed Sven.

"My good widow—please. We have no means to pay you. We were on our way into slavery because we could not pay the ransom, until the good Baron d'Ibelin intervened. There's no way we can repay—"

Mariam waved Godwin's protest aside. "You look like a strong man to me, and I'm sure you can make yourself useful with the team and—more important— guarding this wagon when we set up camp. That's all I ask—oh, and your name."

"Sven!" the boy spoke up for the first time. "Sven Godwinsen. My Dad's the best armorer in all Jerusalem," he declared with fierce pride. "He made the Baron of Ibelin's sword!"

"Godwin Olafsen," his father introduced himself more modestly.

"Ah, yes, I think I've heard of you," the widow decided, frowning slightly as she tried to remember. "Didn't you take over the armory behind St. Mary Magdalene? The one that used to belong to Ibn Adam?"

"Yes, exactly. He made me his heir and we moved in four years ago. I took over the shop and my wife looked after him in his old age."

"Where is your wife? And didn't you have daughters?" The widow looked around, confused.

"I scraped together the money for their ransom, but there wasn't enough left for us," Godwin explained.

"Good heavens! Here, have some of this!" She handed him the basket and took the reins back. "There's a half chicken in there and a loaf of bread, and at the very bottom there is some marzipan, as I promised."

Godwin could not resist her invitation a moment longer. Sven and he had not eaten since breakfast, and that had been scanty. He readily found the chicken and brought it out. Between them, he and Sven pulled it apart and ate the moist flesh from the bones. The bread followed, and then the marzipan. The look on Sven's face as he bit into the marzipan was so expressive of delight that Mariam laughed out loud. "Well, I can see how to make *this* young man happy!" she declared with obvious satisfaction.

"Forgive us," Godwin begged as he wiped his fingers on his hose. "That was the best meal we've had in a long time."

"I can see that," Mariam quipped, with a smile that assured them she was pleased rather than offended.

"And yourself? You're traveling alone?" Godwin asked. Now that the growling in his stomach was stilled, the ache in his back was easing, and the surprise was fading, he looked at his benefactor more closely. She was fat and wearing widow's weeds, but she was not an old woman by any means. She also spoke French with a heavy accent and wore her wimple like the Syrian women did, ending on the top of her head and trailing down her back.

"Femme sole, as you say in French," she confirmed matter-of-factly.

"You husband died at Hattin?" Godwin ventured, although the woman hardly seemed overcome by grief, as one would have expected had her husband died so recently.

Mariam laughed in answer. "Hattin? If he'd lived to fight at Hattin, he would have been eighty-two! No, he died more than a decade ago. God rest his soul."

"And children?"

"All dead and buried; two died in the womb, to be precise, and the other two within days. I'm not what you call a good breeder."

That surprised Godwin, as she looked the picture of health in her hefty way.

"I wasn't always like this," Mariam read his thoughts. "When I was married, I was just a wraith of a girl, all skin and bones and not an ounce up here," she continued, patting her fleshy breasts with an easy familiarity that made Godwin feel awkward. He looked away, embarrassed, but a moment later caught himself sneaking a look at them again. They were quite phenomenal, actually. He cut off the inevitable thought about how exciting it would be to see them naked, and distracted himself by asking Sven if he needed a drink of water.

Sven shook his head. "It would wash away the taste of the marzipan," he explained, and the adults laughed.

Mariam continued with her story as if she hadn't been interrupted. "By the time I was ripe for breeding, my husband couldn't get it up anymore. He was sixty by then, so one can't be too surprised."

"You never thought of remarrying?" Godwin asked, calculating that ten years ago Mariam would have been quite a young woman.

"What? And give up running the shop the way I like to? No, young man, I never gave it a moment's thought. Since my husband died, I've nearly tripled the turnover, doubled the profit, expanded my product line, and won the best customers. I was the preferred purveyor to the Patriarch and the palace both. My marzipan delicacies in the shape of the the Holy Sepulcher, St. George killing the dragon, and even the martyrdom of St. Stephen have been praised by high and low—and yielded me a very pretty penny indeed. I had no less than five apprentices in the shop."

"Where are they now?" Godwin looked around, expecting to see them in a second wagon or at least walking along beside.

"Stupid me," Mariam declared, "I hired only girls. Cheaper and better workers, I said to myself, and so they were. Good girls, every one of them—and every one of them still a maid under her father's care. When the surrender came, it was their fathers that decided their fate, and not one chose to head for Tyre." She shook her head—whether in disgust or despair, Godwin couldn't tell.

Godwin hadn't had a choice. If he had, he would have chosen Jaffa, because it was closest and offered the best prospects of finding a ship bound for the West. His ten years in the Holy Land had led him to the very brink of slavery; it was time to go home. "Why did you choose Tyre?" he asked Mariam.

"I'm Syrian, young man. Not just Syrian Christian. My family only moved to Jerusalem from Homs after King Fulk offered incentives to Syrian settlers in order to repopulate the city you Franks depopulated in your first assault. I myself was born in Jerusalem, but my parents, aunts, and uncles were all born in Syria. While most of my apprentices came from Palestinian families prepared to relocate in Ascalon or any of the other coastal cities, I'll feel much safer behind the walls of Tyre. But I will have a hard time getting started—unless you'd like to try your hand making marzipan, young man?" she addressed Sven jokingly.

Innocently, Sven took her offer seriously and declared instantly, "I'd like that, ma'am!" And then he turned to his father on his other side and asked, "May I, Father?"

"We'll have to see about that," his father equivocated.

The column made camp roughly six miles north of Jerusalem that night. They left the wagons and carts on the road, unhitched the draft horses and offloaded the pack animals to let them graze hobbled, while the people built campfires and cooked the food they had brought. It was roughly one hundred miles from Jerusalem to Tyre, and most people had brought provisions for ten to twelve days.

The Baron's knights rode up and down the length of the camp, checking that all was in order. In the distance the Sultan's cavalry, which shadowed them on both flanks, could also be seen making camp for the night.

Godwin was surprised when the Baron's squire rode up to inquire if he had any provisions. "My lord says you are to join us, if you don't."

Godwin glanced at Mariam and then shook his head. "Thank my lord for his kindness and for thinking of me, but I've found a friend and will travel with her."

"As you wish," the squire answered indifferently, and swung his horse around, anxious to get out of the saddle and rest himself.

Godwin watched him ride away and then stepped over to the wagon to check on Sven. The boy was out cold, snuggled contentedly in a corner of the wagon between several bags of flour, raisins, candied fruits, and spices. He was covered by the softest blanket Godwin had ever felt. In sleep, Sven's face was completely relaxed and beautiful.

Godwin couldn't resist brushing the boy's long blond hair out of his face to look at it closely for a moment. He loved this boy more than anything in the world. More than his wife, who had deserted him, or his little girls—although the realization that he would never see them again still made his heart heavy. He found it impossible to remember, much less understand, all that had happened to him in the last forty days.

He felt someone beside him and found Mariam holding out a mug of ale. "Come; it will help you sleep as well," she suggested.

Godwin nodded and returned with her to the little fire.

"I expect you'll try to rejoin your wife and daughters after we make Tyre," Mariam remarked conversationally.

Godwin started visibly, then shook his head grimly.

Mariam looked surprised, but held her tongue, not wanting to probe.

"You have to understand," Godwin murmured, staring at the weak flames licking at the sticks stacked together. "My wife . . ." He licked his lips and swallowed. "My wife had a secret store of coins. Not enough to pay my ransom, but she could have paid for Sven, if she'd wanted to. Instead, she kept the money for herself."

"Christ have mercy on her soul!" Mariam exclaimed, crossing herself and glancing over her shoulder at the wagon. "She—she would—she *abandoned* her own son—or wasn't he her own?"

"He's her son, all right," Godwin answered grimly. "He's her son, but she hates the sight of him."

"That can't be!" Mariam protested instinctively. "He may be lame, but he's a good boy. Didn't I hear he helped you in the smithy?"

Godwin nodded. "He worked the bellows better than any apprentice I've ever had. He's a good boy, and he's bright. But he'll never make an armorer, and who else will ever take him in?"

"I will. I told you. He can work in a kitchen just fine. Put him on a bench behind the table and he can work there all day long."

"Would you really give him a chance? A job, I mean. I may be free, but I have nothing. I have to start all over again from the bottom."

"Hmm." Mariam bent forward to scrape some of the embers closer together and then lay another stick on the fire. "Seems to me that if we can find the right place, we could share an oven, which would save a lot of money on firewood. In a besieged city like Tyre, there won't be an abundance of wood, and it'll probably sell dearly."

"I sold my tools to raise my wife's ransom," Godwin admitted glumly. "I've no means to start up a shop again."

"Well, I've got some silver, if it comes to that. And I wouldn't underestimate the Baron of Ibelin's patronage, either. He's a good man, I'll give him that, but I daresay when he paid your ransom he had an eye on keeping a good armorer with him as well. I think if you approach him for assistance, you'll find him receptive."

Godwin looked over at Mariam with a crooked smile. "I hadn't thought of that. I'm not very good with business, I guess. If I hadn't repaired weapons for free, or if I'd sold rather than given the Baron that great sword I made for him, I could have paid my ransom ten times over. My wife was furious with me."

"Well, I can understand that," Mariam admitted, nodding. "It would have driven me to distraction, too, if my husband had been squandering his services. That's another reason I never wanted to marry again—but that doesn't mean we can't try to help each other. My advice is free!" She laughed at that, upending her mug to finish her ale before pouring another portion.

Tyre, November 22, 1187

Georgios had been serving the Baron of Ibelin for roughly three months, and he had never seen him look so grim. Not even during the siege of Jerusalem. But now, with the city of Tyre at last in sight, Ibelin looked as if he had turned to stone.

Georgios cast him a nervous sidelong glance. His cheeks were hollowed out and his eyes sunken in his skull. His hair, which had been a dark, lustrous brown before Hattin, now had a startling white strand that began at his temple. His lips were badly chapped and his face unshaven.

"Damn him!" Ibelin spat out, making Georgios jump. "He's not lowering the drawbridge."

Georgios looked back toward Tyre and at last noticed what the baron had seen moments earlier. The city was maintaining its vigilant stance, as if the approaching fifteen thousand people were an enemy army rather than Christian refugees. The bridges over the widened moat, which effectively turned the peninsula on which Tyre stood into an island, were both firmly raised; the gate and postern were shut. The ramparts were manned, and the late afternoon sun glinted on the helmets of the soldiers on the wall walk.

Without a word to his squire, Balian put spurs to his aging palfrey and sprinted forward, leaving the slow-moving, lumbering column of refugees in his wake. Georgios was left kicking his less agile gelding to try to catch up. Ibelin galloped to the very edge of the moat and drew up sharply, shouting up at the walls even before his horse had come to a complete halt. "This is Balian d'Ibelin! I have some fifteen thousand Christian refugees from Jerusalem. I demand that the gates be opened at once!"

Silence answered him, although Georgios could see men scurrying this way and that, apparently seeking instructions.

Ibelin cursed under his breath in a steady stream, threatening Conrad de Montferrat with various kinds of torture, mutilation, slow death, and damnation. Finally a voice called out from the walls of the city, "Just a moment, my lord! My lord of Montferrat will be here shortly!"

Ibelin swung his horse on forehand to look back at the column of refugees he had been commanding for eleven days. It was still far behind, moving at its snail's pace, but very visible to the men up on the walls of Tyre.

"He knows exactly who we are and what we want," Ibelin snarled to his squire without looking at him. "He'll have had spies out watching for us ever since he learned from Sir Bartholomew the terms of the surrender."

"Ibelin!" The call came faintly from the closest gate tower.

"Montferrat?" Ibelin answered, narrowing his eyes against the sun and trying to identify the man who had addressed him.

"The same. I'm lowering the footbridge. You may enter alone."

"I'll tear out his jugular with my own teeth!" Ibelin answered under his breath to Georgios, his eyes fixed on the gate opposite. As they watched, the narrow wooden bridge from the postern jerked slowly down from its upright position to the horizontal. Ibelin jumped down from his horse and flung the reins over its head to hand them to Georgios. "Wait here!" he ordered as he strode in the direction of the bridge, which had just settled on the dusty soil this side of the moat.

Ibelin was wearing helmet and hauberk, but his legs were encased in knee-high, suede leather boots rather than the heavy and uncomfortable chain-mail chausses he wore for battle. His short-sleeved surcoat was particolored—red on the right and bright marigold on the left—and it was studded with crosses in the contrasting color. Made of fine Gaza cotton, it rippled and flowed as he strode angrily across the bridge.

As he approached the far side of the bridge, a man emerged from the narrow, peaked-arch door of the postern. Georgios could see only that he was wearing a purple surcoat with what looked like gold trim. Ibelin recognized the well-formed and attractive face of Conrad de Montferrat, who bore a striking resemblance to his elder brother William, Queen Sibylla's first husband.

The latter bowed (a little mockingly, Ibelin found), but Ibelin did not return the courtesy. Instead he roared in a harsh, strained, and raw voice, "What the hell do think you're doing keeping your gates shut! I have fifteen thousand refugees who have lost practically everything they owned and have been on the road eleven days. They need to get inside these walls before dark so they don't have to camp out another day! We only have a few more hours of daylight as it is! You shouldn't be wasting time with whatever goddamned formalities these are!"

"If you're finished?" Conrad answered with raised eyebrows and an air of superiority.

"What's that supposed to mean?" Ibelin snapped back.

"I'm simply asking if you're done ranting, so I can get a word in edgewise."

"What the hell is there to say? Lower the goddamned bridge and open the gates!"

"No."

For all his bluster, from the moment he realized that Tyre was remaining on the defensive even after the column of refugees was in sight, Ibelin had been expecting exactly this answer. It was anticipation of Montferrat's refusal to admit them that had ignited Ibelin's rage. He was not surprised by Montferrat's "no," and the confirmation of his suspicions had a chilling effect.

Balian d'Ibelin was an exceptionally tall man. He took two steps closer to Montferrat to stand towering over him. "Say that again!" he ordered in an ominously soft voice.

"I obviously don't need to," Montferrat countered, backing up a step so he was not so directly under Ibelin's glare—and nose. "You heard me the first time, and you understood me. This city is already overcrowded, and at any moment the Saracens may decide to resume their assaults. We're already under siege, cut off by both land and sea. We cannot—I repeat—cannot admit fifteen thousand more refugees, most of whom are women and children."

"You're saying you intend to deny women and children refuge, after all they have suffered already?"

"Yes, that's exactly what I'm saying. Unless I have been misinformed, the terms of the surrender of Jerusalem were that those who could raise their ransom were free to depart Jerusalem with what goods they could carry and proceed unmolested to Christian territory." Sir Bartholomew had evidently reported the surrender terms faithfully. "Well," Montferrat made a flippant gesture with his hand in the direction of the north. "Let them proceed to Tripoli! Tripoli is not under siege!"

"Tripoli is damn near a hundred miles away! These women and children have already traveled that distance to get here. They are exhausted—emotionally and physically. They need rest and security."

"They would have neither in Tyre," Montferrat answered bluntly. "Salah ad-Din is close on your heels. According to my scouts, he is no more than two days behind you with his whole army. He plans to finish the job of conquering the Kingdom of Jerusalem by capturing this city—the last in the entire Kingdom to hold out. The battle for Tyre will start at the latest three days from now, and anyone inside this city will be subject to the dangers of siege engines and assaults—neither of which are my definition of peace and security. Furthermore, the longer we resist the assaults, the more we consume our supplies. Even without your fifteen thousand refugees, we will run short of food within three months. With your fifteen thousand, it will be more like three weeks! I can't—and won't—take that responsibility!"

They stared at one another. They were both hardened veterans of battles and siege warfare, and they recognized that they were well-matched equals. Ibelin had fought at Montgisard, on the Litani, at Le Forbelet, in the sieges of Kerak, and finally at Hattin before taking over the defense of Jerusalem. Montferrat had a reputation from the interminable wars between the Holy Roman Empire and the Holy See. More recently, he had almost single-handedly won the decisive battle that defeated Alexios Branas' rebellion against the Greek Emperor, and then had brought spirit and determination to the demoralized city of Tyre, saving it for Christendom. As they faced each other now, it was Montferrat who softened his stance first.

"You have but recently been in my shoes, my lord. You know what I'm talking about. The commander of a city under siege sometimes has to make hard decisions—decisions that will surely seem heartless and cruel to the clerics and chroniclers that come after us. But *they* do not know the sound and smell of battle, whereas you, Ibelin, are a fighting man. You know what I'm saying is true. I *cannot* afford to admit fifteen thousand women and children to this city when I am about to be blockaded by sea and invested by land. I *cannot* reduce our fighting capacity or chances of holding this city as long as all hope of regaining the Holy City depends upon our ability to hold Tyre. Tyre must hold out long enough for reinforcements to arrive from the West."

Ibelin knew that Montferrat was right. He recognized it both intellectually and in the marrow of his warrior bones. Montferrat was right—but how could he go back and tell the people he had led here that they were not welcome? He found himself arguing, "Not all those fifteen thousand refugees are women and children. There are over three hundred men among them who helped hold Jerusalem. Men who stood in the breach when the walls came down and fought Salah ad-Din's thousands to a standstill."

"And *they* are welcome in Tyre!" Montferrat was quick to agree. "Anyone who can contribute to the defense of this city—first and foremost, yourself—is welcome. But I cannot and will not admit noncombatants."

"Most men—or should I say honorable men—fight for their wives and children, not for pay or glory."

"The fighting men may bring their wives and children into the city," Montferrat made another concession, "but not their sisters, brothers, parents, and cousins. Fighting men and their immediate families only—and, of course, your household." He smiled as he said this, hoping it would mollify Ibelin.

Ibelin just stared back at him with a look between hatred and despair. Then he nodded and turned away.

Hardly anyone in the refugee column slept that night. There was too much commotion as families argued among themselves, women complained, children cried, and old men raged. Eventually people started sorting themselves out, and those remaining in Tyre extricated themselves from the main column.

To Ibelin's astonishment, most of his own household opted to continue to Tripoli. They had had enough sieges for a lifetime, the cook explained emphatically, speaking for his entire staff. Likewise, the laundresses were badly shaken by their near encounter with slavery and insisted on continuing. Sir Constantine announced his intention of going all the way to his relatives in Constantinople, and even the Ibelin marshal, the Ethiopian Mathewos, opted to continue to Tripoli.

"The girls are terrified," he explained, nodding in the direction of his daughter and daughter-in-law, both of whom had been widowed in the last days of Jerusalem's defiance. "Beth cannot bear the thought of facing another siege, and I want to give my grandson a chance to see Ethiopia."

Ibelin reminded him that his younger son was with the Dowager Queen in Tyre, but Mathewos shook his head. "Eskinder is seventeen. He's old enough to find his own way, and I'm sure he will be proud to fight with you, but my duty is to the girls and my infant grandson."

As the sun crested the eastern mountains and the refugee train slowly rolled into motion again, less than five hundred people, fighting men and their families, remained behind. Ibelin found himself with just thirty-two of the youths he'd knighted in Jerusalem, his squire, and the faithful Sir Roger Shoreham with his two surviving sons, Father Michael and Edwin, the latter with his wife and family.

The widow Mariam was among those seeking admittance to Tyre and sat on her wagon, nervously biting her lip. She knew Montferrat had explicitly said only the immediate families of fighting men would be admitted to Tyre, and she didn't qualify. She was just hoping no one would notice, much less enforce, the requirement. She was determined to stay in Tyre, because she didn't trust the escort remaining with the refugees now that Ibelin was staying here; none of the fighting men continuing to Tripoli commanded the unquestioned obedience of the others—much less of Salah ad-Din.

Mariam looked nervously across at the score of remaining wagons, and noticed Edwin Shoreham's German wife staring at her. Mariam nodded curtly, but the woman didn't return it. Instead she started talking to her husband and pointing at Mariam. He called to his father. Sir Roger Shoreham rode over to his son and daughter-in-law, and a moment later looked over his shoulder at Mariam.

"I've been betrayed," Mariam muttered, her lips pressed together in fury. What harm did it do anyone—much less Mistress Shoreham—for Mariam to enter Tyre? It wasn't any skin off her nose! Damn her!

Shoreham trotted over to Mariam and pulled up. He cleared his throat awkwardly. "Ma'am, only the immediate families of combatants are allowed to enter Tyre. Your husband is—ah—dead and buried. I'm afraid—"

"I'm her husband," Godwin announced, stepping over to stand directly at Shoreham's stirrup.

Shoreham looked at Olafsen in confusion. "But—I thought—"

"Mariam and I are plight-trothed," Godwin insisted. "We'll seek out a priest as soon as we're in the city."

Shoreham frowned in obvious disbelief, and glanced over his shoulder at his daughter-in-law.

"You take me and my betrothed with you to Tyre, or I'll continue to Tripoli!" Godwin threatened.

"What's going on?" Ibelin demanded, riding up beside Shoreham, his expression forbidding and his tone impatient.

"Master Olafsen is insisting that the good widow here be admitted as his family although they aren't married, my lord. In fact, Olafsen has a wife and two daughters, who joined the column headed for Jaffa. My daughter-in-law was quite friendly with her and knows that Godwin wasn't able to pay his or his son's ransom because he worked for free throughout the siege, and—"

"And gave me a valuable sword," Ibelin interrupted. "He may be a bad merchant, but he's a good Christian. He's part of my household, and if he wants this good widow to come with him, then she is part of my household, too. It's as simple as that. This is no time for bickering and pettiness, Sir Roger. Tell your daughter-in-law that from me!" He nodded once to Mariam, and then swung his horse around and took up his position at the head of the little column.

"God bless him!" Mariam exclaimed, staring after his back and crossing herself.

"Amen to that!" Godwin seconded her sentiments as he scrambled up beside her on the wagon, adding, "And, of course, you needn't fear I'll try to make you my wife in fact."

Mariam looked over her hefty arm at him with an unreadable expression. "Can't, seeing as you have a wife already. Still, it might be wise to pretend otherwise in Tyre, if you don't mind. These are uncertain times, and a woman alone is more vulnerable than a woman with a man. Mistress Shoreham can't be everywhere, and if we stay clear of her and act like husband and wife, who's to know differently?"

"We can stay together," Godwin assured her with a smile at Sven, who grinned back in relief.

The sun was halfway up the sky and the last of the wagons headed for Tripoli had receded into the distance before, with shouting and waving, the drawbridge over the outermost ditch slowly started to descend. As it clunked down on the dusty bank at the near side of the deep sea-water ditch, the gates of the outer defensive wall swung open. The Marquis de Montferrat, flanked by squires with fluttering banners and accompanied by the Dowager Queen of Jerusalem, rode out onto the lip of land at the base of the outermost wall.

As Maria Zoë watched Balian slowly emerge from the approaching column, taking distinct and individual shape as he drew nearer, she was conscious of emotional strain unlike any she could remember. It was neither pure joy nor sheer fear and trepidation—but something between the two. When she had left Jerusalem, she had not believed she would ever see him alive again. When Sir Bartholomew brought her the unbelievable news that Balian was not only alive but would soon be joining her in Tyre, it had seemed too good to be true. She had lived with the irrational fear that something would still go wrong. But here he was, only a few feet away from her—and he looked ravaged.

Not that he looked that way to strangers, she supposed. He rode at the head of the column, upright and unbent, with his squire carrying his banner on a vertical lance behind him. His armor didn't gleam, but it was clearly in good order, and his surcoat might not glitter with gold as Montferrat's did, but it was brightly dyed and proudly displayed his arms. The stallion was gray at the muzzle but he held his head up and pranced, showing his breeding. No, Maria Zoë thought to herself, to a stranger her husband looked every inch a proud, fearless, and undefeated baron. But to her he looked—changed. Frighteningly changed.

Ibelin crossed the drawbridge at a controlled pace, and he stopped directly in front of Montferrat, who bowed and announced in a voice intended for posterity: "My lord, I am honored to receive you and the other gallant defenders of the Holy City into my city of Tyre!"

For a moment it seemed as if Ibelin wouldn't dignify him with an answer, but then he remarked in a lower voice, thick with bitterness, "I hope you are satisfied, my lord. I bring you 33 knights, 18 crossbowmen, 3 Greek engineers, 69 archers, and 146 able-bodied men prepared to join the defense of Tyre—and their immediate families."

This memorized message delivered, he at last shifted his eyes to his wife. She had donned her Greek finery for this occasion, a purple gown with broad bands of gem-studded gold embroidery at the hem and neck. The long, open sleeves were lined with cloth of gold, and her veils, draped loosely over her head to cross under her chin and hang down her back under an embroidered crown-like hat, were made of sheer, gold silk. She had never looked so regal as now—when she, too, had lost her kingdom.

Their eyes met, and he saw concern bordering on fear in her dark eyes. He lifted his lips in an effort to reassure her, but already the Marquis de Montferrat was inviting them into the city with sweeping, dramatic gestures. More important, the rest of the train was waiting impatiently behind him. Ibelin urged his horse forward and Montferrat fell in beside him on his left, his wife on his right. She reached out a hand and he took it for a moment, squeezed it, and then let it drop as they passed into the outer gate.

Beyond this first wall was a second, shallower, evil-smelling ditch, beyond which was a second wall. Rather than a central gate and protruding gatehouse, this wall had three flanking towers that provided complete crossfire for two smaller gates offset from the outer gate they had just passed through. The Marquis led through the gate to the left and across the narrow "killing ground" between the two walls to the massive barbican protecting the entrance through the last and highest of Tyre's landward defenses.

As they entered the dog-legged barbican the noise from the city reached them, and when they emerged out of the darkness of the stone building they were met with thunderous cheers. The street ahead was lined with people three to four deep, while men and women waved from the windows of the upper stories. Both the Marquis and the Dowager Queen cast a quick glance at Balian to see his reaction to the tumultuous reception, and neither liked what they saw. Ibelin appeared completely indifferent.

The crowd had started chanting "Ib-lin! Ib-lin!" led by Ernoul and some of the other squires of his household, who had managed to place themselves close to the gate. Ibelin raised his hand to acknowledge the cheer, but his face remained impassive—as if it were chiseled in stone. A chill ran down Maria Zoë's spine as she watched him.

Montferrat raised his voice to be heard above the noise, "You would appear to be well loved, my lord!" He was wearing a smile to conceal his own intense displeasure. He did not like to see crowds this enthusiastic about anyone but himself.

Ibelin shrugged, "I expect they've had little to cheer about of late."

"But they *are* pleased to see you, Balian," Maria Zoë assured him anxiously.

Ibelin glanced at her and then back at the crowd, recognizing Ernoul, Eskinder, and some of the others. He nodded, but he did not smile.

Montferrat deftly guided his horse to the right, effectively herding the others toward the archiepiscopal palace. The crowd lined the street, still cheering—until with a screech of nearly hysterical joy, a woman discovered her husband among the men behind Ibelin. Soon other citizens and refugees experienced their own reunions, most completely unexpected, while others searched the column in increasing despair and fading hope. With each yard, the column was disintegrating into the crowds and the cheering died away, replaced by the gabble of hundreds of people talking at once.

At the archiepiscopal palace Montferrat had gathered the dignitaries of Tyre: the leading merchants and sea captains of the Italian communes, the Bishops of Beirut and Sabaste—refugees like so many others—the officials of the Archbishop's household and other senior clerics, the city's guild masters, and the knights who had washed up here. Ibelin acknowledged his own men, the men he'd led off the field of Hattin but left behind when he went to Jerusalem, but his expression remained sober. Indifferently he let Montferrat introduce him to the leading citizens of Tyre, nodding and thanking them as Montferrat slowly guided him to the high table. Here Isabella was waiting, and she (Maria Zoë noted with relief) at last drew a wan smile from her stepfather by rushing forward and kissing him enthusiastically on both cheeks. Maria Zoë was too busy watching her daughter and husband to note Montferrat's sour face at the spectacle.

Montferrat indicated that Ibelin should sit in the place of honor to his right with his wife on his far side, while Isabella was seated to Montferrat's left. As soon as they were seated, trumpets sounded, and liveried servants paraded into the hall laden with platters of food. Other servants came forward to offer bowls to wash their hands, towels to dry them, and then wine to go with the food being laid out before them.

"Tell me, my lord," Montferrat opened, "just how in the name of our Sweet Savior did you ever convince the Sultan Salah ad-Din to allow the citizens of Jerusalem to buy their freedom? He'd publicly vowed to slaughter the entire population, and the Saracens had already breached the walls when you finally sought to negotiate. By then, Salah ad-Din already had you! Jerusalem was no longer defensible."

"True, but I still had nearly a thousand fighting men. I told him that before we sortied out to kill as many of them as possible, we would first slaughter our women and children, denying him slaves, and—more important—we would destroy the sacred monuments of the city. I promised to chisel away the rock in the Temple of God, known to them as the Dome of the Rock, until there was nothing left of it."

His audience was staring at him wide-eyed: Montferrat in admiration and Maria Zoë and Isabella in horror.

"I wasn't bluffing," Ibelin added. "I would have done that if he had denied me terms. I think," he added softly and chillingly, "I would have enjoyed doing it."

Maria Zoë and Isabella looked at one another.

"I also heard you managed to destroy several of the Sultan's siege engines," Montferrat pressed him, clearly intrigued. "How did you do that with no trained fighting men in the entire city?"

"With the courage of the lepers of St. Lazarus," Ibelin answered. He added into the astonished stillness, "They volunteered to sortie out of the St. Lazarus postern and set fire to the siege engines attacking Tancred's tower. They knew we could not leave the postern open and that they would all die, but they took pots of Greek fire with them and set them ablaze. This served as a diversion for me and my knights to sortie out of the Zion and Jehoshaphat Gates to attack the siege engines. Speaking of my knights, I am now a pauper with no income and cannot possibly pay the thirty-two knights who chose to come to Tyre. I presume you will assume the costs of their maintenance?" It was clearly not a question, and Montferrat was not inclined to quibble. He'd brought a fortune out of Constantinople, most of which had not belonged to him, and he had no need to pinch pennies—at least not when it came to fighting men. He nodded and glanced out into the hall where the knights Ibelin had brought to Tyre had taken seats at the lower tables with the other guests.

The conversation continued with Montferrat, and occasionally the ladies, asking Ibelin questions, while course after course was served. Meanwhile, musicians had taken their place in the gallery and jugglers were entertaining between the tables. The atmosphere at the lower tables was relaxed and good-natured, with volleys of laughter and occasional singing punctuating the continuous babble of men talking. Yet even the excellent wine, of which he partook very sparingly, failed to make Ibelin unbend.

It was midafternoon before the banquet was over, and Ibelin, accompanied by his wife, stepdaughter, and household knights, was free to make his way to the home he'd never seen. Sir Bartholomew led the way through streets that were now nearly deserted, as a cold, drenching rain had swept in off the sea. Montferrat graciously provided both ladies with voluminous cloaks to protect their gowns, but the men were soaked by the time they reached the expropriated residence.

Sir Bartholomew led the party to the back entrance for ease of stabling the horses, and as Ibelin led his horse in out of the rain he was ambushed by Eskinder. "My lord!" the Ethiopian youth asked anxiously, taking the bridle of Ibelin's horse but standing still and confronting his lord. "Where is my father? Where are my sister and Beth and Menelik?"

Maria Zoë saw her husband stiffen as if he'd been hit, but his face remained an impenetrable mask. "Your father, sister, and Beth with Menelik did not wish to endure another siege. They chose to continue to Tripoli, and from there to Ethiopia."

"And Dawit?" Eskinder demanded. "Sir Bartholomew said he was killed in the siege, but I have a right to know more. How and when did he die?"

"Yes, you do," Ibelin agreed solemnly. "Everyone should hear the news, for it was after the Saracens had breached the walls and I had gone out to negotiate with Salah ad-Din that some Saracens managed to take the northeastern tower. They planted the Sultan's banners on it, and Salah ad-Din pointed to them, mocking my attempts to negotiate by scoffing that 'one did not negotiate for a city one already held.' In that moment a Christian counterattack flung the banners and the Sultan's men down off the walls. We saw them fall, and I could answer that the city was not yet his." He paused to lend his words greater weight before continuing, "It was Dawit who led that desperate attack against the men already on our walls."

A murmur of awe and appreciation surrounded them, and several men crossed themselves.

"On the very last day, the last hour . . ." Eskinder murmured in numbed horror.

"Dawit gave his life for—" Ibelin broke off. He had been about to say "for Jerusalem," but that was not true. When Dawit died, Jerusalem was already lost. "For sixty thousand Christian lives."

Eskinder stared at him, and around them everyone else had fallen so still and silent that they could hear the rain splattering on the cobbles of the street outside.

Ibelin continued, "If he had not made his attack—if he had failed—none of us would have survived in freedom," Ibelin told them. "Not one man, woman, or child. Dawit gave his life for his father, sister, wife, and son. I cannot believe that he regrets that choice."

A murmur of assent followed, and many crossed themselves again as they commended Dawit's soul to God.

"And Gabriel?" It was Ernoul who asked the next question. Like Eskinder, he knew already from Sir Bartholomew that Gabriel was dead, but he too wanted more of the details.

"Gabriel was with me until the night before the surrender. That night we made a last sortie in the hope of reaching the Sultan's tent and killing him." Ibelin paused. Had he really hoped to reach the Sultan's tent? No, that had been a fairy tale for the others. He'd hoped only to die honorably rather than face humiliation, slavery, and possibly torture. "We were overwhelmed by the Sultan's cavalry and forced back through the Jehoshaphat Gate almost as soon as we sallied forth. Unfortunately, Gabriel's horse went down in the confusion, and he fell into Saracen hands. I had hoped to ransom him after the surrender had been negotiated, but Salah ad-Din told me personally that Gabriel had refused to accept imprisonment and requested execution. I suppose at the time he thought our situation was hopeless and preferred a quick end to the prospect of slavery." Ibelin paused, thinking for the hundredth time of Gabriel's dilemma and regretting again that he had allowed this to happen. Out loud he said simply, "He was very proud."

Ernoul remained stunned in place as Ibelin and his lady continued toward the passageway to the house. Gabriel had been Ernoul's only friend when he came to the Ibelin household as an incompetent and unwilling squire. Gabriel had saved Ernoul's life at Hattin, dragging him onto his own horse, after Ernoul had been severely wounded and was about to fall between the horses to his death. Gabriel had tended Ernoul's wounds and loaded him on a sledge behind his horse to get him from Hattin to Safed and then Tyre. And it was only because Ernoul was still recovering from his wounds that Gabriel had gone with their lord to Jerusalem, while Ernoul stayed behind in Tyre. The news of his heroic death left Ernoul feeling very cold and lonely.

The sound of voices echoing in the passage from the stables alerted Balian's children to the fact that their father had evaded their ambush at the front door and taken them by surprise from the rear. With a cry of outrage, John ran across the inner courtyard and flung himself at his father just as the latter reached the kitchen entrance. The little boy collided with his father so hard that the tall man staggered slightly. Then he realized what had hit him and closed his arms around his son like a drowning man his rescuer.

As Maria Zoë watched, her husband seemed to crack, and tears began flooding down his face as he clung to his son. Then Helvis and Margaret and Philip caught up with John, and he let go of John to try to embrace them all. Margaret and Philip were jumping up and down with excitement, while Helvis cuddled up against her father.

Then one of his tears splashed on Helvis' cheek and she looked up to ask, "Why are you crying, Daddy? Aren't you glad to see us?"

"Christ!" Balian gasped and broke down altogether.

Maria Zoë gently but firmly pushed her bewildered children apart and took Balian in her own arms. "It's all right, my love. You're home safe."

Balian couldn't answer, but he held her to him—and the children stood around gazing up at him, silenced and sobered by the sight of their father crying, while the household looked at one another in both concern and sympathy.

Slowly, Balian got hold of himself and released his grasp on Maria Zoë. Taking a deep breath, he turned to Helvis and smiled at her through his wet face, reaching out to stroke her silky curls as he reassured her. "Yes, sweetheart, I'm glad to see you. You see, tears can be a sign of joy as well as sadness."

John immediately stepped forward to take his father's hand and assure him, "I know that, Papa. I cried when we learned that you were alive and would come to us."

"Thank you, John." Balian wanted to ruffle his hair but thought better of it, and patted his shoulder instead.

"Come, let me show you our new home," Maria Zoë urged, cognizant of the household staring at them. She slipped her hand through her husband's elbow, leaving John on his other side. With the other three children in their wake, Maria Zoë led Balian through the kitchen, introducing the local staff. Then she guided him through what had been the merchant's showroom and now housed the squires, and then darted through the rain across the inner courtyard and up the stairs wrapping around the courtyard to enter the house again on the first floor. Here Maria Zoë pointed out the interior stairs leading to the third floor, but led instead through the hall to the solar that stood at right angles to the hall over the showroom below.

Someone had thought to light a fire here, and the room was warm compared to the rest of the house and lavishly furnished with the carpets and cushions Maria Zoë had loaded on their precious brood mares when she left Jerusalem. Because they occupied many fewer rooms in this modest merchant house than they had at the Ibelin palace, the room was almost as well furnished with rugs, chests, tables, and cushions as an Arab house.

Maria Zoë led Balian to an armed chair before the fire and sent John to fetch wine for his father. "We just ate," she told him, "so there is no need to bring snacks, but have Ernoul or one of the other squires help you—"

"I can do it myself!" John answered, insulted, and ran off with Philip at his heels.

Balian sat and took Margaret on his lap, while Helvis settled herself at his feet.

"You're going to stay with us now, aren't you, Daddy?" Margaret asked, snuggling into the crook of his shoulder.

"Yes, sweetheart," Balian promised her.

It was after dark before Maria Zoë could convince the children that they needed their supper and then had to go to bed. "Your father will still be here in the morning," she assured them.

Fortunately, they had been so excited the night before that they had hardly slept and were now falling asleep on their feet. Still, they insisted their father join them for supper and see them to bed. Balian sat with them in the kitchen as they had their light evening meal with their cousins, and then escorted them up to their bedrooms, which they now shared with Isabella, Eschiva, and Eloise.

Eschiva and Eloise had greeted Balian when he brought the children to have supper with their own, and they stayed with the children, so Balian and Maria Zoë could be alone together at last, Isabella discreetly withdrawing. Because the bedroom was cold and damp on this rainy night, they returned to the solar, however, while Ernoul was sent to get the bedroom fire going and then prepare a bath for his lord.

Maria Zoë moved her chair closer to her husband's and took his hand in hers. He gripped it so hard it hurt, and she let out a little whimper in protest.

"I'm sorry, my love." He eased his grasp at once and looked over at her. "My God, you're more beautiful than I remembered. You must be the most beautiful woman on earth." He smiled at her for the first time. It was only a soft little smile, but it reached his eyes and moved her to stand up and come to kiss him. He reached up and pulled her down into his lap to kiss her hard and long.

They kissed until Maria Zoë pulled back to remark, a little embarrassed, "I'm much too heavy for you now." She started to get up.

He shook his head and held her fast. "No, but I stink. I haven't had a bath in twelve days."

"No matter. Ernoul's preparing one now."

He kissed her again, more tenderly than passionately, and then she laid her head on his chest as Margaret had done. "Was what you said about Dawit the truth?"

"Yes, every word of it. But it isn't the siege that has embittered me. We fought well. Men, women, and even children. Franks, Syrians, and Armenians. The sacrifice of the lepers was terrible—but it was inspiring, too. Daniel said to me, "This is what King Baldwin would have wanted," and he was right. They left their rotting bodies behind to be reunited with Christ, whole and beautiful as angels. And when I faced Roger after Gabriel's capture, he too believed we were all doomed and that they would soon see each other again in heaven.

"No, it isn't the siege that angers me—it was what followed. When I negotiated with Salah ad-Din, I knew the city was full of refugees, as many as forty thousand people, who had fled their homes with only what they could carry with them. And most of them were women with children. It was clear that many of them would be incapable of finding five dinars for themselves and two per child. Think of it! A widow with four or five children needed fifteen dinars! Where were poor women to find that kind of money? I told Salah ad-Din that, but he answered that the Church or the treasury of the Kingdom would have to pay their ransoms. I managed to talk him into accepting a lump sum of thirty thousand dinars for ten thousand paupers—not knowing where I'd come up with money like that—and knowing that ten thousand was only a portion of the poor.

"But I still was not prepared for what followed. It was a nightmare. To be sure, the Grand Hospitaller didn't even let me finish speaking before he promised the full sum of thirty thousand—contingent on the agreement of the other brothers, but that was never really in doubt. Furthermore, the Hospital paid for the freedom of every soul in its care: the men and women in the wards of the Hospital, the old people in the hospice, and the children in the orphanage, too. But the Templars whined and prevaricated about the money they had being "deposits" that they could not release without breaking their word and sacrificing their honor—which they weren't prepared to do. Eventually they gave me a couple thousand dinars that they collected by selling off equipment and wine. But the worst was Heraclius!" When he said the name, Balian's entire face twisted with contempt and hatred.

Maria Zoë instinctively stroked his arm, both in sympathy and to calm him.

"That bastard! That egotistical, selfish, corrupt bastard would not donate a single dinar for the poor! His wealth, he claimed, wasn't his. It belonged to the Church. He wasn't saving it for himself, he protested—his hands dripping jewels. He was only saving it for future generations! I came so close to hitting him, I had to walk out. Just turned my back on him and left him standing!"

Maria Zoë said nothing, just stroked his arm in sympathy until he had calmed himself enough to continue.

"I next tried to convince Salah ad-Din to give me more time to raise a ransom for the poor by appealing to the Pope, but he turned me down—so when the forty days were up, I didn't have enough for all the poor. I had to watch as roughly fifteen thousand Christians marched off to slavery—and Heraclius left the city with four wagons loaded to the brim with gold and silver plate, chalices, altar crosses, and reliquaries!" Balian was working himself into a rage at the memory of it, and Maria Zoë again stroked his arm to calm him, but knew better than to speak.

"He didn't even have the decency to look the people he condemned to slavery in the eye! He stole out of the city by the David Gate, turning his back on the women who will be ravished and the children brutalized because of him! But I had to watch them trudge out. . . .

"You wouldn't believe it. I was sitting there beside the Sultan, his men around us already making jokes about what they were going to do with the women, and I recognized amidst the new slaves the very man who had made my sword. Oh, that's right, you don't know about it. A Norse armorer had heard that I had returned to Jerusalem without a sword and made a new one for me." Balian had removed his heavy sword hours ago, when the children were still with them. He now gently pushed Maria Zoë off his lap, stood, and retrieved the sword from where it was leaning against the wall. Holding it horizontal in his hands, he pulled the blade partway out of the sheath to reveal the bronze etching on the blade: Defender of Jerusalem.

"That's beautiful!" Maria Zoë exclaimed, and held out her hand to take it from Balian as he added, "Look at the pommel, too—the crosses of Jerusalem on one side and Ibelin arms on the other. Furthermore, it's extra long—made specially for me. But unbeknownst to me, the man couldn't raise the money for his own ransom! He *gave* me this, Zoë—refused any kind of payment—but couldn't raise his own ransom when the time came. He paid for his wife and daughters, but had not enough money to buy his own freedom or that of his crippled son. I saw him in that column, carrying his son on his back—"

"Oh, Balian, surely you could have found twelve dinars—" Maria Zoë interrupted.

"But what of the others? There were fifteen thousand of them!" Balian retorted in angry anguish. "While the Sultan's men brought the armorer out of the crowd, I begged Salah ad-Din again to let me stand surety for all of them. I begged him to hold me while I wrote to the Pope and the Kings of France and England for more money—"

"Balian!" Maria Zoë gasped, horrified by what this would have meant.

"But he refused," Balian answered, shaking his head grimly, his gaze no longer in the room or on his wife but back in Jerusalem. "By then the armorer and his boy were in front of me. Naturally, I begged Salah ad-Din to let me buy them. Again he refused, saying they were a gift from him. His brother al-Adil at once spoke up and asked for a gift of a thousand slaves—and, emboldened, I asked for the same number. Salah ad-Din granted both our wishes, so we saved another two thousand souls. . . ."

Maria Zoë put down the sword and pulled Balian into her arms as she insisted earnestly, "You did the best you could."

"But it wasn't enough!"

"Let God be the judge of that."

"I have nothing to give my sons!" Balian cried out, breaking free of her embrace and turning his back on her.

"Oh, Balian! You can't mean that?" Maria Zoë answered reproachfully.

"We have nothing, Zoë," Balian turned back to face her, his face limp with defeat. "Ibelin, Ramla, Mirabel—all overrun by our enemies."

"Yes, like Nablus and the rest of the Kingdom. But you have more important things to give your sons than *land*!"

He stared at her blankly as if she were mad.

"You can teach them that a brave man leads by example and that a Christian lord sacrifices his treasure for the sake of the poor. You can help them understand that nobility is not material wealth, but the ability to disdain greed and self-interest for the sake of others. Most of all, you can show them that courage is not mere fearlessness in the face of physical danger, but rather the ability to face whatever fate God grants us with equanimity, perseverance, and faith in the goodness of God."

Balian smiled at her sadly. "It sounds to me like they will learn all that from *you*, not me, Zoë."

"No!" Maria Zoë contradicted him. "They won't! They need you, too. Even if you can give them not a single dinar, Balian, you can give them most precious gift of all: you can give them a father's love."

Pulling her back into his arms gratefully, Balian capitulated. "Yes, you're right, Zoë. I can do that."

Chapter 4

Aleppo, November 28, 1187

THE SOUND OF THE VOICES BEYOND the door, followed by the turning of the key and the screeching of the door on its hinges, attracted the attention of all the prisoners. Some sat up or even stood. "Too early for dinner," someone remarked warily.

The door clunked against the wall as it was shoved back by a strong arm, and Humphrey de Toron walked in wearing a clean kaftan and smelling of balsam soap. He was growing a beard now and wore a turban as well as a kaftan. He looked every inch the elegant young Muslim scholar—except for being blond. "Come to try to convert the rest of us?" Haifa snarled, and had the satisfaction of seeing Toron wince.

Toron recovered rapidly, and replied with dignity, "No, I would not attempt something so futile. Nor do my clothes denote a change of religion—"

"No, just a willingness to toady to our jailers," Aimery de Lusignan sneered, emerging from the darker reaches of the dungeon. He too was bearded, but not by choice.

Toron turned to the Constable. "My letter to the Sultan has yielded fruit," he announced bravely. "Queen Sibylla is to be allowed to go to Tyre, and the Marquis de Montferrat is to accompany us."

"Me?" The aging Marquis reared up on his pallet. "Why me?"

"I don't know for sure," Toron admitted, "but Imad ad-Din hinted that your son Conrad might pay your ransom."

"Ah, Conrad." The old Marquis smiled at the mention of his son's name. Conrad was his second son, but after his firstborn came out to Jerusalem to marry Sibylla and died there, Conrad had been his greatest asset in the wars against the Holy See. Except for that unfortunate incident when he'd rebelled against the Archbishop of Mainz, he'd been a powerful ally, a natural leader of men, fearless in battle, and a charmer in council. For the others in the room he remarked, "He married Emperor Isaac Angelus' sister, you know, and was raised to the position of Caesar. He certainly has the funds to buy my freedom."

"Put in a good word for the rest of us, would you?" Caesarea suggested bluntly.

"You can be sure of it, my good lords. For all of you. All I need is to get word to Conrad. He's a good boy."

There was little love lost between the old Marquis de Montferrat and Sibylla of Jerusalem. Her affection for Guy de Lusignan, his son's successor, was, to put it politely, excessive, and the aging Marquis had heard enough rumors about Sibylla's neglect of his grandson to think her a poor mother as well. Nevertheless, no adherent of chivalry could be completely unmoved by Sibylla's current state. She was clearly suffering some kind of stomach ailment, and although she was traveling in a litter, they had to make frequent stops for her to seek out a toilet. Furthermore, Sibylla looked ghastly. She had puffy eyes, splotchy skin, and cracked lips.

Because of Sibylla's condition, the little caravan made very slow progress along the road from Aleppo to Hama, Homs, and finally Baalbek. They stopped at caravansaries every night, the Sultan's Mamlukes unceremoniously expelling all other guests to make room for them. Their slow pace afforded the Marquis the opportunity to bathe at public baths, visit barbers, and have his surcoat washed several times along the way. He had also been given a change of underwear. All this encouraged him to think his fortunes were about to change for the better.

Just beyond Qal'at Subaiba, Sibylla's condition took an abrupt turn for the worse. She started groaning and then crying out in pain. The lady traveling with her, a native Syrian chosen by their jailers to accompany her, looked genuinely alarmed and insisted they get her to a doctor immediately. Being in the middle of farmland as far as the eye could see, the best the escort could do was to get her to one of the typical adobe peasant farmhouses. Here a brood of children stood around gawking and getting underfoot as the Sultan's Mamlukes commandeered everything.

Sibylla was carried inside and the women of the household closed around her, while one of the Mamlukes galloped back toward Qal'at Subaiba for a doctor. After that, they waited while the Queen of Jerusalem screamed in obvious agony inside the mud hut. As the day dragged on, intermittent rain showers made the wait even more miserable.

Eventually the screaming stopped, to be followed by sobbing. Montferrat thought he heard Sibylla call for Guy several times, but he couldn't be sure. Eventually the doctor arrived, disappeared inside, and returned, shaking his head. There was nothing he could do. It was all over.

"What?" Toron asked.

"She has miscarried a child," he announced, looking at the two Franks significantly but refraining from further comment.

They spent the night and the next day there to give Sibylla time to rest and cry herself out. Then they set off across territory that had once been Christian but was now controlled by the Sultan of Egypt and Damascus.

There had been no time to move new settlers in, and Montferrat found himself wondering whether or not the lands had already been divided up among the Sultan's emirs. In any case, most of the villages were deserted and the towns nearly abandoned, except for remnants of the Jewish and Muslim populations that had returned once the initial hostilities died down. Here and there they passed through villages full of native peasants who greeted the escort with deep bows, and praising Allah a little too enthusiastically for Montferrat's taste. He suspected they were Syrian Christians trying to pass themselves off as Muslims. They encountered some shepherds who likewise made a great show of being Muslim, but the Marquis noticed large numbers of straying farm animals. These had apparently been left behind when their owners fled. Packs of dogs roamed at large, too, and many farms lay unnaturally fallow. Montferrat hated the sight of fallow fields; gray and bleak in the November rains, they whispered "famine" to his old ears. Whoever controlled this land in the future would first have to live on imported foodstuffs for some time to come, and that took money.

They had been traveling almost two weeks before they finally reached the coastal plain. By that time, Montferrat's old bones were aching badly from the days in the saddle and the damp cold. Yet when the towers and walls of Tyre came into sight, his heart leapt in pride. Even in the gray and drizzling rain, Tyre looked magnificent to his tired old eyes. It stood defiantly flying the crosses of Jerusalem, while surrounded by a thousand bright-colored tents and a seething mass of Saracen soldiers: The Sultan's army was besieging it.

The little party of Franks was escorted through the camp, eliciting only mild curiosity, but the old Marquis noted many things. First he sensed that the mood in the camp was glum. This was not an army full of confidence, raring for a fight or on the brink of triumph; this was an army that was bored, discouraged, and tired. Of course the rains had an impact on morale, and the paths between the tents were a morass of mud. Indeed, everything seemed soggy and dirty.

The Marquis de Montferrat had been at enough sieges to know what it was like. He understood that a besieging army didn't have to suffer outright defeat to reach a state of demoralization. However, he noted keenly that many men were nursing wounds, too, and they loitered together, bandages on their arms, legs, and heads, while others hobbled about on crutches or held their arms in slings. That spoke volumes: these men weren't just tired, dirty, damp, and bored—they had been badly mauled in one or more assaults on the city. The thought made him proud of the defenders, and he smiled to himself.

Eventually they were brought to a sumptuous tent decorated with sayings from the Koran. Toron showed off his knowledge of the language by reading several aloud, to the disapproval of Montferrat. While Sibylla was taken to a separate tent clad in plain black canvas that huddled behind the Sultan's green-and-gold tent, Humphrey and the Marquis de Montferrat were taken directly inside. Salah ad-Din was absent, but they were told to sit down on the floor to await him. Water was brought for them to wash their hands and drink.

Roughly a half-hour after their arrival, a large party of horsemen arrived and with a flurry of commands, men rushed to take the horses and others to report the arrival of the visitors. A moment later, the Sultan swept into the tent followed by a half-dozen of his men. The Mamlukes went down on their faces, and Toron imitated them, but the old Marquis simply got to his feet.

The Sultan was not particularly tall, and he was no longer thin, if he ever had been. His beard was sprinkled with white and the lines on his face were deeply carved. "Ah, Monsieur de Montferrat, we meet again," he opened in Arabic, so the Marquis had to wait for Toron's translation before replying with a stiff bow. The last time they had met had been immediately after the catastrophe at Hattin, and the Marquis had been subjected to the spectacle of the Sultan personally decapitating the Lord of Oultrejourdain. To be sure, the slaughter of the Templars and Hospitallers that followed had been even more appalling, but that did not, in Montferrat's mind, wipe out the Sultan's own barbarism.

At the moment, however, Salah ad-Din was playing gracious host, indicating that Montferrat should sit down again, praising Toron's command of Arabic with a gracious smile, and snapping his fingers for refreshment. Montferrat, mindful of the fact that hospitality provided protection, gratefully accepted the Sultan's mint-laced sherbet and some almonds as well. While the Sultan and Toron exchanged flowery pleasantries and smiles, Montferrat admired the beautiful furnishings of the Sultan's tent: Turkish carpets, silk cushions, low tables inlaid with ivory, lamps with bright-colored cloisonné decorations.

Finally the Sultan turned directly to Montferrat and, through Toron, addressed him. "I'm pleased to see you looking so well, my lord," he told the old man, and Montferrat bit back the inclination to snap, "No thanks to you!" He bowed his head instead. "It would be my pleasure to have you with me as guest for a while longer, but I suspect you would prefer to join your own family."

Again Montferrat bowed his head in agreement, but the hope he had carried in his heart from the start of this voyage swelled his chest and made his blood run faster.

"I daresay it may have escaped your notice, seeing that you were so far away and cut off from the world in Aleppo," the Sultan continued through Toron, "but your son Conrad is now in command of the Frankish forces holding Tyre."

"What?" The Marquis could hardly believe his ears and, to be sure he had not misunderstood, asked: "Conrad? Here?"

The Sultan smiled and assured him, "Yes! Just beyond the walls of Tyre. Not more than a mile away at this very minute."

This was, indeed, marvelous news. Conrad, his father thought, had always been audacious, but this was truly an exceptional demonstration of both daring and filial devotion. To leave the safety of Constantinople and come voluntarily into the lion's den took a degree of arrogance that was not to everyone's taste, but the old Marquis burst with pride at the thought. It was like Conrad, too, he thought indulgently, to seize command at once, whether it was his place or not. He smiled to himself.

"I suspect that you would like to be reunited sooner rather than later, so if you have refreshed yourself from your arduous journey," the Sultan continued with a gesture toward the empty water goblet, "I suggest we go." He smiled as he stood.

The Marquis was so eager he almost fell over as he tried to get up too rapidly. Toron caught him with a beaming smile, and they went out together.

Horses were waiting for them. They remounted and rode through the camp, then out onto the field before the castle. Halting just out of bowshot, the Sultan signaled his men to wave a white parley flag. On receiving an answering signal from the outer gate, they started forward in a small group: the Sultan, two of his emirs, four Mamlukes, the Marquis, and Toron.

They rode to the very edge of the first salt-water moat and halted there. On the massive main tower above the closed drawbridge archers stood at the ready, while a man in gleaming armor with a well-polished helmet leaned out. The Marquis's old heart was pumping so fast it was almost painful. It was recognizably his dashing son Conrad!

The Sultan gave instructions to Toron, who raised his voice and shouted across the distance in French. "The Sultan Salah ad-Din sends his greetings and presents your father, William Marquis de Montferrat!"

If the man on the ramparts was pleased, relieved, or surprised, he was too far away for them to tell. From this distance he seemed completely impassive.

"We are here," Toron continued, "to return your father to you."

"On what terms?" Conrad shouted back, and his father felt his heart sink. The question made it clear there had been no negotiations in advance. This wasn't the final act in his release—it was the first.

"Why, what do you think?" Sultan sounded surprised. "The surrender of Tyre!" he answered through Toron.

The Marquis gasped when he heard Toron translate the terms and cried out: "He can't do that!"

Father and son were of the same mind. Conrad's "No!" reached them even as his father spoke.

The Sultan responded by drawing his sword with a loud hiss and brandishing it over the Marquis' head. The old man again saw the execution of Reynald de Châtillon in his mind's eye, and started to recite the Pater Noster.

"Surrender Tyre, or your father dies!" Toron shouted out at the Sultan's bidding.

"My father is an old man! Look at his white hair! He has lived long enough!" Conrad retorted. "I would rather kill him myself than surrender this city to you! By God's grace, I will hold Tyre for Christendom until help comes from the West! May God receive my father's soul with the grace!" As he spoke, Conrad grabbed a crossbow from the nearest archer and aimed it at the party addressing him—whether at his father, the Sultan, or Toron was irrelevant.

"Well said!" the Marquis of Montferrat shouted back at his son. "Well said, my boy!"

Salah ad-Din was furious enough to backhand the old man so hard that he swayed in his saddle and his nose gushed blood, but he put away his sword. Then he swung his horse around and galloped back to his camp, leaving Toron and his escort to bring the worthless prisoner back with them.

December 14, 1187

Balian and John sat side by side upon an elaborately carved oak chest, with Balian's chain-mail hauberk spread across their four knees. Balian had a brush with metal bristles in his right hand and was demonstrating the short, vigorous strokes necessary to clean the rust off the armor. "You've got to push down a little so the bristles get right between the rings. Like this. See? Now you try." He handed the brush to John, who with great concentration tried to imitate his father's motions.

Under the boy's vigorous but inept assault, the heavy hauberk started to slide off their laps. As he grabbed it with his small fist to pull it back in place, the lower part of the large metal shirt sagged down, revealing a long gash.

Maria Zoë, glancing up from her own needlework to enjoy the sight of her husband and son together, caught her breath. Leaving her needlework behind, she walked over the pair. "That cut," she said, narrowing her eyes as she measured the distance from the shoulder to the gash, "was below your rib cage!" Sword thrusts that penetrated armor below the rib cage endangered a man's innards and were often fatal.

"It drew blood," Balian admitted, "but wasn't deep enough to leave a scar."

"When?" Maria Zoë demanded sternly, as her son looked up at her with large eyes that reflected growing understanding.

"Last sortie," Balian replied dismissively, and immediately distracted attention from the subject of the wound by announcing, "I have an idea. Let's take this hauberk to Godwin Olafsen for repair. His wife" (Balian consciously dignified Mariam with a status he knew she did not enjoy to shield his young children from knowledge of an illicit relationship and shield Godwin and Mariam from disapprobation) "is a pastry and sweets maker—"

"Oh, can we go, Mama? Can we?" Helvis and Margaret had already jumped up, dropping their needlework, Margaret from disinterest in the tedious task of stitching and Helvis because she loved sweets.

"We haven't had any sweets *in ages*," Philip added so solemnly that the adults burst out laughing.

Moments later they all left the house together, disdaining horses because Balian assured them they could walk. "They need the exercise," he explained to Maria Zoë as the boys rushed ahead down the cobbled street. "It's not good for boys their age to be cooped up all the time."

"You're right," Maria Zoë agreed. "But they don't like letting you out of their sight. Tell me when they get on your nerves."

"I will, and they aren't." Although he had been with his family three weeks now, Balian still felt he could not get enough of them.

Maria Zoë squeezed her hand more firmly on his elbow and briefly leaned her head on his upper arm. "Thank you for being so indulgent," she murmured.

Balian looked down at her, surprised by her tone.

"You know," Maria Zoë started cautiously, "I didn't tell them you weren't coming with us when we left Jerusalem, which was the main reason I insisted on them all—even John—traveling in the litter. They didn't find out you were still in the city until we stopped for the night. When John learned that, he screamed furiously at me and ran away—swearing he would go back to be with you. When I tried to stop him, he turned on me, hitting out with his fists and screaming insults."

Balian stiffened with disapproval.

"The escort was clearly amused and impressed by his fiery spirit. The commander came over to assure me that his men would watch over him carefully, but that it was better to let him burn out his anger. Reluctantly, I followed their advice, and an hour or two later John crept back into the camp and buried himself under his blanket. The blanket was shaking so violently that I didn't know if he was crying or shivering with cold. I went over to cover him with a second blanket, and then I sat beside the blanket and tried to explain your decision."

Balian looked at her in wordless anguish.

"I said that you loved us too much to let us die when there was a means of escape—but also too much to leave us a legacy of shame. I told him you had no choice, as an honorable man, but to defend Jerusalem. I explained that had you slunk away to safety, leaving Jerusalem and the other Christians in captivity, that you would have thrown away something more precious than life itself—your honor."

"Did John understand that?" Balian asked with a glance toward his son, who was currently scuffling with his younger brother.

"He never answered me directly, but he eventually went still and fell into a deep sleep. We never spoke of it again."

"And the others?" Balian pressed her.

"All reacted in their own way. Margaret started wetting her bed again. Philip has been particularly rebellious, and Helvis took to prayer."

"Do you think Helvis is suited to a religious vocation?" Balian asked, glancing at his eldest child, who was still the most timid of the four.

"Perhaps, but it's too soon to tell."

"Yes, of course." Balian was thinking that he had nothing with which to dower either of his daughters, and that their future was therefore bleak. To distract himself he suggested to his wife, "Tell me the gossip from Eschiva."

The infuriated Sultan had put the Marquis de Montferrat in chains, but he had gallantly released Queen Sibylla. Balian cynically noted that Salah ad-Din knew perfectly well that she enjoyed neither respect nor support among the defenders of Tyre. Her presence in the besieged city was nothing but an awkward burden. "He's sent us a gift he knows we didn't want," Balian summed it up.

No one, however, had been less pleased by the arrival of Queen Sibylla in Tyre than Eschiva. As the wife of the Constable of Jerusalem, it was her duty to serve the Queen, particularly since there were so few other ladies of rank in the city. Balian had not been included in the ensuing drama, but the house was too small and crowded for secrets. Balian knew that Isabella had spiritedly advised Eschiva to refuse Sibylla's summons, reminding her of Sibylla's earlier slights and insults. "She's a selfish bitch!" Isabella declared emphatically, earning reprimands from Eschiva but (notably, Balian thought) not from her mother. Eschiva had dutifully gone to the Queen, reminding Isabella, "She was in Aleppo. Maybe she'll have news from our husbands."

Maria Zoë sighed. "Are you sure you want to hear all this feminine gossip?"

"Absolutely," Balian assured her.

"Well, we can start with the fact that dear Sibylla never left the comfortable apartments put at her disposal and could not say a word about Aimery's condition."

"Selfish bitch!" Balian spat, echoing his stepdaughter's sentiments.

"She could report, however, that my dear son-in-law has managed to ingratiate himself with his jailers and is accorded totally different treatment from the others. He is housed separately, has access to the baths and other conveniences, and now dresses like an Arab scholar, while spending most of his time with one of the Sultan's secretaries."

Balian was gazing at his wife with an expression somewhere between outrage and disbelief. "Tell me you jest."

Maria Zoë slowly shook her head. "Sadly, I do not. And it gets worse. He escorted Sibylla and the Marquis de Montferrat here and did the translation at the negotiations with Conrad. Conrad didn't know him, of course, and assumed he was a blond Mamluke." Since Mamlukes were bought or captured as boys, many were blond.

"Jesus God! Has Humphrey converted?"

"No, not according to Sibylla, but now comes the real news: while in captivity with Guy, Sibylla managed to get herself pregnant—"

"Holy Mother of God!"

"Which was why Guy ordered her to leave him, in the hope that the child she was carrying would be born in freedom—"

"That's the first sensible thing Guy's done since he set foot in the Kingdom," Balian commented.

Maria Zoë smiled cynically and continued, "However, Sibylla lost the baby on the way here."

Balian said nothing. That was good news as far as he was concerned. He did not want to see Guy's claim to the throne strengthened by a child, particularly since he did not think a child born to two such parents would amount to much. It would probably combine Sibylla's stupidity with Guy's cupidity, he thought.

Maria Zoë was continuing, "Understandably, Sibylla is still deeply dispressed. She's convinced herself, though there is no way of knowing so early in the pregnancy, that the child was a boy. She variously blames Guy for sending her away, the Sultan for the arduous travel, and God for abandoning her."

"Everyone but herself, it seems."

"Quite, but, it seems, Conrad's brother William wrote Conrad rather intimate—and none too complimentary—details about his marriage to Sibylla. Furthermore, he accused Sibylla of being a bad mother and all but murdering his brother's child. It escalated into a huge fight, with Sibylla screaming hysterically and Conrad shouting insults back. Eventually Sibylla started screaming that she wanted to go back to Guy—which, of course, Conrad flatly refused to let her do."

Ahead of them the children had come to a T-intersection and were loudly demanding directions. Maria Zoë and Balian dropped their conversation and joined the children. Taking a daughter by each hand, Balian led the way to the glassmakers' quarter of Tyre.

Glassworking was a luxury that a city under siege could not afford, and the glassmakers had boarded up their workshops and either left the city or taken up arms in its defense. Two of these workshops, side by side, had been leased out to Godwin and Mariam for their respective trades, but the accommodations on the floors above were long since occupied to overflowing by other refugees. The couple and Sven therefore lived in the vaulted storerooms behind the workrooms.

The smell of cinnamon and apples greeted them as they approached the pastry shop, and Helvis dropped her father's hand to run forward, her sister and Philip at her heels. Mariam had already taken on two apprentices, and they manned the wooden counter, wearing crisp white aprons and neat white head scarves. They did not recognize the Ibelin children, but the arrival of the Dowager Queen produced palpable excitement. Their chatter brought Mariam out of the back, bright red and sweating from working near the oven. She at once wiped her hands on her apron and came forward to greet her exalted customers. Soon she was busily ordering her best for the Ibelin children.

Balian left his wife and younger children to the sweets, and with John in tow went next door to the armory. Godwin was at work at the anvil, while a hired youth worked the bellows of the forge. The armorer was concentrating so hard that he did not immediately take note of his visitors, and Balian gestured for John to be quiet and watch. "A skilled armorer is an artist," he told his son in a low voice, inaudible to Godwin over the roaring of the forge.

Godwin's hammer clanged down and the blade of the sword he was working rang. There was rhythm to his blows, and the sword seemed to sing in counterpoint. Catching his father's enthusiasm, John watched wide-eyed until they were both disturbed by men bursting into the forge from behind them.

"Godwin!" a man roared, followed by a flood of words in an incomprehensible tongue that was both staccato and melodic. Godwin was startled from his concentration and turned to look over his shoulder at the intruders.

The new arrivals surged past Balian and John, and John instinctively shrank back toward his father. These were big, powerful men in leather armor, and most of them had axes at their hips as big as ox heads. More to the point, they looked as if they'd just come out of a fight with a collection of cuts, bruises, swelling eyes, and bloody chins. A couple of them were nursing real wounds under oozing bandages as well.

Godwin saw Balian and John surrounded by the tattered, stinking, fighting men, and his eyes widened. "Haakon Magnussen! Don't you know whom you just shoved aside?" he called out in French. "That's my lord of Ibelin!"

The man directly beside Balian stopped short, turned, and looked straight at Balian. "Well," he grunted in passable French, "you're the first man out here that I don't have to look down on." He might have been referring to Balian's height, which put them eye to eye, but Balian had the feeling that he meant it figuratively instead.

"My lord, Haakon Magnussen commands the Norse snecka out in the harbor."

"The one that ran the blockade five days ago?" Ibelin asked back.

Salah ad-Din had resumed the full-scale siege of Tyre on November 26, only four days after Balian and the other refugees from Jerusalem arrived, but it had not been until December 10 that the Egyptian fleet had arrived offshore and instituted a sea blockade as well. Tyre, which until then had been able to receive supplies, reinforcements, and news, was now completely cut off from the rest of the world by land and by sea. Only one ship had slipped past the Egyptian war galleys: a Norse snecka, which had somehow evaded the Saracen ships in the dead of night.

"The same—and we would have run the blockade again last night in the opposite direction if that son-of-a-Pisan-whore Montferrat hadn't stopped us! The Queen of Jerusalem promised us one hundred gold bezants to get her out of this piss-pot and land her safely at Tripoli, but Montferrat somehow got word of her intentions. His men ambushed us on the quay before we could even go aboard, and two of my men were killed in the ensuing struggle. May his putrid soul rot in hell! I came here to fight Saracens, not Pisan sailors and French archers!"

"What happened to the Queen of Jerusalem?" Ibelin asked, cutting through the grumbled curses of the Norsemen's men, who were echoing their commander's sentiments.

"Montferrat's men put a sack over her head—literally—and carried her off kicking and screaming. Well, they silenced her fast enough. Stuck something in her mouth, I presume, or just knocked her out. I was too busy keeping myself from getting gutted by those Pisan bastards to notice much more than that she suddenly went silent."

Balian didn't like the sound of that, although part of him couldn't help noting that Sibylla's death would solve a lot of problems. "Thank you for the intelligence," he told the Norseman with a nod of his head. Then, turning to Godwin he noted, "These customers have more urgent need of your services than I, it seems, but when you have time, let me know. My hauberk is in need of repair."

"Of course, my lord!" Godwin readily agreed, and turned to take the ax Magnussen was handing him.

Balian turned to leave, but his son was gazing at the Norsemen with a wonder that was not to Balian's liking. These men might all wear crosses, but to Balian's mind they were little better than Vikings. "Come along, John!" he ordered sharply, and firmly pulled the boy away from their evil influence.

Tyre, Christmas Eve 1187

The rains had let up, replaced by a "cold snap" that was far above freezing but still seemed chilling to the inhabitants of Outremer. The grooms were bundled up in the warmest clothes they owned, and the horses were exceptionally frisky. Ibelin stepped out into the alleyway beside the house to get out of everyone's way while they tacked up the horses. His household had been invited to a Christmas feast hosted by Montferrat at the archiepiscopal palace. Dinner would be followed by midnight Mass at the Cathedral of the Holy Cross. The very name seemed like mockery to Balian as he waited in the silent street under the glittering canopy of the night sky.

It hardly seemed credible that just a year ago he and Maria Zoë had celebrated Christmas in the Church of the Nativity at Bethlehem. They had been avoiding Sibylla and Guy's court, and instead of going to the traditional Christmas court at Jerusalem, they had accepted Guillaume de Hebron's hospitality to spend the Christmas season in Hebron. They had taken Helvis and John to experience Christmas in Bethlehem for the first time—never thinking it might be the last time as well, for all of them. Just as they might never see Jerusalem or Ibelin again. . . .

Balian sighed and tried to shake off his memories. What did Ibelin and Jerusalem matter, when it was beginning to look as if their very lives and freedom were in danger? Even if the city was not yet feeling the effects of the siege too intensely, the situation was getting increasingly untenable. Montferrat, to give credit where it was due, had confiscated the bulk of the city's warehouses to ensure grain was neither wasted nor sold at usurious prices, but he had in the past purchased important staples such as wine, olive oil, and salt from Cyprus. Those supplies were now cut off. Furthermore, Godfrey had confided to Balian that Mariam's sugar supplies, brought with her from Jerusalem, would also soon be depleted. She'd used almost everything she had left for the Christmas sweets that would be served tonight. It was safe to assume that the situation was similar for others who had come to Tyre with all their stores. In short, with each passing day the number of people dependent on the rations Montferrat doled out increased, and those reserves were drawn down faster and faster. Balian had already heard rumors that some taverns were getting short of both ale and wine.

Meanwhile, and more important, Salah ad-Din had stepped up his assaults on the city's defenses ever since Conrad had refused to surrender the city in exchange for his father's life. Each time an assault failed, the Sultan paraded the aging Marquis de Montferrat before the walls, dressed in nothing but rags and heavy chains. Just yesterday, after yet another failed attack, the Saracens had not only paraded the old man, they had chased him with whips until he stumbled over his chains and then made him crawl. Salah ad-Din clearly hoped to soften the heart of the prisoner's son.

Ibelin was relieved that Montferrat had remained obdurate so far, yet he found the spectacle heart-rending nevertheless. The sight also reminded him how much they would all be at the Sultan's mercy if no help came from the West before one of the Sultan's assaults succeeded. At least in Jerusalem, he had known that Maria Zoë and the children were safe. . . .

"What are you thinking, Uncle Balian?" Eschiva's voice startled him from his thoughts, and he turned to smile guiltily at his niece.

Eschiva was wrapped in a leather cloak lined with otter fur that fastened at her neck with a heavy silver brooch. She wore a wool scarf wrapped around her head to keep her ears warm, and wool mittens on her hands. She slipped one of her hands through his elbow and asked earnestly, "Do you think the Count of Tripoli will send a second relief effort?"

Four days ago, the lookouts on the northern watchtowers of Tyre had watched in frustration as ten galleys sent from Tripoli to break the blockade had encountered such ferocious headwinds that after fighting wind and waves for almost a day, they had given up and turned back.

"Hard to say," Balian answered honestly; "it will depend on how much damage the ships sustained. I'd say the chances are high that they will need substantial repairs and a refit before they can put to sea again."

"And Antioch?" Eschiva asked in an almost inaudible voice.

Balian looked down at her sharply. Eschiva's face was very strained, and it struck him that it wasn't just enduring Sibylla's whining and complaining or concerns for her captive husband that was eating away at her youth and substance. "Wouldn't you have thought my father would have made *some* effort to come to our rescue?" As she put the thought into words, the tears were in her voice, though not on her face.

Balian's brother, Eschiva's father, had preferred to abdicate his baronies rather than pay homage to Guy de Lusignan. As a highly respected nobleman, however, he had been welcomed at the court of Prince Bohemond of Antioch. He no doubt felt Hattin vindicated his judgment of King Guy, but it was hard to understand how he could also turn his back on his daughter and grandchildren. "It *is* odd," Balian admitted cautiously, "that we have heard nothing from him, but I would not assume he has forgotten us." He knew this was Eschiva's fear.

"No?" Eschiva asked, with an expression that suggested she thought he was trying to coddle her.

"I fear Barry may be seriously ill or already dead."

"Or maybe he's just married again and doesn't care about us anymore," she put her suspicions into words.

"You are being unfair, Eschiva," Balian told her sternly. "Barry desperately wanted a son and because of that he slighted you—I don't deny that—but he loved you, too."

"Maybe. And Aimery, do you think he loves me?"

This conversation was taking unpleasant turns and becoming increasingly uncomfortable for Balian. He was prepared to speculate about and defend his brother's feelings, but felt considerably less qualified to talk about the Constable's. He avoided a direct answer by asking instead, "Why do you doubt it?"

Eschiva shrugged, not meeting his eyes. "He had affairs, you know."

"He's certainly not having affairs now," Balian shot back, adding, "If there is one thing a man needs when in captivity, it is the assurance of his wife's fidelity. I'm sure Aimery is clinging to the thought of you and yearning for a reunion. His current situation will make him regret every dalliance all the more intensely, because he knows you alone can bring him home."

"Can I, Uncle Balian? Can I bring him home? How? I'm utterly dependent on your charity." Eschiva was close to tears again, and Balian recognized that she was close to breaking down. She was usually so self-effacing, dutiful, and calm that one tended to forget she also had a fragile heart and overly strained nerves. In response, he put his arm around her shoulders and pulled her close. "Eschiva, you aren't charity! You are as much a part of my family as Isabella or my own children. Together we will find a way to obtain Aimery's freedom."

"And Humphrey's?" Isabella asked pointedly, as she emerged from the stables leading her mare.

Eschiva immediately stepped back out of Balian's embrace, as if she were ashamed of the moment of weakness she had shown, and hurried back inside to get her mare. Isabella came up beside her stepfather and looked up at him. "What about Humphrey?" she asked again pointedly.

"Humphrey's mother has the means to set him free!" Balian answered in exasperation. "I don't!"

Isabella's lips narrowed and she snapped back, "Stephanie de Milly would rather see Humphrey *dead* than surrender Kerak—and so would you!"

"Isabella!" It was he mother's commanding voice. "Don't use that tone of voice when speaking to my lord of Ibelin!"

"But it's true, Mama!" Isabella spun around on her mother. "He doesn't care about Humphrey. He never has!"

"Humphrey has done precious little to win my lord husband's respect," Maria Zoë replied firmly. "And this is no night to pick a fight with anyone. We should be celebrating the birth of our Savior, not squabbling like spoiled children."

Eloise had followed Maria Zoë out of the house, while Georgios was bringing Balian's stallion, so the conversation came to a natural end, but the tension lingered in the air as they mounted up and started down the street to the clatter of hooves on cobbles.

The archiepiscopal palace was well lit by torches along the outside wall and in the courtyard. The horses were taken from them and led across the street to a livery, while young boys carrying lanterns led the arriving guests in relays up to the main hall. The Dowager Queen of Jerusalem and her daughter Princess Isabella were immediately ushered to the high table, where they were greeted with great gallantry by Conrad de Montferrat. Isabella was placed to his left because her half-sister Sibylla, as the reigning Queen of Jerusalem, was already seated to Montferrat's right. Since the Archbishop of Tyre had sailed to the West with the news of the defeat at Hattin, the highest-ranking prelate in Tyre was the

Bishop of Beirut. He was seated on Isabella's far side, while Ibelin was accorded the dubious honor of sitting on Sibylla's right hand with his wife on his other side, flanked by the Bishop of Sabaste, another refugee.

Maria Zoë detested Sibylla—and vice versa—so the ladies exchanged only the barest of outward courtesies, while Isabella and Sibylla made a show of touching cheeks for the people at the lower tables—although anyone who could see their expressions could easily read the dislike they bore one another.

Given the atmospherics at the high table, Eschiva was relieved to find she and Eloise were relegated to the lower tables. Eloise sought a place with some nuns, while Eschiva sat next to Sir Bartholomew. He gallantly helped her over the bench and reached down the table for wine, which he poured into her waiting glass goblet. Eschiva had lived with Balian and Maria Zoë as a child and had known Sir Bartholomew since then. She had only come to *value* him, however, since her arrival in Tyre. When the Sultan had sent his bodyguard to escort Maria Zoë and Isabella out Jerusalem, she and her children had gone with them. It had all happened so fast and unexpectedly that no one had really been prepared for suddenly being refugees in Tyre. The ladies had been grateful when the knights who had escaped Hattin with Uncle Balian rallied around them and provided not just protection but a sense of household and support. No one had been more of a source of reassurance and comfort in those uncertain weeks before Uncle Balian joined them than Sir Bartholomew.

"Did you get the children settled, my lady?" Sir Bartholomew asked with a gentle smile, one that suggested he knew Eschiva bore the brunt of keeping the youngest members of the household happy. These, with the resilience of youth, were more excited by the prospect of Christmas treats and caroling on the morrow than worried by the continued siege and the repeated assaults on the city. The assaults took place far away on the eastern walls, after all—and only John, who had questioned his father mercilessly about it, seemed to understand the implications of the word "blockade."

"As best I could, sir," Eschiva answered, adding, "It's kind of you to ask."

"A grandfather's indulgence," Sir Bartholomew answered sadly, and Eschiva caught her breath. While the children might rejoice, Christmas was clearly having a melancholy effect on the adults. Evidently, Sir Bartholomew had been thinking of his own lost family on this high feast day. "If only I didn't know what the Arabs do to slave children," he added, confirming Eschiva's intuition.

It was now her turn to offer comfort. Summoning her own waning courage, she laid her hand on Sir Bartholomew's arm and declared firmly: "Hope is *not* lost, sir. The captain of that Norse snecka—that man over there—says that when he put in at Messina to take on water he heard that King William of Sicily is building a fleet to come to our aid. Furthermore, King William had personally sent messengers to his father-in-law of England, demanding a vigorous response. We need only hold out until next summer, and we are bound to be reinforced by the finest knights in Christendom."

"You do well to remind me of it," Sir Bartholomew answered, before sighing deeply and admitting, "But all I can think about is that my grandchildren will not even hear the bells this Christmas, much less see the mummers and dance carols. Nor will they sup on stuffed goose, baked apples, and frumenty," he continued, waving in the direction of the platters being brought in from the kitchens. "Indeed, I can't be sure they will not go hungry. On this sacred day they may be burdened with labor while their stomachs growl from emptiness. It takes my appetite away," the old knight admitted, pushing his trencher away and sighing deeply.

Eschiva shuddered and was at a loss for words. She sympathized far too intensely to utter stupid protests or offer facile assurances that all would be put right. Even if they received help from the West, who was to say it would be sufficient to liberate the lost territories? And even if they retook Jerusalem, that did not ensure the restoration of the captives. These were now scattered across Syria and Egypt, the property of the men who had served in the Sultan's army but often held land as far away as Alexandria or Mosul. As for Sir Bartholomew's daughters, Eschiva knew that the damage had long since been done. They had by now been raped so often that even if they were treated kindly, they were effectively whores. Unpaid whores, she corrected herself, without even the dignity of wages.

"I'm sorry," Sir Barthomew pulled himself together. "I have no right to ruin your Christmas dinner."

"Yes, you do," Eschiva answered, meeting his sad eyes. "That is what this feast is about: the birth of the loving Christ who teaches us to share our burdens and give what comfort we can. I will pray for your daughters and their children tonight. I will beg Christ to reach out to them and all the children who have been taken from Him against their will. *We* cannot help them tonight or in the short term, but perhaps *He* can. I'm sure He will find a way to at least give them comfort."

Sibylla retired early, unable to tolerate either the happiness of others when she was herself so miserable—or the way Conrad was openly making love to her half-sister. It would have shocked her to hear that most people who remembered her at Isabella's age found Isabella's behavior nothing short of saintly in comparison with her own. Isabella kept her eyes down modestly when Conrad addressed her, and she blushed more than once at the remarks he whispered in her ear. She certainly could not be heard giggling, nor did she snuggle up against his thigh, or lure him under the mistletoe—all things that Sibylla had done frequently in the years after the death of Conrad's brother William but before her marriage to Guy de Lusignan.

Sibylla remembered none of that. She saw herself as a virtuous wife, suffering humiliation after humiliation at the hands of her hated brother-in-law—if the brother of a dead husband still rated the term. Furthermore, she was the reigning Queen of Jerusalem, but Conrad de Montferrat treated her hardly better than an unwanted guest, an impoverished widow perhaps, tolerated out of charity. Isabella, on the other hand, was waited on hand and foot, her merest whim read from her eyes before they could reach her lips. Her wine cup was never allowed to become even half empty, while her plate remained full to overflowing no matter how much she ate. Her every word was greeted with smiles, while her inane small talk was treated like brilliant repartee.

No, Sibylla couldn't take it a moment longer. She stood abruptly, but had to shove back her chair loudly before Conrad even noticed and reluctantly got to his feet. Slowly the rest of the room likewise noted that their Queen was standing, and resentfully also rose.

Sibylla spun about and stalked out to the solar. As the door clunked shut behind her, she heard Conrad urging everyone to sit and resume the feast. They didn't care in the slightest that their Queen had been snubbed and humiliated. They didn't care that she had just lost a baby—the heir Jerusalem so urgently needed. They were all a bunch of stupid pigs! Bursting into tears, Sibylla fled to the chamber Conrad had reluctantly put at her disposal, utterly alone in the world she had made for herself.

Shortly before midnight, the Bishop of Beirut withdrew to prepare Mass. The tables had been cleared earlier and now the flow of wine ceased altogether. The guests washed their hands in the offered finger bowls, and as the bells chimed, they filed out of the banquet hall and crossed the courtyard to the Cathedral.

Eschiva took Sir Bartholomew's elbow, and they stood side by side in the nave while the Mass was read almost inaudibly before the high altar. Eschiva did not need to hear the Mass. She was intent on saying prayers: first for Aimery's health and release, next for the safety of her children, and then for Sir Bartholomew's daughters and grandchildren.

As the Cathedral canons filed out at the end of Mass and the crowd slowly shuffled for the exit, Conrad de Montferrat grabbed Ibelin by the arm. "A word with you alone, my lord, if I might?"

Ibelin looked at the Marquis with raised eyebrows, but then gestured for Maria Zoë and Isabella to go ahead and nodded to Monferrat. The latter pulled him out a side door into the cloisters, abandoned at this hour and crisply cold.

"My lord," Montferrat opened formally, "I'm not sure if you realize just how precarious our situation is."

"How should I know? You've been miserly with information," Ibelin noted caustically with raised eyebrows.

"And you've made yourself scarce!" Conrad snapped back. Since the day of his arrival, Ibelin had not once sought an audience with Montferrat, nor had he offered his sword to the city.

"I'm a refugee like thousands of others," Ibelin replied with a shrug. "What else should I do but look to my family's welfare?"

"You might try to *assure* their welfare by assisting in the defense of this city!"

"By recognizing *you* as my overlord?" Ibelin inquired with a hint of mockery in his voice. "I may be a pauper, Montferrat, but I'm not a mercenary."

"You can't mean to say you recognize that brainless peahen as your Queen!" Montferrat fumed, gesturing vaguely in the direction of the apartment he had assigned to Sibylla.

"Sibylla of Jerusalem is a crowned and anointed queen," Ibelin answered soberly, before adding with an acid hiss, "She is also a duplicitous usurper. No, I don't serve Sibylla or her jackanapes husband—not anymore."

"Whom do you serve, then?"

"I try to serve Christ," Ibelin admitted, and any hint of arrogance that might have been implicit in the words was utterly negated by his tone. It was late, and Balian was feeling the hopelessness of his situation more intensely than ever.

Montferrat considered the man opposite him and weighed his words carefully. "Surely," he started cautiously, "you recognize the need to hold this city for Christ?"

"Yes, I do."

"Then help me!" Montferrat flung out his plea like an order.

"How?"

Montferrat dropped his voice, "Listen to me! I may have put on a feast tonight, but our reserves are almost at an end. If we can't break the blockade within a fortnight, we'll have to start shortening rations. I was prepared for the Sultan's army to return, but I never thought he'd cut off my lifeline to Cyprus! Christ knows, the Syrians are no seamen. And we've beaten the Egyptian fleet so often in the past, I never thought they could choke us like this. Now Tripoli has failed me, too! We've got to break the blockade—soon. That or overrun Salah ad-Din's camp and force him to lift his siege."

The latter was so obviously fantastical that Ibelin focused on the former. "Why don't you ask your friends the Pisans to help you out?"

"Have you taken a look at their ships?" Montferrat shot back. "Merchant-men, all of them!" he explained. "There's not a war galley among them. They have constructed makeshift hide screens on their skiffs to turn them into archery platforms, and using these they tried to capture one of the enemy galleys. They are not cowards, Ibelin, but in the end all they did was lose a dozen men."

Ibelin nodded. Ernoul, who frequented the harbor taverns, had told him about this incident. "So, what do you think *I* might do? I'm no sailor."

"I know, but there's no denying that you command the respect of the men from here—from Outremer. Certainly you have the loyalty of the men you brought from Jerusalem. They have been idle ever since they got here—"

"Hardly," Ibelin interrupted. "They all take their turn on watch—"

"Ha! I thought so!" Montferrat sounded triumphant. "You are keeping an eye on them."

Ibelin could not deny that and fell silent, unsure where this was going.

"Listen, we need to set a trap for the Sultan's ships. Lure them into a sense of complacency and then attack. If we could somehow convince them that there were riots in the town, perhaps? Or spread rumors that the rich are going to make a break for safety and then lower the chain across the harbor entrance? If we did that, maybe they could be lured into a position where we could attack them with small boats in confined waters, or at least lure them inside the range of our crossbowmen on the harbor walls."

Ibelin considered Montferrat with reluctant admiration. He was undoubt-edly cunning, and this plan was clever. "Let me think about it," he answered at length.

"What do you mean?" Montferrat asked tensely. "Will you help me or not?"

Ibelin paused long enough to see just how urgently Montferrat wanted his help, and then nodded. "I'll help you, but this plan is far from ripe. We need to refine it. I'll think about it and get back to you."

"Soon!" Montferrat insisted, already sounding more imperative than he had a moment earlier.

"Soon," Ibelin agreed, and then he nodded and took his leave.

Chapter 5

Tyre, December 26, 1187

ANY SHORTAGE OF WINE AND ALE was not yet noticeable in the narrow alleys behind the dockside warehouses. Here Christmas was still being celebrated in ways not sanctioned by the Church, and often in excess. The alleys, never particularly savory places at the best of times, smelled particularly foul—as many customers, unaccustomed to excess, had vomited into the gutters.

Four hooded men picked their footing carefully to avoid the puddles of piss and several unconscious drunks as they moved between the shabby buildings by the port. Detouring around one of the men lying in the gutter, one of the men collided with a pair of drunks coming the other way. The latter took instant umbrage and snarled, "Watch where you're going, dunce!"

The insult instantly drew steel, and for a moment naked blades flashed in the dim light filtering from the shuttered windows of the buildings lining the alleyway. But the companions of the men who'd drawn intervened to calm tempers, and each party went their separate ways.

Around the next corner, the four men reached the establishment they were looking for and slipped out of the crisp darkness of the winter night into the murky light of an overheated tavern. A fire was booming in a large fireplace, spilling smoke into the room, and the tables were lit by cheap tallow candles that also smoked badly. The smell of stale ale and spilled wine mixed with the fatty smell of candles, but the scents oozing from the kitchen were not displeasing. Furthermore, a hefty woman was diligently wiping off the tables with a wet cloth in an effort to keep things moderately clean. As harbor taverns went, this was one of the "better" places.

The four hooded men found a place at a vacant table and sat down warily, looking suspiciously at their surroundings—at least three of the four men did. The slightest and youngest of them, on the other hand, was obviously familiar with both his surroundings and the landlord. He raised his hand and waved for service, and the proprietor came over with a smile. "Where have you been keeping yourself, Ernoul, my lad? I've had customers asking for you."

"I've been busy," the squire answered with evident pride. "The Marquis asked me to sing at his Christmas feast."

"Pays better than my customers, eh? Better watch out, though—got competition these days." Then without further explanation the landlord moved on to business by asking, "So what are you and your friends drinking?"

"What wine do you have?" one of Ernoul's companions asked.

"Red and white," the tavern owner answered simply.

After a baffled moment of silence, one of the new customers asked pointedly, "From where?"

"Haven't a clue. Found it in a barrel in the warehouse out back. Didn't seem to have an owner, so I adopted it."

Silence greeted this announcement. It was too cheeky to be credible, but eloquently expressed the tavern-keeper's intention not to reveal the source of the wine he sold. The landlord put a point on his position by concluding, "it's your choice, sirs; you can drink it—or not."

"White," one of the men ordered, while two of the others opted for red and Ernoul ordered "the usual."

"Anything to eat?" the landlord asked next.

"What have you got?"

"Umbles and leek stew, or kidney pies."

The guests placed their orders and then leaned back to settle in—without, however, removing their hoods. The landlord brought their drinks and they tested them skeptically, only to be pleasantly surprised. They were speculating among themselves about the origin of the wine when another figure slipped into the tavern. The body hidden by the voluminous but filthy and tattered cloak was far too small for the garment, suggesting the latter had been made for someone else altogether. The newcomer approached the landlord, received a nod in reply, and then threw back the hood to reveal the long, braided hair of a girl. With a deep breath, the woman turned to face the tavern from the serving counter, and a moment later she lifted her head and began to sing. Her voice was so clear and beautiful it made every man in the room turn to stare at her, none faster than Ernoul.

This singer was not the usual tavern wench. She was neither buxom nor bold. Indeed, she kept her cloak clutched around her as she sang, revealing nothing but her face, while her eyes consciously avoided those of the customers by singing to the beams of the ceiling. The contours under the ragged cloak and the tiny, bird-like fingers that clutched it together suggested the girl was all skin and bones, with enormous eyes in a face too thin and triangular to be pretty.

After the initial surprise, most of the men returned to their respective conversations, but Ernoul could not tear his eyes away from the girl with the beautiful, melancholy voice—not even when a party of six other men loudly entered the tavern.

These men were clearly regular customers, and they called their orders to the landlord even before they settled at a table. Ernoul's companions immediately stood to approach them, but Ernoul was too entranced by the singer to move. The girl had finished singing and was going from table to table holding out a tin cup in the hope of contributions. Ernoul was appalled to see that most of the customers just shook their heads or pointedly turned away. He started frantically digging in his purse.

"Ernoul!" one of his companions called.

"Coming!" he answered, stepping over the bench while still digging with his fingers in the bottom of his purse.

Behind him, one of his companions addressed the newcomers: "Haakon Magnussen?"

The blond Norseman kicked over his stool and sprang to his feet in a fluid motion, his hand already reaching for his ax. But as he unfolded to his full height and realized the man opposite him was just as tall as he, his pose relaxed. A smile seeped across his weathered face, and he bowed his head slightly. "Monsieur d'Ibelin, we meet again."

"May we join you?"

"I don't believe I know your companions," the Norseman replied with a significant look at the two men flanking Ibelin, both of whom were broad-shouldered and wearing hauberks and swords.

"Sirs Bartholomew and Galvin, and the lad over there is my squire Ernoul."

"Ah, the boy with the golden voice. We need to teach him a few Norse drinking songs. Sit down." The Norse captain indicated empty stools at his own table.

While his lord and the knights sat down at the Norseman's table, Ernoul dropped every coin he had into the girl singer's battered cup, whispering in breathless enthusiasm as he did so, "You have the voice of an angel! What's your name?"

"Thank you, sir! Thank you!" The girl was bowing and clutching her cup to her chest as if afraid someone might take it from her or she might spill the contents. Her tone of voice and the look on her face could have been no more fervent if he had just saved her life. "God bless you, sir!"

"Ernoul, bring our mugs over here!"

"Your name, angel? Please!"

"Ernoul!"

"Coming, sir! Your name, angel?"

"Ernoul!"

Ernoul grabbed the mugs and hurried over to the other table, but he was looking over his shoulder at the girl singer. He thought he heard her say "Alys" but he didn't catch her last name.

As he joined his companions, his lord was saying in a low voice: "Last time we met, Master Magnussen, you boasted you could run the blockade again."

"That was no boast. I can run it anytime I want," Haakon Magnussen retorted.

"Then why stay here?"

"We came here to fight Saracens and regain the Holy Sepulcher, not run away!" The Norseman's words were seconded by his men, many of them thumping their fists on the table for emphasis.

"Then you would favor an attack on the Sultan's fleet?"

"One to ten?" Magnussen raised his eyebrows.

"Those are the usual odds here in Outremer, sometimes less, sometimes more. I've led charges often enough against cavalry ten times as strong. But of course, I know nothing about naval warfare."

"Obviously," Magnussen replied.

"Then I have my answer," Ibelin answered in a level tone as he started to get to his feet.

Magnussen clamped his hand on Ibelin's forearm and stopped him in mid-motion. "What does that mean?"

"The Marquis and I want to break the blockade. We thought if we could plant rumors in the enemy camp of growing disaffection and then simulate riots by the harbor, we might be able to lure the Sultan's ships closer. Salah ad-Din knows this city is most vulnerable from the sea, and he knows that if he could penetrate the harbor with his ships, our landward walls with their towers, moats, and barbicans would be worthless. If we could lure the Sultan's ships into the confined waters of the outer harbor and then strike them, we thought we might have a chance of destroying one or two. That would then reduce the odds to something more favorable, no?"

Magnussen snorted and gestured for Ibelin to sit down again. "And you say you don't understand naval warfare? But the outer harbor isn't good enough. There the Saracens could still bring their greater numbers to bear and force us onto the ledges. We need to lure them into the *inner* harbor, and that means dropping the chain."

It was Ibelin's turn to raise his eyebrows. "That sounds risky."

"It is—but nothing would be better designed to lure the enemy into a sense of complacency. Furthermore, if morale *were* to crack in the city, then people would try to flee by sea, and to do that the chain has to be lowered. Load a Pisan merchantman to the gills with ballast so it appears to be carrying hundreds of passengers, then have it demand the lowering of the chain. Ideally we would make it appear that they are violating orders from Montferrat, and panicked people would throw themselves into the water to try to swim to the ship. If the Saracens are smart, they'll ignore the bait and make a dash into the harbor—at least, one or two of them will. If they do that, we'll take them, clear their decks, and turn them against their former masters."

"You have enough men to do that?" Balian asked skeptically.

"Not enough men to man ships for a long voyage—but we don't need to have relief crews, just a fighting crew. I could man three galleys with my own men and volunteers."

"So, best case, we capture two additional galleys, and the odds become eight to three. Is that good enough to chase the blockaders away altogether in a second engagement?"

"Maybe."

"Are you willing to try?"

Magnussen looked around the table at his men. Most of them were nodding. One or two were clearly enthusiastic, but a couple of the others, led by a man of obvious experience, appeared to voice objections. Magnunsson switched to Norse and a short but lively discussion ensued. Ibelin had no choice but to wait with simulated calm. At last Magnunsson turned back to him and declared in French: "We'll do it—provided you and the Marquis provide the diversion and the Pisan bait."

"I'll see what we can do," Ibelin agreed, getting to his feet and holding out his hand.

Magnussen took it with a smile and closed his grip. "The usual odds, eh?"

"In the name of God and with His grace."

Tyre, December 31, 1187

Ernoul was no longer any good for fighting; his shoulder was too weak. So while Ibelin with his knights and men-at-arms took up positions at the main landward gate, ready to fight off any assault by the Sultan's troops, Ernoul stayed down by the harbor. His job, Ibelin told him, was to help create the impression of panic and chaos among the civilians, while Montferrat with the bulk of the garrison stealthily took up positions around the harbor walls and in the towers controlling the chain across the harbor mouth. Meanwhile, the Pisans and the Norse prepared to play their respective roles.

Ernoul was happy to foster the illusion of panic and found ready helpers among the tavern-keepers to whom he explained the plan. His main interest, however, was in finding Alys. She had to live down here somewhere, he told himself, probably among the refugees housed in the warehouses. Thus while going from tavern to tavern to explain the idea of creating the appearance of panic, he was also looking for Alys.

"We want to make it look like the rich have bought off the Pisans—"

"As they probably have!"

"—and the poor are trying to stop them. We want to have men shouting at each other! Brawling a little, even—"

"That shouldn't be hard!"

"—and it wouldn't hurt to have a hysterical woman or two. Do you know someone we could dress up as a wealthy merchant's wife who could act like she's trying to flee?"

"Oh, my Bess would love that role—I'll just have to be sure she doesn't really bolt!" the man laughed.

"She could have a daughter with her and be hysterical about what might happen to the poor girl—"

"Aw, don't need that. Bess will make a fuss about her own virtue—such as it is." He guffawed at his own joke.

"But it wouldn't hurt to have a younger girl with her. What about that girl who was singing here the other night?"

"Who? Oh, you mean Alys? No idea where she sleeps. Probably with whoever fed her last, eh?" The tavern-keeper laughed again at his own joke and Ernoul turned away, disgusted. He was sure Alys wasn't like that. You could tell just by looking at her.

As darkness fell, Montferrat ordered several bonfires lit in a square close behind the port. From beyond the walls, it would be impossible to tell the smoke wasn't from burning houses, and the ringing of bells added to the impression that fires had broken out. Meanwhile more and more people converged on the harbor, and an atmosphere of excitement hardly had to be simulated; the growing tension was so tangible even the dogs started barking frantically. Soon Ernoul couldn't decide how much of what was happening was play-acting and how much was real.

Two Pisan merchantmen lay alongside the quay and while some people tried to board, sailors fought them off, provoking outraged protests that grew in volume as the stars started to fade with the dawn. Then one of the wealthiest Genoese merchants made an appearance on the quay. He rode up on a brightly caparisoned palfrey and began loudly cursing the Pisans as traitors and cowards. While probably part of the script, this action was well designed to provoke fury among the Pisans, and soon genuine fighting broke out between Pisans and Genoese—an occurrence for which it generally took little excuse anyway.

By then the stars were bleached from the sky by the approaching sun, and the features of the people crowding the harbor began to emerge out of the retreating darkness. Ernoul at last located a figure that he thought might be Alys. A slight form in an oversized cloak was cowering near the doorway to one of the warehouses. Dodging the brawlers, Ernoul darted across the head of the harbor and plunged recklessly into the growing crowd of women and children collecting on the fringes of the fight. "Alys!" he called, craning his neck to look beyond the women nearest him. "Alys!"

Sure enough, the figure turned her face in his direction, and it was Alys. She was all frightened eyes in a pale face. "Alys!" Ernoul called again as he shoved his way through the other spectators until he was right before her. As he reached her, however, she seemed to shrink back and looked over her shoulder as if seeking a route of escape.

"Alys! Don't you recognize me? I'm Ernoul. The troubadour. We met five days ago at the Pig's Head!"

Suddenly her face lit up as she remembered his generous tip. "Oh! Yes!" But instantly it clouded again as she asked urgently, "What's happening? Has the Marquis surrendered? What is to become of the poor? We have no money for passage or ransom! We'll all be enslaved!"

"No, of course not. This is just a ruse!" Ernoul assured her with a dismissive gesture toward the brawl on the quay, where the Pisan ship was starting to cast off, while the Genoese merchant shouted insults from behind a row of Genoese archers with locked arms protecting him from shouting Pisan sailors.

Alys' expression dismissed Ernoul as mad, and she started to turn away. He caught her arm. "Seriously!" Ernoul had to shout to be heard. "Lord Balian and the Marquis—" His words were cut off by outraged shouting. Someone had started screaming hysterically: "They're lowering the chain! They're lowering the chain! The Pisans! They've bribed the men on the tower!"

Dozens of voices picked up the refrain: "They're lowering the chain! They're lowering the chain!" A stampede of desperate and furious young men surged past, shoving the women out of the way, causing many to stumble and stagger.

Alys was flung into Ernoul's open arms, and he enclosed her in them protectively, while around them the crowd became more agitated than ever.

Women were screaming, "Stop them! Stop them!" to encourage the men already rushing for the tower controlling the harbor chain. Yet other women had become completely hysterical, shrieking in terror, tearing their hair or falling on their knees in frantic prayer.

Alys struggled a little against Ernoul's embrace, but he stroked her bony shoulders, noting in shock that he could feel every vertebra in her back. He tried to soothe her. "Hush, hush! There's nothing to fear. I won't let anything happen to you!"

"Kill the bastards!" The call was one of anguish as others let out a collective groan of disbelief. By craning his neck (without loosening his hold on Alys), Ernoul could just barely see the Pisan merchantman surge forward as the harbor chain sank down into the depths and she was free to sail out.

The angry mob reached the foot of the tower and started hammering at the locked door. So many of them were screaming curses or vehemently promising murder that it took the crowd several minutes to realize that two and then three Saracen galleys were shooting into the harbor. When someone spotted them, the level of hysteria and volume of screaming increased feverishly.

The crowd started to run in the opposite direction. Some men howled in outrage and others screamed in terror. The people still at the head of the harbor began to flee up the streets away from the port to seek cover deeper inside the city, just as the first volley of arrows hissed off the ramparts and clattered on the decks of the Saracens.

Alys was so terrified she put her head down and closed her hands over her head as she sought to make herself as small as possible. Ernoul held her closer than ever, the feel of her bony hips against his own igniting an involuntary reaction from his loins even as his eyes were transfixed by the drama unfolding around him.

There were now five Saracen galleys inside the little harbor, but he was distracted from them by a flurry of shouting and pointing that drew his attention to the harbor chain, which was now being raised again. As he watched, the last Saracen recognized the danger and tried to back out, but failed to reverse direction fast enough.

An instant later, with the chain in place, the Norsemen let out a blood-curling shout, and their snecka shot out of its hiding place behind the breakwater and crashed in among the Saracens.

Ernoul had never seen anything like it. The Norsemen crowded the deck, their axes in their hands, their blond or ruddy hair flowing out from under their helmets. (They wore leather or scaled armor that ended at the base of their necks without chain-mail coifs.) As the Norsemen came alongside the first of the Saracen galleys, men poured over the side of their ship and leapt onto the oars of the Saracen galley. The Saracens at once started to pump or wave their oars to throw the Norsemen off, but the latter wrapped their legs around the oars and hauled themselves forward with their arms until they had reached the side of the ship. Here they hauled themselves up over the gunnel, screaming their war cries and wielding their axes. Gaping in wonder, Ernoul registered that the Norsemen must have practiced this maneuver hundreds of times, learning the hard way by being dunked repeatedly in freezing water—just as he had so often bitten the dust of the tiltyard. There was more than courage on display here: this was competence of the highest level.

While Ernoul admired the men crawling up the oars, the Norsemen on the other side of the ship had flung out a handful of grapples to snare another Saracen galley. They had hauled it beside their own ship and were now springing aboard. As the Norsemen thus took control of two Saracen ships at once, the archers concentrated on the remaining three, pumping so many volleys of arrows onto their decks that they were soon carpeted with corpses and blood.

At last, even the uninitiated of the population began to comprehend what was going on. Outrage was transformed into wild enthusiasm. Men who had been running away turned and surged back toward the quay, waving their weapons and shouting encouragement to the Norsemen. Ernoul heard voices shouting (more than singing) in unison: ". . . *We are alive, Salah ad-Din. We are alive and cannot die!*"

"They're singing my song!" he exclaimed excitedly. "Alys, they're singing my song!"

The Pisans, meanwhile, had launched their modified skiffs and were deftly weaving amidst the apparent chaos, firing their volleys of arrows directly into the oar-decks of the galleys from sea level. Once they were convinced sufficient damage had been done, they started to board three Saracen galleys that had not been taken by the Norsemen.

The Norsemen, in the meantime, had slaughtered the Egyptian crews. The bodies of the dead, dying, and wounded were unceremoniously flung into the harbor, and Norsemen took their places on the bloody oar-banks. Magnussen signaled emphatically for the chain to be lowered as he pointed his captured galley at the harbor entrance.

Along the quay people started cheering and singing in scattered groups: "*The day will come, when we will win! When we will take Jerusalem!*"

Even Alys risked lifting her head to see what was going on. To Ernoul's relief, she didn't let go of him as she did so, but clung all the more determinedly.

For a second time that morning, the chain sank below the waters of the harbor. By now, however, it was broad daylight, and the light of day revealed an inner harbor choked with corpses and slowly turning red.

The first of the captured Saracen galleys shot forward, propelled by oars manned by Norsemen. The second captured galley and the Norse snecka followed within minutes. Within another quarter-hour, the remaining three Saracen galleys had likewise been cleared of their original crews. These, now manned by Pisan sailors, turned to follow the Norsemen, determined not to be outdone in valor. Those left on land could only crane their necks or climb up the walls to see what was going on in the outer harbor.

Ernoul and Alys were not among them. They had no desire to join the crowds or see more slaughter. Instead, Ernoul took Alys by the hand and led her away from the noise, commotion, and violence. He wasn't sure where he was going, only that he wanted to take her away from all that, to someplace safe and quiet. Alys followed him unprotestingly, not sure why she trusted him. She just did.

Ibelin had barely three hundred men and just forty-six knights to hold the landward defenses. With that number he could not hope to man all three walls with their six towers and the barbican. Although his first instinct was to man the outer wall and retreat as and when necessary, Montferrat insisted that they abandon the barbican and first wall altogether in order to reinforce the deception. The lack of defenders on the barbican, Montferrat argued, would give the Saracens further "proof" that at least some of the population was trying to escape the siege by ship.

This, however, put Ibelin and his men in an uncomfortable situation. From the the second or middle wall, they could not see into the Saracen camp as well as from the first wall. Furthermore, leaving the massive modern barbican undefended went against Ibelin's instincts as a warrior.

From the walls on the eastern edge of the city, it was impossible to know what was happening at the harbor. Although they'd seen the fires and heard the church bells during the night, they knew these were part of the ruse. The first indication that Montferrat and Haakon Magnussen had been successful was a rider who galloped into the Saracen camp from the direction of the beaches south of the city. Soon there was a visible wave of growing agitation in the Saracen camp, and Ibelin thought (but couldn't be sure) that Salah ad-Din and his staff rode out of the camp heading for the beaches south of Tyre.

More riders and then a mass exodus of troops in the direction of the beach finally convinced Ibelin that some sort of sea battle must be raging outside the harbor, and that suggested that Haakon Magnussen had managed to break out with one or more ships.

Before he had a chance to send someone back to the harbor to find out what was happening, however, horns and shouting warned Ibelin of a Saracen attack on his own position. A very large force under the banners of al-Adil poured out of the camp toward the narrow causeway that separated the city of Tyre from the mainland. Cursing inwardly, Ibelin and his men could only watch helplessly as the enemy advanced up the causeway without meeting any resistance. No one manned the barbican to fire crossbow bolts at them, and they quickly realized the barbican was empty. Triumphant shouts marked the Saracen discovery, and a moment later they surged forward with new élan and confidence.

Although the barbican gates were locked and barred, the absence of defenders on the ramparts made it comparatively easy to scale the walls. Siege ladders were simply stood up against the walls, and men ran up the rungs like sailors hurrying to hand sail in a gale. Soon hundreds of men were spreading out along the top of the outer wall, pumping their arms in the air triumphantly and shouting "Allahu Akbar!"—as if they had already taken the whole town.

"Wait and see what happens next, laddies," Sir Galvin muttered in a low guttural French, heavily accented by his Scottish roots. His massive hand opened and closed on the thick handle of his battle-ax as he kept his eyes fixed on the enemy collecting jubilantly on the wall opposite.

Ibelin's gaze was fixed farther afield, to where a messenger was clearly being sent to fetch reinforcements from the troops that had flooded toward the shore. Al-Adil thought he'd discovered the city's door open, and he was sending word to his brother to forget whatever was happening at sea and come take the unprotected prize.

Meanwhile, however, the Saracens who had already taken possession of the barbican were using their siege ladders and the interior stairways to descend onto the bank behind the first wall facing the moat. Although the drawbridges were raised, it didn't take the enemy long to realize their siege ladders were long enough to bridge the moat. They lay these horizontally over the muddy water and started to cross their improvised bridges with careful steps.

"Should I take them out, sir?" Sir Roger Shoreham, commanding Ibelin's archers, asked eagerly. He was a superb commander of archers, and held a crossbow at the ready in his own arms.

Ibelin, however, shook his head without taking his eyes off the approaching enemy. "Let them think there's no one here a little bit longer. When we start firing, they'll abandon those precarious ladders and bring up something more substantial. The more of them we lure over now, the more we'll be able to slaughter in the killing ground," he indicated the narrow ledge at the base of the wall, "before they can bring up reinforcements."

"Aye, aye, my lord," Shoreham answered dutifully, but he looked dubiously over the edge of the ramparts and fingered his crossbow lovingly.

Around him the other knights and men-at-arms squirmed uneasily. It was against their instincts to let the enemy get any closer without any effort at self-defense.

Fortunately, the Saracens were concentrating so single-mindedly on crossing their precarious improvised bridges that they didn't see the many heads that popped out between the merlons as defenders unable to bear the suspense tried to see what was happening. Sir Galvin was starting to tap the stone flooring with the ball of his foot, and Sir Bartholomew was humming Ernoul's tune as if to school himself in patience, before Ibelin finally nodded and said to Shoreham, "Open fire."

Shoreham had been leaning his back against a merlon to disguise his presence. In a single motion he spun around to stand in the crenel, lifted the crossbow to his shoulder, and pulled the trigger, while shouting at the top of his lungs: "OPEN FIRE!"

Along the whole length of the middle wall and from the flanking towers, archers followed his example. The effect was devastating. The Saracens who had gained a foothold on the shelf below the wall were almost instantly slaughtered or wounded, while the men on the ladders lost their footing in their surprise and fell into the moat. The screams of the falling mingled with the groans, cries, and curses of the injured.

The attackers still on the far side of the moat reacted rapidly, however. They dived or ducked for cover and then started returning fire furiously.

Ibelin kept his attention focused on what was happening beyond the first wall, and saw a commotion there. In a short space of time, the inner wall was manned by Saracen archers, and now a fierce duel developed between the defenders, who had the advantage of height, and the attackers, who had the advantage of numbers. Although the Frankish archers at first seemed to be holding their own, Ibelin watched with a sense of déjà vu as a wagon rumbled up from the Sultan's camp and he recognized Saracen sappers. These were the men who had brought down the wall of Jerusalem and forced him to surrender. Now they were prepared to lay down broad bridges.

Indeed, it took them no more than an hour to get their bridges in place, protected by men with heavy rectangular shields and extra-heavy helmets.

Although Ibelin tried to set the bridges on fire with burning pitch, it was soon evident that the Saracen sappers had used green wood, possibly treated with some material to make them virtually fireproof. Without Greek fire (and Ibelin had none), he was helpless.

Once the bridges were in place, the Saracens rolled up a heavy battering ram and started hammering away at the northern gate of the middle wall. The battering ram itself was well protected by animal hides soaked in vinegar, and its deployment against the northern gate had been dictated by the wind direction. A strong northerly breeze came off the Mediterranean. This ensured that Ibelin's archers, shooting into the wind, could rarely hit their targets. Shoreham finally ordered them to stop trying in order to save ammunition.

The blows of the metal-tipped ram against the studded door were so powerful that they shook the wall from end to end and down to the foundations. Each blow vibrating under the feet of the defenders rattled their nerves a little more. Since they could do nothing to stop the battering ram, it was only a matter of time before the Saracens would break through into the middle line of defense. They had no choice but to pull back to the third and final line of defense: the city wall.

Ibelin could feel the glances from his knights and archers, and he could feel their increasing nervousness. Command, he reflected dispassionately, was mostly about timing. Timing and nerves. But this was a situation where they would gain nothing by delaying, he decided, and nodded once. "Pull back."

Because his instinct, once the decision was made, was to run for the safety of the next wall, he forced himself to wait almost immobile until the last of his men were safely across the rearward drawbridge. Only then did he duck down into the spiral staircase that led to the westward exit. Sirs Bartholomew and Galvin, waiting at the foot of the drawbridge, gave the order to start lifting it up as soon as the three of them broke for the main gate. As they entered the gate, the drawbridge crashed into place behind them. They started up the stairs, panting from the exertion of their dash.

The archers were already in position all along the length of the wall, and the knights were spaced out roughly ten feet apart. Ibelin settled down to wait as the sun crept up the sky and the hammering of the battering ram continued rhythmically. It was hard to judge the time of day, because the church bells had been silenced on Montferrat's orders. Nothing was to seem "normal" on this day, he had insisted.

Ibelin frequently looked over his shoulder at the city as he waited. It lay eerily still at his feet. He knew rationally that tens of thousands of people must be waiting anxiously inside its jumble of buildings both proud and humble.

Many, no doubt, were praying for a positive outcome to today's risky stratagem, but from here he could see nothing stirring, not even a stray cat. Straining his ears, he tried to hear the sound of fighting from the harbor, but all he heard was the waves on the north shore and the hammering of the battering ram. Sweat trickled down his face from his already soaked arming cap and drenched the armpits of his shirt under his chain mail.

Then, with a slow, crunching sound Ibelin would never forget, the door of the northern gate gave way and a cheer went up from the Saracens. Soon they could be seen rushing foolishly out of the shattered gate—to be instantly skewered by a dozen of Shoreham's archers.

"Well done!" Ibelin called over to Shoreham, and saw the Englishman nod, a subtle but unmistakable smile of pride on his face. It was good to see him smile, Balian reflected, after losing two of his sons in the defense of Jerusalem.

But too soon the Saracens had redeployed their bridges. Fortunately, the main gate to Tyre was a dogleg and the battering ram was too long to make the turn. Ibelin was impressed that the Saracen sappers didn't waste time trying to deploy it, apparently having judged by eye alone that it would be worthless. Instead, more siege ladders were brought forward and the Saracens flung these against the wall, as arrows and boiling pitch poured down on them from the ramparts overhead.

Sir Galvin was the first to note that the ladders were too short. This wall was about ten feet higher than the middle wall, which was twenty feet taller than the outer wall. The siege ladders that the Saracens flung against it all landed a good twelve feet or more short of the top. The gap was too great for a man to bridge, and when they tried to decrease the angle of tilt to reach higher, the ladders simply toppled over backwards, sending the men on them into the moat or to their deaths. "Got wee ladders just like your dicks!" Galvin shouted gleefully. "Too short to be any use!"

Around him the archers jeered at the enemy and the knights cheered Sir Galvin—until Ibelin called them to order. "Don't be fools! They've still got the sappers down there!"

The young knights who had been with Ibelin in Jerusalem sobered at once and looked fearfully over the battlements, but Sir Galvin, who had not, scoffed. "What good are some bloody moles? The water will fill any hole they try to dig. They'll all drown like the rats they are!"

Ibelin raised his eyebrows eloquently, but inwardly he wondered if he was losing his nerve. Maybe Sir Galvin was right. Jerusalem, after all, was in semi-arid country, and you had to dig deep to reach water. Here the water lay close to the surface, and any attempt to dig might indeed only end in the tunnels flooding. Maybe. He cautiously peered out between two merlons to try to see what the sappers were up to at the foot of the wall. An instant later a well-aimed arrow sliced across the top of his shoulder, singeing him.

He dropped down instantly, grabbing his left shoulder with his right hand, and was shocked to see blood glistening on the palm of his leather mitten. At this range, Saracen arrows were usually harmless.

Sir Bartholomew was beside him, waddling forward on his haunches to keep below the rim of the wall. "How bad is it?"

"Nothing serious."

Sir Bartholomew ignored his words and conducted his own inspection of the broken links in Ibelin's chain mail that were oozing blood. "That was no Saracen arrow. Someone down there has a crossbow! Traitor!"

"Maybe. Maybe some Turk has learned how to use one of the many they've captured in the last six months. One crossbow won't defeat us. The sappers might."

"I'll get something to stanch the bleeding."

Ibelin supposed he ought to say "no" and scoff off the need for any assistance, but the pain was surprisingly sharp, as if his bone had been nicked. Damn it! He didn't need this.

Shoreham was beside him with a water skin. "Here," he offered the still-cool water laced with just a hint of wine. While Ibelin drank, Shoreham called over his shoulder: "Fetch my lord's squire and tell him to bring wine and bandages!"

The few squires who had survived Hattin and Jerusalem had been deployed at the narrow arrow slits in the flanking towers rather than on the wall walk. These positions offered the most protection, and firing from the arrow slits required less skill. Ibelin thought of countermanding Shoreham and telling him to leave Georgios at his station, but he felt strangely lamed. He leaned his head back against the wall and closed his eyes for a moment.

With his eyes shut he seemed to hear more acutely. Men were shouting, cursing, and praying as they variously loaded their bows, took aim, or fired. Men also panted from exertion as they wound their crossbows to the ready or drew them taut with the stirrup. Farther away the Saracens were also shouting orders, curses, encouragements, and threats. And beyond all that was the wind and the waves. A gale seemed to be blowing up. Balian wondered how that would affect the naval engagement.

Georgios thumped down beside him, a concerned expression on his face. "My lord?"

"It's nothing serious," Ibelin answered, forcing himself to smile.

"It's the sappers, my lord!" Georgios answered, even as he untied the cord

of Ibelin's aventail and slipped a quilted square of cotton into place over his
bleeding upper arm. Ibelin gasped in pain as the squire pressed down briefly
on his wound to stanch the bleeding. Then, gritting his teeth, he asked, "What
about the sappers?"

"They're using pickaxes to hack away at the wall right at the base. We can
see what they're doing, but we can only reach them from one or two of the
windows. They're well protected, of course, with shields. If we could sortie
out—"

"No!" Was that the pain speaking? Or the fact that the last sortie in Jerusalem
had been so disastrous? Was he completely losing his nerve?

"But, my lord, if we don't—"

"Georgios! Listen! We *will* sortie out," Ibelin told him firmly, "but not until
there are enough of us to make a difference. That is not you and a score of other
squires! Where's Sir Galvin?"

"Here, my lord." The big Scotsman sank down on his heels to be at Balian's
level.

"We need to get word to my lord of Montferrat that we are at risk. We've
held half of Salah ad-Din's army for half a day now, but we need reinforcements.
I don't know what's happening at the port, but unless he is fighting with every
last man to hold it from being overrun, he needs to spare us everything he can.
Tell him that."

"Yes, my lord."

"And tell him the sappers are chipping away at the inner line of defense."

"Yes, my lord."

Ibelin nodded. "Go now."

"Yes, my lord."

"My lord!"

Balian reeled as he realized he'd passed out and was being shaken awake. His
head felt as heavy as a mace, and he could hardly tear his eyes open. He managed
to crack them enough to see light, but then they fell shut again.

"My lord!" The voice was right in his ear. He could feel and smell the
man's breath, but he couldn't recognize the voice. "That arrow was probably
poisoned!" The man was already getting an arm under his shoulder and knees.
"We need to get you to a surgeon *now!*"

Ibelin's eyes rolled back in his head, and he lost consciousness again as
Godwin lifted him in his arms and clattered down from the battlements.

Tyre, January 3, 1188

"He's coming to, my lady!"

Balian struggled to open his eyes, frowning unconsciously at the effort. He sensed and smelled his wife before he saw her. She leaned over him, kneeling on the edge of the bed in a waft of lavender. "Balian?"

"What happened?"

"Someone tried to assassinate you, my love," she answered steadily. "But we think we managed to drain off enough of the poison."

"Your lady is being modest, my lord," Sir Bartholomew's baritone rang out. "She sucked it out of the wound herself."

"Every Comnena is taught how to deal with poison," she brushed it off.

"Which didn't make it less risky," Eschiva pointed out, coming to stand beside Maria Zoë, her eyes seeking reassurance that her uncle was indeed lucid.

"I assure you," Maria Zoë insisted, "I was *not* at risk. Sucking blood is simply unpleasant; I'm sure half my reaction was just nerves."

"She was so ill, we feared we would lose you both," Eschiva corrected firmly.

Balian looked up at his wife with increased admiration. She was no longer what one would call a stunning beauty. Her facial skin was starting to sag and her waist had thickened, but she was still attractive and, more important, intelligent and intensely loyal. She was—even penniless—his greatest asset. She was what God intended woman to be when he took a rib from Adam's side and gave him not a slave but a helpmate. He reached for her hand and she took it, smiling with relief. With each moment, however, he was regaining lucidity, and his thoughts went at once to where he had been when he lost consciousness. "The sappers—"

"Montferrat slaughtered them," Sir Bartholomew told him with evident satisfaction. "Along with three thousand or more of the enemy as he drove them all the way back to their camp."

"What were our casualties?" Balian asked next.

"Very light. I don't know the exact number of those with Montferrat, but of our men we lost only one knight, Sir Anthony, no squires, and three archers."

"What about wounded?" Balian pressed him.

"Aside from you, my lord, nothing that couldn't be patched up easily."

"Sip this carefully," Maria Zoë urged as she put a silver chalice to his lips.

Balian took a sip and immediately protested irritably, "That tastes terrible!"

"It will calm your stomach," his wife answered reasonably.

"My stomach isn't upset," he countered.

"But it will be, if you try to get up too fast."

Balian didn't answer directly, but he asked querulously, "What happened at the port? Did Magnussen succeed in breaking out?"

"He did more than that, my lord!" Ernoul moved into his line of sight, looking rather disheveled, for he'd been keeping a vigil along with Sir Bartholomew, Maria Zoë, and Eschiva. Excitedly, he related the outcome of the ruse and ensuing naval battle. "He and the Pisans between them managed to take five of the Saracen ships after they'd entered the inner harbor. Then they chased the others so hotly that the crews preferred to beach their own ships rather than face Magnussen's men! They scrambled ashore to save their lives, while swarms of Saracen horsemen rushed down to the shore's edge, threatening to stop our men from coming ashore and taking the ships, but the Norsmen and Pisan landed anyway. Quite a melee ensued!"

"That was when our messenger got through to Montferrat," Sir Bartholomew continued, "and he called off his men to come to our aid. They sortied out of the main gate and drove the astonished Saracens all the way back to their camp!" The old knight felt understandably smug about this outcome.

"But the best part is," Maria Zoë took up the narrative, "the next day Salah ad-Din dispersed his army. They just packed up their tents, loaded their camels, and plodded away with their tails between their legs."

"Seriously?" Balian couldn't believe his ears.

"Yes!" his wife, squire, niece, and knight assured him in unison, and he let his eyes sweep across them one after another, seeking the slightest indication of embarrassment suggesting deceit. Yet they were all beaming at him.

"The siege has been completely lifted," Bartholomew declared. "We've sent patrols as far as twenty miles inland without running into any enemy. Reginald de Sidon has taken command at Belfort as well and holds it for Christ. Perhaps more important, two of the Pisan ships sailed for Cyprus to spread the word that it was safe to send supplies again. Meanwhile, we've sent out foragers. The Saracens have picked the immediate vicinity clean, but we found some stray cattle."

"And some of the refugees have moved outside the walls, too," Eschiva told him, "preferring tents to the squalid conditions down by the port."

"My lord of Montferrat has won a great victory," Balian concluded.

"Not Montferrat alone!" Maria Zoë protested loyally. "You played your part."

Balian smiled cynically. "Do you honestly think he's likely to mention it?"

"Does it matter? We know what you did. And our enemies know your worth as well."

"What do you mean?"

"The Saracens wouldn't bother trying to assassinate someone inconsequential. That poisoned bolt was meant for you and you alone." Maria Zoë met his eyes as she spoke.

"You're sure it was meant for me?"

"Olafsen collected the spent arrows and conducted a very thorough investigation. There was not one other crossbow bolt anywhere. Only one was shot, and it was shot at you with a poisoned tip. That's convincing evidence to me," Maria Zoë replied firmly.

Balian had to concede mentally that she was right, but he was not yet sure what to make of it. Usually, only kings were the target of assassins. . . .

Chapter 6

Tyre, March 1188

"I CAN HANDLE HIM! I CAN handle him!" John insisted furiously.

It was a beautiful, sunny day, and Balian was taking a patrol into the surrounding countryside for forage and reconnaissance. John had asked not only to come along, but to ride Balian's aging destrier, Centurion.

The request wasn't completely unreasonable. There had been no sign of the enemy since January. Many refugees had moved outside the walls of Tyre and were gradually building a substantial (if indefensible) town of adobe, wood, and stone on the mainland. Ibelin, meanwhile, had fenced off pasture for his horses and was trying to keep them and his knights fit and trained. They had a riding ring for training the young horses, a tiltyard to hone their own skills, and an archery range for the archers. John came out with the men every day and had ridden Centurion in the ring many times.

With the loss of their land, neither Ibelin nor Maria Zoë had any income, but they still had substantial expenses. Maria Zoë had cleverly exploited the insecurity of the ruling despot of Cyprus (a distant relative who styled himself "Emperor of Cyprus" and claimed to represent the "legitimate" Emperor against the usurper in Constantinople) to sell her coronation crown at an enormous price. Her crown had come from the Imperial treasury in Constantinople, was Greek in style, and had been part of her dowry. Sibylla, naturally, had been crowned with the traditional Latin crown of Jerusalem, and Maria Zoë had retained possession of her crown—until she sold it to Isaac Comnenus.

The proceeds of this sale would keep the whole household clothed, fed, and equipped for at least six months, but Balian had been quick to point out that she had only one crown to sell. Maria Zoë countered that she next planned to sell to the Cypriot "Emperor" her jewel-studded coronation robes for his wife or daughter. But the sale of his wife's jewels could never be more than a stopgap, and Ibelin was obsessed with finding a sustainable means of maintaining his family and household. He placed his hopes in his horses.

Trained destriers often cost a knight's annual income, even in the West. Good destriers commanded an even higher price in Outremer, because many horses failed to survive the rigors of sea travel or the climate and conditions once they arrived. As a result, many a rich and powerful nobleman—and many more knights—found themselves without a mount in Outremer. A knight or noble without a horse was worthless. New arrivals had been known to pay half a fortune for little better than a broken-down nag.

There had been a steady stream of promises of help from the West, and some early recruits, like Haakon Magnussen, had already trickled in, but Ibelin hoped that when the Mediterranean opened again for long-range traffic, the trickle would become a flood. If he could have several first-rate destriers ready for sale, he calculated, the combined proceeds from Maria Zoë's jewels and his horses would to get them through a full year or more. After that, it was a matter of breeding and training more colts indefinitely.

The barony of Ibelin had had a good stud, and Shoreham and Maria Zoë between them had rescued the bulk of the brood mares and some of the older colts. Although they had lost some of the older stallions and mares and the youngest foals (those not able to travel at the pace or distance required), they had the makings of a good herd.

That said, Ibelin had lost his younger destrier, and he and all his knights had lost their palfreys at Hattin, so they were themselves very short of horses. The bulk of his grooms had preferred to continue to Tripoli and Antioch, so Ibelin, his knights, and their squires had to do the training themselves. Not all of them were suited to the task.

With Ibelin concentrating on training two promising three-year-old colts, exercising Centurion had fallen to the eager John. Balian had been pleased to discover that John not only loved horses, but was a natural rider. He seemed glued to the saddle (once he managed to get into it), and he had rapidly developed a rapport with the old warhorse, who (Balian swore inwardly) was more docile and calm for John than ever he had been for Balian.

Still, Centurion had always been prone to shying when confronted with something unexpected or new. The first time he'd seen the sea almost a decade earlier, he'd nearly killed both Balian and himself in his panicked about-face and bolt across the dunes near Ibelin. Furthermore, this was a reconnaissance patrol, and there was always the risk of running into the enemy. With the weather improving, Salah ad-Din, too, might feel it was time to resume the offensive. For a start, Salah ad-Din was known to be besieging Belfort Castle, which still held out under Reginald de Sidon.

"The only way to find out if John can handle Centurion in open country is to try," Eskinder suggested (unhelpfully, from Balian's perspective).

Balian snapped back, "It was because Ernoul couldn't handle Thor that I was late to the rendezvous at Le Fevre, which led to the massacre at the springs of Cresson, which in turn led to—"

"The fall of the Kingdom, no doubt," Sir Bartholomew interrupted with a wink at John. "We know. It was all Ernoul's fault. But now there's no kingdom left to lose. Let John come along. The sooner he learns about reconnaissance, the better."

"We can bring him home at the first sign of trouble," Sir Galvin chimed in.

"Please, my lord!" John pleaded earnestly, using the formal "my lord" as he always did in front of his father's knights, and stroking Centurion's neck.

There was no point threatening punishment if something went wrong. If something went wrong it would bring a catastrophe worse than any punishment. Fearing that he was losing his nerve and turning into an old woman, Ibelin reluctantly agreed.

John beamed at him and scrambled up on the mounting block to fling himself into the saddle. Ibelin signaled for Eskinder to bring him one of the colts he was training, and within minutes they were riding out onto the road, a party almost fifty strong. They wore hauberks but no chausses, and although they rode with their coifs over their heads, their helmets hung from their pommels. They were not expecting trouble, but they were prepared for it.

They rapidly left behind the large, flat apron around Tyre, still scarred by the perimeter ditches and improvised mud walls of the Sultan's army. The entire area was littered with discarded equipment and broken weapons. It had been a trampled morass throughout January, but it was now sprouting grass, a testimony to how rapidly the land recovered on this fertile, coastal plain.

As they turned onto the road leading north to Sidon, Beirut, and Tripoli, the footing became harder, enabling the company to take up a trot. John rode between his father and Sir Bartholomew. Centurion, used to leading, snapped irritably when the younger horse edged a little ahead of him. The young stallion flattened his ears and snapped back, causing Centurion to squeal and swing his haunches for a kick.

"Get your horse back under control!" Ibelin ordered his son sharply, "Or I'll send you right back to the stables!"

"But—" John started to protest, then he clamped his mouth shut. Still glaring at his father, he bent and told Centurion: "Behave yourself, or we'll both be sent home!"

The knights around them laughed, but Ibelin did so ruefully. He'd always talked to Centurion, too.

"The outer town is growing up very fast," remarked one of the younger knights, looking over his shoulder at the improvised city spreading north along the coast.

"I've heard some of the refugees who first continued to Tripoli have returned," another knight reported. "They prefer to live out here where they have more space and can plant kitchen gardens. They figure if Salah ad-Din returns, they'll still have time to get back inside Tyre."

Ibelin reflected inwardly that all that depended on how suddenly and stealthily the enemy attacked. But that was not his problem, he told himself, turning his attention to the countryside around them. It was green from the winter rains and already going wild—although some men had found plows and draft horses and were starting to till the coastal plain all the way to the banks of the Litani. It was good, fertile soil—just as at Ibelin, Balian reflected—but it was very late for planting, and success would depend on late rains.

At this thought he searched the skies, and registered that rain might indeed be in the offing. It was certainly worth trying to farm, he reflected. While the land belonged to the Archbishop of Tyre and the men tilling it would owe him rent, the prices they would command with their harvest—if they had one—would more than compensate them.

Ibelin was so distracted by the men attempting to cultivate the soil so late in the season that Sir Galvin saw them first. With a grunt of alarm he called out, "Riders! Coming down the Litani from the east!"

"And wearing armor!" Sir Bartholomew added, seeing the glint of sun on steel.

Sir Galvin was already reaching for his helmet, while Ibelin cursed inwardly. He'd known better than to bring John. His instincts had been right. He had to start trusting them again. Aloud he only barked, "John, go back!"

"But, my lord—"

Ibelin backhanded his son so hard that the boy reeled in the saddle and came up with a bleeding nose.

"Back, now!" Ibelin ordered a second time.

Resentfully John turned a reluctant Centurion around, so angry that he kicked and jerked unnecessarily.

Meanwhile the other knights donned their helmets and Sir Galvin reported, "Twenty to thirty is my guess."

"They've got a banner. Can you decipher it?" Sir Bartholomew asked the younger knight, while Ibelin shaded his eyes and tried to answer the same question.

"The shape is not Saracen," Ibelin decided out loud. "The banner is Frankish—but that might be a ruse, of course."

"Or they may be knights from Belfort," Sir Bartholomew suggested cautiously. "They're coming from the right direction."

"They would have had to ride through Salah ad-Din's army to get here. . . ."

Ibelin reached for his own helmet and pulled it on, making it fast before declaring: "Let's go find out."

They picked up a canter, leaving a dejected John struggling to keep Centurion from following.

The riders coming toward them had evidently seen and recognized Ibelin's troop, for they too took up a canter. The two parties of horsemen closed at a good rate, and Ibelin soon distinguished the banner of Sidon. The armor of the riders was likewise Frankish, yet it wasn't until he could see their faces that Ibelin was fully convinced this was not a ruse.

Both parties drew up, and Ibelin was face to face with Reginald de Sidon. He had known Sidon all his life. Sidon and his elder brother Hugh had been friends, and Sidon had married his brother's widow. Sidon was roughly twenty years older than Balian, and fast approaching sixty. He had been one of a handful of knights, and the only other baron, to break out with Tripoli early in the Battle of Hattin. He had gone to Tyre, but he had been badly demoralized, and it had been rumored (although Ibelin had never been convinced) that he had intended to surrender the city. The arrival of Montferrat had, at all events, turned the tide. Sidon had left Tyre to defend his inland castle of Belfort, which lay on the border between the baronies of Sidon and Galilee. Ibelin had not seen him since.

The sight of the older man shocked him now. Ibelin knew he too had aged—he had white streaks in his hair, and his expression had hardened—but Reginald de Sidon looked like an old and broken man. He could hardly sit upright in his saddle, his shoulders hunched, and curiously he was not using his stirrups. Instead he let his feet hang loose. His hair had thinned so much that half his scalp was exposed, and his eyes were sunken in a colorless face with a scraggly red-grey beard.

"My lord of Sidon!" Ibelin exclaimed, in both salutation and shock.

"Ibelin! Thank God it's you!" Sidon choked out in a voice that was gravelly and breathy, as if he'd been shouting or drinking all night. "I beg your hospitality."

"What I have is yours, my lord, but I have almost nothing. My lord of Tripoli—"

"I don't think I can make it that far," Sidon gasped out. "I need—rest. Please!" He reached out a gnarled hand and laid it on Ibelin's arm.

The wrist, exposed because he had reached out, was raw and bleeding between new scabs formed over similar wounds. Ibelin stared at it and then lifted his eyes back to Sidon in a horrified question.

"He tortured me, Ibelin. Hung me from my wrists and put burning irons to the soles of my feet. I tried to bite my own tongue out rather than give in, but I—I broke. I ordered the surrender of Belfort."

"Salah ad-Din ordered this?" Ibelin asked, horrified.

"Yes, the 'chivalrous' Salah ad-Din himself," Sidon confirmed.

"But how did you fall into his hands?" Ibelin asked, still confused.

"He tricked me. Gave me a safe-conduct, and then broke it."

A shudder went down Balian's spine. He too had trusted in a safe-conduct from Salah ad-Din. This could have been him. Out loud he announced, "We'll get you back to Tyre and into the care of my lady and household. How many are with you?" He lifted his eyes to count the men riding with Sidon.

"There are just eighteen of us left. Most made for Tripoli and Antioch," Sidon explained.

A click woke Sidon from his doze, and his eyes snapped open to take in warm sunlight flooding through the thick, yellowish panes of glass set in the window. The room was small by castle standards but elegantly appointed, with glazed green and white tiles in a checkerboard pattern and green-trimmed wooden paneling on the walls. Best of all, the box bed built into the wall was soft and cozy.

Following the sound, Sidon saw a serving girl backing into the room carrying a tray. She was dressed neatly in a blue wool gown with a starched and bleached linen surcoat, while her hair was saucily braided with what looked like bright satin ribbons. They were a bit cheeky for a serving girl, he thought disapprovingly—until the girl turned around, and he realized it was Ibelin's eldest daughter Helvis.

He tried to right himself in his bed, combing at his hair with his fingers and pulling the sheets up to cover his skeletal body. "What are you doing carrying trays about, my child?" he asked as she advanced to set the tray down on the little table beside the bed.

"Mama says we're poor now and we all have to do our bit," Helvis answered firmly without a hint of shame or sorrow. "I don't mind helping," she added cheerfully. "Didn't Christ teach us to be humble? Would you like me to pour ale for you? Mama keeps the wine for afternoon and so there's only ale for breakfast. Well, the babies get milk, of course, and John still drinks it, too, but I hate milk. I prefer ale, or sometimes the cook presses oranges and lets me drink the juice. Or lemons with sugar, only we're all out of sugar. Daddy says we have to hope ships come from Cyprus with sugar when the storms are over."

Sidon let Helvis chatter away, completely content to listen to her prattle. She seemed so full of hope and optimism, despite her words, and it buoyed up his own spirits.

". . . and I really wanted to adopt her," Helvis was explaining with childish earnestness, "but Mama says she will not have a dog in this little house. She says I have to wait until we have a proper palace or castle again, but Daddy says we may never have a castle again. What do you think?" Helvis suddenly looked at him with her bright amber eyes. "Do you think we'll ever defeat Salah ad-Din and recapture Ibelin?"

Sidon was spared the need to answer by the arrival of Queen Maria Zoë, who swept into the room, having apparently caught some of what Helvis had been saying. "Helvis!" she called sharply. "You were told to see if my lord of Sidon wanted some breakfast, not to talk his ear off with your idle chatter! My lord, I beg your forgiveness. Helvis—"

"Has been a delight, my lady!" Sidon assured the child's mother. "She has brightened up my morning and made me want to face the world again. You and Lord Balian must be very proud to have such a bright, cheerful, and devout daughter. "

His words made Helvis blush and look down, embarrassed. Maria Zoë gave her eldest child a startled look, but then smiled and inclined her head to Sidon. "If she was not getting on your nerves . . .?"

"Not at all," Sidon assured her.

"And you are feeling better this morning?"

"Very much, thanks to you and your lord's kindness. The salve you had for my feet enabled me to sleep for the first time since I was tortured. The pain tormented me so much this past week that at night I could do nothing but thrash about in agony."

The floorboards creaked and Ibelin loomed up behind Maria Zoë. Maria Zoë looked over her shoulder at him and reported, "My lord of Sidon is feeling better for a good night's sleep."

"And your daughter's cheerful wakening," Sidon added, smiling again at Helvis.

Ibelin entered the room, giving his eldest girl a rueful smile. He had always harbored secret fears that God would mark her in some way because she had been conceived in sin before Maria Zoë and he had received the sacrament of marriage. But God seemed to love her best in some ways, blessing her with an even temperament and innate optimism. She was the most obedient of his children, her younger sister Margaret being prone to temper tantrums and the two boys being, well, boys: generally rambunctious, mischievous, and occasionally defiant. She was physically timid, too, afraid even now of horses, but she was self-confident and precocious when it came to household tasks and book learning. This had led him to believe she might prefer a life in the Church. Without a dowry for her, however, it would be hard to find a convent willing to take her. Her best prospects lay with the Hospital, but Ibelin was reluctant to let her join an order that was so much at the forefront of the struggle. He could not—or did not want to—picture Helvis dealing with hundreds of mutilated and dying men in a city under siege. . . .

For the moment he said only, with a smile to his daughter, "I'm glad she could cheer you. She's good girl."

"You may go now, Helvis," her mother told her pointedly. Helvis bobbed a quick little curtsy to Sidon before darting out the door, embarrassed by so much praise.

As the door clunked shut behind her, Ibelin turned his attention from his daughter to his fellow baron. "When you're well enough, I'd be interested in talking to you about Salah ad-Din. Your men say you were a guest in his camp almost a week before seeking to return to Belfort and triggering the arrest and torture."

"I'm well enough to talk now," Sidon assured him, sitting up even straighter and indicating a chair.

Both Maria Zoë and Balian accepted his invitation and sat down, Maria Zoë on a chest by the door and Balian on a chair by the bed.

"What may interest you most," Sidon opened without further prodding, "is that Salah ad-Din is attended only by his own slaves and his brother al-Adil. Most of his emirs have dispersed, and I overheard remarks that suggested Salah ad-Din was annoyed and disgusted with what he felt was a lack of zeal on the part of his subjects. 'They think the war is over just because we hold Jerusalem,' he scoffed, adding, 'Until we have driven the last enemy of Allah into the sea, we have not finished the task He has set us!' To which his brother answered, 'And who failed to take Tyre?' Then they noticed I had entered the room and instantly dropped the conversation."

"Do you think he is driven by religious zeal, or greed?"

"Both. He sees our presence as an insult to Islam, but he also wants control of the remaining ports—and Antioch—for the income and prestige they would bring him. He will certainly try to take Tripoli, which he sees as much weaker than Antioch."

"And Tyre?"

Sidon frowned. "He burned his fingers here once already, and would rather focus on other targets first. If he can wipe out every other Frankish city and enclave, then, he thinks, Tyre will fall like a ripe fruit into his hands. So for now he'd rather concentrate on Antioch and Tripoli. He even restored half of Sidon to me—not Belfort, of course, but he had his scribes draw up a grant that granted me Sidon as my *iqta*."

"As a ploy to get you to surrender Belfort?" Ibelin asked, confused.

"No, after he'd tortured me. When I cracked and ordered my garrison to surrender, he had me cut down and taken back to his camp. There he visited me and announced that he felt guilty about breaking his word to me. He asked me to forgive him, and I said something rude. Then he offered me half my barony back, if I would accept it as an *iqta* with him as my overlord."

"Did you accept?" Ibelin asked.

Sidon shrugged. "What did I have to lose? Half from him who holds it is better than everything from a man who should never have been King in the first place, and is now himself a prisoner."

"You swore an oath to Salah ad-Din?" Ibelin pressed him.

"I did, for half of Sidon—but after what he did to me, I don't trust him. Still, for as long as it suits him, I may be able to hold the city and surrounding lands. We could settle some of the refugees there, maybe. . . ." His voice trailed off as he awaited the judgment of his peer.

Ibelin was torn. Taking an oath of fealty to the man who had destroyed the Kingdom seemed treasonous. But wouldn't he have done it for Ibelin? He might well have—to have something to give his children. The bitterness he felt at having nothing for them was laid bare when he answered acidly, "So, the only baron of Jerusalem who may hold a handful of land is a man without heirs to give it to. No doubt Salah ad-Din thought of that *too*, when he made the grant."

"No doubt," Sidon agreed steadily, his eyes fixed on the younger man and seeing deeper than was comfortable, "but he may have miscalculated. I am a widower. I could marry again, and I'm not impotent *yet.*"

"You can have your pick of every maid and widow still in freedom. As the only man with any property, you will be much sought after," Ibelin noted bitterly.

"True," Sidon agreed, "but in the circumstances, I can't afford to marry for fancy. I need a girl who brings me fighting men likely to help me retain that precarious—fiefdom."

"Fighting men clog this city."

"And who commands them?"

"Montferrat."

"Funny. It wasn't Montferrat that found me, was it?"

"Don't be deceived, Reginald," Ibelin warned. "The men with me are men with nowhere else to go, loyal out of habit."

"There are no better men then that—except the men who command such loyalty. Do you think I'm blind and deaf? Tripoli and I broke out of Hattin, but we failed to open a breach large enough for any infantry to follow. What fighting men are here, are largely men who survived because of your breakout, not mine. They know that."

"That's very true, Balian," Maria Zoë seconded Sidon before her husband could, in modesty, deny the claim. Then she asked Sidon pointedly, "Where is this leading? What are you suggesting?"

"That a marriage to your daughter Helvis, Madame, would be the best means of uniting the few resources left to us and possibly securing the future of both our houses."

Maria Zoë had already guessed what Sidon was thinking, and was not disinclined in principle, but she noted practically and firmly, "Helvis is not yet ten."

"And I don't yet control the coast or city of Sidon. We can make the marriage contingent on me actually taking control. This is about an alliance to secure your husband's support in taking it." He glanced at Ibelin, who appeared lost in thought.

"I will not allow my daughter to marry before she is fourteen," Maria Zoë told him firmly, "whether you control Sidon or not."

"Fair enough," Sidon conceded, "but give me a chance in the meantime to convince her that marriage to an old man need not be a terrible fate."

Ibelin took a deep breath, and Sidon and Maria Zoë looked to him expectantly. The way Balian saw it, although Sidon did not control his fief, his chances of doing so eventually were significantly greater than his own prospects of regaining Ibelin. It also made sense for the two barons of Jerusalem still in freedom to join forces and work together—a partnership that need not be, but was not harmed by, a marital alliance. As for Helvis, it was an advantage that she was too young to have formed affections for someone else. If she knew her fate sooner rather than later, she was more likely to accept it. "What you propose makes sense, Reginald. Let us plan on it, and, God willing, it will be so."

Aleppo, May 1188

"Tell me about Ibn Barzan," Imad ad-Din remarked casually, gesturing for his guest, Humphrey de Toron, to help himself to the delicacies spread on the table before him. They were seated cross-legged before a beautifully carved table inlaid with ivory. They were made comfortable by thick cushions and cooled by fans worked by two slave boys standing behind them.

"My wife's stepfather?" Humphrey asked uneasily. It wasn't that he didn't know whom Imad ad-Din was asking about, or that he was uncomfortable talking about his fellow barons. Imad ad-Din and he had discussed the hated Reynald de Châtillon and both of the Lusignans at length. He had even told Imad ad-Din everything he knew about Reginald de Sidon during Salah ad-Din's siege of Belfort. But Ibelin was different. Isabella loved her stepfather, and part of Humphrey still craved his approval. After all, Ibelin wasn't a brute like Châtillon; he *should* have understood Humphrey better. That he didn't increased the intensity of Humphrey's confused feelings. Part of him wanted Ibelin's respect, but another part of him wanted revenge for Ibelin's contempt. He wanted to prove to Ibelin, more than to anyone else on earth, that he wasn't a weakling or a fool. But he didn't know how to do that.

Sensing his reluctance to talk about this particular topic, Imad ad-Din deftly changed the subject. "The Sultan has decided to release the Templar Grand Master."

That grabbed Humphrey's attention. He started so violently that he spilled some of the lemon-water he was drinking. He looked hard at Imad ad-Din as he asked, "Why?"

Imad ad-Din shrugged and tried to appear casual as he reported, "The Sultan offered him his freedom if he would deliver the castle of Darum."

"As an exchange?" Humphrey asked, flabbergasted. "The castle for his freedom? But that is against the Templar Rule!" he protested, remembering how Master Odo de St. Amand had refused a prisoner exchange for his freedom. St. Amand had declared that a Templar could not be ransomed in flesh any more than in gold—much less for the betrayal of one of the last strongholds in the Holy Land still in Christian hands!

Imad ad-Din shrugged. "Don't your Templars swear absolute obedience to their Master?" Humphrey nodded. "Well, Ridefort ordered the garrison of Darum to lay down their arms and surrender the castle to the Sultan, so they did."

"But—but—" Humphrey could not grasp it. Darum was strategically vital, lying across the caravan route from Egypt to Damascus. It was inconceivable to him that a Templar—any Templar—would consider his own freedom more important than the defense of the Holy Land. Such a trade was in violation of their entire ethos, their very purpose for existence. He had long hated Ridefort, but this seemed the ultimate act of perfidy and cowardice both. "How could he?" Humphrey burst out helplessly.

Imad ad-Din shrugged. "How am I supposed to understand the actions of your religious fanatics? They are not rational and so not comprehensible. I only know that the garrison at Darum laid down their arms and marched out. We have put our own soldiers in it, and so we now control the entire coast from Alexandria to Tyre." He sounded smug even to Humphrey, who liked to think of him as a friend. Humphrey was spared further discomfort by the unexpected arrival of an old eunuch.

The man burst into the room so abruptly that Imad ad-Din scowled and opened his mouth to rebuke the slave, but the slave had already flung himself at his master's feet and gasped out: "If you wish to see the daughter of Ayyub alive, you must come to her at once, Master. For the women say she will surely not last much longer."

The expression on Imad ad-Din's face changed instantly. All anger vanished, replaced with shock. "But she is young and healthy!" he protested.

"She was two days ago when she started her ordeal, but she is also very thin and fragile. The child will not come, and her strength, the women tell me, has been bled away until she can fight no more."

Humphrey wished himself at the other end of the earth, conscious that no half-stranger (as he was) had the right to witness this intimate moment.

Imad ad-Din was in shock, and various emotions seemed to be warring in his breast, reflected by a tortured expression on his old and usually serene face. "Little Aisha!" Humphrey heard him gasp out, and tears flooded his fading eyes. Then he frowned and his expression became fierce. "No!" he shouted. "NO! I don't believe it! I won't accept it! Send for my sister, the wife of Moussad, at once! She will know what to do better than the stupid geese here!"

Beatrice prayed to God for forgiveness as she brought the filthy linens to the laundry for the umpteenth time. Some part of her Christian soul knew she ought to feel pity for a fourteen-year-old struggling to bring her baby into the world, but Aisha had been too heartless and selfish a mistress for Beatrice to feel anything but satisfaction. Imad ad-Din's other wives were all older women, women he had married in his youth, women who had borne him several children and were each in their own way both weary and wise. Not one of them had been *kind* to Beatrice, but they had not been *cruel*, either. They recognized that she was a slave because of misfortune beyond her control. For them it was simply the will of Allah that she had to accept, no less than they did.

Aisha, on the other hand, had come to the household after the death of Imad ad-Din's second wife. At thirteen she was still very young, but she had rapidly recognized that her sixty-something husband was smitten with her. He had lavished gifts on her, unable to deny her any wish, and neglected his other wives in his eagerness to savor her charms. The knowledge that she was the master's favorite rapidly went to her head. She relished showing the other wives that she could get whatever she wanted, while they were rebuked for their "greed" and "covetousness" if they asked for the smallest thing. She ate in front of them the ice and figs they had been denied, and she laughed and stuck out her tongue when the First Wife tried to rebuke her.

To the slaves she had been even worse, of course. No one ever pleased her, and she threw temper tantrums that included not only throwing things at whoever offended her, but also scratching their skin with her excessively long nails or spitting on them. She had taken particular pleasure in mocking Beatrice, calling her "my lady slut" and "my lady whore," asking how many men it had been the night of her capture. Was it three or four, or maybe even a dozen or a score? What had it been like having so many different men inside her, one after the other? Had she been able to climax for them all? Her questions had been so shocking that the First Wife had intervened, chiding Aisha for immodesty and sending Beatrice away to spare her further indignity. But Aisha had pursued the game whenever the others were out of hearing.

Beatrice straightened and put her hands to the small of her aching back. "Christ forgive me," she muttered, "but I hope she *dies*, and her little Muslim brat with her!" With a sigh she reached for the clean linens, stacked neatly on shelves outside the laundry. She had stacked them there herself after taking them down from the line this morning and folding them exactly as instructed. (When she first came, she had often been slapped or kicked for doing things the Frankish way.) As she took the clean sheets, she was reminded of the effort that went into making them so—something she had not appreciated in her former life. Clean linens had simply been her right as a lady, and laundresses were an almost unseen part of the household. They were generally widows or other poor women who were allowed to sleep in a dormitory and eat at the bottom of the table in exchange for keeping clean the underclothes, bedclothes, and table-cloths of their lord, his family, and his retainers.

But just this morning she had stood for hours over a cauldron full of boiling water, stirring the clothes as the steam drenched her in sweat and scalded her hands. The lye soap stank and stung, and the smell of it up close almost choked her. The skin of her hands was permanently red and rough from exposure to the damp heat and lye steam. She avoided looking at them now, because they made her sad. Once, she had loved her long-fingered hands, adorned with rings. . . .

Entering the long, dingy corridor between the laundry courtyard and the harem, she was startled when the delivery door suddenly crashed open and people poured inside. They were chattering Arabic much too fast for her to understand it (although her command of the language had improved from the rudimentary Arabic of her former life to serviceable Arabic now). An elderly woman was removing her veils, now that she was inside, and handing them off to the woman behind her as she questioned the eunuch leading her toward the harem. She was dressed in very rich robes decorated with strands of gold, Beatrice noted with wistful envy. Most notable, her tone of voice was commanding; she was obviously a First Wife in some important man's household, Beatrice concluded.

The next instant, Beatrice was distracted by the realization that the woman trailing her, who had also removed her veils, was blond! More than that, she looked familiar. "Jesus God and all his saints! Constance!" she called out in utter amazement.

The woman spun about, startled, and then let out a cry of recognition so piercing it stopped her mistress and the eunuch in their tracks. They turned back angrily and saw the two Frankish slaves fall into each other arms. A moment later they were chattering in French, oblivious—and utterly indifferent—to the disapproval of the others.

"Beatrice! Beatrice!" the newcomer gasped, clinging to her. "I never thought I would see you again! Oh, sister! What of your children?"

Beatrice clung to her younger sister as tears streamed down her face. "Don't ask. Let us instead be thankful for this moment."

Constance was crying, too. Her heart-rending wails came from the depths of her being as she folded her head upon her sister's breast and sobbed like a little child. She did not see the look of astonishment on her mistress' face, much less hear the sharp question from the eunuch demanding an explanation.

"She is my sister," Beatrice told him, meeting his glare firmly. "You may flog me till I die, if you like, or kick me till my guts spill out my mouth, but you will not stop me from holding my own sister!"

"Leave them!" Constance's mistress snapped. "We have more important things to do!" She swept on in to see to her sister-in-law, leaving the Christian slaves alone in the hall.

Tyre, July 1188

"My lord," Ernoul started earnestly. He was dressed in his best, scrubbed down and newly shaved. He had evidently been lying in wait for Ibelin to return from training (an activity Ernoul no longer engaged in).

Ibelin was sweaty and dusty from the tiltyard, and annoyed because the colt he had been training had been in an ornery and stubborn mood. He had been ready to kill it for dog meat—if he hadn't been so desperate to sell it for a profit to some unsuspecting newcomer. Then again, he couldn't afford to get a bad reputation. . . . "What is it, Ernoul?" His tone reflected his mood: irritable and impatient to wash up.

Ernoul was usually sensitive to people's moods, but he'd been waiting too long and was too wound up. "My lord, I—I want your permission to marry."

"Marry? You are a penniless squire, who stands to inherit nothing, and won't ever again lift a sword in jest or anger. The very food you eat at my table is charity! You are in no position to marry, and that's an end of it."

"Yes, my lord, I understand, but Alys—my wife, I mean my wife if you'd let me marry her—would help out. She'd earn the keep for both of us, I promise."

"Alys, did you say?" Sir Galvin had come in behind Ibelin with the other knights of the household. "That little dockside whore?"

"She's not a whore!" Ernoul protested vehemently. "Just because she sings in taverns doesn't mean she sleeps with customers!"

"She's sleeping with you, isn't she?" Sir Galvin noted with a little smirk that was more approving than the reverse, but Ernoul sprang forward and thrust his knee at Sir Galvin's groin. It was a defensive tactic he had learned in taverns since he'd lost the strength in his shoulder and arm. Sir Galvin, although taken by surprise, was fast enough to avoid the full impact of the blow, and lifted his fist to strike back.

Ibelin stopped him with a hard blow to his chest from his own balled fist. "Enough! Both of you! You're in my house, not a tavern! Begone, Sir Galvin, and mind your own business!"

Sir Galvin shrugged and stalked away. He felt unjustly rebuked, since Ernoul had attacked him, but he reminded himself that he was in Outremer to do penance for killing a man in a drunken brawl. Part of that penance undoubtedly entailed suffering moments like this. . . .

Ernoul remained standing before Balian, his face red with indignation and his eyes blazing with pent-up anger.

"Is it the singer?"

"She's not a whore!"

"We don't need another singer in this household, Ernoul," Ibelin told him flatly, adding ominously, "I can't afford the one I have."

"She would make herself useful! I promise you, my lord! And if I don't marry her, my lord, she'll—she'll starve. I swear it, my lord." Ernoul's face was flushed not with anger so much as the sheer intensity of his emotions. Balian was reminded of Gabriel, who had also flushed bright red when he was agitated about something. Christ, of the five youths he'd trained to knighthood, he'd lost one at Hattin and three in Jerusalem. Ernoul had always been the least promising of the lot. He should have gone into the Church. Balian sighed and shook his head in regret for all the young men who had been so hopelessly lost this past year. Then, dodging the decision, he told Ernoul, "You'll have to put your case to my lady. She runs this household, and I will not impose anyone on her." Then he continued on his way to the courtyard to wash himself down.

By chance, Maria Zoë caught a glimpse of the couple from her window. She had told Ernoul that she would make no decision without meeting his intended bride, and Ernoul had promised to bring her for an interview the following morning. Maria Zoë had risen early as she always did, had heard Mass with Balian at the little Church of St. Helena around the corner, and then they had broken their fast with the household before the knights headed for the tiltyard and paddock. Maria Zoë then checked on the nursery (run efficiently by Eschiva aided by Eloise) and the classroom (where Fathers Antonius and Michael were less effectively in command) before retiring to her bedchamber to go over the household accounts. Isabella usually joined her there, doing needlework or reading. Conrad de Montferrat had loaned her a beautifully illuminated copy of Chrétien de Troyes' *Erec et Enide*, and she could not seem to put it down.

Maria Zoë had paused to look over Isabella's shoulder when a barking dog drew her attention to the street. That was when she saw them. The girl was hanging back, and then balked altogether, shaking her head from side to side. Ernoul was pleading with her, but she just kept shaking her head. Then she dropped her face in her hands and broke into tears. Although the couple was on the far side of the street, her sobs were so violent that Maria Zoë could see her bony shoulders shaking, and when Ernoul put his arms around her protective and comforting it melted Maria Zoë's heart.

"Isabella!" She turned to her daughter.

"Mama?" The teenager looked up, frowning in annoyance at the interruption.

"Tell Helvis to go down and tell Ernoul that I don't have time to see him right now. She must tell him to wait at St. Helena's until I send for them. Then come back and help me change."

"Can't—"

"Isabella!"

"Yes, Mama."

The Church of St. Helena was very small and very poor, but it had once been richer, and it was still adorned with a beautiful mosaic that depicted St. Helena discovering the True Cross. At this time of day, between Prime and Terce, it was quite empty. The priest had gone to get himself a bite to eat at a nearby cook shop.

"Ernoul, I *can't* face her!" Alys tried to explain. Although she spoke only in a breathy whisper, the acoustics of the church betrayed her, and she could be heard clearly throughout. "Look at me! I've no stockings at all, and my feet are bursting out of my shoes. My skirt's ragged at the hem and has patches at the knee from when I fell and tore it during the siege. My surcoat is stained, and I stink of sweat and grease and spilled ale. How can I face a *queen*? I can't!"

"But you want to marry me, don't you?" Ernoul tried to reason with her. "You want to escape the taverns and the other men."

"Of course, I do! Oh, Ernoul!" She laid her head on his shoulder and clung to his hand. "Isn't there any other way? Couldn't you take service with someone else?"

The couple took no note of a widow in black, her veils completely covering her face, who came in to light a candle and then say some prayers.

"Who would take a squire with a worthless shoulder? I can't raise a sword, or even look after highstrung horses anymore."

"But you can sing! We can both sing! Couldn't you go to the lord of Montferrat and ask to be employed as his minstrels? We could sing every night in his hall."

"No! I can't!" Ernoul retorted angrily. "I owe fealty to my lord of Ibelin! I'm not some hired workman! I'm a squire, his liegeman, his vassal." Worlds were clashing; Alys came from a class that did not live by oaths of fealty, it worked for wages.

"Well, then, couldn't we make a living together some other way? I know how to make soaps that smell sweet, and I can shave and trim hair. If we just had a shop of our own—"

"Where are we to get the money for rent? And what am I to do while you cut other men's hair?" Ernoul snapped back, his voice raised in his mounting anger.

"Children! Have you no more respect for a house of God than to bicker like this? You are so loud, you drown out everyone else's thoughts and prayers!" the widow admonished, getting up from her prayers and turning toward Ernoul and Alys.

Ernoul gasped, because he had recognized Maria Zoë's voice, but Alys only thought he was ashamed of being publicly rebuked.

"Forgive us, Madame!" Alys hastened to defuse the situation. "Please!" She held her hands with the palms pressed together as in prayer. "We meant no disrespect. I swear it."

"I see that you did not, child, but I'm *not* so sure about your *gallant* here. Leave us, young man! I wish to speak to your maiden alone."

The word maiden brought a flush to Alys' face, and she was on the brink of protesting when Ernoul said, "If you can talk sense to her, Madame, then I will gladly leave her to you. She will not listen to me, though I have only her best interests at heart and love her more than life itself."

"Just leave us alone." The widow gestured imperatively for him to go.

Only after the heavy wooden door of the church clunked shut behind Ernoul did the widow address Alys again. "So, from what I heard—quite against my wishes—you want to marry that young man—though I can't see why you would want such a puny youth with a twisted back—"

"He doesn't have a twisted back!" Alys rushed to Ernoul's defense. "He was wounded at Hattin! A Saracen crushed his shoulder and collarbone! But that doesn't make him worthless! He sings like an angel and he can compose poetry and lyrics—"

The widow waved her silent. "Be that as it may, he apparently has no means to support you, so marriage is out of the question."

"Oh, no, Madame! Please don't say that!" Alys was on the brink of tears again. "There *has* to be a way!"

"Why? If that particular young man can't support you, then find another. This town is overflowing with young men!"

"But you don't understand, Madame!" Alys pleaded. "My dad and my brothers, all three of them, they never came home from Hattin! My mother was always poorly, and the flight from Acre did her in. She died last fall. I found an apprenticeship for my little sister with a silk-maker, but she wouldn't take me. Said I was too old to learn a new trade."

"How old are you?"

"Sixteen, Madame."

"And what trade did you learn?"

"My dad was a saddler, Madame, and my mum's dad was a barber. She taught me to cut hair and make soaps, sweet-smelling soap and saddle soap.

I helped clean the stirrup straps and the underside of the saddles. My mum and me, we did the needlework on the cloth my dad stretched over the seat, pommel, and cantle of his saddles. I'm good with a needle, Madame; I could do lovely designs with lions and stags. Things gentlemen like on their saddles."

"Did you look for work with a saddler here?"

"Of course, Madame—but just like my mum and me, their wives and daughters do the needlework. They sent me away."

"How, then, have you earned your daily bread?"

Alys looked down at her hands and said almost inaudibly. "I sing."

"I see. Where?"

Alys didn't answer at first, but then she looked up and declared almost defiantly, "In taverns, Madame. But it's not what you think!"

"What do I think?"

"That I'm a whore! That's what they all think! Except Ernoul. He's the only one who understands that I *don't* want that! It's just the only—the only way I could earn enough to pay for a bed and bread. If you knew how many times I'd gone hungry because I wouldn't—wouldn't *do* it. Some men buy you a meal and then just expect it of you, but the worst ones set the meal in front of you and then don't let you take a bite until you've kissed them and—and—they've had you!" There was a bitterness in her words that chilled Maria Zoë to the bone. The expression of repulsion and hatred on Alys' face told her that she had paid that price for a meal more than once, but the almost skeletal thinness of her arms spoke of how often she had refused.

"And does your young man know—about the times you had to earn your dinner with more than a song?" she asked softly.

"I—I don't know." Alys' voice was so soft it was almost inaudible. "I've told him I don't want to do it. I've told him how hard it is to earn enough by just singing. He saw me all beat up once because a customer wanted me to pay my meal that way and I refused. But, you know, I think he must know that I couldn't always—that I sometimes didn't have the strength. . . ."

They were silent for what seemed like a long time, and noises from the street filtered in: a cart on the cobbles, a dog barking, a man offering to grind knives, and a man selling fresh lemons.

Maria Zoë was lost in thought. She was thinking that she had probably never sat beside a whore before, but she did not feel defiled. Indeed, she had far more sympathy with Alys than with Queen Sibylla. Surely, in the eyes of God, a woman's motives, and her alternatives, must be considered. Christ had set the example by forgiving—not stoning—the woman taken in adultery. "If you married your young man, would you sleep with any other?" She asked.

"Of course not! Why should I?" Alys protested—then, realizing she was speaking to a widow, she added, "Unless I was widowed and wed again, of course."

"But what if your young man cannot earn much of a living and you are both poor. Wouldn't you be tempted to supplement your income?"

"Just because we're poor? No, of course not! My dad was a good saddler, Madame, but we were seven, and there never seemed to be any extra. Most people would have called us poor. I can stand being *poor*. But—have you ever been *hungry*, Madame? Really hungry? So hungry it feels like the walls of your stomach are sticking together? I never knew what hunger was until this winter. . . ."

They fell silent again, and then the Maria Zoë nodded and sighed before declaring pointedly, "You are as much a victim of Hattin as your young man— and all the dead and captives. This is Guy de Lusignan's doing—and Sibylla's for making him King in the first place!" The bitterness in her voice took Alys by surprise—as did the criticism of people so exalted. Where she came from, you begged God's blessings on the King and Queen, rather than blaming them for fate.

Before Alys had recovered from her amazement, the widow announced: "So. I am going to take a chance with you, Alys. I will tell my lord husband to give his permission to Ernoul to take you to wife, and my daughter and I will see that you have something decent to wear for the occasion—and thereafter," she added, with a smile Alys could hear even though her face was still veiled. Still she couldn't make sense of what the widow had said.

"Do you know Ernoul, my lady?" Alys asked.

Maria Zoë flung back the veils to reveal her face as she nodded and announced, "I am Queen Maria Zoë Comnena, Lady of Ibelin, and you have nothing more to fear—provided you keep your word and are a dutiful and faithful wife to our Ernoul."

Alys was so overwhelmed she almost fell over backward in her haste to get up from the bench and drop to her knees. As her knees hit the floor, she started kissing Maria Zoë's hands and babbling, "Thank you, Madame—I mean, my lady—I mean—you will never regret it. I swear it, my lady!"

Maria Zoë helped her back to her feet with a smile. The essense of woman could not be defined by her sexual activity alone, she told herself, and everyone deserved a second chance.

Chapter 7

Aleppo, May 1188

ACCORDING TO THE LINES SCRATCHED ON the wall beside his pallet, Aimery de Lusignan had been in the dungeon of Aleppo nine months and eleven days. That was more than three times as long as his last imprisonment, but the presence of the other lords had helped both pass the time and ease his inner terror, while the thought of Eschiva and the children gave him a powerful incentive for living. The little girls were still babies, but Hugh had been a rambunctious four-year-old when he left home. He wanted to see them all again—especially Eschiva.

Aimery was certain that his wife Eschiva loved him. Not the way Sibylla loved Guy, with an unseemly and blind sexual passion, but with dignity and loyalty and reason. If they were ever reunited, Aimery promised Christ for the thousandth time, he would never again betray her in adultery. He closed his eyes as he swore this, and imagined Eschiva's face smiling in greeting, relief, and thanks.

"Aimery! Aimery! Have you gone deaf? The Commandant has sent for you!"

His eyes flew open and he saw the moldy bricks of the arch over his head. Then he rolled on his side and struggled to his feet. He was stiff and weak from too much lying on the stone floor, with only the thin straw pallet between him and the damp. He was still wearing the clothes he'd been wearing at Hattin, though he'd removed the chain-mail parts for greater comfort. The shirt and braies were saturated with sweat and other bodily fluids discharged over the last nine months, while the surcoat was so filthy that his arms were no longer readily identifiable.

He made his way forward slowly on his stocking feet, both because his body was stiff and because he was wary of what their jailers might want of him. The closer he got to the door, the more he had to screw up his face against the unaccustomed light streaming in from beyond the dungeon. Not that this was the brightness of day: it was only the corridor leading out of the dungeon. Nevertheless, it had windows at the far end, and these were so bright that Aimery could not look at them directly.

The guards at the door grabbed Aimery by the arms to hurry him along as soon as he came abreast of them. They were talking in Arabic, but Aimery had never learned more than a few words and phrases of the language. He certainly could not understand the flood of words that broke over him now, but he didn't like the tone of it. The guards shoved him forward, not harshly but impatiently. They prodded him in the back as if afraid of a rebuke if they took too long. Aimery did not think he had any reason to want to hurry, but hanging back would clearly earn him only blows or kicks.

He scrunched up his eyes against the increasing light and his breath became short from the unaccustomed exertion as he was half led, half dragged along corridors, through halls and eventually up a stairway until they abruptly stopped before a guarded door. The guards opened it at a bark from Aimery's escort, and he was thrust into the room. Here, to his utter amazement, he found himself standing opposite his younger brother.

Guy de Lusignan looked much better than Aimery. He was clean-shaven, for a start, his shimmering blond hair was neatly trimmed, and he wore a beautifully woven kaftan with stripes of green. Furthermore, although the chamber was simply appointed, it was lit and aired by two windows, which provided welcome cross-ventilation in the Syrian heat. The tiled floor was scrubbed and cool, and on the simple wooden table under one window stood a bowl of pomegranates and figs.

"Aimery!" Guy exclaimed as his brother came to an amazed stop just inside the door. "You look horrible. And you stink."

"What do you expect after nine months in a dungeon?" Aimery snarled back.

"You don't have to be aggressive," Guy reproved. "It's not my fault you were in the dungeon."

Aimery took a breath to remind his arrogant younger brother that it was very *much* his fault that *any* of them were in a dungeon, but he was too weary of this fight. He just sighed and asked, "So, you sent for me?"

"Yes. I have very important news to share, and need to talk things over where the others can't hear us. But you *really* stink." Guy's face was twisted with revulsion. "And—are those *lice* in your hair?" he asked, drawing back in horror.

"Very likely," Aimery agreed, scratching his head; the mere mention of the insects made his scalp itch.

"Henri!" Guy called out in the direction of the door to the adjacent chamber. "Henri!"

"Your grace." Henri d'Ibelin appeared in the wooden doorframe between the two rooms of the King's suite and bowed his head.

"Call the guards. Tell them I can't speak with a man in this state. Have them take my brother down for a bath and shave, and tell them to find him some clean clothes. Really, this is unacceptable!" His tone was more petulant than commanding, but Aimery narrowed his eyes. His brother was acting like a man in a position to give orders, and that had not been the case the last time they'd met.

Henri, who spoke Arabic very well, opened the door and addressed the guards waiting outside. Aimery watched their reaction alertly. One bowed deeply and the other ran off, apparently to seek guidance from an officer. Aimery could detect no particular surprise at his brother's request. He looked back at his brother. "What's happened?"

"I'll tell you as soon as I can stand to be within three feet of you," Guy answered, withdrawing a little farther. Then, softening his insult with a little crooked smile, he added, "All I will tell you now is that it is good news. Very good news, in fact."

"For you, or for all of us?" Aimery asked skeptically. He had never met another "king" who thought so singularly of himself alone. When he remembered how King Baldwin had tortured himself in his suffocating mask, dragging his rotting body around in the heat and the sand for the sake of his subjects, the contrast between the selfless leper and his selfish brother made him want to weep—or vomit.

"You'll see!" Guy countered with a self-satisfied smile, leaving Aimery no choice but to gratefully accept the bath and change of clothes.

The bath was very thorough. Aimery was taken to a bathhouse outside the citadel but only a stone's throw away from it, and turned over to the professional attendants. These men made no faces at his appearance or smell—but they made him strip naked in a small courtyard, doused him in cold water, and then scrubbed him down with horsehair brushes and sea sponges before letting him into the actual baths. After he'd been allowed to lie in the steam room for a half-hour to sweat out even more of the dirt, they soaped him down again, scraped the suds and dirt off him, and oiled him. Then he was given a loose cotton kaftan and cheap, new sandals, before being led to a barber who removed his beard and most of his hair. Feeling better for the bath but naked in the kaftan that billowed around him and let the hot breeze tease the bare body underneath, he was taken back to the citadel and his brother's tower suite.

"Ah," Guy greeted him, "that's much better. Now come sit here at the table and share the fruit and bread. No wine, I'm afraid, but soon."

"Meaning?" Aimery asked, as he cautiously sank onto the wooden chair opposite his brother. The table and chair were of Frankish manufacture—probably captured somewhere, Aimery noted mentally. They had evidently been brought to furnish the King of Jerusalem's prison tower as a courtesy. They enabled him to sit upright at meals in the Frankish fashion, rather than lounge at a low table like their jailers.

"Meaning," Guy answered, beaming with pride, "I have secured our release!"

"*Our* release?" Aimery pressed him, afraid to rejoice too soon. He could not overcome his mistrust and resentment of a brother who had never once protested the conditions in which his fellow prisoners were kept.

"The Sultan has generously agreed that I may take ten other captives with me. That's what I wanted to consult you about. Which of the others should I pick?"

"Slow down," Aimery urged. "You are to be set free? Just like that? Was a ransom paid? By whom? How could Hugh come up with a king's ransom?" His brain had started racing once the news penetrated his defenses.

"No ransom at all," Guy replied smugly. "Don't you remember? The Sultan promised to set me free if I talked the garrison of Ascalon into surrendering—and then broke his promise."

"As I recall," Aimery remarked carefully, "you *suggested* surrender to the garrison if they had no reason to expect relief in the short term, but you did not flat-out order them to surrender the town."

"That was because I wasn't sure they would obey me. I thought by giving them an excuse to say no, I wouldn't expose my own weakness."

Aimery raised his eyebrows, surprised, but relieved that his brother at least *recognized* that he did not command much respect among his subjects. Out loud he merely remarked, "Evidently the Sultan was not impressed by your sincerity."

Guy shrugged. "No matter. Sibylla has been bombarding him with letters accusing him of dishonor for not keeping his word, so he has offered to release me, in exchange for an oath to quit the Holy Land and never take up arms against Islam again."

"That's all?" Aimery asked, flabbergasted.

Guy beamed and opened his arms in a gesture of openness. "That's all!"

"And have you? Taken the oath, I mean?"

"Not yet. We'll have to go by way of Damascus, and I've already been told a priest will be in attendance. But then, Salah ad-Din has promised, we will be escorted to Tripoli."

Aimery was still trying to absorb the implications of all this. His brother was prepared to renounce his kingdom and sail away to the West. At first that seemed mind-boggling. Then again, since there was only one city of the Kingdom left, maybe, in practical terms, Guy was not sacrificing very much. But how on earth would Sibylla react? It was *her* kingdom, after all. Then again, she was so selfishly enamored of Guy that she would probably follow him anywhere. A woman stupid enough to choose voluntary imprisonment would surely run off to the West without a second thought. But what about the others? The barons and bishops born and raised here? And what about the tens of thousands of settlers? The latter certainly didn't have wealthy brothers back in France to whom they could return. And what about the Holy Land itself? Were they going to just turn their backs on Jerusalem, Bethlehem, Nazareth, and all the other holy places? What about the native Christian population, whose oppression under Muslim rule a hundred years ago had ignited Pope Urban's pity and sparked his appeal to liberate them? Were they all to be abandoned?

As he sat there in the citadel of Aleppo, facing the prospect of freedom only on the condition of abandoning the Kingdom he had adopted fifteen years earlier, Aimery was astonished to realize that he did not *want* to return to France. He was *not* willing to turn his back on the Holy Land. He *wanted* to fight for it. "Will we all be expected to swear the same oath?" Aimery asked anxiously.

Guy looked surprised by the question and answered indifferently, "The Sultan's letter didn't mention anything about that. I shouldn't think so."

Aimery smiled cynically. He supposed that in his brother's mind, the rest of them were so unimportant that their oaths were superfluous. Very likely, Aimery reflected, the Sultan shared the same view. What danger were men without land, without vassals, without tenants or the means to pay mercenaries? What danger were men who could hardly afford to buy a warhorse or new arms to replace those forfeited at surrender?

Aimery was beginning to see the logic behind the Sultan's apparently generous offer. Salah ad-Din probably calculated that the bulk of his prisoners could not raise a ransom, since he now controlled their lands, so there was little point in continuing to hold them. He either had to kill them, which would have been dishonorable and against Sharia law, enslave them, or set them free. While enslaving them was within his right, he appeared to have sufficient respect for his former opponents as noblemen not to exercise this option. For that Aimery was intensely grateful. He was even grateful for the Sultan's presumption of his inability to cause him trouble. The Sultan clearly thought he had won so completely that he could afford to be generous. But by the grace of God and in the name of the Father, the Son, and the Holy Ghost, Aimery swore to himself, we will show him he is wrong!

His brother, meanwhile, was cutting into a pomegranate and prying it open over a glazed pottery plate. With his thumb he started to break the ruby-red kernels out of the leathery skin as he explained to his brother, "I've been given just two days to decide whom to take with me, and I'm only allowed to take ten other prisoners, but there are eighteen prisoners of note. Oh, and I'm taking Henri, so there's really only nine others I can take. You, of course, and the Bishop of Lydda. Then I was thinking of Caesarea, and the poor old Marquis de Montferrat." The Marquis had been returned to them after Salah ad-Din had abandoned his siege of Tyre at the start of the year. From him they had learned that Conrad de Montferrat commanded the defense at Tyre, and also how the Sultan had tried to force him to surrender the city by humiliating his father before his eyes. They had been shocked by what the old man had gone through, yet heartened by the spirited defense of Tyre and the capture of half the Sultan's fleet.

"But I can't decide about the last five. Bethsan? Scandelion? Hebron, perhaps?"

"I'm not sure Hebron would leave without his son; or he might give his place to his son," Aimery remarked with respect. Hebron was the kind of man who thought of others first, and he would probably put the freedom of his son and heir ahead of his own freedom.

Guy was continuing, ticking off the barons held in captivity at Aleppo, "Then there's Nazareth, Jubail, Haifa, Toron—"

"You can't pick Toron!" Aimery interrupted sharply.

"Why not?" Guy asked innocently.

"Haven't you seen or heard *anything*?" Aimery asked back in exasperation. "Toron's been given favored treatment by the Sultan's secretary—and you can be sure there's a reason! If he hasn't converted, he's been giving them intelligence. Whatever he's been doing, he deserves no reward from *you*. I wouldn't trust him farther than I can throw him." Only as he said it did Aimery realize just how much he hated Humphrey de Toron for the special treatment he had received: for his baths, clean clothes, clean water, and good food. He accepted that his brother had been treated better; Guy was, like it or not, an anointed king. But Humphrey was just one of them, a baron of considerably lesser importance than Caesarea, and younger than all of them.

"Well," Guy agreed amiably, "he's off the list, then. Who else is left?"

Together the brothers Lusignan chose from among the remaining prisoners and passed these names to the commander of the citadel. It was he who would remove the lucky men from the dungeon, see that they were cleaned up and provided with clothes, and house them separately for the last night of their captivity. Aimery, for the first time, was allowed to share his brother's accommodations.

Damascus, June 1188

The magnificence of the Sultan's palace in Damascus could hardly be described. It wasn't that the Franks didn't have silks, gold and silver, ivory, glass, and mother-of-pearl, but the sheer abundance of these materials and the Saracen love of intricate and detailed decoration made each room a kaleidoscope of color and luxury unlike anything most of them had ever seen. Brightly glazed tiles in vibrant turquoise, aqua, and blue set off carpets of red, gold, and cream. Cushions clothed in shimmering red and orange silks and adorned with golden tassels were tossed upon the bright floor. The intricately carved tables were inlaid with ivory and mother-of-pearl, and even the plaster on the walls had been cut away in elaborate geometric designs that intersected and intertwined. Over everything, running along the length of wall about ten feet above the floor, was a broad band of blue tiles containing verses from the Koran engraved in gold.

The palace was intended to impress all who visited, and it did not fail to do so. While Guy kept muttering about the amount of gold and silver and the wealth they represented, Aimery was more unsettled by the number of fountains that ran perpetually, filling round and oblong pools surrounded by magnificent gardens overflowing with blooming flowers. That said to him that the rains had been exceptionally good this past winter (while he was in a windowless dungeon unable to judge for himself). In short, neither drought nor famine was likely to curb the Sultan's thirst for further conquest.

Equally disturbing was the number of fine soldiers: both the uniformed Mamlukes and the peacock-like emirs dressed in silks glittering with jewels. Salah ad-Din had put his entire power on display here, Aimery concluded, and it was daunting.

The audience chamber itself was huge, with a high ceiling composed of three rows of small domes supported by pillars so fine they hardly seemed suited to supporting the weight of the roof. The windows were covered with lattice-work shutters that let in the light and a breeze, yet kept out much of the heat.

As intended, by the time the Frankish prisoners had been brought through the series of magnificent rooms to the foot of the dais on which the Sultan sat surrounded by a brilliant cast of courtiers, the prisoners were thoroughly intimidated. Most of them went down on at least one knee in reverence, and only Aimery's firm grip on Guy's forearm prevented him from doing the same. "You're a king!" Aimery hissed in his brother's ear, while dropping to one knee himself. Guy, confused and unsure of himself, bowed stiffly but deeply.

The Sultan asked something, and Henri d'Ibelin spoke up, explaining to the others, "He asked if any of us speak Arabic."

"You aren't the only one," Haifa reminded him a little sharply.

"But better that I serve the lowly role of interpreter than you, my lord," Henri countered deftly with a smile.

Haifa shrugged, and let Henri serve as their interpreter.

Henri extended the Sultan's greetings (which were formal but not warm), and then the Sultan gestured to a man behind him, who bowed, withdrew, and returned with a bent old man. Translating, Henri explained, "He says this man was the abbot of the Convent of the Holy Trinity in Edessa and has been his prisoner for forty-five years." The man bowed deeply to Guy de Lusignan, but his expression was bewildered and his eyes were opaque with cataracts. At another snap of the Sultan's fingers, another man emerged, and he advanced carrying an object that made every Christian in the room gasp. It was the beautiful jewel-studded golden reliquary that had been created to carry a fragment of the True Cross. The Franks had last seen it on the field of Hattin. They had seen it cast down by angry Saracen soldiers, trampled, and ground in the dirt.

The Bishop of Lydda dropped so abruptly to his knees that the sound was jarring, and Hebron hissed, "That's only the case. We don't know the Cross is still inside."

The Sultan seemed to understand what was happening without translation, for he snapped another order, and the young man carrying the reliquary opened the latched door to hold it toward the Christians. Now all the Franks went down on their knees, ignoring the sneers and shaking heads of the Sultan and his court.

Henri alone spared the Saracens a glance. He understood perfectly how much they despised the Christians for revering a piece of wood. To them this was pure idolatry, and proved that the Christians had primitive beliefs. They did not understand that, far from revering a piece of wood, the Frankish lords revered the abstract concept it symbolized: Christ's sacrifice for mankind. The barons of Jerusalem knelt from shame because they had failed to protect Christ's homeland, symbolized by this piece of wood.

The Sultan was impatient. He had other important business. He ordered Guy de Lusignan to come forward, lay his hand on the reliquary, and take the required oath. Guy, feeling more uncomfortable than ever, awkwardly got to his feet, and advanced to stand in front of the Mamluke holding the True Cross. He was ordered to kneel by the "abbot" and place his right hand on the reliquary.

"Swear," the Sultan ordered through Henri d'Ibelin, "that you will leave

Syria, cross the sea, and never again take up arms against the followers of the Prophet Mohammed, may peace be upon him and his name."

"I'm supposed to wish the Prophet Mohammed peace?" Guy balked.

"No, just swear you will leave Syria, cross the sea, and never again take up arms against Muslims," Aimery hissed.

Guy looked doubtful, and Aimery held his breath, the very stench of the dungeon suddenly vivid again. After comparative comfort and freedom during the last fortnight, he could not bear the thought of a return to the darkness and mold of the dungeon. Don't balk, he silently begged his brother. Take the damn oath! Take it!

Guy shrugged his shoulders, laid his hand on the reliquary, and loudly declared, "I swear—"

"In the Name of Father and the Son and the Holy Ghost—" the abbot (evidently well prepped for his role) interrupted.

Guy gave him a disgusted look, but dutifully recited ". . . in the name of the Father and the Son and the Holy Ghost, that I will leave Syria, cross the sea, and never again take up arms against the followers of Mohammed." Then he stood again and glared defiantly at the Sultan.

Salah ad-Din stared at him, and his courtiers stared at their Sultan. Aimery started praying silently again, terrified that the Sultan was about to change his mind or demand further conditions. When Salah ad-Din spoke, however, it was only to remark, "Now we will see if you are an honorable man."

Henri translated, and Guy visibly bristled.

Again Aimery found himself pleading silently to his brother to keep his mouth shut. Just don't say anything, he urged him mentally.

One of the men behind the Sultan—Henri didn't recognize him—scoffed that the word of all Christians was worthless. Another added, "These pig-eaters have no honor." The Sultan hissed them silent, adding: "We will see."

"As we saw with Ibn Barzan," a young man, whom Henri took to be one of the Sultan's seventeen sons, muttered sullenly.

"You bark like a puppy," his father told him. "When you grow up you will learn—I hope—to know the difference between a man like Ibn Barzan and this man who calls himself a king."

"What did he say?" Guy asked Henri uneasily.

"He just told his son that he was too young to speak up on an occasion like this."

"Then we're done?"

"Yes." Henri bowed deeply to the Sultan, received a gesture of dismissal, and bowing again, told the others they should withdraw backwards for three steps before turning to depart.

Tripoli, County of Tripoli, July 1188

By chance or design, the released barons of Jerusalem entered the County of Tripoli exactly one year after their crushing defeat on the Horns of Hattin. It was July 4, 1188. The Sultan's escort stopped but signaled them to continue into a deserted village at the foot of Mount Lebanon.

In the village the doors swung uselessly in the wind, testimony to the fact that they had been broken open by force—whether before or after their owners had departed was no longer relevant. The skeletons of a half-dozen horses near the village entrance suggested, however, that there might have been some sort of skirmish.

From there the released prisoners rode across largely abandoned country-side. Now and then, in the distance, they saw shepherds with flocks. They also came across a few tilled fields, but no sign of the men who cultivated them. After riding for almost two hours, they came to a vineyard. The wine stalks were half concealed in weeds, but underneath the weeds the shriveled grapes of last year's crop still hung unharvested. They stopped to collect some of the raisins and drink from their water skins. The stillness was eerie, and they soon pressed on.

Not until they were about ten miles from the city of Tripoli did they encounter concentrated agriculture. The orchards around Tripoli were evidently well tended, and the vineyards here were in good condition. The men and women they passed stopped to stare, clearly unsure who these men were. Aimery supposed they made an odd impression, mounted on poor Arab horses but wearing chain mail and ragged surcoats. Certainly they had no banners to proclaim who they were, no squires to attend them, and no weapons, either. They were a sorry lot, he concluded, too sorry to even provoke alarm.

Yet somewhere along the way someone had taken the precaution to send word of their approach to the city. About two miles outside Tripoli, with the city walls already in sight, a handful of knights rode up in a cloud of dust and blocked the road. The barons of Jerusalem were not worried. They advanced steadily, straining their eyes to see if they could recognize any of the men ahead of them—and wondering when they would be recognized.

"That's William of Tiberius." Haifa was the first to put a name to a face. As he spoke, the young man spurred forward to draw up directly beside Guy de Lusignan, a look of amazement on his face. "My lord King? Is it really you?" Even as he asked, his eyes swept across the other faces and he nodded to each of them in turn. "My lords. Marquis. Have you all been set free? Without a ransom?"

"As you see," Guy answered for them, while the others merely nodded.

William twisted in the saddle and called back to his brother. "Ralph! Ride at once to the citadel and tell the Queen of Jerusalem her husband is approaching! Eustace, tell my lord Bohemond that the King of Jerusalem and other barons of the Kingdom have been released and will soon reach the city!" Only then did he turn back to Guy and bow his head to him. "Welcome to Tripoli, my lords."

They approached the city at a leisurely pace to give the messengers time to announce their approach. This afforded them time to learn from their escort what had happened in Tripoli since Hattin. William of Tiberius informed them that his stepfather, Raymond of Tripoli, had died within months of the disaster at Hattin. He suggested his stepfather had died of a broken heart, for the loss of the Kingdom he loved so well and had served so long. Aimery thought he detected an undertone of reproach for the king who—against the advice of Tripoli—had led them to that disaster. Aimery's eyes lingered on his brother as Tiberius spoke, but if Guy heard the same undertone in Tiberius' words, he ignored it.

Tiberius continued, explaining that lacking sons of his own, Raymond had, on his deathbed, bequeathed the still independent and rich County of Tripoli to the Prince of Antioch. Here Aimery raised an eyebrow, thinking that Tiberius and his brother must have felt slighted. They had been exceptionally loyal to their stepfather, and they had lost their inheritance (the barony of Galilee) immediately after Hattin. They had every reason to expect their stepfather to bequeath his county to them. But if young Tiberius resented the turn of events, he disguised his feelings well. He reported without apparent rancor that the Prince of Antioch had sent his second son and namesake, Bohemond, to assume control of Tripoli.

Setting aside Tiberius' personal feelings, Aimery supposed Tripoli's decision made strategic sense. To entrust the County of Tripoli, with the important coastal cities of Tripoli and Tortosa, to the only Latin Christian monarch still in control of his territory was more rational than to try to defend it with the limited resources of the County alone. Nevertheless, Aimery had little reason to hope the Prince of Antioch would be particularly generous to the Lusignans, while his younger son was an unknown quantity, a man Aimery could not remember ever meeting.

By the time they reached the city, word had spread that King Guy and "other prisoners" had been released and were approaching. People poured out of the shops, workshops, and houses to get a look at the arrivals. The mood was more curious than jubilant. Although here and there someone raised a lukewarm cheer, it did not catch on. Most onlookers remained silent or muttered remarks to their neighbors. It certainly didn't feel like a homecoming, at least not to Aimery. Rather, he sensed wariness and disapproval in the crowd. He imagined the onlookers thinking: Who are these men, and why have they been set free while tens of thousands remain in slavery? Weren't these the very men who had led the others to an unnecessary defeat?

Aimery was acutely conscious that they were in Tripoli, and the Count of Tripoli had broken out of the encirclement. If only he had been reinforced (as Aimery had urged and begged his brother to do), then many more men would have been saved. It would still have been a defeat, of course, but maybe enough of them could have broken free to at least defend the major cities. If a hundred knights instead of a handful, if thousands of sergeants rather than scores, had followed Tripoli out of the trap, they would surely have been able to hold Acre, Jaffa—and Jerusalem itself.

Riders were coming toward them from the direction of the citadel, and Guy drew up in astonishment. The small party approaching the released prisoners was led by Queen Sibylla, wearing her crown and a splendid silk brocade cloak of red and gold, flanked by the new Count of Tripoli, Bohemond of Antioch, and—to Guy's astonishment—his older brother, Geoffrey de Lusignan.

"That's Geoff!" Guy exclaimed in amazement to Aimery. "Where did he come from?"

"Lusignan," Aimery answered, despairing of his younger brother's intelligence.

Guy frowned in annoyance and snapped, "I know that! I mean: what's he doing here?"

"I expect he's come to help you regain your kingdom," Aimery surmised.

"I've sworn to not even try," Guy pointed out.

"But the rest of us haven't," Aimery reminded him.

Guy was no longer listening. Instead, in a dramatic gesture he spurred forward. Once he had closed the distance, he flung himself from his horse and grasped his wife's stirrup. "Sibylla!" he called out for the audience of onlookers. "Beloved! My queen!"

Sibylla responded with equal pathos. She was riding sidesaddle in the Greek fashion and so easily slid down to fall into Guy's embrace. "My lord," she babbled, "my sweet lord! How I have prayed for this moment! To embrace you again in freedom!"

There in full view of the public, who were now straining and craning their necks to get a glimpse of this "historic" moment, they kissed each other on the lips.

Aimery grimaced at the unseemly display, so unbefitting a king and queen. Beside him the Bishop of Lydda muttered something about "wanton passion being the root of civil ruin," by which Aimery presumed he meant Sibylla's passion for Guy being the ruin of the Kingdom. Amen to that!

Meanwhile, however, Geoffrey had nudged his horse beside Aimery's, and his bright blue eyes were penetrating and hard. Like all the Lusignans he was blond and attractive, with regular features that included a square chin and a slender nose. Guy might be the prettiest of the four brothers, but Geoffrey was unquestionably handsome in a hard, hawkish way. "So, you at least got yourselves out of the dungeon."

"No thanks to you," Aimery snapped back.

"Hugh was prepared to pay *your* ransom," Geoffrey replied, referring to their nephew, the son of the eldest of the four Lusignan brothers, and, since his father's death, the ruling Lord of Lusignan and Count of la Marche. "He could hardly be expected to come up with a king's ransom, however." Geoffrey shrugged to underline his helplessness, and he kept his eyes fixed on Aimery. "We have much to talk about," he concluded.

"Indeed. Have you brought troops to regain the Holy Land?"

"Hugh sent me as an advance guard, if you like: twelve knights and a hundred men-at-arms. He'll bring the bulk of our forces with King Henry."

"King Henry is coming to the Holy Land?" No one had told the prisoners that.

"King Henry, King Philip, and the Holy Roman Emperor have *all* taken the cross," his brother answered, surprised that this momentous news had not penetrated the walls of the citadel at Aleppo.

Aimery crossed himself in gratitude. He had never imagined there might be *that* strong a response in the West. Hadn't these same monarchs all refused to come to Jerusalem when Baldwin IV begged them to do so three years ago? Baldwin had offered them the keys to the Kingdom, foreseeing the disaster Guy would be, but not one of these powerful Western leaders had been willing to come then. They had not even been prepared to send one of their sons!

But then Aimery had to laugh inwardly at his own indignation. When Baldwin IV had made that offer, he and Guy had been desperately afraid Henry of England just *might* send one of his troublesome sons to challenge Guy's right to the throne. Aimery had calmed Guy's nerves (and his own fears) by arguing that the Plantagenets were too preoccupied with their fratricidal quarrels to come to Outremer, and he had been right. But now, when it was too late, when the Kingdom was already lost, they were coming. It could only be God's doing, he reminded himself—hastily making the sign of the cross in gratitude and awe.

"I expect it will be next year before they actually set off," Geoffrey continued practically. "They have to regulate their affairs and organize their forces first. The Holy Roman Emperor will come by land, I hear, but both King Henry and Philip of France plan to come by sea. King Henry's building his own fleet."

"Christ! That will take forever! Don't they recognize how urgent the situation is?" Aimery answered, as his euphoria over so much support met the reality of waiting a year or more to see it.

"What's the rush?" Geoffrey asked back, his eyes narrowing slightly. "You've already lost most of the Kingdom."

"Of Jerusalem, yes, but Tripoli and Antioch are still threatened!" Aimery shot back. "You can't seriously think the Sultan will leave them be? When we left Damascus we could see the troops flooding in. He's clearly preparing a new offensive against us."

"Indeed? Then we have even more to talk about," Geoffrey concluded. He turned his attention from Aimery to Guy, who had finally finished greeting his wife and was approaching his elder brothers.

"Geoffrey!" Guy called up. "Sibylla tells me you are the harbinger of a great host that is gathering to relieve the Holy Land!"

"So I am," Geoffrey agreed, swinging down from his horse to embrace his youngest brother. Then everyone remounted and they continued to the citadel, where a hasty welcome feast was being prepared.

Tripoli, July 1188

"You did *what?*" Geoffrey asked Guy in disbelief.

Guy shrugged, but looked shamefaced, while Sibylla gaped at him literally open-mouthed. The Lusignans had withdrawn to the solar after dinner and were among themselves.

"Half of Christendom is coming to your aid, and you've abandoned your kingdom!" Geoffrey shouted in outrage.

Afraid someone would hear, Guy gestured for his brother to quiet down.

"I'm not going to be quiet!" Geoffrey roarded back, louder still. "The most powerful rulers in Europe have pawned their crown jewels and taxed their subjects to the bone to raise a mighty force for the rescue of Jerusalem, and the *King* of Jerusalem is going to sail away with his tail between his legs?" Geoffrey had worked himself into a rage, and he was shouting so loudly that even Aimery winced.

"I don't understand," Sibylla interrupted, frowning in evident puzzlement. "An anointed king can't just set his crown aside. What is given by God—"

"God had little to do with it!" Aimery snapped. "You stole the throne and you know it!"

"I am the rightful Queen of Jerusalem and Guy is my husband!" Sibylla answered stubbornly, sticking out her lower lip and pulling herself to her full height—which to a half-starved Aimery hardly looked greater than her breadth. She had put on a lot of weight this past year and was very round and flabby.

"You needed the consent of the High Court to be crowned, and the Templars and I made damned sure the High Court court didn't have a chance to meet before Heraclius went through with that sham coronation—and even that was on the condition that you divorce Guy!"

Geoffrey's eyes darted from Aimery to Sibylla and back and then he broke in. "Right or wrong, Guy's been crowned, anointed, and acknowledged King for two years!"

"Go out in the streets, Geoff, and ask how many of the men out there are prepared to follow *King* Guy anywhere!" Aimery answered bitterly, pointing to the window. In the stunned silence that answered him, he added, "And as for God, ask if what happened to this kingdom since Guy was crowned was truly His will. If so, then I say it was God's punishment for Guy usurping the crown!"

"This is a pointless discussion!" Geoffrey snapped. "Half of Christendom is on its way here to regain the Holy Land. Guy—King or not—has no business departing! If no one else, our nephew Hugh expects him to be here leading the fight, and so does our liege lord, King Henry!"

"Oh, since when have you become so respectful of King Henry?" Guy sneered.

"Since he gave us back the Marche, you fool!" Geoffrey snapped.

"Don't talk to my husband like that!" Sibylla protested.

"I'll talk to my brother any damn way I like!" Geoffrey snarled at Sibylla, before turning on Guy again. He took a step nearer and jabbed his finger at Guy's chest. His eyes glinted with fury, and Aimery could remember the way he'd always bullied them as children. "You are going to stay here and fight Salah ad-Din whether you like it or not! Anything else would disgrace the Lusignans in the face of the whole world—not to mention the living God!"

"I swore an oath on the True Cross!" Guy protested, but his discomfort was reflected in the high pitch of his voice.

"Get me a priest!" Geoffrey ordered Aimery. "Any priest! But the Bishop of Tripoli or Lydda would be a good start!"

Aimery understood Geoff's intentions and went willingly. Although he was himself still not certain Guy was the best man to lead this fight, he was determined to fight for his adopted country. Furthermore, he appreciated Geoffrey's point that, bad as Guy was, his running away now would discredit him even further—and so the whole family.

Aimery eventually found the Bishops of Lydda and Tripoli sharing a flask of wine at the archiepiscopal palace. After he explained the situation, they agreed to return with him to the citadel. Altogether it was about an hour before he returned to the solar with them. Here they were confronted by the sight of Sibylla in tears in the window seat, while Guy stood literally backed into a corner, looking as harried as a rabbit.

Geoffrey had his back to the door, so Guy caught sight of the worthy bishops first. He called out to them in relief. "My lords! Come help us out!"

The churchmen exchanged a wary glance, but advanced deeper into the room with practiced dignity.

"My brother is insisting I break my oath to Salah ad-Din," Guy exclaimed, stepping around Geoffrey to come to the center of the room, "but you were there, Lydda, you saw me swear on the True Cross!"

"I did indeed, my liege," Lydda answered, and Aimery cocked his ears at the use of "my liege." Lydda could just as easily have used the more generic "my lord." Instead, by choosing to emphasize his subordination to Guy as his King, he was signaling support for Geoffrey. "And I saw that the oath was extracted from you under duress. It was your only means of securing not just your own freedom, but that of your brother, myself, and other nobles. Such an oath is no more valid than if a mother were forced to swear something to free her children, or a wife to free her husband." He smiled in the direction of Sibylla.

"And you agree with that, my lord bishop?" Guy asked the Bishop of Tripoli in astonishment.

Tripoli was more ambivalent, weighing his head from side to side before answering cautiously. "It is certainly true that an oath taken under duress is invalid, as my worthy colleague suggests. On the other hand, it could be argued that in the absence of physical force, duress was not in play. After all, your life was hardly in danger—"

"Of course our lives were in danger!" the Bishop of Lydda interrupted hotly, with a look of reproach at his fellow bishop, who had not suffered Saracen imprisonment. "Our brother-in-Christ was hacked to pieces before my very eyes!" Lydda reminded them in a voice explosive with outrage. His entire face was distorted by the horror he was reliving. "The sword sliced him open at the junction of his neck and shoulder, and stuck fast halfway to his heart! His life's blood gushed out all over the wagon! When they seized the cross from me and flung it to the ground, his blood poured down on me! I *wore* his blood for damn near a year!" the Bishop rasped out. There was so much fury and pain in his voice that it stunned and silenced the other men in the room.

Aimery noted mentally that the Bishop of Lydda was not used to the violence and gore of the battlefield as were the rest of them. That made his experience at Hattin all the more traumatic. They had all worn the blood from Hattin in captivity, but for Aimery and the others, most of that blood had been from men they'd killed to stay alive. He conceded that wearing the blood of an unarmed friend would have been considerably more disturbing.

Only after the Bishop of Lydda appeared to have calmed himself and regained his composure did the Bishop of Tripoli suggest in a gentle voice, "I did not mean to suggest you were not *ever* at risk, brother—only that King Guy was not in imminent risk of death when he took the oath to renounce his kingdom."

"He did not renounce his kingdom!" Lydda retorted sharply, still agitated. "He promised to go overseas and never take up arms against the Muslims again."

"Is that right?" Geoffrey looked to Aimery for confirmation.

"Yes, that's right."

"Then all Guy has to do is take a boat to an island out in the harbor somewhere," Geoffrey gestured contemptuously in the direction of the sea, "and then return. As for not taking up arms: he need not raise his *arms* against the Muslims— we can do it for him. His sword arm wasn't all that effective anyway," he sneered.

Aimery was about to point out that Guy was much more dangerous making decisions than fighting, but thought better of it. The Holy Roman Emperor and Henry of England were on their way, and they were not the kind of men who would bow to the likes of Guy de Lusignan or his opinions—whether he was technically King or not. They were both highly successful strategists and brilliant battle commanders. The bigger problem would be to get them to cooperate with one another, Aimery surmised.

"Yes, of course!" The Bishop of Tripoli clearly liked this solution that did not entail outright violation of an oath, while Lydda huffed, "He can do that, too, for all I care, but I say his oath is invalid anyway."

"Then we are in agreement?" Geoffrey demanded, looking from one brother to the other and then to the bishops. "Guy will make a symbolic crossing of the sea, but he doesn't leave the Holy Land. He *acts* like a king, whether he is one or not! And without taking up arms himself, he leds the rest of us in a campaign to regain Jerusalem. And that's an end of it!"

Tripoli, July 1188

And then the Sultan came.

Not alone, but with his entire army.

Guy fumed that his "release" had been a mockery. "Like a cat with a mouse," he suggested indignantly, "he let us go, only so he could take us prisoner again."

"Don't assume defeat!" Geoffrey rebuked him.

Guy frowned and ended the conversation.

Sibylla was considerably harder to silence. She wrung her hands and complained tearfully about not being able to take another siege. "Jerusalem, Tyre, and now this. I can't take it," she whined.

"Then sail away," Aimery advised, with a dismissive gesture in the direction of the port.

"Where would I go?" she asked back blankly.

"Cyprus. Constantinople. Rome, for all I care," Aimery told her bluntly.

"Stop it!" Guy protested. "First you tell me I *can't* run away, and then you suggest Sibylla should. She's the Queen of Jerusalem."

"Really? I hadn't noticed."

"Aimery, you aren't being helpful," Geoffrey observed from across the room. While he shared Aimery's assessment of both Guy and Sibylla, whether he liked the pair or not, they were who they were.

Aimery shrugged and wandered to the window to get another look at the army that was still assembling battalion by battalion and setting up their tents on the plain around the city. From this particular window he could not see the Sultan's tent, but he hardly needed to. Spread out before him were at least a dozen emirs with fluttering banners, and the sunlight glinted on the tips of lances and the burnished surface of helmets. Salah ad-Din was so endlessly strong, Aimery reflected.

A loud knock on the door made Aimery jump and turn.

A pageboy stood flushed in the doorway. "My lords! I've been sent by my lord of Tripoli. He says ships have been sighted offshore, approaching fast."

"Ours or theirs?" Geoffrey snapped, even as Aimery opened his mouth to ask the same question.

"We don't know yet," the page admitted.

"Oh, my God!" Sibylla wailed out. "It's Tyre all over again. He's brought up the Egyptian fleet to cut off our escape and prevent supplies from getting in!"

The three men looked at her. Guy's expression was sympathetic, Geoffrey's indifferent, and Aimery's contemptuous. Then Geoffrey suggested simply, "Let's go find out."

They were not alone in this intention. The Sultan's army was still gathering and the activity in his camp was entirely peaceful: tents were being erected, latrines dug, field canteens set up. There was consequently no need to man the walls beyond posting lookouts, and everyone, garrison and citizen, was free to head for the port. The Lusignans found that men-at-arms, priests, laundresses, and other knights and ladies were all streaming out of the citadel and down the hill toward the city.

Being mounted, the Lusignans overtook most of these, but the streets of the city were already flooded with people. The crowds only thickened as they reached the narrow headland that jutted out from the coast to the west. Everyone was being jammed together here, and the horses became more a hindrance than a help. Certainly, calling out "Make way for the King of Jerusalem" got them nowhere. People turned and stared at Guy and his brothers, but no one made way for them.

Geoffrey pointed toward a stairway leading up to the wall walk, and they forced their way across the flow of people to the wall. Here, they tied the horses at the foot of the stairs and climbed up.

Again they were not alone. The walls were already lined with people, all straining to see the approaching ships. The Lusignans were not hesitant about ordering people out of their way or shoving them aside, but given the sheer drop to the street below on the inside of the wall walk, they still had to be cautious; it took time to reach the narrow western salient.

Here, of course, the crowds were thickest, and it was only with shouting and insistence that they forced their way to the very front, joining Bohemond of Tripoli. The latter acknowledged them with a nod of his head before returning his attention to the sea.

The sun was low in the sky, making identification of the ships more difficult. Sunlight bathed the surface of the water, which was ruffled by a light breeze. It danced off the shifting surface, creating a constant glitter. In other circumstances it would have been beautiful. The bright sunlight, however, turned the ships to silhouettes, and the profile of Frankish and Saracen ships did not differ sufficiently for landlubbers to easily distinguish one from the other.

All that was certain was that this was a huge fleet. By now the leading three ships were close enough to be shortening sail, but beyond them were eighteen vessels clearly identifiable as galleys against the light. Behind them were an innumerable number of dark spots that slowly grew and took shape, while yet more dark specks emerged out of the glittering horizon. People kept calling out the numbers they thought they had counted: twenty-nine, thirty-six, forty-two.

"Does the Sultan have that many ships?" Guy asked his brothers in awe.

Geoffrey grunted ambiguously, because he didn't know. Aimery reminded his brothers, "He has the means to build them, and has had the winter to do so."

A commotion drew their attention to the right. "There! There!" A man was shouting so shrilly he sounded like a hysterical woman. "A cross! There's a cross on the sail!"

They all looked back at the approaching fleet, squinting and shading their eyes with their hands.

A second shout went up. "Holy Trinity! It's true! They have crosses on their sails."

But still many doubted. They strained their eyes even harder. Then the lead ship swung into the wind to hand the mainsail—and in that moment, as the sail slowly sank, scores of onlookers simultaneously saw the unmistakable imprint of a black cross on the white canvas.

The cheer that went up was deafening to those in the midst of it. It spread down the length of the wall like rolling thunder, and tumbled to the streets below like the roar of a waterfall. People waiting anxiously in the shadow of the wall recognized the tone more than the content and started shouting and cheering.

From across the water, faint but unmistakable, came an answering cheer. The crews and passengers of the first crusader fleet to reach the Holy Land since Hattin realized with relief that they had made landfall at a Christian-held port. They were fifty galleys sent by the King of Sicily carrying five hundred knights and thousands of archers and men-at-arms.

Tyre, August 1188

A pain stabbed through her belly so sharply that Mariam gasped and dropped the kindling she was trying to bring over to the fireplace. The small logs clattered loudly on the tile floor, and the noise brought Godfrey from the forge with an angry admonishment: "Mariam! I've told you before! Let the apprentices do the heavy lifting!" The sharpness of his voice sprang from his concern, and his face was furrowed with worry.

Although the pain was ebbing, Mariam was too alarmed by it to even retort. She just stood trying to catch her breath, and Godfrey crossed the distance between them to collect the dropped kindling, set it beside the fireplace, and lead his woman to a bench against the wall. "Mariam, you need to see a doctor— or a midwife."

She reached up with the back of her hand to wipe away a tear of pain—and fear. She knew she was with child, and she knew she was too old, too fat, and too full of sin for this to end well. Godfrey closed his powerful hand around her plump one. His hand was black with soot, hers white with flour. The callused feel of his hand on hers only made her cry harder. She loved him so much, she could not even pretend she regretted the sin they had committed. She had found in his arms such ecstasy and such comfort. Yet if she did not learn to repent what she had done, she would burn forever in hell—and as a pastry mistress she knew something about the torments of intense heat. That frightened her almost as much as the pain of childbirth itself.

"Let me get you some water," Godfrey offered helplessly. He understood Mariam's fears, and he shared them. He lost sleep trying to think what he could do to help. Was there some sacrifice he could make that would please God enough to forgive them? What could a poor, near-penniless armorer do that would please God that much? Since the siege of Tyre had lifted, the demand for his services had plummeted, and they were almost completely dependent on Mariam's bakery to keep them in food, firewood, and clothing. (Sven was growing like never before, now that he ate at Mariam's table and worked in her shop rather than his dad's.) Godfrey had literally nothing he could give away to the Church to appease God's anger.

Mariam pulled herself together. As he brought her the water, she smiled up at him. "I'll be fine, Godfrey. These pains are normal."

Godfrey didn't believe her, and she read his disbelief on his face. Before she could speak again, however, they were interrupted by Sven coming from the shop. "Mama! Mama!" he called as he swung himself forward on the crutches. "Mistress Alys has come for the things you made for the Dowager Queen."

The Ibelin household would be celebrating the first communion of their younger daughter Margaret, and Queen Maria Zoë had ordered marzipan treats in the shape of Ibelin and Jerusalem crosses. Mariam had worked most of the previous day on the order, and Sven himself had painted them this morning. They had made more than the Queen requested and would be sharing the rest with their own guests this evening, for Haakon Magnussen and his mate had promised to bring fresh fish and wine for the privilege of a homemade meal and Mariam's sweets. Godfrey suspected that the Norse seafarers needed the sweets far less than Godfrey needed the fish and wine, but they always made it sound the other way around.

Alys trailed in Sven's wake. Mariam had first met Alys when Ernoul brought her with him throughout the spring, spending whatever pennies he had to buy her a meat or cheese pie. She'd been in rags, a frightened wraith with eyes far too large for her face and hands as tiny as a bird's. Mariam had overheard some of her apprentices making incensed remarks about "honest girls" not serving "whores," and she'd taken Ernoul aside to ask him about Alys. He had defended her reputation with an insistence that rang a little false in Mariam's ears, but then, who was she to judge another woman? She was, after all, living in sin with and pregnant by a man not her husband.

Today was the first time she had seen Alys since Ernoul had taken her to wife. While Alys would never be a beauty, her whole face radiated joy as she entered. Mariam couldn't help smiling at her. "Now, isn't that a pretty gown!" she exclaimed, knowing how much Alys had been ashamed of her rags. By the look of it, the Dowager Queen and her daughter had dug into their own clothes chests to find suitable clothes for Ernoul's bride. The shift was simple but of good-quality linen, and the surcoat was brightly-dyed cotton. It being August and very hot, the latter was sleeveless, but it was a bright marigold yellow trimmed with red ribbons that laced up the sides.

Alys brushed the front of the dress with the palms of her hands in wonder, her eyes beaming with pride. "Ernoul likes this one best, too!" she admitted, "but I have *two* shifts and *three* gowns. And look at my shoes!" She lifted her skirts six inches and thrust out a foot in Mariam's direction, showing off soft leather shoes with a strap. "And I have stockings now, too!" Alys added for good measure, hitching her skirts a little higher.

Mariam nodded approval, and then because she still didn't feel well enough to stand, she signaled Alys over to her. "Come, show me the wedding ring."

Alys danced over with her hand held out, and Mariam held it to examine the simple gold band she wore on her left ring finger. The ring was not adorned by any stones, engraving, or other ornament, but that did not detract from its value in Mariam's eyes. She knew from Godfrey that Ernoul had sold his sword to obtain the money to pay for it himself. His sword, he reasoned, was of no use to him with his shattered shoulder, and he hadn't wanted to marry his Alys with a ring given him by his lord or anyone else. Mariam respected that.

The ring inspection over, Mariam pulled herself to her feet to fetch the box in which the marzipan was stacked, but Godfrey angrily gestured for her to sit down again and on her directions fetched it himself. Alys was pulling out her purse to pay when Haakon Magnussen and his mate, Eric Andersen, pushed into the crowded kitchen.

On a hook Eric held a fish large enough to feed a dozen people, and Haakon had a small cask over his shoulder as they swept in. Salt had crystallized on their eyebrows and turned their hair to stiff strands, but they were clearly in good spirits.

"You'll never guess what's happened now!" Magnussen declared, as he clunked the cask down and righted himself to stand with his hands on his hips. He was too eager to share the news to wait for Godfrey to ask about it, so he continued. "King Guy has been set free, and the King of Sicily has sent a fleet of fifty galleys, crammed full of fighting men."

"Where did you hear that?" Godfrey asked, coming forward to take the fish from Andersen and fling it down on a large wooden cutting board.

"We ran into a merchantman running down the coast from Tripoli. It should dock in a few hours. On board were a bunch of people who'd been in Tripoli when the fleet arrived, and some Hospitallers who'd crossed over with the Sicilian fleet. They said King Guy and ten other noble prisoners have been released."

"Which others, sir?" Alys asked, knowing even after her short stay in the Ibelin household how anxious both Eschiva and Isabella were about their respective husbands.

"I didn't catch the names," Magnussen admitted. He was unfamiliar with the geography of the Holy Land and except for place names he'd heard in the Bible, he recognized no titles.

Alys knew the Ibelins would want to meet the ship so she handed over payment in a hurry, and ran all the way back to the Ibelin residence.

Aimery stood at the railing of the poop, trying not to get in anyone's way as the crew maneuvered into the harbor. The trick was to reduce the weight on the ship enough to avoid collisions with the other ships at anchor, but not lose maneuverability or become becalmed too far from the shore to cast a line. This was a difficult maneuver in the cramped and crowded inner harbor, and it entailed many incomprehensible (to landlubber Aimery) bellowed orders and much rushing this way and that by the barefoot sailors as they hauled on one line, then heaved on another. The progress seemed painfully slow, and the heavy ship appeared to glide at a snail's pace.

"It seems to take forever, doesn't it?" a Hospitaller sister standing at the rail beside him remarked out loud, echoing his thoughts.

"It does," Aimery agreed, glancing over at her. She was no longer young—probably over forty, he judged—but she was handsome and had a proud bearing. "Your first trip to the Holy Land?" Aimery inquired, more to distract himself from the nerve-racking slowness of their progress than out of genuine interest.

The Hospitaller sister started in surprise and then cast Aimery a smile. "No, my lord Constable. I was born in Outremer. The last year on Sicily was my first time away from it in my life, and even that was too long. I thank God with all my heart that I have been allowed to return. This is home to me, and I hope He gives me the grace to die here—in freedom and in Christ."

The fact that she recognized him, although Aimery felt he had changed greatly in his year's imprisonment, made him ask uncomfortably, "Should I know you, Madame?"

"No, there's no reason why you should. My name is Sister Adela, and I ran the women's ward of the Hospitaller establishment in Nablus. The Dowager Queen liked to include me in major feasts when she was there. I saw you at the high table with my lord of Ibelin several times, but there's no reason you should have taken note of me."

"How did you come to be in Sicily?" Aimery asked, his hunger to understand what had happened while he rotted in the dungeon of Aleppo awakened interest in the nun.

"After Hattin we evacuated the Hospital at Nablus for Jerusalem, and I was there throughout the siege. When it ended, the Hospital was charged with leading one of the three columns of refugees, the one to Jaffa. At Jaffa, transport to the 'nearest Christian land' had been promised by the Sultan, but we insisted on transport to a *Latin* kingdom, unsure what our fate might be if we landed in Cyprus or Constantinople under the new Emperor."

Aimery had heard reference during the last two weeks to the defense of Jerusalem by his wife's uncle, the Baron of Ibelin. Most people spoke of it with awe, despite the ultimate failure to hold Jerusalem for Christ. He asked cautiously now, "The loss of Jerusalem is a terrible blow. It must have been hard for you to witness the surrender."

"Hard?" Sister Adela looked at Aimery as if he were half mad. "I have never been so conscious of the living God in all my life! They had already breached the wall, you know. They were throwing assault after assault through that breach, and thousands remained outside just waiting their turn. We were out of Greek fire, too. We had fought for a week—women, children and priests alongside what men were there—and we could not fight anymore. But slavery, at least for us women, is truly a fate worse than death. I was trying to decide if I should kill my sisters to save them from that, taking the sin upon my own head, when people started shouting that the Baron of Ibelin had talked the Sultan into sparing us all. Despite the fact the walls were breached! Despite the fact that his banners had briefly waved over the northeast tower!

"That, my lord Constable, could only have been the Grace of God. Who else could have inspired the Lord of Ibelin with words to soften the Sultan's heathen heart? Who else could have inspired a man of such renown on the battlefield to put the welfare of the poor ahead of his honor as a knight? It was a miracle—or as close to one as these old eyes are likely to see." She pointed with her two index fingers to her eyes before adding, "What followed was less pretty, of course. People scrambled to find the ransom payments by any means, including theft, blackmail, extortion, and prostitution. And some rich men—including prelates of the Church—preferred their own wealth to the freedom of the poor. But there were also acts of great charity and generosity," she added more mildly.

Aimery nodded, wondering what Eschiva had experienced. The nun's tale reminded him that he was not the only one to have suffered this past year. Eschiva, too, must have gone through hell. She would have been frightened for herself and their children as well as for him. She would have witnessed that short but brutal siege—and then this unsavory scramble to escape slavery. He suddenly realized he didn't even know what the ransom payment had been, much less where Eschiva would have found the means to pay it for herself and their children.

"Sister," he turned to the Hospitaller nun tensely, "have you any news of my wife, Eschiva? I've had no word from her since Hattin. Is she safe?" In all that time in prison, when he had clung to images of Eschiva, it had never occurred to him that she might have suffered some misfortune in the catastrophe that had enveloped them.

"She accompanied the Dowager Queen and Princess Isabella when they left Jerusalem before the siege," Sister Adela reassured him. "And I believe," she added, gently touching Aimery's arm, "that's her with the Queen and my lord of Ibelin now." Adela pointed to the quay, which was now only yards away as the ship glided alongside.

Aimery's heart stopped. He had imagined this moment a thousand times or more—yet it was so different than he had pictured it. In his imagination there had always just been the two of them. They had both been on foot, and they had come together to embrace in relief and gratitude. Instead, here he was on the raised deck of a ship, surrounded by strangers, and she was ten feet below him on a crowded quay, a worried look on her face as she futilely searched the passengers crowded in the waist of the ship.

Aimery raised an arm and waved, but the lump in his throat prevented him from getting out a single sound. She was—there was no word for it. He was not objective enough to see if she was aged, thinner or fatter, or anything at all. All he registered was that she was truly here. Alive. Well. His.

"Excuse me," he muttered to an understanding Sister Adela, as he grabbed the railing of the ladder to drop down from the poop to the waist in a single leap. There he had to fight his way through the other passengers pressing together to cross the gangway. He unabashedly ordered people out of his way, until at last he could haul himself onto the gangway and cross it with long, hurried strides. As he jumped down onto the quay, she ran towards him, her veils streaming out behind her.

"Aimery! Aimery!" The next instant he had her in his arms and was clinging to her as if his life depended on it. As perhaps it did. "Aimery!" she gasped again, her head on his chest, and he bent to kiss her on the lips, with a mental apology for disdaining his brother for doing the same thing only a fortnight ago.

Behind Eschiva, Isabella collapsed into her stepfather's arms as she realized that Humphrey wasn't on the ship.

Chapter 8

Tyre, May 1189

THE NEWS THAT KERAK HAD FALLEN reached Tyre via the garrison, remnants of whom washed up in the taverns there after receiving a safe-conduct from the Sultan. They had withstood the siege for nearly two years. Their supplies had been getting low, and then somehow the water had become contaminated. They had started dying like flies then, and when the Lady of Oultrejourdain herself succumbed to the disease, the backbone of the resistance was broken. Isolated by the siege, the garrison had not heard about the great crusade now gathering. Without hope of relief, resistance seemed pointless. When the most senior of the surviving sergeants put it to the vote, not one man had advocated holding out any longer—as long as they were granted their lives and freedom. The offer had been made to the emir commanding the Sultan's siege force and had been accepted. They had to leave their weapons behind, but had been allowed to take any other belongings they could carry, along with their women and children.

Squires from the Ibelin household brought the news of Kerak's surrender to their lord, and Balian broke the news to Isabella. She jumped up, her cheeks flushed with excitement, and then stopped. "And Humphrey? What about Humphrey?"

"There was no mention of Humphrey, Bella. He was not at Kerak, so he was not included in the surrender."

"But Salah ad-Din *always* offered to release him in exchange for Kerak," the teenager protested hotly. "From the start, that was *always* his demand!"

"I know, but Humphrey did not deliver Kerak to him," Balian reminded her carefully. "The garrison did."

"But what's the point of keeping him a prisoner any longer? He doesn't have anything else of value!" Isabella remonstrated.

"Montreal," her stepfather countered softly, referring to the other stronghold of Oultrejourdain that still held out.

"Salah ad-Din can't expect Humphrey to surrender that as well!" Isabella objected, but she sounded foolish even to herself and at once fell silent, crestfallen.

Her mother slipped an arm around her waist and drew her closer, kissing her temple. "With Stephanie de Milly dead, there's no reason the garrison at Montreal will hold out much longer, either," she suggested softly. "I'm sure Humphrey will soon be released." As she spoke she looked to her husband. "Surely you could send word to the Sultan inquiring after the Lord of Toron?"

"I can't see what good it would do. He was trying to assassinate me eighteen months ago," Ibelin retorted.

"We don't know it was the Sultan," Maria Zoë countered. "It might have been his brother, or just one of his emirs who had a grudge against you. Besides, no one is asking you to go personally. We can send Sir Bartholomew or Ernoul."

Balian shrugged and admitted, "I could try, I suppose." He did not sound particularly willing, much less eager.

"Please do," Maria Zoë answered pointedly, stroking Isabella's arm. She understood her husband's contempt for Toron—yet it was hard to watch her daughter, who should have been a blooming seventeen-year-old, becoming more and more morose and depressed.

Isabella hadn't chosen Humphrey. She'd been taken forcibly from her mother and stepfather at the age of eight, sent to live in the bleak quasi-prison of Kerak, and denied the right to even visit her mother for three years. Then at the age of eleven, before the age of consent, she had been married to Humphrey de Toron, a youth four years her senior. Humphrey had been chosen for her by Maria Zoë's bitterest enemy and rival: King Amalric's first wife, Agnes de Courtenay. Isabella's marriage to Toron had been intended to ensure that Isabella remained under the control of people who would prevent her being used to depose Agnes' children, Baldwin and Sibylla.

What no one had reckoned with was that the children, Humphrey and Isabella, would fall in love with one another. Isolated in the brutal atmosphere of Kerak, where the Lord of Oultrejourdain terrorized his own men and Humphrey at least as much as he preyed on Bedouin and attacked the Sultan's convoys, they had turned to one another for comfort. They had become best friends long before they were old enough to consummate a marriage. Indeed, Isabella had confided to Maria Zoë, their marriage had still not been consummated when

Humphrey left for Hattin. Humphrey's affection for Isabella was so manifest, however, that Maria Zoë felt confident that her son-in-law's restraint was motivated by respect for his bride's tender age.

To her husband she suggested gently, "Isabella has a right to know what Salah ad-Din intends to do with her husband now that he has Kerak. There must be some way you can request news of him."

Balian capitulated. "I'll ride out to the border and make contact with one of the Sultan's patrols."

Humphrey was appalled to realize he had not recognized where he was until he saw the silhouette of Toron Castle in the distance. He'd taken a fond leave of Imad ad-Din ten days earlier. He'd then been escorted to Damascus, where he'd had a brief, unsatisfying interview with Salah ad-Din. The Sultan had seemed distracted and disinterested, bluntly telling Humphrey he was no longer of any value as a prisoner because both Kerak and Montreal had surrendered.

In Damascus, Humphrey had been turned over to a troop of Mamlukes commanded by a red-headed young man who called himself Khalid al-Hamar, Khalid the Red. They took Humphrey across the upper Jordan at Jacob's Ford. The ruins of the castle King Baldwin had tried to build here a decade earlier reminded Humphrey of a butcher's yard. Like the bones of dismembered beasts, the masonry lay tossed about the valley floor in disorderly heaps, bleaching in the summer sun. Around these disjointed ruins, the dry weeds of summer waved and whispered in the dusty breeze. The only sounds were the screeching of the crickets and the rustling of the grass, while the only living creatures inhabiting the ruins were snakes and scorpions. Overhead, however, vultures circled, as if they still hoped to find food in the shallow pits where a thousand defenders had been dumped without proper burial.

Humphrey had shuddered in the heat, and then had sweated through the night because they camped among the ruins of the accursed castle. It was said the Templar commander of the unfinished castle had flung himself into the flames of the breached walls, and Humphrey was certain that his damned soul lurked here still, a ghostly testimony to the Christians' humiliation. Each time he heard a footfall or the rustling of a snake in the grass, his imagination conjured up the image of the Templar—his skin burned black but his robes still a pristine white, with a cross of blood upon his breast.

The next day, at some indefinable point, they had crossed into Humphrey's hereditary lordship of Toron. Yet although he had spent the happiest years of his life here, a carefree boy in his grandfather's care, he did not recognize it. Nothing looked familiar now that it was abandoned and uncultivated. Not until he saw his grandfather's castle perched on the side of the mountain slope, far off to their left, did he know for sure where he was.

Khalid al-Hamar pressed on, leaving him lost in miserable memories of his last visit here. That had been after his marriage to Isabella, and five years after his grandfather's death. During the five years of his minority, Toron had been controlled by his mother's third husband, Reynald de Châtillon, the Lord of Oultrejourdain. Humphrey had hated Châtillon from the moment they met. The man was the antithesis of his grandfather—brutal, unscrupulous, cold-blooded, and self-serving. He had no morals and no pity. He'd tried to bludgeon courage and skill at arms into Humphrey while plundering his inheritance. He had stripped Humphrey's castle, too, leaving him nothing but the bare bones.

In a castle stripped of furnishings and surrounded by gardens trampled to bare earth, he and Isabella had frozen through one winter, but by spring Humphrey had been glad to surrender the barony of Toron in exchange for a money fief and a comfortable house in Jerusalem. Isabella had been far from happy with his decision, however. She'd said a money fief was for men of base birth, and had indignantly reminded him she was a princess. It had been their first serious fight, Humphrey remembered morosely.

The memory of that clash cast a shadow over Humphrey, and he took no notice of where they were riding. He hardly even noticed the increased alertness of his escort when they drew near the unofficial border between Saracen-controlled territory and the land held tenuously by the Franks from Tyre. Because there were no fortresses or even fortified manors along the improvised border, Frankish control of the countryside could last only as long as the Sultan was engaged elsewhere. Patrols of Franks and Saracens constantly probed each other's strength. Yet the very fact that Frankish forces could come this far ensured that the area closer to Tyre was partially protected and could be cultivated.

As the afternoon wore on, Khalid appeared to become increasingly unsure of himself. He led down one track and then another. Twice he halted and examined a map. The day seemed to be slipping away from them, and Humphrey was starting to feel nervous. Then a shout of alarm drew everyone's attention to a puff of dust in the distance. After staring at it, Humphrey made out a dark, moving shape at the head of the dust cloud.

"Riders," Khalid announced, and drew up. The others halted behind him, squinting into the bright but low afternoon sunlight. At last Khalid was satisfied and declared "Ibn Barzan," gesturing for them to move forward again.

Not until this moment did Humphrey realize his captors had arranged to release him directly into the hands of his wife's stepfather. That did not give him much time to prepare. His thoughts were in turmoil as they picked up an easy canter and the figures in the distance took on an increasingly definable shape.

Ibelin was riding at the head of a small troop. His squire held his cleft banner aloft, a red cross pattée on a marigold field; the banner snaked and writhed in the wind. Ibelin himself was fully armored. The chain mail molded to his arms and legs glimmered in the sun; his torso was covered by a surcoat made of a light material that billowed out from his back and fluttered away from his legs in the wind created by cantering. He wore an open-faced helmet with nose guard rather than visor. The stallion he was riding was a powerful chestnut with energy to spare, although dark with sweat in the summer heat.

Humphrey felt himself getting nervous at the mere sight of the Baron of Ibelin. Damn him! He looked so supremely self-confident. So proud and unbroken. Free.

And why shouldn't he? *He* hadn't surrendered at Hattin. He had led his knights right through the lines of the enemy. He had delivered them—and thousands of infantry who followed in the wake of that breakout—from that field of blood, death, and shame.

Humphrey remembered how Ibelin had shouted at the Constable, pointing to something. The Constable had shook his head, but laid a hand on Ibelin's arm in a gesture of affection or condolence, before nodding and gesturing for him to go.

Ibelin had gathered his knights around him, and the squires had pressed in close behind them, drawing their swords. With a shout, Ibelin had couched his lance and put his spurs to his aging grey destrier. The old stallion had sprung forward with amazing energy after two days without water, and the little troop of heavy Frankish cavalry had crashed into the mass of Saracen light cavalry, hemming them in from all sides. Like a lethal wedge, Ibelin had pierced the wall of Saracens and driven deeper and deeper into that mass of murderous enemies. Then the Saracens had surged into his flank, and abruptly Ibelin had changed direction. In a split second, Ibelin and his men were galloping east rather than north. As they thundered down on the Saracen foot soldiers, the latter parted in sheer terror. If they didn't, they died, trampled under the Frankish horses. Meanwhile, the Frankish infantry that had been cowering on the southern hill rushed down the slope to follow Ibelin's charge. Humphrey remembered watching in awe as Ibelin disappeared over the edge of the cliff facing the Sea of Galilee, and the infantry followed after him like lava pouring over the edge of a volcano.

Humphrey remembered that, and remembered feeling amazement and envy, without once thinking about following. Why not? Why hadn't he joined the squires of Ibelin, Ramla, and Nablus? Why hadn't they *all* followed?

Too soon, the gap torn by Ibelin and his knights was filled again with hordes of enemy. The flow of human lava stopped. Those, like Humphrey, who had not dared to ride with that last charge found themselves trapped on an ever-shrinking island in the sea of Saracens. They were surrounded by the corpses of men and horses, while beyond them on the hill, the Saracens hacked the Bishop of Acre in two and flung down the True Cross. It landed in dirt that had been turned to mud by the blood of the martyrs defending it.

That image terrorized Humphrey's dreams at night. Although what followed had in many ways been worse. . . .

There was no more time for memories, however. Ibelin reined his horse to a walk, and Khalid al-Hamar did the same. Signaling their men to stay where they were, the leaders on both sides advanced to meet in the space between them. They bowed their heads to one another and conversed in Arabic. Then Khalid gestured with rotary motions of his arm for Humphrey to come forward.

Humphrey's mouth was dry, his palms wet. He was so close he could see Ibelin's face, his dark, penetrating eyes on either side of his nose guard. Ibelin was an exceptionally tall man and he rode a tall horse, which only made Humphrey feel even smaller and more ashamed.

Ibelin did not smile as they came abreast of one another. He nodded his head in greeting with a formal "my lord of Toron," and then without further comment swung his horse around on his haunches in an unthinking display of horsemanship. He guided his horse off the road and rode to the rear of his troop as his knights turned their own horses around to follow him, their order now reversed. Then, without a word, Ibelin picked up a canter again. Humphrey, on his aging Arab packhorse (that was all they'd been willing to give away with him), had a hard time keeping up with Ibelin.

They rode like that for at least a half-hour, or so it seemed to Humphrey. Ibelin made no effort to converse with him, although he did moderate his pace when he realized Humphrey's nag could not keep up with his own stallion. Finally, however, they came to a small stream banked by still-green grass and wildflowers. Here Ibelin drew up, and then dropped his reins on his horse's neck to let his stallion wade into the desultory, muddy waters and drink. Humphrey and the others followed his example.

Ibelin shoved his helmet up by the nosepiece and bowed his head to wipe sweat off his face on the inside of his surcoat. Then he hung his helmet on the pommel of his saddle and reached up to untie his aventail. With the flap hanging down, he shoved the chain-mail coif and arming cap off his head, revealing his sweat-soaked dark hair. Ibelin's squire squeezed his horse forward to offer his lord a water skin.

Humphrey started. The youth was familiar, but it took him a moment to remember where he'd seen him before. Finally he recalled that this young man had been nothing but a groom in the Ibelin stable in Nablus.

Ibelin saw his surprised look and remarked dryly, "Ernoul's shoulder and collarbone were broken at Hattin, so he can no longer serve me in the field. Gabriel gave his life at Jerusalem—as did Dawit and Daniel." He paused and then remarked in what almost passed for a friendly tone, "We can't make Tyre tonight, so we'll spend the night at an abandoned sugar mill a little up the road."

The well-watered coastal plain southeast of Tyre had been one of the centers of sugar-cane production before Hattin, and stone refineries still dotted the countryside. No doubt Salah ad-Din and his emirs had no interest in destroying something of no military value to their enemies but of potential economic value to themselves—whenever they finally set about organizing this conquered territory for their own benefit. The sugar cane itself, however, had died of thirst when the mill-powered irrigation stopped. Starved of water when the people fled with their mules, the cane had grown and then toppled over to lie like a huge mat across the countryside, slowly parching in the Palestinian sun. The irrigation ditches had gradually dried up and the water reservoirs were little more than stinking, mosquito-breeding ponds, at best a third of their original volume.

The dried cane made good firewood, however, and the squires were sent out to gather up bundles of it, while two of the knights took crossbows and went in search of dinner. Small game and wild chickens were abundant throughout this abandoned landscape, Humphrey was told.

Ibelin untacked his horse himself and hobbled him. Taking his saddlebags, he led Humphrey into the vaulted hall of the derelict sugar factory. Although someone had removed any jars containing molasses, a number of empty jars remained, surrounded by broken shards of pottery; apparently, someone searching for sugar had systematically broken all the sugar molds. The well, however, was still (or again) functioning, and Ibelin went there first, pumped water over his hands, and splashed it on his dusty face. Then he filled a bucket with water, which he brought to his horse. Humphrey awkwardly followed his example, although the silence was increasingly taxing his nerves.

Returning inside the stone structure, Humphrey noticed now that straw had been heaped up in the corners, and under the bronze vats originally used for boiling the crushed cane there was evidence of recent fires. There were even brass oil lamps on shelves around the old millstone. This had been converted into a table, where Ibelin set out the bread, cheese, and sausage that he'd been carrying in his saddlebag.

At last, Ibelin sat down on a bench on the wall of the mill and gestured for Humphrey to sit beside him. Cautiously, Humphrey did. Ibelin took a wineskin from his saddlebag and offered it to Humphrey. "It's not very good," he warned as Humphrey took it tentatively. "One could call it the bitter harvest of Hattin, but at least we *had* a harvest last fall. And the sugar mill closest to Tyre is operational again as well. We're still dependent on imports from Cyprus for wheat, oats, and barley, but we're self-sufficient in vegetables and fruits, and we produced surplus olive oil this spring."

Humphrey sipped at the wine, wondering why the Baron of Ibelin was talking like a farmer when there were so many more important topics they ought to have been discussing—starting with Isabella.

"Hattin has changed everything," Ibelin seemed to answer him. "We are no longer a kingdom, but an outpost. A vulnerable outpost. Our very survival is predicated on the defenders having enough to eat and clean water to drink. And no man is what he was before. Everyone must prove his worth in the world as it is now—after Hattin."

"What are you trying to say?" Humphrey bristled defensively.

Ibelin shrugged, either to diffuse Humphrey's anger or to take the edge off his words. "The Constable reports you were given favored treatment."

"Did he tell you I'd converted to Islam, too?" Humphrey sneered.

"Did you?"

"No, of course not! But it's the kind of slander the others spread about me. They're all hypocrites! *They* would have welcomed a bath and a change of clothes just as much as I did. They *all* would have accepted 'special treatment,' if only it had been offered them." Humphrey upended the wineskin and drank in gulps to drown his anger.

"Undoubtedly," Ibelin answered steadily, only sipping at his own wine. "But they didn't make Guy de Lusignan King, did they? They didn't put the Kingdom in the hands of an arrogant and incompetent fool. They, with me, tried to *prevent* the catastrophe that put you all in Saracen hands in the first place."

"Are you blaming me for Hattin?" Humphrey asked, flabbergasted. He was acutely aware that he had not played a particularly heroic role in the disastrous battle, but he hadn't ever felt to blame for it, either. King Guy had been in command; all the decisions had been his—including the failure to reinforce either Tripoli or Ibelin when they broke out of the encirclement.

Ibelin shrugged. "If you hadn't betrayed your wife to go crawling on your belly to Guy and Sibylla, the High Court of Jerusalem might have stopped Guy from becoming King at all. We could certainly have ensured he never commanded the feudal army of Jerusalem. Instead, *you* would have been crowned King, and *you* would have commanded us. Would *you* have ignored the counsel of your barons and led your army away from the springs of Sephorie?"

Humphrey stared at Ibelin in shock. Of course he wouldn't have done anything so foolish! He would never have dared to defy the collective wisdom of men older and more experienced than himself. But no sooner had the thought formed than Humphrey's blood ran cold—because he *had*.

When word reached the High Court that Sibylla had had herself crowned Queen of Jerusalem without the consent of the High Court, and had furthermore crowned Guy as her consort against the wishes of her supporters, the High Court had voted to crown Isabella in Bethlehem as a legitimate rival. Humphrey had been horrified by the thought that they would use his wife as a counterweight to Sibylla and that he, as her husband, would be part of their plan. Humphrey had seen only the risk of civil war in a kingdom with two crowned and anointed queens (and their respective consorts). He had believed he was saving the Kingdom from disaster by robbing the High Court of their weapon: himself. He'd slunk away in the dark of night to go to Jerusalem and he'd paid homage to Sibylla and Guy. In so doing, he had foiled the plot to crown Isabella queen and had ensured Guy was recognized as king. He had never regretted that, because not once had he made a connection between his refusal to challenge Sibylla and Guy's coronation in 1186 and the defeat at Hattin. Now that his wife's stepfather had made the connection, however, Humphrey found the thought chilling.

Before he could recover from this new revelation, Ibelin put another question to him. "So tell me: if you did not convert to Islam, why *were* you treated differently from the other prisoners?"

Humphrey was relieved to have the conversation diverted away from his responsibility for Hattin, and answered readily, indeed with a trace of pride. "Because I write fluent Arabic. I wrote the letter to Salah ad-Din requesting Sibylla's release, and the Sultan's secretary was impressed with my command of Arabic. He wanted to meet me, saw the condition I was in, and took pity on me. That was all." Humphrey helped himself to more wine.

"Really?" Ibelin asked with obvious disbelief. When Humphrey didn't answer, he continued, "If that had happened once, I might have believed you, but Aimery says you met with Imad ad-Din roughly once a fortnight. What were all those subsequent meetings about?"

Humphrey was flushed—whether from the unaccustomed wine, from shame, or from anger was unclear—but his lips had a stubborn set. "We just talked," he told Ibelin obstinately.

"About what?"

"Philosophy, religion, literature, all kinds of things!" Humphrey gestured as if to brush flies away as he remembered talking about his fellow barons. "It's not as if I didn't learn things of importance, too!" he defended himself.

"Like what?" Ibelin pressed him.

"That the Sultan dotes on his eldest son al-Afdal, for example, but many of the emirs find al-Afdal arrogant and shallow. And many of the Sultan's men are tired of *jihad* and want to have time with their families. And there have been rebellions against Salah ad-Din in northern Syria."

Not uninteresting, Ibelin noted, but he wasn't prepared to admit that to this youth who deserved so much blame yet refused to even understand his failures. "And what did Imad ad-Din learn from you?"

"That I hated Reynald de Châtillon!" Humphrey burst out. Then before Ibelin could pose another question, he lashed out, "You don't know what it was like!"

"You forget my brother Hugh spent years in a Saracen prison, and Barry was held for a half-year, and Aimery was with you; he's told me a great deal."

"That's not what I'm talking about," Humphrey insisted passionately, the now unfamiliar wine clearly speaking. "I'm talking about the slow slaughter of 250 Templars and Hospitallers! Before our very eyes! And I'm talking about slave markets glutted with Christian women. Why, Imad ad-Din even offered me the services of one of his slaves! He thought to overcome my resistance by assuring me she was Christian! All it did was add to my revulsion!" Humphrey spat this out so furiously that Ibelin was taken aback, and a silence fell between them.

At last Ibelin asked, "Did you get her name?"

"Of course not! What good would it have done? I'm sure she would not want anyone who had known her before to see what she has become. Besides, I refused the services offered, so I neither saw nor spoke to her."

"I doubt Imad ad-Din understood such admirable restraint."

"No, he didn't. No one does. You don't, either, do you?"

"You think *I* would have raped a Christian woman simply because she had been degraded and humiliated by the Saracens?" Ibelin asked sharply, his cheeks flushed from his effort to restrain his own fury.

Humphrey saw he had gone too far, and hastened to retreat. "No, that's not what I meant. I just meant—I just meant—you don't understand!" he ended helplessly. That was the whole problem: Humphrey did not think anyone understood him. Except Isabella. The thought of her made his throat constrict, and he felt tears in his eyes. He swallowed hard. "Is—is Isabella well?" he asked.

"Isabella is the only reason I'm here," Ibelin answered honestly, his hostility to Toron simmering just below the surface. "She has been inconsolable since your capture, and as soon as word came of the surrender of Kerak, she insisted I seek your release."

Humphrey looked up at Ibelin with a sudden light of hope in his eyes. "Then she has not forgotten me?"

Ibelin remembered fleetingly that Christmas dinner with Conrad de Montferrat and other meetings since. Conrad was clearly attracted to Isabella, and he was a very charming man when he wanted to be. But Isabella was far too loyal and innocent to have been diverted by Montferrat. To Humphrey he answered firmly, "Not for a moment."

The answer sent a wave of relief through Humphrey so powerful that tears flooded his eyes. The return of the squires with the kindling, however, distracted Ibelin's attention, and soon afterward one of the knights returned with a hare. Ibelin rose to help prepare their dinner, and the time for intimate conversation was past. The conversation had not been to either of their liking anyway, and they made no effort to repeat it.

Tyre, June 1189

The group of men were gathered in the solar of the Ibelin residence, standing closely around the small mosaic-topped table on which Ibelin had spread out a map. The map was not very high quality—"sketch" might have been a better word for it—but it was a means of jostling the memory of the men collected in the room. Besides Balian d'Ibelin, they were Reginald de Sidon, Aimery de Lusignan, and Humphrey de Toron. Conrad de Montferrat was also present, but he had no knowledge of the terrain between Tyre and Sidon anyway, so he was more an observer than a participant in the discussion.

"The distance from here to Sidon is almost exactly forty miles," Reginald declared, stretching his hand over the map, his thumb on Tyre and the tip of his little finger on Sidon. He had recovered remarkably well from his ordeal, Ibelin thought. No scars had been left on his wrists, and those on the soles of his feet were well hidden. His hair was still thin and almost completely gray, but he had recovered his proud bearing. In the tiltyard he could still take on most of the younger knights with at least a fifty-fifty chance of staying in the saddle—and that was good enough for a man of sixty, he'd assured Ibelin. A joust with Ibelin himself he consistently declined, with a smile and the assurance that he didn't need to eat any more sand.

"More important," Aimery took up the conversation, "we control the territory all the way to the Litani, and no Saracen has dared set foot across the river since I've been here."

"But we've often seen their patrols beyond it, and once or twice they've let their horses drink from the far bank," Ibelin reminded them.

"Patrols, yes," Sidon declared, straightening up, "but nothing to indicate they're in a position to occupy everything from the Litani to Sidon. As Aimery points out, the distance that might be contested is at most thirty miles, not forty. Furthermore, Salah ad-Din *gave* me Sidon."

For the last three weeks, Reginald had been trying to convince the others that they should try to retake Sidon and so extend Frankish controlled territory. There were good reasons for doing so. As Ibelin had outlined to Toron on his return from captivity, Tyre was not self-sufficient in food, and it could not be unless they controlled more farmland. It made sense to expand along the coast, where the land was most fertile. Expanding to the north had the advantage of reducing the distance to Tripoli, the next Frankish state. Furthermore, Sidon was a good port, once the home of important shipyards, and the local inhabitants had been renowned shipwrights for centuries. Regaining control of those and reopening the shipyards would enable the Franks to gain control of the sea, more important than ever since Antioch, Tripoli, and Tyre were currently separated from one another by the enemy on land. Reginald de Sidon, of course, had the added interest of regaining his own lordship.

At the mention of Salah ad-Din's promise, Ibelin looked annoyed. "You told me from the start you didn't take that seriously."

"Yes and no," Sidon prevaricated. "I think it was an empty gesture—but if we don't call his bluff, we can't expose his duplicity. He can always claim he *would* have kept his word, that all I had to do was go to Sidon."

"Whatever Salah ad-Din said or meant, we have to assume we're moving into hostile territory," Aimery countered. "The question is: do we have enough knights, Turcopoles, and men-at-arms to take control of the coast from the Litani to Sidon? What is the status of Sarepta? Do we know if anyone is living there now? The state of the defenses? And what of Sidon itself? Is it correct that the walls were razed and it is no longer defensible?"

They all nodded. Ships passing from Tripoli to Tyre and back had been able to report that Sidon's walls had been dismantled and the castle itself scandalized—the ramparts leveled, the gates torn out, and fire set to the storerooms so that great smoke stains pointed upwards from the windows. The shipyards, on the other hand, appeared to be intact, only abandoned. Sailors further reported that the city was inhabited by what they guessed were a few hundred people, mostly native Syrian fishermen and their families.

Sidon explained, "Sarepta surrendered without a fight and the citizens fled to Sidon. The town was plundered and the walls slighted. Sidon's defenses were more thoroughly dismantled, but that is good from our point of view," he argued, "since it means the Sultan isn't going to hold it against us. Once we reach Sidon, we can reconstruct the defenses—if not around the whole city, then at least around the inner harbor area."

"I don't doubt that. The issue is, can we establish control of the road from here to there?" Aimery returned to his earlier point.

"Well, if we can rebuild the fortifications at Sarepta and leave a garrison there as well, we should be able to establish control over the road," Sidon argued. "We have enough fighting men here at Tyre capable of garrisoning both cities. The orchards around Sarepta are plentiful and valuable in themselves, while the fishing harbor is also useful. I think once we've taken control, we'll find plenty of volunteers to hold it."

"Once we've established control and rebuilt the defenses," Ibelin modified.

"And what if we can't?" Aimery asked. "What if the Saracens send a large force against us that cuts us off from Tyre after we've moved up the coast?"

"Haakon Magnussen says he can keep pace in his snecka. If we get into trouble, he can bring word back here and either recruit reinforcements or, in the worst case, bring the Pisan fleet to take us on board and return by sea."

There were grunts of approval at that plan.

"So," Aimery moved to the next issue, "How many knights, Turcopoles, and sergeants do we have for this expedition?"

"I can't allow you to reduce the strength of the garrison," Montferrat interjected himself into the conversation for the first time. He'd been leaning against the wall, his arms and ankles crossed casually. Now, as the others turned to look at him, he righted himself, uncrossed his legs and arms, and assumed a quasi-belligerent pose.

Ibelin, Sidon, and Lusignan stared at him with unreadable expressions, while Toron looked shocked and slightly outraged. Before Montferrat could explain himself, however, Ibelin turned to Sidon. "You have eighteen knights. I have fifteen. The three of us—or four, if you're with us, Toron?" He tossed the question casually in the direction of his stepdaughter's husband.

"Of course, my lord," Humphrey answered at once, conscious that failure to participate would be seen as cowardice, treason, or just plain inadequacy. At twenty-one he could afford a reputation for none of these, and Isabella would not forgive him if he didn't defend his honor.

Ibelin continued, "Maybe one or two of the knights who have come from the West in the last year will join us as well. Altogether, I think we can count on roughly forty knights. As for Turcopoles, archers, and other infantry, we'll have to see what we can recruit."

The others nodded agreement. There wasn't really a question in any of their minds that it was worth trying. They were tired of doing nothing. It was time to start fighting back.

Although they had felt the need for action themselves, they were still somewhat overwhelmed by the response of the commons. As soon as word leaked out that Ibelin, Sidon, and the Constable were going to lead an expedition to try to retake Sidon, men started clamoring for inclusion. At first Ibelin thought they were just eager for wages. Annoyed that it hadn't been made clear from the start that there would be none, he sent word around that the only "wages" would be plunder. The stream of applicants did not diminish in the least.

When they mustered on June 1, they found one hundred eighteen Turcopoles (on a motley collection of mostly bad horseflesh), close to a thousand archers, and roughly six hundred pikemen, supplemented by a few hundred youth with clubs and other improvised weapons. The backbone of this force, Ibelin soon discovered, were men he'd led off the field of Hattin. These were experienced fighting men, and they trusted his leadership. Perhaps most important, however, almost all these men had lost their families in the subsequent collapse of the Kingdom. These men were desperate to start fighting back.

Ibelin entrusted Sidon, who spoke excellent Arabic, with command of the Turcopoles, and gave him the task of forming the vanguard. He turned the knights including Toron over to Aimery, and tasked him with commanding the heavy cavalry, which would form the rear guard and reserve. He took command of the infantry himself. That he was in overall command had never been questioned by the others.

They left Tyre on June 3, having spent a day in camp organizing, checking weapons and supplies, and ensuring that everyone had enough water and rations. On June 4 they reached the Litani and camped on the south bank. The following day, they crossed the river and immediately progress slowed dramatically. They found the road had washed out in several places, apparently during the heavy rainfall of the past winter. The little force only covered six miles that day, but at least they had seen no Saracens. On June 6 they covered a further nine miles, reaching the ruins of Sarepta.

In the crusader era, Sarepta had always been dominated by the Church. It was a bishop's seat and had housed the headquarters of the Carmelite order. The largest shrine had been St. Elijah, as this was the site of the biblical miracle in which he had raised a widow's son from the dead. The Saracens had trashed the great church and burned something inside, leaving it a blackened hulk. The large number of pig bones in the ashes suggested that they had burned the entire pig population as an expression of contempt and hatred. The sight saddened and embittered the Christian troops, and Ibelin heard much muttering among his men, vowing revenge. They spent the night in whatever buildings they could find that were still more or less intact, the leaders enjoying comparatively comfortable quarters in the cloisters of the Carmelite monastery. Although the flower beds had gone to seed, the well had not been poisoned, and the cloisters provided shade and tranquility.

No sooner had they left Sarepta behind, however, than they attracted the attention of an enemy patrol. Sidon led his Turcopoles in a dash to try to cut off the Saracens and ensure their intelligence did not reach anyone, but the horses of the Turcopoles were inadequate to overtake the fleeter horses of the Saracen reconnaissance.

They had to expect resistance of some kind now, and Ibelin was made uneasy by the fact that just beyond Sarepta, the road turned inland to skirt some higher bluffs that dropped precipitously into the sea. For the first time since setting off, they were going to be out of sight of Haakon Magnussen's ship.

The march along the dusty road in intense, cloudless, windless heat was all too reminiscent of Hattin, and Ibelin saw his own disquiet reflected in the grim expressions on the faces of his men. He ordered Sidon to divide up his Turcopoles into multiple patrols and sent them ahead in sweeping reconnaissance. "Don't just watch for the enemy: note every well, every orchard, every stream and fishpond. If we need to take up defensive positions, I want it to be where there is water," he ordered. Then he kept the infantry marching at as brisk a pace as possible. He did not relax until the shore came into view again, shimmering silver and gold in the afternoon sun.

By dusk they were still a mile away, but Ibelin would not let his troops rest until they'd reached the beach. With relief, he located Haakon Magnussen's snecka ghosting along the shore several miles to the north on the dying breeze. The Norseman dipped his banner once to indicate he had seen them, and then ran out his oars and returned to drop anchor opposite their position.

They camped that night on the sandy shore. The soothing sound of waves slowly sweeping in and out across the sand lulled most of the men to ready sleep after the exhausting, tense day. Ibelin, Sidon, Toron, and the Constable stayed awake longer, however, while the crickets chattered in the tall grasses of the dunes and the gulls cried overhead. They were now just seven miles from the city of Sidon, and Reginald said the substantial but unfortified town of Ghaziye lay only a mile or so inland. This was—or had been—a major olive-oil manufacturing center surrounded by olive orchards.

Ibelin didn't like the sound of that. "Are there springs there?"

"Yes, it's lush countryside," Sidon confirmed, thinking of how beautiful and prosperous the town had been with its limestone houses set amidst green orchards. Ibelin was thinking that such a town might serve as the perfect base for Saracen troops.

He was not happy to be proved right.

They had barely broken camp and started up the road on the final leg toward Sidon when the enemy appeared in force. Sidon, commanding the advance guard, immediately drew up and sent for Ibelin, the Constable, and (as a courtesy) Toron. By the time the others arrived, Sidon was able to report that the Saracen force was composed exclusively of mounted archers—no infantry or lancers—and was, he estimated, almost five thousand strong. They counted at least eighteen banners, but in the experience of the Frankish leaders, the size of a Saracen battalion could vary from two to three hundred. By their equipment, Sidon and Ibelin concluded they were Turkish regulars. They were blocking the road in a large, dense mass, daring the Franks to continue.

This put the Franks at a disadvantage. In a defensive situation, their comparatively large infantry force would have provided the horsemen with cover, and all they would have needed to do was hunker down, let the enemy exhaust themselves in futile attacks, and then launch a mounted counterattack. Sidon and Ibelin agreed the Saracens would be mad to do them the favor of attacking—but hoping for good luck or the Grace of God, they drew up into a defensive position and waited.

The sun crawled its way up the sky. Flies and gnats plagued them. The horses stamped in irritation. They sweated and thirsted, and their only comfort was that the enemy was in exactly the same situation. Late in the afternoon, they elected to withdraw back to the beach. Here they could refresh themselves and their horses while retaining a defensive posture. The Saracens shadowed them and camped within sight but out of bowshot. Judging by their campfires, they numbered closer to six thousand than five thousand.

"What if we were to retreat to Sarepta and establish ourselves there?" Aimery de Lusignan suggested. "The harbor is in good condition, and holding the territory from the Litani to Sarepta would still be a step in the right direction."

Ibelin agreed, although Sidon was deeply disappointed at the thought of pulling back. "We can't just scuttle back to safety like curs!" he protested. "We should at least probe the mettle of enemy."

The other three men gazed at him mutely. Toron was sweating badly and kept trying to wipe his palms dry on his surcoat, leaving streaks of sweat on the skirts.

"If the knights charge with the Turcopoles in their wake, we might be able to break through."

"Maybe, and then the Turks will close ranks again, and we'll be separated from our infantry. Then they can slaughter us separately at their leisure," Aimery speculated.

Sidon frowned fiercely, but he didn't contradict him. Both men looked at Ibelin.

"Even if we could break through with our entire force, the number of Saracen units out there suggests that Salah ad-Din intends to hold onto this territory. In short, we have called his bluff, and his promise to you was worthless," Ibelin noted dryly. He would have preferred to be proved wrong in this as well. This wasn't just Sidon's inheritance they were fighting for, it was Helvis' future. "The fact that we got this far, however, suggests also that we might indeed be able to hold Sarepta and the land between Tyre and Sarepta. That would give us a second port, substantial fertile land, and more defensible and comfortable housing for many refugees. Taking control of Sarepta, rebuilding the defenses, establishing a garrison there, and cultivating the coastline from the Litani to Sarepta are not insignificant accomplishments."

Sidon growled something and stalked out of the meeting. Balian and Aimery exchanged a glance.

"Do we retreat tomorrow, then?" Humphrey asked.

"No, we take our time. Keep the enemy guessing about our intentions. I propose moving out tomorrow night after darkness. There will be almost no moon by then. If we move with sufficient care, we could be halfway back to Sarepta before they notice we've gone."

The Constable and Toron nodded agreement, and Ibelin went in search of Sidon to convey their decision. He also had Sir Roger Shoreham pass the word to the archers and the other infantry, before signaling to Haakon Magnussen the need for parley. The Norseman lowered a small boat and had himself rowed ashore, so Ibelin could explain the situation.

On the night of June 9, the Franks quietly packed up their few belongings and retreated by cover of darkness. Despite having failed in their objective, the mood among the men was, Ibelin thought, remarkably good. They had escaped the boredom of waiting for the brewing crusade and were encouraged to have come this far. They were not really eager to attack a force roughly three times their size in territory where they were essentially isolated. Their overall concurrence with the decision taken by their leaders was expressed in the disciplined fashion in which everyone maintained silence and moved efficiently.

The march back to Sarepta was considerably easier than the march out. The night was cool and they were rested, but as they came within sight of the ruined town they were discomfited to see Saracen banners fluttering from the tallest remaining buildings. Now their only option was to keep marching back south whence they'd come. This felt more like a "cur scuttling back to safety with his tail between his legs" than Ibelin was comfortable with.

They skirted the town of Sarepta in the half-light of early dawn and were already a mile to the south when the rear guard shouted a warning. Ibelin at once reined his horse around and cantered back to the Constable.

Lusignan had turned the knights around to face what was following them: a force of what looked like four to five hundred horsemen. And they weren't just ordinary horsemen: they were the Sultan's Mamlukes. "They must have seen us slink by," he commented as Ibelin drew rein beside him.

"Maybe they just want to herd us back to the Litani," Ibelin suggested.

"Maybe."

They couldn't keep marching indefinitely, not after the sleepless night, so Ibelin sent Sidon and his Turcopoles ahead to find a defensible position in which to camp. Meanwhile the Constable and his knights formed a protective screen across the road, leap-frogging forward in relays to keep up with their infantry.

Just beyond one of the tributaries to the Litani, the Turcopoles found what they thought was a defensible campsite. Abandoned vineyards slanted down toward the shallow stream, serving as a break to any cavalry charge, and at the top of the slope was a large citrus orchard that provided both shade and cover for archers. The stream itself ensured the horses had drinking water.

The flagging infantry perked up at the prospect of rest. Within an hour the leading units were already across the stream, which while fordable, slowed them down. As the infantry spread out to cross the stream all along the bank, the Saracens launched an attack on the rearguard.

Ibelin supposed that the Saracen commander shared their assessment of the campsite—or simply wanted to imitate on a small scale the success King Baldwin had had at Montgisard. At that battle in 1177, King Baldwin had pounced on Salah ad-Din's invasion force when it was making camp for the night on the banks of a river—and obliterated it. Shouting for the archers to get across the stream and start providing covering fire from the far slope, Ibelin spun his destrier around and galloped back to join Aimery de Lusignan, with Sidon and his Turcopoles at his heels.

In the short time it had taken for Ibelin to give his orders and turn back, the Constable and his knights had been completely enveloped by the enemy. Although they were still fighting in a tumultuous melee, around the edges Turkish horsemen were streaming past, shouting war cries and raising their bows to fire at the retreating Frankish infantry. Ibelin made a split-second decision to try to cut the Constable and his knights free rather than try to stop the Turkish archers rushing to attack his infantry. He had to trust Shoreham to organize his archers to protect the infantry.

A moment later he crashed into the seething mass of confused combat and started felling his opponents with his sword. Sidon was right beside him, doing the same thing. The Turcopoles, though less well armored than the Frankish knights, were on very equal footing when fighting mounted Turkish archers in close combat. By closing before the Turkish archers could use their bows, they robbed them of their greatest tactical advantage, and with half the Turks rushing past them to attack the Frankish infantry, the odds were swinging in favor of the Frankish/Turcopole cavalry.

It took Ibelin and Sidon at most half an hour to hack their way through to the Constable and the other knights, but by then the intensity of the Saracen opposition was waning. Ibelin could not spare a glance over his shoulder, but he could clearly hear screams that were not just battle cries, much less ululations of triumph on the part of the Saracens. His peripheral vision, furthermore, registered movement in the direction of Sarepta. It might just be riderless and panicked horses, or it might indicate that at least some of the enemy had already abandoned the attack.

With a well-trained slashing stroke that harnessed gravity to the strength of his sword arm, Ibelin brought his sword down on the back of a man's head. Ibelin's sword, the words "Defender of Jerusalem" engraved in bronze in the fuller of the blade, sliced clear through the back of the man's helmet, sank into his neck, and cut his spine in two. Blood spurted from the ruptured artery as the corpse slid from the terrified horse, and Ibelin drew up beside Sir Galvin. In the protection of the Scottish knight's great mace, Ibelin risked looking back over his shoulder. He was both relieved and amazed to see that the Turks appeared to be in headlong flight. It wasn't just a few of their number who were fleeing northwards; apparently they all were—at least those not pinned to the earth by the crossbow bolts coming in steady volleys from the far bank of the stream.

Around the Frankish/Turcopole cavalry, the Turkish horsemen were beginning to understand that their fellows had been routed, and they were looking for
ways to disengage. On the edges, they were spinning their mounts around and
pounding the flanks of their horses with their heels, but in the thick of the melee
it was not so easy to escape. The Constable was killing men with chilling pro-
ficiency, and Ibelin saw on his face a fury he could not remember seeing there
before Hattin. Sidon, on the other hand, was flagging, his age or the aftereffects
of his torture sapping the strength from him. Ibelin saw his blows fall ineffec-
tively, and one Turk and then another used that weakness to dart away. Sidon
just slumped in his saddle, relieved to be alive. Even Sir Galvin had stopped
fighting as their opponents melted away before them, spurring their horses in a
frantic bid for escape.

Ibelin was on the brink of deciding they had won the engagement, when
out of nowhere Sir Bartholomew launched himself after the retreating Saracens.
He flung himself half out of his saddle in an attempt to wrap his arms around
one of the most tenacious of the leaders, a Mamluke with a flaming red beard,
and drag him from his own saddle onto Sir Bartholomew's own. This rude and
targeted attack on the troop leader had the appalling effect of rallying the already
routed enemy. With shouts of alarm and outrage, the captured Mamluke's men
not only rushed to his rescue, they screamed for support. From where he sat,
Ibelin saw Saracen horsemen sit back, haul their horses around, and come to the
rescue of their embattled comrade. He registered that the red-headed Mamluke
was either very popular or very important. It took only a few seconds for Sir
Bartholomew to be surrounded, and then to become completely lost from view
as the enemy rained blows on him from all sides.

Ibelin shouted and spurred his destrier into the fray, lashing out in a frenzy
with "Defender of Jerusalem." Sir Galvin and a half-dozen other Frankish
knights joined him. They cut and hacked their way into the enemy, but the
Saracens were already falling back before them, their comrade rescued.

As the enemy withdrew again, Ibelin saw Sir Bartholomew fall onto the
neck of his horse and then tip forward even farther, to sink slowly off his stallion
and land in a heap beside the horse's front feet. From the way his body fell and
sprawled, it was obvious he was either dead or unconscious. His stallion stopped
dutifully beside him, dropping his head to sniff at his immobile rider. The horse
was covered with cuts, bleeding and favoring his off foreleg.

Ibelin drew up beside Sir Bartholomew and flung himself out of the saddle to
go down on one knee beside the older knight. Confused memories filled his brain:
Sir Bartholomew steadying his nerves on the Litani, standing by him like a rock
at Le Forbelet, flanking him as they crashed over the cliff at Hattin to slide and

scramble in a cascade of sand and rubble down the slope toward Lake Tiberius. Dear God, how could You grant him escape from Hattin to die here? Pointlessly. In a skirmish that would never be remembered? Ibelin mentally asked God.

Ibelin removed Sir Bartholomew's helmet, and the older man's head flopped to one side. Ibelin pulled off his chain-mail mitten, freeing his fingers so he could untie Sir Bartholomew's aventail and slip his hand inside to feel for a pulse. Around him the other knights gathered, Sir Galvin dismounting to go down on one knee beside Ibelin, anxiously awaiting his report.

Ibelin was startled to feel the flutter of a pulse beneath his fingers, and called out, "He's alive! Does anyone have water?"

At once Aimery handed him his own water flask, and Ibelin slipped his hand behind Sir Bartholomew's head to lift it before pouring water onto his forehead in a slow dribble.

Sir Bartholomew sputtered and shook his head, as if coming back to life. As his eyes registered the crowd around him, he grunted and shook himself again.

"Are you all right?" Ibelin asked him.

"I've been better," the older knight growled, but the very way in which he now started to pull his feet under him and reached out his hand for Sir Galvin to help him up was answer enough. He was undoubtedly bruised and battered, but he'd sustained no serious injury or wound.

As Sir Galvin braced himself and hauled Sir Bartholomew to his feet again, the others started to disperse, their attention now directed to Sir Roger, who was advancing with the archers in good order. They also began to take stock of what they had achieved. Since Sir Bartholomew was not dead after all, they had sustained no fatal casualties among the knights. In fact, aside from one dislocated shoulder, a couple of broken bones, and the usual collection of bruises and sprains, they were fine.

Ibelin heard Sidon ask about the casualties among the infantry, and Shoreham answered that they were "few, my lord"—whatever that meant exactly. But as the others drifted in the direction of their campsite, eager for water, food, and rest, Balian focused on Sir Bartholomew.

Now they were alone except for Sir Galvin, who was still supporting his friend. In his mind Balian was reliving the older knight's absurd attack on the red-bearded Mamluke after the enemy was already routed. "What the hell was that all about?" he demanded of the older man.

Sir Bartholomew dropped his head and looked down at his feet. "My daughters and grandchildren," he muttered in misery, the full implications of his failure overwhelming him now that he'd recovered from the surprise of his own survival.

Into the stunned silence around him, he added, as if his lord and friend might not fully understand, "I recognized that Mamluke, he seemed in high favor with Salah ad-Din. I thought I might have been able to exchange him for my daughters and grandchildren."

Balian caught his breath—the image of the fifteen thousand women and children who had been marched into slavery because they could not raise a ransom suddenly vivid in his mind's eye. He felt his throat constrict, too, and for an instant was paralyzed by his sense of guilt.

It was Sir Galvin who put his arm around Sir Bartholomew's shoulders and promised, "We won't forget them, Bart. We'll get them back. I promise you on my soul!"

Tyre, August 1189

The high-pitched squealing of excited children drowned out the knocking at the door to the street, and Mariam had to knock several times before one of the Hospitaller sisters answered. Sister Patricia was Irish by birth, with bright red hair (now hidden by her wimple) and pale, freckled skin that a decade in the Holy Land had been unable to darken. She smiled at the sight of Mariam loaded down with boxes, and backed up into the courtyard of the little orphanage.

The orphanage was a simple structure consisting of four vaulted chambers around a small cobbled courtyard. Here the children were playing some game with wild enthusiasm on the part of the elder children and confused but excited running and shouts on the part of the younger children. Built of mud bricks covered with a layer of dirty white plaster, the orphanage was one of the buildings that had sprung up over the last eighteen months outside the defenses of Tyre.

The arrival of Mariam caused a small sensation. Every now and then she brought to the orphanage the things she could no longer sell. At the sight of her, the children dropped their game to crowd around, jumping up and down and clapping in excitement or asking eagerly "What have you brought us?" "What have you got?"

Mariam and Patricia together shooed the children out of the way, to enter the kitchen tract. Here Mariam set her packages down on the solid central table with a sigh of relief. Sweat was dripping from her red face, and she dabbed it dry with the skirts of her apron.

"Today must be the day for visitors," Sister Patricia announced cheerfully, peering into the packages as eagerly as any of the children might have done. "The Dowager Queen and Princess Isabella arrived only a few minutes ago and are with Sister Adela," she told Mariam.

"Ah, yes," Mariam nodded. "Alys mentioned that the Dowager Queen was born on the feast of St. Helena and likes to do something charitable to commemorate the day. Do you know what she brought?"

"Nothing that I know of," Sister Patricia answered honestly. "Or anyway, nothing tangible. I think she said something about employment for one or two of the boys."

Employment was a scarce commodity in Tyre, particularly for youth with no family connections, so Mariam nodded approvingly. To be sure, many of the children here were not true orphans in the sense that they still had living mothers, but they had all been abandoned by relatives unwilling to look after them, and so unwilling or unable to place them in apprenticeships. Not a few were the children of whores, abandoned by mothers who had taken to the streets in the aftermath of Hattin.

"I heard some of the glassmakers are reopening their workshops," Mariam told Sister Patricia. It was not good news for Godwin and herself, because they were being evicted, but it would surely create some more jobs, she thought.

"I hadn't heard that. I'll be sure Sister Adela knows, so she can talk to the glassmakers about giving some of our charges a chance. Meanwhile, I think Queen Maria Zoë said something about grooms. I gather Lord Balian's horsebreeding is flourishing and Queen Maria Zoë wants to give the orphans a chance."

Further discussion was cut short by the arrival of Sister Adela with the Dowager Queen and her daughter.

"Ah, Mistress Olafsen!" Sister Adela greeted the pastry mistress with a warm smile, and Mariam blushed and became flustered. She usually made her deliveries to Sister Patricia, and was uncomfortable with Sister Adela because her sense of gratitude toward the Hospitaller sister bordered on adulation.

When Mariam had been brought to childbed this past year, she had, as expected, stood on the brink of her grave. The child was born dead and the hemorrhaging wouldn't cease. Godwin frantically begged her to confess and repent, but she insisted she did not regret any part of their relationship. So Godwin had gone to the Bishop of Beirut, confessed to bigamy, and asked to be flogged publicly in order to appease God. The Bishop had obligingly turned Godwin over to the secular authorities, and the Marquis de Montferrat had had no qualms about a public flogging. But although Mariam's bleeding had stopped, she had still been slowly sliding into her grave, unable to repent.

Then suddenly the Dowager Queen had appeared with Sister Adela in tow. Sister Adela went down on her knees beside Mariam's bed and announced, "Godwin's first wife is dead. He is free to marry you, and says he wants to." Behind Sister Adela, Godwin had declared in a choked voice that this was true. "All you need do is repent past sins and accept his offer," Sister Adela had coaxed.

Mariam had broken down. A priest was brought, and she had confessed and been married without leaving her bed. After that she fell into a deep sleep, and while she took weeks to recover fully and had she lost close to twenty pounds, she had been on the mend from the moment she confessed. She was convinced that Sister Adela had saved both her life and her soul.

So was Queen Maria Zoë, watching now as Mariam tried to go down on her knees to the Hospitaller sister, who stopped her and told her to sit down instead. Maria Zoë had strong suspicions that Sister Adela had made up the whole story about Godwin's first wife being dead. It had all been too propitious: the way she "remembered" the woman's death only after learning Mariam was on her deathbed. Furthermore, when Godwin asked about his daughters, she had looked startled and then told him glibly that they had been adopted by a childless couple after their mother's death. Too neat and pretty for reality, Maria Zoë thought. Yet she admired Sister Adela all the more for taking this sin upon her head for the sake of making three people—Mariam, Godwin, and poor Sven—very happy.

Perhaps she had done it for Sven more than anyone, Maria Zoë reflected, watching as Sister Adela deftly drew attention to Mariam's boxes and exclaimed enthusiastically about how happy she made the children. "Sister Evangeline frequently admonishes me that more bread and fewer sweets would be better for their health, but it seems to me that happiness is the best nourishment of all— after faith, of course."

Sven had been as close to death as Mariam, and that from sheer grief. During her illness he had refused to leave her side and could hardly be persuaded to eat. Maria Zoë herself had witnessed him begging a half-conscious Mariam not to abandon him, promising to be "good" and never talk back to her ever again, if only she would live. It was as if he saw her dying as a personal rejection.

Separately, Sister Adela had noted to Maria Zoë that "Godwin may have committed bigamy and Mariam adultery, but Sven is an innocent lamb," adding indignantly that his real mother had selfishly kept the cash that would have saved Sven from slavery to buy herself and her daughters things in Sicily. "Can you imagine that?" she'd asked Maria Zoë, her eyes blazing with indignation. "She preferred pretty clothes to her son's freedom! She will burn in hell for all eternity for what she did! Just as your husband will find God's blessings for saving Godwin and Sven."

"I wish my lord believed that," Maria Zoë had answered honestly. "For he still feels guilty for those he could not save."

"That is to his credit, my lady, but our Lord is more generous than we mortals."

Not for the first time, Maria Zoë was left feeling privileged to know this woman, although at times she also made Maria Zoë feel ashamed of her own worldliness. Even today, as she offered two youths jobs at the Ibelin stud, she had found herself ashamed by how carefully she calculated what they could "afford" when Sister Adela pressed her to take a third boy as well.

Of course Sister Adela had won, but Maria Zoë still felt guilty for her own resistance and her lingering resentment at the price of hiring a third groom in their present circumstances. She was far too worried about her family's material well-being for the good of her soul, she admitted—but she couldn't stop herself. She lay awake at night mentally going through the accounts, adding up income and outlays, turning over one scheme after another to raise more cash without detracting from the dignity of either her husband or her eldest daughter. Having Humphrey to outfit in accordance with his station did not help, Maria Zoë reflected, although thankfully Aimery had talked Montferrat into providing separate accommodations for his small family and wages in exchange for doing homage to Montferrat as lord of Tyre.

Her thoughts were interrupted by children bursting into the kitchen, all shouting at once. They seemed to be saying something about "Saracens" or "army," and then Maria Zoë's blood ran cold as she heard the sound of bells clanging in alarm. She felt the grip of terror and spun about on her daughter. "Isabella! Get back inside the walls at once!"

"What about you?" Isabella countered—not because she was reluctant to go, but rather because she was unprepared to leave her mother outside the city.

"Don't argue with me!" Queen Maria Zoë snapped back. "Hurry!" She grabbed Isabella by her arm and shoved her out the door into the courtyard.

The image unfolding in the courtyard was enough to make her heart falter. Children were running away from the door in evident terror, and angry men's voices could be heard in the street. Then the door crashed open and armed men spilled into the courtyard. Their arrival was so forceful, it took Maria Zoë a moment to recognize Conrad de Montferrat.

The Marquis caught sight of her at almost the same moment she recognized him, and he strode toward her ordering: "My lady! To the fortress at once! Your husband sent a rider back from his patrol reporting that a large armed force is approaching from the north. My lady, I *insist* that you come with me!" This last command was addressed not to Maria Zoë but to Isabella, and was underlined by Conrad taking the younger woman's arm.

Even as he started dragging Isabella toward the exit, she looked back over her shoulder at her mother. "Mama!"

"Go!" Maria Zoë ordered, following both to convince Isabella she was coming and to be sure Isabella was indeed taken to safety. Montferrat's men were holding his stallion just outside the door, and before Isabella knew what was happening, the Marquis lifted her up off the ground from behind. At that point she stopped all resistance, found the stirrup with her left foot, and grabbed the pommel as she flung her right leg over the cantle. Montferrat swung himself up behind her, took up the reins, and with his men clearing the streets for him, he clattered away as fast as he could ride in the confined alleyway.

As Maria Zoë turned around, she found herself face to face with Sister Adela. "You must get yourself to safety as well, my lady," Sister Adela advised.

"Not just yet," Maria Zoë answered. "We need to get all the children safely into the city first."

Beyond them in the streets of the shanty town, panic was spreading. Some people were shouting the news, others were screaming hysterically or crying, and everywhere dogs were barking. People streamed toward the causeway that led to the city gates, while others frantically tried to collect the few belongings they had managed to scrape together over the last two years.

"Madame, please ride to the gate and hold it open for the rest of us! I fear Montferrat will order it closed long before half these people are inside!"

Maria Zoë shared Sister Adela's opinion. Montferrat would close the gates as soon as he decided it was militarily prudent—and those outside be damned, as far as he was concerned. So she nodded agreement and hastened to retrieve her already much alarmed and fractious mare. As she swung herself into her saddle, her eyes met those of one of the boys selected as a groom. He was staring up at her with a silent plea in his eyes. "I can take one of the children up behind me," she offered to Sister Adela, "and if one of your sisters can ride a hot horse, they can do the same on Isabella's mare."

"Take Philippe!" Sister Adela agreed at once. "And can you also take an infant on your lap?"

Maria Zoë nodded, and while boy eagerly scrambled up behind her with a breathy and clearly excited "Thank you, my lady!" Sister Adela handed her a squalling infant.

Maria Zoë's mare was unnerved by all the people shouting and running. She fretted and pranced, flinging her head up and down to try to get free of the bit. Maria Zoë, riding one-handed with the infant in the crook of her left arm, found herself praying to St. George not to let the mare get away from her. More than once she shied sharply, and the boy behind her clung frantically to her waist to stay on.

As they emerged from the narrow alleyways of the outer town to a point where they could see the causeway, it was evident that the crush of people trying to cross the causeway was too great. There was a serious risk of people being trampled underfoot. People were shoving and pushing already. It would take only the slightest spark to set off a real stampede. Maria Zoë's mare had no intention of joining that seething mass of humanity, and Maria Zoë couldn't blame her. She drew up and looked about for some alternative.

Coming down the road from the north at a fast pace was a band of riders, and Maria Zoë felt a surge of relief when she recognized the banner of Ibelin. Turning her mare away from the causeway, she rode instead to intercept her husband.

Halfway there, he recognized her and spurred ahead of his men. "We've got to get the orphans inside!" she shouted toward him, forestalling any questions.

He did not answer her, turning in his saddle instead to shout: "Take over the causeway and establish order!"

Sir Galvin nodded and led the others past Ibelin and his lady. Meanwhile, Balian turned back to tell Maria Zoë, "There are well over five hundred horse and probably ten times that number on foot approaching from the north, but they're marching under the crosses of Jerusalem."

"What?" Maria Zoë asked, and then she caught her breath. "Guy de Lusignan?"

"Maybe, or a ruse. We're not taking any chances."

"Yes, that's my brother—or rather, both of my brothers," Aimery told the Marquis. He was standing beside Ibelin and Montferrat on the ramparts of the outer gate of Tyre. Since Salah ad-Din had broken off his siege a year and a half earlier, Montferrat had rebuild and reinforced this gate, and they had a good view down to the men assembled on the causeway. These were led by Guy and Geoffrey de Lusignan, the Bishop of Lydda, and Queen Sibylla, the latter riding in a horse litter bedecked with white and gold hangings.

"Open the gates to your King and Queen!" Guy de Lusignan called up, in a voice that was weakened by distance and partly blown away by the breeze off the sea.

Monferrat did not hesitate for a second. He leaned forward between two of the parapets and shouted a decisive, "NO!"

"This is King Guy and Queen Sibylla!" Guy answered, apparently still convinced they had not recognized him.

"I know who you are, Lusignan!" Montferrat shouted back. "But you're not welcome here, and I have no intention of letting you in!"

Ibelin was watching the exchange from the crenelation next to the one Montferrat was standing in. He was gratified by the look of utter disbelief on Lusignan's face. Guy's mouth dropped open, and then he turned to his wife and brother. A flurry of consultations took place, inaudible on the battlements. Finally, however, Geoffrey de Lusignan raised his voice and shouted: "Are you denying the city to the rightful King of Jerusalem?"

"Rightful king?" Montferrat called back. "Who says that? What I see is a usurper who lost his stolen kingdom at Hattin. He's got no right to Tyre, since he would have lost that, too, but for me!"

"He is the anointed King of Jerusalem!" Geoffrey de Lusignan shouted. "If you don't obey him, you commit treason!"

"How? I never swore an oath of fealty to him!"

The indignation on the causeway was palpable, and on the tower the Constable stalked over to Ibelin to demand sharply, "Speak up, damn it! I can't, because I've bound myself to Montferrat. But you didn't, so say something!"

"Why?" Ibelin asked back, turning a cold gaze on the Constable. They stared at one another.

"Because you *did* take an oath to my brother!"

"I did, didn't I? I didn't have the backbone *my* brother did. I was too worried about my lands and my wealth, and look where it got me? Your brother repaid our loyalty by losing every goddamned inch of his kingdom! If that isn't God's judgment on his usurpation of the throne, I don't know what is. As for speaking up, I'm just a landless knight with no authority here. Go argue with Montferrat if you don't like what he's doing." Ibelin gestured in the direction of the Marquis in his blue velvet surcoat, glittering with gold trim.

Aimery looked from Ibelin to Montferrat. The Marquis was shouting yet another negative reply, to another demand for admittance. Quite aside from the oath he'd sworn, Aimery recognized that trying to argue with Montferrat would be futile. He was lord of Tyre, and had no reason whatever for letting in trouble in the form of a man who called himself king but had no kingdom, much less a woman who should have been a queen but was only a pathetic wife to her utterly discredited husband.

The worst part of it, Aimery admitted, was that he agreed with Ibelin and Montferrat both: his brother did not deserve to be admitted here. It would have been better for them all had he died at Hattin—or better yet, before he had led them to such an unnecessary defeat in the first place.

Chapter 9

Tyre, early September 1189

MARIA ZOË HAD EXPECTED ISABELLA'S MOOD to improve after Balian went to so much trouble to secure her husband's release from captivity, but if anything she acted more erratic than ever before. Before, she had been moody and depressed; now she was short-tempered and prickly. While her tone of late had often been sharp or sarcastic, now she was screaming outright. "I'm a married woman! I'll do what my *husband* wants, not what my *mother* tells me!"

"And your *husband* wants you to live in a war tent surrounded by rude soldiers and whores?" Balian interjected sharply, cutting off both his wife and stepdaughter by adding derisively, "If Toron thinks his lady should sleep in the refuse outside a city under siege, he's not only a fool, he's a lout!"

Having been refused entry to Tyre, Guy de Lusignan had continued down the coast with his little band of volunteers and audaciously set siege to the city of Acre. Acre had been the economic heart of the Kingdom of Jerusalem. It had a large harbor, and the city's prosperity had been reflected in large and luxurious residences for the King, the militant orders, and the various merchant communities. Furthermore, it was so well fortified that its surrender without a fight just days after the disaster at Hattin had been a major blow to the Christian cause. As in the Holy City, the remaining citizens had been *willing* to defend it, but unlike in Jerusalem, they had not found a champion to organize that defense. Instead they had been betrayed by Queen Sibylla's maternal uncle, the ever unready and militarily incompetent Count of Edessa. He'd been too "ill" to take part in the Battle of Hattin, and after the news of the defeat reached him, he had preferred to abscond to Antioch with his riches rather than try to defend Acre. Although the burghers had rioted in protest, they'd had no real alternative but to accept Salah ad-Din's terms: abandonment of Acre in exchange for their lives and movable property. With the Christians thus expelled, Salah ad-Din had repopulated the city with an Egyptian garrison fiercely loyal to him. The latter had been allowed to bring their families (or at any rate, women) and were served by merchants and tradesmen from Egypt. Guy de Lusignan and his forces had set up camp surrounding Acre by land, and the Pisan fleet had left Tyre to set up a sea block as well.

When yet more ships, loaded with volunteers from Friesland and Denmark, arrived in Tyre headed for the siege of Acre, many of the fighting men collected in Tyre decided to travel with the Danes and Frisians to likewise join the siege. An alarming number of women were planning to go with them. While this was hardly surprising in the circumstances, Isabella's announcement that she intended to go with her husband shocked both Balian and Maria Zoë.

"You just hate Humphrey!" Isabella flung back furiously at Balian. "I'm not the only lady joining the siege! Sibylla's there already, and—"

"That in itself should tell you how stupid the idea is!" Maria Zoë jumped back into the fray. "When has that brainless peahen ever had a sensible idea?"

"She may not be very bright, but she loves her husband, and so do I! Humphrey and I were separated too long. I refuse to be away from Humphrey another day. I'm going with him, whether you like it or not!"

"Stop shouting at your mother and answer us like an adult!" Balian ordered his stepdaughter in a voice that broached no contradiction, even from the furious teenager. Beet-red with indignation and eyes blazing with resentment, she clamped her teeth together and faced him defiantly—but silently—as he asked: "Whose idea was this? Yours or Humphrey's?"

"Humphrey *has* to join the siege!" Isabella exploded. "If he doesn't, everyone will call him a coward or, worse, a traitor—just because he can speak Arabic so well and had won the trust of Imad ad-Din. He's got to join the siege and show he's as determined as anyone to regain Jerusalem for Christ."

"That wasn't my question," Balian remarked dryly, "but since you are unwilling to discuss this in a civilized manner, I will take it up with my lord of Toron directly."

"Balian—" Maria Zoë tried to interrupt, but he waved her silent so imperiously that she was stunned into obedience. Isabella took advantage of her mother's discomfiture to flee.

Balian found Humphrey in the squire's hall getting a final fitting for his new hauberk. The Sultan had not seen fit to restore Humphrey's arms or armor on his release. This meant that Humphrey needed to be completely re-equipped—an expensive proposition at any time, but particularly burdensome when Humphrey himself was penniless and Ibelin's resources were limited. Humphrey, of course, swore he was only "borrowing" the cost of his arms, armor, and horses, but Balian never expected to see a penny of the money he "loaned." He shouldered the costs without protest, however, because in his mind it was a debt he owed Isabella for being too weak to prevent her marriage to Toron in the first place. He had failed to stand up to the insidious intriguer Agnes de Courtenay a decade earlier, and now Isabella was hitched to a spineless coward. To refuse to outfit Humphrey would have humiliated her further, a humiliation she did not deserve.

"My lord, could we have a word in private?" Balian addressed Humphrey, but the armorer took the hint at once. Godfrey announced he'd take the hauberk back to his workshop for a few final adjustments and return with it the next day. Bowing to Ibelin and Toron, he beat a hasty retreat, leaving Humphrey eyeing the older man guardedly.

"Your lady announced this morning that she intends to travel with you to Acre. That came as a great shock, given the appalling conditions that generally prevail at sieges. You can't seriously intend to expose your lady to such risks, can you?"

"It was her idea," Humphrey declared defensively. "She said we have been separated far too long already, and she can't bear to be apart again."

"That is an understandable reaction on the part of a young woman deeply in love with her husband, but it also reflects her complete ignorance of what a siege is actually like. You, on the other hand, should know better and should forbid her from accompanying you."

"How can I forbid her?" Humphrey demanded indignantly. "She is a princess, and she has been a patient and dutiful wife throughout the years of my captivity. To forbid her to come with me would only cause her great grief and unnecessary pain."

"A lot less pain than becoming sick with dysentery, scurvy, or any of the other illnesses common in siege camps!" Balian snapped back. "Not to mention the risk of being burned by Greek fire, skewered by arrows, or crushed by boulders."

"Do you think I'm too stupid to keep her out of the range of the enemy's archers and siege engines?" Humphrey bristled, and Balian's silence was answer enough. Humphrey tried a new tack. "Queen Sibylla is already there with her infant daughter, despite being pregnant again. If the Queen of Jerusalem is prepared to endure the hardships of a siege camp, why should I object if my wife chooses to do the same?"

"Queen Sibylla voluntarily took herself into Saracen captivity," Balian reminded him pointedly.

"But Isabella *wants* to come," Humphrey repeated helplessly, his tone more whining than defiant.

"And I say *again*, she doesn't know what she's talking about," Balian insisted, adding, "Do you love your wife so little that you care nothing for her health and safety?"

Humphrey fell silent, his gaze cast down in evident sorrow. After a moment, he looked up and met Balian's eyes with something akin to pleading in his own. "Would you speak to her, my lord? I can't talk sense to her, but maybe you could."

Having already tried that, however, Balian decided instead to engage the assistance of his niece Eschiva. For three years Eschiva had been a doting and attentive elder sister to Isabella. Furthermore, Eschiva was in a similar position to Isabella, since Aimery, like Humphrey, had been held captive after Hattin and now planned to join his brothers at the siege of Acre. On the other hand, unlike Isabella, Eschiva had no intention of following him. She readily agreed to try to talk sense to Isabella.

Eschiva took her eldest children, Hugh and Burgundia, with her, knowing that Isabella was very fond of both children, and as expected she was welcomed with great enthusiasm by Isabella. After fussing over the children for a bit, Isabella gave them an illuminated book to keep them happy and asked Eschiva to help her pack. "I know I can't take too many things," she admitted excitedly, "but I need to keep myself from getting bored, too. And of course, I want to make things as comfortable for Humphrey as possible. I want to make a little home out of his tent!" she declared with naïve enthusiasm.

"Are you really so sure you should go, Isabella?" Eschiva asked cautiously. "Aimery says siege camps are terribly unsanitary and stink most of the time. He said that no matter how much the lords try to enforce discipline, some of the men are always too lazy to go to the latrines and just, you know, *go* in the alleys between the tents. He says the whores ply their trade very blatantly as well, and you can hardly avoid coming upon men engaged in fornication, even in broad daylight."

Isabella's happy and friendly mood vanished instantly. She righted herself and stood with her hands on her hips and a sullen expression on her face. "Did my mother send you here to lecture me?" she demanded hotly.

"No!" Eschiva could honestly reply. "I haven't spoken to your mother about this at all. I just—I just can't understand why *any* lady would want to live in a siege camp."

"Is it so hard to understand that I want to be with my husband?" Isabella snapped back, desperation coloring her voice. "Don't you understand? It's *impossible* to lead a married life here under my mother's nose. And you know how much my stepfather looks down on Humphrey. Humphrey feels like Lord Balian is always looking for something to criticize. I—I just want to be *alone* with Humphrey."

"In the middle of a siege camp?" Eschiva asked back, flabbergasted. "Isabella, there are going to be close to ten thousand men at the siege of Acre by the time all the reinforcements flood in!"

"Yes, but Humphrey and I will have our *own* tent!" Isabella countered. "And with all the others doing what they please, who is going to notice what Humphrey and I are doing?"

Eschiva was too stunned by this irrational reasoning to find an immediate response.

"Don't you see?" Isabella abandoned defiance and pleaded for understanding instead. "Humphrey's too—shy. I mean, he can't—not *here*—" she gestured to the small room around her, which was squashed between Maria Zoë and Balian's chamber and the chamber used for the Ibelin children and their two tutors, "he's too *shy*."

It was not a very private environment, Eschiva conceded. Even now they could hear, muted but unmistakable, the voices of the Ibelin children squabbling next door. Yet Eschiva was certain it was still better than a siege camp. She opened her mouth to say this, only to register that Isabella had crumpled up beside the bed and was sobbing miserably into her hands.

Eschiva sank down on the floor beside her, reached out and took Isabella in her arms, while her two children turned to stare at the odd sight of an adult crying. "Sweetheart!" Eschiva exclaimed, stroking her arms. "Sweetheart, what's the matter? What's troubling you so?"

"I've been married for *six years*, but I'm yet to become Humphrey's *wife*."

"Of course you're his wife," Eschiva answered incomprehending. "Why half the Kingdom of Jerusalem was witness to your wedding!"

"I'm not talking about the ceremony! I'm talking about consummation!" Isabella gasped out. "The marriage has never been *consummated!*"

Eschiva was stunned by this confession. Eschiva had been married (with Church dispensation) to Aimery at the age of eight. He'd been a complete stranger and twenty years her senior. She had fallen instantly in love with him as only a little girl can when faced with a dashing knight who seemed straight out of a fairy-tale. By the time he deigned to consumate their marriage, however, she was a nubile teenager in a far more ambivalent state of mind. For the first year of marriage if not more they had been two awkward strangers sharing a bed. She had always envied Isabella going to the bed of man who was already her best friend. But if that bed was a chaste one? It was a strange thought. Just what was the basis of marriage? Mutual respect or the carnal act?

The latter was something men engaged in all the time without the slightest interest in or respect for their sexual partner and that made friendship the more important part of marriage in Eschiva's eyes.

But Isabella was wailing, "What's wrong with me? Why doesn't Humphrey love me?"

"Humphrey? But he dotes on you, Isabella. He's so attentive and kind. I've never seen a more perfect, gentle knight than your Humphrey." Eschiva spoke with conviction because there had been periods in her marriage with Aimery when he had been none of these things, treating her more with indifference than affection, and pursuing affairs with other women. It seemed to her that Humphrey's kind of love, particularly if it was chaste, was very rare and valuable.

"Yes, but he turns his back on me in bed," Isabella insisted, evidently not content with chaste love. "Why doesn't he want me, if he loves me?"

Eschiva could not imagine any reason why Humphrey would not want to consummate his marriage with Isabella. Isabella had a delectable body, slender but well-shaped, and she had a beautiful face with golden eyes and auburn hair. Certainly Conrad de Montferrat looked at her with desire, and Aimery, despite being extraordinarily attentive, affectionate and devoted since his release from captivity, had remarked with studied neutrality that Isabella had grown into a "stunning beauty."

Nor was there any reason to think that Humphrey took his pleasure elsewhere. On the contrary, Humphrey seemed to be comfortable only in Isabella's presence, preferring to stay at her side even when the other men removed to the far end of the hall to talk of war. Indeed, as Aimery had noted with disapproval, Humphrey preferred to read a book than hunt or exercise at the tiltyard. "It's no wonder he's worthless on the battlefield," Aimery had scoffed, "since he does nothing to hone his fighting skills."

In short, Eschiva had no answers, and was reduced to cooing meaningless reassurances. "I'm sure he just needs time. No matter what our husbands pretend, Hattin and the subsequent imprisonment has been traumatic for them. Aimery still has nightmares so terrible he thrashes about violently or groans and cries out in his sleep." None of this explained why a healthy young man like Humphrey should disdain his nubile young wife, however—so Eschiva found herself saying, quite against her better judgment, "You are probably right that being here under your mother and stepfather's gaze isn't the right atmosphere.

Humphrey must feel constantly watched. Going to the siege of Acre is probably the right thing, after all."

Isabella at once pulled free of Eschiva's embrace to fling her arms around her instead. "I *knew* you'd understand!" she declared with great relief and a surge of affection. "You're the *best* friend I've ever had. I'm so glad you came. Promise you'll pray for me—pray that I get with child soon. If that happens, I can come right back here!"

"Of course, sweetheart," Eschiva assured her, glad to have something she could honestly pray for.

Acre, October 4, 1189

The worst thing was the flies. Isabella had gradually become accustomed to the stink, and by never venturing beyond the cluster of baronial tents, she could avoid unwanted encounters with whores and their customers. She had even adjusted to the plain fare and sour wine, but she could not get used to the flies.

They were everywhere and they were persistent, tenacious, cloying. Even moving was not enough to shake them off, and swatting at them only drove them away for a second. If Isabella lay down to sleep, they lighted on her face and clustered in her eye sockets and the corners of her mouth. Sometimes they tried to crawl up her nose. She hated that so much she had taken to wrapping a gauze shawl around her face when she went to bed. That in turn made it hard to breathe and made her sweat, so that after a few moments she tore it off again, a process that was repeated again and again until she eventually fell asleep—always conscious of Humphrey patiently suffering beside her without once making any attempt to help, much less take her in his arms.

The whole thing was an utter disaster. Humphrey was no more interested in her here than he had been in Tyre. Why should he be? She hadn't had a bath since they'd arrived, and her clothes were washed by camp followers in a muddy stream. The results were shifts that came back damp, crumpled, and hardly cleaner than before. Isabella swore that her "clean" clothes smelled worse than her dirty ones. Meanwhile, her hair was oily and hung in strands if she removed her wimple, and her lips were chapped from chewing them so much.

Her self-pity was so great that she wanted to cry or scream half the time, and the other half of the time she was frantically trying to think of some way to return to the safety and comfort of Tyre without actually admitting to her mother and Uncle Balian that they had been right. If only Sibylla would decide to return home, or some other miracle would happen . . .

Instead, after food supplies had run so low that the common soldiers started fighting among themselves and covetously eyeing the horses of their betters, Geoffrey de Lusignan had convinced his brother King Guy that they should attack the Saracen army that was now besieging the besiegers. Salah ad-Din had sent an army to hem them in, and they were surrounded by some twenty thousand Saracen fighting men. As a result, they were unable to forage and hunt in the surrounding countryside and were instead utterly dependent on the trickle of supplies that arrived by sea.

The Saracens had made several attacks on the camp, forcing the Franks to dig trenches around it and build palisades with the masts and beams of their ships. The Saracens' favorite tactic was to attack the outer perimeter and, after the Franks rushed to repel the attack, to sortie out of the city to attack the inner perimeter—or vice versa. Either way, the Franks ended up fighting on two sides at once, and Isabella, Sibylla, and the other ladies could only cower in their tents, listening to the screams, shouts, and clanging of weapons as the fighting swirled around them.

Sibylla tended to become hysterical if the sound of battle came too close, an emotion that rapidly transmitted itself to her infant daughter, who then started squealing two octaves above normal human speech. Admittedly that was unlikely to happen today, because King Guy and both his brothers had remained behind to guard the camp. On the other hand, Isabella disliked both Guy and Geoffrey too much to spend time with them when Humphrey wasn't with her. That's why she'd chosen to remain behind in their own tent.

Things had gone well at first. She'd been able to clearly decipher a shout of "Dieu St. Amour" as the Templars led the attack, and even a dull roar of surprise from the Saracen camp as the Knights of Christ struck just after dawn. Isabella gauged the continued success of the Frankish attack by the simple fact that the sounds of battle rapidly receded. After about an hour Edith, the girl Isabella had hired to run errands for her (especially to take her clothes to the laundresses), arrived, stuffing flatbread into her mouth. "We've completely overrun their camp!" she declared enthusiastically, her mouth still full. "Dietrich says there was more food and plunder there than in all of Hamburg!" (Dietrich was the German pilgrim Edith was sleeping with at the moment.) "Mounds and mounds of hot bread, just out of the oven!" She held up what was left of the bread she was eating, and then opened her apron to show more. "Can I store this here where no one's likely to steal it?"

Isabella nodded.

"Dietrich nabbed some chickens, too," she next told Isabella proudly. "Can I bring them, too?"

"No! I don't live in a henhouse!" Isabella answered irritably.

"I didn't think so," Edith grinned. "Just asking. But we have some other stuff. I'll go get it." Then she was gone again.

When Edith didn't return quickly, Isabella started to get nervous. She tried to convince herself that plundering took time, but the longer she waited, the more Edith's absence seemed ominous. Isabella's discomfort was reinforced by the sound of horns and trumpets yowling in the distance. Isabella cursed. Her mother could read trumpet signals, but she had never taken an interest in the art. Now she would have given her favorite book for that knowledge. As it was, she couldn't tell if the Frankish lords were rallying their troops for a new assault, blowing retreat, or begging for assistance.

Unable to stand the suspense, Isabella pushed aside the tent flap and stood in the entry, trying to figure out what was going on. To her dismay, she saw men running around and shouting in what looked suspiciously like panic. She was momentarily reassured by the appearance of a Templar galloping up to the royal tent, but when King Guy, his older brothers, and their knights left the royal tent to mount up a moment later, she realized the Templar had brought a plea for assistance.

Isabella liked to think of herself as brave, but the sight of the King and his knights galloping through the camp in the direction of the external perimeter sent a chill down her spine. Obviously something had gone terribly wrong, and now she and the other women were defenseless.

Automatically she looked toward the city walls. What she saw froze her blood. The defenders of Acre were ululating as if in victory. Apparently from their higher elevation they could see what was happening, and it was clearly to their liking; in short, it was not going well for the Franks. Worse, a great deal of activity soon unfolded that suggested the garrison had no intention of watching passively. Drums started pounding inside the city, and something about the rhythm made Isabella's blood run cold. "Oh, my God," Isabella whispered to herself, "they're going to attack us now that the King and his knights are gone."

Screams answered her. Not shouts of command or challenge, but blood-curdling screams of terror, rising in pitch until they were cut off abruptly. Women were squealing like stuck pigs. Isabella heard, or imagined she heard, someone crying out, "Help! Help us! God—"

She fled back inside her tent, but the sounds of the assault followed her. Isabella looked frantically for someplace to hide. There was no place. Flee! She had to flee! How? Where? They were completely surrounded! The ships! She had to get to the ships drawn up on the beach, those few that hadn't been dismantled to build the palisade. . . .

Isabella grabbed her purse, the functioning part of her brain telling her that money was her best, indeed her only, weapon. Money could buy her protection, perhaps, and passage. Nothing else mattered.

As she stepped outside again, however, the sounds had changed subtly. The pitch of the screams was lower, the tone more angry than terrified. She caught the clang of weapons on the wind. Someone was offering resistance after all.

But was it enough? Isabella hesitated, a little ashamed of her instinct to flee. She glanced toward the royal tent. There was no sign of Sibylla fleeing. Surely if they were in great danger, Sibylla would be the first to flee? But maybe she just hadn't heard what was going on. Sibylla often got herself into a frenzy of hysterical prayer that blocked out all other sounds.

In confusion Isabella looked in the direction of the beach, then toward the city and back again. She was concentrating so hard on trying to make sense of the sounds ahead of her and decide what she should do that she was taken by surprise when loud shouting erupted behind her. Spinning around with her heart beating in her throat and a cry on her lips, she saw four men staggering toward her tent, carrying a fifth between them. The man leading was the man she thought of as Uncle Balian's "watchdog," the aging Sir Bartholomew. She was certain he had been sent to keep an eye on her and she'd resented his presence from the day she had discovered him in the camp. In the next instant, the realization that he and his companion Sir Galvin were carrying a limp Humphrey between them negated all her resentment at being spied upon.

"Oh, my God!" Isabella cried out, rushing forward.

"He's not dead!" Sir Bartholomew assured her—but if that was so, he was so badly wounded he was unconscious. Two squires were following the knights, each carrying a leg. Humphrey not only hung limply between them, his surcoat was soaked in blood, dripping a trail of it behind him.

The four men pushed their way into the tent, almost tearing it down in the process. Something crashed inside as they knocked it over. Sir Bartholomew was giving orders to "put him down there" and Sir Galvin was shouting for "wine and water." As Isabella entered, Sir Bartholomew was drawing Humphrey's helmet off and opening his aventail to make it easier for him to breathe.

Isabella choked on the stench of shit and the sight of blood. For a moment she quailed. She knew what her duty was: to kneel beside her wounded husband and clean him up, bandage him, nurse him back to health. Indeed, she *wanted* to do that. Yet as she watched, Sir Galvin pulled up Humphrey's hauberk, exposing a long, vicious wound running down his ribcage to his side, leaving his entire abdomen awash in blood. Isabella felt faint. For a moment she found herself thinking, "I can't deal with this. I *can't*!" She had never wanted her mother more than she did just then.

But her mother was a hundred miles away, and Humphrey's lifeblood was pouring out of his side onto the floor of the tent. "How do we stop it?" she cried out to her stepfather's knights in despair, instinctively bunching up the front of her outer gown to press it against Humphrey's wound.

"That's a good start," Sir Galvin remarked dryly. "Do you have linen here? Heavy linen?"

"There!" she nodded with her chin. "In that trunk. That's where all our table linens are." Idiot that she had been, Isabella had brought table linen with her, imagining life in a siege camp was similar to a grand hunt, where you had a fine meal at the end of each day. Twice, in that distant age before Hattin, she'd accompanied the court on a lion hunt, and she had always loved those evening meals alfresco. . . .

Meanwhile, she found herself almost gagging on the smell of her husband's shit and sweat and blood. Only her shame at her reaction made her swallow down her revulsion.

Sir Galvin had found the linen and brought back a large cloth, still neatly folded and pressed. He gestured for Isabella to pull back, taking her now blood-soaked surcoat away from the wound. Then he bent and pressed the linen cloth firmly onto Humphrey's side. After a moment he looked over his shoulder at Isabella and urged, "Hold this firmly in place." After she had taken over, he demanded of his squire, "Did you find any wine?"

"Yes, sir."

"Bring it here," he ordered. Then he turned again to Isabella to assure her, "It may look bad, but it's unlikely to be fatal. Unless he starts frothing at the mouth, his lung wasn't punctured. Watch for that, but meanwhile hold that cloth in place until we can sew him up and stop the bleeding."

Numbly Isabella nodded, grateful to the older knights for their instructions. She would not have known what to do on her own. In a daze, she simply did what she was told, all the while keeping a fearful eye on Humphrey's mouth for the telltale sign of frothing blood. Later she remembered no specifics of what she'd done—just the smell, the sweat dripping down her face, the horrible clammy feel of Humphrey's skin, and the flies. Always the flies.

Isabella didn't come to herself until she heard Sir Galvin bark at Humphrey's squire, "Don't just stand there! Remove his soiled braies and clean him up!"

A moment later she felt powerful hands under her armpits, and Sir Bartholomew was dragging her to her feet. She had been on her knees so long that they were stiff, and her feet had gone to sleep. She cried out in surprise, but Sir Bartholomew seemed to know what had happened, for he carried her to a chest and set her down. Sir Galvin handed her a goblet brimming with wine. Isabella was shaking so badly that she sloshed half the wine down the front of her gown, but what difference did it make? The gown was completely ruined with blood, some of which had already dried and crusted, some of which was still wet and a vivid red.

Only then, as she sat on the chest, clinging to the goblet with both hands to try to steady them, did she realize the tent was full of men. Indeed, half the barons of Jerusalem appeared to have gathered here, still wearing sweat-soaked surcoats and chain mail dull with dried blood. As she stared at them in a semi-daze, Scandelion pushed into the tent, asking about Humphrey. Isabella registered with a degree of wonder and shame that although these men were often critical of her husband, they appeared to care about his survival, too. Assured that Humphrey was not fatally wounded, Scandelion nodded and then announced, "Ridefort is finally on his way to meet his Maker."

"Dead?" asked William de Hebron the Younger, wanting absolute certainty.

"No doubt about it! Decapitated. The Saracens are parading his head on the end of a lance."

"May God forgive him his sins, for I cannot," Caesarea exclaimed without dissembling, "Today was the third time his idiocy cost the cause of Christ dearly!"

"May God grant the Templars the wisdom to elect someone of better judgment and character," added Haifa, thinking ahead already.

William de Hebron was more hot-tempered, adding angrily, "He wasn't the only one responsible for today's disaster! Where the hell was our *king*?" The word 'king' was said with so much derision and sarcasm that it was obvious he did not consider Guy de Lusignan deserving of the title. "The Templars may have rushed too far too fast and fallen into the age-old trap the Saracens always spring on the foolhardy—but if the rest of the army had maintained discipline rather than disintegrating into mindless, plundering rabble, we could have fought through to the Templars' relief. We might then have taken the day after all!"

"You can't blame half-starving men from seizing food when it is offered them on a silver platter—sometimes literally!" Bethsan noted wearily.

"Nor do I! Not when there was no one *leading* them. But I *do* blame our *king* for staying back in camp rather than providing that leadership!"

"What I don't understand is how King Guy could first justify not taking command of the attack by the need to defend the camp against a possible sortie from Acre—and then abandon the camp when it was most vulnerable! If he'd done what he'd said he was going to do, it might have been unsatisfactory, but it would have been conscionable. Instead, he changed his mind in the middle of everything, and we damn near lost the camp as well as the battle."

"Just like Hattin," Haifa observed. "He vacillates, changes his mind more quickly than a rabbit, and cannot carry through any plan at all."

"How many more defeats are we going to let that man—that *usurper*—jam down our throats?" William de Hebron angrily asked the other men in the room. "How much more can we afford to lose?"

The tent flap was pulled open, and Aimery de Lusignan stepped in. The look he cast William de Hebron suggested he had overheard his treasonous statement, but he refrained from comment and simply remarked, "I've come to inquire after my lord of Toron."

"He's lost a lot of blood, my lord," Sir Bartholomew answered with a glance in Isabella's direction, "but he should pull through."

"I am glad to hear that. He fought bravely, if foolishly." Aimery's gaze fell on Isabella. "My lady, the Queen asked if you needed any assistance—and I must say, with all due respect, that you look very much like you could use some sisterly care. May I escort you to the royal tent?"

Isabella was in no state to protest. She might detest Sibylla, but she did desperately need a change of clothes and at least a sponging down, as her husband's blood had blackened her fingernails, smeared her forearms, and dirtied her face and neck when she'd wiped away sweat with her bloody hands. She set the empty goblet down on the chest and got unsteadily to her feet. Sir Bartholomew took her elbow and helped her across the tent to Aimery, who took her other elbow and led her out.

The men in the tent remained respectfully silent as the dazed and bloody princess crossed between them to the exit. No sooner had the flap fallen closed behind her, than Caesarea growled, "Hebron is right! We're the fools for following the man."

"We all took oaths to him. Have you forgotten?" Bethsan reminded them all.

"How could I forget? But so did Ibelin, and I don't see *him* here," Haifa noted.

"Would that he were!" Haifa retorted. "If anyone could have rallied the rabble today, it would have been him. They trust him, after what he did at Hattin."

"*Our* men trust him; the pilgrims don't know him from Adam," Caesarea countered. "It was the Germans and Danes who broke ranks first. They weren't listening to any of us, and I doubt they would have listened to Ibelin, either."

"We have to put our faith in the Holy Roman Emperor and the Kings of England and France. Once they arrive, Guy de Lusignan will be of no consequence," Scandaleon suggested.

"And until then?" Hebron asked.

"You won't see me risking my neck or my men for Lusignan. I'm pulling back to Tyre." It was Haifa who spoke, but none of the others contradicted him. Nodding grimly, they dispersed.

Tyre, December 1189

The death of the Saracen ship kept the city entertained for almost two days. She first hove into view on the afternoon of St. Nicholas, battling against a strong southerly gale. She clawed her way to windward, making only a couple hundred feet per tack, but was almost beyond the city when a sudden gust almost capsized her, making her fall off and run before the wind, losing almost all she'd gained in a day of hard sailing.

As darkness fell, the exhausted crew threw out a sea anchor and tried to ride out the storm. By dawn the following morning she was down by the starboard bow, and wallowing in the troughs rather than riding the waves. Apparently some of her planking had been reamed during the fight to windward the day before or during the night.

By noon, the sailors were throwing crates of cargo and provisions overboard to lighten her. People from the shanty town north of Tyre streamed down to the beach to try to retrieve the objects thrown overboard—and watch the nautical entertainment.

At dusk on the second day the ship was still afloat but only barely so, and by dawn of the third day it was obvious she was beyond rescue. As the sky lightened behind a heavy overcast that was still spitting sporadic rain showers, the crew hauled in the anchor, set a rag of sail on the boom, and turned toward the shore with the intention of beaching her to save their lives.

Word of the impending wreck spread rapidly. People rushed up onto the walls to watch, while those in the shanty town flooded to the shore, eager for salvage. Although the wind had abated, the breakers were wilder than ever. The ship, waterlogged already, foundered in the crashing surf and started to break up a good hundred yards offshore.

Sailors began to jump overboard, and were caught in the raging surf. Observers saw men upended and rolled over many times by the ravenous waves before they sank permanently beneath the frothing surface. Only a handful of men, those who managed to hang on to some part of the ship long enough to reach the rocky beach, survived. Two were killed as they staggered ashore. The others, terrified by the murder of their colleagues, started shouting in Arabic that their master would pay a ransom. "Who's your master then?" An Arabic speaker shouted out, raising his arm to hold back his revenge-thirsty companions.

"Rashid ad-Din Sinan!" The shipwrecked men shouted back. "Rashid ad-Din!"

"You'll hear him referred to as 'The Old Man of the Mountain,'" Ibelin patiently explained to Montferrat.

"Meaning?" the Italian asked back with raised eyebrows. A man had arrived earlier in the day, claiming to represent Rashid ad-Din Sinan and seeking an audience with Montferrat. After a highly unsatisfactory meeting, in which—despite the man's apparent command of French—Montferrat had the feeling the emissary and he were not communicating in the least, Montferrat had sent for Ibelin. They were seated now in the lovely solar of the archiepiscopal palace, whose tall northern windows looked out at the glistening sea breaking at the base of the wall below. The floor was paved with bright glazed mosaics depicting the Garden of Eden, complete with lifelike snakes and lizards lurking among palms, figs, and apple trees. The groin-vaulted ceiling overhead was plastered and painted with stars.

"He's the leader of a Shia sect, headquartered in the mountains west of Tortosa." Ibelin gestured vaguely out the glazed window toward the north.

"Shia?"

"Yes—Muslim heretics, if you like. The Fatimids were also Shia, but this sect is more radical. They follow the teaching of an imam, who they claim teaches the only legitimate interpretation of the Koran. That naturally makes them anathema to the rest of the Islamic world. They have been rigorously persecuted by the orthodox Muslims. To avoid obliteration, they retreated into the mountains and have built, I am told, spectacular, impregnable fortresses there, but I have never seen them personally. They are reputed to be exceptionally fanatic."

Montferrat snorted. "The Saracens are all fanatics!"

"Not really. Indeed, far from it," Ibelin observed dryly, finding himself

annoyed at having to explain all this. Montferrat, with all his experience in Constantinople, he felt, ought to know better. He continued, "However, this sect
is too weak to fight their opponents openly, so they have developed the tactic
of targeting the leaders. When they want to weaken their enemies, they send
out men who blend into the surroundings of their intended target. Once these
men have won the trust of their enemies and ingratiated themselves enough to
have unfettered access to their intended victim, they murder him. Raymond of
Tripoli's father was murdered in this way, and it is rumored that they came close
to killing Salah ad-Din."

"But they're Muslims. Why would they want to kill Salah ad-Din?" Montferrat wanted to know, gesturing irritably for one of his servants to put another
log on the fire that blazed in the fireplace on the far side of the room.

"Because," Ibelin answered as patiently as possible, "Salah ad-Din is Sunni,
for a start. Second, he brought down the Fatimid Caliphate. Third, he per-
secutes Sinan's followers in his territories, and finally, Salah ad-Din brought
an army to root out the entire sect from their mountain refuge. However, the
Sultan's close escape from death at the hands of a man who had infiltrated his
bodyguard appears to have dissuaded Salah ad-Din from attacking them again."

"I see, but what right has the man to send demands to *me* to pay *him* restitution for the loss of his ship, cargo, and crew? I didn't cause them to wreck! Furthermore, I'm holding the captain and four other crewmen captive. He ought
to be offering to pay *me* ransoms, not demanding restitution! That's what the
captain promised."

Ibelin considered this calmly and remarked, "The Old Man of the Mountain
is nothing if not arrogant and audacious. He once claimed to be interested in
converting to Christianity just to win the trust of King Amalric. Ultimately, his
right to make demands is based on his *ability* to eliminate those who anger him."

"Nonsense!" Montferrat dismissed him. "If Salah ad-Din can't break the
defenses of Tyre, how does this Rashid think he's going to do it?"

"He doesn't dream of doing it. He doesn't need to. If you don't give in to his
demands, he will view you—not Tyre—as his enemy."

"And how is he going to attack me if he can't take Tyre?" Montferrat countered, gesturing expansively to the room around him, but indirectly including
the powerful walls that had withstood all assaults so far.

"As I said, by sending men out to kill you—assassins, we call them."

"He may be able to infiltrate the ranks of the Sultan's bodyguard with his
men, but he can't disguise his fanatical Muslim followers as Christians," Montferrat retorted contemptuously. "Why, they'd betray themselves just by what
they eat—or rather don't eat—and by praying all the time."

"The Assassins follow different rules," Ibelin warned.

"Well, then, they'll be discovered the first time they have to go to Mass."

"I doubt it. These men are very clever and very well trained."

"I can see *you've* been intimidated, Ibelin, but I'm not so easily cowed."

"Well, my lord," Ibelin answered evenly, although he was inwardly seething, "I'm far too long in the tooth to bristle at every insult to my courage, but consider the fact that I have nothing to gain by urging you to be wary of making an enemy of Rashid ad-Din, while you have everything to lose by not heeding my advice."

"I'm not going to pay some damned Muslim heretic restitution for a ship that just happened to go aground under my nose! The poor people who salvaged things from that ship have already lost their homes and livelihoods, and I don't begrudge them taking what they could from the sea. As for the sailors, most of them drowned. While the murder of the other two was unfortunate, it's hardly a cause for demands like these. One thousand gold bezants! The man's crazy!"

"Possibly," Ibelin concurred, "but that only makes him more dangerous. Now, you've heard what I have to say. You can take my advice or leave it." Ibelin got to his feet and stepped down from the window seat, which was lined with marble benches. As he crossed the chamber, one of the young deacons who served Montferrat brought Ibelin his cloak. He thanked the cleric for it and swung it over his shoulders. Only at the door did he pause and look back to warn Montferrat one last time. "Think twice, Montferrat. The Old Man of the Mountain makes a far better friend than enemy."

Chapter 10

Siege camp at Acre, mid-October 1190

Sibylla was finding it hard to breathe. That triggered panic—but the more she panicked, the more she sweated, and the harder it was to breathe. It felt as if a dead weight were sitting on her chest, pressing down, and her shoulders hurt her terribly, as if she'd been lifting something heavy.

She let out a cry and thrashed in her sweat-soaked bed. Her eyelids were far too heavy to lift, so she cried out again. Where was everyone? Why wasn't someone cooling her brow with wet cloths or offering her chilled water to drink? She could feel the flies crawling on her arms and face. Someone should have been waving them off. Had everyone abandoned her? She cried out again.

"Hush, my lady." The male voice was calming but unfamiliar. Sibylla struggled to open her eyes and squint at the world around her.

The voice apparently belonged the monk bending over her bed. He was tonsured and wore the black robes of the Benedictines. When he saw Sibylla's eyes slit open, he held out a wooden cross with a silver crucifix upon it. "Here, my lady, hold this. It will comfort you."

Sibylla was far too weak to protest, but she frowned. Her head was throbbing, and the pain in her shoulders seemed to be getting worse, while the weight on her chest was surely a thousand tons. She was so weak, and the air was so heavy. . . .

"Your daughters are dead, my lady," the priest told her in a low, solemn voice, now that she was holding the crucifix.

"Which daughter?" Sibylla gasped out, trying to lift her head from the pillow and opening her eyes wider.

"Both, my lady," he answered steadily.

"Both? How is that possible?" Sibylla wailed. "How can God do this to me?" She started flinging her head from side to side. "No! It can't be true! You're lying to me! Where is the Patriarch? I demand to see the Patriarch!" She might be a shapeless slab of sweat-soaked fat, but she was still the Queen of Jerusalem.

"The Patriarch, my lady, is dead. We buried him at Prime this morning."

"Heraclius?" Sibylla gasped out, going instantly still in horrified disbelief. Since she had been fourteen and had come to her brother's court, Heraclius had been the churchman she loved and trusted best. As a maiden she had been jealous that the strikingly handsome priest had been her mother's lover, and she had fantasized about luring him away from her mother's bed to her own. She had used him as her confessor, too, knowing full well he could not condemn sexual appetite, since he had so much of it himself. He always obligingly set only light penance for her sexual escapades—most of which had been more imagined than real, until she slept first with Ramla and then with Guy. After she'd fallen in love with Guy, all her sexual dreams had centered around him, of course, but Heraclius had remained her sympathetic confessor. She could confess to him her desire, her obsession, and all the violations of Church law with respect to timing and position, because she knew he enjoyed hearing what she did in bed. And, of course, he'd crowned her queen when half the bishops and all three archbishops were balking.

"Yes, my lady," the Benedictine answered steadily. "As I said, we buried him at Prime. We'll bury your daughters and your uncle Edessa at Vespers."

"Uncle Joscelin?" Sibylla was spinning now, dizzy with disbelief. "He's dead, too?" Was everyone who loved and supported her dead? How was it possible?

"He died during the night, my lady. We found him dead this morning."

"My God! My God! How can this be?" The pain appeared to be spreading out from her shoulders, down her arms, and the weight on her chest was crushing her.

"Thousands are sick with the fever, my lady," the black monk reminded her. "Thousands."

But Sibylla didn't care about the others, the commoners, the soldiers and whores. What were they compared to Heraclius, Uncle Joscelin, and her two little girls? Sibylla started weeping as the news sank in. Her little girls, her bright-haired little girls, the gift Guy had given her since his return. She'd wanted sons, of course, for Jerusalem, but Guy had not reproached her for only giving birth to girls.

"Guy!" she called out, half lifting herself off the pillow. "Guy!" She was suddenly terrified that Guy, too, had died, and she gasped in a voice constricted by pain and breathlessness, "Where's my lord husband? Where is King Guy?"

"He is seeing to the funeral arrangements of your daughters, my lady."

"Good Guy," she murmured, falling back onto the pillow exhausted and dripping sweat again. But now her heart was palpitating, and she let the crucifix fall to press both hands over it in alarm. It was too much! Heraclius, Uncle Joscelin, and her little girls. All she had left in the whole world was Guy. Why did God hate her so? Why did He take away everything she loved? Hadn't she suffered enough already?

She flung her head from side to side. She did not know where to turn for help or comfort, and the pain was becoming unbearable. It was everywhere now.

The black monk retrieved his crucifix, and firmly pressed it into her hands again. "You would do well to confess your sins, my lady. Your time is nigh."

"What?" She tried to sit up, but the strain was too much. She sank back on the pillows, and the sound of her pulse pounded in her ears. It felt as if her heart were thrashing about in her chest trying to get free.

"Confess your sins, my lady," the priest urged insistently.

"No, no! What have I done to deserve this? I am Queen of Jerusalem."

"And where is Jerusalem now, my lady? Is Mass still read over the grave of our Lord Jesus Christ? Can pilgrims still bring gifts to the Church of the Nativity? Are not both shrines besmirched and befouled by the followers of the false prophet Mohammed?"

"But that's not my fault!" Sibylla wailed, her heart beating faster than before. It seemed to be pumping so much blood into her veins that she was sure her head would soon burst apart.

"In your coronation oath you swore to protect the Holy Sepulcher, yet it is trampled under the feet of infidels. And you swore, Madame, to protect the people of Jerusalem, but tens of thousands now groan under the yoke of Saracen masters. Christian maidens are deflowered and debauched by Muslim men while their fathers and brothers watch in helpless agony, chained to the oars of Saracen galleys and driven with whips to the stone quarries or the infamous tin mines. All because of *you*, Madame."

"No, no!" Sibylla reared up to scream at him in furious protest. Her eyes widened, and her eyeballs seemed ready to pop out of her head. She clutched at her heart between her massive breasts, and her tongue protruded as she gasped for breath that would not come. Then she blacked out. Five minutes later she was dead.

Tyre, mid-October 1190

Alys was singing solo while Ernoul accompanied her on a harp. The over-crowded hall of the Ibelin residence was so still one could hear the rain pattering on the closed shutters. Alys had always had a beautiful voice, but when she was a half-starved girl straining to be heard above the squabbles and laughter of sailors and soldiers, it had often been lost amidst the ruder noises. Nor did a ragged beggar command the same respect as a young woman dressed, as she was now, in a gown of saffron-colored cotton under an embroidered surcoat of carmine. Her hair was modestly covered by a wimple, and the neckline of her gown was so high there was no skin exposed between veils and bodice. No one coming upon her here for the first time would dream that in the past she had been taken for a whore. But mostly it was the elegant accompaniment of the harp that made men think of royal courts rather than taverns. Ernoul had mastered this new instrument to an exceptional degree.

Alys was singing a song of grief for a lover gone to an early grave. Ernoul had composed the song himself, but he'd told his audience it originated from a great Western troubadour, knowing they'd be more impressed that way. The combination of text and performance had captivated everyone. Nanny Anne was dabbing her eye with her sleeves and sniffling, while several squires were looking decidedly lovesick. Even the more jaded members of the household were so absorbed by the song and the singer that a loud hammering on the door below was ignored at first. Only when male voices started shouting for admit-tance did Ibelin gesture irritably for one of the squires to go and see who it was. The mood, however, had been shattered. Alys ended the song abruptly, reaching for a glazed pottery cup filled with wine.

The shouting and pounding moved from the street into the courtyard, and the occupants of the hall turned to look in alarm toward the entrance as they heard multiple pairs of feet pounding up the courtyard steps towards the first floor. An instant later a half-dozen men burst through the screens into the hall, bringing with them the cool, damp air of the outside, the smell of wet wool, and the sight of glistening conical helmets, for the rain made the steel shine.

"My lord!" The leader of the intruders was the ruggedly handsome Norseman Haakon Magnussen, and he was followed by a half-dozen of his men. He paused, both to catch his breath and to be sure he had everyone's attention. Then he announced: "Queen Sibylla of Jerusalem is dead!"

The hall erupted. Men wanted to know how and when. Women crossed themselves and called down blessings on the dead. The children began asking each other what was going on, and the dogs started barking. Ignoring them all,

Magnussen crossed the distance to the high table with long, loping strides that still bore the rhythm of the sea. On the dais, both Ibelin and his lady had sprung to their feet. As Magnussen reached them, Ibelin asked in disbelief, "You're sure of this? The Queen is dead?"

Magnussen met Ibelin eye to eye. "She succumbed to a fever that is sweeping through the camp and has claimed the lives of both her daughters, her uncle, and the Patriarch as well."

"Holy Mother of God!" Maria Zoë gasped. "What of my daughter? The Lady of Toron?"

"She was well, last I heard, my lady," Magnussen assured the Dowager Queen. While Maria Zoë crossed herself in relief and added a prayer for Isabella's safety, Ibelin handed the Norse captain his own goblet of wine, which the Norseman downed in a single draught.

"You say the Queen *and* her daughters are dead?" Ibelin pressed Magnussen, as the Norseman handed back the goblet. "And the Patriarch, and the Count of Edessa?"

"Exactly."

That was, with the exception of Aimery de Lusignan, everyone who had supported the usurpation of Sibylla and Guy in 1186, Balian calculated, stunned. He had rarely seen such ruthless evidence of Divine Justice, albeit later than he would have liked. It even made sense that Aimery, who had repented that usurpation, had been spared. Then, alert as a hunting lion, he asked sharply: "And King Guy?"

"He's well, my lord. No sign of *him* getting the fever when I left."

Ibelin absorbed that, and asked in a calmer voice, "When did the Queen die?"

"She died two days ago, my lord. As soon as I heard, I put to sea. We had a following wind and current and rowed whenever conditions permitted. I doubt any man alive could have beat me here."

Ibelin smiled at that and readily agreed. "I believe you, Master Magnussen. Sit down;" he indicated the chair beside his own, adding, "you must be hungry," and he beckoned to Georgios to bring a place setting and food for the Norse captain. The latter gestured for his own men to take seats at the lower tables, where they were already surrounded and assaulted by questioners.

"Tell me everything you know," Ibelin urged, lowering himself into his chair but leaning forward in his seat. Behind him, his lady remained standing, far too agitated to resume her seat, yet determined not to miss a single word.

"Despite all that has happened in the last year, the situation in Acre has not fundamentally changed since the siege started, my lord," Magnussen began.

It had indeed been an eventful year. Three great and powerful kings who had taken the cross had died: Henry II of England, William II of Sicily, and most devastating of all, Friedrich "Barbarossa," the Holy Roman Emperor. The latter had been advancing through Asia Minor at the head of a mighty host coming to the relief of the Holy Land, when he had drowned while crossing a river. His death led to the almost complete disintegration of his army. Many of his vassals and their men simply turned around and headed home via Constantinople. Only about ten thousand continued on to Antioch, where they then halted. Montferrat had been forced to travel north to implore Friedrich of Swabia, the new commander, to bring his men south, but although Friedrich had come with most of his remaining knights, they brought a force of just five thousand men—one-tenth of the number who had set out from the Holy Roman Empire.

Meanwhile, at the siege of Acre, a combined Frankish assault on the beleaguered city by land and sea had resulted in nothing but thousands of casualties. Likewise, an attempt to drive Salah ad-Din off the heights surrounding the siege camp had ended in bloody failure. Adding insult to injury, an Egyptian fleet had succeeded in breaking through the Frankish blockade to relieve the Saracen garrison.

Morale was further undermined by the fact that the command of the land forces around Acre splintered more with the arrival of each new contingent of troops, from Friedrich of Swabia with the remnants of the German crusade, to the Counts of Champagne and Flanders with the advance guard of the French. The French did not recognize the primacy of Swabia, the Germans were contemptuous of the French, the Danes and Frisians recognized no authority at all, and the Pisans and Genoese, who had worked jointly in the sea assault on Acre, had since fallen to bickering again.

Magnussen was summarizing. "The arrival of new fighting men is offset by the casualties incurred either in the near perpetual skirmishing or through illness. The latter has been most deadly this past month."

"What is it? Dysentery?" Maria Zoë wanted to know.

The Norseman shrugged; he was no doctor. "It ignites a high fever and it kills fast, but it is not dysentery. Something else. It's taken the life of Friedrich of Swabia in addition to the Patriarch, Queen Sibylla, her daughters, and Edessa. Furthermore, supplies are running short again, and the winter storms haven't even started yet. Things are only going to get worse, not better."

"And still no word of the French and English Kings?" Ibelin asked, exasperated.

"They have both reached Sicily, my lord, but it is too late in the year to sail east now. I had that news from a Sicilian mariner who arrived only the day before Queen Sibylla died. He also reported that the young English King made a huge fuss about his sister's dower being sequestered and the lady herself confined against her will by King Tancred. He described King Richard as hot-headed and arrogant, and did not think he got on well with the French King."

Ibelin found himself wondering how much more bad news he could bear, and his expression reflected his grim mood. They had put so much hope and trust in the relief armies that the Holy Roman Emperor and the French and English Kings had promised to bring east—but the German army had dis-integrated, the French were dying like flies while their King tarried, and the English had yet to arrive at all. Furthermore, the English King, far from being the formidable Henry II, was now Richard of Poitou, a man with a bad repu-tation. He had rebelled against his august father and driven the good King to an early grave. Ibelin had no reason to think well of King Richard.

On the other hand, the death of Sibylla and her daughters, he reminded himself, was surely a divine sign. Sibylla had never exercised her authority inde-pendently, much less intelligently. She was little more than the conduit for passing royal power to her husband and heirs. But with her daughters dead, her heir was her half-sister Isabella.

Balian glanced over at his wife. Her expression was worried, her brows drawn together, her eyes turned inward. He guessed she was far ahead of him in considering the implications this death had for all of them.

"Master Magnussen," Ibelin turned to his guest. "Make yourself at home, but forgive me if I withdraw with my lady wife."

"Of course, my lord." The Norseman nodded curtly to the Dowager Queen. He found her rather intimidating and never felt fully comfortable in her presence—in large part because he was more attracted to her than was good for him.

Ibelin offered his arm to his wife. Together they made their way down the hall and up the internal stairs to the only room in the house where they had a shred of privacy: their bedchamber.

No sooner had the door clunked shut behind them than Maria Zoë declared, "Isabella is now the rightful Queen of Jerusalem."

"I know, but I very much doubt Guy de Lusignan—much less Geoffrey de Lusignan—is prepared to acknowledge that, and you'll find no one among the barons of Jerusalem willing to pay homage to Toron. He burned his bridges when he left us in the lurch at Nablus."

"Isabella said he fought very bravely and that all the barons showed him great respect after he was so badly wounded."

"We're not barbarians, Zoë. I'd have treated him kindly, too, if he'd been willing to return here during his recuperation. But being *nice* to a man when he's wounded is not the same thing as vowing fealty to him as King."

"You're saying you'd rather have a man *known* to be an incompetent ass than a youth who—"

"Has proved himself treacherous? Yes. Remember, he didn't just betray us at Nablus; he was thick as thieves with the Sultan's secretary Imad ad-Din."

"And he has been fighting the Saracens ever since he returned. You don't seriously think he is the Sultan's man, do you?"

"No; I think he's a spineless, self-pitying youth who has none of the qualities essential in a good king: courage in word and deed, good judgment, decisiveness, a sharp understanding of men and how to lead them, and the charm to inspire loyalty. Humphrey is indecisive, weak-willed, afraid of responsibility, retiring, and humorless. Sibylla's death is a God-sent opportunity to place the future of Jerusalem in the hands of a man capable of regaining it. We cannot squander such a chance by putting the crown on the head of a man who has already proved himself inadequate!" The heat of his emotions made Balian's tone sharp and far less polite than usual.

Maria Zoë was silent for a few moments. Her opinion of Humphrey had never been quite as low as Balian's, but her views were colored by the fact that Isabella loved him so much. She knew Isabella would be loath to part from him. But Maria Zoë was a crowned queen, and she had been raised in the imperial court of Constantinople. In power politics there was little room for affection. Indeed, a princess' love (not to say lust) for an unsuitable man had plunged them into this abyss in the first place. If Sibylla had married the Lord of Ramla instead of the woefully inadequate Guy de Lusignan, the army of Jerusalem would not have been lured onto the plains behind the Horns of Hattin, and the Kingdom would still exist today.

"So," Maria Zoë concluded, "if Isabella is to be recognized as Queen by the High Court of Jerusalem, she will have to set Humphrey aside —as Sibylla so singularly failed to renounce Guy."

"Exactly," Balian confirmed, "and she'll have to do it before, not after, the coronation. After Sibylla's betrayal, no one will accept a mere promise. She'll have to divorce and remarry a man acceptable to the High Court *before* she is crowned."

"And who do you think that might be?" Maria Zoë wondered out loud.

Balian shook his head and sighed. "I haven't a clue at the moment. Sidon's single. We could dissolve his betrothal to Helvis to clear the way for him to marry Isabella."

Maria Zoë frowned. She liked Reginald de Sidon, but she did not see him as exceptional enough to be raised above his peers. Besides, he was over 60. "Bohemond of Antioch?" she suggested instead.

"Maybe," Balian agreed at once. "That would unite Tripoli and Jerusalem—but even better would be Raymond of Antioch. That marriage would unite Antioch and Jerusalem, but I'm not sure if either prince of Antioch can be lured south to take part in the siege of Acre. Then again, there's also no reason why they should. The decision to besiege Acre was another of Guy's harebrained ideas that made little tactical sense. It would have been far more rational to retake Sidon, Beirut, and Gibelet in order to re-establish continuous control of the coast from here to Tripoli."

"Yes," Maria Zoë agreed absently. She generally left military tactics to her husband, but conceded, "It's a pity Montferrat did not support your effort to recapture Sidon. Which reminds me of Montferrat. He's very likely to put himself forward as a candidate for Isabella's hand."

"Montferrat?" Balian frowned. "Why?"

"He is not a humble man," Maria Zoë observed dryly. "I think he fancies a crown—and Isabella."

Not for the first time, Ibelin was struck by his wife's political acumen. She had gauged Montferrat perfectly. Within hours of learning of Sibylla's death, Montferrat made a call on the Ibelins. Notably, Montferrat did not send for Ibelin, as he had so often done in the past. Instead, he rode to the Ibelin residence with a large retinue. He had also gone to the trouble to dress in his best finery, including a feathered cap and a sable-lined velvet cloak. Montferrat's changed behavior drove home to Ibelin that his own status had changed overnight with Sibylla's death. He might only be the titular baron to a lost lordship in a kingdom that had almost ceased to exist, but he was also stepfather of the sole legitimate heir to that kingdom.

Montferrat's retinue was left on the ground floor, and Montferrat was escorted to the solar on the floor above. Since there was no door separating the solar from the hall, the area was not secluded, but it offered comparative privacy. Georgios and Ernoul provided wine, nuts, and dried fruits and then positioned themselves at the juncture with the hall to prevent others from coming near enough to eavesdrop.

Montferrat bowed deeply to Maria Zoë Comnena, kissed her hand, and opened in Greek. "It never ceases to amaze me, my lady, how you defy the laws of nature to look as young and radiant as a maiden! It is always a pleasure to look upon your face."

"And it never ceases to amaze me that men think a compliment on a woman's looks is the best means to ingratiate themselves," Maria Zoë answered in French, to ensure her husband understood what she was saying. "I am wise enough to know flattery when I hear it, my lord, and old enough to resent being patronized. You are here on account of my daughter Isabella, the rightful Queen of Jerusalem, not to make me empty compliments. Please, sit down, so we can discuss the situation like rational human beings." She indicated a chair at a round mosaic table before the hooded fireplace, then seated herself between Montferrat and her husband. Her high-necked purple gown was embroidered with gold, and her long, flowing sleeves, lined with shimmering gold silk, cascaded on either side of her chair. Balian had to suppress a smile at Montferrat's evident consternation, for she was indeed both beautiful and regal at that moment.

The handsome Italian was unused to having women dismiss his gallantries, but he bowed his head graciously and took the seat offered. He slowly sipped the wine Ibelin poured for him, using the time to recover his composure. Then he set down the enameled glass goblet, smiled, and made the best of a bad start by admitting, "Indeed, Madame, I am here about your daughter. It will not have escaped your notice that I was enchanted by her from the day we met, and I have been distressed by her enforced absence. I most certainly would not have subjected *my* tender and noble wife to a siege camp—if I had one. But my marriage to your kinsman has been dissolved at her behest, leaving me solo." He paused, apparently expecting some comment. When none came, he was forced to continue. "With the death of her sister, Isabella's safety is more important than ever, not for herself alone but for the Kingdom she embodies. She should not remain exposed to the dangers of disease and enemy action any longer. She must be brought to safety—back to Tyre—at once."

"Just how do you propose to remove my daughter from her husband, my lord?" Queen Maria Zoë replied.

Montferrat cleared his throat. "My lady: as you said yourself, your daughter is the rightful Queen of Jerusalem. Her husband by rights should be King, but Toron is clearly neither inclined to nor suited for such an exalted position— certainly not in the present crisis. For the good of her kingdom, your daughter must set Toron aside and marry a man capable of regaining her kingdom for her."

"The laws and customs of the Kingdom of Jerusalem are very clear on the subject of the marriage of a princess designated as the heir," Ibelin interjected. "The selection of a female heir's husband is reserved to the High Court of Jerusalem. King Baldwin IV ignored the laws and customs of the Kingdom when he allowed his sister Sibylla to marry Guy de Lusignan without the consent of the High Court. If Isabella were to set aside her current husband, who was likewise selected without the consent of the High Court, then it will be the High Court of Jerusalem, not her mother or I, who selects her consort."

"Regaining Jerusalem will require the help of all of Christendom," Montferrat answered solemnly, meeting Ibelin's gaze. "A man with close ties to the most powerful kingdoms of the West would, therefore, be ideal."

Ibelin could hardly deny that, so he conceded, "True enough." Then he asked, as if he didn't already know the answer, "Did you have someone in mind?"

"I'm first cousin to Friedrich Barbarossa, late Holy Roman Emperor, first cousin to Louis VII, father of the ruling King Philip II of France, and nephew to Duke Leopold of Austria, who now commands the remnants of my cousin's German crusade since Friedrich of Swabia has also died. Nor should you forget that the High Court found my brother William a suitable husband for Sibylla, when she was heir to the throne. Last but not least, I have demonstrated my commitment to the Holy Land by my presence here these last three years, and I have demonstrated my ability to defeat the Sultan in battle."

"Then you wish to sue for Isabella's hand?" Ibelin concluded, their eyes locked.

"Yes, I do." Montferrat's face was flushed by the intensity of his emotions. The fire burning in the grate was reflected in them—a purely physical coincidence that nevertheless underlined the ambition smoldering inside.

"I will put your proposal to the High Court," Ibelin answered, adding realistically, "or at least those members of it present in Tyre."

"Do they constitute a quorum?" Montferrat immediately wanted to know.

"As close to one as we can get in the circumstances," Ibelin assured him.

Montferrat appeared to think about challenging that, but then thought otherwise. "Do I have *your* support, my lord of Ibelin?" he asked instead.

"I haven't decided yet. I need more time to think," Ibelin told him honestly, with a significant glance at Maria Zoë.

His gesture reminded Montferrat of her immense influence in this delicate matter, for who better than a mother might be trusted to influence a gullible young woman? Montferrat turned to Maria Zoë and leaned forward, exerting all of his charm. "And you, Madame? Do you support my suit?"

Maria Zoë, like Balian, had not yet decided what was best for either her former kingdom or her eldest daughter. Montferrat's arguments, however, could not be dismissed lightly, and she personally preferred the "fresh blood" that Montferrat represented over any of the local lords, including Antioch. Montferrat's ties to the Holy Roman Empire and to France were indeed invaluable. Maria Zoë calculated that England was likely to side with Lusignan in any case, since Guy's brothers were vassals of the English King. King Richard, particularly since he was young and new to his crown, would most likely feel bound by these feudal ties to support them.

"I want the crown of Jerusalem, Madame. I don't deny it," Montferrat continued earnestly in his deep, melodic voice. "But I also want to make your daughter a cherished and beloved wife, something Toron has never done. And I want to make her a mother, something Toron's not inclined to do, either."

Maria Zoë recoiled at these words and tossed a frown to Balian. How could Montferrat possibly know about Isabella's disappointment in her marriage bed?

"I'm a man of the world, Madame," Montferrat continued in a voice so low Maria Zoë was not sure even Balian could hear. "I recognize a sodomite when I see one, and that is what your son-in-law is. A man who prefers boys to women."

Maria Zoë shuddered at the thought. She had been raised to view sodomy as one of the most heinous sins imaginable—far ahead of fornication or even adultery. She did not like to think of someone as kind as Humphrey favoring such unnatural pleasures, nor facing eternal damnation because of it. And yet . . . Such proclivities might explain his behavior. She looked to Balian for help.

"We understand your suit, my lord," Ibelin announced neutrally. "We will put it to the members of the High Court here in Tyre and let you know the outcome of our deliberations."

"I hope you mean to do that soon, my lord. We have no time to waste."

"Indeed," Ibelin agreed. "No time to lose at all."

Tyre, late October 1190

It was a measure of Ibelin's increased status that no one objected to him summoning a session of the High Court; on the contrary, they hastened to comply with his summons. The barons and bishops took over the church of St. Helena, and their knights guarded the entrances and the streets around. In addition to Ibelin himself, representing not just Ibelin but his brother's baronies of Ramla and Mirabel and his wife's dower of Nablus, the secular lords present were the Prince of Galilee and the barons of Haifa, Sidon, Scandelion, Caesarea, Sebaste, and Hebron. Conspicuously absent were Toron and Oultrejourdain (both baronies held in personal union by Humphrey), Tripoli, now held by Bohemond of Antioch, Caymont, which was vacant, and Beirut and Nazareth, whose lords had remained at the siege of Acre after the other barons left.

It was the lords of the Church, however, that had the greater role to play if Isabella was to be freed of Toron and allowed to remarry. With the Patriarch dead, the senior churchman of the Kingdom was the Archbishop of Tyre, but he was still in the West. The Archbishops of Caesarea and Nazareth were at the siege. The slaughtered Bishop of Acre had not yet been replaced, and this left the Bishops of Lydda, Bethlehem, Hebron, Sebaste, and Sidon to represent the heads of the Latin Church in Jerusalem. That was five of the nine bishops, but the absence of all three archbishops meant they did not represent a majority of the ecclesiastical lords on the High Court—unless the Archdeacon of Tyre's claim to represent his Archbishop was accepted.

After the Bishop of Bethlehem had led them in prayers, begging the Almighty's grace and blessings on their deliberations and decisions, Ibelin opened the proceedings by reminding his peers of the death of their Queen and her daughters. He then asked if there was agreement on who her heir was. Isabella was named at once, but Lydda noted that Guy had been anointed King and would therefore have the right to reign until he died, arguing that Isabella was the heir apparent, not the Queen.

This view was immediately challenged by the secular lords, who unanimously rejected Guy. "He should never have been King in the first place!" Haifa insisted, backed forcefully by Tripoli's stepson William of Tiberias, now nominally Prince of Galilee. The fact that Guy had been crowned without the approval of the High Court was brought up next, followed by the reminder that Sibylla had lied to most of the bishops in the room about her intention to set Guy aside and take another consort. All these painful past defeats ignited new indignation. When Hattin was mentioned, immediately followed by descriptions of Lusignan's equally terrible leadership in the siege of Acre, the mood became so hostile to Lusignan that the Bishop of Sebaste felt compelled to remind the assembled lords that they were here to discuss the succession, not indulge in diatribes against Lusignan.

"The point, my lord Bishop," Ibelin noted into the ensuing pause, "is that the secular lords are not prepared to acknowledge Guy de Lusignan as King of Jerusalem. He ruled by right of his wife only, and she is dead. Her half-sister Isabella, the daughter of King Amalric, is the rightful Queen of Jerusalem."

This time no one contradicted him, but the Bishop of Hebron pointed out, "In that case, Humphrey of Toron is by right of his wife the next King."

This provoked a roar of indignant contradiction and protest, particularly from those who had been imprisoned with him, including Haifa, Hebron, and Galilee. As Ibelin had predicted, the barons were just as unanimous in rejecting Humphrey as they had been in rejecting Guy. The notion of taking oaths of fealty to Humphrey was compared to lunacy, heresy, and treason. But the bishops were troubled by the fact that Humphrey had been recognized as Isabella's husband for eight years. Marriage was a sacred vow, they reminded the assembled lords, and it was for life. Much as they sympathized with the reluctance of the barons to bind themselves to a man unlikely to lead them well, the laws of the Church were sacred—and explicit: a man could not set aside his wife, nor a woman her husband, for any reason whatsoever—not infidelity, nor infertility, nor even heresy and sorcery. "Unless you can demonstrate that Isabella was not rightfully married to the Lord of Toron in the eyes of the Church, her marriage cannot be dissolved," The Bishop of Hebron declared solemnly.

This statement was greeted with sullen silence. The men in the room knew this was Church law, and they resented it bitterly; it stood in the way of their desperate need to find a competent man capable of leading the Kingdom in its hour of need.

"Isn't consent a condition of marriage?" Ibelin spoke into the silence.

"Of course," the bishops agreed almost in unison.

"What is the age of consent for women?" Ibelin asked next.

"Twelve," came the answer from several voices at the same time. By now, however, half the barons were sitting up straighter in the choir seats they had taken; their frustration was already giving way to anticipation.

"Isabella was eleven when she was wed to Toron," Ibelin reminded them.

Suddenly everyone seemed to be speaking at once, going back into their memories aloud, calculating Isabella's age on their fingers. Her marriage had been infamous because it took place at the Castle of Kerak in the middle of a siege by Salah ad-Din. The feudal army that would normally have gone to the relief of Kerak had refused to march until Baldwin IV removed Guy de Lusignan as regent. Guy was dismissed, but the march was further delayed by Baldwin IV's decision to crown his nephew co-monarch to ensure no future interregnum. Most of the men in the room had been in the army that eventually marched to the relief of Kerak, arriving almost a month after the wedding had been celebrated in the besieged castle. They knew the date: November 1183. Isabella, however, had not been born to King Amalric until 1172. She could not yet have turned twelve.

The mood among the barons turned jubilant, but the bishops responded with chagrin. Such a marriage should not have been allowed at all. The Bishop of Lydda turned on Ibelin. "So why did you let this fraudulent marriage take place? Why did you stage this mockery of a holy sacrament?" he asked indignantly.

"Because," Ibelin answered steadily, his eyes fixed on the bishop but his voice pitched for the entire room, "I was not there." He paused to let this sink in, and then reminded them, "I was in Jerusalem—with most of the rest of you.

Isabella, on the other hand, was being held prisoner in Kerak—as she had been for three years. Her mother and I had nothing to say about this marriage. Furthermore, her marriage to Toron, who had turned fifteen, was her only chance to escape the clutches of Reynald de Châtillon!"

Châtillon's reputation was dark enough for this answer to subdue even the bishops. Châtillon had once tortured the Patriarch of Antioch into giving him money—money he used to finance a raid on the peaceful Christian island of Cyprus. Châtillon was a man of violent tempers, insatiable greed, and infamous brutality. No one doubted that he could impose his will on a child.

The matter of Isabella's non-marriage to Toron settled in their minds, the High Court turned its attention to who would be the most suitable candidate for Isabella's next husband. Ibelin brought forward the new Count of Tripoli, the heir to Antioch, and Montferrat, and then sat back to listen to the debate. Within a half-hour it was clear that Montferrat's unquestioned capabilities as a fighting man and commander gave him the edge over his younger rivals. No one had anything negative to say about the sons of the Prince of Antioch—but Montferrat was here, he was proven, and he had put in his bid. Perhaps most damaging of all, it would take time to send to Antioch or Tripoli and inquire if the young men in question were willing to marry Isabella of Jerusalem. A positive answer was by no means assured, because with Isabella came responsibility for her occupied and beggared country. A bird in the hand . . .

Chapter 11

Siege camp at Acre, early November 1190

ISABELLA WRIGGLED DEEPER UNDER THE COVERS and snuggled closer to her husband. The winter storms might not have struck yet, but the nights were getting damp and chilly. Humphrey lay with his back to her, but he did not protest when she slipped her arm around his chest. They were both wearing nightshirts, of course, but Humphrey's had become bunched around his waist in the course of the night, and Isabella could slip her hand under the edge and stroke his naked side. She was seeking the distinctive but familiar feel of scar tissue.

The horror of that day when Sirs Bartholomew and Galvin had brought Humphrey to her half-dead would never be completely blotted out, but the months of nursing him back to health had done much to restore their relationship. Humphrey had been so helpless and so thankful for her care. He had apologized a thousand times for bringing her here and he had urged her to go home, saying his squire could care for him. But whenever he slept, he had clung to her, and sometimes when passing through that twilight zone between rest and wakefulness he had kissed her passionately.

Isabella was *sure* that it was just a matter of time before he overcame whatever demon was making him impotent. A year in a siege camp had overwhelmed any last vestiges of sexual innocence. She now knew more about sex than she, as a princess, really needed or wanted to know. It had become clear to her that Humphrey's failure to make love to her had less to do with a lack of *desire* than a lack of *ability*. Since he was otherwise a healthy young man, however, his sexual incapacity (Isabella thought) could only be the work of demons. She had convinced herself that prayer would eventually defeat them.

Meanwhile, however, the siege continued. The killing and dying, the stench, the flies, and the boredom. Most recently the fever had terrorized them, and Isabella had begged Humphrey to quit the siege. His answer had been that she could go, but he would not abandon his King. Then Sibylla had died and she had been needed to help wash and wrap the corpse, while Humphrey was one of the men who comforted a stunned and grief-stricken King Guy. Isabella didn't like Guy, but she could not deny that he had been shattered by the loss of both his daughters and his wife within forty-eight hours. That crisis, too, had brought Humphrey and Isabella closer together—only for them to fall out more hotly than ever over her claim to the throne.

Tonight Isabella wanted reconciliation, and the fact that Humphrey was holding her hand against his chest encouraged her. She risked leaning forward to kiss him on the shoulder. When he did not react, Isabella reasoned that he might not have felt her lips through his nightshirt. She tried nuzzling his shoulder with her nose, and was annoyed by men talking loudly outside. This was no time for that, she thought irritably. It was still dark.

The voices sounded angry. Probably some squabble over a whore, she told herself, resigned to such things after a year in the camp. Suddenly the immature voice of Humphrey's squire pierced her consciousness. "But my lord's asleep!" he protested.

"Not alone, I warrant," came a gruff answer that elicited laughter.

Isabella didn't like the sound of that. She lifted her head to listen more intently.

"No, he is with his lady," the squire answered manfully, although Isabella could hear fear in his voice. Who on earth could be threatening the boy, here in the middle of the night in the the Frankish camp? And why?

"*Queen* Isabella, you mean," another voice—pinched, nasal, and clerical in tone—corrected the squire.

Isabella was astonished to hear herself referred to in that way. She had laid claim to the title shortly after Sibylla's funeral, and it was because Humphrey had batted the notion away like a tiresome fly that they had quarreled. Humphrey insisted that Guy had been anointed and that he'd paid him homage. He told Isabella she should "stop hankering after a crown that will only cause you grief," adding: "You should have grown out of those girlhood fantasies."

It had been these last words that lacerated Isabella, and she had withdrawn from Humphrey—indignant, resentful, and hurt. However, no one in the camp at Acre had so much as whispered that she should be queen, leading her to reluctantly conclude that Humphrey was right.

Meanwhile, beyond the curtain of the tent, Humphrey's squire was reacting in bafflement. "Queen? But—"

"Get out of our way, boy," a new voice cut off the frightened squire. Although the voice was calm, it was sharp and foreign. It was also so threatening that it made Isabella's heart race. She sat bolt upright in bed grabbed her husband's shoulder to shake him away. "Humphrey!"

He groaned and stirred, but before he came to himself, men tore aside the curtains that enclosed their bed and loomed over them. They were all strangers, big, burly men (or so it seemed in her terror), and wearing armor. Their helmets glistened in the light of torches, held by men behind them, but their faces were lost in shadow.

"My lady Queen?" The pinched voice of the foreigner who had spoken before issued from one of the men standing over the bed. He was dressed just like the others, in a chain-mail hauberk and a nasal helmet, so what he said next confused Isabella more than ever. "I am the Bishop of Beauvais, and I am here to remove you from this tent and this bed."

"Why? What is going on? Humphrey, wake up!" Isabella shook Humphrey more vigorously than before. He groaned in inarticulate answer.

"The validity of your marriage has been cast in doubt and must be decided before an ecclesiastical court. Until a decision is reached, you must refrain from all contact with this man—"

"What? What?" Humphrey was at last coming to consciousness, but already it was too late. The armored Bishop flung back the covers, took hold of Isabella's upper arm, and started pulling her from the bed.

"No! Stop!" Isabella resisted. "Humphrey!"

"What's going on?" Humphrey croaked out in a sleep-heavy voice as he sat up, frowning.

By now, however, a second man had hold of Isabella around the waist and was physically dragging her off the bed. Isabella was horrified and stunned to feel the arm of this strange man around her near-naked body. She was wearing nothing but her nightshift. She flushed with shame and went rigid with mortification as his hand accidentally brushed against her breasts.

"My lady! Here!" A young man who had been hanging back stepped forward and, tearing his cloak off his back, covered her with it. Although he too was a stranger, the gesture was both chivalrous and protective and Isabella was grateful to him. The cloak he offered, furthermore, was thick and so voluminous that it offered sufficient cover to restore her modesty. In taking the cloak, however, she had been separated from Humphrey, and the martial Bishop of Beauvais was hustling her out of the tent, while other men hemmed in a protesting Humphrey.

At the tent entrance were more men. Isabella quailed and tried to stop. The Bishop closed his vise-like grip on her arm and pulled her forward impatiently.

"No!" Isabella raised her voice. "I demand to know where you are taking me!"

"You have nothing to fear," the young man who had provided the cloak assured her, coming up on her other side. His mere presence was calming and comforting. "I swear on my honor, my lady," he continued earnestly, "no harm will come to you." Although—or perhaps because—he was very young, Isabella believed him. He was not particularly tall, and certainly not as heavy-set as most of the other men around her, but he was attractive, and something about him seemed inherently trustworthy. Furthermore, outside the tent the sky was graying and she could now see he was dressed in very expensive armor, the kind only French noblemen wore, with gold links forming patterns in the mail. "I am Henri, Count of Champagne, my lady," he introduced himself as he met her eyes. "You can trust my word."

"Yes, Monsieur," Isabella agreed, taking a deep breath. "I trust you—and it will be on your head if something happens to me. But I can go nowhere without shoes." She pointed to her bare feet.

"Fetch her shoes!" the Bishop ordered, and one of the men disappeared back inside the tent. A moment later he returned with two of her shoes, which Isabella bent to slip on. When she righted herself, she nodded. Clutching the cloak around her, she let the Bishop of Beauvais and the Count of Champagne escort her through the camp to the French quarter.

The French contingent had been growing steadily and was now the largest in the siege camp. At the heart of the French camp were the baronial tents. The largest tent belonged to the highest-ranking of the most recent arrivals, the Duke of Burgundy. His tent was flanked by the tents of the counts of Flanders and Champagne. Isabella, however, was taken to yet a fourth tent. This smelled of incense, and as soon as she slipped inside she saw an altar and clerical vestments. Her arrival caused a commotion, as monks scurried to safety and curtains were drawn across these sections of the tent.

The Bishop of Beauvais paused and announced to Isabella: "My lady, you are to remain here in my tent until an ecclesiastical court determines the validity of your marriage to the Lord of Toron. You will be well guarded by my own knights and those of the Duke of Burgundy. They will prevent Toron from trying to seize you by force."

"What about—" Isabella started to protest, but then something stirred in the shadows, and a figure separated itself from the darkness. Isabella could hardly believe her eyes. It was her mother. "Mama!" She ran to her instinctively. How often since her foolish arrival here had she fantasized about returning to the safety of her mother's arms! How often had she longed and prayed for her mother to come and rescue her!

For a moment they clung to one another, but then Isabella's brain overcame her instinct and she pulled back to ask: "Mama! What are you doing here? Do you know what's happening? They're trying to separate me from Humphrey!" Even as she spoke, it dawned on Isabella that if her mother was *here*, in the Bishop's tent, she was on the side of the men who had abducted her. "You can't be making common cause with these men!" she protested, already starting to get angry. "How could you?"

"Listen to me, Isabella," Maria Zoë admonished firmly. "Your marriage to Humphrey has never been valid. You were not of the age to consent—"

"Maybe I wasn't then, but I am now!" Isabella countered furiously. "I love Humphrey! Why can't you accept that? Why can't *anyone* accept that? I love him!"

Maria Zoë was conscious of the large audience staring at them, and she imperiously told the men to leave. "This is between my daughter and myself, my lords. Leave us."

The young Count of Champagne cast Isabella a concerned look, while the Bishop of Beauvais seemed reluctant to take orders from anyone, but Maria Zoë met the Bishop's eyes with an uncompromising expression. "My lord Bishop, that was *not* a request."

"Your grace." He bowed deeply and, grabbing Champagne by the arm, shoved him out of the tent in front of him.

"Mama, I can't believe you've done this!" Isabella turned on her mother as soon as the strangers were gone.

"Isabella, calm down. Here, have some wine—" Maria Zoë tried to offer her a chalice filled with red wine.

"No, I don't want wine! I want an explanation of what is going on!"

Maria Zoë set the chalice down again and opened, in a cool voice that was intended to get Isabella's attention and force her to respond less emotionally, "As I believe you know, your sister Sibylla is dead."

"Yes, I was *here*, remember?" Isabella retorted snippishly.

"That, my dear child, was entirely *your* choice. I think you remember well enough how strongly your stepfather and I warned you against coming to a siege camp. We urged—no, *begged*—you to remain in Tyre. Don't come to me with your self-pity at being here."

Isabella clamped her lips together in furious helplessness because, of course, her mother was right.

"With your sister's death," Maria Zoë continued, taking a deep breath to check her own anger at her daughter's intransigence, "you have become the rightful Queen of Jerusalem."

"But Guy is already anointed, and Humphrey says . . ." Isabella's voice trailed off.

"Yes?" Maria Zoë prompted with raised eyebrows.

"Guy is still King. Everyone still addresses him that way."

"As long as no one challenges him, he will certainly try to retain that status. And as long as no one challenges him, everyone will accept the status quo." Maria Zoë paused to let this sink in before continuing. "A man willing to steal a crown is unlikely to abandon it easily. But that changes nothing about your right. You are the rightful Queen of Jerusalem, and the High Court is willing to recognize you." As she spoke, Maria Zoë watched her daughter very closely. Isabella caught her breath and straightened her back. Although it was hard to see in the half-light, Maria Zoë also thought she flushed, as if with a surge of excitement.

"Have they met already?" Isabella asked, and the breathlessness in her voice confirmed her mother's intuition: Isabella welcomed this news with all her heart.

"Yes, your stepfather summoned all the lords, sacred and secular, in Tyre. That was the majority. They are prepared to recognize you as their queen, Isabella. On one condition." She stopped.

"Condition?" Isabella asked sharply. Her frown indicated she had already guessed what it might be.

"That you set Humphrey aside."

"Why?" Isabella lashed out. "Why? What do they have against him?" Isabella's questions were flung out more in protest than inquiry, but her mother was ready to enlighten her.

"Because, Isabella, your husband betrayed them at Nablus, when they last agreed to make you queen. Have you already forgotten?" Maria Zoë knew perfectly well that Isabella had not. Still, she continued in an uncompromising voice, "They offered to make him king then, Isabella. Young and untried as he was, they were prepared to crown him king and do homage to him. All he had to do was accept. But he wasn't man enough—"

"That's not true!" Isabella protested hotly, ever ready to defend her husband's courage. "He just wanted to prevent a civil war—"

"What? So Guy could lose the *whole* Kingdom rather than just part of it?" Maria Zoë snapped back, rapidly losing control over her temper.

"How can you blame Humphrey for what Guy did?" Isabella demanded self-righteously. "It's not Humphrey's fault that Guy turned out to be such a disastrous king. No one could foresee Hattin four years ago."

"No one?" Maria Zoë asked sarcastically. "The whole High Court foresaw it, for God's sake! Why do you think they opposed making Guy king in the first place? Why do you suppose they were prepared to pass over Sibylla and make *you* queen? Why, even Guy's own brother Aimery saw it, but at the time he was too greedy for his own gain to oppose it, just like Edessa and Heraclius. In fact, the only one *fool* enough to think Guy might make a competent king was Humphrey de Toron."

"Humphrey's not a fool!" Isabella protested furiously, tears of frustration and confusion streaming down her face.

Maria Zoë considered her daughter distantly and finally remarked, "I would like to comfort you, Bella. I can see how hurt, confused, and miserable you are. But, frankly, I'm afraid of your rejection. You have thrust me aside too often in the last years for me to risk taking you in my arms—as much as I long to do so. It seems that when Agnes de Courtenay took you from me as a child of eight, she succeeded more profoundly than I thought possible. It seems you are no longer my daughter, after all."

Isabella gasped, and her blood turned to ice. She had no memories of her father whatever. Her earliest memories were being with her mother in a convent, a world in which everything revolved around her. And then her mother and she had moved to Nablus and from there to Ascalon, the latter with Uncle Balian. Uncle Balian had been a wonderful addition to her life because he had made it so much more exciting. He had introduced her to tree climbing and swings, taken her out on boats, and taught her to ride. Life had been lovely until one day the Baron of Oultrejourdain's men had come and taken her away from that personal Garden of Eden. They'd taken her into the desert and beyond the Dead Sea to a horrible, bleak castle on the edge of Sinai: Kerak. There she'd been subjected to the heartless and vindictive regime of the Lady of Oultrejourdain, while Humphrey was brutalized and humiliated by his stepfather, Oultrejourdain himself.

Isabella had been eight years old. She was utterly helpless and terrified. She wanted to run away, but how do you escape from one of the most heavily garrisoned castles in the world and then cross the notorious desert surrounding the Dead Sea? A girl? Alone? At the age of eight? She'd prayed for rescue, but Oultrejourdain had prohibited her mother and stepfather from visiting. They had defied him three times, and once Uncle Balian had come on his own, but in between those times, day in and day out, she had had only one friend: Humphrey.

Humphrey had been as miserable as she. He had wanted to escape, too, but he had nowhere to go. His "home" was where they were. And his kin were the very people who were making their life hell. He had begged Isabella, and she had promised, never to leave him. But Isabella had made that promise with the certainty that when he came of age they would escape together, and she would be reunited with those she loved: with her mother and stepfather. She had wanted to take Humphrey away from *his* world and *into* hers.

Of course, things hadn't worked out like that. Humphrey had been uncomfortable with her parents. He claimed Uncle Balian looked down on him. Isabella had resisted believing it, but she could not overlook the fact that her husband was not happy in Uncle Balian's company. So she had followed Humphrey wherever he went, and physical distance had grown between herself and her parents.

Yet that deep-seated, almost visceral, sense that "home" was with her mother and Uncle Balian had not seriously diminished. It had been reinforced dramatically when Uncle Balian had rescued her from Jerusalem after Hattin. And it had been only natural that she await Humphrey's release from captivity with her mother and Uncle Balian. When Humphrey was finally released, almost a year after the others, he had come to her and them.

Yes, she had come with Humphrey to Acre, because the tensions between Humphrey and Uncle Balian had been worse than ever, but the horrors of the siege camp had only reinforced her sense that "home" and "safety" were with her mother. She had made her bed and had been prepared to sleep in it, but she had never stopped trying to find a way to go home—to her mother and stepfather—without quite admitting she'd been wrong. How often had she imagined that she heard Uncle Balian's voice and jumped up full of joy, thinking he had come to rescue her from this hell hole just as he had once rescued her from Jerusalem? Not once had she imagined that her mother and stepfather might reject her.

With cold clarity as the light of a gray dawn seeped into the strange tent, Isabella realized that her mother might *not* always be there for her. Worse: she abruptly recognized that her mother might not always *forgive* her. With naked brutality, Isabella remembered how rude and selfish she had been; her temper tantrums and her (usually overblown and unfair) accusations of treachery and cruelty echoed in her head. She had flung insults at her mother and stepfather; she had screamed and rejected their advice with utter faith in her impunity. Suddenly it dawned on her that she was *not* immune after all.

Isabella noted how tired her mother looked, how *aged*. Her mother had always been beautiful. She was the beautiful Greek bride admired by the whole world; she was the lovely young widow who had captured the heart of a brave knight. But she was thirty-six now. Older than Sibylla had been at her death. She'd brought five children into the world, too, and that was now reflected in the solid width of her waist. And yet, she hadn't looked this old a year ago, Isabella's mind protested. Had she?

"Mama?" Isabella asked uncertainly. Had they really become strangers in just a year?

"Yes?" Maria Zoë's voice was strained but controlled, always the queen.

"What do you mean? Why aren't I your daughter anymore?" There were tears in Isabella's voice.

Maria Zoë was aware of nearly overwhelming exhaustion and a sense of futility. Isabella was her firstborn, and her sex had been such a disappointment to her father (who needed an heir other than his leper son) that he had taken little interest in her. Isabella had always been hers—hers alone. When Agnes de Courtenay had engineered Isabella's marriage to Humphrey and taken her away at the age of eight, it had nearly killed her. The most horrible fight of her entire marriage to Balian had been because she blamed him for not doing enough to prevent King Baldwin from taking her daughter away. She had gone so far as to confront the Queen Mother publicly, calling her a bitch in heat. All for Isabella. And what was Isabella now? A self-willed and foolish woman who rejected not only good advice, but the good intentions of those who loved her best.

To Isabella she said simply, "You have rejected me and my advice ever since Humphrey returned from captivity. You have made it clear to me, and your stepfather, that you place Humphrey ahead of everything else."

"Isn't that what a wife is supposed to do?"

Maria Zoë took her time and considered her answer carefully before she spoke. "A wife, perhaps, but not a queen. I am a princess of the Eastern Roman Empire, Isabella. I was taught at a very early age that my duty was to that Empire, and that the interests of the Empire would always take precedence over the stirrings of my heart. I thought I had taught you that, too. That you are not a woman—you are a queen. Sibylla failed to understand that, and we can see where it led us. I always blamed Agnes for that. I always thought my daughter carried my blood as well as the blood of Jerusalem. I thought *my* daughter understood her duty—as a queen. At Nablus, you seemed ready to pick up your burden. You seemed determined to be a better queen than Sibylla. At fourteen, you seemed more mature than now."

Isabella winced inwardly and remarked bitterly, "Everyone tells me I'm acting like a child—Humphrey because I have 'childish fantasies' about being a queen, and you because I'm so 'childish' as to think a wife should be loyal to her husband."

Maria Zoë drew a deep breath. "Well, if you do not want us to look on you like a child, Isabella, then you must start acting like an adult." She took a gauze shawl striped white-on-white by the weave and wrapped it around her head and shoulders before adding in a weary voice, "Since you do not seem to value my advice, I will leave you to make your own decision. You are safe here. The Bishop of Beauvais has guaranteed that no one but the clerics involved in the case will be allowed access to you. Of course, you will not be allowed to leave this tent until the ecclesiastical tribunal has ruled on the validity of your marriage, either. Think well, Isabella." Then the Dowager Queen swept past her daughter and out into the new day.

Siege camp at Acre, mid-November 1190

Humphrey knew what he was facing. No, the *whole siege camp* knew what was going on. His mother-in-law and her husband had engineered this entire plot so they could take Isabella away from him and marry her to Conrad de Montferrat. They had always looked down on him, and never accepted that he was good enough for, much less good *for*, Isabella. As for Montferrat, it was obvious that all he cared about was the crown of Jerusalem. He was a grasping, greedy, arrogant bastard, and an ignorant adventurer as well. Humphrey hated him with all his heart, and the sight of him in his expensive clothes, surrounded by a large entourage, made Humphrey's blood boil.

At least Montferrat would not be admitted to the trial. The church court was exactly that: a court presided over by the Papal Legate, Hubert the Archbishop of Pisa. The other judges were the Bishop of Beauvais representing France, the Archbishop of Mainz representing the Holy Roman Empire, the Archbishop of Canterbury representing England, and the Archbishop of Nazareth representing Jerusalem. These worthy bishops were seated in a long row against the canvas wall that divided the tent, while lesser clerics sat at flanking tables set at right angles to the row of bishops and prepared to record the proceedings. All that was as it should be, Humphrey thought, but he was less comfortable about the crowd of secular lords who were standing behind the lesser clerics on the sides of the room, apparently spectators. It was particularly galling to see Ibelin there, come to see him humiliated! And it hurt to see William of Tiberius, whom Humphrey had sometimes thought of as a friend. Telling himself they did not matter, Humphrey focused his attention on the five clerical judges. He went down on one knee before them and bowed his head.

The Archbishop of Pisa addressed him. "Humphrey, Lord of Toron, you are summoned here before this court to testify on the validity of your marriage to Isabella of Jerusalem. Do you swear upon this sacred relic, that you will speak only the truth before us?" A priest was holding a reliquary covered with jewels set in gold.

Humphrey dropped his second knee, placed his hand on the reliquary, and answered firmly, "In the Name of the Father, and the Son, and the Holy Ghost, I do."

"Humphrey, do you solemnly swear that you are Humphrey, son of Humphrey, and Lord of Toron in the Kingdom of Jerusalem?"

"I do."

"Is it correct that you have been cohabiting as man and wife with Isabella, Princess of Jerusalem?"

That sounded like a trick question to Humphrey. He answered steadily, "It is true that Isabella, Princess of Jerusalem, and I have lived together as man and wife ever since our wedding."

"Where and when were you allegedly married?"

"Isabella and I took vows of marriage to one another publicly at Kerak on November 18, 1183. There were hundreds of witnesses," Humphrey added testily, casting an angry look at the spectators, several of which, like Ibelin's younger brother Henri, had personally attended that wedding. Why didn't they speak up?

"November 18, 1183," the Papal Legate repeated, gesturing to the clerks to record that.

"Yes," Humphrey confirmed.

"And how did this marriage come about?"

"As most marriages come about," Humphrey answered, trying to curb his irritation. "My guardian, the Lord of Oultrejourdain, and Isabella's guardian, King Baldwin IV of Jerusalem, betrothed us."

"When did the betrothal take place?" the Archbishop of Mainz asked.

"Three years earlier."

"How did the Lord of Oultrejourdain come to have guardianship of you?"

"He was my mother's third husband."

"And King Baldwin's right to dispose of Isabella in marriage?" the Archbishop asked, purely for the record.

"Isabella's father died when she was two. Her nearest male relative was King Baldwin, her paternal half-brother," Humphrey explained.

"How old were you at the time of your betrothal?"

"Eleven—or twelve. I don't remember the exact date. It was the summer of 1180. I was born on the Feast of John the Baptist."

"And how old was Isabella?"

"Again, it depends on the exact date of the contract, which I do not know—but she was born on the Feast of St. Athanasius."

"July 5," the Bishop translated, and again indicated that the date should be recorded. "Anno Domini 1172?"

"Yes," Humphrey confirmed.

"So she was at most eight, but possibly still seven, at the time of the betrothal."

"Yes," Humphrey confirmed, frowning and resisting the temptation to say, "What of it?" Some children were betrothed while still infants.

"Did Isabella come to live with you and your family after the betrothal?"

"Yes, she did."

"Did she come willingly?"

"No, of course not," Humphrey readily admitted. "She was taken from her mother against her will and over the strong objections of her mother. She had lived all her life with her mother, and Kerak was a strange and forbidding place. I hadn't liked coming there after my grandfather's death, either. Neither Isabella nor I were happy in Kerak. Oultrejourdain was a brutal and vicious lord!" Humphrey's hatred of Oultrejourdain was so intense that he still could not speak of him with equanimity.

"And your lady mother?" the Archbishop of Canterbury asked in a shocked voice.

"You obviously never met her, my lord Bishop. My mother was a good match for Reynald de Châtillon!"

Some of the men in the audience laughed, earning a frowning rebuke from the clerics, but Humphrey felt for the first time that some of the men here were on his side. He breathed a little easier.

"In the time after the betrothal and before the alleged wedding, did you have contact with Isabella?"

"Of course! We shared a trencher at meals and spent as much time together as possible."

"But you did not know her carnally?" the Archbishop of Mainz asked, with a curious look on his face and an ambiguous tone.

"Of course not! We were both children!" Humphrey answered indignantly, flushing.

"Who made the decision for the two of you to marry in November 1183?" the Bishop of Beauvais leaned forward to ask.

"Oultrejourdain, as far as I can tell," Humphrey said with a shrug. He really didn't know who had decided or why the marriage had been set for that date.

"You were by then fifteen," the Archbishop of Pisa intoned.

"Yes," Humphrey affirmed.

"And Isabella?"

"She was—eleven." Humphrey stumbled a little as he spoke, because he too knew that the canonical age of consent was twelve.

"So she was under the age of consent," the Archbishop observed dryly. "Can you tell me why, then, the marriage should be considered valid? Why you should be deemed married to a woman who could not consent?" the Archbishop pressed Humphrey.

"Because she *did* consent!" Humphrey met the Archbishop's eyes. "With all her heart and all her mind! Isabella consented of her own free will! No one forced her! I swear it!"

"You lie!" The challenge came from the spectators, and everyone in the room turned to stare at the speaker. It was Henri d'Ibelin, and Humphrey's heart sank.

Henri stepped forward and announced, "I was at Kerak, my lords. I served Oultrejourdain—as these men can all attest. I personally witnessed the cruel way in which Princess Isabella was bullied into submission. I had many opportunities to see how frightened she was, how desperately she wanted to escape. Why, she outright begged me to help her escape and bring her to my brother, the Lord of Ibelin, her stepfather. Last but not least, I was there at the wedding between Toron and the Princess Isabella. The castle was under siege from Salah ad-Din. Siege engines were pounding us. Soon the threat of starvation and disease hovered over us." Each word was like a nail in Humphrey's coffin, because they were all true—even if they didn't make her an unwilling bride. "Isabella was a frightened child," Henri insisted, "cowed and intimidated by Oultrejourdain and his cruel lady. The betrothal and marriage—all of it—was against the wishes of Isabella and her noble mother," Henri d'Ibelin ended forcefully.

Humphrey answered hotly, conscious of how precarious his situation was: "It may have been against the wishes of her mother, but it was not against the wishes of Isabella herself! You are speaking for your brother the Lord of Ibelin!" Humphrey accused Henri with a hate-filled glare at Balian, who was (Humphrey thought) hypocritically holding his tongue. "You speak for him, not Isabella," Toron flung at Henri d'Ibelin. "Isabella had come to love me in the three years we were together at Kerak. She consented!"

"You lie!" Henri insisted, and dramatically threw his leather gauntlet onto the floor of the tent in front of the bishops. "I'll prove it before God with my own body!"

Humphrey stared in horror at the flung gauntlet, and then his eyes lifted to Henri d'Ibelin. Henri, even more than Balian, was a hardened fighting man. This was a man who'd helped defend a borderland against a numerically superior foe for decades. Worse, Henri d'Ibelin had been the leader of Oultrejourdain's Red Sea raids, in which he'd led some three thousand cutthroats on an orgy of blood and rape against unarmed Arab merchantmen and pilgrims.

Unseen behind the canvas that divided the tent, Isabella sat, straining her ears. Her heart was pounding in her chest, and her hands were sweating. Over the last three days, while the tribunal was being prepared and the bishops gathered, she had inclined more and more to her mother's advice. She had increasingly come to believe she must accept her destiny as Queen. The sound of Humphrey's beloved voice and his description of their joint childhood, however, had shattered her resolve. How could she sacrifice Humphrey for a crown? Not just for a crown, but for something as abstract as Jerusalem? It wasn't as if the Kingdom were rich and powerful. It hardly existed at all. Should she give up the man she loved for a dream? A hope?

But the silence on the other side of the canvas wall was killing her. "Fight for me!" she pleaded silently with her husband. "Humphrey, please! Fight for me!"

Humphrey looked at his challenger, and he knew he didn't have a chance of winning. Henri was much more skilled at arms. He was bigger and stronger. Only God could give him a victory over such a challenger, and why should God do that? When had God ever been on his side?

"My lord of Toron," the Archbishop of Pisa spoke up in a firm but almost gentle voice. "This knight has challenged you to judicial combat to prove that Isabella of Jerusalem did indeed consent to her marriage. Do you accept the challenge?"

Isabella held her breath and pressed her hands together. "Humphrey!" she begged more intently than ever before, "if you love me—*as you love*—take it up. Please! God is on our side! God knows I do love you! God knows I wanted you then as now!"

But the silence from the other side of the canvas was deafening. It was all Isabella could do to stifle her sobs as tears flooded down her face. She clutched at the edge of her chair in desperate misery.

The Archbishop of Pisa spoke again. "My lord of Toron, is this your last word? Do you admit that you lied when you said the Princess of Jerusalem consented to the sham marriage with you?"

Still Humphrey did not answer. He *could* not. They were all against him, and they had conspired to take Isabella away from him. Sir Henri was Lord Balian's tool. He knew he had lost, but he would not—under oath—lie, either. Wearily, his face petrified with bitterness and grief, he got to his feet, turned his back on the tribunal, and walked out of the tent. He was utterly alone in the world. He had lost his only friend: Isabella.

Maria Zoë had sent Rahel to attend on Isabella. The aging waiting woman put cold packs on Isabella's face to bring down the swelling of her eyes, and although these eyes were still bloodshot, Rahel's expert use of powder, rouge, and eyeliner had done much to restore Isabella's appearance. By the time she entered the tribunal chamber to face the five judges (there were no spectators now), she was composed.

Unlike Humphrey, Isabella was offered a chair, and water was brought to her as well. The Archbishop of Pisa accorded her all the deference due, if not a reigning queen, then a lady of high standing. For the sake of the record, Isabella too was asked her date of birth, the age she was at her betrothal (eight), and her age at the wedding ceremony in Kerak (eleven). From the looks that passed between the judges, it was clear to Isabella that four of the five men had already made up their minds, and that they viewed her marriage to Humphrey as invalid. The one holdout was the Archbishop of Canterbury, and it was equally clear to Isabella that the irascible old man was getting on the nerves of his fellow bishops.

"So, can you tell us your feelings when you were taken from your mother's house and sent to Kerak?" the Archbishop of Pisa asked solicitously.

"I was in shock, my lord Bishop. I had never dreamed something so terrible could happen to me. I had been a very spoiled little girl." She smiled wanly at this description, and the churchmen smiled back, her confession winning their sympathy.

"Did you protest what was happening to you?"

"I did. I was very insolent and disobedient to the Lady of Oultrejourdain. She had to discipline me many times."

"Did she beat you or otherwise abuse you?"

"I often had to forfeit meals, but her preferred method was to lock me in the crypt, which frightened me greatly because I believed some of the bodies there had not received Christian burial and that their souls still haunted the underground caverns."

That surprised the clerics enough to raise eyebrows, but it was not relevant to the case, so the Archbishop resumed his questioning. "When you were told you were to wed Lord Humphrey, did you protest?"

"No, my lord Bishop."

"Why was that?" The Archbishop of Pisa sounded surprised.

"Because by that time I had lived three years at Kerak and had learned not to defy the Lady of Oultrejourdain directly." Isabella paused, her heart pounding from nervousness, and then added, "And because I had come to love Lord Humphrey."

"Love him?" the Archbishop of Canterbury asked sharply, his nose for sin already sniffing for illicit sexual activities.

"Like a brother, my lord Bishop." Isabella turned and looked the Englishman in the eye. "I trusted Lord Humphrey, because he was the only one of my future in-laws who had ever been kind to me. I knew that I would be safe with him."

"Then you consented to the marriage!" the Archbishop of Canterbury declared triumphantly.

"I did not know that I had a choice, my lord Bishop," Isabella told him bluntly. Her lips had firmed, her chin lifted. The slaughtered Lord of Oultrejourdain would have recognized her pride and laughed to see her defiance turned against the worthy bishops rather than himself.

"When removed from your husband's tent early last Saturday morning, you protested vehemently, I am told," the Archbishop of Canterbury insisted sternly. "And you told your mother that you loved your *husband*." Canterbury made it sound as if he had caught her in an act of blatant perjury.

Isabella was not intimidated by the English cleric. "My lord Bishop," she answered in a voice that was only patient on the surface, "I have for the last seven years lived as man and wife with Lord Humphrey. As I noted only moments ago, even when we were children he was always good to me. That is true to this day. Lord Humphrey has never given me cause for grief—unless you count being taken captive at Hattin and leaving me a virtual widow for two long years. I have come to love Lord Humphrey deeply, even more than I loved him as a child. Furthermore, on the morning I was removed from his tent I was taken by surprise. I had no idea what was at stake, what the cause of complaint against us was." She paused, and the defiant set of her jaw and the flash of anger in her eyes would have made Reynald de Châtillon applaud, because he detested all clerics.

"Over the last week," Isabella continued in a voice that was now as sharp as a sword blade, "the issues at stake have been explained to me at length and in great detail." She paused to look from one judge to the next, meeting their eyes. "And I have had much opportunity to pray." The bishops murmured their approval.

"Just as it is a simple biological fact that I was below the age of consent when my marriage to Lord Humphrey was celebrated in public, it is also a biological fact that I am still a virgin. Lord Humphrey is impotent, and I see now that this was God's way of sparing me the sin of bringing a child into the world out of wedlock."

This answer caused a stir among the bishops. They whispered among themselves in evident agitation for several minutes before the Archbishop of Caesarea turned to her for confirmation. "You are saying your marriage with Toron has never been consummated, my lady?"

Isabella took a deep breath, faced the Bishop, and declared, "Yes, that is exactly what I am saying—and you are welcome to send a doctor to verify that fact."

The bishops started whispering among themselves again, and Isabella thought she heard the word "sodomite" fall. It made her wince, and she had to swallow down her sympathy for Humphrey. She did not really believe he liked boys, but he had not been *able* make her his wife, and he had not been *willing* to fight for her. He had simply turned his back and walked away. He had turned his back once too often.

The Archbishop of Canterbury was still blustering. "In the eyes of God, this was a marriage!"

"Without consent or consummation? Maybe you still sell girls like chattels in England," Beauvais sneered, "but in the civilized world there is no marriage without consent—much less consummation!"

"This is all a plot by Montferrat to steal the crown!" Canterbury croaked out furiously, conscious that his new young King needed the support of the Lusignans and would be ill pleased to find Guy de Lusignan deposed in favor of a relative of his bitter rival, the French King.

"What does Montferrat have to do with this?" the Archbishop of Mainz wanted to know. "It's a clear-cut case of canonical law."

"You've *all* taken bribes from Montferrat!" Canterbury countered, screeching hysterically. "You're all his creatures!"

"And you're the toady of Richard of Poitou!" Beauvais shouted back. While Nazareth indignantly protested his innocence, and the Archbishop of Mainz tried to calm tempers, the Archbishop of Pisa had the presence of mind to tell Isabella she could go.

For the next three days the Church council deliberated on the case. The Archbishop of Canterbury stubbornly prevented the church tribunal from announcing a decision one way or another. But on the evening of the third day he took to his bed, railing against the greed and jealousy of the princes, the slothfulness of the knights, and the immorality and licentiousness of the common soldiers. He was heard to say that God must rebuke them all, for he had grown stiff and weary from being a "voice in the wilderness." The next morning he was dead.

They were saying Masses for the English Archbishop's soul when the remaining four members of the Church council summoned Isabella to inform her of the judgment of the tribunal: her marriage to Humphrey de Toron was invalid. She was in the eyes of God free to marry any man of her choice. Isabella thanked the churchmen with dignity and withdrew to pray.

That same evening Isabella asked the Bishop of Beauvais to allow her mother and stepfather to visit her. The Bishop was reluctant at first, but after thinking it over he agreed.

Just as the muezzins were calling the garrison of Acre to prayers for the last time that day, the loud whispering of priests warned Isabella that her mother and stepfather had arrived. A moment later a thin voice called out, "My lady of Jerusalem? The Lord and Lady of Ibelin are here to see you."

"They are welcome," Isabella answered, getting to her feet.

The curtain was pulled aside by the hand of an unseen servant, and Isabella was face to face with her mother and stepfather for the first time since the night she'd been dragged from Humphrey's bed.

Her mother's face was so strained she looked vulnerable—a look totally at odds with her usual regal composure. Even during those horrible days immediately after news reached them of the disaster at Hattin, when they had no idea whether Lord Balian was alive, the Dowager Queen had not looked this fragile and frightened.

Balian's expression, on the other hand, was wary, even slightly hostile. He was gripping his wife's elbow as if he were holding her up, and Isabella realized that he was here to support his wife emotionally as well as physically. He evidently feared that Isabella was going to hurt her again, and he was here to defend his wife against his stepdaughter.

Isabella's sympathy for both of them was instantly ignited, and she ran forward to fling her arms around her mother. "Mama! Mama! Please forgive me! I didn't mean to hurt you! I know I have, but you have to believe me, I didn't *mean* to. I'm sorry. I can't tell you how sorry I am!" Her words came out in a flood, and Isabella could sense how her stepfather relaxed in relief.

Maria Zoë, however, had been so wounded by their fight earlier that she had been crying and reproaching herself for days. Her composure shattered instantly, and she broke down into tears, returning Isabella's embrace and clinging to her as she stammered, "It's my fault, too! I should never have let them take you away from me! I should have gone to the King myself! None of this would have happened if I had protected you from Agnes de Courtenay."

Balian stiffened, taking it as criticism, but Isabella opened her arms to pull him into them as well. Hugging him, too, she declared, "You did the best you could, Uncle Balian! I know you did! And you visited me as often as you could," she reminded him.

Then, drawing back a little, she looked from her mother (who was now wiping the tears from her face) to her stepfather (who was looking strained) and declared firmly, "I don't want to think of Kerak, or Oultrejourdain. That is part of the past. It is time to think of the future. Please," she indicated that they should come and sit down at a crude little table with two folding chairs flanking it; these were the only furnishings of her tent-chamber beyond the bed and a wicker chest for clothes.

Balian took his wife's arm again and escorted her to one of the chairs, but he remained standing behind it so Isabella could take the other seat. When Isabella was seated, she announced, "You will have heard that the Church council has declared my marriage to Toron null and void?"

Her mother and stepfather nodded solemnly.

"The Archbishop of Pisa also told me I was free to marry whomever I please." Again Maria Zoë and Balian nodded warily. They had been talking all afternoon about what Isabella was likely to do. Would she insist on marrying Humphrey as an adult, or would she agree to set him aside?

Isabella answered with a question: "That is not strictly true, is it?" She looked Balian straight in the eye as she said this.

"No," he answered candidly, "not if you want to be recognized as Queen of Jerusalem."

Isabella nodded and drew a deep breath. "As is right and proper, the High Court has chosen for me, have they not? It is their wish that I marry Conrad, Marquis de Montferrat."

"Yes, that is correct," Balian confirmed.

"But as the brother of my late sister's former husband, some would say we are related within the prohibited degrees. Don't you think?"

"They might," Balian admitted, tight-lipped and defensive. "But he's the best we've got. This is about the survival of your kingdom."

"And there are more serious canonical obstacles than that," Maria Zoë noted dryly. Surprised, Isabella looked over at her mother, and Maria Zoë continued, "Montferrat was married according to Greek rites to Theodora Angela, the sister of Emperor Isaac Angelus. He *claims* she has since renounced him, but I have been unable to verify it. My ties to Constantinople are not what they once were. I cannot in honesty assure you it is true, but we know for a fact that she is still alive."

"So Conrad may still be married to someone else, which would make his marriage to me bigamous, and make me nothing but a concubine?"

"If it is true that his marriage to her has not been dissolved," Maria Zoë added, "which it very well may be, since neither Emperor Isaac Angelus nor his sister Theodora has any reason to want her marriage to Conrad to continue in force."

"And you still think I should go through with this?" Isabella asked, a little shocked.

There was a moment of embarrassed silence, when both Balian and Maria Zoë hoped the other would answer. Then Maria Zoë reached across the table and took Isabella's hand as she said, "If you are not going to marry Conrad de Montferrat and seek to regain your kingdom, then why leave Humphrey? You could remarry him—your choice this time, and as a consenting adult."

They gazed at each other, woman to woman, while Balian went rigid with tension, holding his breath in horror at the thought. He knew Maria Zoë thought as he did, but he could also see that her heart, not her head, was guiding her now.

Isabella had one last moment of doubt. She thought one last time about doing just that, but she could not. Humphrey had not been able to make a woman of her, and he had not been willing to fight for her. She didn't believe he was unnatural or cowardly, so there had to be some deeper reason.

The afternoon of prayer had revealed to her an answer. She met her mother's eyes squarely as she explained, "Mama, I think Humphrey has always known he was not suited to be king. That is why he always tried to persuade me that I couldn't—and shouldn't *want* to—be Queen. He always called my aspirations "foolish" and "childish." He did that to make me not want my inheritance.

"At the same time, he knew it was my destiny—and that is why, in the end, he let me go. He didn't fight for me. It was Humphrey as much as the Church tribunal that set me free to remarry. This marriage is for Jerusalem, but you need not be afraid that I dread it or fear it. I'm proud to do my duty for the good of my realm, but I'm also ready to become a woman, Mama. I have been ready for a long time."

Siege camp at Acre, November 25, 1190

Rahel and Edith had spent much of the morning trying to brush dust and creases out of the embroidered silk gown Queen Maria Zoë had brought with her. It consisted of a long-sleeved kirtle made of cloth of gold, over which a sheer, high-waisted white silk surcoat embroidered with the crosses of Jerusalem was worn. The silk was so transparent that the gold kirtle glimmered through. The neckline was a band of heavily embroidered silk depicting the crosses of Jerusalem in a continuous band. The long, pleated sleeves were of the same silk as the surcoat and unlined, so that they too were transparent. At her hips, Isabella wore a belt studded with amethysts that hung down from the knot to her knee. On her head she wore nothing, and her hair had been brushed for nearly an hour so that it gleamed a reddish brown. Maria Zoë brought out a pair of large, elaborate amethyst earrings, which had been a gift from her own mother on the occasion of her marriage to King Amalric of Jerusalem.

Maria Zoë bent and kissed Isabella on her forehead, then wordlessly threaded the earrings through her daughter's earlobes and helped her to stand. Rahel held the curtain open for them, and they exited into the main section of the tent and from there out the main flap into the daylight.

Several large canvas mats had been spread over the muddy ground to create a kind of improvised porch. The Archbishop of Pisa waited, attended by the Archbishop of Nazareth and the Archbishop of Mainz. Around the canvas porch a large crowd had gathered. The Lusignans were conspicuously absent, of course, but the sacred and secular members of the High Court of Jerusalem were jostling with the most prominent of the crusader lords: the Duke of Austria, the Duke of Burgundy, the Counts of Flanders and Champagne. . . .

Isabella's eyes met those of Henri de Champagne for a moment, but she quickly looked away. His gaze was filled with far too much sympathy, as if he felt she were in need of it. She focused instead on Conrad de Montferrat, who stood at the front of the crowd and at the sight of her, stepped onto the canvas. His eyes were fixed on her face, his expression tense. He was like a lion focused on his prey, she thought to herself. Then he smiled and bowed to her gallantly, and the lion was banished from thought.

The Papal Legate signaled for the principals to come and stand before him. They turned their backs on the crowd and stood side by side. They weren't touching, and yet Isabella was acutely conscious of Conrad's presence. They bowed their heads as the Papal Legate raised his hand and blessed them, making the sign of the cross with his upraised fore and middle fingers. He called down God's blessings on their heads and on their union. Then he took Isabella's hand

and placed it in Conrad's. Each in turn repeated the marriage vow after the Papal Legate, and then the Archbishop pronounced them man and wife. A cheer went up from the crowd as they turned to face them.

Behind her, the Archbishop of Nazareth called for silence. "My lords! Queen Isabella of Jerusalem!"

Another cheer went up, and again the Archbishop called for silence. Isabella glanced toward her mother, who nodded once, and then watched as her stepfather gestured for silence from the men around him. Stillness spread until the entire crowd waited with bated breath in anticipation.

Isabella raised her head and projected her voice as far as she could. In the open air, that was not as far as she would have liked. To her own ears her voice sounded frail and high. "My lords! I stand before you, the last surviving child of King Amalric of Jerusalem. In my veins flows the blood of both Jerusalem and Constantinople. I claim by right of that blood the throne and crown of the Kingdom of Jerusalem!"

They interrupted her with cheers of "Long live the Queen!"

But again Ibelin quieted them so that Isabella could continue. "My lords, it is our duty to see that the Kingdom is resurrected from the ashes that it now is. Our duty is to see it restored to its former dignity!"

This time their cheers were tinged with desperation.

When they had calmed down again, she continued, "My lords, I pray that one day I can be anointed in the Church of the Holy Sepulcher—"

They interrupted her to cheer again, drawing courage from their dreams, and she had to wait again before continuing.

"But until that day, I beg you to demonstrate your support for me by taking the oath of homage due to me as your Queen."

Ibelin, of course, had been instrumental in suggesting she make this demand, and he moved promptly to lead his fellows. He was thus the first to go down on one knee before his stepdaughter and offer her homage for Ibelin, Ramla, Mirabel, and Nablus. When he stood and backed away, his place was taken by William of Tiberius for Galilee—whose enthusiasm was even greater than Ibelin's, because he was younger and more easily inspired with hope. After that came Haifa and Sidon, and then each of the other lords of the defunct Kingdom. Their expressions varied from euphoric to sober, but no one hung back, until only one man was left. Toron was here after all, and he stood at the edge of the canvas staring at the woman he loved with an expression of such profound anguish that Isabella's heart bled for him.

Yet even so, she could not feel regret. Faced with his silent misery, she saw what Oultrejourdain had seen a decade earlier, and what Ibelin and the High

Court had seen since: a young man of fragile beauty, fine emotions, and great intelligence—utterly unsuited to reign a kingdom won, held or lost with blood.

"My lords!" She raised her voice over the chattering that was spreading through the already dispersing crowd. "My lords! My lord of Toron was as blameless as I in our unfortunate, invalid marriage. Therefore, it is only right that all the properties he surrendered to my brother at the time of our presumed marriage now be restored to him. As Queen, I hereby restore to him the baronies of Toron and Châteauneuf, for him and his heirs to hold in perpetuity, as soon as we have regained control of them."

Her words were greeted by general indifference. The Western lords were getting bored, while the lords of Outremer were more concerned with regaining their own baronies than those of the ineffectual Toron. People at the back were talking among themselves as they turned away. Beside her, Montferrat had taken hold of her elbow to propel her inside the tent for the wedding Mass.

Isabella and Humphrey stared at one another for one last moment and one last silent exchange of thoughts. Humphrey shook his head. "I don't want Toron," his eyes told her. "I want you."

Isabella shook her head in answer. "No, Humphrey," she told him mentally. "You want the little girl from Kerak. You don't want Isabella, Queen of Jerusalem."

Montferrat was anxious to leave Acre. He had said from the start that he did not want Isabella in a siege camp, and although the weather was unseasonably mild at the moment, it was late November; the winter storms were overdue. They had to be expected shortly.

As soon as they had taken the sacrament together, Montferrat hustled Isabella, still in her wedding gown, to a Pisan dromond waiting at the improvised quay of the siege camp. Magnussen's ship was also lying alongside, Isabella noted, and she was pleased to see that her mother had already gone aboard, while her stepfather was on the quay giving instructions to Sir Bartholomew.

The captain of the Pisan ship greeted Isabella at the foot of the gangplank with profuse courtesy and not a little excitement. Then he led her aboard his ship to a waiting cabin that was cramped but luxuriously appointed. Silk hangings covered the walls, hiding the planking, and bright cushions spilled from the bunk onto the carpeted floor. Isabella noted that her chest of belongings was already waiting for her here, evidently transported while she was at her wedding Mass.

Isabella thanked the captain, but said she would stay on deck for now. The captain agreed readily and led her up onto the poop, but here he asked her to stay at the poop rail. She nodded agreement, while Conrad assured the captain he would "keep her out of the way."

Already the main deck was alive with sailors—some hauling in the lines cast off from the quay, others climbing dexterously up the ratlines, and still others flinging halyards and sheets off the belaying pins in preparation for setting sail. The bow of the ship was slowly pushed away from the quay by a tender. When the bow pointed roughly forty-five degrees away from the shore, the sailors began chanting and hauling together on the halyards. The heavy booms of the lateen mainsail jerked upwards a foot or more at a time. The sail flapped loudly, spilling the wind and rattling the rings around the mast until the upper boom of the lateen sail reached its position. Once the halyard was secured, the captain ordered the sail sheeted in and the helm put over. Wind filled the mainsail, and the ship surged forward so forcefully that Isabella could hear water gurgling along the hull.

As they glided away from the shore, she noted that the sea air was sharply cooler than the stagnant air of the siege camp. It smelled fresh and clean, too. Isabella took a deep breath of it and pulled her cloak closer around her shoulders.

"Are you cold, my lady?" Conrad asked. Without awaiting an answer, he drew her inside his cloak, pressing her close to him, his arms around her belly.

It was the first time he had done more than take her hand or elbow, and Isabella felt a rush of blood in her veins from head to foot as he enclosed her. She instantly recognized that although clothed in courtesy, his gesture was more predatory than protective. She was in the arms of a near stranger, yet he had the right to hold her. Even more shocking: through the back of her dress she could feel his hard male organ. He was aroused, and they were both fully clothed!

She stiffened and tried to pull away from him, but Montferrat laughed and held her tighter still. Then he bent to whisper in her ear. "There's nothing to be afraid of, my love. It will soon give you pleasure you cannot yet imagine. It will give us *both* pleasure."

"Not here; not on this ship!" Isabella protested in near panic.

"Why not?" Conrad answered, surprised. "All those soft cushions and the sound of the water under the hull will make it particularly delicious."

"But, but —it's so public."

"Not as public as here on deck," Conrad answered, amused and not displeased by her modesty. He had married a virgin, after all. Then he bent and spoke so directly into her ear that his warm breath curled up her eardrum, sending waves of nearly unbearable tension through her nervous system.

"Because if you don't let me take you to the cabin soon, I'm going to lose control and make love to you right here."

Her cheeks burned so brightly, Montferrat was sure he would scald himself by touching them. Amused, he murmured in her ear, "You thought I married you for a crown, but that's not so. I married you for what we're about to do." Stepping back and releasing her, he gestured with a gallant bow toward the gangway leading down to the cabins. "My lady, I believe it is getting too chilly on deck. May I suggest we go below?"

Isabella, while nervous, was not seriously disinclined. As she descended the gangway, she registered that she had traded a friend for a lover—and she prayed that it was a good trade, one that would bring her happiness as well as being the price of her crown.

Chapter 12

Coast of the Levant,
January 1191

IBELIN SAW THE WAVE COMING AND braced himself for its collision with the hull. He tightened his grip on the rail and then ducked and turned his back into the spray as best he could. The water cascaded down on him, drenching him further. He was already soaked through to the skin, and his clothes clung to him, while the salt was starting to crust on his eyebrows and face.

They had been fighting this storm for thirty-some hours, and he could feel his own strength and willpower draining away. He had to keep his mind on his goal. The siege camp at Acre was completely dependent on supplies brought by sea. At this time of year, when the Mediterranean was closed to shipping from the West, that meant supplies from Cyprus and Tyre. Unfortunately, the Cypriot tyrant Isaac Comnenus had been bribed by Salah ad-Din to keep his ships in port. Montferrat, on the other hand, had promised to send grain, oil, wine, and other desperately needed foodstuffs to the beleaguered Frankish camp at Acre.

The little supply fleet consisted of four busses, crammed to the gills with the promised food, and six galleys to defend them from Saracen attack. While there had been no sign of the Saracens, they had been fighting headwinds ever since they passed Scandelion. The galleys could butt their way into it to a certain extent by the force of their oarsmen's arms, but the busses were forced to tack. They'd clawed their way another ten miles down the coast, and then the wind had veered to the west and had begun to blow a gale.

If they stayed too close to the shore, they risked being wrecked on the underwater shoals and rocks that dotted the coastline, but if they stood off too far, they were caught in a strong southern current that swept them backward. They sought to navigate the middle ground between these extremes—but as the crews became increasingly exhausted, the risk of error grew. One of the busses was already lagging so far behind it was almost out of sight behind the intermittent rain squalls.

With dusk rapidly approaching, Ibelin grimly faced the fact that he was losing hope of being able to complete this voyage. If only there were some friendly port to run to! Someplace they could have sheltered and waited out the storm. But there were no ports, and the coast itself was too straight to offer even a bay or a cove in which to shelter offshore. Being no seaman himself, Ibelin relied completely on the advice given him by Haakon Magnussen, and the Norseman had told him they could not hope to weather the storm on sea anchors. "Nothing but a slow death," he'd shouted above the wind hours ago.

But how much longer could they keep on trying?

Georgios, looking like death warmed over, was trying to make his way along the deck to his lord. As Balian watched, the squire slipped on the wet planking, and he was sent sliding into the gunnel by the lurching of the ship as it plunged down the back of the next wave. Water pouring over the bow added insult to injury by all but drowning Georgios in a frothing, seething whirlpool as he struggled to pull himself back onto his feet. Ibelin was too busy watching his squire to see the next wave until someone shouted.

Glancing right, he caught his breath and clutched the railing with both hands, too terrified to even pray, much less look away. It loomed up over their starboard bow. The ship started to lift on it, but the wave was stronger and faster. It broke, smothering the prow of the ship. The weight of the water hitting the deck sent a shudder through the timbers right down to the keel. The bow went down. Water washed completely over it and the deck tilted dangerously.

Ibelin was certain they were sinking. With horror he registered he had not confessed since leaving Tyre, and he found himself frantically begging God for forgiveness, even as the froth on the bows started to pour to either side. Agonizingly slowly (or so it seemed), the deck re-emerged out of the depths. Still winded by panic, Ibelin turned to find Magnussen.

The Norse captain was standing beside his helmsman, his expression unreadable, but his eyes narrowed against the wind and flying spray. Then, as if sensing Ibelin's gaze, he turned his hawk-like face in his direction and shook his head once.

Ibelin tried to cross to him, but lost his footing on the violently pitching deck and fell hard. Without anything to clasp or haul himself up with, he could not regain his feet, and had no choice but to crawl the remaining six feet to Magnussen. With one arm looped around the stern railing, the Norseman reached out a hand to help him stand up again. "How much more can we take?" Ibelin asked.

Magnussen shrugged. "The *Storm Bird*" (that was his ship) "can ride it out, but I'm not so sure about the *Santa Anna*." With a thumb he indicated the Genoese galley off their port quarter.

Now that Ibelin's attention had been drawn to the *Santa Anna*, he realized she appeared half-sunk already. Water was so deep on the main deck that the oarsmen were knee deep in it, and it sloshed from side to side as the galley wallowed in the waves. Ibelin felt as if he were watching dead men, because he could see no hope of the ship making shore safely. That was what the *Santa Anna* was attempting to do. She had fallen off the southerly course the rest of them were holding and had turned her bow to the southeast instead. This was a course that avoided turning broadside to the waves, but would eventually take her onto the shore.

All those men were on his conscience, Ibelin told himself. He had brought them out here, and he had not given the order to put about in time to save them. If he, too, were to meet his Maker in the next hours or days, it would be with their deaths on his hands. He had led men to their death before, of course, when he took his knights, Turcopoles, and men-at-arms to fight—on the Litani, at Le Forbelet, at Hattin. But that was different. Those men had been called up in defense of the realm. They had been fighting for their families, their way of life, their God, their very survival. And now?

Of course the men at Acre needed the supplies, but did they need them so desperately that men should die bringing them? All because that idiot Lusignan had taken it into his head to lay siege to a city he needn't have lost in the first place? There shouldn't *be* a siege of Acre. If all the men and beasts that had already been lost in the mad siege of Acre had instead been collected at Tyre, they could have retaken Sidon and probably Beirut as well, Ibelin calculated. Thousands, maybe as many as ten thousand men, had already died in the siege of Acre. For what? For Lusignan's pride!

Shouting broke into his thoughts and Ibelin looked up sharply. Magnussen had turned around, following the outstretched hand of his forward lookout, who was pointing aft.

"Oh, my God!" Balian gasped. As he watched in helpless horror, one of the busses slowly rolled over onto her side, exposing her broad bottom and keel. She didn't fully capsize, but lay on her beam ends, her sails full of seawater, while the waves broke on her belly. Screams came faintly across the water.

"If we put about, could we rescue anyone?" Ibelin asked Magnussen.

"Maybe."

"Run up the signal to disperse and sail independently," Ibelin ordered.

That produced a nod of apparent approval before Magnussen called out the order, and one of his men started to make his way along the deck to the mainmast to hoist the signal flag.

"Do you want me to attempt a rescue?" Magnussen asked next.

"I want you to, yes, but I'm not ordering you to."

Magnussen smiled faintly at that. "You *couldn't* order me, my lord." Their eyes met, and Magnussen added, "But we'll give it a try." Then he lifted his voice and started giving orders in Norse.

Two days later they limped back into Tyre. They'd lost two ships with nearly all hands, and all the ships that made Tyre were damaged more or less severely, including Magnussen's *Storm Bird*. Ibelin himself was nursing numerous bruises, and his skin was chapping on his neck and wrists from never being dry. He had not been out of his clothes since they left port six days earlier, and salt completely coated his face and had turned his hair stiff and white. He had never in his life been so glad to see Tyre, yet he dreaded Montferrat's reaction. He had lost nearly one hundred men, two ships, and tons of grain for nothing; the army at Acre had not been resupplied as Montferrat had personally guaranteed.

He was relieved, therefore, that Monferrat had not come down to harbor to meet him. Any recriminations would be made in private. His wife and eldest children, however, had come to meet him, escorted by most of his knights.

Helvis broke into a bright smile and started waving excitedly as soon as she saw her father. John said something to her sternly, but she just stuck out her tongue at him before jumping down and running to Balian's arms. "I knew you were safe!" she declared loudly. "I knew God wouldn't let anything happen to you!"

"Helvis! That's blasphemy!" Balian told her sternly.

Helvis just smiled at him knowingly, smugly confident that she knew God's will, and slipped her arms around his waist. He melted at once and placed an arm over her shoulders.

Meanwhile John had reached his father, too, and said more solemnly, "When the storm struck, Sir Galvin and I kept a vigil on the south tower."

"Well done, John," Balian praised him. He could not get over how mature John was. So many fathers had trouble with their heirs—youths who were spendthrift or irresponsible, lazy or dull. John was none of that. He acted much more responsibly than most eleven-year-olds, Balian thought proudly. But mixed with his pride was sorrow, because he knew that most eleven-year-olds had not lost their inheritance and faced two sieges.

Finally, he could turn to Maria Zoë. She just stood there, the expression on her face one of relief mixed with lingering anxiety. He reached out, caught her hand, and took it to his lips. "My lady," was all he said in public.

Magnussen watched from the deck of his ship. It would be wrong, he told himself, to call his emotions jealousy, for he did not begrudge Ibelin his happiness, but he did sometimes wonder why some men were granted so much domestic joy and others so little. It was one thing to say that the Lord determined each man's place and there had to be both rich and poor, farmers and lords, priests and fighting men. But within those roles, why did some men enjoy so much more love?

The crowds on the quay were starting to disperse, as Ibelin and his entourage started in the direction of his residence. Magnussen's crew was efficiently making the *Storm Bird* secure, putting a harbor stow in the sail, coiling the ends of the running rigging, and fastening the covers over the hatches. There was a lot of work to be done to repair the damage to the starboard rail, to replace lost oars and their shattered tender. They needed to pump out the bilges and measure the rate she was taking on water, then search for damage to the hull. They had to clean and scrub and get her ship shape again. But not now, not tonight. Tonight every man-jack of them, except the watch, of course, needed shore leave.

Magnussen turned to his mate, Eric Andersen. "Have you set the watch?"

"I'm taking the first watch myself, Haakon. Go ashore."

Part of him thought he ought to refuse, thought he ought to be the responsible captain, but today he felt a burning need to get drunk. So drunk he had neither memories nor dreams anymore. "I owe you one," he remarked to his mate, and then swung himself over the side of his ship and onto the quay with a single, easy leap.

His mood was such that he shied away from the dockside taverns, where he could expect to encounter most of his crewmen. Today, tonight, he wanted anonymity. He wanted to be among strangers, men who did not know his past, men who did not even know his reputation. He moved deeper into the town, consciously ducking into the side alleys, avoiding the main thoroughfares, the wider streets with the more respectable establishments behind proud façades of stone. The mud and wattle buildings crushed behind and between the stone buildings were better harbors on a night like this.

He put his nose into one or two such places, but they were too empty as yet. It was early for drinking oneself to oblivion. Annoyed, he looked around, not knowing what he was looking for, and spotted a pack of youths careening around the corner and starting toward him. They were excited, shouting to one another, laughing even as they ran, but in a sinister way. The leader of the pack was clutching something to his belly, and Magnussen was pretty damned sure that whatever it was, it wasn't his.

On an impulse, he stuck out his leg to try to trip up the little thief, but the youth was agile. He managed to half-leap, half-shy away from the foot, and shouting crude insults, he kept going with his friends in his wake. One of the boys, trailing the others, was carrying a pair of crutches. Not that he needed them. He was fleet on his feet. He held the crutches over his head like a trophy.

"Little piss-pots!" Magnussen thought to himself. "They've robbed a cripple!" For a second he was torn between the impulse to chase after them, and the instinct to go to the assistance of the victim. Although there were a half-dozen youths, he didn't doubt his ability to take them all on. But he also judged that if he did, blood would flow, and—thieves or not—they were young to die. So he hurried instead to the corner and looked in the direction from which the pack of thieves had come.

Collapsed in the gutter, sobbing, was a little bundle of misery. Magnussen started forward briskly, and halfway there recognized the crippled son of Godwin Olafsen. He covered the remaining distance in half a second. "Sven! Sven! What are you doing in this part of town? What happened? Blessed Mother Mary!" The boy's face was bruised, his nose streaming blood, and the palms of his hands were torn open. Magnussen guessed that the thieves had knocked or yanked his crutches away, tumbling him onto the rough cobbles. Once he was down, they'd probably kicked him a couple of times in the gut and face, and when he was "softened up" they'd robbed him.

"They—they took—everything," Sven wailed, confirming Magnussen's suspicions.

"What did you have with you?" Magnussen asked, wondering about chasing after the thieves after all, though by now they could have disappeared into some cellar.

"Everything!" Sven insisted, sobbing for breath and crying.

"Come, let me get you back home—"

"NO!" Sven screamed.

Magnussen stared at him uncomprehending.

"I'm not going back! Never! I hate them!"

This made no sense at all to Magnussen. He would have given—well, not his health, but just about anything else to have had parents like Sven's. His own father would have been more likely to leave a crippled son for the wolves than look after him the way Godwin had. Christian charity was only skin deep in men like Magnus Haakonssen, Haakon's father. Magnussen was in no mood to discuss things in the street, however. It was getting dark and the gutter was foul with waste and sewage.

"I'll take you to the orphanage, then," he announced simply. Then he bent and heaved the cripple into his arms. Sven was no longer all skin and bones, but he was still no great burden for the Norse captain.

At the orphanage, Sven was taken in hand by Sister Patricia, who insisted on Sven stripping off his stinking clothes and washing himself at a trough. She sent the clothes for washing and gave him a simple kaftan to wear before taking him to get some hot stew from the kitchens.

Magnussen was preparing to leave when Sister Adela intercepted him. "Captain! I'm so glad you found Sven. Godwin and Mariam have been frantically looking for him for two days now."

"Why?"

"He ran away."

"So I gathered, but why? What child could want for better parents?"

Sister Adela smiled faintly. "He got in a fight with Mariam and started calling her very unkind things. His father threatened to take a cane to him—as he richly deserved, given what he'd said. He screamed at his father that his mother had been right to hate him. It was an ugly scene."

Magnussen stared at her. He'd had fights like that with his father, too. His father didn't just *threaten* to hide him. "Did Olafsen hit him?"

"Yes, he did, and that night he ran away."

Magnussen shrugged. "He'll get over it."

"No, he won't. You see, Mariam's pregnant again, and this time she's sure all will go well. Sven's afraid that if she has a child of her own, she'll not care for him anymore. That's what's behind this."

It sounded understandable to Magnussen. "Can you take him in, then?"

"Master Magnussen, I have enough trouble feeding the children that *need* me without taking on boys whose parents are perfectly willing and able to look after them. He can stay the night, of course, but I want you to talk to him. He idealizes you—almost as much he does the Baron of Ibelin. You must try to convince him he cannot run away from his destiny. Convince him he must be brave."

"I really just want to get drunk."

Sister Adela smiled so brilliantly that Magnussen fell instantly in love with her. "I know you do," she told him as he stared at her, dazed, "but you are going to discover that it is much *more* fun helping Sven, and with him Godwin and Mariam. Furthermore, I guarantee you it won't give you a hangover, either."

Tyre, April 20, 1191

The French fleet dwarfed everything Eschiva had ever seen before. They could not all fit in the harbor, so they lay at anchor offshore. From here they looked like an untidy orchard of masts stretching in every direction as far as the eye could see. Eschiva and Isabella stood on the rooftop of the archiepiscopal palace, where they'd come to get a better view of the French fleet than was possible from the windows. The sight was overwhelming. There had to be tens of thousands of troops and thousands of horses aboard those ships. For the first time since Hattin, Eschiva started to seriously hope that Salah ad-Din might be defeated and driven out of her homeland.

Isabella stood beside her, the wind fluttering the ends of her veils, and she was biting her lower lip nervously in a gesture Eschiva had known (and admonished) since childhood. "Bella, stop biting your lower lip. It makes you look very common," Eschiva advised in her elder-sister voice.

Usually that annoyed Isabella, but today she only cast Eschiva an imploring look. "But I'm *so* nervous, Eschiva! Conrad says we have nothing to worry about. King Philip is his nephew and apparently they met several times, but *look* at that!" She pointed to the French fleet riding at anchor, with hundreds of brilliant pennants fluttering from the mastheads and tiny men walking the decks. "The King of France commands all that!" she continued. "All that and more, because he has castles and cities, men and knights and nobles, at home in France as well. And all we have is this one city."

Eschiva thought it did Isabella credit that she was acutely aware of how little, indeed insignificant, her "kingdom" was. Eschiva also recognized, however, that at the moment Isabella needed encouragement. Isabella had learned courage in adversity from her childhood imprisonment at Kerak, from her husband's captivity, and most recently from the necessity of leaving Humphrey for Montferrat. She was determined and brave when she set her heart on something, but she had not learned *confidence*. So Eschiva answered firmly: "Isabella, it's not about what you *possess*, it's about what you represent. You *represent* Jerusalem."

Isabella turned to look her oldest, best, and arguably only friend in the eye. "You think I can do *that*? Think what it means!"

Eschiva hesitated, conscious of just how great the burden was, but then she nodded solemnly. "Jerusalem is the birthplace of Christianity, and as such it is the homeland of *all* Christians. You are the guardian of the hearth of Christendom."

"Me?" Isabella found herself saying, torn between awe and a sense of unreality. "I'm nineteen years old. Surely the guardian of the hearth of Christendom ought to be a venerable old crone."

Eschiva had to laugh at that, relieved that despite her nervousness Isabella had not lost her sense of humor. Indeed, ever since her marriage to Montferrat, the moody teenager had been replaced by a young woman full of joie de vivre. That came, Eschiva knew, from being well loved, and she respected Montferrat for that—no matter how much she disliked him personally. In answer to Isabella, Eschiva quipped, "Bella, believe me, men *always* prefer a pretty young woman over a venerable old crone!"

Isabella giggled and glanced sidelong at Eschiva. These last months married to Conrad had been so exciting and enlightening. She had always thought she understood what "consummation" and "fornication" meant, but Conrad had taught her otherwise. There was so much *more* to it that she had ever imagined. She had often been tempted to talk to Eschiva about it. Had she experienced these things with Aimery, or was Conrad special? He was so well traveled, and he admitted to learning many things in the Greek empire. Which made Isabella wonder if her mother knew these things—but she would have *died* before she asked her mother, *Queen* Maria Zoë Comnena, about her sex life!

"Come!" Eschiva drew her thoughts back to the present. "You need to prepare to meet the King of France."

"Oh, holy Jehoshaphat!" That was one of Isabella's favorite sayings from when she was a little girl. She'd found the word very strange the first time she was taken to the Ibelin palace at the corner of the Street of Spain and Jehoshaphat Street, and she had insisted on saying it over and over. Eschiva was glad to hear it on her lips again. "You're right! What time is it?"

"I have no idea, but it must be almost Sext."

"Oh, dear. He's due at Nones."

"Yes, so let's go back inside."

Protocol demanded that the Queen of Jerusalem and her consort meet the King of France at the quay as he disembarked. This was because neither Isabella nor Conrad had been crowned or anointed. A small but brilliantly painted and gilded barge with eight banks of oars and sixteen oarsmen brought the King of France into the harbor from his large, comfortable buss that lay offshore. Trumpets on the forecastle of the barge blared out a fanfare as the barge passed over the lowered chain. This was answered by a trio of trumpeters on the tower controlling the chain. As the barge then maneuvered closer to the quay, a second fanfare intoned, answered this time by the heralds on the quay beside Isabella and Conrad.

Isabella glanced at her husband nervously. He had never looked more magnificent to her than he did now. He was outfitted in his robes as a Greek "Caesar." Maria Zoë had given Isabella one of the gowns she'd brought from Constantinople; it was stiff with seed pearls sewn in patterns across her breast, and heavy with turquoise stones along the hemline. Isabella glanced toward her mother and stepfather, who headed the barons of Jerusalem, lined up behind Conrad and herself to receive the King of France. Her mother nodded encouragement and Uncle Balian smiled at her.

Conrad, sensing her nervousness, laid his left hand over hers, which held onto his right elbow. "You look absolutely stunning, my love," he assured her in a low voice, even as he watched the approaching barge alertly, trying to identify the men Philip had selected to accompany him. "My fear is that Philip will be enchanted," he continued rather absently to his wife, "indeed, smitten—which would be quite dangerous, since he is a widower at the moment and might take it into his head to steal you away."

"He would have no chance, my lord," Isabella assured her husband with a smile, warmed and flattered by his compliments.

"Wait until you meet him, my dear," Conrad teased, confident that Philip II was no threat to his position in Isabella's heart.

Isabella turned her attention back to the approaching barge, straining to distinguish the King of France from the other men crowding the sterncastle of the barge. At least three of the men were bishops in ecclesiastical regalia, and the tallest man was quite plainly dressed in an open-faced conical helmet, apparently more bodyguard than noble. That left only two other men, one dark and one fair. The dark-haired man was slighter and less impressive than the fair-haired one, but he appeared to be wearing a crown. The longer Isabella looked, the more certain she became that this rather nondescript young man was (disappointingly) the King of France.

Moments later the barge glided alongside the quay. The oarsmen raised their oars to the vertical in a flashy display of seamanship as a new fanfare of trumpets sounded. The man Isabella had been watching descended from the sterncastle, made his way to the waist of the ship, and crossed the gangplank that had been run out to the shore. As he stepped ashore, Conrad disengaged from Isabella and strode forward. These movements were carefully choreographed, and Isabella knew exactly what her husband planned to do next. "Cousin!" he called out in a booming voice. "Welcome to the Kingdom of Jerusalem!"

Isabella stood tensely where he had left her, awaiting the outcome of Conrad's gamble, for they had no way of knowing if Philip of France was prepared to endorse Conrad as king—or if he would incline to the interpretation that Guy was still king because he had been anointed. To Isabella's immense relief, Philip of France opened his arms and offered first one and then the other cheek to Conrad. Finally, pulling apart, he said loud enough for all to hear, "Cousin, it pleases me to find you here. Your lady?" Philip had already turned to look at Isabella.

Both Conrad and her mother had instructed her not to dip her knee. As Queen of Jerusalem, she was King Philip's equal. "Smile," had been her mother's advice. "No man can resist a beautiful woman's smile, and it will break any tension."

Isabella did her best, but Philip of France's gaze was unsettling. He seemed to be taking her measure in a very calculating way, as if he were ticking off points: age, height, weight, hair color, eye color, bloodlines, income. . . . He did smile, but there was nothing spontaneous about it. It was calculated, just as his approach was calculated. He took her hand and held it almost—but not quite—to his lips, as he inclined his head slightly. "Madame la Reine de Jerusalem. *Enchanté.* You are indeed as charming and attractive as my dear friend Philip of Dreux told me." The words did nothing to settle Isabella's instinctive discomfort; Dreux was the Archbishop of Beauvais, and she would never forget the way that churchman, dressed in full armor, had torn her from Humphrey's bed and tent. She did not regret setting Humphrey aside for Conrad, but that didn't mean she could forgive Beauvais for the way it was instigated.

Isabella fell back on the lines she had drafted under her mother's tutelage. "Jerusalem welcomes you, my lord! We have prayed for this day ever since God withdrew His grace from the usurper Guy de Lusignan at the Battle of Hattin. With your help, my lord, we trust we will regain God's favor and triumph over the enemies of Christ."

"Indeed, Madame, that is why I am here," the King of France announced dispassionately as he raised her hand to his lips a second time. Then, laying her hand over his own, he nodded and indicated she should lead him down the line of her barons, introducing one after the other, with Conrad in their wake.

When the principals were out of hearing, Balian turned to his wife, speechless. Their eyes met. He had been their last hope, this young King of France, and he had managed to disappoint them in just moments. There was no fire in this king, no passion, no determination. Just cold calculation. He was here, Balian sensed, for his own purposes—and he would leave the moment his purpose was fulfilled. He was not here for the love of Jerusalem, and he would abandon Jerusalem without so much as a backward glance. Ibelin shuddered in the warm sunshine.

May 11, Limassol, Cyprus

Aimery's brothers were quarreling again. Guy was convinced that leaving the siege camp at Acre amounted to "desertion" and that while they were away, Conrad de Montferrat was likely to come down and take command. Geoffrey caustically reminded Guy that three years ago he had been prepared to run away to France and had to be talked into the siege in the first place. Before Guy could recover from spluttering, Geoffrey added that with the arrival of Philip of France, everyone else was outranked. "The only man capable of confronting Philip of France is Richard of England. We need his support, and we need it now! Nothing else matters."

"I don't know why you think the Plantagenet whelp is going to be any help to us!" Guy countered. "He's not yet thirty—and every time he had trouble in Aquitaine, he had to beg his father, the old King, to come help him out. He'd have lost it ten times over if King Henry hadn't come to his aid, and then he betrayed the old man and pledged allegiance to the same damned Philip of France who is our worst enemy. By God!" Guy was working himself into a proper rage. "He's a dupe of the damned King of France and will do whatever he says!"

"You don't know what the hell you're talking about," Geoffrey countered.

"I'm only repeating what you told me yourself—"

Aimery could stand the bickering no longer. Closing his ears to their squabbling, he left the sterncastle by the stairs to the main deck and strode across it to haul himself up onto the forecastle instead. Here the air seemed fresher and cleaner and the motion of the sailing ship more pronounced. The bows rose and fell regularly on the moderate swell, making a low hissing and snarling sound. As they pushed down into the water of the trough, the water frothed and danced around the bows, only to fall away as they rose on the next wave. Beyond the rail, emerging ever more distinctly from the haze, was the looming presence of their destination: Cyprus.

Aimery supposed he must have sailed past Cyprus on his way to Outremer almost twenty years ago, but he had no memories of it. He'd forgotten how high the mountains were, and how big the island was, too. At the moment it seemed to stretch to the horizon in both directions, and because the wind was blowing from the southwest, they were still hours from their destination. Limassol was another ten or fifteen miles west of here, so they had to tack, and while each port tack brought them close to the island, the starboard tack took them out to sea again as they clawed their way westward.

Aimery strained to remember everything he knew about Cyprus. A part of the Eastern Roman Empire, it had been overrun by the Muslims in the mid-seventh century, but it had been liberated by Constantinople more than a hundred years before Jerusalem. It was so rich that it had attracted the greed of Reynald de Châtillon, who had made an attempt to capture the island. He was driven off by a fleet sent by Emperor Manuel I, and the incident had done much to disgrace him in the eyes of his peers—but he'd brought home a great deal of loot. After the death of Manuel I and the usurpation of Andronicus, Cyprus had broken away from the control of Constantinople. For the last five years it had been ruled by a man from a cadet branch of the Comnenus family, Isaac, who styled himself "Emperor." The Lady of Ibelin, herself a Comnena, had exploited his vanity and craving for legitimacy to sell him the crown and gown she'd worn at her coronation as Queen of Jerusalem, but his attitude toward the Latins was on the whole hostile. There had been numerous reports of pilgrim and merchant ships being seized and their cargoes confiscated while their crews and passengers were killed, enslaved, or held for ransom. Most recently, Isaac Comnenus had taken bribes from Salah ad-Din to stop supplies from reaching the siege camp at Acre.

"Look at that!" Henri d'Ibelin broke into Aimery's reverie. He had joined Aimery on the forecastle and was now pointing to the west, squinting into the early afternoon sun. Aimery followed his finger and realized the shimmering sea was dotted with black objects that could only be ships anchored offshore.

"It must be the English fleet." There was no mistaking the awe in Henri's voice, for they could see no end to the fleet. "It looks even larger than the French fleet!"

Aimery nodded. Henri was right, and like his wife when she had seen the French fleet, Aimery began to hope Christendom had gathered sufficient force to defeat Salah ad-Din.

"Have you ever met the English King?" Henri asked casually, turning away from the vista before them to stand with his elbows on the rail as he concentrated on Aimery.

"I think I did. I mean, I must have. We both attended the second coronation of Henry the Young King, shortly before I left for Outremer," Aimery admitted. "Richard was still a youth, fourteen or fifteen at the time."

"And?"

"He was tall for his age, and very good in the tiltyard. There was a tourney the day before the coronation because his elder brother loved them so much. Henry the Young King, was a lion on the tourney circuit, but only because he surrounded himself, literally, with a clique of knights who were the best veteran tourney fighters in France. Richard, I remember, was unhorsed by his brother's knights and treated a little contemptuously, but, by God, he was fighting his own fight, not letting others do it." Aimery, as a younger son himself, had identified strongly with Richard at the time and had admired his spirit. To Henri he continued, "But all eyes were really on the Young King, and although he was very precocious, he was also hotheaded and self-important. His father did him the honor of serving him at table, and he claimed it was 'only right' since his father was the son of a count, while he was the son of a king. I don't think that went down very well."

"No, not terribly tactful," Henri agreed, but then he laughed and admitted, "but it's probably the kind of thing I would have said if I were in his shoes. I've never been accused of too much respect."

Aimery laughed dryly at the remark. He had never liked this Ibelin overmuch. He was uncomfortable with the knowledge of how ruthless he'd been as Oultrejourdain's man, and Eschiva said his wife was little short of terrified of him. Yet he had to admire his tenacity ever since he'd attached himself (like a barnacle) to the cause of Guy de Lusignan. Aimery was certain his only motive was self-interest. For one things, his servility had gained him accommodations with Guy while the rest of them rotted in the dungeon. Still, he had proved useful at Acre. He'd taken on the role of ensuring that nothing happened to Guy in the many engagements in which Geoffrey and Aimery too often led and got ahead of their more cautious brother. Aimery didn't know of any specific incident in which Henri had saved Guy's life, but he'd seen the way his brother relied on the younger Ibelin with increasing gratitude. There was an almost alarming dependency in Guy's relationship with Henri d'Ibelin, Aimery thought. But Sir Henri's loyalty had been cast in doubt by his testimony before the Church tribunal investigating Isabella's marriage to Toron.

Seeing they were alone (except for a sailor with a weight to check the depth now and again), Aimery could not resist asking, "What the hell were you doing helping Montferrat dissolve Isabella's marriage?" As he spoke, Aimery automatically looked over his shoulder to be sure Toron, who was traveling with them, was out of hearing. Reassured that Toron was nowhere in sight, he added angrily, "If you'd kept out of it, maybe she'd still be married to Humphrey, and Montferrat wouldn't have a ghost of a claim to the throne! What you did was little short of treason—indeed, it *was* treason."

Sir Henri shrugged and put on his insolent smile. "What you all seem to forget is that Isabella is my stepniece—just as I am *your* uncle-in-law," he reminded Aimery with amusement. (Sir Henri was, as Aimery preferred to forget, his wife Eschiva's uncle, no less than Lord Balian was.) "I was at Kerak all the years she was imprisoned there, and I happen to know her and Humphrey very well. She deserves better."

"You know as well as I do that this isn't about what husband Isabella *deserves*. It's about the crown of Jerusalem!"

"Ah. Yes. The kingdom your brother lost. And then agreed to renounce. And is now tearing apart."

"Christ on the cross, man! My brother trusts you more than any man alive—including me—and you can stand there saying he is to blame for where we are? If I tell him what you just said—"

Sir Henri cut him off with a laugh. "Save your indignation, Aimery! You've said the same things to his face—and so has Geoffrey. I'm not deaf, you know! So don't get on your high horse and pretend otherwise. I serve your brother just as you do, because he's our best chance of recovering some shred of land and income. That's why I pushed for him to focus on Acre: it's so rich and there are many money fiefs to be had, if we could just expel the Saracens and take control of the harbor. We don't need to hold a lot of land if we control Acre."

"And by helping Montferrat lay hold of Isabella, you diminish our chances of ever seeing any spoils! What do you think Montferrat will throw us if *he's* crowned king?"

"Maybe more than your brother, since he's more likely to actually *conquer* something that he can give away."

"You're not making sense! Whose side are you on?"

"My own, of course. To *your* brother, I am one of the few men who never makes recriminations and always openly supports him. But if he loses, *my* brother will be the first baron of Jerusalem, and—in case you haven't noticed—Balian's got this old-fashioned notion of honor and family ties. But just to be sure, I helped free Isabella from the boy puppet, and I wager she's so grateful for a real man in her bed that she'll reward me without any urging from Balian."

Aimery snapped for words, and in the silence they heard a faint voice calling: "Ahoy! Ahoy there!"

Both men followed the sound, and looking over the railing. Dancing on the waves they saw what looked like a fishing smack. A moment later, Sir Henri realized it was an oared skiff much farther from shore than was either normal or prudent.

The men in the open boat were drenched and one man was bailing, but a tall, broad-shouldered man was standing in the bows with his hands cupped around his mouth, shouting at them.

Henri and Aimery both stepped up to the rail, and Henri waved in answer.

"Where do you hail from?" a voice asked in French. It was faint at this distance but carried on the wind.

"We're out of Acre, bound for Limassol," Henri answered, and Aimery thought cynically that Henri's months on the Red Sea had made a partial sailor out of him.

"Limassol? Why?" the man in the skiff wanted to know.

"We bring King Guy of Jerusalem for a rendezvous with King Richard of England!"

"King Guy is aboard?" the man shouted back in apparent disbelief.

Aimery pointed to the banner of Jerusalem flying from the masthead, while Henri dutifully called out the answer. "Aye, aye! Can you give us news of King Richard?" Henri asked back.

Aimery saw the man in the bows of the ship lurch a little as he lost his footing on the pitching and rolling deck of the skiff, but he recovered rapidly and answered. "He's beaten the hell out of Isaac Comnenus and accepted the homage of half the Cypriot nobility. King Guy is welcome!" Then he turned, gestured to the helmsman, and sensibly plopped himself down in the forepeak as the skiff turned to one side, lay briefly broadside to the waves with half the oars flailing in the air, and then continued swinging around to show them her stern. As the oarsmen started pulling again in unison, the man sitting in the prow, now facing aft, lifted one hand and waved cheerfully at them, indifferent to the spray falling over his red-blond hair. Aimery started.

"Do you think that's possible?" Sir Henri asked, disbelieving. "I mean, why would King Richard attack Isaac Comnenus—and if he did, could he really defeat him so fast?" Henri was torn between amazement and skepticism as he watched the skiff set a direct course for Limassol while they continued, hard on the wind, on an oblique tack.

"I think it must be true," Aimery admitted, a little perplexed, "because you just exchanged words with Richard Plantagenet himself."

"What?" Henri spun about and stared at Aimery as if he were mad.

"The man in the bow. I'm almost certain it was Richard."

"Are you daft? That man was dressed no better than any sailor. Besides, what the hell would a king be doing out in an open skiff? Christ! He could drown in an instant."

"Richard was never one to shun risks," Aimery pointed out.

"But—but—" Henri turned to stare after the skiff, but the people in it were now nothing but lumps of darkness against the sunlit sea. "A king . . ."

King Richard was nothing if not magnificent. His crown was heavy and jewel-encrusted. His cloak was trimmed with ermine. The snarling leopards on his surcoat were stitched in gold. His sword belt was of enameled panels, but the pommel of his great sword held a cabochon garnet. And without the slightest doubt he was, Aimery noted with amusement, the man in the boat. Indeed, the King himself acknowledged the fact with an amused smile when it was Aimery's turn to bow to him. He remarked dryly, "We have met before, my lord, at my brother's coronation, no?"—adding a wink.

Aimery would have liked him for that alone, but Richard's wholehearted and uncompromising support for Guy was both heartening and heartwarming. He'd even gone so far as to pledge the Lusignans financial support, immediately turning over two thousand silver marks from his treasury, along with some of the loot he'd captured on Cyprus, which included cutlery of purest gold.

It turned out, furthermore, that they had arrived on the eve of the King of England's marriage. While still on Sicily, the Queen Mother of England, the infamous Eleanor of Aquitaine, had brought the daughter of the King of Navarre to be her son's consort. They had, however, arrived during Lent. So the lady, accompanied by Richard's sister, the widow of King William of Sicily, had sailed with Richard's fleet. Unfortunately, a terrible storm had struck the fleet shortly after departing Sicily, and it had been scattered. While King Richard had managed to round up most of the ships and reassemble the fleet at Rhodes, the Queens' vessel and three others had been blown all the way to Cyprus. Two had wrecked, but the others, though storm-damaged, had anchored offshore.

Fortunately, the Dowager Queen of Sicily and the knights with her were familiar with Isaac Comnenus' reputation and had resisted all invitations to come ashore—a decision reinforced by news that the survivors of the wrecked ships had been robbed and imprisoned. King Richard had arrived with the rest of the fleet just when Isaac was becoming threatening. Richard's request for the restoration of the goods plundered from the ships had been answered insult-ingly, and the hotheaded Plantagenet had responded by launching an assault from small ships against the fortified shore. It should have been suicidal.

That it was not, both puzzled and fascinated Aimery. While Guy played elaborate court to the widowed Queen of Sicily (with far too obvious an eye to cementing his surprisingly easy alliance with the English King), and Geoffrey did his best to solidify support among Richard's far more skeptical and semi-hostile barons, Aimery asked one of the less exalted knights, a Poitevin he had known slightly in the past, to show him the battlefield.

Standing on the shore and looking out at the rolling swells that broke regu-larly upon it, Aimery shuddered. The Cypriots had held all the cards. They had *terra firma* under their feet to enable steady archery, while Richard's archers had been forced to fire from the bouncing decks of little boats bobbing in the waves. The Cypriots had also erected barricades along the beach that gave them cover, and had their horses ready to ride down anyone unlucky enough to come ashore.

The English had no horses, no cover, and no steady firing platform. The knight who excitedly related the details of the battle noted that King Richard had been the first to jump over the side of his boat and wade through the sucking surf to reach the shore. In full armor, wading up the incline of a beach with a strong undertow was dangerous even without being under enemy fire. Aimery could not imagine many men leading such an assault. Châtillon might have been capable of it, but he doubted even Montferrat could have pulled that off. Certainly not Guy . . .

Richard's example had, of course, forced his barons, knights, and men-at-arms to follow. They had charged the Cypriots, hunkered down safely behind their barricades, and put them to flight. The self-proclaimed "Emperor" had fled on a fleet horse, as had most of his nobles, but there had been considerable slaughter among his foot soldiers. At the end of the engagement, there were scores of corpses on the beach—and not one of them belonged to a man in King Richard's pay. No wonder he was called "the lionheart," Aimery concluded.

Chapter 13

Acre, June 8, 1191

IBELIN JOINED THE FRANKISH ARMY BESIEGING Acre with twenty-nine knights, their squires, eighteen crossbowmen, and five hundred sergeants. He could easily have found more men had he been able to pay them, for the news that he was recruiting had produced a flood of applicants. Even after his arrival in Acre, men who had been with him at Hattin or Jerusalem sought him out, anxious to trade their current paymasters for a billet with a man they trusted. But Balian was operating on borrowed money and could not afford one man more, unless (or rather, until) casualties made way for new faces. Isabella had advanced him the money for recruiting troops from revenues Montferrat had turned over to her. Ibelin presumed that Montferrat knew what she was doing, but he preferred not to ask.

Montferrat had also raised a small army of one hundred knights and two thousand sergeants, with which he too joined the siege at Acre. Everyone expected that the arrival of the English King with his large force would ring in the decisive battle for Acre, and with it a campaign that would lead to the recovery of Jerusalem.

When word spread that the English King's fleet had been sighted, Ibelin with his knights and men joined the rest of the army as it surged toward the shore. It was late afternoon and the sun was low on the horizon, already distended and discolored by haze. It cast a sheen of bronze on the calm surface of the Mediterranean, but the heat it emitted had only marginally diminished. Many of the crusaders were obviously suffering from that heat. They stank badly, their shirts and gambesons soaked in sweat. Ibelin was only partially sympathetic. He'd endured too many snide remarks about "effeminate local lords"

who preferred silk to wool to feel sorry for fools who did not adapt to their surroundings. Admittedly, many of these men could not afford to outfit themselves
in silk or even the light cotton fabrics of the region, but too many of them took
perverse pride in their own intransigence.

At the shore, the army spread out along the edge of the sea as everyone
tried to get a good view. The excitement was palpable. Trumpets sounded, pipes
wailed, bells rang, and drums pounded. Although the ships were silhouetted
against the sinking sun, it was not hard to tell which carried the English King.
His snecka not only flew the English royal standard, it surged ahead of the other
ships in a commanding fashion. As it drew near, people started shouting to one
another: "There he is! There he is! Look! On the forecastle!"

Sure enough, the King of England, a golden crown fitted over his chain-
mail coif, was standing at the forward rail of his snecka, waving his arm in great,
slow sweeps of majestic greeting. The crowd went wild. Men cheered, clapped, or
chanted "Richard! Richard!" Others hugged one another and danced little jigs.

Ibelin was not impressed. The display reminded him of Guy de Lusignan,
who likewise had a fondness for dramatic gestures and royal trappings. It was
important for a king to be conscious of his dignity. A degree of pomp, ceremony,
and display of wealth was essential to retaining the respect of one's subjects and
one's enemies. But this was little short of theatrics. Then again, he reminded
himself, Richard of England might be showy, but he must also have some substance, or he wouldn't have been able to seize the island of Cyprus and subdue
all resistance in a mere fifteen days.

News of the English King's complete subjugation of Cyprus had reached the
siege camp at Acre almost a week earlier. French noblemen, sent to Cyprus by
the King of France to urge the English King to join the siege of Acre in all haste,
had returned with the amazing news that King Richard was master of the entire
island. It seemed that after Isaac had reneged on a promise to join the crusade,
the English King had turned on the Greek usurper, putting him to flight and
taking control of the entire island with no casualties. The French returned
to Acre with the news, but the English King had delayed his own departure
another week in order to establish an administration that would ensure revenues
and provisions from Cyprus flowed to him in support of the crusade.

A commotion to Ibelin's right drew attention to the French King with his
entourage. Philip, too, was wearing his crown, and he was well attended by the
highest of the French nobles, including the Duke of Burgundy and the Count of
Champagne. Sadly, the Count of Flanders had recently died of what the crusaders
called "Arnoldia" or sometimes "Leonardia." The crusaders considered the disease
highly contagious, and it could certainly be lethal. Even when it didn't kill, it

caused men's hair and fingernails to fall out, while painful mouth ulcers made it difficult to eat. The crusaders universally blamed the climate of Outremer, but Ibelin was skeptical, since no natives ever seemed to catch it—not even if they had contact with crusaders suffering from it. He personally suspected that it was more the result of crusader diet than the climate. The crusaders scorned many of the native dishes (at least initially), and Ibelin suspected that the things he had learned to eat as a small child protected him now from this illness.

As the crowd parted respectfully for King Philip, Ibelin caught a glimpse of his face. It was carefully controlled—too carefully controlled. The rumors of bad blood between the Kings of England and France seemed confirmed in that look alone.

With a great fanfare and shouts to clear the beach, the King of England's snecka prepared to run itself aground. Those gathered on the shore could hear the drumbeat setting the pace for the oarsmen, while the oars churned the water beside the galley into white froth. Then, with a terrible, screeching crunch, the keel struck the shore. Like a snarling dragon, the high prow thrust itself half a dozen yards onto the beach before it came to rest. A loud shout of triumph went up from the crew and was answered by a cheer from the observers on the beach.

Almost at once, the King of England (who had wisely descended from the forecastle for the beaching itself), put a hand on the forward railing and flung his feet over the side of the ship, to land with a single lithe motion on the beach. It was an athletic feat that not many men could have equaled in full armor. Although Richard of England appeared to lose his footing slightly as his feet hit the small, rolled stones of the beach, he had the presence of mind to disguise it by falling on both knees and crossing himself, as if giving thanks for setting foot in the Holy Land.

The crowd went wild with approval, and a group of churchmen struck up the Te Deum. Although the latter could have been a means of expressing King Richard's apparent gratitude for finally reaching the land of Christ's Passion, it sounded more like praise for King Richard's arrival—a response that seemed grossly exaggerated to Ibelin. From the grimace on King Philip's face, furthermore, Ibelin suspected the French King shared his feelings. A king to the core, however, Philip Capet dutifully advanced to meet Richard Plantagenet with open arms. The two kings embraced, kissed each other, and then, arm in arm, turned to wave to the crowd. Around them people continued to rejoice with cheers, clapping, song, and dance. After letting this go on a bit, the kings and their entourage began pushing their way through the crowd to King Philip's tent.

Not too surprisingly, the rejoicing in the crusader camp continued well into the night, as one after another of the English King's galleys beached and skiffs were launched from the larger ships, each carrying various noblemen and knights. Wine flowed in the tents of the wealthy, and ale flooded the more squalid quarters of the commoners.

Ibelin was in no mood for either. "If I were Salah ad-Din or al-Asadi Qara-Qush," he referred to the commander of the Saracen garrison in Acre, "I'd make an attack right now, before the bulk of the Plantagenet's men have disembarked and while the rest of us are drunk on alcohol and self-delusion."

"Maybe we should keep watch," Sir Bartholomew suggested practically.

Ibelin glanced at the men around him. "I don't mean to ruin your evening."

Sir Galvin shrugged and grunted. "It would be ruined a lot more by a Saracen attack that we didn't see coming."

Ibelin looked to Sir Roger Shoreham, who commanded his archers and sergeants. "Sir Roger, do you think you could find a half-hundred men willing to stay sober tonight?"

"Without difficulty, my lord," Shoreham answered. The men who signed on with Ibelin were natives to Outremer. They had lost their homes and livelihoods after Hattin. They were fighting for their families and their future. That didn't mean they were immune to the pleasures of the flesh, but they were on the whole more sober and focused than the newcomers, for whom the crusade was mainly an adventure or a chance to prove themselves.

Ibelin nodded. "Good; then let's go reinforce the watch along the northeast salient for a bit." This was the sector that offered a view of both the eastern walls of Acre and the heights to the west on which Salah ad-Din's army lay encamped.

There were no churches with bells in the siege camp at Acre, and that made it hard to measure the passing of time. Ibelin was aware only of growing weariness, and he paced to keep himself from dozing off entirely. Eventually Sir Galvin suggested he take a nap, but when he sat down with his back propped up against the wall of the palisade, sleep evaded him. His nerves were too on edge. So he returned to the wooden wall walk, pausing now and then to look out through the arrow slits.

Abruptly he started, shaken awake out of a sleep that had overcome him unawares. He looked up at the faintly graying sky, alarmed on the one hand to think he'd fallen asleep, and on the other because a nearby noise had startled him out of it. Holding his breath, his hand on his hilt, he strained to hear again what had woken him. A moment later he realized there were footfalls on the steps almost directly below him.

He spun about to face the exit from the stairwell just as a tall, broad-shouldered man emerged from it. The newcomer was hooded and alone, which made Ibelin uncertain at first, but when he strode over to the railing and looked out toward the enemy, just four feet from where Ibelin was standing, Balian was no longer in doubt. Even without his crown, Richard Plantagenet, sometimes called "Lionheart" by his admirers, was an imposing figure. He was as tall as Ibelin, but considerably more muscular. He wore a thick but close-cropped beard. His face was square and divided vertically by a strong, straight nose. His forehead was both broad and high, accented by his straight eyebrows. His mouth was a firm, straight line over his solid but not projecting chin. Altogether it was a harmonious face, and far more than handsome. The Lusignans were blessed with fine good looks, but unlike them, this face was strong. At the moment it was dominated by eyes that drew together as they searched the distance. Ibelin noted with approval that the English King was obviously still sober and still alert at this hour of the night—and that he was here alone to assess the enemy. Those facts spoke well for him.

"Welcome to the Holy Land, my lord King," Ibelin drew attention to himself.

Richard turned sharply to look at the man who had spoken, apparently surprised to be addressed so directly and familiarly by a man he had taken for a mere sentry. "Have we met?" he asked pointedly.

"No, I've been keeping watch all night."

"Who are you?"

"Ibelin."

The English King started in recognition and burst out indignantly, "The man who contrived the scandalous sham separation of my cousin Isabella of Jerusalem from her lawfully wedded husband!"

Ibelin frowned. He did not like—or think he deserved—to be reduced to an intriguer. Furthermore, he did not view Isabella's separation from Toron as a "sham." In dismay he asked back pointedly, "Who have you been talking to, my lord? Humphrey de Toron?"

"Among others, yes. Do you mean to deny it, my lord?" the King retorted, thrusting out his chin belligerently.

"Deny that I helped end Isabella's shameful relationship with Toron? Why should I? Isabella was eleven years old when she wed Humphrey, and he knows it as well as I do. Did you ask him whether he was willing to fight for his bride?" Ibelin paused only barely long enough to give the English King a chance to answer before continuing. "He was given the chance to prove she was his wife in judicial combat, but he quailed before such a prospect. He did not even take up the gage. That should tell you something about both the justice of his cause and the man himself.'"

The English King was quick to abandon a lost argument and declared instead, "Montferrat is a bigamist! He has a wife living in Constantinople!"

"Who has renounced him." Ibelin countered, sticking to this story even if there was justifiable cause to doubt it, but he added, "Had we known the King of France was widowed—or that your betrothal to Alys of France was not set in stone—we might have waited for either of you," Ibelin suggested provocatively. "We did the best with what we had. Whomever Isabella wed was to be our king, and we need a king capable of fighting for her kingdom. Montferrat can; Toron cannot."

"You already *have* a crowned and anointed king!" Richard countered, starting to get genuinely annoyed with this impudent upstart.

"If you're referring to Guy de Lusignan, who *lost* the Kingdom at Hattin, his claim to the throne was extinguished with his wife's death." It angered Ibelin that the English King was being so partisan and pigheaded. So much depended upon him, and yet here he was rejecting everything the High Court had done to eliminate the rot that had led to the fall of Jerusalem four years ago. If the English King insisted on supporting Lusignan, whether out of bigoted support for a vassal or merely to spite Philip of France, it would divide them when they needed unity. Everything depended on this crusade being a success. They had at last pulled together a force large enough to challenge Salah ad-Din's dominance, but that force had to be used effectively in support of the common cause if it was to have chance of defeating him. That meant they could no longer tolerate Lusignan's stubborn refusal to accept his fate. Ibelin tried to underline how untenable Lusignan's position was by noting, "You'll find not one single baron of Jerusalem—except poor Toron—who supports Lusignan."

"The barons of Jerusalem?" the English King scoffed in response. "The pack of you together don't control so much as an acre of land!"

"We control no less than your once and would-be king!" Ibelin reminded him indignantly.

"In your shoes, my lord," Richard advised ominously, narrowing his eyes as the muscles around his jaw tensed, "I would be more respectful toward those who have come to recover the lands *you* lost through *your* sins!"

Now Ibelin was truly angry. He'd had enough of this logic, and he was not afraid to say so to the King of England. Looking the Lionheart straight in the eye as he spoke, he asked: "Why, my lord King, do you *truly* think our Lord is so *petty* or so *cruel* as to punish all of Christendom for the sins of so few?"

Richard avoided the question and dismissed Ibelin with an imperious, "You've been warned once, Ibelin. Don't make me warn you again."

Acre, June 22, 1191

Eschiva had delayed as long as she could, pleading first that little Hugh needed to be better outfitted for his new life as a page to the King of England, and then that their daughter Helvis had a fever. She could not delay indefinitely, however. Aimery was relentlessly demanding her "immediate" appearance. They had been getting along so well since his release from captivity that she wanted to please him. Yet she hated the thought of serving two strange queens in the cramped quarters of a ship.

She had served as lady-in-waiting to queens before, of course. She had served both Sibylla and Isabella. But they were kin. She had hated the first and loved the latter—but either way, she had been related to them, and that had given her a measure of protection, at least in her own mind. The women she was being sent to serve now were utter strangers and had no reason to be kind to her. But Aimery was right, too. Ever since the High Court of Jerusalem had thrown their weight behind Conrad de Montferrat, the prospects for all the Lusignan brothers had dimmed. Only Richard of England stood between them and complete ignominy—after all these years.

The galley in which she traveled down from Tyre lay alongside a rickety wooden pier that had apparently been built in haste to help offload the English fleet. There was no one to meet them, of course, because they'd had no way to get word to Aimery of the exact date, time, or even the name of the vessel on which they would travel. So they paid a boy to run into the camp and find him.

Hugh, meanwhile, was agog at the sight of the siege camp, and he couldn't stand still long enough for her to give him last instructions. How was he ever going to take to the discipline of being a royal page? She'd asked herself that a hundred times already, however, and for the hundredth time she heard Aimery's answer in her head: He'd better learn fast.

He would, she told herself. Hugh was as quick of mind as he was fair of hair. He'd inherited the Lusignans' bright blond locks and their intense blue eyes, and was a very pretty boy. He was still two months shy of his ninth birthday, but he was starting to grow, and he was already as agile as a monkey. He'd talked the sailors into letting him climb aloft, and she'd nearly had a heart attack when he called down to her from high overhead. He was quick to laughter, too, and he

had a lovely voice. Maybe that would please the English King, who had a reputation as a troubadour.

"Madame?" It was the voice of Maria Zoë's faithful servant Rahel. After the
surrender of Cyprus, Richard of England had taken Isaac Comnenus' only child,
a daughter, into his "care" (or as a hostage, some would say). Maria Zoë suspected that Isaac's daughter wouldn't be able to speak a word of French, much
less Latin, and would be totally bewildered and isolated in Richard's household.
She had therefore suggested that Eschiva take Rahel with her, since Rahel would
be able to translate for the Cypriot princess turned prisoner. Maria Zoë had also
guessed that Eschiva herself would want a familiar face and friend in this difficult and unsought-for situation.

"Yes, Rahel?"

"I think the King is coming. There." Rahel was pointing at the shore.

Eschiva caught her breath and turned to follow her finger, expecting the
already legendary Lionheart to be striding toward them. She unconsciously
started fussing with her veils and wondering if she was presentable as she
searched the crowds clogging the landing stage. Surely people should have been
giving way before the King of England? Then she caught sight of her brother-in-
law Guy, and realized that was who Rahel was referring to. Poor Guy—he was
mounted and wearing a flashy surcoat over his expensive armor, but no one was
taking any note of him. If it hadn't been for Uncle Henri, he might have made
no progress at all. Henri d'Ibelin, however, was not above using his sheathed
sword to knock people out of the way, and the insults and threats he liberally
distributed made some men move aside resentfully.

At last the way was clear, and Guy jogged the last few yards to jump down
on the quay, tossing his reins to Henri. He had evidently seen Eschiva, because
he waved to her before bounding onto the gangway. They met in the waist of the
ship, where he bent and kissed her rather exuberantly on both cheeks. "Dearest
sister! What a pleasure to see you!" Eschiva could not remember such a warm
reception from her haughty brother-in-law. "Where is that fine boy of yours?"
Guy asked next, already looking about for a nephew he usually ignored.

Eschiva turned toward the bows where she had last seen her son and called
out, "Hugh!"

"Sir Henri will take him back to the King of England's tent on my horse,"
Guy explained, "while I accompany you to the buss housing the Queens of
England and Sicily."

Hugh caught sight of his uncle and dropped out of the standing rigging to
greet him with an exaggerated bow he'd been practicing ever since he'd learned
he was to serve the English King. He ruined the effect, however, by giggling

as he straightened. Guy, evidently in a good mood, laughed with him before remarking, "You'd better learn your manners, Hugh. They say the Plantagenet roasts rude pages for breakfast! He has a terrible temper, you know."

Hugh laughed, obviously unconvinced.

Sir Henri, having tethered the horses, joined them on the deck, and Eschiva went on tiptoe to return his perfunctory kiss on the cheek. His eyes had already found Hugh. "Come along, young man!" he urged, gesturing toward the quay and the horses. "Life is about to become a great adventure."

As if to punctuate his words, a large boom followed the end of the sentence, making Eschiva and Rahel both gasp.

"That's just 'Bad Neighbor'—the King of France's largest siege engine. It throws stones the size of Hugh here! The Accursed Tower is starting to crumble a bit under its attention."

"How *is* the siege going?" Eschiva asked.

Sir Henri shrugged. "Well, at least we've got the siege engines. And with all these ships, there's no chance of the Saracens slipping supplies into the garrison by sea. They're truly cut off from all aid now."

While this was not bad news, it did not sound like victory was just over the horizon. "What about the Kings of France and England?" Eschiva inquired; everyone in Outremer had put so much hope on their arrival.

"Sick," Sir Henri replied simply.

"Sick? Both of them? What is it?" Eschiva was instantly alarmed for Hugh's health, and was on the brink of declaring she would not let him go ashore to serve a man with some illness.

"Arnoldia. Nothing to worry about. Ibelins don't get it. The French King has lost all his hair, and the Plantagenet is starting to lose his as well. He could probably deal with that, as he does not appear particularly vain, but the forced inactivity is making him very irritable. He snarls at everyone just like a wounded cat. If you're clever, Hugh," Henri addressed his nephew, "you'll slip lime sherbet to the King. It will sting the sores in his mouth and he's likely to throw the bowl at you, but the Samaritan doctors swear it helps cure Arnoldia."

"Be off, Sir Henri; the ladies and I have to continue." Guy dismissed his knight without rancor but in an obvious hurry.

Eschiva had no choice but to bid her eldest child a hasty farewell. It was better that way. He was clearly more excited about the siege and all the adventures he was about to have than about his mother's admonishments to be "good" and "careful." What more could she possibly say to him now? His father, two of his uncles, and his great-uncle Henri were all there to look after him. It was time to let go.

Meanwhile Guy was giving orders for the galley to back away from the quay again, and directing it toward a large buss that flew the royal standard of England from the masthead. Only after they had cast off did he give his attention to his sister-in-law again. "Where is Aimery?" Eschiva asked.

"Ah." Guy evaded her eyes. "He and Geoffrey felt it was important that the Lusignans support the French King."

"Yes, of course, but why couldn't he meet me? I would have liked to at least *see* my husband—"

"Yes, yes, of course. If we'd known you were arriving this afternoon . . . but we honestly didn't hear you'd docked until they were already committed. The French King ordered an assault, you see, but was too ill to lead it himself—"

"Christ in heaven!" Eschiva exclaimed, turning back to look at the siege camp in horror. "You mean—"

"Oh, you can see nothing from here," Guy explained cheerfully. "They're focusing on the part of the wall that has already been weakened by our siege engines. More to the east."

Eschiva could only stare at Guy. Both his brothers were apparently risking their lives at this very moment, and he found nothing odd in the fact that he, the "King," was not with them while they fought for his kingdom. She would never learn to love this man, she thought resentfully, and yet she and her family were harnessed to him by bonds of blood.

"Eschiva, I wanted to use this time together to be sure you understand your role," Guy declared, blithely ignorant of his sister-in-law's resentment. It was bad enough that the man was a selfish fool, Eschiva thought, without him presuming to tell her what to do! But Eschiva, as usual, kept her opinion to herself, and Guy continued: "The Queen of Sicily is a widow in need of a new husband, and kings don't grow on trees. I'm sure she fancies me, actually, but the more I know about her interests and tastes, the easier it will be to win her. You know, does she like hawking or hunting? Or does she prefer books? Does she play an instrument? Or is she very pious? Find out if she craves relics; I'm sure I could find something to impress her, if she does. Or is she more interested in silks or jewels? Anything you can find out that will make my suit easier."

Eschiva nodded. Aimery had warned her that Guy had hopes of seducing the English King's sister. He'd slept his way to the crown of Jerusalem, after all— why shouldn't he hope to secure his fortunes with another bedroom conquest? If the King of England gave his sister to Guy in marriage, he would be locked into the alliance with the Lusignans by ties of kinship, and that made it much less likely that he would withdraw his financial and military support at a later date.

The galley rapidly covered the short distance to the large buss that rode lazily at anchor. The ship was manned by a skeleton crew capable of handing a sudden storm or another emergency, but otherwise it had been converted from a transport vessel into a floating palace for the Queens of England and Sicily. By living here, they were spared the squalor and dangers of the siege camp.

King Guy was announced, and the ship's captain duly lowered a ladder for them, because the freeboard of the buss was substantially higher than that of the galley. While sailors held the ladder steady, Eschiva hitched her skirts up into her belt and took hold of the sides of the ladder. Guy followed behind her to catch her if she made a misstep. Rahel and the servants followed with the baggage.

By the time Eschiva reached the deck of the buss, the queens had come on deck to greet the newcomers. There was a bevy of seven women, to be precise, but two women led the way arm in arm, and Eschiva rapidly guessed they were the principals. One of the women was tall but very slim, with fair skin that had burned bright red in the sun and pale eyebrows that suggested fair hair hidden under her silken wimple. The other was very petite and dark, with smoldering black eyes that reminded Eschiva of some of the Saracen women she had seen.

Eschiva dipped her knee in a deep curtsy before the two women, bowing her head. "My ladies: my lord husband, Aimery de Lusignan, suggested you might appreciate the company of a lady born and raised here in Outremer, and" she gestured for Rahel to come forward, "the services of a lady who speaks Greek as fluently—"

"Deo Gracia! Gracia, ma dame!" the little dark lady exclaimed with exuberance, and then turned and gave a rush of orders to one of her ladies.

Beside her, her taller companion laughed, then extended her hand to Eschiva with a smile. "As you can see, we are sorely in need of someone who speaks Greek! And I, for one, am desperate to learn more about Outremer! I am woefully ignorant, and my beloved brother is annoyingly sparing with both his presence and his intelligence!"

"Your brother begs your understanding, my lady. He personally asked me to assure you he thinks of you constantly—" Guy's pretty speech was silenced by a withering look from the Queen of Sicily.

"We were told my brother was seriously ill—too ill to receive us. Were we misinformed, my lord . . . king?" Eschiva winced at the tiny pause Joanna Plantagenet inserted between "lord" and "king," making it clear she did not view this man as an equal to her brother or her late husband.

Guy was flustered by her directness, and Eschiva watched him without sympathy. He'd had it so easy with Sibylla. She'd been a silly teenager, so susceptible to flattery. Guy was babbling something about King Richard being on the mend, but not wanting to endanger his lady wife or his beloved sister. The

Queen of Sicily nodded as if she accepted his explanation but without, Eschiva thought, any indication that she liked the messenger. Eschiva wondered if Guy recognized her indifference and that was why he wanted her help—or if he was deluding himself about his charms, just as he had deluded himself about his skills as a leader of men, a diplomat, and everything else?

Meanwhile, the Queen of England had finished giving her instructions to her lady, and turned back to address the new arrivals. "My lord king," she addressed Guy de Lusignan, "please give me the latest word from my lord husband and the siege. We can hear the crack of the siege engines even from here—by night as well as by day—and sometimes shouting reaches us faintly over the water, too. But what of my lord husband? Has the fever broken yet? You know I protest most vigorously against being kept here, away from his side, when he is so ill!"

Eschiva liked the sound of that. The Queen of the English might be small and delicate of build, but she had spirit.

"You remind me of my own dear, late Queen, Madame," Guy answered with a bow; "she too could hardly bear to be separated, coming to me even in captivity." Eschiva winced, thinking it was not wise to remind the present company that he had been a captive—or of the debacle that had led a king into captivity. She noted, however, that while the Plantagenet raised her eyebrows in evident disapproval, the Queen of England nodded vigorously. "Quite so, my lord, as would I, if—God forbid—my lord husband were to fall upon such misfortune. So it is all the more unjust that with only a mile separating us, I am kept a virtual prisoner here."

"Madame, I will convey your indignation, but I assure you that your husband's knights are only obeying his orders."

"I don't doubt that for a moment," the Queen of Sicily intervened, and Eschiva had the feeling that this was an argument the women had had among themselves more than once. "My brother hates being coddled. All Plantagenets do. I'd like to have seen the man brave enough to tell my father he should let a woman near him when he was sick! Fortunately, my mother didn't have a coddling bone in her body. Richard is exactly like my father. When he's sick, he wants to crawl into a cave until he's feeling better. Now, my lord king, we have kept you long enough from the business of regaining your kingdom." She held out her hand for him to kiss in a gesture of such definitive dismissal that Guy de Lusignan had no choice but to dutifully kiss her hand and then Queen Berengaria's. Both queens stood graciously at the rail, waving goodbye until he was well out of hearing.

Meanwhile the Queen of England's lady had returned, leading a little girl by the hand. She looked no more than nine or ten, and while she appeared to trust the lady with her, she also looked generally frightened and unhappy. Rahel at once stepped forward and spoke to her in Greek, producing wide-eyed wonder followed by such a flood of words that all the women around them laughed.

Rahel could only nod, saying again and again, "*ne, ne*" in reassurance to the girl until the latter paused for breath and Rahel explained, "Mesdames, Sophia wants me to thank you for your many kindnesses, and she begs you not to be angry, but she says she wants to go home to Cyprus, and would you please tell her what has happened to her father, and—well—she has lots of other questions, too." Rahel concluded.

"Poor thing! I'm sure she has!" Queen Berengaria agreed. "But first," she turned to Eschiva, only to stop in embarrassment. "Forgive me, I didn't catch your name."

"Eschiva, my lady."

"Wonderful. Eschiva, we are truly delighted to have you join us. Now, what do you think, Joanna? Where shall we put them?"

The Queen of Sicily took over. "Let's have—was it Rachel?" she interrupted herself to ask.

"Rahel," Eschiva corrected.

"Let's have Rahel move in with Sophia, and Nina can join me, while Eschiva takes her cabin. Nina, will you show them where to put their things, help them settle in, and then bring them to join us for dinner?"

The ship's captain had fixed a heavy canvas over the entire sterncastle that kept it in shadow all through the day. Only in the early morning and late afternoon did the sun's rays slant in under the canvas onto the spacious raised deck. The combination of shade and breezes from all directions made this a very pleasant space. It was also comfortably furnished with tables, chairs, and chests.

When Eschiva joined the other ladies of the household, she found that water for washing her hands waited on a sideboard and that the table itself was set with Egyptian pottery. The buff terracotta, with green patterns painted under a transparent glaze, was very popular throughout Outremer because it was cheap and could easily be replaced. Eschiva found it made her feel more at ease than if the two queens had been using expensive silver plate. The meal itself consisted of local flatbread and grilled fish garnished with herbs, onions, and lemon juice.

Eschiva was offered a seat directly beside the Queen of Sicily and opposite the Queen of England. It was the latter who, after insisting she have some of the wine and help herself to the food, asked her with apparently sincere interest to "tell us all about yourself!"

Eschiva was not used to being the center of attention, much less having the undivided attention of two queens. At first she didn't know what to say, and stammered about being "no one special" and having "nothing much to tell."

"Well, have you children?" Queen Berengaria countered eagerly.

"Four," Eschiva declared proudly. "Hugh is almost nine, and I brought him with me to serve your lord husband as a page."

"Ah! I will look for him—if ever I am allowed off this ship!" Berengaria sent her sister-in-law a reproachful look.

Eschiva deftly returned the conversation to safer territory. "Burgundia is seven, Helvis is five, and the baby, Aimery, named for his father, is two."

"You are very lucky!" Berengaria assured her. "I hope—may the Holy Mother hear my prayers and have mercy on me—to have a nursery overflowing with a baby every year!"

Eschiva sensed, however, that this topic was not so safe after all, since the Queen of Sicily's only child had died very young. She looked rather sad as her sister-in-law of just one month declared her grand plans for a full nursery. Eschiva changed the subject again. "But I had no brothers, as you both have. I would have loved to have brothers!"

"Ah, but then you would not have been an heiress," the Plantagenet pointed out immediately.

Eschiva shrugged. "I don't think being an heiress is such a fine thing. It isn't as if my father ever treated me as such. On the contrary, he wanted a son so desperately that he set aside my mother to marry again." Eschiva immediately had the sympathy of her audience. It was something all high-born women feared: the consequences of the failure to produce a male heir. "And then, when my baby half-brother died, he nearly killed himself from grief."

"Who is your father?" Queen Berengaria asked gently.

"My father is dead," Eschiva answered; the bitterness that he had died without ever coming back to see her made her voice unconsciously harsh. "He was Barisan d'Ibelin, Baron of Ramla and Mirabel, but he renounced both—" She cut herself off in horror as she realized she'd been about to admit how much her father hated her brother-in-law, the very man who was now courting the widowed Queen Joanna.

Fortunately, her audience was distracted by his name. "Ibelin? Isn't that the man who tore poor Queen Isabella from her husband's bed?" Queen Berengaria exclaimed in shock, while Queen Joanna asked indignantly: "Ibelin? You can't mean the man who treacherously set up Conrad de Montferrat as a rival to King Guy?"

Eschiva looked from one woman to the other. They were obviously outraged by Isabella's marriage to Montferrat, so when she shook her head and explained, "No, that was my Uncle Balian, " both queens looked distinctly relieved.

Queen Berengaria exclaimed immediately, "I *knew* you couldn't be closely related to such a monster!"

Eschiva could have left it at that, passively distancing herself from her uncle to avoid unnecessary association with a man the queens evidently despised without meeting. But it irritated Eschiva that Guy, in his egotistical pursuit of a crown (and a new queen), had felt he had the right to disparage a better man. Even Aimery admitted privately that Uncle Balian was more intelligent and more courageous than his brother. "My ladies," Eschiva broke into their side conversation about how despicable Ibelin was. "I was told I had been sent here, among other things, to explain a little more about Outremer."

"Indeed!" they agreed in unison, looking at her expectantly.

"Well, one thing you need to understand is that my uncle, Balian d'Ibelin, is a highly respected man, and because he is so highly respected, he is also very influential."

"But how can a man—" Berengaria started indignantly, but Joanna silenced her emotional outburst with a gesture. Then, settling her pale but intelligent eyes on Eschiva, she urged, "Go on. Tell us more."

"Uncle Balian was one of the few Frankish lords who did not allow himself to be captured at Hattin. He fought his way off the battlefield, and in so doing he punched a hole in the encircling Saracen army that enabled almost two hundred Frankish knights and three thousand Christian foot soldiers to escape. Ask any man from Outremer whom they trust more, Ibelin or Lusignan, and you will hear only one answer: Ibelin."

Berengaria caught her breath on the brink of protest—but the Plantagenet frowned, her eyes still fixed on Eschiva, and forestalled her with a "Go on. What more can you tell us?"

"Uncle Balian led those three thousand fighting men to the most defensible city in the Kingdom, and it was as much because of them as the fortuitous arrival of my lord of Montferrat that the city was able to hold out against Salah ad-Din. For what would Montferrat have done without men to man the walls?"

"Indeed," Joanna Plantagenet agreed dryly.

"But while Uncle Balian and his knights and men were safe behind the walls of Tyre, his wife, his four young children, his stepdaughter Isabella, and I were all trapped in Jerusalem." Eschiva paused. "I do not think that you can imagine what it was like in Jerusalem."

Berengaria crossed herself and muttered something in her own tongue.

Then, switching to French, she declared, "With God's grace, I hope that I *will* see the Holy City with my own eyes."

"I wish that for you with all my heart," Eschiva assured her sincerely and earnestly, because for Berengaria to tread the streets of Jerusalem it would first have to be reclaimed for Christ by the forces now gathered on the shore. "But that is not what I meant," Eschiva continued. "I meant that I'm not sure you know what it was like here in the Kingdom of Jerusalem after Hattin. You see, with the army destroyed, the Saracens swept across the entire Kingdom, pillaging and burning—and killing, raping, and enslaving any Christians that fell into their hands. Because King Guy had called up all able-bodied men for his army—the army he led to destruction on the Horns of Hattin—all the towns and castles were denuded of their garrisons."

Eschiva realized how much bitterness was in her words only after they were out of her mouth. But she could not regret what she had said, regardless of how much it was in her self-interest for Queen Joanna to marry Guy. Instead, she continued her narrative. "One after another, the cities fell: Ascalon, Jaffa, Acre, Caesarea, Sidon, Beirut. As the Sultan's army swept along the coast, people fled their homes, taking whatever they could carry, to seek shelter in Jerusalem. Normally there were about twenty thousand inhabitants in Jerusalem. During the pilgrim season, there were sometimes twice that many people there. But after Hattin, more than forty thousand refugees found their way to Jerusalem. Most of those refugees were women, children, and churchmen. There were fifty women and children for every man in Jerusalem, Mesdames. And most of those men were little more than boys, grandfathers, or men in holy orders. We collected there, Mesdames—but what chance did we have against the victorious armies of the Sultan Salah ad-Din?"

The two queens were staring at her, transfixed by her story. They had heard Jerusalem had fallen. They had heard the Saracens were trampling disrespectfully upon the sites of Christ's crucifixion and resurrection. They had felt grief and outrage and determination to reclaim the lost city. But they had never before given a thought to the *human* drama, to the fate of women like themselves.

Berengaria's nerves broke first. "What happened?" she asked urgently.

"Uncle Balian came."

"With his three thousand men?" Joanna asked.

"No. Alone. Well, with one squire."

Berengaria and Joanna looked at one another, uncomprehending. "What do you mean? How could one man make any difference? And why didn't he take his troops to relieve Jerusalem?" Joanna asked critically.

"Three thousand against sixty thousand, Madame? And leave Tyre, the only port still in Christian hands, undefended? Without Tyre, how could the kingdoms of the West have helped us? The Sultan had defeated an army of twelve hundred knights and twenty-five thousand men at Hattin; do you think three thousand might have crossed a hundred miles without being forced to battle? And if confronted, do you think they could have avoided being crushed?"

Berengaria was convinced and nodded, but Joanna raised her eyebrows and noted, "My father was known for moving at lightning speed through enemy territory. It can be done. And to save Jerusalem, it *should* have been done."

"If it would have saved Jerusalem, Madame," Eschiva answered steadily, "you are right. But they could *not* have saved Jerusalem." Reading Joanna's arched brows correctly, she hastened to add, "I do not claim to understand military matters, Madame, but I was there. With sixty thousand residents crammed into the city, Salah ad-Din didn't have to *fight* at all. All he had to do was surround the city and wait for us to die—of poor hygiene, illness, hunger, and thirst. With three thousand more mouths to feed, the water and supplies would have run out sooner and disease spread faster."

"But my brother told me it was defended—and it fell in just a matter of days, although it took months to take it during the First Crusade," Joanna pointed out disdainfully.

"In 1099, the civilians had been expelled and it was manned by elite Egyptian troops, while the forces of Christ were too decimated by their long pilgrimage to even surround the city. Four years ago, the Sultan's army was so numerous it surrounded the city like a sea, and the defenders consisted of just eighty new-made knights, churchmen, tradesmen—and women. That the city fell in days is no wonder; that it fought at all, that it inflicted so many casualties that the Sultan grew cautious, and that despite that fierce defiance, the bulk of the citizens were allowed to go free in the end—*that* was the miracle."

Berengaria crossed herself, but Joanna wanted to know, "And how *was* that possible?"

"Because of Uncle Balian. As I was telling you, he came with one squire and a safe-conduct from the Sultan to remove his family." For the first time, Eschiva sensed that she'd impressed the Plantagenet. Joanna knew her father would not have sought a favor from the King of France for her mother's sake. Nor would William have done it for her. "However, the Patriarch and the burghers were determined not to surrender Jerusalem. They preferred a martyr's death, and they had told the Sultan so. In turn, he had vowed to take the city by storm and put all to the sword, or carry them away as slaves. Now, these same men who had defied the Sultan begged my uncle to remain and take command of that futile last defense."

Berengaria grasped her rosary, identifying with this decision to die for one's faith, but Joanna was impatient. "But that didn't happen. There was a surrender," she protested indignantly. "Tell us what happened. You said you were there."

"Well, not during the actual siege and surrender," Eschiva conceded a little sheepishly.

"How did you get out?" Berengaria asked, amazed.

"The Sultan sent some of his own men to escort Uncle Balian's family out of Jerusalem before he laid siege to it, and—"

"*What?*" the two queens exclaimed in unison. Joanna elaborated with the question, "Why would the Sultan do such a thing?"

"Oh, Salah ad-Din is very savvy. He'd just made a treaty with the Greek Emperor, and he thought it would be awkward to have one of the Emperor's kinswomen trapped in a city he intended to take by storm. He didn't want Queen Sibylla there, either. He wanted a free hand to deliver a bloody lesson to anyone who defied him. He didn't want the embarrassment of his troops defiling queens or former queens."

"I see about Sibylla, but what did that have to do with your uncle?"

"Uncle Balian is married to the Dowager Queen of Jerusalem, the Greek princess Maria Comnena."

"Oh!" Joanna Plantagenet was startled by this news; Berengaria was just confused. The latter asked, "But hadn't your uncle just broken his word to him? Surely the Sultan wanted to punish him more than anyone!"

"Not really. The Sultan understood that Uncle Balian had no choice. He really *did* have no choice. Tante Marie summarized it simply: What sort of man, she asked, would walk away from sixty thousand helpless refugees begging for help?" Eschiva paused. "Well, my uncle was *not* the sort of man to do that. He stayed and organized a defense—with women and priests—that was so effective that the Sultan had to abandon his assaults after five days, call in sappers, and undermine the walls. It was only after the walls came down that my uncle surrendered. You think he should have sought martyrdom?" Eschiva asked Joanna provocatively. "Well, the *men* would all have been martyrs, and the *women* would all have become harem slaves. Even now, more than twenty thousand Christian women live as the slaves of Muslim men because they fell into the hands of the Saracens."

Berengaria gasped and covered her mouth in horror, while Joanna's lips tightened.

"Not just lowborn women suffered that fate," Eschiva continued. "The Sultan might have spared queens, but the daughters of one of my uncle's knights were taken from their estates near Ibelin and have never been heard from since.

When Jaffa fell, all the Italian burghers' wives were divided up among the conquerors. The Convent of the Sacred Heart at Hebron fell completely into Saracen hands, and all the nuns are now the sexual toys of their Muslim owners." Berengaria was clutching her rosary beads in distress, and Joanna looked grim.

"One day perhaps you will meet Sister Adela," Eschiva continued. "She was the head sister at the Hospital in Jerusalem during the siege. She now runs an orphanage in Tyre. She told me that her greatest fear throughout the siege was that the men would get their martyr's crown—while she and the sisters of the Hospital would spend the rest of their lives in a Turkish brothel."

"Holy Mother of God! Our good Lord would not let that happen!" Berengaria protested.

Eschiva looked sharply at Berengaria and told her bluntly, "He let it happen to the sisters of the Sacred Heart at Hebron. That it did *not* happen in Jerusalem is due entirely to the negotiating skills of my Uncle Balian. For the sake of the women and children, he sacrificed his martyr's crown and found a means to extricate as many people as possible."

"I daresay he was thinking of his own skin, too," Joanna noted cynically.

"No, my lady," Eschiva corrected the Queen of Sicily almost sharply, "for he offered up his skin for the sake of those who could not pay a ransom!"

Joanna caught her breath at that. Neither her fathers nor brothers, much less her late husband would have done that—risked their own freedom for the poor.

"How did he escape?" Berengaria wanted to know.

"The Sultan knew his troops were restless from being denied plunder, and the fifteen thousand Christian women and children too poor to pay a ransom were his means of paying them off. He did not want my uncle, nor any ransom he might have been able to raise in a year or two of begging. He wanted those female bodies for his troops."

"All right," Joanna conceded, "you have made a case that your uncle is a military leader, an adroit negotiator, and a man of exceptional charity. I take your point that his actions have won him respect and influence among his countrymen. Yet you also admit that he broke his word to the Sultan, *and* he has also broken his oath of fealty to King Guy. Finally, he has callously, not to say brutally, forced Queen Isabella into a bigamous relationship with a man who cannot legally be her husband. Whatever his other virtues, I'd still say those are the actions of a treacherous and unscrupulous man."

Eschiva took a deep breath and then a sip of wine before answering. "I see that you have made up your mind about my uncle without even meeting him, so I will say no more in his defense. However, I would like to tell you more about Queen Isabella."

"You know her?" They sounded so surprised that Eschiva almost snapped back at them in irritation. She caught herself in time, remembering that they had no reason to know about her family ties, and reminding herself she knew almost nothing about their families, either.

Patiently, Eschiva explained, "When my father set aside my blameless mother so he could marry again, the last thing he wanted on his hands was a 'useless' daughter. After all, his hopes were that he would soon have many sons to displace me altogether. But he couldn't entomb me alive in a convent, as he did my innocent mother, because I'd been married since the age of eight to Aimery de Lusignan. Aimery, however, had taken very little interest in me, and although I was thirteen when my mother was set aside, my marriage was not yet consummated. I would have been quite abandoned if Uncle Balian had not taken me into his family. He had only recently married, and Isabella was his stepdaughter. We lived like sisters until she was betrothed by the King to Humphrey de Toron. She was taken from us and forced to live in the fortress castle of Kerak, on the edge of Sinai, with the truly brutal and unscrupulous Reynald de Châtillon. You must have heard of him? He once tortured the Patriarch of Antioch just to extort money from him."

Berengaria crossed herself again and muttered something under her breath as she shook her head in shock and disapproval.

"Isabella and I became particularly close, however," Eschiva continued, "after Hattin, when we both found ourselves again living on my uncle's charity while our husbands rotted in Saracen dungeons. We had no money for ransoms, after all. At least I didn't. And even after Aimery was free and we took our own lodgings, I spent most of my days with Isabella and Tante Marie, Uncle Balian's wife."

"Wait." Joanna was beginning to put two and two together. "Didn't you say your uncle's wife was a Greek princess? A dowager queen?" Eschiva nodded. "But then she must have been King Amalric's widow, and so Isabella's mother?"

"Yes, didn't I say that?" Eschiva was sure she had already mentioned this fact, but Joanna's expression suggested that she had not taken it in, so she added, "She is a Comnena. She is the great-niece of Emperor Manuel I."

While Maria Zoë's Greek heritage would not endear her to many of the crusaders, Joanna had lived long enough on Sicily to see the world in shades of gray. Furthermore, precisely because Sicily had so often been at odds (if not at war) with the Greek Empire, she knew just how rich and powerful it was. It dawned on Joanna that if this "Ibelin" was married to the Dowager Queen of Jerusalem, then he had a legitimate interest in the affairs of his wife's kingdom. Joanna was beginning to suspect that Guy de Lusignan and Humphrey de Toron had been very misleading in their depiction of the "abduction" of Isabella. "One more question. Toron claimed that Isabella was torn from his bed—literally—against her wishes, and forced into this marriage with Montferrat completely against her will. As her friend, is that how you would describe it?"

"Madame, Isabella and Humphrey lived together at Kerak as children. She loved him very much. But she was below the age of consent when she married him. Five princes of the Church, including the Papal Legate, ruled that her marriage to Toron was invalid. After the Church council came to this conclusion, the worthy bishops explicitly told her she was free to marry anyone she pleased. She *could* have married Humphrey. All she had to do was renew her vows with him as a consenting adult to thereby become his wife in the eyes of the Church. She chose not to do that."

"Why?"

"Because with her sister's death she had become Queen of Jerusalem, Madame. I'm sure no one knows better than you that a queen does not follow her heart; she marries in the best interests of her kingdom. Humphrey de Toron—well, you have met him, have you not?"

Joanna and Berengaria exchanged a look.

"He is not suited to be King of Jerusalem. Conrad de Montferrat is."

"But you already have a King!" Berengaria protested. Eschiva noted, however, that Joanna Plantagenet, far from nodding, was twisting her wedding ring on her finger.

"Guy lost his kingdom *twice*, Madame." Eschiva focused on Berengaria as she explained, but her words were meant more for Joanna. "First *physically* on the Horns of Hattin, and a second time *morally*, here at Acre."

"What do you mean by the latter?" Berengaria asked, frowning more from concentration than displeasure.

"I mean that Guy brought his wife and his two little girls to live in a siege camp where disease, scorpions, poisonous snakes, and enemy action all take a daily toll. When he did that, he demonstrated a disregard for the health and safety of his wife—his queen—that God rightly saw as culpable. My Uncle Balian would never dream of bringing his wife, much less his young children, to a siege camp! Nor would my lord husband. And nor, it seems, would *yours*." She paused to let this sink in before adding, "I know you are upset to be kept 'imprisoned' on this ship, Madame, but believe me, it shows that King Richard wants you near but *safe*. It is a measure of his respect for you that he did *not* take you into that camp," she gestured over the side of the ship, "as my brother-in-law did with his wife and queen. Guy's negligence was more than a personal tragedy: it carried political consequences. Guy only wore the crown by right of his wife, and he lost the *legal* right to that crown—and in my opinion as a wife and mother, the *moral* right to it as well—when he squandered the lives of his wife and daughters out there." Again she pointed over the side of the ship to the siege camp of Acre, slowly sinking into shadow as the sun set.

In the stunned silence they could hear the steady pounding of the French King's siege engines, and a moment later the more distant wailing of the Muslim call to prayers in the city itself.

After a moment, Joanna roused herself. "I think we are very fortunate that you have joined us, Lady Eschiva. We are going to learn a very great deal from you."

Eschiva looked down at her hands, embarrassed. She had said her piece, and part of her felt calmed for finally having candidly said what she felt, yet had never before dared say out loud. But part of her felt guilty, too. She had, in her defense of her family and her feelings, betrayed her husband and his brother.

Chapter 14

Acre, July 10, 1191

THE NEWS THAT THE GARRISON AT Acre was offering terms spread like wildfire through the siege camp. By the time Ibelin left his tent to follow the summons from the French King for a council of war, men by the thousands had converged on the royal tents. Ibelin's knights had to force a way through the crowds for him. The constant conversation made the whole camp hum and buzz like a disturbed beehive. Men were squabbling, speculating, gesturing, demanding, posturing, and just plain standing around dumbfounded.

"Does this mean we won't get to plunder it?" one man asked a companion resentfully, only to receive the rude reply, "Of course not, dumb-ass, but it means we won't have to bleed anymore, either, and can move on to Jerusalem!"

That put things in a nutshell for the crusaders, Ibelin supposed, but things were not that simple for the men of Outremer. This explained why so many of them—sergeants, squires, and Turcopoles—had clustered around his tent and moved with him through the camp, conveying by their presence how much they expected of him.

The French King's magnificent blue-and-gold tent loomed out of the chaotic surroundings, the long fleur-de-lis banner floating on a light breeze from a pole projecting out of the roof. Before Ibelin could enter, however, a weathered man, in an elegant but much-worn surcoat over sagging chain mail, caught his arm. "My lord, remember, those are *our* homes in there! I don't know what condition they're in, and I realize that nothing movable is left, but the substance—the wells and gardens, walls and floors—is intact. We want our houses back, my lord."

"What is your name, sir?" Ibelin asked politely.

"My name is unimportant. I speak not for myself but for the citizens of Acre, specifically for the Commune of Pisa."

Ibelin nodded. "I understand, *signore*."

"This isn't just about Acre," another man piped up, latching on to Ibelin as he tried to move forward again. "What happens here will set a precedent. If they're allowed to plunder the places they recover from the Saracens, we'll have been robbed twice!" The speaker this time was a younger knight in torn and much-repaired armor under a faded and patched surcoat.

Again Ibelin nodded and repeated, "I understand." The man dropped back.

Ibelin had reached the entrance to the French King's tent. Sergeants in fleur-de-lis surcoats formed a barrier to keep the masses out, while royal household knights asked for the name of each man and checked the names against a list before letting anyone inside. Ibelin had been invited; his knights had not. He nodded to them to indicate he would proceed alone, but as he turned to cross the threshold into the tent itself, Sir Bartholomew croaked out, "Balian." Ibelin turned and waited, but Sir Bartholomew couldn't find words. He just swallowed, his eyes pleading.

Balian reached out and grasped his shoulder. "You don't have to remind me, Bart. Not a night goes by when I am not tormented by their plight. God grant me words to make the others understand. Pray that He does." Sir Bartholomew nodded mutely, his face strained, and Ibelin entered the French King's tent.

Although this was enormous, larger than any tent Ibelin had seen before, it was already crowded. The number of people crammed inside, combined with the effects of the afternoon sun and the absence of a breeze, made the atmosphere thick and stifling. Ibelin felt himself begin to sweat as he wormed his way past the lower-ranked commanders—the Danes and Frisians, the Pisan and Genoese captains, the bannerets of England and France—to the inner circle, which consisted only of barons.

The Kings of England and France were both seated on large armed chairs representing thrones. The Dukes of Austria and Burgundy had also been provided with chairs, but neither Guy nor Conrad was seated. Instead, the rival kings of Jerusalem looked flushed and agitated, as if they had already clashed. The Count of Champagne cast Ibelin a vaguely relieved look as he entered, and William of Tiberius pushed his way through some of the English lords to reach Ibelin's side. "King Richard tried to expel Montferrat," he hissed under his breath, "and Philip answered that if Monferrat left, then Guy must also—"

"Is everyone of note here?" the King of England interrupted the exchange in a loud voice.

"I'm awaiting the Bishop of Beauvais," Philip countered, harvesting a derisive snort from the King of England.

Ibelin exchanged a look with Reginald de Sidon, who had also made his way through the crowd to stand with him. Pagan de Haifa, William de Hebron, and the other lords of Outremer were one by one congregating around him, although Conrad himself was evidently reluctant to leave his position just to the left of the French King.

Philip of France did not look particularly well. Although he had recovered from Arnoldia sooner than the English King, he was still completely bald, and his face and hands were covered with unsightly sores. Richard of England, who had been more intensely sick, seemed to have recovered more completely. There was already a coppery fuzz covering his scalp and chin, while his forehead and nose were tanned. Ibelin had to admire the fact that before he was fit enough to stand, Richard of England had had himself carried out to the battle lines in a litter so he could fire a crossbow at the defenders of Acre on the ramparts. While his efforts were materially insignificant, their effect on morale had been tangible. He had demonstrated to a demoralized army that he was back and fighting, his spirit and determination unbroken by the debilitating fever. Particularly significant was the fact that he did not disdain the "lowly" crossbow. By taking the weapon of sergeants in his own hands, the King of England had demonstrated a solidarity with the common soldiers that Ibelin had never seen in a king before—unless one counted that moment of defiance when Montferrat had fired a crossbow at the men escorting his father to demonstrate his determination to hold out. Guy de Lusignan wouldn't have taken a crossbow in his hands to save his life, Ibelin thought, with a disgusted look at the former King.

Guy was flanked by his brothers, both of whom overshadowed him even here inside the tent. Guy was dressed in silk; his brothers wore chain mail. That, Ibelin decided, said it all.

At last the Bishop of Beauvais arrived and followed King Philip's gesture to come and stand directly behind his throne.

"Can we begin now?" King Richard asked impatiently.

"Yes, go ahead. You have a louder voice," the French King conceded. It was not a compliment.

"My lords." King Richard raised his voice, and the general gurgle of conversation faded out. "The garrison of Acre offered to surrender the city of Acre in exchange for their lives and their weapons—"

"What? We are to just let them walk away and fight us somewhere else? I can assure you my Emperor did not die so that we could let these vermin walk

away, leaving behind a ruined shell!" It was the Duke of Austria who had the
temerity to interrupt the King of England in this tone.

"You can be sure, my lord Duke, that I didn't come all this way for such a
pact, either!" the King of England snapped back. "I wasn't finished. We rejected
those terms, the King of France and I. We demanded, in addition to the surrender of Acre, two hundred thousand gold pieces, the return of the True Cross—"
That produced a cheer from the men standing farther back—"and we rejected
the right of the garrison to retain their arms."

"Do they have two hundred thousand pieces of gold?" the Duke of Burgundy
asked, startled.

"No—the Sultan will have to provide the gold as well as the True Cross."

"So how do we know he'll keep the terms of the agreement?" the Duke of
Austria wanted to know.

Again the King of England looked annoyed. "We will retain hostages."

"How many?" the Austrian wanted to know.

"I think that is still open to negotiation, if we are in agreement with the
overall outline of the terms."

"No," Ibelin answered bluntly, firmly, and loudly.

The King of England snapped his head around to glare at him, and the
King of France raised his eyebrows in surprise, while both Lusignan and Montferrat frowned. From the corners of the tent came whispers of unease as people
asked one another who had spoken and what was going on.

"Just what objections do you have?" Richard Plantagenet demanded irritably.

"That there is nothing in this agreement about Frankish captives, my lord.
Hundreds of knights, who have since lost their land and so their ability to raise
a ransom, are still in captivity. Thousands of women and children are enslaved
because we have no means to purchase their freedom. There can be no agreement that does not take those Christian souls into account."

"Amen, my lord! Well said!" This vocal support came from the Archbishop
of Nazareth and was seconded at once—not just by the other prelates in the
room, but by most of the lords of Outremer. Hebron even murmured a heartfelt, "Thank you, Ibelin," in his ear.

The Kings of England and France exchanged a surprised look, and con-
ferred in whispers together before Richard spoke for them. "Fair enough; we'll
add that to our demands. How many?"

"One freed captive for every single Saracen we let go free from Acre," Ibelin
answered emphatically, earning a chorus of approval this time.

Richard and Philip exchanged a look. Philip nodded and Richard shrugged.
"Why not?" the King of England replied. "Anything else?"

"No, my lords," Ibelin conceded.

"Good. So be it."

The council was over, and everyone started to disperse. Ibelin turned, anxious to get out of the stale air of the tent as soon as possible. Around him his fellow barons were congratulating him, thumping him on the back, and jabbering in elated tones. It took a few moments before they noticed that Ibelin himself was not joining in their high spirits. "What's the matter, Balian?" Sidon asked as they reached the fresh air outside the tent at last.

"We don't have a deal yet," Ibelin snapped back. "All we have is an offer. Let's see what al-Asadi Qara-Qush says before we congratulate ourselves."

They had their answer by nightfall, and the man to bring the news to Ibelin's tent was the Bishop of Lydda, the newly elected Patriarch of Jerusalem. He was accompanied by a tall, thin man with thinning gray hair and a long beard, whom Ibelin had seen in the King of England's entourage. The Patriarch introduced his companion as "Robert de Sablé, an Angevin knight close to the King of England."

The latter knight nodded his head curtly before adding, "The *old* King of England, to be precise, and a friend of William Marshal. He spoke well of you, my lord."

Ibelin was pleased to hear mention of Marshal, a man he respected. To Sablé he remarked, "I'm sorry he did not join this crusade. I would have been pleased to see him again—and grateful for his lance."

"King Richard felt his wise head and strategic competence was needed in England. The King's chancellor is an intelligent churchman, but brains alone will not hold a kingdom together, particularly since King Richard's younger brother has distinguished himself only by betraying his father."

"As did King Richard," Ibelin pointed out, his disapproval barbed.

Sablé weighed his head from side to side. "Richard rebelled against his father openly after significant provocation; John did so behind his father's back without any cause but a fear of losing. There is a difference."

Ibelin recognized that was true and nodded, but he still found it hard to believe that Richard had no loyal and competent barons he could trust to keep his brother in check other than Sir William Marshal. Unlike most of his peers, Marshal had firsthand experience of fighting in the Holy Land. His experience with the weather, terrain, and above all, the tactics of the Saracens made him more valuable here, advising his king, than back in England. It was hard not to wonder if the King of England feared being overshadowed by a knight like Marshal. To his guests, however, Ibelin simply offered seats, while asking Georgios to bring wine.

The newly elected Patriarch dropped heavily onto the stool offered, and Ibelin heard the distinctive chinking sound of chain mail. He was apparently wearing a hauberk under his ecclesiastical robes—and who could blame him after seeing his colleague cloven in two at Hattin? The Angevin knight, although older, moved with the controlled strength of a man who'd worn armor all his life, yet he wore a large wooden cross around his neck, and he nodded to Father Michael as if to a brother when the latter, assisting Georgios, brought him wine.

"Before we get to the negotiations with the Saracens, there is something else you should know," Sablé announced. "Ever since my wife died five years ago, I have longed to join the Knights Templar—but first the Old King insisted that I stay with him, and then King Richard urged me to assist him in organizing this crusade. Yesterday King Richard announced that he would allow me to join the Templars, on the condition that the Templars elected me their Grand Master."

There had always been rumors that the Templars could be bought by men of wealth and power. Certainly Gerard de Ridefort's election had seemed highly irregular and stank of undue Lusignan interference—but for a man to go from complete outsider to Grand Master without serving a single day as a Templar knight or officer seemed particularly egregious. Ibelin made no attempt to disguise his disgust, remarking acidly, "I believe the word for that is simony."

"Yes," Sablé agreed, without even wincing. "I agree with you—but to save my honor, should I anger a powerful king and deny the Knights Templar the island of Cyprus? King Richard has told the Templars that he is prepared to sell them Cyprus, with all its wealth and strategic value, in exchange for one hundred thousand bezants—and making me Grand Master."

"Why are you telling me all this?" Ibelin answered, thinking that he would prefer not to know about corruption on this scale.

"Because regardless of what you have every right to think about me, my objective, should I become Grand Master of the Temple, is to serve the interests of Christ, not the King of England. That is why I sought out my brother in Christ, the good Patriarch here," he smiled toward the former Bishop of Lydda, "why I have consulted with the other bishops of the Kingdom of Jerusalem, and why I have come to talk to you. I was impressed, my lord, by your concern for the Christian captives—"

"Thirteen thousand women and children marched off to slavery before my very eyes because I couldn't raise their ransoms!" Ibelin burst out, the fury and anguish in his voice taking both the Patriarch and Sablé by surprise. Ibelin drew a deep breath to calm himself, before adding more softly but no less intensely, "I *saw* them, my lords; I saw those women and children, their faces marked by shock and grief and *terror* of the future. And they saw me sitting beside the

Sultan and his emirs, on a fine horse in glittering armor. If they hate and curse me to this day, I cannot blame them, but I was helpless. Absolutely helpless! The Sultan flatly refused my offer to stand as surety for their ransom. He didn't want me—he wanted those women as rewards for his troops. Only gold would have been a substitute, and I had none.

"Your predecessor, on the other hand," Ibelin turned on the new Patriarch, "slunk out of the Jaffa gate laden with enough gold and jewels to have bought all of them their freedom!" Ibelin paused, gratified by a gasp from the hapless new Patriarch. He softened his tone a little to note, "You were not there, my lord, I do not blame you—but where now are all those precious crosses, croziers, cups, and plates Heraclius 'rescued' from Jerusalem?" The new Patriarch's eyes widened with recognition, and Ibelin continued mercilessly: "When you eat off the plates and serve communion in the chalices, remember the women and children who paid for them with their honor, their freedom, their health, and their very lives!" He spat it out so vehemently that the newly elected Patriarch visibly winced.

"Now tell me," Ibelin turned to the future Templar Master, "What did al-Asadi Qara-Qush answer to our demand for captives?"

"He offered 250 highborn—"

Ibelin let out an expletive so crude that both his companions started, and then competed with one another to assure him that the King of England had reacted almost the same way. "It was agreed that the number of released captives would equal the number of Saracen hostages: twenty-five hundred."

Ibelin looked from one to the other, and they waited tensely. Sablé, personally, had thought it was a good number, and the Patriarch had assured him that the news was good. Only Ibelin didn't look like he thought so. Finally he commented, "Well, it is better than none, and better than 250. Yet it is, I estimate, less than 10 per cent of the Christians in captivity. I know for a fact that thirteen thousand Christians went into slavery at Jerusalem. At Jaffa it was between five and six thousand. We lost seventeen thousand men at Hattin; assuming no more than half of those were killed, that makes another eighty-five hundred men of fighting age. Across the Kingdom, others were taken without grand sieges or surrenders: simply overrun on the roads, seized in their scattered rural manors and homes, like Sir Bartholomew's daughters with their entire households, or dragged from defenseless establishments like the sisters of Sacred Heart at Hebron, and, of course, driven from all the villages along the Jordan valley. I think we can safely assume another five to seven, maybe even ten, thousand Christians were taken in such places. How many does that make? Over thirty-two thousand, in any case. And now, after four years, we may see twenty-five hundred again?" He nodded grimly. "Yes, it is better than nothing, but it will not ease my nightmares—and, my lord Patriarch, it would not make it easier for *me* to eat upon the gold plates Heraclius took with him from Jerusalem."

The former Bishop of Lydda swallowed and assured Ibelin, "I will melt it down and give it to the poor, my lord. I swear it." Ibelin looked at him hard and nodded; at least for the moment, he thought, the churchman was probably utterly sincere.

Aleppo, July 1191

No one owed explanations to a slave. Beatrice was used to that. Yet the tone and urgency of the eunuch in charge of the harem, when he told her to pack her things and come with him, alarmed her nevertheless. She did not dare ask him what was going on, nor did she protest that she had next to nothing to pack. The gown and surcoat she had been wearing when she was captured had long since been turned into rags for scrubbing floors. The shoes she had worn then had been lost, along with her stockings. Her veils had been used to gag her while they raped her, and then to wipe the blood and semen from between her thighs before being discarded. All her other possessions were "gifts" from her new masters: discarded bits of clothing, used sandals, broken combs. The bundle she reported with was so pathetic that it earned a sneering look from the eunuch as he shoved her out the door into the hands of a Mamluke.

Beatrice quailed. It had been soldiers who raped her, and the sight of Saracens in armor brought back all those horrible memories. Her mouth went dry, and her knees started trembling so violently she had to steady herself against the wall. She wished she had some means of covering her face and body, but slaves did not rate hijabs, much less abayas or any other form of honorable cover.

Fortunately these horsemen were not currently in the mood for recreation, and this stinking Christian slave woman with shorn head and callused hands was hardly appealing, anyway. They could afford pretty young whores from a reputable establishment. Meanwhile, they were intent on bullying Imad ad-Din's steward into surrendering his other *faranj* slave.

"He was enslaved when Edessa fell. He's not one of the captives from Hattin."

"So what?" the Mamlukes retorted. "Our orders were to round up as many *faranj* as possible. No one said anything about them being from Hattin."

"The man must be over seventy," the steward muttered disapprovingly. "What good is he to you?"

"He doesn't have to be any good to us. Just bring him!"

The fact that Imad ad-Din's haughty steward capitulated before this arrogant soldier made Beatrice more frightened than ever, and when only a few moments later the gardener was shoved out the door, stumbling on the shallow steps, she caught his arm as much to comfort herself as to stop him from falling.

"What is happening?" he asked, baffled and no less frightened than she. "What is going on?"

"I don't know, father," Beatrice answered in French. Her fear was echoed as she muttered a second time, "I don't know."

The Mamlukes bound their hands together and tied a rope around their waists, and then led them behind their horses. They were pulled, stumbling and dazed, to a large administrative building near the center of the city, and there shoved into a vaulted chamber already crowded with other slaves.

As her eyes adjusted to the dark, Beatrice registered that everyone in this room was speaking French. The Mamluke's words echoed in her head: they had orders to round up *faranj*—Franks. Although she dared not guess the purpose, Beatrice was seized with hope: maybe, just maybe, her children would also be here! Her sister certainly was, and already Constance was pushing her way through the crowd. The sisters embraced warmly, and then Beatrice introduced Constance to Father Francis. Constance kissed his hands, while Beatrice asked if she knew what was going on.

Constance shook her head. "It was all so sudden. I had no warning at all."

"Your daughters?"

Constance shook her head again, before focusing on her sister's companion. "Father, please hear my confession! Please! I have—"

Father Francis took Constance and gently led her toward a more secluded corner, leaving Beatrice in the center of the room searching for her sons. It was four years since she had seen them last. Would she even recognize them? Bart would be fifteen now, Amalric fourteen, and Joscelyn, her baby, would be ten! She could not imagine him as a ten-year-old. Dear God, she prayed, let them be here. Let me find them. But then she reminded herself that she did not know the purpose of this assembly. Maybe they were being collected only to be slaughtered as the Templars and Hospitallers had been— bound and helpless! She immediately amended her prayer, begging God to bring them here *only if it would not lead to greater harm and suffering.*

Another "batch" of captives arrived and were thrust into the chamber with curses and shouting. Some of the newcomers trampled on those in the room in their hurry to escape the blows and insults hurled after them. One youth, who stumbled and fell as he was thrust into the room, instantly curled into a ball, his hands over his head to protect it from the blows he expected. The gesture spoke volumes about what he had endured, and Beatrice felt her heart go out to him. The woman he'd tripped over tapped him on the shoulder, and although they were too far away for Beatrice to hear her words, she could read the woman's gestures and expression: she was assuring the youth he had nothing to fear. The boy tentatively lifted his head to look at the strange woman, and Beatrice felt as if her heart had been ripped out of her breast. "Bart!" she screamed. "Bart!"

He flinched, hunched down, and looked around to see who was calling. His pose was so defensive that it made Beatrice weep. Bart had never been a timid child; the firstborn and heir, he'd tended more to arrogance and impudence. Beatrice stepped over people, pushing and shoving, utterly unconscious and indifferent to their looks of sympathy—for there was not one person in that chamber who did not sympathize. As she got closer, Bart recognized her at last, and he struggled to his feet. "Mother?" he asked in disbelief. "Mother? Is it really you? Can you have survived?"

He had hardly grown in four years. His body was skeletal and his legs were strangely misshapen: the knees turned out and the ankles bent awkwardly inwards. Although the effect was bowed legs, the deformity could hardly have come from riding, as there were no muscles on his legs at all. As Beatrice took him into her arms, she found herself screaming silently in inner rage. He was all skin and bones. He was as fragile and light as a bird. The youth who should have been the heir to a fiefdom, a knight-in-making, was nothing but a stunted boy, as bony and awkward as a street urchin. "Oh, Bart! What have they done to you? What have they done to you?" she asked, more rhetorically than literally.

"I was sold to a carpetmaker, Mother," Bart answered soberly. "I make carpets." As he spoke he looked down at his hands in shame. "And you, Mother? I saw—I saw—"

She put her finger to his lips and shook her head. "Don't speak of it. We both want to forget. It's over. Come, I've found your Aunt Constance and—"

"Mama! Mama!" A strong, piercing voice reached them from the doorway, where more prisoners were been herded in. Before Beatrice had time to orient herself, she was swept into an exuberant clasp by a youth so strong and tall that Beatrice was disoriented. Unlike his elder brother, Amalric was clearly in the best of health; he'd grown inches since his capture and was tanned and muscular. "Bart!" he gasped out as he saw and recognized his brother. He eased his embrace of his mother to gape in horror at his elder brother.

Bart looked down, ashamed, but his brother growled, "They'll pay for this, Bart! They'll pay for what they've done to you and Mama!"

"How can you make them pay?" Bart lashed back, his back hunched and his face sullen. "You're a slave! You no less than me and Mother!"

"Not for long!" Amalric answered, and before his mother could warn him not to assume anything, he declared exuberantly, "Haven't you heard? Acre has fallen to the Kings of France and England! They came with hundreds of ships and thousands of men and mighty siege engines! They took Acre, and the Sultan has agreed to free twenty-five hundred Frankish captives in exchange for the lives of the garrison! We're on our way to freedom! And the first thing I'm going to do is take service with the King of France, and then I'm going to kill Saracens— more Saracens than anyone else on earth!" Amalric declared emphatically. The hatred in his vow made his mother shudder.

Acre, August 15, 1191

Berengaria was finding it very difficult to decide what to wear. On the one hand, this would be one of her first public appearances before the entire Christian army as Queen of England—but on the other hand it was a solemn religious event, since no relic was more sacred than the True Cross, stained with the blood of Christ. Not to mention the fact that as a young bride who had been given so little opportunity to be with her husband, she was very anxious to please him most of all. Her Spanish ladies were fretting and fluttering about, as concerned with their own appearance as hers, with the exception of Doña Esclarmonde, of course. The latter would have preferred to see her charge in a convent rather than wearing a crown, and was piously advocating a sackcloth as the only attire suitable for such an occasion.

Berengaria was relieved by the appearance of the Queen of Sicily, dressed in state robes and wearing her crown. "We must hurry, Ria," Joanna Plantagenet urged, already familiar with her sister-in-law's tendency to be late to everything. "Today, no matter how much he loves you, my brother cannot afford to wait for you. The Sultan has agreed to the exchange at noon, and even a moment's delay on our part would be an excuse to say we violated the terms of the agreement."

Berengaria hated being rushed, but she was equally conscious of the need not to displease her husband. While gesturing irritably for her ladies to bring her coronation gown, she protested to Joanna, "Salah ad-Din has postponed the date three times already! I don't understand why my lord husband is so tolerant of his excuses!"

"Because so much is at stake. It was the garrison of Acre that agreed to the terms, and the Sultan made it clear he finds them excessive and difficult to fulfill. He only grudgingly agreed to honor them out of respect for his men, who are now our hostages. Richard feels it is only fair to give him more time to meet the obligations his subordinates committed him to."

Berengaria cast Joanna a peeved look that expressed her frustration with her sister-in-law's impeccable logic. Sometimes Berengaria wished the woman would just be irrational and emotional, like normal women. Today, for example, she did not want to think about all the good reasons for the delays; she wanted to complain a little without complaining about her husband. Richard Plantagenet was everything a woman could dream of in a husband. He was highborn, handsome, rich beyond measure, brave, educated, witty, and courteous—and almost always busy with someone or something else. Berengaria sighed and picked up her mirror again.

Joanna at once swept over and took it from her, placing it firmly face down on her table. "You look *lovely*, Ria. All you need now is your veils and crown. Then we must go."

Berengaria accepted her sister-in-law's injunction, and snapped her fingers at her ladies for her embroidered veils. "Tell me, Joanna, what do you make of the Marquis de Montferrat's refusal to be here today?"

"Well, the important thing is that he returned the French King's half of the hostages—otherwise the deal could not have gone through at all." To the scandal of all of Christendom, Philip of France had announced his intention to return to France shortly after the surrender of Acre. Everyone, including his own nobles and bishops, had been dumbfounded. He pleaded illness, said he'd fulfilled his pilgrimage vows, blathered about his infant son being vulnerable, fussed about Acre being a sufficient conquest, and generally made himself the object of contempt. Acre was an important staging ground for the reconquest of the Holy Land, but it was not and never could be the final objective of this massive military undertaking. Even the poorest and most illiterate soldier and camp follower knew that. No one believed the King of France was so stupid as to have spent the resources of his kingdom for the sake of taking a city with no direct relation to Christ at all. So speculation about why he *really* wanted to go home had been rampant ever since his announcement a month earlier. Some claimed he wanted to regulate the complex inheritance of the Count of Flanders, others that he intended to remarry, and still others—among them the Plantagenets—that he planned to attack the Angevin Empire while King Richard was in the Holy Land.

Whatever his reasons, his departure put Conrad de Montferrat in an awkward position, since the King of France's support for his claim to the crown of Jerusalem had been an essential counterweight to the King of England's unstinting support for King Guy. Philip had ostentatiously accorded Montferrat the courtesy owed a king and had even shared his booty with him—including 1250 of the hostages held as a guarantee that the Sultan would fulfill the terms of the surrender agreement. When Philip of France departed the siege camp, Conrad de Montferrat had taken those 1250 hostages with him to Tyre. It had taken two embassies of high-ranking dignitaries to convince him to return the hostages so that they could be exchanged today for the captives, the ransom money, and the True Cross. But no words could persuade Montferrat to return to the siege of Acre himself.

"Lady Eschiva says he is not pleased with the agreement my lord husband struck with Philip of France before the latter's shameful departure," Berengaria remarked, testing the reaction of her sister-in-law. She was sitting stiffly on her stool while her ladies affixed her crown over her veils, pinning the latter carefully in place to help ensure that it did not slip.

"I daresay he was not, since the agreement recognized Guy de Lusignan as King of Jerusalem as long as he lived, making Conrad no more than his heir. Conrad cannot bring himself to bow to Guy, and that is the main reason he removed himself to Tyre. Nor did it please him that my brother named Guy's brother Geoffrey Count of Jaffa and Ascalon—should those coastal cities and their environs ever be recovered. Conrad rightly recognizes that Geoffrey de Lusignan is a far more formidable opponent than Guy. No one takes Guy seriously anymore, but Geoffrey is not a man to be ignored."

"But why not Aimery? I felt most distressed for our friend Eschiva that her husband was overlooked in the settlement." Berengaria had come to the point that interested her most, and her tone was more impassioned than before. "Sir Aimery has been in Outremer longer than either of his brothers. He was a good constable, so everyone says, and he suffered captivity with his brother after Hattin. Why wasn't he even mentioned in the settlement?" The English crown now fixed in place, Berengaria turned to look at her sister-in-law as she asked this question earnestly.

Joanna was used to Berengaria asking her questions she could answer, but this was one she couldn't. She was as baffled as her sister-in-law, and she shook her head. "I don't know. I honestly don't know. I share your sympathy for dear Eschiva. She has endured so much—and always the poor relation, always 'in waiting' on someone else, always living on charity from her brother-in-law or her uncle. It seems most unfair, particularly as Aimery de Lusignan strikes me as both braver than Guy and wiser than Geoffrey. Geoffrey, you know, was implicated in that horrible attack on my mother! According to her, Guy wielded the lance that killed the Earl of Salisbury from behind, but Geoffrey was in command."

"I've never heard of this!" Berengaria declared, wide-eyed. "What happened?"

"Not now! We must hurry!" Joanna countered, taking her sister-in-law by the arm, to rush her out of her chamber and down to the courtyard where their horses and escort were waiting.

Berengaria and Joanna descended by a covered stairway to a cobbled courtyard, where their escort of Poitevin knights waited impatiently for their arrival. The escort was commanded by Aimery de Lusignan, and Eschiva had gone ahead of the queens so she could have a few minutes with her husband.

At the sight of the queens, Aimery helped his wife into her saddle, and the other men started mounting, while grooms led the queens' mares forward. Berengaria had a very pretty white palfrey, a gift from King Richard shortly after their arrival in Acre. She was a captured Arab with a dish face, very dainty feet, and beautiful manners. She never kicked or bit, but waited as docilely as a dog for Berengaria to mount. Joanna's mare was a pretty chestnut, less eye-catching but lively and intelligent. Aimery swung himself into his own saddle and, riding over to the queens, respectfully asked them to fall in on either side of him. Joanna answered that she would instead ride behind with Eschiva, and in this order they rode out of the gate.

Once in the street, Joanna was alarmed by how empty the city seemed. "Are we very late?" she asked Eschiva.

"No, not very. We should still make the muster in time." As she spoke Eschiva glanced toward the steeple of St. Mark's in the Venetian quarter, which rang the hours like a ship's clock, marking each half-hour. "It only just struck seven bells, a half-hour before Sext." Ahead of them Aimery picked up a trot, and they urged their horses forward to keep up with him.

Despite Richard of England's efforts and expense to rebuild Acre's shattered defenses, the city still had the shabby feel of a garrison town. Neither the Saracen nor the crusader army had come with the intention of making it a pleasant or habitable place; for them it was simply a means to an end. Although the burghers of Acre had appealed to the King of France for the restoration of their property, and the French King had ordered it done, the restoration had been on the condition that they billet troops with them as long as the army was present. That meant that the houses, shops, and markets were used overwhelmingly by men who had no interest in their substance or state of repair.

Men pretty much tossed their rubbish where they wanted, pissed where they wanted, and scratched their names on any inviting surface in a perverse desire to "immortalize" themselves. The owners had much to complain about, and found little sympathy after the principle of property restoration had been established. In these circumstances, they did not send for their wives or children, waiting instead for the plague of crusaders to move on. As a result, the only women in Acre were the the queens and their ladies, the laundresses with the army, and whores—lots of whores. There were so many of the latter, in fact, that Joanna and Berengaria were usually discomfited when they ventured into the streets of Acre. Today, however, even the whores were gone.

As the queens emerged from the city gate, it became clear where everyone had gone. The entire Frankish army was drawn up in ranks and files under the bright, fluttering banners of their leaders. The clergy in their vestments (but barefoot as a symbol of humility) were drawn up in processional order behind the army, and the women clustered around the fringes in an excited, jabbering mass. At front and center of the army, the banner of England flapped lazily from a converted mast mounted on a mobile platform. This placed the English banner above the others, including those of France, Austria, and Jerusalem itself. Berengaria felt a little uneasy about the latter, since the crosses represented Christ and the Apostles, while Joanna was reminded that the Duke of Austria had already made quite a fuss about his banner being tossed down from the walls of Acre after its fall. Because Richard and Philip had agreed to share the spoils of all they captured fifty-fifty, acknowledging the claims of the Germans was awkward. On the other hand, the Germans had been at the siege longer than either the French or the English, and the Duke of Austria was offended and had declared his intention to return to the West as a result. Joanna did not think her husband would have been so abrasive or insensitive to another nobleman's pride—but then, William wouldn't have led assaults on enemy beaches as Richard had done at Limassol, nor would he have fired crossbows at the defenders of Acre from a litter. Richard was like no other king, she concluded; he made his own rules.

By the time the queens reached the cluster of men around King Richard that included King Guy, the Dukes of Burgundy and Austria, and the other senior nobles, the bells were ringing Sext from all across Acre. That there were bells to ring was little short of a miracle. The Arabs had trashed the churches on taking control of the city four years earlier—disfiguring the crucifixes, smashing the statues of the saints, burning or hacking the altars, and melting down the bells. On learning of the latter, the bellmakers' guild in Tyre had called all their members together and set to work forging two dozen bells, which had been sent to Acre and installed only the previous week.

While the bells were ringing, the Frankish leaders scanned the heights surrounding the city, on which the Sultan's army was still encamped, searching for signs of movement. The common soldiers did the same. Now and again someone thought they saw something, calling out or pointing only to be disappointed. The sun was very hot and seemed to grow hotter as they waited in the open, while the flies were increasingly bothersome. The horses stamped, shook their heads, and swished their tails in growing annoyance.

King Richard's face was so grim that Berengaria did not want to draw attention to herself. He looked as if he were about to explode, and she had heard terrible things about his temper. If nothing else, his father had in a rage inadvertently brought about the murder of an archbishop, and that was a terrible thing indeed.

Her husband's voice barked, and Berengaria started. A moment later, Humphrey de Toron rode up beside the English King and bowed from the waist. Berengaria could not hear what her husband said, but Toron bowed again and then spurred his horse across the empty plain, galloping alone toward the enemy camp.

"That is very brave of him," Berengaria noted to Aimery in a low voice, so as not to draw attention to herself.

Aimery snorted and then cast her a sideways glance. "Humphrey has nothing to fear. He made very good friends with the Sultan's secretary while in captivity, and he speaks Arabic like a native. Some claim he converted—"

"Holy Cross! Surely not?" Berengaria crossed herself at the mere thought of having dined and conversed with a man who might have abrogated the True Faith to follow the false prophet Mohammed.

"No, he didn't go that far," Aimery conceded, shaking his head. "But he admires much about their culture, their food, medicine, literature. He flatters them with that and they like him for it—like a poodle." That was not a compliment.

"You do not like my lord of Toron," Berengaria concluded.

Aimery shrugged. "I might have liked him more if he hadn't been playing chess with Imad ad-Din in fragrant gardens, waited on by slave girls, while I rotted in a dungeon," Aimery admitted acidly. Berengaria mentally noted something else she had to ask Eschiva about at the right time.

This time was obviously not right, however. Several of the lesser commanders had lost patience and rode forward to find out what was going on. Berengaria hadn't yet learned to recognize all the men in her husband's service, much less the French, German, and Italian crusaders, but she did recognize the Count of Champagne and the Lord of Ibelin.

Champagne, she knew, was in the odd position of being nephew to both Philip of France and Richard of England, because his mother was Eleanor of Aquitaine's daughter by Louis VII of France. Champagne had come out to Outremer in the French King's service, but had transferred his allegiance to the King of England because he'd run out of funds and the Plantagenet had been willing to advance him a loan, while the Capet had not. Berengaria knew, furthermore, that Champagne was a devout crusader, seriously concerned about the recovery of Jerusalem, and no one had been more shocked and outraged by the French King's defection than the young Count of Champagne. He had personally come to Berengaria to express his shame at his uncle's ignoble decision to return to France, and although Berengaria was alert to men trying to win her husband's favor by pleasing her, his distress had struck her as very genuine. In fact, if she hadn't been so mesmerized by her husband, she would have found herself very attracted to the Count of Champagne. He was in his early twenties, after all, a slender, elegant man with fine blond hair and a sunburned face.

Ibelin, in contrast, although tall and lean, was dark of hair and skin and looked all of his forty years. His eyes were sunken in his regular face, and he had a dramatic gray streak running from his right temple. He was a handsome man, in his way, Berengaria conceded, but she still couldn't overcome her initial mistrust of him, instilled by the story of how he'd taken his stepdaughter away from her lawful husband just so he could make the Marquis of Montferrat King of Jerusalem.

Her husband was talking to Ibelin now, and she wished she could have heard what they were saying. Whatever it was, it did not make her husband happy. His stallion was swinging his haunches from side to side, his ears flat back on his head, his tail lashing. Berengaria knew enough about horses to realize the rider's fury had been transmitted to the horse.

Berengaria was beginning to get very hot, and she didn't like the way she was sweating in her expensive coronation robes. Furthermore, the weight of the crown was becoming very uncomfortable, and her brow was so wet with sweat that it was starting to trickle down behind her ears. It was obvious that something had gone wrong—again—and she wondered how much longer they were going to wait out here in the sun. She glanced at Aimery and then twisted a little to look at Joanna. The latter shook her head in a mute warning to do and say nothing.

At last Humphrey de Toron emerged out of the distance and cantered back to the waiting host. As he drew in opposite the King of England, it was clear from his face alone that he brought bad news. Berengaria risked urging her horse nearer so she could hear him as he announced, "I'm sorry, my lord King. The

Sultan of Egypt and Damascus regrets the inconvenience, but he has still not been able to find the designated twenty-five hundred captives or the gold—"

"Does he take me for a fool?" the King of England burst out. "He's been playing me out for three weeks now, and all he has to offer me are lies! Damned lies!" Richard swung his horse around and galloped straight through his host, leaving it to his commanders to pass the word.

The King of England was not the only one outraged and distressed by this latest betrayal. Throughout the city of Acre, priests had prepared a procession to honor the return of the True Cross. Men from above the Artic Circle (like Haakon Magnussen) and from Scotland, England, France, and Flanders, men from the Rhineland and the Palatinate, from Normandy, Lombardy, and Sicily—indeed, from every part of Christendom—had assembled this day to receive the Cross on which Christ had been crucified. The ransom money went to their leaders, but the Cross was theirs. Just as Christ had died for their sins, His Cross belonged to all of them. It had been the thought of the Saracens insulting, beating, and urinating on the Cross that had motivated many of them to leave their homes and take up arms against the infidel. The promised return of the Cross had compensated them emotionally for being denied the right to plunder Acre. But now the Cross was denied them, too. It had been promised today, and it had not come. The Saracens had played a trick on all of them, sitting up on their hill and laughing as the Frankish host waited gullibly in the burning August sun. The more they thought about how the Sultan had played their leaders for fools, the angrier the Christian soldiers became—with the enemy and with their own leadership.

The mood was increasingly explosive. Brawls broke out across the city, and the shouts of angry men hurling abuse punctuated the night. Ibelin and his men were billeted near the customs house close to the harbor, and he set an extra watch, both as protection and to keep his men out of trouble. After his second inspection he returned to the hall, and his eyes swept across the scene of men drinking in sullen silence. Sir Bartholomew was missing.

"Where's Sir Bartholomew?" he asked, in a sharp voice loud enough to wake them all from their individual thoughts. No one had an answer. "When was the last time anyone saw him?" he asked next, receiving worthless answers such as "He was at the muster." "Damn it!" Ibelin shouted. "No one lost more today than Sir Bartholomew. We need to find him!"

Sir Galvin roused himself from his wine-soaked lethargy with a growl. "I think I might know where he might be," he confessed, shaking his head to clear it of drunkenness.

Sir Galvin led his lord to a small and rather poor Augustine establishment only a few blocks away, but they found the door locked and barred. They pounded on it, but got no answer. Sir Galvin stood stupidly on the doorstep, swearing he was sure this was where Sir Bartholomew said he was going.

Apparently all they could do now was comb the streets, the taverns, and the wharves, Ibelin though resentfully. Resigning himself to a sleepless night of searching, he took a deep breath and was about to turn away when the monastery door cracked and a feeble voice called out, "Sirs? Can we help you?" It was hardly surprising that the monks were keeping a very low profile in Acre tonight. Few monks had risked returning to the city at all, and the Augustines of Acre were notoriously reclusive.

"We're looking for one of my knights, Sir Bartholomew d'Auber."

"Are you the Lord of Ibelin?"

"I am."

"Come!"

Ibelin exchanged a look with Sir Galvin and followed the monk's invitation into the church. The monk closed and bolted the door behind the visitors before leading them to a cloister. Tall cypress trees loomed up in the corners of the small garth, and the leaves of citrus trees clustered around the well at the center rustled in the light breeze. There were no lanterns or torches, and it was hard to see where they were going. Once Sir Galvin (still a little drunk) tripped as his foot fell into a hole in the pavement, and the monk apologized, explaning, "The Saracens tore up all the graves in the walkway—anything with a cross on it—and threw the bones somewhere." Sir Galvin crossed himself, and Ibelin shook his head in sympathy.

The monk led them to a bench on the far side of the cloister where a man sat hunched over, his elbows on his knees, sobbing into his hands. It was Sir Bartholomew.

The old knight did not seem at all surprised by the arrival of his lord or his friend. Nor did he stop weeping. Even as Balian laid an arm over his shoulders and Sir Galvin laid a hand on his knee, he did not react in any way. He just kept sobbing, his tears falling on the pavement between his worn boots like heavy drops of rain.

Balian had no idea how long they sat like that. Eventually the tears dried up and the sobs stopped, but Sir Bartholomew did not straighten or lift his head. "I'm nothing but a broken old man," he told Balian. "A worthless, broken old man."

Ibelin wanted to assure him that this was not the case, but before he could formulate his thoughts into words, Sir Bartholomew continued. "I intend to stay here, my lord. I don't want to set foot outside these walls ever again. Maybe if I spend the rest of my days in prayer, I will learn to forgive God what he has done to my daughters and grandchildren. Maybe if I do nothing but fast and pray, I will learn to stop cursing Him. Maybe."

Ibelin and Sir Galvin exchanged a glance over Sir Bartholomew's back, and then Ibelin turned to see if the monks had overheard the words.

Instead he heard a loud hammering at the church door and raised voices.

"I'm looking for the Lord of Ibelin!" an imperious voice shouted through the heavy wood as one of the monks hurried by.

Ibelin stood, ordering Sir Galvin to stay with Sir Bartholomew a while longer. "Let him stay the night here, if that's his wish. We can come again tomorrow or the next day to find out what he really wants."

Sir Galvin nodded, while the angry man demanding Ibelin pounded more furiously on the outside door.

Ibelin reached the nave of the church as the monk cracked open the door to ask what was going on. "The King of England commands the Lord of Ibelin's presence at once! I've been looking all over for him!" the angry messenger shouted at the innocent monk.

"I'm here," Ibelin answered, slipping out of the church door and back into the streets. By now there was a lurid light over part of the town, suggesting that someone had set something on fire. The shouting coming from that section of town was both angry and frantic, a combination of aggression and panic.

"We can ride double!" The man who'd fetched him indicated a tethered horse that was already skittish from the smell of smoke and the flickering light rising from the fires to the northwest.

Ibelin did not object. He could well imagine it had taken more time to find him than the King of England expected, and he was likely to be displeased. Fortunately, the horse the messenger was riding was a sturdy and powerful mount capable of carrying two, at least the short distance to the royal palace.

Torches were burning in abundance at the king's headquarters, and there seemed to be more people coming and going than usual—but that was hardly surprising given the circumstances. Ibelin's escort was apparently well known, however, for they were readily granted admission and were soon pounding up the shallow limestone stairs two at a time. Ibelin was led down a long corridor, and finally at the end of a hall, double doors were thrown open and he was waved inside.

As was to be expected, the King of England was not alone, but nor was this a council of war similar to the one held in the French King's tent at the time of the surrender of Acre. There were less than twenty men here, and nearly half of them were prelates. Of the commanders, Burgundy, Champagne, Leicester, and the Lusignans stood out, as well as Sablé, already wearing the robes of the Templar Master, and the Hospitallers' new Master, Garnier de Nablus, as well. Curiously, Humphrey de Toron was also here, looking like a whipped dog, Balian thought.

As Ibelin entered, the Plantagenet was prowling the room like a caged lion, growling and snarling, while the bishops sat on edge looking even more nervous and ill at ease than the fighting men. At the sight of Ibelin, the Lionheart stopped and fired words at him as readily as he might have fired a crossbow. "Ibelin! We've been waiting for you. I want your opinion. Is the Sultan's claim that he can't find twenty-five hundred Frankish captives credible?"

"Not in the least," Ibelin answered without hesitation, and he was gratified to see both Garnier de Nablus and Robert de Sablé nod agreement. "I estimate that more than thirty thousand Franks were taken captive after Hattin. While they will be dispersed across the Sultan's territories, and some will have been sold to the Bedouins, it should not be difficult to pull together a tenth of that number."

The King of England snapped at the embarrassed-looking English bishops. "See! Just what I told you! Now," he swung back on Ibelin, "what happens to the captives if we kill the hostages?"

Taken aback by the abruptness of the question, Ibelin started slightly. He looked around at the other faces; all gazed back at him expectantly. Rather than answering immediately, he asked cautiously, "My lord King? Did I understand you correctly? You intend to slaughter the hostages?"

"I haven't decided yet," the Plantagenet growled back. "But it's a possibility. First of all, I don't like being treated like a fool who can be cheated, tricked, and mocked. The Sultan needs to learn that Richard Plantagenet is a man he has to take seriously. Second, I can't waste any more time here in Acre; I need to open the campaign to retake Jerusalem, and that means taking the army down the coast. I can't spare men to guard twenty-five hundred Saracen fighting men on the march, and leaving them here would be inviting a Saracen attack at my back to free them and regain Acre. Third, there is the small issue of the slaughter of 250 helpless Templars and Hospitallers, which should not be completely ignored as if we did not care about our own men. Fourth, the siege of Acre has cost Christendom heavily. I've been told that no less than six archbishops, including the Archbishop of Canterbury, twelve bishops, forty counts, and upwards of five hundred other noblemen, have died in the siege of Acre, while thousands of good Christians of humble birth have given their lives. Last—and most important—because of those losses and the Sultan's broken promises, those men out there are furious and need an outlet for their anger." He pointed toward the windows lit up by the orange glow of fire, although it appeared a darker shade now, as if the fires were being put out. "We don't want the troops to take out their fury on the innocent people of Acre, do we? No, we don't," he answered himself, "and we don't want them killing each other, either. I say the rightful outlet for their anger is the Saracens, who not only pray to a false God but follow a deceitful and duplicitous Sultan. Now, my lord of Ibelin, I want an answer from you: what will the Sultan do to the captives if we kill the hostages?"

After the arguments just listed for the execution of the hostages, Ibelin was amazed that the English King had given any thought at all to the fate of the captives. For that he was grateful.

"Well?" the English King demanded impatiently.

"My lord, the bulk of the captives are women and children, and they are by and large the property of various subjects of the Sultan. He will have had to pay compensation to their respective owners to take away their property. If they have lost their value to him as a means of regaining the hostages, he will be anxious to avoid the expense of paying for them; he will return them to their respective owners."

"You don't think he would slaughter them in revenge?"

Ibelin thought hard, knowing how much hung on what he was about to say. When he answered, he glanced at Toron. "I'm not saying the Sultan is not capable of such an act of barbarism. He burned the women and children of his Sudanese guard alive in their homes—and then broke his word to their men as well, slaughtering them after they had surrendered their arms and left Cairo—"

"You say that about a man who treated you so chivalrously!" Humphrey de Toron burst out angrily. "Tell King Richard how he treated *you* after *you* broke your word to *him!*" Toron added challengingly.

The crusaders swung their attention from one "poulain" to the other, evidently entertained by the tension between Ibelin and Toron.

"I doubt the King of England is terribly interested in the courtesies the Sultan showed a princess of the Greek Imperial family," Ibelin answered evenly. "The point is that the Sultan is capable of slaughtering women and children and of butchering helpless prisoners. But he is also capable of restraint. It depends entirely on where he sees his self-interest in a particular situation. My estimate, my lord," Ibelin turned his attention away from Toron to again address the English King, "is that Salah ad-Din would rather restore the slaves to their owners and spare his treasury the costs of compensation—but I could be wrong."

Richard Plantagenet met his eyes and held them for a moment. Then he nodded grimly. "We execute them tomorrow in full view of Salah ad-Din's army.

We'll need troops to hold back any attempt by Salah ad-Din's troops to rescue them, and we'll need volunteers to carry out the executions. I will not *order* any man to kill unarmed prisoners." The last remark was directed at his bishops, who were shaking their heads and looking distressed.

The response of the fighting men was more relieved than censorious. "I don't think you'll lack for volunteers," Burgundy remarked dryly, and Leicester nodded agreement.

"And you, my lord of Ibelin, where will you be?" King Richard asked provocatively.

"On my knees praying that I am right, your grace."

Chapter 15

Coast of the Levant,
August/September 1191

THE FRANKISH ARMY, HAVING ASSEMBLED OUTSIDE of Acre, set off in marching order to regain Jaffa on the eve of the feast of Saint Bartholomew. Neither Balian nor Sir Galvin had been able to dissuade Sir Bartholomew from remaining behind in the monastery of St. Sebastian at Acre. He was, after all, over seventy, and he deserved his rest. Balian would have felt easier, however, had he believed the old knight would indeed be happier praying rather than fighting. . . .

The King of England had taken considerable care in the deployment of his polyglot troops. The King's standard, raised on a mast and set on a wheeled platform covered with iron (to protect it from Greek fire) was guarded by an elite squadron of knights and marked the center of the entire force. The battalions, made up of men speaking the same tongue under their respective bannerets, marched in blocks, with the archers and footmen on the landward (eastward) side, protecting the knights, who in turn protected the baggage train, which trundled along the coastal road with the sea on their right to the west.

This was a sensible modification of the typical marching formation of the Franks. Prior to Hattin, the knights in Outremer rode in the middle of a square, completely surrounded by infantry. But that formation presupposed ready access to provisions at regular intervals and hence no need for a cumbersome baggage train. With the loss of the Kingdom and so the castles and cities at which the army had replenished supplies, they needed to take their provisions with them. This circumstance dictated the English King's formation, and Ibelin was impressed that King Richard also ordered his fleet to sail down the coast within sight and signal range of the land army.

The Templars and Hospitallers alternated in the positions of vanguard and rear guard. Immediately following the van came the Angevin and Gascon troops of the English King, then King Guy and his brothers with the Poitevins, followed by the English and Normans, who usually defended the royal standard. The Italians and natives of Outremer came next, led by the remaining barons of the lost Kingdom, including Ibelin, Sidon, Haifa, Caesarea, Hebron, and Galilee. The larger part of the second half of the army was composed of the French and Flemings, supplemented by the smaller contingents of Danes, Frisians, Czechs, Hungarians, and what was left of the Germans.

On the second day of the march, the army had to pass through a defile where the mountains pressed in on the road for roughly two miles, narrowing it to the width of a single cart or three knights side by side. Because they were familiar with the route and knew this was coming, the commanders from Outremer interspersed the knights and infantry with the baggage, so that each cart was protected by on average six knights and a two dozen infantry.

They were already several miles beyond this bottleneck when Haifa, commanding the last block of troops from Outremer, saw the French knights following him suddenly reverse direction and start galloping to the north again. He sent word of what had happened to the Normans around the standard, and one of the Norman knights galloped forward to inform the King of England, who was riding with the van. In less than a half-hour, the King of England came galloping past the rest of the army with forty knights of his mobile reserve.

The knights and men of Outremer held to their positions doggedly and continued marching southwards. They were relieved when a couple hours later the English King and his knights trotted back toward the front of the column, looking no less numerous than when they'd galloped north. It was only when they made camp that night that they learned how close the Saracens had come to cutting the army in two. It seemed that the French under the Duke of Burgundy had sent their knights through the defile first, followed by the infantry and then the baggage. The result was that the knights got far ahead of the infantry, and the baggage train, lacking leadership, snarled itself hopelessly. Saracen scouts had reported the situation, and Turkish cavalry had swept down upon the French baggage train. The slaughter and plunder had been going on for some time before the French leadership realized what was happening and sent knights back to extricate the baggage.

Ibelin was not present at the meeting between the King of England and the Duke of Burgundy, but the latter returned to his troops flushed and grim-faced. Thereafter the formation was better maintained, and the army moved forward in short, easy stages. Which is not to say the march was uneventful. They were frequently harassed by small bands of Saracens that darted out from the larger mass of enemy forces shadowing the Frankish host. The main body of the enemy moved at the same pace as the Franks just a few miles further inland, but light Turkish cavalry took advantage of their mobility to launch repeated niggling attacks. They employed the typical Turkish tactic of riding within bow range and firing off their missiles, only to spin about and gallop away if anyone challenged them.

King Richard gave very strict orders not to break ranks, and warned that any knight who disobeyed would be stripped of his horse and spurs and forced to walk with the baggage train. The archers were given permission to return fire, but only if the enemy was well within range and if they could keep up with their troop. This meant that if they stopped to fire, they had to run to catch up again. The result was an army that kept plodding forward with arrows sticking out of the armor of the knights, the trappers of the horses, and the shields of the infantry. From above, it would have looked like a giant caterpillar bristling with stiff hairs.

Of course, some men were poorly armored or unlucky enough to take an arrow in a vulnerable spot. Furthermore, the farther the army advanced, the more the enemy risked coming in close. At times they fired at ranges that could penetrate even the best armor. Casualties started to mount, but King Richard repeated his orders not to be provoked. It helped that he had also provided for mobile first aid in the form of wagons with medical supplies manned by brothers of the Hospital, and that the seriously injured were taken out to one of the galleys that served as a floating hospital.

Ibelin noted, however, that the attacks never came near to the intensity of the attacks on his rear guard during the march to Hattin. By comparison, these were nothing more than annoying attempts at provocation. The great mass of the army was more tormented by marching in the heat of a Palestinian summer than by the Saracens. Quite a few of the crusaders succumbed to heat stroke and had to be carried on the baggage carts until they recovered, often to the derision of the local men. At night, when they camped, it was the tarantulas and scorpions that plagued the army. Once the crusaders discovered tarantulas could be scared away with loud noises, there was never a peaceful night there-after. The men of Outremer, on the other hand, were much more disturbed by the density of the scrub brush that had grown over the road as they approached

Caesarea. Remembering how busy the road had been and the traffic it had once supported, its present state of neglect depressed them.

Caesarea itself was even worse. Unlike Acre, Salah ad-Din had not placed a garrison here, and so there had been no attempt to preserve the substance of the city. On the contrary, the Sultan had demolished the walls and towers and set fire to the houses, leaving them gutted and filled with blowing ashes and charred, collapsed beams. Although the Roman aqueduct that brought water nine miles from the Crocodile River to the city had not been demolished, the harbor had been scandalized, with a large ship carrying stones sunk in the inner harbor to choke it up and close it to shipping. The English fleet had to offload on the back side of the mole.

Ibelin had been skeptical about this operation at first, because the English fleet had a dubious reputation at best. It was common knowledge that it had been late for its rendezvous with the English King (who had travelled over land to Marseilles) because the sailors had run riot in Lisbon while stopping there to take on water. Their rampage had been so excessive and caused so much damage that the authorities had thrown the bulk of the sailors in jail. The commanders had been forced to pay large ransoms to get their crews released.

At Caesarea, however, the English sailors managed to offload supplies from the off side of the quay with remarkable efficiency. This was important because by then the army had been on the march ten days, and men carried only ten days' rations in their kit. Most men's rations were thus running short. The arrival of the English fleet with both food and reinforcements met with great enthusiasm, and the bulk of the army crowded the little harbor, tripping over each other in their eagerness to get their share.

Ibelin chose not to take part in that free-for-all, and instead sent his men in search of fresh vegetables in the abandoned gardens beyond the walls. Because of the aqueduct, Caesarea had previously produced a surplus of a variety of vegetables in irrigated fields. Ibelin's men found that although the gardens had gone wild and were overgrown with weeds, they could still harvest beans, watermelons, and cucumbers.

After Caesarea the Saracens increased the pressure. They sent in larger, more determined attacks, although they still avoided a set battle. By September 3, however, the attacks on the rear guard had grown so intense that the Templars and French lost large numbers of horses. Sir Roger Shoreham, pointing out the scores of carcasses dragged into the camp so the common soldiers could enjoy fresh meat for a change, remarked to his lord, "If we'd brought the colts from your stud with us, you could have made a fortune selling them today."

Ibelin answered ruefully, "I will never make a man of commerce, Shoreham. When I see all those fine animals destroyed, I am filled with sadness. It would break my heart to send my colts, each so full of life, loyalty, and personality, to such a slaughter, much less to see them cut to pieces by greedy infantry." Shoreham, who didn't particularly like horses, looked at his lord uncomprehending, and Ibelin added, "I wish my wealth still came from pomegranates, grain, and almonds, as once it did." Hearing the sadness in his voice, Shoreham realized how much his lord missed Ibelin and all that had been before Hattin.

Later that same night, William of Tiberius sought out Ibelin. "Toron's disappeared," he announced indignantly and without preamble.

Ibelin raised his eyebrows. "I can't say that's much of a loss. What did he bring, a handful of crossbowmen?"

"Two dozen, to be precise, and paid for by Lusignan, who gets *his* money from the English King. I think they were all Armenian mercenaries formerly in the service of Isaac Comnenus. But that's not the point; *they're* still here. Only Toron is gone."

Ibelin shrugged. "Even less loss, then. Don't worry about Toron."

"I think he's a traitor," the titular Prince of Galilee answered bluntly.

"To whom?" Ibelin retorted. "He hates Montferrat—and me—for taking Isabella away from him, although he would neither fight for her nor honor her as a queen. But he's loyal to Lusignan to a fault and eats out of the King of England's hand."

"He's never been the same since he returned from Saracen captivity," Tiberius countered. "He wears kaftans as soon as he removes his armor, and he eats sitting cross-legged."

"But I've seen him drink wine. I don't think he's abandoned the True Faith."

"I didn't say he had, nor does he have to in order to be a traitor. The Sultan has Jews and Syrian Christians in his service, too," Tiberius pointed out.

Ibelin thought about that and nodded. "You're right, but what could Toron tell Salah ad-Din that he doesn't already know? The Sultan knows the size, composition, and leadership of our army already. He knows our marching order simply by reading our banners. As for our intentions, it doesn't take a genius to realize the ultimate objective is Jerusalem, and Jaffa is the closest port."

Tiberius nodded unhappily, accepting that Ibelin was right. In his head he could almost hear his late stepfather saying something similar.

"Don't worry about Toron," Ibelin repeated, laying a hand on Sir William's shoulder. "He can do us no harm."

Tiberius took a deep breath. "But at some point Salah ad-Din has to try to stop us. I'm not happy having to pass through the forest of Arsuf tomorrow."

"True, the forest offers a degree of cover for an ambush. Indeed, it would be the ideal place for *us* to ambush *them*, since our archers could take up fixed positions using the underbrush and trees as cover. But short of trying to set the whole wood on fire—which is harder than it sounds—I doubt that Salah ad-Din is even tempted to fight there. The forest robs the Turks of their most effective tactic: fast attacks by mounted archers. No one can ride fast through a forest, so the mounted archers lose their mobility—not to mention that they would have to shoot through the trees. The risk comes when we turn inland and lose touch with the fleet. As long as we have the ships with us, we have supplies, lines of communication, and a means of both rapid retreat and rapid reinforcement. The tricky part comes when we're more than a day's march from the coast," Ibelin predicted.

Arsuf, September 7, 1191

Ibelin was wrong. To be sure, there was no ambush in the forest of Arsuf, and they had a day of rest after passing through, but as they prepared to march out the following morning, they found that Salah ad-Din had moved his army down from the heights and was blocking the road. The unavoidable confrontation had come much sooner than expected.

The order was given to prepare for battle, and men took particular care with preparing their arms. They also took care of their souls, seeking out one of the many priests traveling with the army. The knights, meanwhile, donned their full armor and prepared their destriers.

Ibelin elected to ride Centurion, the elder of his two destriers and the horse that had brought him safely through Hattin. It was not a sentimental choice; Centurion stood a far better chance of dying today than his rider did. Balian didn't like that thought, because Centurion was a friend and a comrade, and it would break his son's heart. But he had to be practical: the stallion was nearing twenty, and his useful life was almost over anyway. The younger stallion, Ras Dawit (King David in Amharic, named in honor of the Ethiopian knight who had died at Jerusalem), was the more valuable and so the less expendable of the two warhorses.

Centurion was tacked up with battle kit. The girth consisted of five chains of steel, encased in tubes of leather and wrapped in canvas sewn diagonally for additional strength. The reins, too, were chains of steel encased in leather and robust cloth. The trapper was of quilted canvas painted with the arms of Ibelin, and reinforced with panels of boiled leather across the chest and over the rump to the tail and down to the haunches. A leather mask attached at the browband and noseband with protruding eye shields protected Centurion's forehead and eyes from blows from above, but did not inhibit lateral vision, since Ibelin trusted his stallion to see danger coming and assist in keeping them both alive by sidestepping if necessary.

Most of Ibelin's knights could not afford so much protection for their horses, but they were personally equipped with chain-mail hauberks, and most with chain-mail mittens for their hands, coifs for their heads, and chausses for their legs, as well as shields and helmets. About half the knights had invested in the newer style helmets with a hinged visor that could be lowered to cover their entire face. The rest still wore helmets with a heavy nose guard but open cheeks. Ibelin favored the old-fashioned helmet when commanding, particularly in defense, because he felt it was important that his men be able to see his face. Today, however, he was just one of thousands of knights following orders, and so he opted for the greater safety of the visored helmet.

While the knights, aided by their squires, armed themselves and tacked up their horses, Ibelin's infantry likewise prepared for battle. Crossbowmen and archers drew extra supplies of bolts and arrows. All ensured that their water skins were full to the brim and that they had something to eat in their belt pouch as well. They donned their protective headgear, whether quilted caps, leather hoods, or kettle helms. Finally, they proudly displayed on their shoulders or chests flannel badges shaped like a yellow shield bearing a red cross pattée, the arms of Ibelin.

The badges had been cut and sewn by the Dowager Queen's women and forwarded to Acre just before they set off on the march. Such badges were more the exception than the rule. Household knights of important lords might wear surcoats and carry shields with the same device, and some of the communes of Outremer had also taken to wearing distinguishing colors or badges to set themselves apart (mostly the Pisans from the Genoese and vice versa, out of rivalry), but the infantry of most armies was made up of an inchoate collection of feudal levies, temporary volunteers, and mercenaries that collected and then melted away without strong ties. It was the Dowager Queen, raised in the Eastern Roman Empire, which retained many more traditions from ancient Rome, who had proposed the badges, because she understood the importance of unit identity. These badges reinforced the pride Ibelin's men felt to be in his pay and service.

Returning from the King of England's command tent, Ibelin was greeted by a cheer. Rather than just acknowledging it and riding on, he drew up. At once the men hushed expectantly. He raised his voice to be heard even in the rear ranks. "How many of you were with me at Hattin?"

Hundreds of hands went up. Without taking an actual count, Ibelin estimated that 90 per cent of his men had raised their hands. "Good. Then you know what to expect. We'll be under attack all day, and will have to keep moving despite that. These won't be the annoyance raids of the past week. Salah ad-Din has drawn up his entire army and intends to fight. We can expect him to send attacks in waves. When they find they can't stop the advance—and they *will* find that, as the Templars and King Richard will ensure that we roll right over anyone stupid enough to try to stand in our way—they'll shift their efforts to the rear. We've been asked to move farther back in the column, immediately ahead of the Hospitallers, who will make up the rear guard today. That means we can expect to be the target of attack starting around midday."

He paused, wondering if he was taxing their patience, but they appeared very attentive—even hungry for more. Not many commanders took the time to tell their infantry what was expected of them. "The key to success is absolute discipline. We cannot—must not—allow a gap to develop between the Hospitallers and ourselves on one hand, or the French and ourselves on the other. Try to march so your shields nearly overlap." He paused again, but he still had their undivided attention. "Have any of you ever heard of the Spartans?" He was surprised that a score of men waved in answer. For the rest he added, "They were ancient Greek warriors with a fierce reputation for never losing a battle. Do you want to know how they did that? By maintaining a wall of overlapping shields. If you try to imitate that, all of us—by the grace of God—may well survive this day. Your line of defense must not break for any reason until nightfall—excepting only at the signal to charge. I'll come to that in a minute.

"First take note: We'll be marching five abreast, and the man on the far left will be bearing the brunt of the direct attacks, but the man immediately beside him will have to march with his shield raised against arrows fired in a trajectory. The middle man is the man who does the shooting, protected by the men on his left, while the man on his right reloads and hands him a cocked bow. At regular intervals, you must rotate functions. If a man is killed or injured, send him to the wagons and shorten—but don't thin—the lines. Do you understand?"

They nodded, murmured, or shouted assent, depending on their nature. These instructions were not new. Ibelin had developed and refined the idea of this order of battle ever since the torturous march to Hattin had cost him one-third of his infantry. Since signing on troops for the campaign, he had drilled his men in the formation, and they had used it daily for the last two weeks. His men, he sensed, were more annoyed than inspired by his reminder of what he expected of them. With an inner sigh, Ibelin admitted to himself that they would either hold or break today based on their own mettle. There was nothing more he could do or say.

He continued to the instructions that were new. "When six trumpets sound the attack—two at the front, two at the standard, and two at the rear—that is the signal for the cavalry to pour out through the infantry for a charge. At the signal, I'll need three gaps for my knights to ride through. One after the first twenty-five rows, one after the second twenty-five, and one after the third. Is that clear?"

"I'll be sure every man knows where the breaks are, my lord," Sir Roger Shoreham assured him, seeing there was some confusion in the ranks.

Ibelin nodded his thanks to Shoreham. Without the veteran sergeant-turned-knight, his troop would be worth half what it was now. "When that signal sounds, the cavalry must attack as rapidly as possible. Everything depends on our blow being delivered as a powerful joint effort. If we attack in ones and twos, we'll squander our strength for nothing. When the signal sounds, open the gaps fast—but not a moment before. I am counting on you. The King of England is counting on you. Christendom is counting on you."

"For Christ and the Holy Sepulcher!" someone shouted from the ranks, and they all took up the shout. "*For Christ and the Holy Sepulcher!*"

As predicted, the initial assaults focused on the front of the army. Waves of Nubians, Bedouins, and then Turks and Kurds hammered at the Frankish host as it advanced. Knowing that their greatest advantage lay in their mobility and numbers, Salah ad-Din did not attempt to actually hold a specific line, but flung successive waves of troops against the Franks. The Templars and the King of England's Angevin and Gascon men put their heads down, their shields up, and kept marching in tight formation. Protected by the infantry, the knights (against their nature) dutifully ignored—as if deaf—the taunts and challenges of the drums, trumpets, cymbals, and the battle cries of their enemies. From their position toward the back of the army, Ibelin and his knights could see the air darken with the volleys of arrows. As they advanced, they increasingly found themselves marching past the corpses of horses, the human casualties having been cleared by their comrades and sent to the wagons.

By noon the focus of the attacks had shifted, however, and came increasingly from the left quarter. The army had been marching three hours without rest, the sun was at its height, and the dust churned up by the repeated attacks made breathing more difficult than ever. They began encountering men from the battalions ahead of them who had collapsed from heat stroke and thirst. Furthermore, as the French and Flemish marching ahead of them started to wilt in the heat and dust, chinks in their defenses resulted in mounting casualties.

In contrast, the Ibelin shield wall was still holding up very well. Riding back and forth beside the inside file, Ibelin caught the occasional joke about "Wait till they start the fires" or "When are they finally going to get off their asses?"

By midafternoon, Ibelin noticed that the Count of Champagne, who commanded the battalion immediately ahead of them, had changed horses twice. He wasn't sure, however, whether it was because he'd lost two horses already or was simply trying to spread the burden among his three horses to ensure he was not riding an exhausted horse when the charge finally sounded. To his credit, Champagne was riding energetically up and down his ranks, encouraging his men and exposing himself to danger.

In his own battalion, no one was joking anymore. They had been marching six hours without a pause. Their throats were parched and their feet sore. Their arms ached from holding up their shields or firing round after round. They were hungry and needed to relieve themselves. Men started to lag or dropped out of rank for a piss. Furthermore, the attacks started coming more from behind them, which made it increasingly difficult to return fire.

Riding to the back of his battalion, Ibelin noticed the Hospitallers were marching backwards in order to return fire without halting. That didn't work very well, as he knew from bitter experience. Men tripped and fell, their aim was bad, and progress was slower than ever. The Hospitallers were under such unrelenting attack, however, that they had no choice, and Ibelin ordered a reduction in the pace of his battalion to prevent a gap developing. Ibelin rode forward to pass the word to Champagne, who at the sight of him at once cantered back to meet him.

"The Hospitallers are marching backwards. We need to slow down," he told the younger, less experienced commander.

Champagne shook his head, not so much in disagreement as distress. "My uncle won't like that. He keeps sending messages to pick up the pace and press onward. He's worried about making it to the designated campground. We can't stop short of Arsuf, where we have abundant water for the horses."

Ibelin found himself asking God why Guy de Lusignan had not had the sense the English King possessed. Here was a Westerner who had only been in the Holy Land three months, yet he had already grasped the essentials of warfare in the Palestinian environment against the mobile Saracens.

Even as they spoke, the Hospitaller Master, Garnier de Nablus, cantered up and shouted at them: "We can't take this much longer! I'm losing horses like flies. We have to fight back!"

"The King will give the signal at the right time," Champagne answered loyally.

"The hell he will! We're at risk of being wiped out!" Nablus snarled back, his face bright red and gleaming with sweat.

"You'd better take that message forward yourself," Ibelin advised; then nodding to Champagne in farewell, he turned Centurion around and rejoined his own men.

"When the hell are we going to charge?" Sir Galvin echoed Nablus' complaint, his ax ready in his hand. "Does the King of England think we can just wear them down without attacking? That's not going to happen. There are too many of them. What the hell is the English King waiting for?"

"I haven't a clue what the King of England thinks," Ibelin admitted, removing his right hand from his soaked mitten to wipe the sweat away from his eyes. His face was caked with dust, as were the faces of all his companions. The sweat from his hair left little rivulets on his cheeks before disappearing in the sheet of perspiration on his neck beneath his chain mail. He reached down for his water skin, took a sip, and then gestured to Georgios to bring water for Centurion as well.

Georgios had just joined them and was leaning out of his saddle with the water bucket for Centurion when an arrow whizzed in and landed with a chink at the feet of Sir Galvin's stallion. The veteran warhorse whinnied and snorted, and Ibelin looked quickly over his shoulder to where the arrow had come from. "Are they moving in closer?" he asked Sir Galvin in alarm.

The Scotsman nodded, muttering his usual obscenities about the sexual organs of their enemy. Ibelin saved his breath, but shouted to his men, "Close up! Shields up!"

As if that first arrow had been the start of a thundershower, a few more arrows pattered down, and then abruptly a storm of arrows rained on them. Ibelin felt one lodge itself in the armor on his left shoulder, while Centurion snorted and bucked in irritation as one pricked his left haunch before falling to the ground.

Some of the men, exhausted already, had been slow to respond, and his troop suffered a half-dozen casualties all at once. Worse: a look at the sky warned that more volleys had been launched.

"Close up!" Ibelin roared at his men, lifting his own shield this time. No less than three arrows thudded into the heavy wooden surface and two bounced off the leather of Centurion's trapper, while Sir Galvin was now wearing an arrow in his helmet like a jaunty feather. Ibelin swung Centurion around to ride back down the length of his battalion, shouting at the men to close up and raise their shields.

"We can't win a battle this way!" Sir Galvin snarled at his side, and Ibelin tended to agree. He would have liked to find out what King Richard was doing and thinking, but the vanguard was far too far away.

The Hospitaller Master, meanwhile, had returned to his battalion looking furious. Certainly the signal was not given to charge, and the pressure on the Hospitallers was, if anything, worse than before. A glance back at the Hospitallers suggested that more knights and Turcopoles were walking than riding. They were leaving a trail of equine corpses behind them, while the Saracens, receiving less and less answering fire, were pressing in closer and closer. For a second time, Garnier de Nablus galloped past on their right.

For a moment, Ibelin had a horrible sense of déjà vu. A voice of panic whispered: It's Hattin all over again! His reason answered sharply: Nonsense! The infantry is unbroken, and the man in command is not a fool! Although he'd only known him three months, Ibelin could not imagine Richard Plantagenet sitting slack-jawed on his stallion and watching with dazed eyes while his army disintegrated around him. There had to be some plan behind all this, he told himself, but he couldn't help wondering if King Richard fully appreciated what was happening here at the rear.

In fact, although it was hard to see through the clouds of dust, Ibelin had the impression that Salah ad-Din's cavalry was dismounting and firing across the backs of their horses. This increased the force and impact of the arrows, effectively overcoming the advantage of armor, but it also made them more vulnerable. If ever there was a time to charge, this was it.

No sooner had the thought formed than a shout of "St. George!" erupted from his left. He turned toward the cry and saw the Hospitaller marshal, a sage and seasoned veteran of many battles, break out of the Hospitaller formation at full gallop with his lance lowered. Almost at once the cry was answered from the right, as a knight broke out from the battalion of Flemings beyond Champagne. Meanwhile, the remaining mounted Hospitallers followed their marshal, lances lowered and a scream of "St. George!" in their throats. Picking up the call a split second later, the Count of Champagne broke through his infantry at full gallop, his horse stretching out its neck, and the banner of Champagne glittering as it fluttered on an upraised lance beside the Count's lowered one. His knights, some of the best equipped and proudest in the army, were so close behind him that the earth trembled.

"Did we miss the signal?" Ibelin asked.

"Does it matter?" Sir Galvin answered rhetorically, closing his grasp on his ax.

"Open the ranks!" Ibelin shouted to his infantry as he fastened his aventail, then dropped his visor and grabbed the lance offered by Georgios. As soon as the path was open, he pointed Centurion at it, leaned forward, and shouted, "St. George!"

Behind him his knights repeated the improvised battle cry, but Ibelin could no longer hear. Centurion was plunging furiously after the knights of Champagne, his ears flat back and his strides so strong he was streaking across the desert. All along the line of march, bannerets with their knights were breaking out of the infantry and streaming after the leaders. The effect was a rolling echelon of compact bodies of knights, each of whom chose a target in the mass of Saracens flanking them. The Franks smashed into the enemy forces not simultaneously, but in a series of mailed punches.

The Hospitallers, of course, struck into the enemy line first, knocking their opponents to the ground and piercing deeper into the Saracen ranks. They rode right over the Saracens who had dismounted to improve their archery. Heads were literally flying through the air as they used their swords like scythes. Riderless horses scattered in panic, adding to the confusion among the enemy.

The knights of Champagne hit the enemy next, and then Ibelin and his knights crashed into the Saracen line. Although this initial impact was dramatic and satisfying, Ibelin was acutely conscious of how rapidly the effect of a charge could dissipate if it lacked sufficient momentum, depth, or energy. The Constable's charge at Hattin had started well, only to get bogged down in the sheer numbers of enemy that closed around the Frankish horsemen. That charge had ground to a halt short of a breakthrough, and they'd lost scores of knights before they could extricate themselves, achieving nothing. Furthermore, at Hattin a breakout toward Lake Tiberius offered the prospect of water, rest, and the promise of survival, whereas now, the depth of the Saracen lines was greater and there was no place to escape *to*. The territory beyond the Saracen army was hostile.

Movement to Ibelin's right caught his eye. He risked looking over his right shoulder. Like a hawk out of hell, the English King was cutting across the dusty plain at a pace so fast it was more like flying low than riding. King Richard had captured Isaac Comnenus' stallion, reputed to be amazingly fast, but Ibelin still found it hard to believe any horse could carry a fully armored man as fast as this—or that any rider would take the risks the King of England was taking by riding at that speed across a plain broken by gullies and scrub brush.

King Richard did not slow his pace even as he sliced into the battle. He skewered two successive men with his lance, tossed it aside, and started hacking his way through the Saracen army with apparent ease. He was not alone. His Angevin, Gascon, and Poitevin knights were in his wake, although the English and Normans remained by the standard. The hole the King punched in the enemy was only the tip of the spear; his knights pried open the entire Saracen host.

Ibelin found himself fighting with the rest in what had become a massive melee. The forward thrust of the charge had gradually diminished until there was nothing but a field full of men and horses wheeling and lunging, leaping, staggering, and falling as they fought in a cloud of dust that thickened with each footfall. Ibelin's lance was long since shattered. The bronze inscription on the blade of his sword, "Defender of Jerusalem," was lost under a coat of blood to the hilt. Blood had splattered over his forearms and left stains upon Centurion's trapper as more than one opponent had fallen headless against his shoulders. Under Centurion's hooves, bones snapped and organs ruptured. There was no mercy on that field.

Gradually and intangibly, Ibelin felt the enemy start to give way. The change was not clear-cut. Some men continued fighting, unaware that their colleagues were already in flight. Some misjudged the moment to break off. Others were so lost in blood lust that they could not stop killing until they were alone and overwhelmed. Certainly no trumpets sounded the retreat. The Saracens, or their morale, were simply slowly crushed by the fury of the Frankish assault.

When there was no Saracen left alive within range, Ibelin rested his sword across his pommel and lowered his shield to take stock of the situation. In the distance all movement was away from the battlefield, as Saracens fled on horse and foot like a herd of sheep suddenly startled by a loud noise. More surprising, when Ibelin looked behind him, he realized that the Frankish infantry had followed the knights onto the field and were systematically cutting the throats of the Saracen wounded and trying to capture the riderless Saracen horses in order to replace their own losses.

Sir Galvin trotted over to Ibelin, his right arm hanging casually at his side, his battle-ax dripping blood. "Now that should have given them a wee something to think about," he remarked smugly.

"Any casualties?" Ibelin asked, opening his visor and trying to find and count his own knights. Although they were somewhat scattered, they were gradually rallying around his standard. He was so used to counting to twenty-nine that for an instant he thought he'd lost someone—before he remembered Sir Bartholomew was still in Acre. It seemed unfair that he was not here to enjoy this moment of revenge.

The trumpets were sounding "regroup," so with a nod, Ibelin gestured for his knights to return to the baggage train, which was still lumbering along the coastal road. As they trotted over the field littered with enemy dead, Centurion had to sidestep more than once, startled several times when a body that appeared dead suddenly moved. Meanwhile some of the infantry was starting to plunder the enemy corpses, and Ibelin had to order them back into formation. Although they had clearly given the Saracens a bloody nose, they needed to reach water before making camp for the night, and there were several hours of daylight left. More ominous, as at Le Forbelet, Salah ad-Din still had thousands of troops at his disposal, and these were rallying a couple of miles away in a long, dark smudge.

A shout from the north alerted Ibelin that a new threat had developed, and abruptly men were shouting and screaming in confusion as a Turkish charge struck the rear guard, seemingly out of nowhere. It smashed into the still decimated Hospitaller ranks, causing men to break and run as at no time previously in the march.

Sidon was suddenly beside Ibelin. He shouted as he rode past with his knights, "Taqi al-Din! He's brought up the Sultan's Mamlukes!"

Taqi al-Din was one of Salah ad-Din's nephews, and without doubt one of his best commanders. Ibelin had encountered him more than once before. He looked around, found Shoreham, and ordered him to take the infantry back to the baggage train, then with his knights chased after Sidon to engage Taqi al-Din. Some of the Hospitallers were still fighting, but with so few horses left they were severely disadvantaged. Furthermore, the troops under Taqi al-Din were the elite Mamlukes of the Sultan's own bodyguard. These men had seen the slaughter the Franks had just inflicted upon their fellows, and they were after blood.

Although the knights of Outremer, Champagne, and Flanders reinforced the Hospitallers, within a short space of time the Franks were embroiled in a desperate fight with roughly equal numbers on both sides. The Franks, however, were disadvantaged because they had no momentum, being on the defensive. Furthermore, they were tired from the day-long march and the battle they had just won against the main Saracen force. Last but not least, the dust and thirst had become almost crippling. Ibelin was conscious that many knights, particularly those from France and Flanders who were least used to the heat, were clinging to their cantles or crouching under their shields without actually fighting. They were trying to withstand the blows of their enemies by the strength of their armor alone. It was a tactic that could work for a few minutes, but not very long.

Then for the second time in the afternoon, a thunderbolt struck from the right. There were no trumpets and no shouting, just an abrupt jarring of the entire picture. Horses staggered, men fell, limbs flew through the air. Ibelin was close enough to see with astonishment the path King Richard hewed through the enemy.

The Mamlukes, however, rapidly recognized who they were fighting, and they turned on him with grim determination. Ibelin supposed they were determined to kill the man who had ordered the massacre at Acre. From their yellow turbans and insignia it was clear these were Egyptian Mamlukes, just as the garrison at Acre had been, and they wanted revenge. At the sight of King Richard, men broke off other fights to converge on the English King, vying for the honor of crossing swords with him. At least two emirs ordered their men out of the way so they could be the ones to engage. There was hatred in the air, Ibelin felt, that had been absent even at Hattin and the siege of Jerusalem.

Despite his prodigious skill at arms, King Richard was so surrounded that he looked hard pressed, and Ibelin was not alone in trying to fight his way to assist him. Henri de Champagne was fighting with more desperation than strength, and the Earl of Leicester and Aimery de Lusignan were pressing forward doggedly. But their aid was quite unnecessary. King Richard killed with his backward strokes as well as his forward ones, and literally struck sparks with the fury of his blows on iron. Nothing hostile was able to get within a seriously threatening range, and after he had dispatched both emirs who had vied for the trophy of the King of England's head, the other Mamlukes became noticeably more cautious.

With that, the momentum of the Mamluke attack was broken, and the Franks could start to push them back. In another half-hour it was over. The Mamlukes had disappeared behind the clouds of settling dust, the western sky was orange, and the Frankish army was again trudging along the coastal road to the designated campground on the irrigated plain outside of Arsur.

Like the other coastal cities that had fallen to Salah ad-Din in 1187 but had been left ungarrisoned, Arsur was an uninhabitable ghost town. The army was ordered to strike camp on the periphery, with the sea protecting the west flank and the city itself the southern. This was an area that had once been both orchard and kitchen garden for the city, and although the Saracens had hacked down the trees four years ago, they had not uprooted them. Most had sprouted new branches and despite the visible scars of their trauma, they were alive, green, and bearing fruit again. This was because whether by design or neglect, the cisterns and irrigation ditches had not been systematically destroyed. They were in poor repair and partially silted up, but they were still functional. The surviving horses of the Frankish host sank their noses down in the cisterns and guzzled greedily.

Leaving Georgios to erect his tent, Ibelin led both his destriers to one of the cisterns. Ernoul told the story that on the eve of Hattin, when the army camped at the springs of Sephorie, Centurion had drunk deeply but Thor, the younger of his two stallions then, had inexplicably refused. Thor had died under him from heat stroke in the midst of the Battle of Hattin, while Centurion had lived to bring him to safety. Patting his shoulder as he plunged his head down and sucked up water in large gulps, Ibelin noticed a bad gash in Centurion's knee. He bent to take a closer look and was startled by the sound of someone shouting, "God and the Holy Sepulcher help us!"

Ibelin looked around, trying to see what was happening. The men around him were already pointing. "King Richard! King Richard!"

Sure enough, the English King was again galloping to the north, and this time he had only a handful of men with him. Ibelin dropped Centurion's reins and grabbed up Ras Dawit's instead, thrusting his foot into the near stirrup at the same time. The young horse, who had done nothing but walk and trot all day, readily answered his heels. As soon as they were clear of the crowds of men around the cisterns, Ras Dawit picked up a gallop and they flew after the King of England and his men, making up ground because Ras was fresh and King Richard's Cypriot stallion was now nearing the end of his strength.

Ahead of them, several hundred Mamlukes, commanded by the now familiar red-bearded Khalid al-Hamar, were causing havoc among the exhausted Hospitallers as the latter tried to set up camp. The mere sight of heavy cavalry rushing to the rescue was enough to scatter them, however. Mounted on fresh native horses, their withdrawal was swift, and King Richard recognized that his own tired stallion had no chance of catching them. He sat back and let his horse fall into a trot and then a walk on a long rein, snorting and dragging his head to express that he'd had enough for one day.

Ibelin and the others likewise slowed to a walk, and Ibelin found himself surrounded by the few knights who had sprinted after their King. "Have you ever see anything like the King's courage?" a Gascon knight proudly asked the despised "poulain."

Ibelin flipped open his visor so that the man could see his face clearly. "Richard Plantagenet is undoubtedly a brave man, but tell me this: would your King have the courage to ride into battle if he could *not* couch a lance? If he could *not* use sword or shield? If, indeed, if he could not even hold the reins of his horse?"

"Huh?" The Gascon looked at Ibelin as if he were mad. "What are you talking about? Of course not! That's—"

"That's what *my* King did. Without the use of arms or hands, he led a force of just five hundred knights and five thousand foot against a Saracen army led by Salah ad-Din that was four times as strong—and put it to flight. That, sir, took a measure of courage far greater than what your King—for all his prowess—displayed today."

The Gascon started to protest, but a voice cut him off. "Well said, my lord of Ibelin," Richard Plantagenet declared. "But tell me this: Who would you rather have fighting beside you?"

Balian had no choice but to concede the point. He bowed from the waist to King Richard.

Chapter 16

Tyre, October 1191

ALYS HAD MOVED UP TO THE position of personal servant to the Dowager Queen of Jerusalem when Rahel had departed with Eschiva. Grateful and used to hard work, she was diligent and eager, always looking for ways to make herself indispensable. The fact that she was good with a needle and understood the care of cloth and leather had proven invaluable, and she had taken the lead in producing the badges for Lord Balian's men. But she was not yet comfortable with protocol. The arrival of the ruling Queen of Jerusalem intimidated and flustered her.

"Madame! Madame!" she cried, running up the stairs from the courtyard. "The Queen has come! The Queen has come!"

Maria Zoë was going through the accounts with Father Angelus when Alys burst in on her, and she gestured for Alys to calm down. Then, turning to the clerk, she asked him to finish for her and verify that what they had locked in the treasury matched the written accounts. "And if John, Balduin, and Philip aren't back by Vespers, you must send Stephan after them, but they are to get no supper except bread and water. They need to learn punctuality." Finally, turning back to Alys, she told her, "There's nothing to get so excited about, Alys. I'm delighted my daughter has come for a visit."

"But, Madame, she came with two knights and four squires, two grooms, and I don't know how many dogs."

"Send the squires and dogs into the lower hall. The grooms are here to take the horses around to the stables, and the two knights can be seen into the hall. Take my daughter to the solar and offer her wine. Then go down to the kitchen and see what light refreshments we can offer. I'll be there in just a few moments."

When Alys had withdrawn, Maria Zoë kicked off the clogs she wore for everyday in the house and slipped on stockings and shoes. She replaced her plain cotton veils with embroidered gauze and started down the stairs. To her surprise, Isabella was waiting at the foot of the staircase instead of in the solar. "Mama!" She kissed her mother on both cheeks and then urged, "Can we sit on the terrace? The weather is so pleasant."

Maria Zoë agreed at once and reversed her steps with Isabella behind her. While the weather was indeed very pleasant, still warm and sunny but no longer humid or blistering as in high summer, she was fairly certain that Isabella's motive for the change of venue was to be out of earshot of her knights. The Marquis de Montferrat was a man very conscious of status and appearance, and he insisted that Isabella never go anywhere in public without a "proper" escort. But whether knights, squires, or grooms, they were her husband's men, not her own. Only the dogs were truly her own, and they trailed behind her now, panting and eager as only healthy young hounds can be.

The rooftop terrace was protected from the sun by a canvas awning, and from the wind by potted yews and oleander that alternated with one another. There were benches to sit on and a small mosaic table on which to set refreshments or books. Maria Zoë sent Alys, who had been trailing Isabella looking distressed and confused, to the kitchen for wine and refreshments before settling herself on one of the benches.

Isabella, she noted as her daughter made herself comfortable on the bench perpendicular to her, was dressed regally. She wore blue silk veils with a gold border, draped so the edge fluttered down her back. Her surcoat was likewise trimmed with gold, imitating the look of a heavy necklace across her breast. The insides of her wide sleeves shimmered, and the undergown was dusted with embroidered stars. While Isabella had always had a flair for dressing well, Conrad's influence was evident in the emphasis on her wealth and status.

The woman beneath the clothes, however, looked strained. Although her skin was unblemished, smooth, and suffused with healthy color, there were streaks of blue under her eyes. Her well-formed rose-red lips were chapped, as if she'd been chewing them. Most of all, her expression was more sober than it had been in the early months of her marriage to Montferrat. Maria Zoë had sensed for several months that the "honeymoon" was over, and she suspected that Isabella was experiencing her first marital crisis.

Just three weeks ago, Isabella had joyously confided in her mother that she was pregnant at last, but this announcement had followed a period of increasing tension between Isabella and Conrad centered on the need for an heir. Maria Zoë surmised that something had gone wrong with the pregnancy and that Montferrat had taken the news badly. Reaching out to Isabella, she asked gently, "You wouldn't be here to tell me I'm *not* about to become a grandmother, would you?"

"How did you guess?" Isabella asked amazed, before looking down at her belly with an expression both sad and angry. "My flux came after all. I don't understand it!"

Maria Zoë sighed. Arguably the worst aspect of being a queen was the pressure to produce male heirs. Her failure to do so had strained her marriage with Amalric—and how different the history of Jerusalem might have been if only she *had* given him a healthy son! Had Isabella been a boy, the crown would have passed from Baldwin IV to her son without question, and Maria Zoë herself, with Balian beside her, would have been regent. But there was no point in thinking about that. She asked her daughter instead, "Is the Marquis very angry?"

"No," Isabella claimed unconvincingly. "Seriously," she stressed, making her mother more suspicious than ever. "It's just . . ."

Maria Zoë had been waiting for it. "Yes?"

"Oh, Mama! What's wrong with me? First Humphrey was impotent, and now, when I have a husband who can hardly leave me alone, I can't conceive! I'm beginning to think God is truly against me—"

"Don't even say it. Humphrey's impotence was not your fault. As for your failure to conceive, there could be many reasons." She paused. At nineteen Isabella was an ideal age for breeding, and she had been married to Montferrat nearly a year, so for all Maria Zoë's conviction, explanations were not readily apparent. She opted to suggest, "We should start by consulting the midwife, of course, to be sure there is no physical impediment, but we cannot exclude the possibility that the Marquis is to blame."

"Oh, I don't think it could be *his* fault," Isabella hastened to say, blushing slightly. "He's so, well, so . . . virile." She turned her head away as she spoke, embarrassed to meet her mother's eyes while talking of these things.

Maria Zoë understood her daughter's shyness and tried to keep her tone clinical. "My dear, no matter how active and well-endowed a man may be, his seed is not necessarily fertile. It takes fertile seed as well as fertile soil to produce new life. I know men tend to forget that, but that doesn't make it any less true. I expect the Marquis is not the kind of man to doubt himself in any context—least of all in bed—so we'll get nowhere suggesting it him. We'd be better off praying to St. Anne. Meanwhile, let me give you some lip salve to heal that chapping. You've been biting your lips again, haven't you?"

"Oh, Mama! It's not just that I'm not pregnant," Isabella burst out, biting her lips as if to stop herself from saying more (and confirming her mother's suspicions).

Maria Zoë reached out and put a hand on her daughter's knee. When Isabella met her eyes she urged gently, "What is it, Bella?"

Isabella didn't find it easy to answer because she was deeply confused. After Humphrey's return from captivity their relationship had been marked by increasingly bitter quarrels that she had blamed on the lack of physical intimacy. But now the pattern was repeating itself, despite the fact that Conrad could not seem to make love to her often enough. If she had learned the hard way that a marriage *without* sex wasn't a marriage at all, she was beginning to think that a marriage based *only* on sex was hardly any better.

She tried to explain things to herself as much as her mother, noting: "Conrad doesn't seem at all interested in what I have to say. He seems to think I'm still a child."

"Ah," Maria Zoë commented. She'd had that problem with Aimery too and nodded knowingly.

"And it doesn't help that he's so—so angry! Not with me. It's not about me at all," Isabella protested defensively. "But he's afraid all his achievements, all he did to rescue the Holy Land, will be forgotten now that the King of England has been so successful. First he took Acre and now Jaffa, and with the conquest of Jaffa the Lusignans' position is stronger than ever. Apparently King Richard wants to revive Jaffa completely, not just use it as a base for the assault on Jerusalem. He's urging merchants and tradesmen to return, and he's brought masons and carpenters down from Acre to ensure the rebuilding is done properly."

"That's wise," Maria Zoë noted, "Whatever makes your kingdom stronger, Bella, is in *your* best interests."

"That's just what I said!" Isabella burst out, "but Conrad told me I hadn't 'a peahen's understanding of politics.'"

"What?" Maria Zoë stiffened sharply. "Were those the words he used?"

"Yes, and it wasn't the first time he's said things like that. He often tells me that I shouldn't worry 'my little brain' about politics, and that I should 'do what I'm good at'—meaning keeping him happy in bed. But I'm not particularly stupid, am I?"

"Of course you're not!" Her mother (as expected) dismissed the notion imperiously. "And even if you were, he should show you more respect!" Maria Zoë's eyes and lips were narrowed as she thought back on her encounters with Montferrat. He had always tried to flatter her with compliments about her body, and had been consistently discomfited by having to deal with her as an intelligent being. Amalric had tended to keep her out of politics, but he had never been dismissive of her opinions, much less overtly insulting. If Conrad was not able to accept that his wife had a brain when he was so dependent on her for his position, what was he likely to do if he was ever anointed king? Maria Zoë found herself beginning to wonder of this marriage had been such a wise thing after all.

Meanwhile, Isabella was trying to explain the tensions that had festered into the most recent clash with Conrad. "Did you hear that Salah ad-Din has torn down Ascalon?" Ascalon had been one of the few cities the Saracens had not demolished during their orgy of destruction in 1187 and 1188. Instead, after the Frankish residents had been expelled, it had been resettled with Egyptians.

"I did receive reports to that effect," Maria Zoë admitted. Haakon Magnussen, whose restless soul could not remain in any one place very long, had been "scouting" (and, Maria Zoë suspected, pirating) along the coast. He'd reported that the Saracens were demolishing the towers and walls.

"That means Geoffrey de Lusignan will get his county. Conrad is afraid of that." Isabella confided in her mother. "Especially since he has no means of gaining Sidon and Beirut—not with all the fighting men following King Richard."

"Ah, yes," Maria Zoë was beginning to understand. After the fall of Acre, the Kings of France and England, in council with the other leaders, had brokered a deal whereby Guy de Lusignan was recognized as King of Jerusalem so long as he lived, and Conrad de Montferrat was recognized as his successor. The deal also named Conrad de Montferrat "Count" of Tyre (to include the lordships of Sidon and Beirut), and Geoffrey de Lusignan Count of Jaffa and Ascalon. While the latter appointment was (ominously from the Montferrat perspective) the traditional fief of the heir to the throne of Jerusalem, at the time it had also been completely fictional, as neither Jaffa nor Ascalon had been in Frankish hands. With the capture of Jaffa by the English King, and Ascalon within grasp, the situation had changed; Conrad had good reason to be unsettled by this increase in Lusignan strength, while his own remained unchanged.

Isabella continued with agitation born of the argument that had spawned this visit, "Conrad wants to negotiate with the Sultan. He thinks he might be able to talk him into ceding Beirut and Sidon without a fight, but he can't go himself. When I encouraged him to try, he called me an idiot and reminded me what happened the last time he'd negotiated with Salah ad-Din."

"Oh? He called *you* an idiot for the fact that *he* threatened his own father with a crow-bow?" Maria Zoë was rapidly losing her patience with her son-in-law.

Isabella forged ahead, determined not to get distracted from her mission. "What I was thinking, Mama, Uncle Balian seems able to talk to Salah ad-Din.

Do you think he might go to the Sultan on Conrad's behalf?" Isabella asked hopefully. "I'm sure if he went he'd be successful, and then Conrad will be grateful to all of us. He has promised to give Beirut to Uncle Balian once he has control of it," she reminded her mother hopefully.

"The Sultan, or one of his emirs, also tried to assassinate your stepfather; have you forgotten?" Maria Zoë reminded her daughter.

"But that was during the siege," Isabella protested. "When he asked for Humphrey's release, he was courteously received."

"*Sir Bartholmew* was courteously received," her mother corrected. But Maria Zoë could also sense how much hope Isabella placed in this mission and she honestly did not know how else to help her daughter. She could hardly barge in on Montferrat and lecture him on how he ought to treat his wife!

She put her hand on Isabella's cheek and then leaned forward to kiss her forehead. Drawing back, she promised with a smile, "I'll ask him. We can send a messenger by the first ship out tomorrow. But remember, I can't promise anything. All we can do is ask if he'll *consider* going to the Sultan on the Marquis' behalf."

Although he had responded to his wife's summons, leaving his men behind in Jaffa under the command of Sir Galvin, Ibelin was far from excited about the diplomatic initiative Montferrat wanted to launch. He heard Montferrat out in complete silence, glancing now and again at Isabella, who sat at the table with them.

Montferrat laid out all his arguments, and Ibelin still said nothing, sipping his wine slowly instead. Montferrat was forced to prompt him: "Well, will you do it?"

"Go to Salah ah-Din on your behalf with these terms?" The very way he put the question made it sound like Montferrat was mad.

Montferrat had ordered Isabella to let him do the talking, but she could not could not keep silent any longer. "Please, Uncle Balian!" she pleaded.

Montferrat thought Ibelin's expression softened when his eyes settled on his stepdaughter. Isabella looked wonderfully soft and lovely at the moment, in garnet and ruby tones that brought out the red highlights in her hair. Conrad was amazed that even after a year of marriage, he still found her as attractive as he had four years ago. Her sexual attraction, however, was unlikely to move her stepfather, and Conrad felt a growing resentment that she had come up with this hare-brained scheme to request Ibelin's assistance.

Ibelin turned back to Montferrat, and the softness had gone out of his eyes. "No, I'm not prepared to take those terms to Salah ad-Din." The eyes he leveled at Montferrat seemed molten with smoldering anger, while the lines around them were very distinct. His jaw, darkened with the first shadow of a beard, was set.

"Uncle Balian!" Isabella cried out in despair. It was not just his refusal to go that wounded her, but the thought of what Conrad would do and say to her the minute her stepfather was gone. Desperation gave her the courage to speak despite Conrad's orders to the contrary. "Think what it would mean if we had peace!" she pleaded. "If we could start to rebuild without fear of losing everything again! If the Sultan agreed to restore Sidon—as he actually promised once already—Helvis could marry and take up her position as Lady of Sidon."

Balian looked at his stepdaughter with sympathy, but then turned his eyes again on her husband. "There is nothing in these terms about the tens of thousands of Christian captives. The King of England was persuaded to include them in the terms of surrender for Acre; I expect no less of you."

"You mean you would go to Salah ad-Din on my behalf if my offer included a demand for the return of Christian captives?" Montferrat sounded surprised, and then shrugged. "I don't see why he should agree to that, but you're welcome to include the demand, as far as I'm concerned."

It was the way he shrugged that angered Ibelin most, but he kept his emotions on a tight rein. "You're right; there is no reason to think he would agree to the release of *all* the captives. How many Saracen prisoners and slaves do we have in Tyre?"

Montferrat shrugged again. "There are some three hundred prisoners in the dungeon that we took when we seized their ships. I have no idea if anyone is holding slaves privately."

Ibelin said nothing, but he was clearly not pleased. He did not like this deal, and he did not like Montferrat's apparent indifference to the rest of the Kingdom, much less the captives. The deal amounted to selling out everything south of Tyre, agreeing not to interfere in the Sultan's war against the crusader army, in exchange for having Salah ad-Din recognize Montferrat's right to hold the County of Tyre (including Sidon and Beirut).

On the other hand, such recognition would have distinct advantages, Balian reminded himself. Salah ad-Din had long vowed he wanted to drive the Christians into the sea. If he could really be convinced to acknowledge their right to *any* territory, it would a victory of sorts. A bloodless one at that.

Ibelin reached for his wine and sipped it again. It was a heavy, sweet wine from Cyprus. Not really his taste at all.

Isabella tried again. "Surely the release of three hundred Christians is better than the release of none. You could specify captives from Ibelin, Ramla, and Mirabel."

Balian studied Isabella. Maria Zoë had told him Isabella's marriage was strained by her failure to produce an heir, and that Montferrat also showed little respect for her mind. He saw what her mother had seen: the circles under her eyes and the frailness of her body. She reminded him of Eschiva in the early years of her marriage. The difference was that his brother had given Eschiva to Aimery, while *he* was to blame for Isabella's marriage to Montferrat. If taking Montferrat's embassy to Salah ad-Din would help her in a difficult situation, it seemed like the least he could do. What was there to lose, really? Montferrat wasn't helping the crusaders anyway, so a promise not to help them did not weaken them in any way. If it secured peace in the north and the return of some of the captives, that was a step in the right direction. The King of England and the powerful forces under his command might still wring a military victory in the south. Last but not least, meeting with Salah ad-Din would reveal something about what he was thinking at this point in time. Unlike Maria Zoë, Balian did not think he was personally in any danger. He was convinced that whoever had tried to assassinate him during the siege of Tyre had done so simply to achieve a military objective, not out of personal hatred.

Ibelin nodded. "All right. I'll take your peace offer to Salah ad-Din."

Isabella jumped up and flung her arms around him in gratitude. "Thank you, Uncle Balian. I knew I could trust you! I knew it!"

Saracen headquarters, Ramla, early October 1191

Ramla had been his mother's inheritance that passed to his elder brother Barry at her death. Barry had immediately taken up residence in Ramla, although Balian remained in Ibelin, and it had been here that all Barry's children had been born. Even after Barry had officially renounced his inheritance and left it along with his infant son in Balian's care, Balian had not moved to Ramla. In Balian's mind, Ramla remained Barry's and Eschiva's home, not his own. But that did not make it easy to see the rooftops flying the Sultan's banners nor find the town flooded with Saracen troops. It wounded him to see the crosses on the churches replaced with crescents or simply discarded, and it ignited a slow-burning fury when he saw the doors to chapels shattered and the insides gutted. By the time he was led to his brother's fine town residence and told this was the Sultan's headquarters, Balian was deeply regretting his decision to come on this mission.

His face impassive, he dismounted from his young bay palfrey and surrendered the reins to Georgios, whom he ordered to stay with the horses while he followed his escort into his brother's expropriated home. At least the fact that Salah ad-Din was using it meant that it had not been subject to wanton destruction, as with some of the other buildings. The architectural substance appeared fundamentally intact. The marble-paved entry hall was gleaming as if freshly washed down, as were the stairs leading up to the main living quarters. In the courtyard the fountain gurgled as happily as ever, while the potted palms had survived defeat and conquest without harm, Balian reflected morosely. The escort indicated that Ibelin should follow him up the stairs, and with an inward sigh he did.

At the top of the stairs was a long hallway paved with glazed tiles. Once it had been lined with carved trunks containing his brother's household goods. Now it was lined with Mamlukes, sentries guarding access to the Sultan. Ibelin was led between the sentries toward his brother's chamber, remembering that horrible day after Barry's son had died and he'd locked himself in his chamber with the corpse in a fit of grief. The anteroom to his brother's chamber was, however, no longer easily recognizable. Frankish chairs and tables had been replaced with rugs, cushions, and low tables. Ibelin was told to wait while his escort whispered to the Mamluke guarding the inner chamber and then withdrew.

The Mamluke rapped on the door in what appeared to be a signal and then resumed his immobile stance, leaving Balian feeling like an awkward intruder. He wondered if the Sultan knew that making him wait here was sheer torture. How could he forget that in this house his brother, crazed with grief, had predicted: *The forces of evil are on the move. They are gathering their troops and sharpening their weapons, and Christ is a powerless man of peace while the gods of war are about to devour us alive.* Balian had not wanted to believe him, but now he stood in his brother's house and the Sultan of Damascus was occupying his brother's bedroom.

Finally the door opened, and a completely veiled woman scuttled out of the room and started down the corridor with her head down and eyes averted. Was it to avoid even the slightest eye contact with a Polythiest? Or was it from shame, because she had been raised to see herself as the embodiment of man's baser instincts, a less worthy soul than all males even in the eyes of God? The sultan emerged, drying his hands on a linen towel, and Balian smiled cynically, thinking how inconvenient Frankish architecture was the maintenance of a harem.

"My dear Balian Ibn Barzan," the Sultan greeted Ibelin with a smile, "please." With a gesture he indicated cushions beside a beautifully carved table inlaid with ivory. "You will appreciate that since it is Ramadan I cannot join you, but I'll have sherbet and refreshments brought for you at once." He snapped his fingers, and a young boy jumped up from a wooden stool in the corner by the door to do his bidding.

The boy was gone too fast for Balian to get a good look at him, but his skin tone had been fair. Balian's stomach wrenched at the realization that he might be one of the many Frankish children who had ended in slavery.

Unaware of what was going on in Ibelin's mind, Salah ad-Din remarked in a pleasant tone, "You are looking much better than the last time we met."

"I should hope so," Ibelin retorted, trying to force levity into his voice; "last time we met I'd been fighting off assaults by your troops for nine days."

The Sultan laughed lightly. "Indeed, but it did you no serious harm, as we see. I seem to find you every place I attack: Tyre, Acre, Arsuf."

"I surrendered Jerusalem; I did not promise not to take up arms against you again," Ibelin reminded the Saracen leader evenly. Balian had nothing to reproach himself with—and if he incidentally disparaged Guy de Lusignan with his words, so much the better.

"Indeed, and I left you your arms." The Sultan indicated with an elegant gesture the sword at Balian's hip, its prominent enamel pommel bearing the arms of Jerusalem on one side and the arms of Ibelin on the other. "But given your unwavering hostility, I was very surprised to hear you had requested an audience."

"It is a very poor general who does not attempt to achieve by other means what will cost him a great deal of blood to achieve by force of arms."

Salah ad-Din laughed. "Who are you talking about? You or me?"

"I am no longer a commander," Ibelin reminded him.

Salah ad-Din only raised his eyebrows in disbelief.

"I am here at the behest of Conrad Marquis de Montferrat, the husband of my stepdaughter, Isabella Queen of Jerusalem."

Salah ad-Din's expression did not change. It was obvious to him that Ibelin controlled his son-in-law, and he found it disingenuous to pretend otherwise. He could only suppose that his pose had something to do with *faranj* laws that allowed titles to pass through females.

The return of the slave boy interrupted further discussion for the moment. The boy was burdened with a large silver tray laden with bowls overflowing with pistachios, almonds, raisins, figs, and dried apricots. A silver chalice already covered with condensation contained crushed ice and a carved ivory spoon. As the boy set the tray down, Ibelin looked at him more closely. He had blue-gray eyes and light brown hair, his skin was coppery red, and he had freckles. He was almost certainly a Frank by birth.

The Sultan saw Ibelin's interest and announced, "Ahmed was born Christian, but he has now converted to the True Faith and hopes to be a Mamluke one day—don't you, Ahmed?"

The boy dropped to his knees and banged his forehead on the floor. "If Allah, praise be to his name, so blesses me, your Excellency!" His voice was more a breathy whisper into the carpet than an affirmation of faith, or so it seemed to Balian. Furthermore, Balian did not see anything particularly praiseworthy in converting orphaned children taken by force from their homes. The boy had been baptized, and he felt certain that Christ would have pity on him. He therefore refrained from giving the Sultan the satisfaction of looking scandalized or upset.

Seeing that Ibelin was not going to react, Salah ad-Din dismissed the boy with a wave of his hand, and he withdrew backwards to resume his station on the stool in the corner by the door, awaiting the next order. Balian reminded himself that life as a page was not much better, and that Eschiva's son Hugh now served King Richard.

"Please, go ahead!" The Sultan urged Ibelin to partake of the refreshments he could not enjoy himself until sundown. "Where were we?"

"I've come to you, your Excellency, with a proposal of peace from the Marquis de Montferrat."

"Ah, yes. Please proceed." The Sultan sat back in his cushions and made himself comfortable. Ibelin mentally noted that the Sultan had gained a lot of weight in the last four years and looked much older than he had at Jerusalem, which seemed odd, given his unbroken series of victories until Acre and now Arsuf and Jaffa.

Ibelin laid out Montferrat's proposal. He included the return of all captives, knowing it was a maximum demand that would have to be negotiated downwards to something more reasonable. The Sultan listened with an impassive, almost disinterested expression, and with each passing moment Ibelin's hopelessness grew. The Sultan, he sensed, was not the least bit interested in his peace terms. Probably not in *any* peace terms, he reflected in discouragement. Not once was there a flicker of interest in his amber eyes. When Ibelin could think of nothing more to say, he fell silent.

Just then the muezzin started the call to prayers. The Sultan excused himself and withdrew into his inner chamber to pray, while the slave boy prayed in place by his stool—bowing, kneeling, standing, and kneeling again in answer to the calls of the muezzin. Ibelin remained sitting, but crossed himself and recited the Lord's Prayer until the voice of the muezzin fell silent. He completed the prayer twice and started a third time before the muezzin fell silent. He finished the prayer in the ensuing silence.

Salah ad-Din returned and settled himself again on his cushions. "Allah has inspired me with wisdom and an answer to your offer," he announced with a smile and hard eyes. "Tell the Marquis of Montferrat that I will gladly acknowledge his title to Tyre, Sidon, and Beirut and withdraw my troops and garrisons from the entire territory between the mountains and the sea that once made up the associated lordships—*after* he has control of Acre and is in a position to surrender it to me."

Ibelin did not react, because now that the Sultan had spoken, it seemed so obvious. Why had he allowed himself to be sent on this fool's errand?

"As for the captives," the Sultan continued, "we will return one captive for each Saracen prisoner you return to us. A simple exchange, one for one—minus, of course the twenty-five hundred that the English King slaughtered at Acre. In short, we'll start counting and return one Christian captive for each Muslim prisoner you return to us only *after* you return twenty-five hundred prisoners to us to make up for the hostages slaughtered so barbarically by your Malik Rik." There was real bitterness in that statement, Balian noted inwardly.

Outwardly, Ibelin nodded, and remarked, "I understand your position, your Excellency. I will report it back to the Marquis de Montferrat faithfully." He bowed his upper body toward the Sultan. "Thank you for receiving me so warmly and for your hospitality." He bowed again, and then uncrossed his legs and began to get to his feet.

A flicker of surprise crossed the Sultan's face. Ibelin's reaction struck him as far too calm, and he began to doubt his earlier assumption that Ibelin spoke for himself. Was it possible he was playing some other game? His spies reported that Ibelin opposed the English King, but he had fought beside him at Arsuf and again at Jaffa. It was very much in Salah ad-Din's interests to keep the Franks divided among themselves. He wavered, wondering if he should offer Montferrat something a little more palatable.

Ibelin was already on his feet and bowing again. "Thank you again for receiving me. I wish you a blessed and peaceful Ramadan, your Excellency."

The parting speech sounded so natural in Ibelin's fluent Arabic that Salah ad-Din found himself on the brink of wishing him the same. He caught himself just in time and, smiling somewhat embarrassedly, admitted, "I find myself wishing we were on the same side rather than enemies. I would have rewarded you far better than your kings. You would be master of a province by now if you were only a Believer."

Ibelin bowed deeply again. "You flatter me, your Excellency—for were I worthy of so much power, then God would surely have seen fit to bestow it upon me."

Salah ad-Din shook his head in bemusement. He wished more of his emirs had so much faith in the Almighty! It was a good thing, he noted with a prayer of thanks to Allah, that this man was not the king of the Franks, because he would have been a far more formidable adversary than either Montferrat or the mad Englishman. Malik Rik was a terrible opponent—untrustworthy and deceitful in negotiation, yet ridiculously brave and indifferent to his personal safety on the battlefield. The combination left Salah ad-Din baffled and uncomfortable, as he found he could neither risk battle nor trust negotiations.

Ibelin did not wait for someone to send for his horses but, familiar as he was with the house, strode around to the back himself. Georgios jumped up at the sight of him and began saddling the horses in such haste that Ibelin asked him, "Is something wrong?"

"I don't like it here. It gives me the creeps," the loyal Greek squire answered simply.

"We can ride another two to three hours before dark," Balian assured him. They could make Lydda, in fact, but he was reluctant to see what had happened to the shrine of St. George, and he didn't want to subject Georgios to that, either. Georgios naturally felt a particular affinity to St. George.

The horses were ready, and Ibelin took his own horse by the bridle and led him out into the street to mount up. He found it satisfying how many of the Sultan's men cast admiring glances at the young stallion. He was aware that the Saracens generally scorned Frankish horses as hulking, ponderous, and lacking in spirit. He had introduced some captured Arab mares into his stud, however, and the cross-breeding produced highly satisfying material for palfreys that did not need to carry the weight of armor or withstand the impact of joust and battle. This particular colt, a fine-boned bay he had named Hermes after the messenger of the Greek gods, was a bit of a showoff who liked to arch his neck, lift his tail, and prance about.

One of the Mamlukes assigned to see them out of the city asked half in jest, "What price do you want for your horse?"

"Five hundred gold bezants," Balian answered instantly, harvesting a laugh at such an outrageous sum.

They passed the Cathedral of St. John, converted now into a mosque, and were on the main thoroughfare leading toward the west when they were confronted by a large troop of Mamlukes coming the other way. Ibelin's party squeezed closer together and moved nearer the houses on their right so the two parties could pass. As they came abreast of the other troop, Ibelin's gaze fell on the blond man riding in the middle of the Mamlukes, and he started violently.

Humphrey de Toron recognized him in the same instant. They stared at one another, their escorts oblivious to the tension that burned the air.

"Tiberius warned me you were a traitor, Toron," Balian snarled at the younger man.

"Traitor? What makes me more of a traitor than you? We're both in the Sultan's camp!" Toron shot back, his face flushed with sheer hatred. He had never hated anyone so much as he hated Ibelin—not even Reynald de Châtillon. The Lord of Oultrejourdain had been a brute who had humiliated, scorned, and bullied him, but he had never betrayed him, never stabbed him in the back, never taken from him the thing he loved most. (Now that he had lost her, that was how Humphrey had come to see Isabella.)

"I'm only here as an envoy for the Marquis de Montferrat—"

"A bigamous, lying usurper!" Toron interrupted to fling back. "What could be more traitorous than that? I represent the legitimate Kings of England and Jerusalem!" Toron was shouting in agitation, while the astonished Mamlukes looked from one *faranj* to the other, uncomprehending, because the exchange was in French.

Ibelin already regretted speaking to Toron. It had been completely unnecessary. He could only excuse his stupid behavior by the inner agitation provoked by his disastrous meeting with Salah ad-Din and the emotions stirred by seeing his brother's home occupied by the Saracens. He shook his head as much at himself as Toron, then looked away and continued riding.

Tyre, October 1191

The Ibelin family was not expecting the return of their lord so soon, and the great hall of the little merchant residence was overcrowded and alive with domestic activity. While Alys and Ernoul practiced a new song in the solar, Helvis and her betrothed Reginald de Sidon were in a window seat playing chess. As an unmarried woman, Helvis did not cover her hair, but she wore it bound up at the back of her head, making her look older than her thirteen years, while her figure was decidedly nubile. Reginald appeared quite taken with her and was happily explaining to her the intricacies of chess. Margaret, on the other hand, had taken a rag, tied a knot in one end, and was wrestling with her new puppy in a rough-and-tumble game that would not have disgraced her brothers. The fact that she *had* a puppy after all her siblings had been consistently denied dogs due to "lack of space" was evidence (they felt) that Margaret was shamelessly spoiled.

Helvis didn't care anymore, because Reginald had promised her "as many dogs as she liked" as soon as they were married, and the boys no longer cared because they were more focused on horses, swords, and jousting. John, particularly, had started training in the lists and was being fitted for his first chain-mail hauberk, while Philip looked on jealously, lying flat on his belly and waving his feet around in the air.

Balian had resisted buying a hauberk for John, arguing that he grew so fast that he'd need a new hauberk every few months, but Godwin Olafsen had offered to exchange each hauberk he grew out of with a new one at no extra cost for the next three years. It was an offer Balian couldn't refuse—although he had first checked with Olafsen whether he could truly afford such a gesture.

"Believe me, my lord," the Norse armorer answered, "the orders for hauberks are unending. I can't keep up with them anymore, and need at least two more apprentices. But ensuring Lord John has proper armor while he's learning his trade is a debt I owe you."

"You owe me nothing, Master Olafsen. God forgive me, you would have gone into slavery if I had not happened to catch sight of you."

"But you *did* secure my freedom, and you also vouched for Mariam, my lord, even though she was not my wife and you knew it. Now, with her at my side, I've made a new life and I'm not a near-starving armorer, but one of the wealthiest burghers of Tyre." This was true. Ever since the crusaders had started flooding into the Holy Land, Olafsen's fortunes (under Mariam's canny guidance) had taken a turn for the better. He had built a large smithy in the new town outside of Tyre, with a courtyard onto which both his own workshop and Mariam's bakery backed. On the second story, over the shops, he had a substantial residence for his own family, his two journeymen, and four apprentices. Mariam employed a nursemaid for her infant daughter and several serving girls in the house, as well as the girls in her bakery. Meanwhile Sven, reconciled by the birth of a daughter rather than a son, was now her principal assistant. Altogether their establishment provided employment to nearly twenty people, and Olafsen had been elected an alderman of the armorer's guild. He was, in short, an established and affluent member of Tyre society.

John stood as still and tall as possible while the armorer slipped the coat of mail over his head, but when he shrugged his shoulders to try to get it to sit more comfortably, he was alarmed by how heavy it felt. He'd been cleaning his father's armor for years, and he thought he was intimately familiar with it. How could it feel so different on his own shoulders? Olafsen was tugging at the hem of the armor and looking with a critical eye at the way it sat. "I think we'd better add five more rings to the girth and ten to the sleeves. You've got very long arms, Lord John."

"That's because he's always snitching other people's things," Philip suggested maliciously.

"Philip! What sort of nonsense is that?" his mother rebuked sharply. She was at the high table going over the kitchen clerk's proposed procurement for the coming week. Looking across the room to frown at her younger son, she saw her husband enter at the foot of the hall.

Because she wasn't expecting him, she let out a startled cry of "Balian!" and jumped to her feet to greet him. Yet even before she had left the dais, she knew something was wrong by the grim expression on his face. She met him halfway down the hall, her sons behind her, and forestalled any comment on his part by asking, "What's wrong? Was the Sultan's answer so terrible?"

"It was—but not unreasonable," he replied. "The Sultan pointed out that Montferrat was not in a position to give away things he did not possess—such as the territories recaptured and held by the English King. He's right, and it was a fool's errand, but what I don't understand and can't accept is that Montferrat told me *to agree to these terms!*"

"But how can you? If he can't give away what he doesn't control—"

"He's willing to make a pact with Salah ad-Din! Willing to make *war* on his fellow Christians! All for the sake of securing his foothold here! Nothing matters to him but holding on to Tyre!"

"Weren't Sidon and Beirut included?" Reginald de Sidon asked, leaving his chess game and his betrothed to join Balian and Maria Zoë in the center of the hall.

"What difference does that make?" Ibelin snapped at his fellow baron. "Salah ad-Din's terms are that Montferrat take Acre! Aside from that being nearly impossible, it would mean an open break—no, open *bloodshed*—between Montferrat's men and the Frankish garrison of Tyre. I'll have no part of that!"

"Of course not!" Maria Zoë agreed, slipping her arms around him in a gesture of support and comfort to try to calm him down. She had not seen him this agitated in a long time, and she did not like the tension she saw on his face or felt in his taut body.

"I don't see the harm in agreeing to those terms," Sidon countered. "We don't have to act on them immediately—just get acceptance in principle that Tyre, Sidon, and Beirut belong to us."

Ibelin twisted free of his wife's embrace to confront Sidon furiously. "Does Sidon mean that much to you? So much that you'd sacrifice Acre and Christian lives?"

"Doesn't Ibelin mean that much to you?" Sidon shot back, with a significant glance toward Helvis, who was watching the exchange in alarm from the window seat.

Balian had to think about that only for a second before shaking his head firmly. "No! I would not go to war with my fellow Christians just to retain Ibelin—or Ibelin, Ramla, and Mirabel altogether, for that matter! Salah ad-Din seeks only to divide us among ourselves so he can conquer us separately—just as he did with his separate peace with Tripoli before Hattin. We must not let him! We must fight together!"

"And you've told Montferrat that?" Maria Zoë asked anxiously.

"Of course!" her husband snapped back.

"And how did he react?" Maria Zoë wanted to know.

"He called me a treacherous bastard and ordered me out of his sight—which was fine with me, as I don't much care for the sight of him, either!"

That was exactly what Maria Zoë feared, at once sensitive to the difficult situation Isabella was now in. She was going to have to find some means of visiting Isabella at the earliest opportunity and possibly building a bridge to Montferrat.

"Look, *I'm* willing to take Montferrat's answer to Salah ad-Din," Sidon insisted, causing Maria Zoë and Balian to stare over at him, the former puzzled and the later angry. "Listen to me!" Sidon demanded. "Agreement is not the same thing as execution. We are already divided among ourselves, in case you haven't noticed, and we should not ignore the possibility that the English King could also make a deal with Salah ad-Din—and who's to say he would not be willing to sacrifice *us* for what *he* has reconquered?"

The question shook Balian to the core. He had not considered that possibility, and he shook his head at once. "I can't believe Richard of England would do that!"

"And Guy de Lusignan?" Sidon asked next.

"Guy—God help us!" Balian shook his head in despair. He could not fathom the man's mind, and so anything seemed possible. Then his blood ran cold, and he admitted, "I ran into Humphrey de Toron in Ramla. He claimed to be there representing the Kings of England and Jerusalem."

"Toron? Who would choose him as an envoy? He eats out of Salah ad-Din's hand!" Maria Zoë exclaimed derisively. Any remnants of sympathy for Toron had been extinguished by Isabella's initial joy in her new marriage. Regardless of any strains in that marriage now—or indeed regardless of whether Montferrat was the right husband for her—the way Isabella had first blossomed after her divorce told Maria Zoë more than she needed to know about what kind of husband Humphrey had really been. In retrospect, she wished she had protested the validity of Isabella's marriage to Toron the minute he had betrayed the barons at Nablus. They could have dissolved the marriage then, and Isabella could have married one of the Tiberius brothers or Antioch's son—any nobleman with the backbone to challenge Sibylla and Guy immediately. Hattin need not have happened, and Isabella would have been happier sooner—and with a man better than Montferrat.

"But he speaks—and writes—exquisite Arabic," Sidon was pointing out.

"And he hates me and Montferrat more than the devil—much less Salah ad-Din," Balian himself noted, only belatedly grasping the danger he was in. He'd let his contempt for Toron blind him. Out loud he admitted, "Even if it were not the King of England's intention, Toron would make a deal with Salah ad-Din that serves us up as appetizers to the Sultan's Mamlukes faster than he'd pray a Pater Noster!" Balian was remembering the vehemence of Toron's emotions in their brief encounter at Ramla.

"The Sultan has a guilty conscience when it comes to me," Sidon countered, recapturing Balian's attention. "He knows he broke his word and behaved dishonorably—and unlike our old friend Reynald de Châtillon, Salah ad-Din takes no pride in being a charlatan. On the contrary, he *likes* to think of himself as a man of honor. He is uncomfortable doing ignoble deeds. I think if I confront him face to face, remind him of his treatment of me, I can shame him into concessions without us having to actually fight our fellow Christians."

Balian shook his head in disagreement. "I doubt it, but I'm not going to stop you from trying. If you offer to go, maybe that will help blunt some of Montferrat's anger. He is so set on this, I fear he'll take his anger out on Isabella."

Maria Zoë caught her breath to hear her husband put her own fears into words, then reached for his hand and squeezed it in gratitude.

"I'll go at once," Sidon declared. As he bowed over Maria Zoë's hand, he assured her, "I have the best interests of *both* your daughters at heart, Madame. I want to see Helvis installed as Lady of Sidon and Isabella crowned Queen of Jerusalem." Turning finally to Balian, he added, "And, no, I won't lead troops against Acre nor fight any man wearing the Cross—certainly not those who left their homes to help us regain ours. I honestly think I can shame Salah ad-Din into restoring what is rightfully mine, while further ensuring that he makes no deal with Lusignan or the Plantagenet that will harm our interests."

Chapter 17

Ramla, early November 1191

THIS WAS NOW HUMPHREY'S FOURTH MISSION to the Sultan on behalf of the English King. That King Richard put so much trust in him was a source of great pride, and Humphrey noted with satisfaction that in consequence of that trust, his status with the Lusignans had increased exponentially. Only Aimery still disdained him, but who cared about Aimery?

Humphrey was impressed that—unlike the Lusignans themselves, much less the bulk of the other crusaders—the King of England valued his mastery of Arabic and his understanding of the enemy. King Richard had grilled him for hours on everything he knew about Salah ad-Din, his brothers, nephews, emirs, tactics—even his wives. While Humphrey, obviously, knew nothing about the latter (and the question revealed the Plantagenet's ignorance of Muslim society), he had been able to provide detailed information about most of the other topics, and the English King had been visibly pleased to find he had such an excellent source of valuable knowledge so near at hand.

Shortly before the Battle of Arsuf, King Richard had explained to Humphrey that he wanted to open the lines of communication with the Sultan. He had confided in Humphrey when none of his other lords were present except the Bishop of Salisbury and Henri de Champagne, explaining that he feared that the massacre of the hostages at Acre, while necessary and justified, had constricted his diplomatic room for maneuver. He noted that the negotiations for the surrender of Acre had sown distrust on both sides—in the Frankish camp because the Sultan had failed to keep his word, and on the Saracen side because there had been no warning of the consequences.

"I should have warned him," King Richard admitted to Toron candidly.

"Given him one last chance to deliver *in the knowledge* of what I would do if he reneged. Now, neither of us trusts the other. Maybe that is the way it will always be, but you yourself said that the Sultan adhered meticulously to the truces he made with Baldwin IV and Raymond of Tripoli. Why not with me?" He'd paused and looked straight at Humphrey as if the question were not rhetorical. Humphrey assured him there was no reason why not, adding "If that's what you want."

"We'd be mad to waste men's lives if we can get what we want without bloodshed! Jerusalem is ours, and I want it back. And not just Jerusalem—every place Christ walked and preached. But now isn't the time to get into details. All I want at this stage is to meet the man face to face, look him in the eye, and let him look in mine. Let each of us take the measure of the other."

That sounded eminently reasonable to Humphrey, so he had nodded his agreement vigorously. If nothing else, he thought to himself, the encounter would dispel the many myths that fogged vision on both sides.

But his first mission to the Saracens had failed. Humphrey had met with Imad ad-Din, who had welcomed him like a long-lost son, insisted on having him to dinner, and housed him in his own tent. Yet he reported the next day that the Sultan absolutely refused to meet with the English King. "Kings only meet after an agreement has been reached," Imad ad-Din explained a little apologetically to Humphrey. "Once a truce or settlement has been reached, then kings meet to exchange gifts and the kiss of peace, but not before." That made sense to Humphrey, too, and he reported this back to King Richard.

The English King had been annoyed, and thereafter distracted by military matters for several weeks. It had been mid-October before he again sent for Humphrey and announced his desire to contact the Sultan again. Salah ad-Din, he reminded Humphrey, had refused a direct meeting but had not excluded talking through intermediaries. He sent Humphrey to the Sultan's court with a request that the Sultan name an envoy to conduct negotiations on his behalf. Imad ad-Din conveyed the request to his master, and then informed Humphrey that the Sultan would allow his brother al-Adil to meet with King Richard.

After delivering this message back to the Plantagenet, Humphrey had been tasked with arranging a meeting between King Richard and al-Adil, a mission that had taken him to Ramla for a third time. Shortly afterwards, the Sultan's brother had met with the English King while Humphrey served as the translator. The meeting had not yielded immediate results, because King Richard had opened with the ridiculous demand for the restoration of all territories ever held by the rulers of Jerusalem since 1099, and homage for Egypt—a demand so lacking in legal basis that Humphrey had been embarrassed to translate it.

To Humphrey's relief, al-Adil had not taken offense—merely smiled and noted that the English King's demands were "somewhat excessive," while suggesting that agreement on something a little more reasonable might be possible. He told them he would consult with his brother.

The most important aspect of the meeting had been that Richard and al-Adil got along with one another, soldier to soldier. Within a very short time they had been bantering, making little jokes, and when al-Adil sent Khalid al-Hamar with a gift of ten valuable camels on the day after the meeting, Toron was very encouraged.

Today he was in Ramla to find out what terms Salah ad-Din was willing to consider. He was also sincerely looking forward to the *iftar* that he would share with Imad ad-Din as soon as the sun went down and the evening prayer ended. Since he had never spent time in Ramla when it was in Frankish hands, he found nothing particularly odd or offensive about seeing the streets crammed with the diverse soldiers of the Sultan's armies. There were black-skinned Nubians with their round shields and naked chests (despite the chill of early November), Berbers in their blue robes, Bedouins and Egyptians in flowing kaftans and white turbans, Turks with baggy trousers and knee-high boots, and Kurds with tight-fitting tunics and painted, spiked helmets. The diversity was significantly greater than in the Frankish camp, but the Saracens had the advantage of all speaking Arabic, Humphrey thought with a twinge of envy. The Christians, in contrast, were divided by their many languages, since only the priests and nobles spoke Latin.

Humphrey made straight for Imad ad-Din's residence in one of the many townhouses of Ramla. Although founded by an Arab sultan in the early eighth century, Ramla had been destroyed by earthquakes and abandoned before the arrival of the Franks. The first Frankish settlers had built on the foundations to some extent, but on a much smaller scale, and the city as it now stood was architecturally Frankish in character. While many of the churches had been converted into mosques, there had not yet been time to build minarets, and the call to prayer came from the rooftops instead. Humphrey had timed his arrival well, and the muezzin fell silent just as he drew up in front of Imad ad-Din's temporary residence.

The porter recognized him and grinned as he bowed to the familiar young Frankish lord and let him inside the dim entryway. A slave woman with shaved hair scuttled for the shadows at the arrival of a guest, the wet rags with which she had been wiping the floors leaving drops of water that gleamed in the light angling in from the courtyard. From deeper inside the house came the enticing smells of delicately spiced dishes—cardamom, cumin, cinnamon, and garlic mixing together with the pungent odor of roasted lamb, grilled goat, baked chicken, chickpeas, carrots, and onions.

Imad ad-Din had spotted Humphrey and hurried forward to embrace him warmly. "I was hoping you would join me today or tomorrow. Come join the feast. Evening prayers are over."

They were soon seated comfortably beside a low table groaning with dishes both sweet and savory. Humphrey washed his hands in the bowl offered by a slave boy, and dried them on the offered linen towel, before accepting the steaming water flavored with hibiscus flowers and sweetened with honey that Imad ad-Din liked now that the nights were chilly.

They spoke at first of personal matters, Humphrey inquiring after Imad ad-Din's sons, and learning he had become a grandfather twice over since they had last met. "Alas, only two granddaughters, but three of my daughters-in-law are still pregnant. Maybe one of them will be more blessed. And you?" he asked gently and delicately. "Have you news to share?"

Imad ad-Din, of course, knew perfectly well that Humphrey's wife had been shamefully taken from him and given to another man. He found the entire incident on the one hand disgusting, and on the other hand satisfying evidence of the Franks' moral depravity. The idea that noblemen might contrive to take another nobleman's wife away from him against his will was mind-boggling. If Humphrey had divorced the woman, that would have been simple and straight-forward, but Humphrey had not. Still, it was far too delicate and humiliating a matter for Imad ad-Din to allude to directly.

Humphrey was grateful for that, although sometimes he wished there were someone he could talk to about the whole sordid affair. While the Lusignans were outraged about the political consequences of his wife's abduction, they also tended to blame him. Geoffrey had said outright, "If it had been *my* wife, I'd at least have taken up the gage and fought for her!" No, Humphrey got no sympathy from the Lusignans. . . .

Seeing his guest was brooding, Imad ad-Din changed the subject altogether. "You will have an audience tomorrow with al-Adil, may Allah smile upon him, but if you like, I will tell you the content of what he will say so you can prepare yourself."

"That would be very kind of you," Humphrey returned gladly to the present. The reminder that he was here on an important mission helped him forget the pain and humiliation of losing Isabella almost a year ago to the day.

"Al-Adil, may God's blessings be upon him, has struck upon a positively *brilliant* idea," Imad ad-Din enthused. "It is a way for both Muslims and Christians to retain hold over the sites holy to our respective faiths. It is a way to bring peace and prosperity back to this troubled land. It is surely a divinely inspired plan, praise be to God!"

Humphrey looked skeptical. "How would it be possible for two peoples so opposed to one another to hold the same territory in peace?" he asked.

"Just as two families who have a blood feud do!" Imad ad-Din answered with a grin of delight. "Through marriage!"

"Marriage?" Humphrey still did not understand, and frowned in his confusion.

"Yes. We know that the English King brought with him a sister, the former Queen of Sicily. As a widow of more than a year, she is now free to wed. Al-Adil, may God bless him, is willing to repudiate one of his current wives to marry her. The King of the English would give to his sister the territories he now controls—Acre, Jaffa, and the coast in between—as her dowry, and al-Adil's brother, the great Sultan, may Allah's blessing be ever upon him, would give the rest of the former Kingdom, including Jerusalem, to his brother as his *iqta*. That way they could rule jointly as King and Queen over all the territories that were once your Kingdom of Jerusalem. Isn't that a brilliant idea?" Imad ad-Din asked, smiling with apparently genuine delight at the idea.

Humphrey was too surprised to know what to think. "Queen Joanna married to al-Adil?"

"Yes, exactly."

"But would she have to convert to Islam?"

"Al-Adil, may Allah bless him, didn't say anything about that. I'm sure it would be far better for her if she did, but if she is stubborn, then it will not be necessary. But what of her brother? Do you think he will see the advantages of such an arrangement?"

Humphrey still couldn't picture it, but the plan certainly had merit if it would work. "Christians would have the right to visit all the holy places without inhibition?"

"As would Muslims."

"And the inhabitants could follow their own faith without being taxed extra?"

"Exactly. Everyone would be free to follow his own conscience. Obviously there are many details still to be worked out, but I can imagine that there could be separate courts for Christians and Muslims and Jews, and mosques, churches and synagogues would all be allowed to operate. The lords would be vassals of al-Adil and hold their fiefs from him, and he would divide them equally among Christians and Muslims."

It all sounded too good to be true to Humphrey, but why shouldn't something good come out of all the horrors that had gone before? Maybe God wanted peace in his homeland. Maybe he would prefer to see it shared, rather than torn apart and fought over. The more he thought about it, the more Humphrey liked the idea, and by the time he met with al-Adil the next day he was already an enthusiastic supporter of the proposal.

Ramla, early November 1191

Salah ad-Din's reaction to his brother's proposal was to burst out laughing.

Al-Adil, who had genuinely liked the idea (not least being King of Jerusalem), was less than pleased by his brother's reaction. "Does that mean you want me to withdraw the offer?" he asked testily.

"Good heavens, no!" Salah ad-Din replied, still chuckling and shaking his head. "Malik Rik will never accept it. It's a great joke. A great joke indeed. How did you ever come up with it?" He looked at his brother with wide, apparently admiring eyes, but al-Adil knew him too well. His brother was saying he should not dream of making himself a king. He was being told not to reach so high, and being reminded that he owed everything to his brother's generosity.

Al-Adil bowed his head to his brother, a slightly bitter smile on his lips. He did not think Yusef was really more intelligent than he; he had simply been at the right place at the right time—and that, reluctantly! Yusef had not wanted to accompany their uncle to Egypt. But what difference did that make now? Today he was the Sultan, and all bounty came from him.

Salah ad-Din, meanwhile, had stopped laughing, and the smile faded from his face. He reached out and grasped his brother's wrist. "Do not misunderstand me, Ahmad. I do not trust these infidels! They are all liars and cheats. They will promise us anything, and then behind our backs they will do the opposite. Look at the garrison of Acre! Fine, brave men who trusted in the words of the Polytheists!

"If I were to die tomorrow, Ahmad," Salah ad-Din continued, "there would be no one to unite the Muslims. Everyone would start fighting among themselves again, and the Franks would again be able to defeat us piecemeal. I must keep this army together until we have thrown the last of the Franks into the sea! We must rid ourselves of this plague once and for all. Now, while we are strong. This proposal of a marriage and an alliance—it is nonsense, and the King of England, as he has been described to me, will recognize that. But we will pretend for a little longer that we take these negotiations seriously, so that they keep talking to us. Meanwhile the weather deteriorates, and we tear down the strongholds they might otherwise use against us."

Al-Adil nodded. He did not entirely agree with his brother. He thought a negotiated settlement had many advantages—not least the lives and treasure saved. But his brother had opened their meeting with a reminder of who was Sultan, and so he saw no point in arguing with him. Instead he simply asked, "And that goes, too, for the offer put forward by the Baron of Sidon?" Only a few nights earlier, Salah ad-Din had put on a lavish banquet for Reginald de Sidon, welcoming him as an ambassador of Conrad de Montferrat. Salah ad-Din had then met with him for several hours the following day in al-Adil's presence.

"Ah." Salah ad-Din sat back and looked more pensive. "The advantage of Sidon's offer is that it sets the Franks against one another—like two dogs fighting over a bone! If I could be sure Montferrat would really fall upon the English King from the rear, I would be inclined to give him his little principality at Tyre and Sidon, maybe even Beirut. But I don't see that Montferrat has the capacity to fight the English King—assuming he really wants to."

"Doesn't he have support from all the Frankish lords?" al-Adil asked, surprised.

"As King, yes; to fight his fellow Christians, I don't think so."

"He has the support of Sidon and Ibn Barzan, at the very least, and we know Ibn Barzan is like a king to them, for all that they pretend it is Montferrat on account of his wife. Montferrat is Ibn Barzan's stepson and his puppet."

"That's what I used to think, too, but it is significant that Ibn Barzan did not return with Montferrat's offer to make an alliance with us against the English King. Ibn Barzan is playing some other game. I don't know what it is yet, but I am certain it does not involve fighting his fellow Christians for the sake of a couple of coastal cities."

"We should try to find out what he is up to," al-Adil warned. "He is a dangerous opponent."

"Is that the reason you tried to poison him?" Salah ad-Din asked, taking his brother by surprise. Al-Adil had not realized his brother knew about that poisoned dart during the siege of Tyre, and it annoyed him that one of his own Mamlukes (for no one else had known about the assassination attempt) was his brother's spy.

Salah ad-Din again built his brother a bridge by not dwelling on the issue. Instead he moved on, remarking, "I have not forgotten what Ibn Barzan cost me at Jerusalem. The worst thing that could happen is for him and the English King to become allies rather than adversaries. Toron assures us that the English

King mistrusts him, and has not forgiven him for dishonoring his cousin by taking her from her lawful husband and giving her to another man. Yet I wonder if Toron is telling us the truth? It was his wife who was taken away, and what did he do about it?"

"Toron is a weak man. We've always known that—which is why he has been so useful to us."

"Yes, he has been useful to us—to the extent that his own emotions do not blind him. From him we learned more about the roots and the depth of the antagonism between Malik Rik and Malik Phil. From his lips we have learned about Malik Rik's alienation of the Germans and his bickering with the remaining French. From Toron we know that the new Templar Master inclines more toward Montferrat than Lusignan, and the Hospitallers the reverse. He has been an invaluable source of information. But does he really know what is in Ibn Barzan's mind, now that they are sworn enemies?"

Al-Adil shrugged. "You've convinced me that he probably does not. What other spies could we use to find out more about Ibn Barzan and his plans?"

"Ibn Barzan has always shown an exceptional concern for the slaves we took after Hattin. You remember? He offered himself as surety for their ransom. Of course, he could never have raised it, so I couldn't accept the offer—but again, last month when he was here he wanted the release of all the captives. Surely we could find one such captive whom we could let 'escape.' If he went to Ibn Barzan, I'm sure he would find employment and could then observe from inside his house."

"We would have to find a slave willing to return to us with the intelligence," al-Adil pointed out.

"Yes, of course: a convert, dedicated now to serving the True Faith."

"I can make inquiries and see if there is a suitable Frankish Mamluke willing to serve us in this."

"I'm sure you will find a suitable young man," Salah ad-Din answered with a smile, adding, "And don't be so sad about 'losing' the crown of Jerusalem, Ahmad. It has never brought its wearers much joy."

Acre, November 1191

Rain showers confined the women indoors, and some servant had been careless with the firewood, allowing it to become damp. Smoke billowed into the room, causing even the dogs to retreat, and Queen Berengaria was indignant.

Queen Joanna, on the other hand, seemed merely depressed. She had wrapped herself in a fur-trimmed woolen shawl and huddled over a book. "I thought there was sunshine here all the time," she complained to Eschiva. "We've had rain for almost a week now!"

"Thank God," Eschiva answered, with a smile intended to cheer up her royal employers. "We need the rains of November to March to refill the cisterns and water our orchards and make the earth fruitful come spring.

"Pilgrims always complained about the heat and sun of the Holy Land," Berengaria took up the theme. "Never about rain!"

"That's because most pilgrims come in the spring and depart in the fall, before the winter storms and rains begin." Eschiva reminded them.

Berengaria nodded, but continued complaining. "This damp cold is terrible! The houses weren't built for it. At least at home we have bigger fireplaces and lower ceilings, and warm wooden floors. These tiles chill my feet right through my shoes!"

There was something to that, and Eschiva noted, "Your slippers are far too thin, my lady. We should try to find you some warmer footwear."

"Do they sell shoes at the souk?" Queen Joanna asked, sitting up a little straighter. Both Joanna and Berengaria found the covered markets of Acre alluring. On a day like this, when they couldn't enjoy being outside, the prospect of being able to shop without being exposed to the rain was particularly appealing.

"Of course!" Eschiva was pleased to have found some means to distract her royal companions from their boredom. "There are dozens of shoemakers in the souk—or at least there used to be. I don't suppose all have come back, but many will have."

The queens looked at one another. "Shall we go and see what we can find?" Joanna asked her sister-in-law.

"Yes! And we can stop for a snack at one of the little cook shops, too. One that sells that delicious grilled flatbread." Berengaria had discovered a fancy for some of the native food.

"And have fresh pomegranate juice." Joanna added. "There's that little corner stand that sells fresh fruit juices, remember?"

Pleased with their enthusiasm for the outing, Eschiva declared, "I'll go warn your knights we will need an escort," and stepped out into the anteroom.

The men of the queens' household were predominantly knights in King Richard's service recovering from illness or injuries. They came and went as men recuperated enough to rejoin the King, and others in need of rest replaced them. As a result Eschiva did not know many by name, and they seemed an interchangeable lot who spent an inordinate amount of time dicing and gambling.

She avoided these young men and instinctively sought out the elderly Norman-Sicilian knight Sir Norbert, one of the few knights who had come with Queen Joanna from Sicily.

Sir Norbert was grizzled and greying, a man of few words, and Eschiva knew little about him beyond his apparent devotion to Queen Joanna. Sir Norbert was filing his fingernails in a window seat, but he put the file away and stood up at the approach of Eschiva. "My lady," he acknowledged her with a slight bow.

"The queens would like to go to the souk for a bit. Queen Berengaria needs some warmer shoes, and—"

The door opened with a bang and they both looked over, annoyed by someone bursting in so roughly. Eschiva's attitude changed instantly, when she recognized her husband. With a cry of surprised delight, she abandoned Sir Norbert and ran to him.

Aimery's coif was gleaming with water, and his cloak was dark with rain. He shoved the coif back off his head and pulled the cloak off his shoulders to shake off some of the water before Eschiva reached him. As he took Eschiva in his arms and bent to kiss her, she exclaimed how cold his skin was. "You're chilled through! Come to the fire." He did not resist as she led him toward the fire, which was struggling in the large fireplace and smoking as much here in the large hall as in the queens salon.

"I've been on the road since daybreak," he explained. "And it's been raining most of the way."

"What brings you, Aimery?" Eschiva asked, certain that he had not come just to see her.

"I've got letters for the queens," he answered, glancing toward the inner chamber.

King Richard had been good at keeping his bride and sister informed of developments. He wrote terse, practical letters for the most part, which clearly disappointed the romantically inclined Berengaria. Joanna, on the other hand, appreciated the fact that if he took the time to write longer, more poetic and flowery letters, they would have fewer of them. "My father never wrote my mother," she'd try to explain to Berengaria. "Even when they were passionately in love with one another," she hastened to add, as Berengaria's face betrayed what she was thinking about the stormy relationship of Henry II and Eleanor of Aquitaine. "He could never take time to write. The best he did was order some hapless clerk to 'write something nice to the Queen'—which, I assure you, produced some of the most hilarious pieces of correspondence you can imagine. My mother saved several of them and shared them with me when I was little, simply because they were so entertaining."

If King Richard had now sent the Constable of Jerusalem to deliver these particular letters, then they had to be particularly important, Eschiva surmised. "Let's take them straight in," she suggested and led her husband toward the inner chamber.

Berengaria and Joanna had been looking for capes or cloaks with hoods to protect them from the rain. One of the chests was open and half the contents already scattered about in the course of their search.

"My ladies," Eschiva called to them as she entered. "My lord husband has brought letters from King Richard."

The queens at once stopped what they were doing and spun about. Berengaria reacted first, running forward eagerly and smiling. "At last! I was beginning to worry he had completely forgotten us!"

Aimery loosened the cords at the neck of his coif so he could slip his hand inside the padded gambeson underneath his hauberk. He extracted two letters. Checking the writing on the front, he identified the letter for Berengaria and handed it to her. She at once spun away, her gown and veils billowing out around her as she moved to the window seat to break the seal and read the letter at once.

Meanwhile Aimery turned to Joanna, the letter for her still in his hand. "My lady, your brother charged me with delivering this and awaiting your answer. I think you will need some time to consider your reply, however, and I hope you will allow me to take my wife from you briefly. We have not seen each other in weeks and would relish a little time alone together."

"Of course, my lord!" Joanna answered with a smile, taking the letter from him. "Eschiva has been wonderful to us and has earned more than a little break. When do you need to return to my brother?"

"I should set out no later than the day after tomorrow, but will not monopolize my lady's time. I have other errands I must also attend to. I will bring her back tomorrow morning, if that is agreeable?"

"I assure you, my lord, we do not begrudge any moment she can spend with you."

Aimery thanked the King of England's sister, and taking Eschiva on his arm, he withdrew. In the antechamber he retrieved his cloak and guided Eschiva down the corridor and steps to the courtyard, where his squire waited with the horses. "I hope we can obtain lodging with one of the religious houses," he told her as he helped her up into his own saddle and then swung up behind her.

As they rode out into the street and the drizzling rain, Aimery wrapped his arms and cloak around his wife to keep her as warm and dry as possible. Eschiva didn't mind the rain at all. It had been at least a decade since they had ridden like this, like lovers, two to a saddle. Nor did she mind that the front of his surcoat was damp, or that the chain mail under it was cold to lean against. She felt loved and young again, and it was almost jarring to have him remind her she was the mother of a boy nearly ten by asking her how Hugh was getting on.

"Queen Berengaria spoils him rotten," she admitted with a little laugh. "He's going to be a terrible charmer when he gets a few years older."

Aimery laughed at that. "Must take after his Uncle Guy."

"Oh, you weren't so bad in your prime, as I recall—or were the rumors about you and the Queen Mother false?" she teased, looking up at him from the safety of his arms.

Aimery snorted. "*You* aren't supposed to know about that, dearest, but since you do, I must confess that it didn't take a lot to seduce Agnes de Courtenay."

Safe in his arms with Agnes de Courtenay long dead, Eschiva could laugh.

"Shall we try St. Sebastian's?" Aimery asked, in no mood to ride the streets a moment longer and pointing to the first monastery that came into view.

Eschiva was in the same mood. The sooner they could get out of the rain and their clothes and into bed together, the better. It mattered to her not at all that it was midday on a Friday. She'd happily do penance for any "sin" involved.

The brothers of St. Sebastian appeared a little flustered by the request for lodging from the Constable of Jerusalem and his wife—but they did have a guest lodge and it did have a room, and within a few minutes, Aimery and Eschiva were in bed behind the heavy damask curtains. They stayed there for hours, making love, dozing, talking, and then starting the cycle again.

It was not until dinnertime that they emerged and took a fasting meal of fish and rice with the abbot, before retiring to their lodgings again with a carafe of wine. Only now did Aimery confide, "King Richard's letter to his sister contains an astonishing offer from Salah ad-Din."

"King Richard has been negotiating with the Sultan?" Eschiva asked, surprised.

"Yes." Aimery paused there. He considered diplomacy a continuation of war by other means, and was fairly confident that the English King saw it that way, too. Only this proposal was different.

"I'm surprised he would share the contents of negotiations with his sister," Eschiva remarked. "I understand he might consult his wife, but you said it was his letter to his sister. Does he trust her more than his bride?"

"No, that's not it. It's just that the Sultan's proposal affects the Queen of Sicily, not the Queen of England."

"How is that?" Eschiva asked, puzzled.

"The Sultan proposes marrying his brother al-Adil to King Richard's sister, and having them rule jointly over a restored Kingdom of Jerusalem."

"That's sheer nonsense!" Eschiva exclaimed dismissively. "You know as well as I do that no woman *rules* anything in the Muslim world. Why, she wouldn't even be his only wife, and she could be repudiated at any time! Surely the King of England wouldn't consider sending his sister into a harem!"

"Frankly, Eschiva, I don't know King Richard well enough to know whether he would or not, but he asked me to deliver the letters personally so you could report back to me his sister's real reaction—not just her formal response to him. Tomorrow I'll drop you off at the palace and go off to do my other errands. I'll collect you again in the evening, and you can then tell me what the Queen of Sicily honestly feels about the notion of becoming Queen of Jerusalem."

Eschiva did not answer. She was not happy about either the proposal itself or the role of spy for the English King, but she did not want to argue with Aimery. They had been so happy together this afternoon, and she wanted it to stay that way right up to the moment he departed. Aimery felt the same way, so he changed the subject; he began telling her about the capture of Jaffa.

Eschiva was surprised by Queen Joanna's welcome. In the months they had been together they had become friends—but Berengaria, with her more flamboyant, hot-blooded temperament, had been the one to throw her arms around Eschiva, or nudge her in the ribs when she was stifling a giggle, or otherwise be affectionate or playful as the occasion warranted. Joanna had retained a reserve that Eschiva ascribed to her widowhood, her imprisonment, and her more serious nature.

This morning, however, the moment Joanna spotted Eschiva, she jumped up and rushed over to her. "Eschiva! I've been waiting for you. Not that I begrudge you time with your husband, but we have to talk!" She already had her hand clasped firmly around Eschiva's wrist, and was all but dragging her to the little chapel that had been built to serve the kings of Jerusalem as a private sanctuary. There was room here for little more than an officiating priest and at most four worshipers. Joanna firmly closed the door behind her to make sure they were not followed, hastily crossed herself in the direction of the Eucharist candle burning over the altar, and then faced Eschiva.

Her face was strained, her eyes bloodshot, and her breath was bad. She looked like she'd had a sleepless night. "You will not believe what my brother is proposing. He wants me to marry Salah ad-Din's brother! A Muslim! He says it would be a way to end the war, the bloodshed, for all time! He says I would rule jointly with this al-Adil, and our children would ensure that the Holy City remained open to Christians ever after. I need your advice, Eschiva. Should I agree to such a proposal? Should I tell my brother to pursue it?" Even more than the way she looked, this agitation, completely at odds with her usual composure, revealed just how distressed Joanna Plantagenet was by this absurd idea.

Eschiva was cautious by nature. Before giving her own opinion, she asked, "What did Queen Berengaria say?"

"You know Ria! She's besotted with my brother. In her eyes he can do no wrong! She says if *he* thinks this is a good idea, then I should be happy to play such a blessed role as "peacemaker"—and that I should count myself lucky to wear the "sacred" crown of Jerusalem as well! But what do I care about another crown if the price is marriage to a—Do you know anything about this al-Adil? What sort of man is he? Richard says in his letter that he met with him, and that he was very cultivated and charming."

"Man to man, no doubt!" Eschiva answered, more sharply than intended. "Nor do I doubt that the Sultan's brother is highly educated, well-dressed, clean, a patron of the arts, and many other admirable things, but he remains a Muslim. Whether he marries you or not, he will retain his other wives and concubines! And don't forget that in Islamic law *he* can divorce you on a whim *without cause* any time he likes. No sooner will your brother sail away than he will be free to cast you off!"

Joanna blanched. She had forgotten that.

"And even if he doesn't, you will have no *voice* in public—maybe not even in private. You will certainly never be allowed to show your face again to any man but him! Oh, my lady, I cannot imagine a fate worse than marriage to a Muslim— unless it is slavery to one! You must not let your brother do this to you!"

Joanna responded by wrapping her arms around Eschiva as she whispered, "Thank you!" It was said with so much heartfelt relief that Eschiva's eyes flooded with tears.

After a moment, Joanna drew back and looked deeply into Eschiva's face. "Thank you," she repeated. "That was the way I *felt*, but I kept asking myself if I was being selfish. All night long I wondered if Berengaria was right, and if the lives of all those men who will die in this struggle weren't more important than my personal happiness. Is it really my *right* to put my own happiness ahead of the lives of all the good Christian men who will die if we reject this settlement?"

"It is not that simple, my lady," Eschiva answered steadily and firmly. "Sharia law does not recognize women as full humans—their word is worth only that of half a man. A woman can not sit or speak in the presence of men outside her family. She can not show her face to men outside her family. In legal suits, she must be represented by her father, husband or son. Indeed, a married woman cannot leave her house without the permission of her husband—even if it is to go only to the baths. How then could your marriage achieve anything so praiseworthy as Christian access to the Holy Places? As I said, al-Adil can divorce you at will—and after he does, then he can also throw the Christians out again. This is a farce. A red herring. Your brother should feel insulted that the Sultan thinks he is stupid enough to fall for such a transparent ruse!" Eschiva was genuinely indignant.

"You are sure of that?" Joanna asked, brightening up for the first time since she had read her brother's letter.

"Of course I'm sure of it—and anyone from Outremer could tell him so. I don't mean the Lusignans—Guy and Geoffrey never bothered to learn anything about their foes—but if you asked my uncle, or Sidon, or even Humphrey de Toron, he would tell you the same thing."

"Oh, Eschiva, you are an angel from heaven!" Joanna embraced her again in boundless relief. "You have not only reassured me that I'm not just being selfish, you have given me the answer I need. I will not protest on my behalf, but point out to my dear brother that he is being hoodwinked! Nothing will better ensure that he says 'no'!

"And then we need to think of ways to entertain him and make him far too fond of me to ever contemplate giving me away against my wishes to anyone! He says in his letter he hopes to come visit us in about a week, and that's a perfect chance to reinforce his affection. If only I knew what would please him most. He doesn't really care about food that much. He loves hawking, but the weather is quite unpredictable."

"Isn't he a great connoisseur of music, my lady?" Eschiva asked tentatively.

"Oh, he adores it! He came of age in my mother's court at Poitiers, and she always had the very best troubadours there. He even writes poetry himself, and he can play the cittern quite well. Do you know of any musicians here that are first class? I can't say I've been much impressed so far," Joanna confessed.

"No, the musicians here in Acre are very second-rate, but . . ."

"Yes?"

"In Tyre, my lady, my uncle has a squire who is not at all bad, and his wife is truly a gifted singer."

"A woman? A respectable woman who sings?" Joanna asked, astonished.

"She comes from a humble background, my lady, but I have never heard anyone sing as beautifully as she. When she sings and her husband accompanies her on the harp, it is truly like the music of the angels."

Acre, late November 1191

Alys had never heard the phrase "stage fright," but it described her state of mind perfectly. She was almost paralyzed with fear, and Ernoul found himself leading her to one of the benches lining the wall and making her sit down. He handed her his lute and went in search of some wine. If she didn't relax, they were going to make a terrible hash of their performance tonight. Ernoul had hopes of impressing the English King and winning a real reward, but all his dreams hinged on Alys performing exceptionally well. At the moment the prospects looked dim.

The hall was so crowded that the air was stifling. King Richard had returned with what looked like hundreds of his fellow crusaders, including the Lusignans, Henri de Champagne, and Hugh de Burgundy. Apparently, based on the conversations Ernoul had overheard, not many women had ventured as far south as Jaffa, and the food supplies were more utilitarian than delectable. As a result, many crusaders had slipped back to the "fleshpots" of Acre, bored and unwilling to remain in the Spartan conditions of Jaffa. Richard and the other lords were here to round them up again.

Kings Richard and Guy occupied the central seats at the high table, flanked by Queen Berengaria on Richard's right and Queen Joanna on Guy's left. Henri de Champagne was beside his aunt Joanna, and Hugh de Burgundy sat beside Berengaria. At both ends of the table were churchmen: the Archbishop of Tyre, who returned from his embassy to the West this past summer, and the Patriarch. Meanwhile, in the hall the servants were clearing away the last of the sweets, and the entertainment was about to begin.

Ernoul looked frantically for an unclaimed goblet, filled it from the nearest pitcher, took a sip himself to steady his nerves, and brought the rest back to his wife. Alys was staring at the high table and breathing heavily. "I can't go through with this, Ernoul," she whispered.

"It's too late to back down now," he told her sternly.

"But they say he writes his own music!" Alys protested, her eyes glued on the English King, who was certainly a sight to behold. He was a tall, broad-shouldered man, dressed tonight in red samite sewn with golden lions, and he wore his crown. His red-gold hair, though still short from his bout of Arnoldia, caught the light from the lamps, and in the Western tradition he wore a neatly clipped beard as well. Above the beard his face was tanned from the Palestinian sun, and it was an unquestionably handsome face, well-proportioned, with strong, straight features. Yet more than his good looks and impressive clothes, it was his reputation for courage that made him so intimidating.

Stories about his daring and his near-escapes from death circulated every-where—even in Tyre. Ernoul knew that once when King Richard had gone hawking with only a few companions, Saracens had ambushed them. King Richard had only escaped capture because one of his knights called out that he was the King. The loyal knight had quickly been seized and carried off for what his Saracen captors thought would be a king's ransom, while the real King escaped.

On another occasion, King Richard had come to the rescue of squires sent foraging for horse fodder. The Templars sent to defend the squires had been overwhelmed by hundreds of Turkish cavalry. Just as the Templars and squires were being led off to slavery and death, some of the King's household knights rode to the rescue. But they, too, were overwhelmed as more Saracens joined their comrades. Hearing their cries for help, the English King sent two of his nobles with their knights into the fray while he armed himself. Before he could join, however, some four thousand fresh Saracens fell upon the Templars, the squires, and their rescuers. Seeing these odds, King Richard's companions had urged him to hold back, saying it would be better if all the others perished than for him to risk his own capture, or death. King Richard, so everyone said, had furiously rebuked them, saying he would not withhold aid to those to whom he had promised it. He then plunged into the fight, and soon put the whole Saracen army to flight. Such were the stories circulating about this king already called the Lionheart.

The palace steward was bending to speak into Ernoul's ear. "The King is ready for you, Master Ernoul."

Ernoul turned to Alys and took the now-empty goblet from her trembling hands. "It's no different than singing for Lord Balian and Queen Maria Zoë, or for the Marquis and Queen Isabella," he tried to assure her.

Alys met his eyes, her lips a grim line, and firmly shook her head as she whispered, "Yes, it is!"

"No, it's not." Ernoul took his harp from her and pulled her to her feet.

Alys was sure she was going to faint right away. Her knees felt like jelly, and she could not seem to put one foot before the other. She *couldn't*. Just then she felt someone slip an arm around her waist and hand her a glass with cool water in it. Eschiva hugged Alys and whispered in her ear, "Don't look at them, Alys. Look at me. I'm going to stand right behind Queen Joanna. Focus on me while you sing. It will be fine."

Alys took a deep breath, and with Ernoul on one side and Eschiva on the other, she advanced to the space before the high table. Eschiva gave her a last hug and withdrew. Around them the room was gradually quieting down in anticipation of the entertainment. It didn't go entirely silent. Particularly at the fringes, people were still talking, and now and again a laugh rang out. Those at the high table, however, were still and attentive. Joanna was leaning on her elbows expectantly. Berengaria was holding on to her husband's hand while looking eagerly at Alys, and King Richard was considering her with lynx-like eyes that seemed to want to eat her alive. Alys caught her breath, and Ernoul whispered, "Look at Eschiva and Aimery."

They were now both standing behind the high table.

Alys focused on the familiar couple, and Ernoul started to play the harp, a series of warm-up chords and scales. Then he gave her the opening sequence of the "Song of Palestine" and hissed (none too gently): "Sing!"

She opened her mouth, and nothing came out. She saw Eschiva clasp Aimery's arm and then nod to Alys and mouth: "You can do it." Alys closed her eyes, and suddenly the sound was there. It was faint and quavered slightly at first, but with each note it grew stronger.

There was applause when she finished, but Ernoul did not give her a chance to flee. He took up another song immediately, one of her favorites, and soon the room was under her spell. Alys was still singing with her eyes closed, but Ernoul risked glancing at the high table and was gratified by the expressions on both queens' faces. They were clearly delighted and impressed. King Richard, in contrast, looked relaxed and pleased, but not particularly captivated.

The applause was greater this time, and Ernoul bowed briefly, but struck up the next song before it had died down. He played the introduction and turned his eyes to Alys with a desperate plea in his eyes. This time she met his eyes and smiled. The fear was behind her. Suddenly they were back on the quay at Tyre, the day they fell in love—only *they* were singing Ernoul's song, together. Her eyes smiled as they held his—and looking only at him, she began to sing as he played.

"Salah ad-Din, you have the grave,"

A gasp went through the great hall, and the King of England started so violently that he splashed wine from his goblet onto the beautiful linen tablecloth.

"And you have made our brothers slaves,
But we survived, we are alive,"

Alys's voice was so clear and true, it rang to the rafters and sent chills down men's and women's spines.

"Salah ad-Din, you have the Tomb

But it is dark, deserted gloom
For Christ is risen! And by our side!"

At the high table, Queen Berengaria crossed herself reverently, and so did the two churchmen. King Richard, at last, was leaning forward, his interest finally piqued.

"We are with Him, we have no fear
Of you, your army, or your emirs.
Christ on our side, we cannot die!"

Around them other men were stirring, and Ernoul now opened his mouth and sang with Alys. Man and wife sang with eyes fixed on one another, and their faces suffused with an inner glow of euphoric joy as the melody mutated slightly.

"Christ is with us, Salah ad-Din.
Christ is with us, we cannot die,
But we will fight you—until you do!"

It was not planned, but there were many men in that hall who knew the song, including Aimery de Lusignan. They could not contain themselves any longer, and as Ernoul and Alys raised their voices for the last verses they joined in, their voices far less melodic or trained, but all the more convincing as they called out:

"The day will come, when we will win
When we will take Jerusalem
For Him, not us; for Christendom!"

"We are alive, Salah ad-Din;
We are alive, and cannot die.
And we will take Jerusalem!"

The applause that followed was thunderous. Men jumped to their feet and were shouting, cheering, and clapping. Alys heard them, but did not dare look away from her husband. His smile was all that mattered, until—with a glance to the high table—he told her, "The King of England wants to meet you, Alys."

Alys gasped and looked to the high table. King Richard was indeed gesturing for both of them to approach. Ernoul helped Alys up the steps, and caught her when she almost fell over backwards in her nervousness as she curtsied.

"You are a remarkable singer, child," King Richard addressed her. "And your husband has the makings of an outstanding musician," he added with a smile to Ernoul, who bowed deeply, more flattered and honored than he had ever imagined he could be. "Tell me, did your husband write that last song?"

Alys nodded vigorously. Her heart was stuck in her throat, and she could not have uttered a sound if her life depended on it.

"I will learn it," King Richard declared firmly, and nothing could have meant more to Ernoul. The King turned to Ernoul, not out of disrespect for Alys, but rather because the King could see the state she was in. "Tell me, what brought you here? Whom do you serve?"

"I was born here, my lord King. My father held a knight's fief in Ibelin, and I served Lord Balian as his squire at Hattin. That's where I got this broken collarbone," he pointed out. Only when his attention was drawn to it did King Richard notice the unnatural slope of Ernoul's shoulders.

"The Baron of Ibelin is a man of many parts, it seems," he observed, sounding not entirely pleased. "In addition to being a good soldier and a dubious diplomat, he is—I see—a patron of the arts. You serve him still?" he asked skeptically.

"Indeed, my lord King. As best I can, but no longer on the battlefield."

"No, that would be a waste of your talents, young man," the English King conceded. "Tell me your name and then name your reward."

Ernoul had hoped for this, and he and Alys had even discussed how high they dared go. Ten bezants? Twelve? Even fifteen? Enough to have a little nest egg of their own, they had decided, insurance against bad times that never seemed too far away since Hattin. But Ernoul could not bring himself to ask for something so materialistic. "My name is Ernoul, my lord King, and all I ask is that you help us regain Jerusalem and the return of the captives. Give us back our homeland and our families." For it was not just Sir Bartholomew's daughters who had disappeared into Saracen captivity, it was Ernoul's old parents, his tutor and all the household of his childhood.

Chapter 18

Tyre, early December 1191

MARIA ZOË COULD NOT HAVE EXPLAINED why, but she was suspicious from the start. The household had been in an uproar, and Helvis in particular had fluttered with excitement. "It's Joscelyn! It's Joscelyn!" she exclaimed, smiling broadly, and breathless with apparent delight (although to Maria Zoë's knowledge she could not have met the boy ever before). "Sir Bartholomew's grandson!" Helvis insisted, adding with breathless excitement, "and he's escaped the Saracens and found his way here."

"Here? Now?" Maria Zoë asked herself. She had never known either of Sir Bartholomew's daughters very well. They had sometimes come for Christmas and Easter courts. Maria Zoë vaguely remembered stopping with one or the other of them once when she and Balian had been caught in a vile thunderstorm on the way home. She knew they both had young children, but the children did not attend on the lord and lady. Under the circumstances, there was no way Maria Zoë would have recognized one of those children now.

The boy who claimed to be Joscelyn d'Auber, the son of Beatrice d'Auber, was a good-looking boy with bright blond hair, blue eyes, and well-formed features and figure. He was certainly of Frankish descent, Maria Zoë conceded, but there was no particular resemblance to Sir Bartholomew. Maria Zoë also found it curious and suspicious that he said he'd "run away" and wanted "to serve the Baron of Ibelin." Surely he would want first to see his grandfather and just be free?

Maria Zoë gave no outward indication of her unease. Instead she sent a squire with a letter to Sir Bartholomew. Meanwhile, Balduin (Henri d'Ibelin's son) was told to give the new arrival some of his own clothes so he could discard the dirty rags he'd arrived in.

The rags, Maria Zoë noted, suited his story of being a runaway slave, but not his tanned and muscular body. For a boy of ten, he was remarkably well filled out, with not a scar on him. He was also astonishingly cocky for having been a slave for four years. Of course he would feel some euphoria to have escaped and then crossed, by his own account, almost a hundred miles of no man's land, living off the rations he claimed to have stolen from his former master, but something about his story just didn't ring true.

Maria Zoë sent for Sister Adela. As a woman who ran an orphanage and had dealt with hundreds of children in various states of distress, Sister Adela would surely have a better feel for what they should expect from a child who had endured slavery for four years and then escaped. Meanwhile, dressed in one of Balduin's shirts, borrowed hose, and low shoes, Joscelyn was taken to the kitchens, and a trencher overflowing with leftovers was placed in front of him. He dug in heartily, while the children clustered around in excitement.

John, Philip, and Balduin pelted him with questions, while Helvis kept giving orders to the cook to bring more food. Margaret sat opposite the newcomer with her chin cupped in her hands and her elbows on the table staring in open fascination.

"How did you fall into their hands?" John wanted to know.

Joscelyn shrugged and stuffed bread into his mouth. "They just overran the manor and took all of us," he answered with his mouth full.

"And then what?" Philip asked eagerly.

"We were tied up and put on a wagon that took us to Damascus."

"Where are the rest of your family?" Balduin asked.

"We were together until we got to Damascus. That's where the slave trader sold us to different masters."

"And you've never seen your family ever again?" Helvis asked in horror.

Joscelyn shook his head, but he didn't seem too upset about it, Maria Zoë thought. Was that normal? He'd been only six when he'd been taken captive and separated from his mother and older brothers. If John and Philip had been taken from her at that age and had lived four years apart, would they too be so indifferent to her, their sisters, and each other?

"What happened then?" Philip asked, more interested in the narrative than in feelings.

Joscelyn shrugged and looked down. "A merchant bought me."

"And what did you have to do?" Balduin asked.

Joscelyn shrugged again. "Look after his things. You know. Like a squire does for a knight."

"How can you compare a squire to a slave?" John protested indignantly. He was looking forward to becoming a squire, and did not want to think his future status was similar to slavery.

"Have some wine," Helvis offered, setting a pottery mug in front of Joscelyn with cut wine.

Joceyln drew back and shook his head sharply.

"It's the good wine," Helvis assured him, "from Cyprus."

"No! I don't want it!" Joscelyn insisted, frowning. "Just water."

"But—"

"Helvis!" Maria Zoë interrupted. "Do as he asks."

Annoyed, Helvis did as she was told, while Philip asked eagerly, "Did he ever beat you?"s

"Only when I did something wrong," Joscelyn answered. "He wasn't bad."

"So why did you run away?" Balduin wanted to know.

Joscelyn frowned. "Because the next master was terrible. You see, the first man sold me to a man who beat me all the time and would hardly let me sleep and gave me almost nothing to eat. I had to get away from him!"

"Was he a merchant, too?"

"Yes, of course—a merchant of weapons!" Joscelyn exclaimed, with strange enthusiasm for the man who had beaten and starved him.

"Why didn't you steal any of them when you ran away?" Philip asked.

"I couldn't risk it—but I learned how to use them!"

"A slave?" John asked skeptically, and his mother nodded to herself, pleased. Even at twelve and a half, John was no fool.

"I did it secretly when he wasn't looking," Joscelyn answered unconvincingly.

It was ringing Nones, and that was when the boys usually went to the Ibelin stud for their afternoon ride and exercise. Even the presence of the exotic runaway slave could not distract them from that. Instead they jumped up, suggesting eagerly that Joscelyn come with them. "Wait till you see the horses!" Balduin told him excitedly.

Joscelyn made a face. "Frankish horses? They're all dead meat!" he sneered.

"Are you crazy?" Philip asked, outraged, while John told him off hotly: "My lord father breeds the finest horses in all of Syria! The Sultan's studs included. He's interbred Arab and Frankish horses to produce the strongest, fastest horses alive!"

"John, don't exaggerate; just take Joscelyn along with you," Maria Zoë suggested, shooing the boys out of the kitchen.

A few minutes later Sister Adela arrived in answer to the Dowager Queen's summons, and Maria Zoë explained what had happened. She concluded with a simple: "The problem is, I don't believe him."

Sister Adela looked surprised. "Why not? Why should he be lying—and who is he, if not Sir Bartholomew's grandson?"

"I don't know the answer to that, but I think he is Muslim, loyal to the Sultan, and here to poison my lord husband."

"Ah." Sister Adela understood. As a Greek princess, Queen Maria Zoë Comnena had been born and raised on intrigue; she was quicker to spot it than mere mortals. Adela asked next, "What do you want from me?"

"To convince me I'm wrong!" Maria Zoë countered with a short laugh. "I'd much rather think that he is Sir Bartholomew's grandson, home safe and sound. It would give poor Sir Bartholomew something to live for again, and ease his conscience a little."

Sister Adela nodded. She too liked the old knight, and thought the safe return of at least one of his five grandchildren might ease some of his pain.

"Come with me," Maria Zoë urged. "They've all gone to the stud."

By the time the women arrived, the boys were already mounted and engaged in a fierce competition that entailed racing, jumping over small obstacles, and attacking one another on horseback. John held a little aloof from the fray. He was significantly taller than his brother and cousin, much less Joscelyn, and since Centurion was with his father, he was riding one of the younger destriers-in-training, a larger and more powerful mount than the ponies his brother and cousin rode. John was making (mostly unsuccessful) runs at the quintain. Philip and Joscelyn, on the other hand, were both ten, and Balduin was a healthy eight-year-old used to playing with his elder cousins.

The women made no effort to interrupt the rough game, although Sister Adela shook her head once and remarked, "I don't know how you can be so calm. I'd be terrified for their life and limb if they were mine."

Maria Zoë laughed. "Believe me, it will only get worse. First they'll get old enough for jousting and tournaments, then they'll go to war and start fighting men intent on killing them. The more they learn here and now in these games of war, the more likely they will be to survive real war." She then drew attention to the paddock, where Philip had his arms around Joscelyn and was trying to drag him off his horse while the newcomer resisted. "Do you see that? That boy is no stranger to horseback, and you can't tell me a slave of a weapons merchant would have learned to ride. Watch him! He's keeping the horse under him with his legs alone, and by doing so, he's escaping being pulled down. I wager if we gave him a bow, he'd be able to hit a target at the far side of the paddock at full gallop."

"My lady! What are you saying?"

"I'm saying that boy's a Mamluke. A slave, yes, but a slave in training as a mounted archer in the Sultan's elite bodyguard."

Sister Adela looked at her askance, still resisting the idea. "Surely not!"

"Look at the way he rides!" Maria Zoë insisted, her eyes still leveled hostilely on Joscclyn as he managed to get his horse to start backing up, and in so doing dragged her son Philip out of his saddle to crash down into the dust. Maria Zoë did not flinch as her son fell, but her eyes narrowed on Joscelyn. "The Sultan has tried to kill my lord husband once before, and suddenly this boy turns up out of nowhere, claiming to be the grandson of one of my husband's closest household knights. Not only does he arrive here, he asks to be taken into my husband's service! We ought to be insulted that Salah ad-Din thinks we are so stupid as to fall for this ploy!"

Sister Adela looked from Maria Zoë to the blond boy, who was pumping his fist in the air in triumph, oblivious to the fact that Balduin was about to launch an attack on him from behind. The eight-year-old charged his horse straight into Joscelyn's, and, dropping his reins, used both his hands to push the newcomer off his horse. Meanwhile, Philip had managed to get to his feet, and he grabbed Joscelyn as he fell. He wrestled him to the ground and, sitting astride him, started hitting him in obvious fury.

Eskinder, the head groom, leaped over the fence, ran out, and tore Philip off his bested opponent. John had stopped in his exercises to watch what was happening, his fractious mount snorting and stamping his foot in impatience.

"What are you going to do?" Sister Adela asked softly.

"See what Sir Bartholomew says—and meanwhile keep the boy, whoever he is, as far away from my husband as possible."

Sir Bartholomew, dressed in the robes of a Augustine monk, was on his knees praying before the altar of the Virgin. When they ushered young Alain into the chapel, the commotion behind him interrupted his concentration. Annoyed, he concluded his Ave, crossed himself, and rolled on his heels to stand up with an unconscious grunt.

Alain was shocked by the sight of him. Sir Bartholomew had always been a well-built man—not as tall as Ibelin, but not short, either. He'd had broad shoulders and muscular arms, the upper body of a man good with sword, shield, and lance. Now he was nothing but sagging skin on fragile bones, for he had been fasting so continuously that he'd passed out several times. Finally, the abbot had felt compelled to order him to eat—and order him to stop flagellating himself as well.

"Sir?" the squire began uncertainly. "I bring a letter from my lady the Dowager Queen." He removed the letter from the inside of his gambeson and held it out.

Sir Bartholomew stared at it with hostility. Why couldn't they leave him alone? He'd served both Ibelin and his lady well, and they had been good to him in return, but now he had to focus on his black, embittered soul. "I don't want to read it," he told the squire bluntly.

"Yes, you do, sir!" Alain countered eagerly. He was the son of a knight of Hebron. He'd had no news of his father since Hattin. He and his mother and sister had taken refuge in Jerusalem, and they had been there during the siege and surrender. Only nine at the time, Alain had not officially taken part in the defense. However, unknown to his mother, he had snuck out several times to help carry water to the defenders, and he'd helped stoke the fires under the pots of molten tar. The siege had been the most important episode in his life—until now. "Your grandson escaped! He made it to Tyre and is now in the household of the Dowager Queen," Alain explained, excited.

Sir Bartholomew stared at him, stunned, until he finally managed to ask, "Bart?"

"No, Joscelyn."

"Joscelyn? But he's just a baby!"

"Six when he was taken; ten now." Alain, at thirteen, didn't think ten was such a "baby."

"You are certain of this?" Sir Bartholomew asked, dazed.

"Read the letter, sir!" Alain urged, grinning.

Sir Bartholomew took the letter at last and broke open the seal almost brutally. He didn't have the patience to read the letter. His eyes flew over the text, seeking the message Alain had already relayed. ". . . claiming to be your grandson Joscelyn . . ." the Dowager Queen had written.

Claiming to be, claiming to be . . . She doubted it. Sir Bartholomew doubted, too, but only in his head. In his heart he believed God had answered his prayers. How long had he been here? Not yet fully four months. He spun around, sank down on his knees, and began thanking the Virgin profusely and passionately.

Two days later they docked at Tyre. Alain was enjoying himself. Sir Bartholomew was so excited, anxious, frightened, hopeful, and full of plans for his grandson he could hardly think straight. Alain had taken care of everything for him: booking passage, packing his things and buying food for the passage, securing a reasonably good place on deck, and on landing, hiring a couple of donkeys that happened to be on the quay.

When they arrived at the Ibelin residence, Sir Bartholomew was almost paralyzed with sudden anxiety. "What if it isn't Josh?" he asked Alain helplessly.

"But it is!" Alain assured him, grinning, paying off the donkeyman, and taking their meager baggage onto his own shoulders.

They knocked and were admitted at once. The squires in the hall greeted Sir Bartholomew cheerfully. He'd been their training master until he withdrew from the world, and he was popular with them because he was better tempered and easier on them than his successor Sir Galvin. "Your grandson's here!" several of them told him at once, and Sir Bartholomew nodded numbly. "Where is he?"

"Upstairs taking his lessons with the other children," they told him in chorus.

Sir Bartholomew nodded dazed. They'd docked with the morning tide and it had not yet struck Terce, so it made sense that his grandson was at his lessons with Lords John, Philip, and Balduin.

Sir Bartholomew mounted the stone stairs that clung to the wall of the interior courtyard leading to the screened passage before the great hall, and then climbed the interior wooden stairs to the second floor. He followed the sound of children's voices competing with one another for attention, and heard the low voice of Father Michael admonishing them to speak one at a time. Outside the door to the improvised schoolroom, he paused and took a deep breath, but his heart was racing and his breathing was shallow. He reached for the handle and only slowly depressed the grip. He gently pushed the door inward, holding his breath unconsciously. As the crack opened, it revealed first Margaret sitting with her arms around her knees, looking rather bored, and then Philip, waving his arm in agitated insistence on attention. Then—it was Joscelyn!

Sir Bartholomew could restrain himself no longer. He burst into the room, his eyes fixed on his grandson as he called out, "Joscelyn!" Joscelyn was big and strong and healthy! He was beautiful! He was perfect! He was alive and free!

And he was staring at his grandfather in fright.

"Joscelyn! Don't you recognized me? It's Grandpapa!"

Joscelyn got respectfully to his feet, but there was no joy on his face. He just stood with his hands at his sides—trembling.

Ramla, December 12, 1191

The Sultan had withdrawn toward the north, disbanding much of his army. What he left behind was sheer wreckage. Ibelin had almost not been able to identify which pile of rubble had once been his brother's lovely house. Only the marble paving stones of the entry hall and the first three steps of the stairway remained in place. The steps led to nothing but broken masonry, shattered tiles, and glass. The wreckage smothered all that had once lived here in rubbish, dust, and ruin.

Rather than living in his brother's home as he had expected to do, Ibelin and his men were forced to strike camp on the plain to the east along with the rest of the Frankish army. Here he encountered outright hostility from the English and Normans nearest the town. Someone called out, "There goes Balian d'Ibelin, as treacherous as a gobelin!" The English and Normans laughed, while a mutter of anger spread through the ranks of his own men. Ibelin was shocked by the hostility of King Richard's men and wondered if he was really welcome. He led his men to set up their tents beside the Templars instead.

They found themselves in what had once been an orchard. The Saracens had chopped down the trees, leaving the stumps. That made it hard to find a level place to erect a tent, much less a place to lie down. Furthermore, because of the recent rains, the plain was a morass of mud, made even more unpleasant by temperatures that hovered only a few degrees above freezing. Men and horses were miserable, the days dark and dingy, and morale mirrored the heavens that sporadically spat snow flurries on them.

Ibelin's tent offered only moderate protection against the wind, and the fire inside struggled in the drafts, blowing the smoke first in one direction and then the next. All his twenty-eight knights and their squires were crowded inside, as much for the warmth of huddling together as for any camaraderie or comfort. They had broken into a new cask of wine, and the squires were squirting the wine into one mug after another and passing the mugs around.

"What's the point of camping here and freezing our asses off?" Sir Galvin growled generally.

"Now that Salah ad-Din has disbanded most of his army, isn't it the moment to strike?"

"In this weather? You've gone soft in the head!"

"My lord!" It was the sentry at the door.

"Yes?" Ibelin roused himself.

"There's a monk here looking for you."

"Send him in."

"He says he doesn't want to come in, my lord."

With a sigh, Ibelin got to his feet and weaved his way between his men, stepping over their outstretched legs to reach the exit. It was close to sunset, and the sky to the west burned an ominous blood red as the sun shot rays through a brief rip in the cloud cover. Ibelin looked around, bewildered, before the sentry pointed to a hooded figure hovering a few yards away.

"Brother?" Ibelin addressed him as he approached the monk.

The man turned, his face still shrouded in the shadows of his hood, and Ibelin felt an instinctive sense of alarm. The monk stood with his hands and arms stuffed up the opposite sleeves. It would be so easy for one of those hands to hold a knife.

"It's me, Balian." The deep voice of Sir Bartholomew blew out of the folds of his hood with a billow of freezing breath.

"Merciful heaven, Bart! What are you doing here still in the robes of a monk? You're welcome to join us anytime, if you want to take up arms again—"

"That's not why I'm here. I've brought you intelligence," Sir Bartholomew interrupted, "but it is something I prefer to share with your ears alone. Will you walk with me?"

Ibelin could think of many things he would prefer to do at dusk on this dreary winter day, but if Sir Bartholomew had come all the way from Acre to tell him something, he had no right to deny him an audience. Ibelin nodded stiffly, and Sir Bartholomew indicated with an inclination of his head that they should walk toward the periphery of the camp. Ibelin fell in beside him, and they did not speak until they had put the last of the tents and campfires several yards behind them.

"Did your lady write about my grandson?" Sir Bartholomew asked at last.

Ibelin hesitated. "My lady did mention in her last letter that a boy *claiming* to be your grandson—"

"Oh, it's him . . . and by all that is holy, I wish it weren't!" Sir Bartholomew cried out in anguish.

That startled Ibelin, and he protested, "But Maria Zoë said he looked healthy and strong. No trace of ill treatment."

"No," Sir Bartholomew admitted. "No, they did not abuse him. They bought his soul with flattery and kindness instead."

So Maria Zoë had been right, Balian thought. "He's a Mamluke?"

"Lord Balian! You should have heard him! He called his mother a whore! A 'filthy Christian pig'—and he told me he never wanted to see her again—or me."

Ibelin heard the misery in the old man's voice, and he felt helpless. He opened his arms and drew the old man into his embrace, but Sir Bartholomew remained stiff, cold, and unresponsive. Balian released his hold, since it was bringing no comfort, and took a deep breath. "If he wanted nothing more to do with you, why did he run away?"

"He didn't. He was sent by al-Adil."

Ibelin drew a sharp breath, Maria Zoë's warnings in his ear. "To kill me?"

"No, just to spy on you—at least for the time being. Who knows when new orders might have come in later?"

"How did you get that out of him?" Ibelin asked, startled less by the content of his words than the fact that he had gained the intelligence.

"Jesus wept!" the old man cried out, loud enough to carry to the edge of the camp, and some of the Templars turned to look at the two cloaked figures silhouetted against the last remnants of the dusk. "He's only ten! They sent a boy to do a man's job, and he got so wound up telling me how important he was and how much better off he was. He scoffed at his older brothers, sneering at them for being slaves—as if he weren't! In his eyes, he—Joscelyn—is going to be a great emir, while his brothers, he said, got what they deserved, as slaves to a carpetmaker and a farrier respectively. He said that was the best they could ever be, because they were "idiots" believing in "idols" and "worshiping vile women!" Balian, he called us all fools for being "polytheists," while he has found the True—" Sir Bartholomew's brittle composure broke and he doubled over, clutching his stomach in agony.

This time when Balian took him in his arms, he sagged into them, shaking with silent sobs. Balian held him, while the wind whipped their cloaks in the gathering gloom, and then he slowly led Sir Bartholomew, still doubled over in pain, back toward the camp.

Before they entered the Ibelin tent, however, Sir Bartholomew righted himself and balked. "No. I'm not going in there. I can't face the others."

"You can't stay out here!" Balian protested. "You're half frozen as it is! You need to sleep by a fire and have a hot meal and wine. I can have Georgios mull some wine over the fire for you."

"Balian." The old man dropped all titles, and Balian remembered when he had been more a mentor than a vassal. "What are we fighting for? Don't you see there's no point anymore? Look around you! This was the most fertile of Barry's estates. Now it's a wasteland. Everything from Beirut to Ascalon is a wasteland! The sand dunes are seeping inland from the sea, and the desert is spreading down from the mountains. We built a kingdom on sand, Balian, on sand and dust! In just four years, there is hardly any trace of us ever being here!"

Balian didn't agree. He couldn't afford to. "Bart, I understand how you feel, but your grief is blinding you. Nothing has been destroyed that cannot be rebuilt. We can irrigate again. We can drive back the desert. The trees have been cut down, but not uprooted. They will bear fruit again. We can make these valleys bloom again."

Sir Bartholomew just stared at him with dull eyes. "Maybe—but you can't give my daughters back their dignity, my granddaughters their virtue, or my grandsons their innocence and faith. This is a futile war, my lord. A futile waste of good lives. I hope you don't lose yours fighting it, for I know you are a good man. When you next write to her, give your lady my best regards as well. Now I will bed down with the Templars. They will give a monk food and shelter without asking questions." He turned and retraced his steps for several yards before heading back toward the Templar pickets. Balian watched him go, feeling chilled to the bone. By the time he started for his own tent, he had numbed feet.

Beit Nuba, Palestine, January 1192

They waited almost six weeks outside of Ramla, while King Richard rounded up stragglers and deserters and (more important) collected supply wagons and supplies. Throughout those weeks the Saracens harassed them relentlessly, particularly anyone who dared to forage for their horses. Various skirmishes developed and there had been steady casualties, but what distressed Ibelin most was the deteriorating weather and the state of the horses. There was inadequate fodder and the horses, particularly the draft horses, were slowly starving to death.

Shortly after Christmas (celebrated in damp misery outside of Ramla), the army received the order to pull out and advance toward Jerusalem. The effect on morale was astonishing. Suddenly the masses of common soldiers took an interest in their clothes and equipment again. Chain mail that had been rusting for weeks was scrubbed clean, leather cuirasses were oiled and waxed, quilted aketons were brushed, and swords sharpened, bows restrung. They even managed to form up in a semblance of order, and they marched that day with purpose and pride, often bursting spontaneously into hymns.

Their high spirits lasted until the next torrential rainstorm hit. This broke over them with so much violence that it swept some of the wagons right off the road, while others became helplessly mired. Horses and mules broke their legs in the chaos and had to be put down. Even men sometimes became so mired in the mud they could not pull themselves free, and lay whimpering in misery until their comrades freed them. Many of the supplies were lost or simply ruined by the rain. As night fell, the rain turned to sleet. The ice storm that night killed hundreds of the already weakened pack and draft horses, and scores of men as well.

As dawn broke, a strong patrol of Turkish cavalry attacked the already lamed army. The Earl of Leicester counterattacked and enjoyed initial successes until the Saracens were reinforced. At that point the Earl of Leicester was unhorsed and many of his men could fight no longer. Fortunately, Andrew de Chavigny rode to his relief, and the Saracens were at last driven off. The English celebrated a victory, but the draft horses were still dead, the supplies soggy slops, and the weather showed little sign of improving.

The humble size of his company and the fact that it was made up of natives were clear advantages for Ibelin. To be sure, they lost one of the destriers in the ice storm when he panicked at a loud noise, fell on the ice, and shattered his knee. They lost two draft horses when the wagon ahead of them abruptly broke an axle and casks of wine crashed down on them, crushing one outright and injuring the other so badly he had to be put out of his agony. But they lost no men, because the natives from Outremer knew Palestinian winters and had come prepared with boots, mittens, and vests lined with sheepskin, as well as woolen shirts and hose. Ibelin had also had the foresight to bring horse blankets, and these had prevented the exhausted draft and packhorses from freezing to death during the night, while keeping the worst of the sleet and rain off their provisions as well.

Despite the lack of casualties, however, morale had reached a low point, and Ibelin heard more and more of his men murmuring about the campaign being pointless. Men also wanted to know where King Richard was; the fact that he was "raiding" and occasionally brought cattle or camels back as loot no longer satisfied anyone.

The bulk of the army straggled into Beit Nuba on the last day of 1191. The Templars had a commandery here, occasionally known as the Castle of the Baths or just the Castle of the Templars. It had been built on the foundations of a Roman fort and was square and regular in plan, with an extensive bath complex that had been restored and well maintained by the Templars. The Saracens had evidently used it as their command post, and it had not been damaged. Because the Templars had formed the vanguard of the army, they had already reoccupied their commandery and had been at Beit Nuba when the sleet and ice storm hit; they suffered no casualties.

Grand Master Robert de Sablé was both shocked and horrified by the state of the main army as it limped, staggered, and dragged itself into Beit Nuba.

Catching sight of Ibelin among the other native contingents, he hurried over to speak with him. "What has happened?" he asked anxiously.

Ibelin told him.

"Please. As soon as you have settled in, join me at the commandery," he urged, and Ibelin nodded glumly.

An hour later Balian was being served hot mulled wine, spiced with cinnamon and cloves and thickened with prune pulp, by a Templar brother. A fire was thundering in the large fireplace, consisting of what looked like the trunk of a tree lying on a base of substantial branches, while twigs and pine cones crackled in the cracks, throwing flames upward. The windows of the room were glazed, and the shutters had been closed over them to help keep the heat inside. As a result, the room was cozy. To Ibelin it felt like the first time he'd been warm in six weeks.

"My lord, thank you for coming. I've asked Garnier de Nablus to join us as well," Sablé announced. Nablus was the Master of the Hospital. Ibelin nodded warily, wondering what this was about.

He did not have to wait long. Nablus arrived, looking chilled through. He removed his wet cloak and handed it to an attentive Templar brother, then went to warm his hands over the fire. The hair fringing his tonsure was turning gray, Ibelin noted, thinking that he didn't remember it that way.

"King Richard has intelligence that Salah ad-Din has occupied Jerusalem with a strong body of troops, presumably his own Mamlukes."

"So it's true," Nablus muttered, looking grim.

"Yes. He's taken firm control of the city and is preparing for a siege. My lord of Ibelin, no one knows better than you how defensible Jerusalem is. Can you give us your assessment of whether Salah ad-Din can hold Jerusalem against this army?"

"As we are now?" Ibelin answered a little incredulously.

Master de Sablé nodded solemnly.

"Of course he can!" Ibelin answered conclusively. "Even if he has only his personal bodyguard and that of his brother, that's close to five thousand crack, battle-hardened fighting men, absolutely devoted to him. That's five thousand more than what I had!" Ibelin added, on the brink of sounding bitter. He swallowed down his emotions and tried to be more objective. "Furthermore, there are no refugees in the city. My understanding is that Salah ad-Din only partially resettled the city, mostly with religious scholars in his new madrassas. Some Syrian Christians have also returned and resumed their trades, but it's a ghost town for the most part. That means he doesn't have a lot of useless mouths to feed, he's got ample supplies of water as these rains replenish all the cisterns, and unless he's been totally negligent—which Salah ad-Din is not—

he'll have packed the storerooms with food, weapons, and ammunition. Ever since the King of France landed last spring, he's known we would eventually make for Jerusalem. He will have prepared carefully and well for a siege."

"Are you saying we have no chance of taking Jerusalem?" Sablé asked, shocked. He had wanted to hear Ibelin's opinion, but he had not expected an assessment as negative as this.

Ibelin shrugged. "We are in God's hands. If He so chooses, we can still take Jerusalem. Plague might break out, or the Sultan could fall ill of a fever and die. Maybe there will be a revolt in Egypt, and Salah ad-Din will decide to sacrifice Jerusalem for Cairo. I'm not a prophet, my lord."

Sablé turned to his fellow Grand Master. "And you, Garnier?" he asked, in a tone that suggested the men had become friends over the last months.

Nablus took a deep breath, looked hard at Ibelin with an expression that was anything but kindly, but nodded and admitted, "Ibelin's right. Short of a miracle, we cannot take Jerusalem—certainly not with that rabble out there. Most of those men have come to pray at the Holy Sepulcher and then go home! Let's suppose for a moment that we actually succeeded; what then? Nine-tenths of the men out there will say their prayers at the grave of Christ, and then rush back to Acre and Tyre to spend the rest of the winter with whores before taking the first ships out come spring. The only men who are going to stay here and *defend* Jerusalem, should it ever be taken, are represented here in this room: the Hospitallers, the Templars, and the men of Outremer."

In the silence that followed, they could hear the fire crackling and hissing. No one contradicted Nablus, but eventually Ibelin asked, "What of King Richard? Will he too return to England?"

"England?" Sablé shrugged. "Perhaps, but his heart is in Aquitaine, and the heart of his domains is Anjou. Philip of France can be counted on to attack him in either place, or in Normandy. He will go back to defend his heritage. I am sure of it. Did you think otherwise?"

Ibelin had not put his thoughts and hopes into words before, and he found it somewhat awkward. Still, the company here was trustworthy, and whatever else one thought of them individually, they were sworn by their oaths when they joined their respective orders to fight for the Holy Land. "King Richard's grandfather was half-brother of King Baldwin III and King Amalric. Richard's father is first cousin to Baldwin IV, Sibylla, and Isabella. A legal case could be made to exclude women from the succession altogether, and declare Richard of England the legal heir to the throne of Jerusalem."

The suggestion took both Masters by surprise. Nablus asked, a little scandalized, "Does your wife know you advocate disinheriting her daughter?"

"No," Ibelin admitted. "I have not discussed this with her or my stepdaugh-ter—but the situation is . . ." he paused, looking for the right word, "desperate. If King Richard could be persuaded to remain here as King of Jerusalem, we would have an honest chance of recapturing our lost territories—and more: of retaining them even after the bulk of the army returns to the West."

The Masters turned to look at one another, and a ray of hope seemed to cast a spark of light into the dark room. "Will you put it to him?" Nablus finally asked his colleague.

"Of course," Sablé agreed. "Of course."

Beit Nuba, Palestine, January 1192

King Richard arrived in Beit Nuba late on January 3. He had successfully ambushed a Turkish patrol that had been lurking outside of Beit Nuba to kill or capture the stragglers still coming in. On January 4, he summoned Balian d'Ibelin.

Balian went warily. He presumed Sablé had informed the King of his sugges-tion, but Toron would also have informed him that Balian had represented Mont-ferrat in negotiations with Salah ad-Din. Balian was unsure what sort of reception he would receive, particularly after the catcalls from King Richard's troops.

King Richard was housed in the Templar commandery, and he had taken advantage of the baths. He was freshly washed, glowing from the scrubbing down and smelling of balsam oil, when Ibelin was admitted. His hair had grown back surprisingly thick and curly after he'd lost it to Arnoldia, and it shimmered in the candlelight, his still-wet beard glistening. He had removed his chain mail and was dressed only in shirt, hose, and a surcoat with exquisite embroidery. "My lord of Ibelin. Welcome." he opened in a firm voice that was neither loud nor soft. "Join me." He indicated a table with a magnificent mosaic surface, the work of Greek craftsmen.

Ibelin bowed his head first, then cautiously took the chair indicated.

"I have to admit, I wasn't sure you would rejoin the army after you left us in October," Richard opened.

"I wasn't sure I would be welcomed back," Ibelin countered.

Richard raised his eyebrows and looked at him sidelong. "Why not?"

"'There goes Balian d'Ibelin, as treacherous as a gobelin.'" Ibelin quoted simply.

Richard snorted and shrugged. "Toron made no secret that you were negotiating with Salah ad-Din on Montferrat's behalf. It didn't go down well with my men."

"Why is it all right for you to negotiate and not Montferrat?" Ibelin asked.

"Because Montferrat represents no one but himself!" the Lionheart snapped back, adding in a calmer tone, "While I am trying to make a deal that would secure the Holy Land for Christ."

"By marrying your sister to al-Adil?" Ibelin's tone was carefully moderate. He didn't want to sound outright mocking—it was rarely wise to mock a king—but nevertheless he wanted to express his skepticism.

The King of England was taken off guard. He had attempted to keep the terms of that particular proposal very secret, especially after his sister suggested to him that it was all a joke and a ruse. "How did you hear about that?" he asked sharply.

"Al-Adil was rather pleased with himself for coming up with proposal; he made no secret of it. Sidon heard of it directly from him."

"Then he was serious?" King Richard found himself asking, his eyes watching Ibelin alertly.

"I'm sure he would have been very pleased to be made King of Jerusalem, with all the land previously held by the Frankish kings. Your sister, on the other hand, would have found herself imprisoned in a harem or simply discarded the moment you sailed away. It would have been a perfect, bloodless way for the Saracens to win the war, reclaim all the territory you have reconquered, get rid of you and the crusaders, and insult you into the bargain."

"What do you mean, *insult* me?"

"A woman's male relatives are *always* dishonored when she is repudiated by her husband, because in the Muslim tradition the woman is always to blame for any marital discord. In short, the Queen of Sicily would have been publicly declared unworthy of al-Adil, and you would have been the laughing-stock of the entire Muslim world."

King Richard was slowly flushing with anger as he grasped the magnitude of the hoax they had been playing on him. "Then it is well done," he said in a tight voice, "that I said I needed papal approval for the match—unless al-Adil converted to Christianity."

"Yes, that should put an end to the proposal," Ibelin agreed steadily. "Al-Adil is no more likely to convert to Christianity than you are to Islam."

"Let us return to your own negotiations, then. You were there on behalf of Montferrat—which is damned near treason to the Christian cause!" The English King's tone had turned belligerent.

"How?"

"He proposed falling on my flank and fighting his fellow Christians!" the Lionheart snarled.

"Not when I was representing him," Ibelin faced the Lionheart down.

"Meaning?"

"I refused to deliver that message, because I could not support it. If we could have secured peace in the north, and then concentrated our forces in the south, then it would have been a peace worth making."

They stared at one another, measuring each other. The Plantagenet broke eye contact first. He helped himself to some of the nuts in a bowl on the table, then looked again at Ibelin. "And what of this proposal that I be crowned King of Jerusalem? Are you serious about it?"

"Utterly."

"Would any of the other *poulain* lords support you?" King Richard asked next.

"Maybe. Probably," Ibelin revised his answer.

"But you agree that an attack on Jerusalem at this time is pointless?"

"It was madness to even make an attempt in winter," Ibelin countered. He added, "I thought you understood that when you argued at Acre that we had no more time to wait on Salah ad-Din. You justified the slaughter of the hostages in part because we needed to start the attack on Jerusalem during the campaign season."

"You have no idea the pressure the French have put on me," King Richard answered in an exasperated tone. The mere thought of the French made him so agitated that he sprang to his feet and began pacing. "I tried to convince them we should use the winter to secure and rebuild Ascalon. In fact, I tried to convince them that the key to Jerusalem lies in Cairo! If we attacked Cairo, we would force Salah ad-Din to abandon Palestine altogether and concentrate his forces in defense of his capital. If we could do enough damage in Egypt, he might even be forced into a treaty that acknowledged our right to Jerusalem and all the lands west of the Jordan for eternity!" King Richard explained his idea forcefully.

"King Amalric used to argue the same thing," Ibelin pointed out coolly. "He made four attempts, you know, and he had the backing of the Greek Emperor and his fleet. Egypt is not easy to conquer."

The Plantagenet looked over at Ibelin with slightly narrowed eyes.

"Yes, my lord King," Ibelin answered the unspoken question. "You are a far better general and a better leader of men than King Amalric. That is the reason I would gladly kneel in fealty to you as King of Jerusalem. But be warned, capturing Egypt is far more difficult than it looks."

"So is capturing Jerusalem. Sablé told me your assessment of our chances."

"My lord King, if I could hold it for nearly ten days with nothing but women, priests, and newly knighted youths, how long do you think the Sultan can hold it with five thousand battle-hardened Mamlukes—and no refugees clogging the streets and eating the rations?"

"Don't misunderstand me," King Richard assured him. "I share your assessment completely! That's why I suggested taking Ascalon instead." He paused, his eyes considering his guest alertly, and then conceded, "We have much in common, you and I. At least we see the situation here in very similar ways. You certainly understand— unlike the damned Duke of Burgundy—that we can't win by force of arms alone. We *have* to negotiate! By God! Anything we can gain without bloodshed is worth twice what we win with men's lives!" He paused and then asked bluntly, "What do you think of Toron as a negotiator?"

"He was in Saracen captivity for roughly two years and in that time became very close to Imad ad-Din."

The King of England started. Why hadn't anyone else told him that? "Are you saying he is in the Sultan's pay?"

"Many of us have suspicions. Some of the barons held captive with him even accuse him of converting."

"No! That's not possible!" King Richard protested. "I've seen him go to Mass."

"And he drinks wine. I do not think he is a secret Muslim, nor in Salah ad-Din's pay. But a man without a backbone makes a poor negotiator, my lord King. He's easily persuaded by whomever he is talking to, and he doesn't know how to call a man's bluff or when to take a stand. Or perhaps he knows *when* to take a stand, but no one takes his 'stand' seriously."

"You stole his wife from him," King Richard noted pointedly.

"First, she was not his wife, as she'd been forced into a marriage before the age of consent. Second, he failed to consummate the fraudulent marriage. And, third and most important, he failed to fight for his wife's right and title to Jerusalem. I can't imagine *your* father failing to support *his* wife's claim to Aquitaine, can you?"

The Plantagenet burst out laughing. "My father not press his claim to *anything* he had a ghost of a right to? He would have taken holy orders first! Not to mention that had he failed to press my mother's claim to Aquitaine, she would have skinned him alive." He laughed again at the thought.

"Isabella is the rightful Queen of Jerusalem—and Toron, who claimed to be her husband, did homage to Guy de Lusignan."

"But you, my lord, are ready to abandon her and her claim," King Richard shot back.

"You don't seem to fully understand me, my lord King."

"Perhaps not. Explain yourself."

"I am fighting for Jerusalem—not just for the city or the Kingdom, but for the people, too, for the Christians who lived here and made it a prosperous land, a land of milk and honey and also of art and knowledge. I will support whatever solution offers the greatest prospect of survival—sustainable survival, in freedom and Christianity—for Jerusalem's people. Lusignan squandered his right to be King because he lost the Kingdom once already, and Toron gave Lusignan the chance to lose the Kingdom by failing to support his wife in the first place. Montferrat, on the other hand, seemed like a better alternative—but I will admit to you, I have been sorely disillusioned by him on many counts but most especially his latest offer to Salah ad-Din. He is, as you said, far more interested in his own position than in Jerusalem or its people. So, what is left? A man who comes from the same House as the last five monarchs of Jerusalem. A man who has already conquered the strategic ports of Acre and Jaffa. A man who can fight Salah ad-Din to a standstill. A man who, indeed, grasps the essential elements of warfare against the Saracens in this environment. I trust you to recapture the rest of the Kingdom and then to hold it—but not in a few months. Regaining the Kingdom will take years. You can restore the Kingdom to its former glory and more—but only if you are willing to take up the burden and stay here the rest of your life."

"Sacrifice the Angevin empire my father built for Jerusalem?" Richard Plantagenet asked intently, his face flushed and his eyes burning.

"Yes. For the Holy Land."

There was tense silence in the little room, and they could hear rain splattering on the shutters over the windows.

King Richard broke the tension. He nodded. "I will think about it, but it is not an easy choice. Not for me. I love Aquitaine, and I have spent the better part of my adult life fighting for it. I need to think—and pray. Meanwhile, tomorrow I will call a council of all the leaders to discuss our current situation. Master de Sablé has agreed to recommend withdrawal to the coast. Can I count on you backing him, my lord?"

"You can count on me, your grace," Ibelin assured him.

King Richard smiled. "Thank you." He held out his hand in a gesture of friendship and respect.

Ibelin hesitated for only a second, and then accepted it with a smile of his own.

Chapter 19

Ascalon, April 1192

ASCALON, TOO, HELD MEMORIES FOR BALIAN. It had been his first command—the first step on the ladder to independence, wealth, and power. It had been here that Maria Zoë had sought him out as a widow, here that they had discovered their love for one another. To Ascalon in 1177, King Baldwin had ridden from Jerusalem with 376 knights to lift a Saracen siege. From Ascalon they had sallied forth together to take the Sultan's army in the rear. That had resulted in the stunning and complete defeat of Salah ad-Din at Montgisard. Balian's memories of Ascalon were good ones.

Nor was the destruction here as complete or as vindictive as it had been at Ramla. The Sultan might have ordered the walls slighted, but he clearly harbored hopes of returning and reclaiming the city. The markets, baths, and houses were largely intact. Only the churches had been systematically plundered and trashed. While King Richard took up residence in the episcopal palace and the Duke of Burgundy claimed the palace of the Constable, Ibelin selected a caravansary near the Gaza Gate that could shelter his entire company and their horses. It was near some baths, and as the weather improved they welcomed the chance to bathe, repair their clothes and equipment, and regain some of their strength. They found their faith returning, too, as they worked together to rebuild the outer defenses of the city.

The vigor with which the reconstruction of Ascalon had been carried out had been impressive. King Richard had set an example by taking his place in the line of men passing stones up from the shore, where they had been tossed down by the Saracens. With the King of England stripped down to the waist as he manhandled one stone after another, no one else dared hold back. They had all pitched in, and under the guidance of master masons from Acre, they had rebuilt the walls at an astonishing pace.

Yet slowly discontent began festering again. On the one hand, the Marquis de Montferrat still refused to make common cause with the King of England, and on the other the French, now out of funds, demanded payment from the English King. King Richard—not unreasonably, Ibelin thought—was only willing to pay men who took an oath to obey him, something the bulk of the French were unwilling to do. By March thousands of French had abandoned the Frankish army at Ascalon, returning to a less arduous and less celibate existence in Acre or Tyre. Furthermore, the interminable rivalry between the Pisans and Genoese had escalated into outright violence, and at one point King Richard had been forced to return to Acre to end street fighting there.

Ibelin, however, refused to get discouraged. As the weather improved, the men remaining at Ascalon became increasingly active. They called their forays "foraging" in search of fodder, but their main objective was to test the enemy's defenses and morale. Surprisingly, they found the Saracen reponse weak, porous, and uncoordinated—which suggested that Salah ad-Din had been unable to keep his full force in the field or was experiencing desertions by elements of his army.

Ibelin managed to capture a dozen camels and more than two score of horses on one raid. That more than made up for their losses of the winter, and he was able to send the best horses back to his stud outside of Tyre. Another raid led by King Richard resulted in the rescue of nearly twelve hundred Christian slaves en route to the slave markets of Cairo. The Saracens escorting the slave convoy had spent the night at Darum and were surprised at dawn by the arrival of King Richard's patrol. Recognizing the King's banner, they had fled to the keep, abandoning their human cargo. King Richard and his knights had freed the captives.

On the return of the patrol, Ibelin had gone at once to see if any of the freed slaves were men or women from Ibelin, Ramla, or Mirabel. However, the bulk of the freed slaves were men captured during the current crusade, and the remainder were from Hebron, Tiberius, and Acre. There were no women among the slaves at all.

The ease with which the Franks were extending their hold in the countryside around Ascalon was highly encouraging, however. Not only was it indicative of Salah ad-Din's waning strength, it also made the prospect of regaining continuous control of at least the coastal plain more plausible. More than once Ibelin found himself looking to the north, imagining he could see Ibelin or smell the blossoms of the now-flowering orchards.

It was an illusion, of course. They were too far away, and Ibelin had been destroyed. On the march south to Ascalon, the army had spent one night in the ruins. The castle had been a gutted hulk, the masonry blackened from the fires that had consumed the furnishings and carpentry. Most of the upper floors, supported by wooden beams, had come crashing down, leaving heaps of shattered tiles in the cellars. Sand had blown in off the dunes, covering the charred wreckage with layers of sifting sand that silted up the troughs in the stables. Only the certain knowledge that Ibelin had been abandoned and that neither man nor beast had been slaughtered here gave Balian any comfort. Roger Shoreham had taken every man, woman, and child out of Ibelin, and the garrison had escorted the little convoy of residents to Jerusalem.

On this fine, sunny day, however, Balian felt an almost irresistible yearning to ride "home." He found himself longing to see if any of his vineyards had survived, and to check on the orchards, too. In the gloom of January everything had looked dead—but, he argued with himself, things might not look so bad on a bright spring day like this. He glanced west toward the sun glistening on the sea, and noted with surprise that a ship was running for the little harbor on a brisk following breeze.

Ascalon's harbor had never been particularly good even in the best of times. It was now barely serviceable. Most of the ships that docked there were fishing smacks or small coastal vessels carrying news from Jaffa and Acre. This ship, in contrast, appeared to be a large oceangoing buss with two masts. As Ibelin squinted at it, the pennant from the masthead snaked out in the wind, and with a start he recognized the King of England's banner. As if a cloud had just blown in front of the sun, Balian shivered with a sense of foreboding.

By evening the news had spread throughout the crusader host: King Richard's brother had risen up in rebellion against him and had chased Richard's chancellor out of the Kingdom. Some of his justiciars and nobles, including the redoubtable William Marshal, remained loyal, of course, but it had come to open warfare between the men loyal to the King and those who had thrown in their lot with his brother. Furthermore, according to the prior entrusted with a letter from the deposed chancellor, the King's brother John had seized hold of the royal treasury, ensuring that Richard would receive no more funds for his crusade, or indeed for any purpose. It was only a matter of time, the prior warned, before the French King took advantage of the situation and attacked in Normandy, Anjou, and Aquitaine. King Richard, the prior continued ardently, needed to return home at once or lose his entire heritage.

The following day King Richard called together the leaders of his army for an urgent council meeting.

Ibelin hoped that the news would sway King Richard to abandon his inheritance in favor of Jerusalem. After all, if he had *already* lost his kingdom to his younger brother, why not stay here? However, one look at King Richard as he joined the other barons and bannerets was enough to dash Ibelin's hopes. They were meeting in the chapter house of the Hospital, a lovely square room with a central pillar from which the ribs of the cross-vaulted ceiling opened like branches of a great tree. King Richard was seated in the central "chair" formed by two stone arms separating off a segment of the stone bench running around the circumference of the room. His nephew Henri de Champagne sat on one side of him, looking as distressed as the King himself, if not more. On the other side was the Bishop of Salisbury, who appeared grim rather than distressed, while the Earl of Leicester was beside the Bishop, looking furious.

The men who had been summoned poured into the chapter house, seeking seats on the stone bench in rough accordance with their rank, and (as always) clustered by language or region of origin. The lords of Outremer were standing as Ibelin joined them, and their faces mirrored his own. They sensed that King Richard had decided to return, and they all feared that the bulk of the crusaders would go with him. Their hope of regaining their homeland was slipping inextricably through their fingers.

The tension in the chapter house was so great that there was hardly any whispering or murmuring. Men fell silent almost as soon as they settled on the benches, and all eyes were directed toward the English King.

Richard Plantagenet looked uncomfortable—more uncomfortable than Ibelin had ever seen him. For the first time he seemed diminished, even chastised. The supreme confidence he had always worn was shaken. "My lords," he opened, getting to his feet, and the last rustlings and mutterings subsided. "Most of you will have heard the news by now, but I will summarize it nevertheless. My brother John, in complete disregard of his own soul, has chosen to rebel against a man who has taken the cross, against his sovereign and his brother all at once." If that was delivered dispassionately, Richard's voice started to getting hotter as he now reported, "He has expelled the royal chancellor and justiciars and seized control of the royal treasury. He has demanded all tenants-in-chief swear allegiance to him as King of England, and he has laid siege to the castles of many men who remain loyal to their rightful King." The outrage in his voice increased further as he announced, "There have been pitched battles in the streets of London and in other towns between men loyal to me, their rightful King, and those supporting my brother, a usurper." By the time he reached this point, there was so much fury in his voice that his words vibrated in the air, and his fists were clenching and unclenching at his sides.

King Richard continued in a voice that rasped, as if he were almost choking on what he had to say. "I took an oath to do all in my power to restore Jerusalem to Christian control. You are my witnesses! I have spared neither my treasury, my strength, nor my blood in that effort. I have regained Acre, Haifa, Caesarea, Arsur, Jaffa, and Ascalon," he reminded them, sounding more like his old self-confident self. But then his voice cracked as he added, "I wish I could do more." He paused; the strain of saying what he was about to say was obvious in the heightened color of his cheeks and the tension around his mouth. "But I cannot. I must go home."

The eruption of protests came not just from the men of Outremer; many of his own vassals and bannerets protested as well. They were all saying the same thing. He was needed here. Their job was not done, their objective not achieved. Jerusalem was still enslaved.

King Richard held up his hand for silence. Reluctantly they curbed their tongues. "My departure need not be the end of this crusade. I do not ask any of you to come with me. Each man must decide for himself what is compatible with his conscience, his vow. Most of you do not face the treachery I do. You can remain and continue the fight for Jerusalem, without risking the loss of your homes. Furthermore, I will continue to finance, at my own expense, three hundred knights and two thousand elite men-at-arms. So the choice is yours. Decide in accordance with your conscience whether to return with me at once, or remain here. You can still win without me," he told them—as much to comfort himself as them, Ibelin thought.

Protests and challenges erupted again. No, they told him in various ways and voices, victory was not possible without him. His leadership, his example, his strategic understanding were all essential to success. It was some time before the Templar Master made his voice heard above the others. "If you depart, my lord King," he addressed his former liege forcefully, "who is to lead the men who remain behind?"

Ibelin suspected that Sablé had intended the question to be a rhetorical reminder of the total disunity in the Frankish ranks, a way of suggesting to the English King that he was indispensable.

King Richard took them by surprise with the answer, "That is for the men who remain to decide—or rather, for the lords of the Kingdom of Jerusalem."

The collected barons were stunned into silence by his words and his tone. King Richard swept his eyes along the line of native barons. "You, along with the militant orders, will collectively bear the burden of holding what we have gained so far, and for continuing the war. I do not presume to dictate to you who should be your king."

Guy de Lusignan started to protest, but King Richard silenced him with a single look and then turned back to the others. "I ask only that you decide *today*, before I leave, and that you swear to uphold whatever decision you make. I leave you to make that decision *now*." Turning to the other side of the room, occupied by the Normans, English, Angevins, and Poitevins, he urged, "My lords, leave the men of Outremer to decide this." Then he strode out of the chapter house, trailed by his own vassals.

Henri de Champagne followed in his uncle's wake even after the others had elected not to test the Plantagenet's temper. King Richard went straight to his waiting palfrey, and as he collected the reins to mount he caught sight of Henri. "I'm in no mood for recriminations, Henri," he warned.

"Nor would I dream of voicing them, uncle," Henri answered, "but—I did want to warn you."

"Of what?"

"That I will stay here. I cannot—" He'd been about to say "walk away" and then realized it might sound insulting. "I think we can still achieve something here, and the Queen . . ." He fell silent, conscious of how foolish he sounded. Ever since that night when he had been witness to Isabella being torn from the warm embrace of her husband and forced against her will to marry another man, he had felt protectiveness toward her. He could not forget how she had been exposed to rude eyes in her nightclothes and practically forced to go barefoot into the night. She was so young and beautiful and vulnerable—a queen in name only, a pawn of the powerful men around her in reality. He had promised her on that night that no harm would befall her, and of course no violence had been committed outright. But how could he know what sort of husband Montferrat was, and what would become of her if the barons chose Guy de Lusignan?

"Which queen are you talking about?" His uncle impatiently brought him back to the present.

"Queen Isabella. What is to become of her if Guy de Lusignan is chosen—"

"Don't worry. He doesn't have a snowball's chance in hell," the Lionheart told his nephew tartly, swinging himself up into his saddle.

Henri gazed up at him, confused. "But you've backed Lusignan ever since you came. . . ."

"Yes, and what has he done with my backing? Has he asserted himself? Made amends for his earlier mistakes? Demonstrated his capabilities? Won the loyalty of his vassals and men? Nothing of the kind! He's done nothing but cower in my shadow and eat out of my hand. If I'd realized he was so unlike his brothers, I wouldn't have backed him in the first place," the Lionheart declared contemptuously.

Henri wasn't so sure. The way he saw it, his uncle Richard Plantagenet had backed Lusignan mostly because his uncle Philip Capet had backed Montferrat, but Philip was now a thousand miles away and the Holy Land needed a king worthy of the name. "You think they will choose Montferrat?"

"Henri," the Lionheart said patiently. "They did before. That's why they made Isabella marry him. Only my pressure and presence forced them to accept the compromise at Acre. When I walked out of the chapter house just now, I was telling them I would no longer stop them from making Montferrat king. The only question I have is how long it will be before the Lusignans come whining to me in protest."

King Richard was surprised that the Master of the Temple reached him before the Lusignans. Robert de Sablé rode into the courtyard of the episcopal palace within the hour and had himself ushered immediately into the King's presence. King Richard just raised his eyebrows.

"It was unanimous, my lord, except for Toron—who backed Guy, of course, with a passionate plea that probably did more harm than good. They detest him at least as much as they do Guy."

"So that at least is done," Richard remarked with a deep sigh. He had not slept all night for praying, and the exhaustion was catching up with him. He could fight a hundred battles without this kind of utter fatigue. Battles made his body tired, so that he fell into a deep sleep, to awake refreshed and invigorated. But this—this sense of helplessness, betrayal, confusion, uncertainty . . . His instinct was to go home and teach Johnny and Philip a lesson, and yet he could not forget Ibelin's suggestion, either. Was it really better to be King of England than King of Jerusalem? His great-grandfather had opted for Jerusalem—but then he'd been only Count of Anjou, not King of England, Duke of Aquitaine and Normandy, Count Poitou, Lord of Maine, Tourraine and Ireland as well.

"There is something else we need to discuss," the Templar Master broke into the King's thoughts in a deep, soft, but penetrating voice.

Richard looked at him skeptically. "*Now*, Sablé?" he asked in warning.

"Yes, now," Sablé insisted.

King Richard sighed and crossed his arms over his chest, as if daring Sablé to have something important enough to demand his attention at this moment.

"Cyprus is in revolt."

"What?" King Richard gasped, his arms dropping instinctively to his sword-belt, his entire body alert and tense.

"Yes; we left too few—and the wrong—men in charge. They tried to impose Latin rites on the entire population, turning out the local clergy—"

"Are you Templars mad?" King Richard challenged, furious. "For God's sake, I took the island so easily largely because I promised them I wouldn't do that! I said everything would remain as it was, except that I'd be their liege rather than that sadistic ass Isaac. I promised—"

"My lord," Sablé tried to calm him. "You are right. I make no excuses for the Templar commanders. They were shortsighted and foolish, and I—I was too focused on things here. I did not exercise proper oversight. I thought our instructions had been sufficiently clear. Evidently they were not. Now the whole island is in revolt, and the Templars are holed up in their house in Nicosia, begging for reinforcements to recapture the island—"

"Not one bloody archer!" King Richard opened, and followed it with profane threats of what the Templars deserved instead. The Lionheart raged because this was the last straw. He shouted and cursed, venting all his pent-up fury with his brother John and the King of France, and indeed with God himself, for allowing his brother and Philip to band together to destroy him while he was on this sacred mission in the Holy Land. He wanted to retake Jerusalem. He wanted to restore the Kingdom's viability. He wanted to humiliate Salah ad-Din. He didn't want to scuttle for home like the vile, cowardly Philip Capet!

But he *had* to go.

And now Sablé was telling him that his greatest conquest, Cyprus—the one thing he thought he had truly achieved for the sake of the Holy Land—was also at risk. Everything he had accomplished at home and here was disintegrating—as if they were no more substantial than sand castles overwhelmed by a powerful wave. Precisely because he could feel things slipping out of his once seemingly powerful hands, Richard raged. He pounded his fist down on the nearest table, making the cups and bowls jump into the air as it shook.

Over the years Sablé had weathered more than one Plantagenet rage, particularly from Richard's father, Henry II. He was not intimidated by this outburst, although he was acutely aware that it was a great advantage to no longer be a subject of the English King. Braving the King's temper, he urged, "Hear me out, my lord. I'm not suggesting we divert troops from Palestine. What I propose is that we, the Knights Templar, return the island of Cyprus to you."

"What the hell am I supposed to do with it?" Richard roared back. "Now, of all times! I need to return to England! Haven't you heard a damn thing I've said all the bleeding day?"

"Your grace, if we restore the island of Cyprus to you, you are free to bestow it on someone else."

"And why should I want to do that?" King Richard demanded furiously. "Cyprus is as vital to the survival of Jerusalem as everything else put together—particularly in the precarious condition it is in now. For Christ's sake! All we control is the coastal strip! Are you all so bloody blind that you can't see that's not enough territory to even feed the Christian population? Nor can the ports of the coast survive unless we control the eastern Mediterranean. Cyprus is the breadbasket and the sentry on the sea lanes to the cities of the Levant! Cyprus must become an invincible bastion from which to launch future campaigns against the Saracens. Why does no one else seem to understand that?" Richard ended, almost in tears from the frustration and the stress.

"We *do* understand—but the knights of my order are better used here in Palestine, fighting on the front lines. On the other hand, someone like Guy de Lusignan, who should never again be allowed to command troops confronting the Saracens, is not unqualified to restore order and then serve as the caretaker of Cyprus. If you give him Cyprus, he will not be tempted to thwart or undermine the authority of Conrad de Montferrat."

King Richard stared at Sablé in astonishment. The idea was so radical that for several seconds he said nothing at all as he absorbed it and then turned it over in his mind. Guy had proved himself a poor leader of men and a terrible military commander. Could he be trusted to restore order and secure Cyprus for the future?

"It's not so much Guy I'm thinking about," Sablé admitted, as if reading Richard's thoughts. "But if you give it to him, his brothers will go with him."

"Ah," Richard was beginning to understand, "and that would kill two birds with one stone. We'd not only keep the troublesome Lusignans from challenging Montferrat and dividing the Franks here in the Holy Land, we'd also keep that rebellious band far away from Poitou—where they would almost certainly ally themselves with Philip of France as they have in the past."

"Exactly."

"But are they capable of getting the situation on Cyprus under control?"

"In my estimation, Geoffrey and Aimery are—provided they restore the Orthodox Church."

Richard did not answer right away. His eyes were unsettled as he thought through various scenarios—but the rage was gone, Sablé noted, and that was good. In the end he said only, "The proposal has merit. I'll think about it."

"No solution is perfect, my lord," Sablé reminded him. "But I think you will find this the best of the options at hand."

Off the coast of the Levant, April 1192

The High Court of Jerusalem selected Ibelin and the Patriarch of Jerusalem to take the word to the Marquis of Montferrat that he had been elected King of Jerusalem. King Richard decided to send the Count of Champagne with them to assure the Marquis that the King of England gave him his full support. The Patriarch disliked sea travel and elected to go overland, despite the fact that the prevailing southerly winds made the journey from Ascalon to Tyre significantly shorter by sea. Ibelin and Champagne, on the other hand, boarded the *Storm Bird*, each accompanied by a half-dozen knights.

The wind was fresh, whipping up whitecaps that frothed and snarled as if in indignation as the Norse ship overtook them, riding the waves down on the following wind. Running before the wind was comparatively comfortable, and despite the speed with which they ate up the miles, the deck was dry and warm. Furthermore, with the oars shipped, men were free to line the rail of the ship and watch the coast of Palestine slip by. Champagne joined Ibelin at the starboard railing.

Balian acknowledged the younger man with a nod, but he was too intent on trying to locate the coast opposite Ibelin to pay him much attention. It was a spot laden with memories. He had often ridden from Ibelin to the shore as a boy, because there was a stretch of beach on which one could gallop wildly without risking harm to horse or rider if one fell. He would never forget the first time he took Centurion there, either; the young stallion had reacted as if the breaking waves were vicious monsters racing to attack him, and he'd fled in panic. And it was here that he'd ridden with John in front of him on the saddle when he learned that King Baldwin IV was dead. Although he'd rarely seen the place from seawards, he wanted to believe he would recognize it.

"You've been a strong supporter of Montferrat," Champagne broke in on his thoughts.

Ibelin turned slowly and reluctantly to look at the French count. On the whole, Champagne had impressed him favorably. He was a conscientious commander careful of his men and their needs, and he was a brave knight. Furthermore, Ibelin had never seen him drunk nor found him gambling, much less whoring as many of the other crusaders did. More importantly, he had been the first to declare he would not return with King Richard, but would remain in the Holy Land and continue the struggle to regain Jerusalem. Ibelin was thankful for that commitment, but he resented his meddling in the Kingdom's internal affairs and was in no mood for a discussion.

"Yes," Ibelin answered steadily, before wearily reciting the facts. "From its founding, the kings of Jerusalem were elected by the High Court. Guy de Lusignan was never elected. He usurped the crown and used his ill-gotten power to destroy the army of Jerusalem and lose the Kingdom. No man should have the right to lose a kingdom more than once—particularly when he had no right to it in the first place."

"I agree with you, my lord," Champagne hastened to assure the older nobleman. "I'm no supporter of Lusignan. I never have been. The Lusignans have an unsavory reputation for being troublesome and grasping. You know Geoffrey and Guy once attacked my grandmother and tried to take her captive?"

"Yes, William Marshal told me that," Ibelin admitted, wondering what Champagne was getting at.

"So, you see, I understand why you oppose Lusignan—but why Montferrat?"

"He was the best man we had at the time," Ibelin admitted. "I said once, and I was serious: if we'd known the King of France was recently widowed or the King of England's betrothal to Princess Alys was not set in stone, we might have offered Isabella to eiter—or both—of them. If King Richard had been married to Isabella and so the lawful King of Jerusalem, maybe he would have agreed to stay," he added morosely.

Champagne shared Ibelin's distress over his uncle's plans to depart and fell silent for a moment. Then he risked speaking his mind. "But what of Isabella? I mean, I saw her the night she was heartlessly dragged from Toron's tent. I understand she consented to the marriage to Montferrat, but how much choice did she actually have?"

"She had the choice between Toron and Jerusalem. It was as simple as that," Ibelin told him bluntly, as he wondered what relevance Isabella's feelings could possibly have for this young Frenchman.

"My mother, you know, was a princess of France, and she had nothing to say about her marriage, either," Champagne noted, "but there are times when I wonder how it is that we, as chivalrous knights, are supposed to protect ladies from harm and violence, when we routinely give young maidens into the hands of husbands they do not choose or want."

Ibelin found himself amused but also attracted by Champagne's reflections. "Chivalry" was a phrase on many of the younger knights' lips these days. While Ibelin did not think the Holy Land had time for it in the present circumstances, it was not a bad thing in itself. Fighting men could always use a check on their tendency to exploit their power, and the Church had tried for centuries to control and redirect the instinctive violence of men raised to arms. If "chivalry" could channel violence into positive directions, so much the better. To Champagne he noted, "As a father, I endeavor diligently to ensure that my daughters will not be forced into marriages with men who will not treat them with the utmost respect, courtesy, and gentleness."

"And Isabella is your stepdaughter," Champagne burst out, an undertone of reproach audible in his voice.

"Indeed. And I reproach myself that I failed to stop her demeaning betrothal to Toron—though I tried. And I reproach myself even more that I did not challenge the sham marriage of a child of eleven. I do not, however, reproach myself for her marriage to Montferrat. Contrary to what men say in the English camp, he is not a monster. He is a highly cultivated nobleman who speaks Italian, French, Latin, and Greek. He is well-read, and you will hardly find anyone more courteous than he—when he wants to be. He was very gracious to Isabella when she first arrived in Tyre, then nothing but a refugee from Jerusalem whose husband and kingdom were in Saracen hands. Furthermore, Montferrat assured Isabella's mother and me that he admired her and would treat her with tenderness. I have every reason to believe he has kept his word. Isabella blossomed after her marriage to him, and she is now expecting."

To Ibelin's surprise, Champagne looked genuinely relieved. "I can't tell you how glad I am to hear that!" he exclaimed. "The image of her that night—it's haunted me. I've felt guilty for not doing more to protect her. But if it is as you say and she is truly happy with Montferrat, then I can rest more easily." He flashed Ibelin an embarrassed smile. "No doubt you are categorizing me as a hopeless romantic!"

Ibelin smiled back. "Perhaps, but there are worse things to be in this ugly world. I'm rather pleased to see that a man who can fight as well as you do can also be romantic."

"Eleanor of Aquitaine's grandson?" Champagne quipped back. "I was nursed on power politics and troubadour lyrics in equal measure."

Ibelin laughed, and then started with surprise at the sound. He couldn't remember the last time he had laughed so simply, without undertones of guilt, bitterness, or irony. Something about the sunshine on the deck of the *Storm Bird* on this April day and the company of the young Count of Champagne had lifted his spirits.

But when he looked back toward the coast, he realized they were already far north of Ibelin, and the shadows slipped back into his heart.

Tyre, April 28, 1192

Isabella was weeping miserably and inconsolably. It wasn't supposed to be like this! This should have been one of the happiest days of her life. Five days ago, the *Storm Bird* had docked in Tyre with her stepfather and the Count of Champagne. They had brought word that the High Court of Jerusalem had elected Conrad king, and that King Richard had accepted their decision and acknowledged Conrad.

The city had gone wild with jubilation, and the stream of well-wishers had been overwhelming. Isabella had lived for two days in a dream of unbounded joy. All the factional fighting was over. The crusaders would acknowledge Conrad, and he would be able to lead them to victory as he had at Tyre. Isabella was even secretly delighted that King Richard was going home, because he would surely have tried to interfere and undermine Conrad's authority.

With great pomp Conrad had gone to the cathedral and, in a voice pitched for the most distant corners of the great church, given thanks to God, adding, "Lord God, You created me and placed a soul in my body. If You judge me worthy to govern Your Kingdom, then see me crowned. But if I am not worthy of this great honor, then strike me down." The crowd had waited with bated breath as he dramatically flung open his arms and lifted his face to the ceiling over the apex of the nave and transept. Light was pouring in and seemed to surround him with a halo. No thunder growled, no lightning struck. The crowd went wild with jubilation.

Everything was so good, so perfect. Why did they have to quarrel? The spark for the fight had been trivial, but the underlying issue was Conrad's continued refusal to listen to anything she had to say about governing the Kingdom they had so long coveted. His tone had moderated after the crusader drive on Jerusalem had failed miserably and the French had withdrawn from Ascalon. Rather than call her a "peahen" he was more likely just to say: "Leave that to me," or "Don't worry your pretty head about that," or "I'll do what's best." But this time he had snapped irritably, "When I need the advice of a pregnant girl, I'll ask for it."

Isabella had flown into a rage, reminding him that "being pregnant" wasn't entirely her fault and that it was, moreover, her primary duty as Queen. She had, she knew, overreacted—but that was part of being pregnant!

The fight had been very ugly, with them both shouting at each other loud enough to frighten the servants away, and then Conrad had stormed off to have dinner with the Bishop of Beauvais, "where he wouldn't have to listen to hysterical drivel," slamming the door behind him.

Isabella had steamed and fumed at first. She paced the beautiful chamber overlooking the sea, and relived the quarrel in her head with embellishments and new arguments. But at some point her anger had turned to despair, and she sank down onto the soft cushions in the window seat, her head against the wall, and wept. Why didn't Conrad want to listen to her? Why didn't he respect what she thought? Why was their marriage all about sex and nothing more?

Her mother's marriage to Uncle Balian wasn't like this. Uncle Balian sought out her mother's advice and usually followed it. Eschiva disliked politics and so spoke rarely about issues of state, but when she did, Aimery took note. Even Reynald de Châtillon had taken Stephanie de Milly's opinions into account some of the time. They didn't always agree on things, but he'd *listened*. How could Conrad, who was so much kinder, so much more refined and civilized, be less respectful of her opinions that the infamous brute Oultrejourdain?

Isabella was left with the answer that it was *her* fault. Her opinions were trivial and shallow, ill-conceived and foolish. Maybe Conrad didn't respect anything she said because she didn't say anything worth hearing? The more she told herself this, the more convinced she became, until she was just blubbering in the window seat, feeling utterly worthless.

The light faded from the sky as the sun sank below the edge of the sea, and the breeze sprang up again from the ocean. From below the window came the sound of waves crashing against the stone base of the city walls. Isabella's tears dried. She got to her feet, stiff and unsteady. Instinctively her hand fell to her belly, feeling for some sign of life. She hoped her weeping did no harm to the precious life in her womb.

Conrad had been so happy when she gave him the news, she reminded herself. He had lifted her off her feet and covered her face with kisses. "A son!" he'd declared. "A son for Jerusalem! What Lusignan could never deliver."

Isabella had not dared to remind him that they didn't *know* it would be a son. She had basked in his happiness, relieved that he was so pleased, and convinced that the strains and squabbles and snide remarks of the previous four months were over. She had told herself that from now on they would live in perfect harmony—at least until the child was born. If it was a girl, the problems would undoubtedly start again, she knew, but she prayed that it would be a son.

And then the news arrived that the High Court *and* King Richard had recognized Conrad as king. She had been overjoyed. It was sheer delight that had made her brain brim with ideas. She'd wanted to appoint royal officials—a constable, a marshal, a chancellor. But Conrad had all but bitten her head off, accusing her of wanting to hem him in. She had backed off. Later, however, she'd suggested that he send word to Salah ad-Din that the treaty they'd made was off. "You can't just break your word. You need to tell him what you're doing and why—just as Uncle Balian did when he decided to stay in Jerusalem," she had argued. Conrad had responded by saying sarcastically, "It may come as a surprise to you, but your stepfather isn't perfect. Leave diplomacy to me; you don't understand it."

She hadn't liked that answer, but she hadn't argued. Instead, the remark had festered, just like his other brushoffs of her opinions. Tonight, when all she'd said was that he ought to discuss a coronation outside of Jerusalem with the Patriarch when he arrived, he'd answered with the cruel quip about not needing the advice of pregnant girls. She had exploded.

She shouldn't have done that. She knew that. It got her nowhere with Conrad and detracted from her dignity. By now the whole palace knew that she and Conrad had quarreled. And everyone would blame her: the hysterical pregnant girl.

A knock on the door startled her and she looked over warily, patting her face to try to determine if it was obvious she had been crying. Surely not in the gathering gloom of dusk, she thought. Yet she still wanted to be alone, so her tone was terse and unwelcoming. "Who is it?"

In answer the door opened and her mother stepped inside, closing it firmly behind her to exclude what appeared to be a crowd of people strangely gathered in the hall. Her mother's expression was so sober that Isabella wanted to crumple up in a corner again. No doubt the servants had gone running to her mother to report that rather than behaving like a queen she was screaming at her husband like a fishwife.

Her mother was advancing through the room, and Isabella looked down, too ashamed of herself to meet her mother's eyes.

Maria Zoë didn't stop until she could enfold her daughter in her arms. She kissed the top of Isabella's head and whispered "Sweetheart," in a voice so gentle that Isabella was instantly terrified. Why was her mother comforting her? "What is it, Mama?"

Her mother didn't answer right away. Instead she guided her daughter gently but firmly to a chest and there turned and pulled Isabella down beside her, her grip still firm around Isabella's waist.

"Mama? What has happened?" Isabella asked again. Now that her senses were alerted, she was aware of the muffled sound of many voices from beyond the door. The whole household appeared to be awake and agitated. Someone was shouting. Hurried footsteps pattered past the door.

"Sweetheart." Maria Zoë took one of Isabella's hands in the hand that was not around her waist. "Something terrible has happened."

"What?" Isabella demanded.

"Conrad was attacked on his way back from the Bishop of Beauvais' residence."

"Attacked? What do you mean, 'attacked'?" Conrad was attacked verbally all the time, but clearly that was not what her mother meant.

"Two men with knives."

"Mama?"

"The crowd killed one on the spot, but the other was apprehended, and your stepfather is interrogating him now."

"But what of Conrad? Where is he? How is he?"

"Bella," Maria Zoë grasped her hand so hard it almost hurt, "he's downstairs in the hall—"

Isabella jumped to her feet, but Maria Zoë remained sitting, holding her daughter's hand so firmly that she could not break away. "Let me go, Mama!" Isabella protested frantically. "I must go to him!"

Maria Zoë nodded but held her fast. "Yes, you must go to him, but not until you are prepared."

Isabella felt as if her blood had turned to ice. She stared at her mother.

"He is dying, Bella. A priest is with him."

Isabella swallowed; her throat had constricted so much she could hardly breathe.

Her mother was speaking softly and calmly. "He fervently wants to see you. He has been asking for you. But—"

"I must go at once!" Isabella cried out and tried again to break free of her mother's grasp, but Maria Zoë held her back.

"Bella, listen to me." She did not raise her voice, and her tone was still gentle, but so intense that it stopped Isabella in her tracks. "These men knew what they were doing. They stabbed him in the stomach and kidney. He is in extreme agony."

"Oh my God," Isabella gasped. "Oh my God." She was overwhelmed with guilt. How could she have quarreled with him about anything, much less for calling her a "pregnant girl"? Tears were streaming down her face again.

Maria Zoë stood and took Isabella in her arms again. She held her tight and kissed her on the head. "Sweetheart, I'll be with you as long as you need me. We'll go down together."

Isabella let her mother guide her out the door, through the crowds of gaping servants, and down the stairs into a hall overflowing with people—friends, retainers, priests, soldiers, and sensation seekers. Isabella recognized some faces, but most seemed to be strangers. They stared at her as her mother cleared a path through the crowd to the center of attention.

They had laid Conrad down on a carpet hastily spread on the edge of the dais in front of the table. A chair cushion had been placed under his head. Blood was everywhere and the stench was vile. Isabella was reminded of that day in Acre when Humphrey had been brought to her wounded. That helped prepare her for the blood and stench. But Humphrey had been half unconscious, while Conrad was very much awake—writhing and grimacing, gasping and stammering words.

The Archdeacon of Tyre was beside him, holding his bloody hand. Seeing Maria Zoë and Isabella approach, he bent and whispered in Conrad's ear. Conrad, gritting his teeth and sobbing to try to get control over the pain, turned his face in Isabella's direction. His eyes were already sunken deep in his skull. His skin was bloodless and glistening with sweat.

Isabella gave her mother's hand a squeeze to indicate she knew what she was doing, and then stepped ahead of her to go on her knees beside her husband, everyone else making way for her in silent respect.

"Is—Is—"

"Shhh! It's all right," she told him, taking his other hand.

He flung his head from side to side, his breathing coming in ragged gasps, almost as if he were gagging. "Don't—don't—deliver—Tyre—aaaagh!" The pain overwhelmed him, and it was all Isabella could do not to writhe in empathy.

She felt her mother's hand on her shoulder, firm and calming. She swallowed down her instinct to scream in sympathy, and squeezed Conrad's hand instead. "It's all right, Conrad. No one is going to surrender Tyre. We have held it all these years. We will continue to do so."

Her words were echoed by a rumbling of affirmative expressions and vows from the men crowded around them. Isabella became aware that many of these men, hardened veterans and detached priests, were openly weeping.

"Let—oh, Christ!" he cried out again, half rearing up off his pillow and clutching Isabella's and the Archdeacon's hands so hard that they both winced. As the pain receded, he panted until he was able to gasp out, "High Court—let them—successor—Christ help me!"

"You want the High Court to name your successor?" Isabella translated his words carefully, her eyes focused on his face.

He nodded, closing his eyes with relief at being understood.

Isabella thought to herself that it was just as well he was in agreement with what would certainly happen regardless, and then leaned and kissed him on the forehead. "I love you, Conrad," she told him gently. "Forgive me, if I ever gave you grounds to be displeased."

"Never!" Conrad gasped out, opening his eyes to look into hers. "Never! Bella Bella, Bella . . ." His voice faded away, and his eyes rolled back in his head.

The Archdeacon leaned forward to feel the pulse in Conrad's neck, and Maria Zoë's hand tightened on Isabella's shoulder.

The Archdeacon crossed himself and started praying aloud. With an audible gasp, people across the room realized what had happened, and started dropping to their knees and crossing themselves. Someone in the crowd began to recite the Pater Noster out loud and others joined in. A woman at the back of the room started wailing.

Maria Zoë slipped an arm around Isabella's waist and pulled her back to her feet. She turned her around and led her through the sea of mourners back to the stairs and up to her chamber. In the back of the Dowager Queen's mind, she noted that Conrad's reign had been the shortest of any King of Jerusalem yet.

Tyre, April 30, 1192

"Rashid ad-Din, commonly known as 'the Old Man of the Mountain,'" Ibelin told Champagne grimly.

The Count had taken ship for Tyre the same hour that the news of Montferrat's murder reached him in Acre. Because of the prevailing winds, he had been traveling overland to bring his uncle the news of the joyous reactions to Montferrat's elevation. On learning that Conrad had been murdered, however, he left his horses and all but one of his knights behind and hired a coastal galley to take him back to Tyre.

His arrival had gone largely unnoticed in a city plunged into collective mourning. The keening of women and the chanting of prayers seemed to float up from the streets and hang over the city like a dark cloud. Black shrouds covered doors and windows, and even cloaked the ships in the harbor. Few people were on the streets, and those who were wore mourning.

Champagne had gone first to the archiepiscopal palace to offer his condolences to the widow, but he had not been admitted. He had paid his respects to the corpse, laid out in state before the altar at Holy Cross Cathedral, and he had lit two candles for Montferrat's soul. Only then had he made his way to the Ibelin residence.

Ibelin had not seemed surprised to see him, and had readily answered his questions, including this one about who could possibly be behind the murder. At Ibelin's answer he asked incredulously, "But why? Are you sure?"

"As sure as one ever can be. I'm the first to acknowledge that confessions under torture are of dubious value. The mob hacked one man to pieces, and the second only escaped a similar fate because he managed to escape to a church. Despite their rage, the men of Tyre weren't ready to shed blood in a church. They dragged him outside with the intent of torturing him to death. By the time I arrived, they had so badly mutilated him that he was hardly recognizable as human. They claimed, however, that he had already confessed to being an assassin in the pay of Rashid ad-Din."

"That doesn't sound convincing to me," Champagne noted dryly.

"Quite right," Ibelin agreed, "but the confession wasn't really necessary. You see, the murder bears the signature of Rashid ad-Din. The men were extremely efficient. They picked a time and place when Conrad was expecting nothing. They delivered fatal stabs almost before anyone knew what was happening. Most important, they were both members of Montferrat's household—"

Champagne gasped in shock, exclaiming in disbelief: "What?"

"That's the way Rashid ad-Din operates. He first infiltrates his trained killers into a man's household and trust, and then they lie in wait until the perfect opportunity presents itself."

"Why would anyone do that?"

"For heaven. That's what Rashid ad-Din promises his supporters: that they will go straight to heaven if they die in his service."

"But what on earth can this Rashad ad-Din have against the Marquis de Montferrat?" Champagne asked, still confused and unsettled by events.

"It may sound trivial, but as we can see, the consequences were not," Ibelin explained. "A couple of years ago, a ship foundered right out there under our noses. The crew turned the bows of the already sinking ship toward the shore and beached her, but I'm sorry to say some of the refugees, keen on salvage and seeking revenge for all they'd lost, killed several of the survivors before the garrison reached the ship. The garrison secured the rest of the survivors and brought them to Montferrat, including the captain. Fearing for his life, the captain promised Montferrat a huge ransom, and Montferrat correspondingly sent ransom demands to Rashid ad-Din. But the Old Man of the Mountain responded by claiming that far from owing Montferrat a penny in ransom for the release of his men, Montferrat owed *him* restitution for the men killed, the ship, and the cargo."

"What sort of arrogance is *that?*" Champagne asked, shocked.

"The Old Man of the Mountain is not short on arrogance. He sees himself as a prophet, but I warned Montferrat to take him seriously. Instead, he summarily executed the shipwrecked men, thereby incurring Rashid ad-Din's enduring hatred."

"You're saying this has nothing to do with the crown of Jerusalem?" Champagne asked, incredulous.

"Nothing at all," Ibelin assured him.

At one level Champagne found that hard to believe, yet Ibelin was a rational man and his explanation made sense. "But the timing . . ." he protested weakly.

Ibelin shrugged. "Ever since Philip of France departed, Montferrat had expected Lusignan to try to murder him. When in public he was usually surrounded by several men-at-arms, men who searched the crowds and scanned the windows and rooftops for possible murderers and sharpshooters. But when the news arrived that King Richard had abandoned Lusignan and bought him off with Cyprus, Montferrat dropped his guard. That was what Rashid ad-Din's men had been waiting for."

Champagne shook his head in sheer disbelief at such profound perfidy, but he no longer doubted Ibelin was right.

"There is something else we must discuss," Ibelin continued in a sober tone.

Champagne looked over expectantly.

"The Patriarch arrived yesterday. He was accompanied by Sidon, Haifa, Caesarea, and Galilee, all of whom came expecting to offer their congratulations to Montferrat. They arrived just in time to learn that he was dead."

Champagne nodded absently.

"We met earlier today to discuss the succession."

"Good God, my lord! Montferrat isn't even is his grave yet! The Queen must be in a state of terrible shock!"

"Her mother is with her," Ibelin answered simply. "But unless you tell me that King Richard has changed his mind about leaving and is now prepared to remain in the Holy Land as commander of the assembled Frankish forces—or better yet, to take up the crown himself—we can't afford to delay. The Queen of Jerusalem is a widow, and she needs a consort who can take King Richard's place as the unquestioned leader of the forces of Christendom in the struggle to regain the Holy Land."

"I've had no word from my uncle," Champagne answered in obvious distress. "I do think this might persuade him to remain, at least until a new King can be elected. He is committed to regaining Jerusalem. No one should doubt that. He's sincerely committed," Champagne repeated, at pains to defend his favorite uncle. "But he can't just let John and Philip rob him of everything his father and he have fought for over the last half-century. They fought for it together far more than they fought each other, although most people forget that. But surely you see that he cannot just abandon his inheritance? He doesn't really have a choice. He has to go home, but he might be persuaded to delay his departure a bit, as long as he leaves before the winter storms shut down the sea lanes back to Europe."

Ibelin let Champagne run on until he had run out of things to say. Then he continued in his somber voice, "We—the Patriarch, Galilee, Sidon, Haifa, Caesarea, and I—discussed possible candidates for Isabella's consort."

Again Champagne shook his head in distress. "It's too soon. You can't possibly ask Queen Isabella to even *think* about a new husband yet. I feel so very, very badly for her!" Champagne's concern and sympathy were written all over his face.

"Which is to your credit, my lord," Ibelin answered. "And also one of the reasons that I raised your name."

"What?" Champagne was taken so totally by surprise that he started physically, and then stared at Ibelin in disbelief.

"Unless I have been misinformed, you are neither wed nor promised."

"Yes, but . . ."

"But what?" Ibelin prompted him. When Champagne remained tongue-tied in sheer shock, Ibelin continued. "You are nephew to both the King of England and the King of France, which will surely assure you the support of the Plantagenet's vassals and the support of Burgundy and his Frenchmen. You have been here longer than most of the other crusaders, and you have demonstrated both your courage and your discretion at the siege of Acre, the Battle of Arsuf, the march on Jerusalem, and most recently at Ascalon. I really can't think of a single reason why you are unsuitable."

Champagne shook his head in continued disbelief, remarking lamely, "But if I accept the crown of Jerusalem, I can't ever go home. What is to become of Champagne?"

"What is to become of Jerusalem if you don't remain?"

Champagne shook his head again. "This is too sudden, too unexpected. I would have to consult my uncle. King Richard must be consulted in any case."

"He very explicitly turned the decision over to the High Court of Jerusalem," Ibelin reminded him.

"Yes, but the High Court isn't here."

"No, but if you agree, the Patriarch, Galilee, Caesarea, Haifa, Sidon, and I will send a joint message to the remaining members of the High Court with our recommendation. We could have an answer in five or six days."

"I must consult my uncle. I will do nothing without King Richard's explicit approval," Champagne insisted still flustered.

"But you will consider it?" Ibelin pressed him.

"Yes—on one condition!" Champagne's tone was urgent, almost desperate. Ibelin waited with raised eyebrows.

"That Queen Isabella agrees freely. I will not have her forced into a marriage she does not want."

Ibelin nodded solemnly. "Agreed."

Tyre, May 2, 1192

The funeral was over, and Isabella was relieved to be back behind thick stone walls, protected from the prying eyes of the curious by more than black cloth. She stripped away the short veil that had covered her face, and then unpinned and unwrapped the rest of the long veils with a sigh of relief. Her mother took the veils from her and set them aside. "I'll send for sherbet," Maria Zoë assured her, going to the door and conveying the request to someone beyond.

Isabella sank down in the nearest chair and took a deep breath of the clean, fresh air coming off the sea through the unshuttered window. As her mother returned from the door, their eyes met. "I don't know what I would have done without you these last four days, Mama," Isabella confessed.

"Oh, sweetheart," Maria Zoë answered on the brink of tears, "what else are mothers for?"

Isabella's lips turned up to indicate she wanted to smile but was still too miserable. "Before Kerak, I thought mothers were for sweets and pets and excursions." She added sadly, "Nothing has ever been the same after Kerak." She leaned her head against the back of the chair and closed her eyes, one hand on her belly containing her precious child, Conrad's child.

Maria Zoë felt as if her heart would break. Isabella was just twenty years old. Although she too had been widowed at twenty, Amalric had not been stabbed to death, nor had she been in love with him. Most important, with his death she became a dowager. His death had freed her to withdraw from public life, to marry the man of her choosing and shape her own destiny. None of those options were available to Isabella.

A timid knock indicated that a servant had returned with sherbet, and Maria Zoë answered it. She brought the tray into the room and set it on the table before Isabella, rather than let the servant in.

Isabella opened her eyes and looked at her mother. "You look exhausted, Mama. I think these last days have been as hard on you as on me."

"No. Hard, but not that hard."

"You spoke to Uncle Balian at length before the funeral. What has the High Court decided to do with me now?"

Maria Zoë was relieved that Isabella recognized her position so clearly. She answered steadily, "The High Court has not had a chance to respond to the changed situation. The members are dispersed."

Isabella nodded wearily but noted, "The Patriarch, Uncle Balian, Galilee, Haifa, Sidon, and Caesarea are a very strong faction. What have they decided?"

"That you must remarry as soon as possible. The Kingdom cannot give you a year of mourning."

"I know that," Isabella answered with a slightly irritated sigh. "My question is: whom do they want me to marry now?"

There was an edge to Isabella's voice, and Maria Zoë hesitated to answer. She and Balian had agreed not more than an hour ago that it was too soon to broach the subject with her. They had agreed she should be given at least the day of the funeral, and perhaps another as well, before discussing the marriage proposal. Since she had raised the subject herself, however, it seemed disingenuous for Maria Zoë to pretend that she did not know what was afoot. "They have a candidate in mind, but he refuses to consider the match unless you are in full agreement," Maria Zoë admitted.

Isabella smiled cynically. "You don't honestly expect me to believe that, do you?"

The cynicism made Maria Zoë sad, and she admitted, "I understand your bitterness, sweetheart. I would probably react the same way in your shoes."

"So, who is it?" Isabella insisted, adding, "It doesn't make it better to drag it out. I'd rather know sooner than later. It will help me adjust."

"I'm not sure if you know him," Maria Zoë started, trying to remember if Isabella had ever met the Count of Champagne. He was, after all, very much in the King of England's camp, and had, to her knowledge, never set foot in Tyre until the day he brought the news that the King of England had abandoned Lusignan. Then she remembered and said out loud, "But he was at the siege of Acre when you were there with Humphrey before the arrival of the Kings of France and England."

Isabella sat up straighter and looked at her mother with a curious expression. "Who?" she asked again.

Before Maria Zoë could answer, there was a loud banging on the door. This was not the timid knocking of a respectful servant hesitant to interrupt, and there was urgency in the knock as well. Maria Zoë turned toward the door and raised her voice to call out. "Who is there? The Queen and I do not wish to be disturbed."

"This is the Bishop of Beauvais with an urgent message from the Duke of Burgundy, Madame!" a deep male voice answered.

Isabella caught her breath. She acknowledged that her divorce from Humphrey had been the right—indeed, the only moral—thing to do, but she still hated the man who had dragged her from Humphrey's bed. "I don't want to see him!" she told her mother sharply. Maria Zoë opened her mouth to protest, but Beauvais strode into the room without awaiting an invitation.

Both Maria Zoë and Isabella jumped angrily to their feet at such an impertinence, and Maria Zoë sharply admonished, "You are not welcome here, my lord Bishop! Nor have you any right to intrude upon a bereaved widow in her chamber. Get out this instant or I will have you removed by force!" It was not an empty threat: the Bishop had evidently bluffed and bullied his way this far, but the uncertain household servants and guards were hovering in the hall in evident agitation. At the Dowager Queen's words, four of Montferrat's men-at-arms took heart and pushed into the room, their hands hooked in their belts and their stance belligerent.

The Bishop of Beauvais was, as usual, dressed in chain mail under a surcoat with crossed bishop's croziers, silver on red, as his motif. He cast a look over his shoulder at the men-at-arms and then looked again at Maria Zoë and Isabella. Isabella looked fragile and frightened, particularly pale against the solid black of her widow's weeds, but Maria Zoë was clearly not intimidated by him. He saw her eyes flicker to the men, and the very subtle but decisive jerk of her head inviting them deeper into the room.

"I have an urgent message for the Queen of Jerusalem," he insisted.

"Then wait in the hall, and the Queen will come when she is ready!" the Dowager Queen told him sharply. "Now, will you go freely or must I have you removed by force?"

"I'll go, but don't keep me waiting too long. The Duke of Burgundy commands ten thousand men, and they are on their way here." With these threatening words he spun on his heel, pushed through the four men-at-arms, who at a nod from Maria Zoë followed him, and left the room. Someone closed the door behind the men-at-arms so that Maria Zoë and her daughter were alone again.

"What can that odious man possibly want of me now?" Isabella asked her mother in outrage.

"I'm not sure, but it is safe to say it is not to offer you his deepest sympathy," Maria Zoë answered sarcastically. "The sooner you meet with him, the better. We'll gain nothing by making him fume, now that we've shown him the door. Sit down and let me put some makeup on you, then we'll change that veil for one with gold trim and fix a gold circlet over it."

Isabella willingly submitted to her mother's efficient makeover. Conrad, too, had been very sensitive to the importance of appearances, and she knew intuitively that her mother was right: she needed to look every inch a queen in the coming interview. Even more important to her psychologically, she wanted to erase the images Beauvais carried in his memory of her with her hair in disarray and her body covered only by a thin nightdress. It was an image fit only for a husband.

Although Isabella and Maria Zoë had withdrawn to Isabella's private apartment immediately after the funeral Mass, a feast had naturally been prepared for the public. Knowing Conrad would want to be remembered for his generosity, Isabella had authorized a large budget and had asked the cooks to "honor my lord's memory." The result was an elaborate spread of roasted and grilled meats, mounds of bread, lentil and green-pea pottages, mushroom pasties, and spring greens garnished with oleander flowers. Since the head table was empty, protocol was abandoned, and the food was offered on heavy sideboards lining the room, from which the guests helped themselves, sitting afterwards at the long benches flanking trestle tables. While the staff had not spared on food, they were more careful with the Bishop's plate and linen, so the tables were bare and only the cheapest Egyptian pottery was used for the serving dishes, while the guests provided their own knives and spoons.

The funeral guests had been surprised by the arrival of the Bishop of Beauvais. His rude insistence on being brought to the widow had aroused both their indignation and their curiosity. Even those who had already eaten lingered to find out what was going on. The hall was therefore quite crowded, with most people discussing animatedly what the Bishop could want.

Beauvais was pacing the dais when the Queen of Jerusalem and her mother emerged from the stairwell. He stopped and started slightly, snorting a little to himself at the effectiveness of feminine wiles. The frightened and exhausted girl he had glimpsed upstairs was now a stately young woman encased in dignity and crowned with gold. He had little choice but to bow deeply over her hand. "Madame," he intoned.

Isabella sank into the central chair on the dais, Conrad's chair, and indicated that her mother should sit at her left. The Bishop was not offered a seat. Instead, Isabella opened, "You wished to speak to me, my lord Bishop."

"Indeed. The news of your lord husband's dastardly murder has shocked us all—none less than the noble Duke of Burgundy. As this is obviously the work of that scoundrel King Richard of England, I have been sent to offer French protection. Even now the French crusaders are on their way to Tyre, so we can take control of its defenses and ensure you are safe from enemies of any sort."

Beauvais was not a man to pitch his voice low unless he was conspiring or seducing, and he had not bothered to lower his voice to deliver this message. His words, therefore, were heard by more than his intended audience, and behind him in the hall they unleashed a flurry of protest.

"We can defend Tyre without any Frenchmen!" someone shouted. "We've defended Tyre longer than you've been here!" someone else noted. "We don't need your damned help!" a third added, while the whole room grew loud with people repeating and commenting on the Bishop's words.

Isabella was relieved by that reaction. It strengthened her own resolve to resist this offer. "As you can hear, my lord Bishop, we have no need of your aid. Thank the Duke of Burgundy, but tell him to spare the exertion of coming here. We are quite capable of defending ourselves."

"My lady, with all due respect, you do not understand the military situation—"

Isabella cut him off furiously. "With all due respect, my lord Bishop, I understand the military situation far better than *you* ever could!" It was bad enough that Conrad had disparaged her opinions when they were in private. She would not tolerate a stranger, a man from France, a bishop, belittling her judgment in front of her subjects. "I was *raised* here, Monsieur. I lived in the border fortress of Kerak. I was there when it was besieged by Salah ad-Din. I was in Jerusalem when the news of Hattin came; I was here in Tyre during the siege of December 1187. I was with my husband at the siege of Acre! Do not presume to lecture to me just because I am a woman!"

A cheer went up from the men in the hall, loud enough to almost drown out Maria Zoë's soft, "Well said." Both gave Isabella courage and she sat straighter than ever, her eyes flashing with righteous indignation.

The Bishop bowed to her in a gesture of mock respect, and then, taking a step closer and looking at her with eyes that were no longer bemused, announced, "Your lord husband held the city of Tyre because my liege King Philip of France granted—"

Isabella didn't have to answer; the uproar from Conrad's retainers and admirers was overwhelming. They shouted the Bishop down, reminding him that Montferrat had saved Tyre before the King of France even knew it was threatened. "We saved Tyre!" they told him. "Tyre is ours!"

Isabella waited until the uproar had died down and then told Beauvais, calmly but very firmly, "Tyre is part of the Kingdom of Jerusalem, my lord. *My kingdom.*"

"You don't seem to understand the danger you are in, my lady. Richard Plantagenet—"

"Has been fighting for and regaining my kingdom, while you and your knights drink and gamble and whore in Acre!" Isabella flung at the Bishop of Beauvais as she got to her feet. She was exhausted and emotionally drained, and she could feel that she was on the brink of losing her self-control completely. Isabella knew herself well enough to know that if she didn't break off this conversation now, she was likely to start screaming hysterically. She did not want to do that in front of her subjects and Montferrat's men, so her only option was to depart *now*—before it happened.

The Bishop sputtered protests and bristled with indignation. "How dare you impute such base—"

"I've heard enough!" Isabella cut him off. "I will *not* surrender Tyre to anyone but the man the High Court chooses as my consort! That was my husband's dying wish, and nothing will convince me to change my mind or do otherwise!" Then she spun about and strode as fast as she could—without running—to the stairwell. As she disappeared inside, a cheer went up from the men in the hall.

The Bishop of Beauvais was stunned. He had not expected any resistance from Isabella. He had seriously imagined she would fall into his arms in weeping gratitude. He found himself face to face with the Dowager Queen, and she was looking bemused.

"Your daughter is a hysterical young woman," he told the older woman, hoping to win her sympathy. They had, after all, been allies in removing Isabella from Humphrey and ensuring her marriage to Montferrat. "No doubt being with child has unbalanced her mind."

Maria Zoë knew her daughter well enough to know that she could indeed appear "hysterical"; she was passionate and spirited, she had thrown terrible temper tantrums as a child, and she had admitted to having violent fights with Conrad. Maria Zoë knew exactly why her daughter had left so precipitously, but she also supported every single word Isabella had said so far and knew that far from being "hysterical," she was being very wise. It was only her method of delivery that had been somewhat flawed. Because Maria Zoë had been schooled at the court in Constantinople, she knew it would have been better if Isabella had kept her temper under control and had dealt with the Bishop in a more restrained fashion, but none of that diminished her support for her child.

"My lord Bishop," she opened in a cool, self-possessed tone, "a young widow whose beloved husband died in her arms after being cruelly stabbed to death can certainly be forgiven for being slightly distraught. A bishop and nobleman, on the other hand, with so little sense of propriety—not to mention so little sympathy—as to burst in upon a grieving widow uninvited is . . ." she hesitated long enough to ensure everyone in the room was holding their breath before she delivered the verdict, "a despicable knave. Save your breath!" She held up her hand and cut off Beauvais before he could open his mouth to voice his protests. "Leave aside the manner in which you burst in here and the manner in which my daughter gave you her answer. All that really matters is the substance of what the Queen of Jerusalem just told you." She paused, made sure the hall was silent with tense anticipation, and then stated firmly and clearly: "She does not need or want your assistance or that of the Duke of Burgundy. Take that message back to Acre."

The Bishop of Beauvais wasn't prepared to accept this answer. "My lady, that is not an option. Tyre must be held at all costs, and a *distraught*" (he smiled condescendingly as he used the word) "pregnant widow cannot be trusted to—"

There was again an uproar from the men in the hall, but Maria Zoë gestured for them to be still. "Cannot be trusted to do what, my lord? Defend her city and her kingdom? You seem unaware that the women of Jerusalem defended the Holy City against Salah ad-Din's whole army for almost ten days!"

"Come now!" the Bishop scoffed. "Your husband was in command—"

"Yes: of women, children, and priests. Turn around and look at the men here! Tyre is not at risk!"

They cheered her as Maria Zoë had rarely been cheered at any time before. After a moment, she signaled them for silence again.

"My lord Bishop, given that the strength of Tyre's defenses is evident," she gestured to the men in the room, "it is equally evident that you are not in the least concerned about the safety of *Tyre*. Your sole concern is obtaining control of my daughter. The Duke of Burgundy, having rejected Sibylla's hand and with it the burden of being King of Jerusalem, now wants to foist his candidate upon my daughter—"

"What do you think we did together eighteen months ago?" the Bishop burst out in exasperation. He couldn't believe that this woman, who had been his closest ally before, was now standing in the way of what ought to be their mutual interest in seeing Isabella married to a man amenable to the King of France.

"Do you honestly not see the difference?" the Dowager Queen asked back in a withering tone. "The Marquis de Montferrat was selected as my daughter's husband by the High Court of Jerusalem, and it is the High Court and only the High Court who will select her next husband. Now, Monsieur, you're welcome to refresh yourself at my son-in-law's funeral feast, but we have nothing more to say to one another."

She stood and turned her back on him, not stopping until she reached the door to the stairwell. There she paused, turned to the men assembled in the hall, and ordered: "Do not let that man upstairs again!" Then she disappeared inside.

A moment later she almost collided with Isabella. "Sweetheart!"

"I wanted to hear what happened next. Thank you!"

Maria Zoë took her daughter by the arm, and together they returned to Isabella's chamber. This time Maria Zoë carefully bolted the door behind them. Then she looked around for wine and glasses, as they were both in need of a drink. Isabella sank down into one of the chairs by the window table.

As Maria Zoë brought her a red glass goblet filled with wine, Isabella met her eyes and asked tensely, "So, Mama, who *has* the High Court selected?"

Maria Zoë laughed shortly before remarking, "All that ridiculous fuss was for nothing, really, as the High Court has chosen someone who will very likely please the Duke of Burgundy well."

"Stop torturing me! Who is it?" Isabella demanded, her nerves very much at the breaking point again.

"The Count of Champagne," Maria Zoë admitted, watching Isabella very closely. To her amazement, a flicker of a smile crossed Isabella's face.

Champagne had accepted Ibelin's hospitality, and it was here that a messenger from his uncle King Richard reached him. Henri stepped into the solar window niche to read the letter in as much privacy as possible, his back to the room in which Ibelin and Sidon were ostensibly going over some papers, Ernoul and Alys were practicing, and Ibelin's sister-in-law and Helvis were spinning. He broke the seal and scanned the letter in nervous haste.

King Richard's congratulations almost leapt off the page, written in his own forceful hand. He even went so far as to praise the wisdom of God in ordaining the twist of fate that gave to the Holy Land a leader of greater merit than either Montferrat or Lusignan. Henri was a little overwhelmed and flattered by the strength of his uncle's support—but on second thought, he wondered how much of it was dictated by Richard's desire to return home. Was the English King just grasping at straws? After all, he'd been willing to back Montferrat, too. Was there anyone Richard would not have accepted? Well, maybe Burgundy, Henri thought whimsically, and then picked up the letter to read to the end. King Richard wrote: "*Of course, Toron is still alive, so if my cousin's marriage to Montferrat was bigamous, then so would be her marriage to you.*"

Henri winced inwardly. He hadn't even thought of that. He folded the letter together again, lost in thought, taking no note of the commotion in the street out front. As he turned back into the room, Sidon and Ibelin were both looking at him expectantly.

"He approves," he informed them simply.

It was rare for expressions to change so rapidly from wary dread to unfettered elation, and rare, too, for two grizzled barons to be so openly delighted. Grinning with relief, they came forward with outstretched hands to clap him on the back. Sidon suggested it would be more appropriate to kneel in homage, and Henri protested vigorously, "Good heavens! Not yet! I've told you I won't go through with this unless Queen Isabella is in agreement. All this does is—" He was struck dumb by the figure standing in the doorway from the great hall.

Isabella was still in mourning, her gown one of thick and impenetrable black Mosel cotton, but the overgown was of sheer purple silk, and so were the veils covering her head and encasing her throat. A circlet of gold crowned her forehead. She was stunningly beautiful, and she was looking straight at him.

Mortified by the fact that he'd been stunned into staring at her, Henri hastened forward to bow deeply over her hand, stammering, "My lady, I came to offer my condolences as soon as I heard the dreadful news, but I was not admitted—not that I'm complaining. I completely understand that you had no wish for visitors—strangers—at such a time, but please accept my deepest, deepest sympathy."

"Your condolences were conveyed to me and were much appreciated," Isabella told him with a faint smile, and then she turned to the others standing or sitting in the solar, all of whom were watching with expressions ranging from shock to amusement. "I would like to be alone with the Count of Champagne," she announced.

Ernoul and Alys scuttled for the great hall, while Helvis and her aunt Eloise dutifully left their spinning—though not without a backward glance from Helvis, who was only persuaded to continue by a firm hand from her betrothed. Ibelin was the last to leave, shepherding the others out and then standing with his back to the solar to make sure no one re-entered.

Isabella advanced deeper into the room, gesturing toward the window niche Henri had just left. "Shall we sit, my lord?"

"My lady!" Henri gestured for her to precede him.

She stepped up into the window niche and sat on the stone bench. He followed her, taking the seat opposite. "My lord, forgive me for taking you by surprise," she opened. "My mother told me that you have been selected by the High Court—"

"Not yet," Henri hastened to assure her. "The full High Court has not yet given their consent to your stepfather's suggestion, and I have told them repeatedly that . . ." He broke off, because Isabella was smiling at him. It wasn't a radiant smile. The strains and horrors of the last week still sat heavy on her face and shoulders; her eyelids sagged from too much crying. Yet a smile from the heart spilled out of her eyes nevertheless, and it took his breath away. In fact, he lost his train of thought entirely.

When he fell silent in sheer uncertainty and embarrassment, she noted gently, "I heard what you were saying as I entered, my lord, and my mother had already reported your hesitation to take on a wife who was unwilling and resentful. We both remember too acutely how we first met to want to endure a repeat of that night."

If he had been tongue-tied before, he was speechless now. The reference to that night in Acre conjured up the image of Isabella in her nightdress with her hair cascading down around her—an image best saved for a woman's husband. At the time he had only been shocked by the rude manner in which the Bishop of Beauvais had proceeded, and the sight had sparked his pity and protectiveness. Now, with the prospect of becoming that husband, the image ignited desire as well. She was a very *desirable* woman.

"I came here to assure you that I am not being forced into this marriage against my will—any more than I was forced to marry Montferrat. I wish that the illegal nature of my marriage to Humphrey had been established without the drama of that night in Acre, but I no longer doubt that it was not a valid marriage in the eyes of God. I married the Marquis de Montferrat in accordance with the constitution and for the benefit of my kingdom. I was, and am, determined not to follow in the footsteps of my elder sister, who by her willfulness and selfishness forced upon the barons of Jerusalem a man unworthy of the crown."

That much Isabella had prepared in advance and memorized on her way here. But Henri was gazing at her with such lovely, soft eyes that she was completely flustered. Neither Humphrey nor Conrad had ever looked at her like this. Humphrey had been too much a brother, and Conrad too predatory. She fell silent in confusion.

Henri reached out, grasped both her hands, and led them to his lips. "You have my utmost respect, Madame—respect and admiration. My grandmother always put Aquitaine first. That's why she married Henry Plantagenet, though God knows it brought her great grief and sorrow. I would not want to be the cause of either. Truly, I would not," he assured fervently and sincerely.

Isabella was more flustered than ever. She had not removed her hands from his, and it felt good that way. His hands were dry but warm, firm but gentle. And then she remembered her baby and drew back with an intake of breath. "My lord . . ."

He waited anxiously. He no longer doubted that he very much *wanted* to marry Isabella—even if it were a bigamous marriage and it meant he had to stay here forever.

"My lord, have they told you—that—that I am with child?" The look in her eyes was so frightened that he wanted to pull her into his arms and comfort her.

"Of course!" he assured her with a smile to calm her fears.

"And you don't mind?" she asked hopefully.

"My uncle Richard thinks that God sent me here to unite the crusaders and lead us to victory over Salah ad-Din, while he returns to secure his heritage. My destiny, he says, is to save your kingdom *now*. That is more than enough for me, my lady. I do not need to found a dynasty. I am content to be Count of Champagne and your consort, Isabella, if you so wish." He meant every word he said, and Isabella believed him.

It was her turn to lift his hands, still clasping hers, to her lips and kiss them. "I do so wish, Henri. I want nothing more in the world than to have you as my husband and consort in the very difficult days, months, and years ahead."

Chapter 20

Acre, July 29, 1192

AFTER ALMOST FIVE YEARS CONFINED TO Tyre, coming to Acre seemed to Isabella like an adventure. For Maria Zoë it was also a relief to take up residence in the spacious, well-appointed royal palace after five years cramped in an over-crowded merchant residence. As Queen of Jerusalem, no one doubted Isabella's right to residence in the palace, but with a fine sense of her own self-interest Isabella had sent word ahead to Queen Berengaria, assuring her and the Queen of Sicily there was no need for them to vacate their rooms or inconvenience themselves in any way; Isabella explained she hoped only that they would not object if she and her mother joined them at the royal palace in Acre. The answer had been the expected: "We'd be delighted."

What was far more astonishing, Maria Zoë thought, was that two ruling queens, two dowager queens, and five adult women could get along so well. Of course, it was no surprise that Eschiva and Isabella fell into each other's arms in hardly containable joy. After that Eschiva had been the bridge between her aunt and cousin and her new friends, the English and Sicilian Queens. Berengaria took an instant liking to Isabella. After carefully and sensitively inquiring about Isabella's feelings as both a recent widow and a young bride, she had been relieved and delighted to discover that the "bride" almost completely supplanted the "widow," and that Isabella was not merely comfortable with her awkward situation: she embraced it. As she explained to an attentive and sympathetic Berengaria, "My marriage to Humphrey was neither valid nor consummated, and my marriage to Conrad was a political necessity, but Henri is totally different! He's not just kind like a brother or passionate like a lover, he's attentive, caring, respectful, *and* loving. I've never been so happy in all my life—well, not since I was seven and living in paradise with my mother and stepfather!"

Berengaria was, furthermore, almost as excited about Isabella's condition as Isabella herself. She bombarded her with questions, delighted by Isabella's openness and willingness to let her feel for the child in her belly. When the baby kicked under her gentle touch, her face lit up with wonder and joy. She admitted openly that she could hardly wait to become pregnant herself—a difficult prospect with her husband almost constantly away.

While Berengaria and Isabella talked of children and husbands, Eschiva, Joanna, and Maria Zoë found common ground in discussing recent political and military developments. King Richard had been persuaded (by whom remained mysterious, although Isabella blithely asserted it was all the work of her new husband) to remain in the Holy Land until the fall and to undertake another attempt on Jerusalem.

While the nickname "Lionheart" suggested impetuosity, King Richard had shown he was very much his father's son by undertaking the campaign in a methodical and highly rational manner, first securing his lines of communication and then expanding Frankish control of the coastal plain. He'd attacked and taken Darum with his own troops before Champagne could arrive with the French, but he'd graciously turned his latest conquest over to Champagne as King of Jerusalem. He next took Castle Rouge, southeast of Hebron, but it was too isolated to hold and he withdrew. However, the feint had been enough to make Salah ad-Din pull back. Soon, in response to the English King's slow but steady advance, the Sultan was systematically giving up more and more of the coastal areas and entrenching himself in the highlands.

Maria Zoë knew from Balian's letters that the English King had at this juncture argued that the key to Jerusalem lay in Cairo, and had tried to persuade his fellow crusaders to turn their back on Jerusalem and strike instead down the Nile. His fleet had been given orders to prepare for the expedition. However, the French flatly refused to go, and the bulk of the other crusaders, be they Danes or Germans, Hungarians or Czechs, had voted with the French. The King of England had been forced to concede. In consequence, the army had advanced as far as Latrun, where they began to collect the materiel, siege engines, and supplies they would need for a full-scale siege.

The Plantagenet used the time to attack the Sultan's lines of communication and supply from Egypt. In late June, Richard's queen and her companions learned from many admiring sources that the King had captured an enormous caravan defended by well over two thousand Saracen troops. The crusaders had seized over twenty-five hundred horses, a veritable boon to the depleted resources of the Franks, and almost five thousand camels. The latter had been loaded with not just food supplies and the instruments of war, but also treasure intended to refill Salah ad-Din's depleted treasury. In fact, in addition to cases filled with gold and silver coins, there had been camel-loads of candlesticks and silver plate, silks, spices, beeswax, perfumes, sugar, and all the luxuries that made the Orient so decadent—or so the crusaders said.

With an appreciation of his wife's rigorous household accounting, Balian had provided a detailed list of his share of the spoils. These included twenty-five horses for the Ibelin stud, five camels as beasts of burden, two thousand gold bezants, five thousand pieces of silver, sixteen bolts of silk, a ton of sugar, five hundred pounds of wax, two hundred pounds of spices, and a long list of various other objects.

Just when all appeared set for the final confrontation over Jerusalem, the queens received word that the Frankish army was again withdrawing to Ramla. Berengaria had been deeply disquieted by the news. She was convinced that something terrible had happened to Richard. "Remember the arrow he took before Arsuf?" she told her sister-in-law. "And, oh, all the other times he was nearly injured or captured or killed? I'm sure he would not have abandoned the assault on Jerusalem unless he was on his deathbed!"

It was hard for the others to argue with Berengaria, because what she said was all too true: Richard had earned the name "lionhearted" because of his complete disregard for his personal safety. Aimery, Balian, and Henri had all attested to their respective wives on more than one occasion that Richard Plantagenet threw himself into the thick of every fight, regardless of the odds. If anyone was destined to die in battle, it was the lionhearted King of England.

Nevertheless, a different image nagged at Maria Zoë: her first husband had died of dysentery while campaigning against the Saracens. A glass of dirty water could kill as easily as a crossbow bolt, a lance, or a sword. Meanwhile, Joanna remembered vividly how her brother suffered from recurring debilitating fevers. What united them all was the conviction that the assault on Jerusalem would not have been abandoned unless King Richard was seriously injured or incapacitated—until he himself walked into the walled garden where they were enjoying the shade of the surrounding arcade on a hot late-July afternoon.

Berengaria saw him first and flew across the flower beds to fling her arms around him. Richard was not alone. As Henri de Champagne emerged from behind him, Isabella followed her friend's example, despite her protruding belly and waddling steps. More surprising was that Aimery de Lusignan and Balian d'Ibelin were also in the King's company—until Maria Zoë realized that they had come precisely because their wives served the King's women. Only Joanna Plantagenet was left out of the ensuing reunion.

When the excitement had died down and it was clear that all four men were in the best of health, the inevitable question came, voiced by the only woman brave enough to put it to the English King—his sister. "But what of Jerusalem?" Joanna asked, baffled. "You were so close!"

"Close enough to see it," King Richard answered in a tone that was grim rather than triumphant.

"Then what happened?" Berengaria asked, as confused as her sister-in-law. She knew her husband was vulnerable to personal injury, but she had come to see him as invincible militarily.

"A council of twenty men voted not to carry out the assault," Richard told the women simply, but his face was guarded and he avoided eye contact with either wife or sister.

"But how? Why? Couldn't you override them or convince them otherwise? I don't understand," Joanna voiced the thoughts of all the women.

"I refuse to lead men to certain and unnecessary death!" Richard snarled back, and added aggressively, "And I didn't come here to be interrogated! I thought I was coming for rest and feminine comfort!"

Berengaria caved in at once. "Of course, beloved! Sit down! I'll call for wine!" She sprang up and ran for the door out of the garden.

Joanna was made of sterner stuff. "We'll be happy to offer comfort once we know what is going on," she told her brother. "You can't just walk in here and expect us to understand everything!"

"Ask Ibelin, then; he was on the council. I was not."

All eyes turned on Balian, and Maria Zoë didn't like what she saw. The last five years had ravaged his face, aging him by ten, but up to now (except for that day when he first arrived at Tyre from Jerusalem) his eyes had burned with determination. Now he looked defeated. "The strategic situation has not changed since last winter," he reminded them with a grimace. "Salah ad-Din holds Jerusalem with an army of seasoned soldiers—not women, children, and priests. And he controls the surrounding countryside, while our besieging army is sixty miles from the sea and our source of reinforcements and supplies. Even if we could capture Jerusalem, we could not hold it, unless all the men with the crusading army were prepared to stay and defend it—which they are not." Maria Zoë thought it was diplomatic of her husband not to point his finger at the King of England as he spoke. "But that doesn't really matter, because there is no way we *could* capture Jerusalem; they've scorched the earth for miles around, poisoned the cisterns, and filled up the wells."

"What? Who?" Joanna asked sharply.

Maria Zoë understood. "Salah ad-Din," she answered for her husband, and then she went to him to take his hand.

Richard was suddenly speaking again, this time so angrily that Henri instinctively slipped his arm protectively around Isabella. "I warned them what would happen! I told them we had to strike at Salah ad-Din's rear, not confront him head-on. Burgundy goaded me. Do you want to hear the latest? He's turned his hand to writing ditties deriding me for cowardice!" the lion roared.

"Pointless, I would think," Joanna noted. "The one accusation that will *never* stick to you is cowardice. Now, a bad temper is something else again. . . ."

To the astonishment of the others, Joanna's quip hit Richard between the eyes. He laughed and turned on his sister with an expression of affection. "That's just the kind of thing Mother would have said. And you're right: I've no right to take out my frustration on any of you. Henri, go frighten the servants into sending us lavish amounts of chilled wine, cold chicken, and—well, a whole feast."

"I'll go," Aimery offered; "they're more likely to be frightened of me than of our turtledove here."

The others laughed, more out of relief that King Richard was prepared to be genial than because of Aimery's remark. Isabella and Henri were too happy to be together to care if the others thought them overly affectionate.

"And where's that squire of yours, Ibelin?" King Richard asked next. "I could use some good music to go with the wine." After that everyone endeavored to be cheerful and distracting.

It wasn't until they retired to their own chamber that Maria Zoë could begin to try to understand what was going on in her husband's head. As so often in the past, she used the bath as a means to relax him into confidences. At this time of year, when the days were oppressively hot, she ordered cool, unheated water. Once the bath was full and Balian had stripped off his clothes with the help of Georgios, she sent everyone away. Alone with her husband, she removed her veils and gowns to sit beside the bath in her sleeveless cotton shift.

She didn't speak as she cupped her hands and poured water gently over her husband's head until his hair was wet. She silently massaged the back of Balian's neck with soapy hands, then stretched her fingers upwards into his long, thick hair. It was still mostly dark, although increasingly streaked with white. She kneaded his scalp with her strong fingers, washing his hair at the same time.

She could feel him start to relax, but she held her tongue except to tell him to raise his head. Then she started soaping his right arm right down to the palm and fingers.

"At Ramla last winter," Balian started speaking at last, "Sir Bartholomew told me there was no point in fighting anymore. He said we'd built our kingdom on sand, and that all trace of us would soon be wiped out by the desert and the dunes." He paused as if waiting for a reaction, but Maria Zoë preferred to let him continue. "I didn't want to believe him." He fell silent again.

Maria Zoë went around to the other side of the tub to wash his left arm and hand. As she worked she gently massaged the muscles of his arm, inwardly admiring the strength in them and their masculine beauty.

Balian resumed. "When my father came to the Holy Land, it was an impoverished backwater inhabited by people beaten down and exploited by their Turkish masters. The people planted the same fields year after year, without variation, and the soil was exhausted. They still used oxen to pull their wooden plows, and there was almost no irrigation. The roads and aqueducts hadn't been repaired since the Romans left; the harbors were silted up. We repaired and rebuilt the Roman roads, bridges, and cisterns. We applied our better farming methods and equipment, we imported draft horses, and we invested in irrigation ditches. We made the desert bloom." He stopped speaking, as if he were seeing again the land of milk and honey in which he had grown up.

"But today things are worse than when we first set foot on this sacred soil. The villages are abandoned, the fields fallow, the cities ruins, and the roads crumbling. The countryside around Jerusalem for twenty miles is nothing but wasteland. There's nothing green as far as the eye can see, and the charred stumps of the olive and orange trees rear up like gnarled hands from hell. Bethlehem has been completely wrecked. The Church of the Nativity sacked." Again he fell silent, but Maria Zoë didn't dare move. She waited tensely for him to continue.

At last he added in a voice that was almost inaudible, "When we passed through Ibelin on the way north to invest Jerusalem, we were attacked by swarms of cincenelles. Swarms of them, Zoë! They were as thick as locusts. The men who didn't cover their faces fast enough soon looked like lepers. It was like a plague. . . . And the wine stalks had all been broken down and trampled. Not one remained. Not one. . . ."

He leaned his head against the back of the bath, his eyes closed, and it took a moment before Maria Zoë realized that tears were trickling down his chiseled cheeks in sheer despair.

Maria Zoë didn't know what to do or say, so she just sat beside the tub with her fingers entwined in her husband's until the tears stopped. Balian still didn't move, however, and she thought maybe he had fallen asleep. When she tried to stand, however, his fingers closed around hers and he urged, "Don't go, Zoë. Say something. Anything."

Maria Zoë thought for a moment and then began to relate in a soft narrative tone, "When I was selected to be King Amalric's bride, my great-uncle sent for me. Now, I may have been 'born to the purple,' as they say in Constantinople, and I had lived all my life in royal palaces surrounded by luxury, but I had seen very little of the Emperor himself. The fact that this was a very important interview was, of course, impressed upon me by my mother, my sister, my tutor, my confessor, and so on. Everyone was very concerned that I was going to do something stupid and that the Emperor would change his mind and choose one of my many cousins as Amalric's wife instead. So was I!" Maria Zoë confessed with a short laugh, which induced her husband to turn up the corners of his mouth slightly without moving his head or opening his eyes.

"I soon discovered, however, that far from being a monster intent on finding fault with me, the Emperor was concerned about instilling in me an understanding of what he expected of me. Among other things, he showed me a beautifully illustrated *Life of St. Helena* that included exquisite pictures of her finding the True Cross and directing the construction of the Church of the Nativity. My great-uncle warned me, however, that *everything* St. Helena had built had been destroyed when the Persians took Jerusalem. Emperor Herakleion had rebuilt the church, he explained, but later the Muslims had set that church on fire. The native Christians, he said, repaired it as best they could, only to have Kalif el-Hakim raze it to the ground. My great-uncle stressed that it had taken a great deal of Imperial gold and influence to convince el-Hakim's successors to let Constantinople finance the reconstruction of even a modest church on the site of the Resurrection. When Westerners came, he explained, they had built a big new church. He didn't call it beautiful, because it was not at all to his taste. He told me he expected *me* to restore to the sacred sites of St. Helena some of the glory that had been destroyed." She paused to see her husband's reaction.

He nodded, which she interpreted to mean she should continue talking. "Yet just as the Emperor was about to dismiss me, he seemed to have second thoughts. With a whimsical smile on his face he reminded me that Christ had not chosen to be born amidst the splendor of Athens or Rome, the greatest cities of his age. He chose a provincial backwater." She paused again, this time to lend her words greater weight. "Then he said to me: 'I always wondered why, until I stumbled upon an account of ancient Sparta. It explained that the Spartans disdained building an acropolis to equal that of Athens—because *they built their monuments of flesh*. Then it struck me: so, too, did Christ. To the extent that we follow in His footsteps, *we* are monuments to Him more magnificent than the most spectacular cathedral."

Maria Zoë paused again and glanced at her husband. He was still sitting with his head tipped back, resting on the padded rim of the bathtub, but his eyes were cracked open, and he was gazing at her.

"I think of that sometimes—"

A furious banging at the door made Maria Zoë gasp and Balian sit upright so fast that water splashed over the edge of the tub.

"My lord! My lord!" an agitated, unfamiliar male voice called through the wooden door. "Come quick to King Richard. Salah ad-Din has laid siege to Jaffa!"

They were all looking dazed. Ibelin's hair was wet. Aimery was half shaved. Henri was still flushed. Only King Richard seemed unflustered. "He must have been waiting for me to leave Jaffa," King Richard speculated. "In any case, according to the ship's captain who brought the news, the Sultan has numerous siege engines and sappers and a very large army. He said he'd counted a hundred emir's tents and put the attacking army at twenty thousand horsemen alone, with God knows how many infantry. That might be a bit of an exaggeration, but we have to assume the worst, and we must respond at once."

The men he had summoned—Champagne, Ibelin, Aimery de Lusignan, and the Earl of Leiscester—nodded grimly. They understood perfectly what was going on. The Sultan was putting them back on the defensive and demonstrating just how fragile their apparent victories had been. If Salah ad-Din took Jaffa, he would isolate the Frankish garrison at Ascalon, make another attempt on Jerusalem futile, and put all their gains at risk again. It was a lunge at the Frankish jugular.

"Just how many men are still in Jaffa?" Leiscester wanted to know.

"About three thousand, but half of them are the sick and wounded at the Hospitaller infirmary there," Richard answered.

"And who is in command?"

Before Richard could answer, the door opened with a loud bang and the Duke of Burgundy strode in, accompanied by the Bishop of Beauvais.

"Ah, there you are, my lords. Have you heard the news?"

"That Salah ad-Din is besieging Jaffa?" the French duke answered. Unlike the rest of them, Burgundy looked unruffled, dignified, and immaculately groomed. "Yes, we've heard it."

"When can you and the rest of the French be ready to march?" King Richard asked back.

"March where?"

"To the relief of Jaffa!" King Richard retorted, his resolve not to lose his temper with this continuous thorn in his side already cracking.

"My lord King, if you think you can ever again command me and my men after your shameful and cowardly refusal to assault Jerusalem—"

"God damn you, Burgundy! I wasn't even on the council that voted to withdraw! None of my vassals were! It was five Frenchmen who agreed with the others—"

"They were bullied and intimidated by the Templars and Hospitallers," Burgundy retorted coldly. "I refuse to take responsibility for your cowardice, and I refuse to—"

King Richard's face was so expressive that Ibelin and Champagne both jumped between him and the Duke of Burgundy before he could strangle the French duke. Champagne held his uncle back, while Ibelin told Burgundy and Beauvais to get out if they valued their lives. Burgundy had seen the same murderous fury in the Plantagenet's eyes, and he fled. Meanwhile Richard was screaming insults at the top of his voice, and Henri was struggling to keep him from following Burgundy; Henri was dragged halfway across the room in the process.

"We don't need the French!" Ibelin shouted, breaking through the stream of oaths from the English King. "The Templars, Hospitallers, and men of Jerusalem are enough!"

Richard stopped screaming and struggling, nodded to Henri that he could let go of him, and turned around. "Can you muster tonight?"

Ibelin took a deep breath. "I'm sure the Templars and Hospitallers can be counted on to muster tonight. I will need a little more time to pull together the contingents of my fellow barons."

Richard nodded. "I will go by ship. It will take at least four days to take an army overland, and I've been told the winds are favorable at the moment. A half-dozen ships of my fleet can be made ready to depart tonight. I will take only Pisan and Genoese archers and my household knights, as my principal purpose is to assure the garrison that help is on the way." And stiffen morale, of course, since the men at Jaffa were largely Richard's men, Poitevins and Normans.

"Let me come with you!" Henri begged, his face flushed with a different ardor from that only the hour before.

"No. Your place is at the head of your troops, Henri," King Richard told his nephew. But turning to Aimery de Lusignan, he added, "As Constable of Jerusalem, Lusignan, you're welcome to join me if you want."

Aimery jumped at the chance. "I will, my lord King."

"Good. Then make ready at once."

Road south of Caesarea, July 30-31, 1192

In the course of the next day, Champagne and Ibelin pulled together a force of nearly six hundred knights, slightly more than that number of sergeants, and almost three thousand infantry. It was composed of Hospitaller and Templar contingents as well as the men in the service of Champagne, Ibelin, Galilee with his younger brother Ralph, Caesarea, Haifa, Hebron, and Bethsan. With Haakon Magnussen's *Storm Bird* keeping pace with them by sea, they took the road south, reaching Haifa at the end of the next day. The third night they spent in Caesarea, which was slowly and hesitantly coming back to life. Where once nearly ten thousand people had lived, several hundred now housed, mostly occupying buildings near the harbor where, presumably, they could flee in the fishing boats clustered along the inner quay. Significantly, they had repaired the Roman aqueduct, and the gardens were again being cultivated, while some of the shops had also reopened.

On the following day, however, shortly after leaving the city, Champagne and Ibelin noticed large bodies of Saracen horse hovering to the east. As they marched south, it was evident that they were being shadowed by a force at least three times as strong as their own. Ibelin found it hard to imagine that Salah ad-Din could field this large an army *in addition to* the one described at Jaffa. He suspected, therefore, that the Sultan, anticipating a relief effort, had split his forces. This seemed particularly likely since the Saracens shadowing them were entirely horsemen. Once Jaffa was invested, the job of assaulting the city lay largely with the engineers, sappers, and infantry, so the Sultan's cavalry there was superfluous. By guarding the road instead, they prevented the Franks from mounting a relief effort.

The Sultan's troops had chosen their position with care and acumen. South of Caesarea the shore road advanced between sand dunes to the west and swamps to the east. This meant that the Frankish army was forced to march in a comparatively narrow column, and the farther south they penetrated, the more their flanks became exposed to the enemy.

At first they adopted the same formation used a year earlier and kept pressing forward, but when they reached the stream crossing known locally as the Locus Magnus, they found the bridge had been destroyed and the enemy was drawn up on the opposite bank. Since the bed of the river was a treacherous mixture of rolled stones and mud, they could not employ their most effective tactic, a charge of heavy cavalry, because they could not risk galloping through it. They would have to advance at a walk and then try to gain momentum on the far side. That meant riding uphill against a barrage of murderous fire. The prospects of success were not particularly good, but Ibelin strongly suspected King Richard would have attempted it anyway.

Champagne, however, had been King only three months. He was loath to risk what amounted to the entire fighting force of his kingdom in a single action. Battle was always risky, the stakes immensely high. Champagne shied from risking a second Hattin. They faced off against the Saracens, drawn up in battle formation on the north bank of the little river, but they did not attempt a breakthrough. Instead they slept in position.

Waking from a shallow sleep with the graying of the dawn, Ibelin rapidly registered that the enemy had not moved, either. As was to be expected, they were still blocking the road south. Champagne called another war council.

"My lord," Garnier de Nablus, the Master of the Hospital, opened, "Salah ad-Din achieves his objective merely by sitting in place. To prevent us from relieving Jaffa, he doesn't need to attack us. If we fail to break through, he has won. We *must* advance."

The Prince of Galilee, William of Tiberius, backed the Hospitaller emphatically, but Robert de Sablé, the Templar Master, pointed out all the advantages the enemy had and the risk that they would founder in the stream, horses twisting or breaking their legs on the uneven ground, while murderous arrows rained down on them. "It's madness to attack here."

"Are you willing to sacrifice Jaffa?" Nablus countered.

"Are you so *sure* you can break through?" Champagne asked him anxiously, his face a picture of uncertainty.

"My lord, we are always in God's hands," the Hospitaller answered stoically.

Champagne shook his head decisively. "We cannot risk the entire army of Jerusalem. It *is* better to lose Jaffa."

That raised many eyebrows, and Caesarea pointed out, "King Richard is depending upon our relief. He has only a tiny force with him. Are you prepared to abandon *him?*"

"Of course not! I'll sail to Jaffa with as many men as possible aboard the *Storm Bird* and bring the word to King Richard of what has happened here. You can send a rider to Acre for more galleys to bring the rest of you."

"And abandon all the horses?" Galilee asked, shocked. Nablus noted that Champagne himself would also be unable to take any horses, adding, "You'll reinforce King Richard by at most a hundred men. That won't be decisive at Jaffa."

"But I'll be able to warn him that we won't be relieving him as soon as he expects."

"If we don't break through, we won't be relieving him at all!" Nablus snapped back, casting a frown at Ibelin for keeping his own counsel.

Ibelin surprised them all by announcing, "My lord of Champagne is right. He, with as many reinforcements as possible, should take ship for Jaffa at once. The rest of us can remain here until more galleys arrive. If nothing else, by staying here we pin down what must be close to half of Salah ad-Din's army. If they are here facing us, they cannot be attacking Jaffa."

Except for Champagne himself, no one seemed at all pleased by Ibelin's suggestion, but with shaking heads and grumblings they accepted it. In feverish haste, Champagne selected his companions—all his own knights and some archers—and headed back up the road for Caesarea.

Ibelin wished him Godspeed and watched him ride away. After the dust had settled, he summoned the others again and announced, "What I suggest we do is withdraw to Caesarea. Then, by cover of darkness, we exit from the postern into the moat and ride along the beach below the coast until we've passed the Saracen positions."

"Can we do that?" Sablé asked. He was the only one not native to Outremer, and he had no idea what the coast looked like from the water's edge.

"If the tide isn't against us," Caesarea answered, glancing over his shoulder toward the Mediterranean. "Otherwise the archers will be wading through water up to their thighs."

"Better wet than dead," Haifa noted succinctly.

The others nodded.

"It would help if some of your Templars manned the walls of Caesarea, my lord," Ibelin addressed Sablé, "to give the impression we are still there in force."

Sablé nodded agreement. "Of course."

Ibelin looked at the others. "Are we agreed, then?" he asked.

Nablus nodded. "It's a good plan—why didn't you raise it earlier?"

Ibelin smiled faintly. "Champagne is our King, and we have sworn to obey him. I couldn't risk him saying no."

"But why would he?"

"Because he was in a hurry to get to Jaffa and join his uncle. This will cost us another day at least—and, if the sea gets up, even more."

Chapter 21

Coast of the Levant, July 30, 1192

RICHARD'S SMALL FLOTILLA HAD BEEN BECALMED off Mount Carmel. They tried rowing the galleys, but the currents were against them, and they could make so little progress that even Richard recognized they were exhausting the crews to no good purpose. He ordered the crews to stand down, while he prowled the decks and did everything but try to row or blow wind into the sails himself. He fumed, cursed, prayed, pleaded, and then fell asleep on deck exhausted, just as the first light air lifted the pennants on the masthead.

Aimery spread a blanket over the snoring King and went to the rail to watch the water slip past the hull as they gradually gained steerage before a very light, but (thankfully) northerly, wind. It was a strange twist of fate, he thought, that he was here and his brothers were on Cyprus. He had fallen in love with Cyprus at first sight, while Guy still growled that it was an insult for the "King" of Jerusalem, and Geoffrey muttered about "ungrateful Griffons and idiot Orthodox." Aimery would have gladly gone to Cyprus to try to restore order, but Guy did not want him. "A lot of help you did me in Jerusalem—always criticizing, nagging, and complaining! I don't need that kind of 'help' anymore. I'd rather have the good Henri d'Ibelin with me," he continued, indicating the knight who had so consistently praised and flattered him over the last five years. Henri had smiled at Aimery like the cat who swallowed the canary. "We'll take Cyprus without you!"

Aimery felt himself getting worked up again. Over the last five years, he had come to hate Guy. He hated him for Hattin, for letting the rest of them rot in a dungeon while he lived in luxury, for the stupidity of starting the siege at Acre rather than taking Sidon and Beirut (which King Richard had wanted to do next, had Salah ad-Din's threat to Jaffa not distracted him). He hated Guy for bringing his stupid royal wife to a notoriously unhygienic siege camp. He hated Guy for trotting around like a spaniel in Richard's shadow. He hated him. Period.

And with time even the complacent, insensitive, self-confident Guy had come to feel that hate and then return it—which had been unimportant as long as Guy was nothing but the nominal King of Jerusalem. But Cyprus! Aimery's heart screamed in frustration. What wouldn't he give for just a small piece of Cyprus! A modest fief he could call his own. A manor on the fertile plain, nestled below the mountains . . .

At some point during the night Aimery sank onto the deck and drifted off to sleep, lulled by the rhythmic hissing of the waves under the hull.

Jaffa, August 1, 1192

A shout from the masthead roused King Richard and Aimery at the same time. Richard leapt up, his wits already collected, while Aimery staggered to his feet still dazed. The sailor in the crow's-nest was pointing, and his voice wafted down to them. "Jaffa's burning!"

The King strode to the forward rail, trailed by every other man on deck, and they all strained their eyes to see what the sailor had seen from forty feet overhead. They held their breaths as the ship raced forward with a good quartering northwest wind. Aimery spared a glance for the rest of the fleet, noting that they were still six ships in tight formation. Men were lining the landward rail of all the other ships as well.

"There it is!" someone shouted, and Aimery looked back toward the shore. A ragged smudge, which might in other circumstances have been only a low cloud, was visible on the horizon. With each passing heartbeat it grew darker, and rose higher.

"Arm!" King Richard ordered, and men scattered to obey.

By the time Aimery returned to the foredeck, the skyline of Jaffa had separated itself from the horizon and was dark against the glare of the morning sun. Smoke was clearly rising from a variety of points across the city, and soon they could make out the tall Saracen siege engines that clustered around it like vicious dogs closing for the kill. Against the morning sun it was difficult to make out the colors on the banners snaking over the walls, but their shape alone betrayed them as Saracen. Jaffa had fallen.

A groan escaped from a score of throats, and King Richard began cursing in a steady, vehement stream. He was cursing himself, and his voice was more anguished than angry. He couldn't seem to tear his gaze away from the city he had rebuilt, the gateway to Jerusalem.

Aimery turned his attention to the vast Saracen camp surrounding the city. It was smaller than he had expected. The colorful tents of the emirs looked like huge, bright flowers on the parched plain, but frowning, Aimery started counting. He got to forty. That was a lot—but not as many as had been reported. Either the messenger had exaggerated for dramatic effect, or some of Salah ad-Din's army was elsewhere.

As Aimery watched, a flutter of activity swept through the camp. Trumpets started blaring, drums pounding, pipes screaming shrilly. The reaction to these signals was anything but disciplined, however. Men seemed to be running every which way all of a sudden. Aimery suspected the Frankish fleet had not only been spotted, but recognized.

He glanced aloft where Richard's banner, a snarling lion passant, flew out from the masthead in the stiff breeze. The lion seemed alive as the wind rippled the long silk. The Saracens knew that banner very well by now, and that meant they knew King Richard himself had returned to Jaffa.

They could also see for themselves that he had only six ships and could calculate, much as Aimery had done in reverse, the size of the Frankish force. Although they undoubtedly overestimated (they would expect fifty knights per ship instead of a total of just fifty-five), it would still be obvious to them that this force was hardly large enough to pose a serious threat to the assembled army of the Sultan. Yet there was every evidence of panic among the men on the shoreline.

"My lord King," Aimery dared break in on the Plantagenet's litany of self-abuse. "I make out no more than forty emirs by the tents," Aimery announced. "I'm going to guess they'll have at most five thousand horse and four or five times that number of infantry. More to the point," Aimery continued, "they don't seem in the least prepared for an assault from the sea."

Richard had turned to look at Aimery when he first spoke up, but now he snapped his head back to gaze at the shore. He stared for several seconds, and then without further comment, ordered the signal raised for the bannerets on the other ships to join him on his flagship.

Within a half-hour the bannerets, and the captains of the Genoese and

Pisan crossbowmen, had gathered in a circle around King Richard. He opened the council with the words: "Sirs, are we going to let that rabble stand in our way of relieving Jaffa? Don't forget that we left nearly all our wounded in the city! Will one of you presume to tell me your life is worth more than that of the men so fiercely besieged?"

The speech shocked the Italians, but Richard's knights had been expecting it. Only one of them had the courage to try to talk sense to their liege. "My lord King, there is no point in throwing yourself at that army with just fifty-five of us and a thousand Italian archers! Jaffa has already fallen, as we can see. You would achieve nothing but your death and ours."

"We do not know that Jaffa has fallen!" King Richard countered.

"They why do the Sultan's banners fly from the city walls?" the man answered.

"But not from the citadel!" Richard answered, and they all turned again to look toward the city. Saracen banners indeed fluttered from the city walls, but the citadel was naked of banners of either friend or foe.

With their eyes all riveted on the city, however, they noticed a man apparently in the robes of a priest waving furiously to them from the base of the wall closest to the citadel. As they watched, the priest ran to the end of one of the harbor moles, tore his robes up over his head, and flung himself naked into the sea.

Several of the men gasped in shock at such a dramatic gesture. Few of them could swim, so a man flinging himself into the turbulent waves breaking at the foot of the mole was the same as suicide in their eyes. Within a few seconds, however, the man's head emerged above the waves, and his arms began to beat the water rhythmically.

"Make for that man!" King Richard ordered the helmsman. The sailor didn't dream of contradicting him or awaiting his captain's orders; he at once put the tiller over. The ship's captain, however, conscious of how difficult it was to take a man onboard from the water, hastily ordered his crew to shorten sail and prepare to maneuver alongside the swimmer.

While most of the men kept their eyes glued to the tiny splashes in the distance that marked the swimmer's slow progress through the waves, Aimery watched the shoreline. More and more Saracen foot soldiers were streaming toward the shore, but Richard's words had been well chosen. They appeared little more than a disorganized rabble—albeit one beating their shields with their swords and shouting dares at King Richard to attempt a landing

The ship's captain stepped up beside King Richard. "My lord, let me lower a boat to rescue the swimmer while the ship withdraws to safer waters. We don't want to get ourselves trapped in the harbor."

That made sense, and King Richard at once nodded agreement. The captain brought his ship into the wind, lowered a longboat manned by six oarsmen, and then sailed to seaward to rejoin the rest of the little fleet. The other five ships were hovering inside the massive rock ledge on which, according to legend, the Ethiopian princess Andromeda had been tied as an offering to a sea monster. The ledge served as a breakwater, providing calmer water while yet far out of range of the enemy's archers.

Meanwhile, the King and his knights clustered on the stern to watch the longboat draw alongside the swimmer. The sailors shipped their oars and with the hull bouncing wildly in the waves, they reached for the swimmer. The gunnel of the longboat almost submerged underwater, and the men held their breath until at last the swimmer was hauled onto the deck. Here he huddled between the oar banks while the crew swung the stern to shore and pulled for their lives. By now scores of Saracen archers were trying their luck with long shots at the boat. The arrows all fell short, but they rained down onto the water of the harbor as thick as a summer hailstorm.

One of the sailors had given the priest his shirt, so that he came aboard the King's galley with bare feet and legs but not fully naked. He was still breathing heavily from his vigorous swimming, the excitement, or both. Since King Richard had been one of the men to offer him a hand over the gunnel into the ship, he dropped to his knees at once and started babbling in an unstoppable rush of words: "My lord King! You are not a moment too soon! They broke through the Jerusalem gate two days ago at noon and brought down ten yards of the adjacent wall. Those of us who could fled to the citadel, but we are too few. My good lord, the Bishop of Bethlehem, went to Salah ad-Din, offering him the same terms as at Jerusalem: that we would pay for our lives with ten bezants a man. Salah ad-Din agreed, but put my good lord in chains, saying he would hold him hostage until the entire garrison had surrendered. Then he sent me back to the garrison (for I had gone with Bishop Randolf) to tell them the price of their lives, and he gave us until Nones to raise our ransoms, but when some of our men took their money out to them, they beheaded them and flung their bodies at the base of the citadel gate, to show us what fate they really intend for us! I fear my dear lord the good Bishop is dead, for surely Salah ad-Din intends to kill us all—"

King Richard had heard enough. Spinning around, he shouted: "Man the oars! We're going in! Raise the signal to beach!"

"My lord King—" One of his knights tried to stop him, but Richard just shook him off like an irritation and started untying the lacings on his chausses. Aimery hastened to do the same.

More than a hundred yards out, the first arrows started raining down on them. These were spent arrows that fell harmlessly on the decks without the force to penetrate anything. The ones hitting the sails (which there had been no time to hand, despite being under oar) clattered down on them as well, making the barrage seem thicker than it was. With each oar-stroke, however, the missiles became more lethal. Nevertheless, the Genoese crossbowmen were lining the gunnel and returning fire with brutal efficiency. By now the enemy was densely crowded on the shore to repel the impending amphibious assault so the Genoese could hardly fire without hitting something. There was no need for careful aim, and they fired as fast as they could load. The screams of the killed and wounded Saracens mingled with their battle cries in counterpoint.

"Brace!" the captain shouted as the bows entered the breakers. Aimery dropped on one knee and clutched the side of the ship. Arrows were raining down thick and fast, with so much force that they stuck upright in the planking of the deck. With a hideous squealing crunch, the ship struck fast, flinging men forward onto their faces. Yet the ship had hardly come to a halt before King Richard grabbed the nearest crossbow off an archer, and grabbing the rail with his free hand, he swung himself over the side of the ship. He fell four feet into the frothing waves, landing groin-deep in the surging surf, and staggered forward until he found solid footing. Then he raised the crossbow to his shoulder and fired before sloshing his way up the steep incline of the beach.

No man could lag far behind such an example, and they were all over the side of the ship as fast as they could. The crossbowman from whom the King had grabbed his weapon reached him as he went to toss it aside, and rescued it from the waves so he could use it himself. Meanwhile the King had already drawn his sword, and then with his left hand he grabbed a Danish battle-ax from his belt. Methodically he hacked his way through the enemy as they collided at the water's edge.

The Franks had two advantages. On the one hand, they'd beached their ships north of the harbor but still close under the city walls, so they were, at most, two hundred yards from the city itself. On the other, the Saracens were singularly disorganized. The men who had filled this space wore the armor of all Salah ad-Din's various subjects: Kurds and Turks, Arabs and Nubians, hairy Mamlukes and black-skinned Berbers. They were all fighting fiercely, screaming in their different tongues and wielding whatever weapons they had, but they appeared to have no plan and no one seemed to be in command.

King Richard made straight for the city gate with the clear objective of gaining the city. Aimery was uneasy about what would happen if the gate was barred from the inside. If the enemy had done that (as they surely *should* have), they might find themselves fighting with their backs to the wall—or have to beat a retreat back to the ships. On the other hand, if they could get inside, they would be less vulnerable. There, even small numbers would be able to control confined spaces using walls as shields. If too hard pressed, they would be able to barricade themselves in one of the buildings, and hope the garrison holding the citadel would sally out to their rescue.

For now Aimery, like the King, was killing two-handed. He had forsaken his shield for a mace he could wield with his left hand while keeping his sword in his right. Although the King still formed the point of their living spear, the knights around him widened the wedge he was thrusting into the body of enemy troops. Behind them the archers spread out to use their weapons more effectively, taking a murderous toll.

Within minutes, Frankish knights were wading through the bodies of the dead and dying, finding it increasingly difficult to get a solid foothold. Yet unbelievably, the pace was picking up rather than slowing. Aimery risked glancing in the direction of King Richard and realized why: Saracens had started quailing and stepping back, reluctant to come within range of the King's bloodied ax, much less try to cross swords with him. As the Saracens drew back, the King lengthened his stride until, abruptly, there was no one between him and the wall. He sprang forward, but to Aimery's astonishment he did not make for the gate. Instead, he ran toward the base of the tower flanking it. Here he wrenched open a postern door that Aimery had not even noticed. "Holy Cross!" he thought—the King of England had the eyes of a hawk as well as the heart of a lion.

The King's knights fought hard to likewise reach the entryway. With the King gone, the Saracens seemed to regain heart, but the Franks had a goal in sight that inspired them to greater effort. Aimery was maybe the tenth knight to gain the safety of the tower. He flung himself through the door, only to be blinded by the darkness after the glaring sunlight outside. There was neither window nor torch inside the base of the tower, nothing but a narrow spiral stairway leading upwards. Aimery joined the line of panting men climbing the stairs in the dark ahead of him. Automatically he started counting the steps.

After forty-six steps, he burst into a room opening off the tower. This was lit by arrow slits and carpeted with bodies and body parts, victims of the men who had been before him on the stairs. With a jolt, he recognized Templar banners still hanging from the rafters and registered two Templar corpses nailed to a side door by the arrows that had killed them days ago. They had entered the Templar commandery.

The English King was nowhere in sight, but the clash of weapons and curses screamed in Arabic were coming from the next chamber. Aimery followed the sound of battle, only to find it almost over. The Saracens inside the command-ery had been intent on plunder and had been taken completely by surprise. They had probably not even noticed the arrival of the Frankish ships, Aimery guessed.

When the last Saracen in sight was dead, the King of England turned and shouted to the men still pouring out of the stairwell, "Raise my banner over the tower!" One of his knights immediately pushed his way against the flow, pulling a banner from inside his gambeson as he went. He regained the entry to the stairwell and disappeared inside. Minutes later Aimery heard faint shouting coming from the direction of the citadel; the survivors from the garrison had seen the banner.

Descending by a larger stairwell at the front of the complex that led into the city, King Richard led his men out into the streets, heading for the citadel. The streets were eerily deserted, but the stench was appalling. From the smashed-in doors, shattered windows, and wrecked furnishings it was obvious the city had been plundered, but except for the men they had encountered in the command-ery, no one appeared to be here anymore—except the dead. There were pig carcasses all over the place, some bloated and ready to burst open, others already spilling their putrid guts and crawling with flies. Far more disturbing, however, was that the pigs were often heaped up beside the bodies of men. Evidently the Saracens had intentionally dumped the "unclean" animals on the corpses of their enemies as a means of insulting them. Everywhere the wine casks had been broken open as well. The smell of stale wine mixed with the putrefying stench of bodies was exceptionally nauseating. Aimery was no more immune than the rest, and ended up vomiting everything left in his stomach into one of the ditches. He was in good company; King Richard, too, had been briefly overwhelmed by the toxic stink.

By the time they reached the Hospital of St. John, they knew what to expect. The patients had been slaughtered on their pallets, and most lay with their throats cut in the blood-stained straw, their eyes glazed in frozen horror at what was happening to them. The brothers of the Hospital, on the other hand, were found in a heap in the courtyard, apparently tossed there by their killers. From the absurd positions in which some lay, it appeared they had been tossed down from the second story—whether alive or dead at the time was no longer consequential. Here, in addition to the dead pigs, the Saracen had taken the time to heap the contents of the latrines and stables over the corpses of their hated enemy.

The survivors, meanwhile, had sallied out of the citadel and joined forces with King Richard's men. This increased the total number of Franks to nearly a hundred knights and about two thousand infantry. King Richard believed that was enough to take on a Saracen army estimated at twenty-five thousand. After what they'd already done this day, however, no one dreamed of questioning him. They just stormed out of the Northern Gate and started killing the already confused and disorganized Saracens.

Jaffa, August 5, 1192

They had built their camp on the same ground the Saracens had used, preferring the risks and discomforts of the open air to the horrors of Jaffa. Lacking horses, they were unable to conduct any significant reconnaissance, so they did not know for sure how far back the Saracens had withdrawn. Was it just beyond the next hill, or back to Ramla, Lydda, or Ibelin? Champagne, however, had meanwhile arrived with the news that the bulk of Salah ad-Din's cavalry was holding the road just south of Caesarea, and this gave them some comfort. Richard surmised out loud that the Sultan's best emirs and troops were with that army, while the less disciplined and less reliable elements had been left to hold Jaffa after the walls were breached. This meant that in the short term, until Salah ad-Din could regroup, they probably had little to fear.

On the other hand, they had to assume that Salah ad-Din would eventually recall his cavalry and rally his infantry in order to renew his assault on Jaffa. They therefore set to work making Jaffa defensible again. The first task was to collect and bury the Christian dead with prayers and respect, albeit wearing scarves wrapped around their mouths and noses to reduce the stench. They also dug a mass grave for the Saracen dead. These they buried with the pigs and other refuse in a large pit at the start of the dunes to the south. Then they started rebuilding the walls as best they could. They had no mortar or time to mix it, but they could put the stones back on top of one another.

The work was exhausting both emotionally and physically, and since most of the wine in the city had been wantonly drained into the gutters by the alcohol-abhorring Saracens, there was little solace except sleep. Benumbed by the images of the last four days, aching from the back-breaking work, and afraid to think what would come next, Aimery stretched out naked in the tent he shared with five other knights of King Richard's household and waited for the mosquitoes to disturb his sleep.

Instead, he fell into a slumber so deep he woke disoriented and utterly confused. He did not know where he was. He did not know the men suddenly shouting and rushing this way and that around him. He couldn't remember the day, the month, or the year. All he knew was that men were shouting on all sides and panic had gripped the camp.

Suddenly King Richard poked his head through the tent flap and roared, "Out! Now! As you are, but with shield and lance! They're almost upon us!"

Richard's knights did not argue and poured out of the tent as they were, although two had nothing on over—or under—their shirts. Aimery was less obedient. He first pulled on his braies and tied the cord tight, then he grabbed his shirt, gambeson, and hauberk and pulled them over his head. There was no time for hose, let alone chausses, however, so he belted his sword and grabbed his shield and helmet as the shouts and screams outside reached a fever pitch.

Following the sound of battle, he found that the knights and men-at-arms had formed an improvised wall around the camp by going down on one knee with their shields held upright before them. They had planted their lances in the earth, the tips jabbing outwards at 45 degrees.

"Position yourselves in pairs so you can fire between the shoulders of the men holding the shields!" King Richard was roaring at the archers. "I want one man firing and one man loading!"

As Aimery fell into place at the end of the still-forming shield wall, the first wave of Saracen horse came thundering toward the other end of the line with hooted challenges and cries of "Allahu Akbar!"

Someone handed him a lance, and he worked feverishly to bury the butt deep enough in the soil for it to be fixed firmly. On his right, horses were squealing and whinnying in panic and pain. Their eyes rolled back in their heads as they refused to impale themselves on the protruding lances, while the crossbows took a terrible toll. As the lead horses crumpled up, spilling their riders in the dust, the horses in the ranks behind spun about on their haunches and bolted for safety, oblivious and indifferent to the efforts of their riders to make them turn back.

Although that first charge broke within minutes, there were thousands of other horsemen milling out of range and preparing to charge. Aimery had no time to return for his hose. The next wave was already rushing forward to test the strength and resolve of his end of the line.

Aimery started saying the Pater Noster by rote. He gritted his teeth together and braced for the onslaught. On either side of him Pisan archers, likewise kneeling on one knee, held their crossbows to their shoulders. No one was giving orders. They fired independently when they thought the Saracens swarming toward them were within range, but as soon as one had fired, he moved behind the nearest knight or man-at-arms to reload, while his companion took aim and fired.

"Steady! Steady!" Aimery recognized King Richard's voice and realized he had come to stand behind their section of the wall, just as he had been at the eastern section when it was attacked. "Make each shot count!" he admonished the archers. "Wait till they're too close to miss."

Aimery took hold of his lance with his right hand to make sure it held firm and steady. Sweat was pouring down his face, although it was still very early morning and not yet hot. His throat was parched and his breathing short. He had never before knelt before a cavalry onslaught. His place had been mounted on a tall horse, lance couched under his arm, whether on the tourney fields of Flanders, the soggy green pastures of Aquitaine, or the hard-baked and dusty plains of Outremer. When he had, rarely, fought on foot, it had been upright with a sword in his hand. He had never before knelt bare-legged in the dirt, crouching behind his shield while hundreds of mounted men charged at him. He had never been so terrified in all his life.

But soon the horses were squealing and whinnying again. This time they were so near he could hear the crossbow bolts thudding into them, and their blood splattered down on him. Horses were falling over sideways, their legs flailing the air until the bolts and arrows embedded in their bellies made them go still. Behind them more horses reared and spun about, dumping their riders onto the heaps of cadavers. Any man who tried to rise was cut down by the arrows that came steadily from behind the shoulders of the Franks holding the shields.

Aimery had no sense of time, but eventually the pressure eased up on his part of the line while a new assault was trying to turn their flank, attacking at the extreme right. Aimery tried to relax his grip on his lance long enough to wipe the sweat from his brow, but his fingers were cramped and he had to pry them open. Nor did he have a surcoat to wipe the sweat on, and the metal links of his hauberk were blisteringly hot.

Aimery glanced over his shoulder, wondering if there was anyone not on the defensive perimeter. To his amazement, he saw that the squires had organized themselves and had drawn water from the springs around which they were camped. They were bringing this forward to the men holding the line. When they reached Aimery, he gulped down the still-cool water and then ordered his squire to bring him his hose and boots.

By midmorning the heaps of corpses before their perimeter were so high they could hardly see over them, and the flies were so thick Aimery was sure he was going to swallow one every time he opened his mouth. The Saracen attacks had slackened, but they had not withdrawn. The Saracen cavalry kept milling about just out of range, apparently trying to decide what to do next. At this juncture someone brought up a string of fifteen horses that had been rounded up in Jaffa.

Not one of these horses looked particularly fit, and none were stallions. They were mares and geldings, long in the tooth, with bog and bone spavins, bowed tendons, and any number of other faults. Aimery suspected half of them were packhorses, and the others merchantmen's docile palfreys. Not one was destrier material. They were terrified by the sight of the dead horses, but not spirited enough to resist the harsh handling of the men bringing them. King Richard walked over and chose the one that looked best. Then he chose fourteen other knights, including Aimery, to join him.

As they filed out from behind the shield wall, the men remaining behind gave them looks of wonder mixed with pity. Aimery simply reckoned there was no better way to die than in the defense of the Kingdom he had come to love, at the side of a king who was already legendary. It was a little like being in Roland's company at Roncevaux, he told himself. It was certainly better than defending his idiot brother Guy!

They had to skirt the corpses of the dead, but once the way was clear, King Richard dug his spurs into the sides of his hack and with sheer force made it take up a gallop. The others did the same, lowering lances as they closed with the Saracens.

Although the Saracens had seen them coming, they were so astonished by the ridiculous charge of fifteen against thousands that they weren't ready. The charge penetrated deep into the enemy, and King Richard so effectively slaughtered everything that got in his way that he rode straight through the massed Saracen cavalry and out the other side. His knights were not so lucky.

The Earl of Leicester's horse broke down on impact and dumped him to the ground. Aimery saw it happen, but he was too busy fighting for his own life to help. A moment later, however, he was amazed to see King Richard come roaring back, leading an Arab horse. He flung the reins at Leicester while he fought back the enemy around them so efficiently that the Earl had time to remount. Aimery had never seen anything like it. A pity he wouldn't live to tell about it, he thought, as he raised his shield to deflect another onslaught.

By now the Saracens had recovered from their astonishment, and they completely surrounded Aimery. All the men who had charged with the King were cut off from one another and hopelessly outnumbered. Aimery fought not for his life—that was lost the moment they charged—but for his honor. When the day was over, the men behind the shield wall and on the ramparts of Jaffa would, he promised himself, report back to Eschiva and Hugh that he had fought ferociously, taking dozens of enemy to the grave with him.

A bad horse, however, was a terrible handicap. The beast simply didn't answer his legs. It didn't swing its haunches away at the touch of a spur to enable Aimery to face incoming enemies, nor did it spring sideways to enable him to evade blows. It certainly wasn't fighting back as his best destrier did. Hamstrung by the unresponsiveness of the beast, he found himself taking blows that he would normally have evaded, and unable to fight back as he needed. Aimery still fought, but he could feel he was losing long before the moment when his horse dropped dead onto its knees, throwing Aimery head over heels to land flat on his back with a horrible thump and the chime of chain mail. His head cracked down on the hard-baked ground, and only his helmet saved him from immediate death.

Even so, the fall was so hard that it winded him and he temporarily blacked out. As he came to, he was surrounded by men pointing their swords at him and shouting. Aimery didn't entirely understand why they hadn't just killed him, but he raised his hands in mute surrender. He'd lost his shield and sword already— either in the fall or wrenched away from him while he was unconscious. They kicked and goaded him, forcing him back on to his feet, and he reeled with dizziness as he tried to stand. 'Christ,' he prayed, 'don't let them torture me.'

One of the Saracens, a particularly burly man with a bushy golden beard (clearly a captured Norseman who was now one of the Sultan's Mamlukes), tied a rope around Aimery's waist that bound his arms to his sides. Tying the other end of the rope to his saddle, he started to lead Aimery off the field. With obvious intent he asked his horse to trot, and after only a few strides Aimery was unable to keep up. He stumbled, fell on his face, and was dragged across the field. His shoulders were held just off the ground by the shortness of the rope, but his hips crashed against each stone and gully. The pain was excruciating and he screamed at each new blow. Why hadn't they just killed him? Why had he let them take him alive? The dust was in his eyes and grinding between his teeth even as he clamped both closed.

Abruptly his upper body flopped onto the ground, and horses' hooves were all around, throwing up more dust. Blood splattered down on him; a fair-skinned hand with blond hairs on the back plopped in front of his face. He tried to squirm around and blink away the tears to find out what was going on, and a knife sliced through the rope holding him. Aimery at once thrust his arms outward to free himself and looked up to see who had rescued him.

King Richard didn't give him a second to say thanks. He shoved him unceremoniously toward the horse he held, and Aimery jumped forward to haul himself up into the bloody Saracen saddle. The King tossed him his own ax, and then they turned together to face the Saracens closing in on them.

Moments later the other knights closed around them—with a frantic desperation that suggested they had feared King Richard lost. Forming up around their King, they were nothing but a tiny island of Franks in a sea of Saracens, but none of the enemy around them was making any attempt to close. King Richard took stock of the situation, looked at the battered knights around him, and pointed back toward their own lines. "Back to regroup."

They dutifully pointed their horses in the direction of the Frankish shield wall—and rode right through the enemy toward their own lines without once having to fight. As they rode out of the Saracen army, a cheer went up from the Frankish lines, loud enough to penetrate Aimery's arming hood and helmet. The Franks behind the shield wall jumped up and down in their enthusiasm, shaking their weapons in the air—at least those that were still there.

When they rode back through the shield wall, they found that roughly half the archers had given up hope when the King of England appeared to have been overwhelmed in his suicidal charge. They had flooded toward the beached ships.

As soon as King Richard realized what had happened, he cursed and flogged his miserable horse into a gallop to chase after them. When he caught up with the hindmost, he knocked the man down with the flat of his sword and kept on riding. At the edge of the water, the King reeled his horse around to face the astonished men who were clustered about or still streaming towards the ships.

The mere sight of the Lionheart alive was enough to persuade most of them to go back—though the King's threats to their heads, throats, and genitals added a touch of urgency to their redeployment. No sooner had they rounded up all the would-be deserters and chased them back to the shield wall than a redbearded Saracen, leading a horse and carrying a white flag, approached.

"Has Salah ad-Din agreed to surrender to me and give back Jerusalem and the True Cross?" Richard roared at the Saracen emissary.

The man looked amazed, shook his head, and indicated the stallion he was holding. "My lord al-Adil," he announced in French, "says it is undignified for such a great king to fight on a gelded nag. He sends you one of his own warhorses as a gift."

The words al-Adil and gift jogged King Richard's memory and he now recognized this was the same Mamluke who had brought him al-Adil's gift of camels during the negotiations the previous fall. Impressed and touched that al-Adil would send him a gift in the middle of battle, he jumped down from his nag to take a closer look at the horse offered. As he put his hand up to stroke the stallion's neck, the horse shied away from him, his eyes rolling back in his head in terror. King Richard clucked at him to steady him, and taking the lead, held it so he could stroke the stallion. The stallion reared up the moment King Richard tightened his hold on the lead, and he released it at once with a laugh. "I've forgotten you name, but you brought me my friend al-Adil's gifts once before."

Khalid al-Hamar bowed his head to King Richard, his hand on his chest. "I am most flattered you remember me, you magnificence," the Mamluke answered astonished.

"Khalid the Red, wasn't it?" King Richard had pulled the name out of his memory because he'd been astonished to see a red-bearded Mamluke, and when told that "al-Hamar" meant "the red" he had noted it. While Khalid looked astonished at his memory, King Richard continued, "Well, Khalid, thank your kind lord, and tell him I deeply appreciate his concern for my dignity, but I fear my appreciation of horseflesh does not allow me to ride a horse such as this."

The Mamluke looked puzzled.

Richard took a step closer and looked him in the eye. "That stallion has a sore mouth, and your lord is trying to kill me with my own vanity. It won't wash. I'd rather ride a mule than a horse in pain. You can leave him here or take him back."

Khalid had orders to deliver the horse, so he opted to leave it, and scuttled back for the Saracen lines.

Richard at last had time to take stock. The Saracens continued to mill about in a large if diminished mass, just out of range. They were, he supposed, waiting for the Franks to get tired and either abandon their defensive posture or thin the lines enough to make the next assault successful. He could not, therefore, let everyone stand down at once, but he ordered every fifth man in the line to fall out and take a short break. When they returned, the man on his right got a break, until all had been given a chance to dress, drink, and relieve themselves.

Meanwhile, realizing that many of the Saracen horses who had lost their riders had been drawn by sheer thirst toward the springs, the squires went to see what horses they could catch there. Confused and unsettled as they were, the horses were skittish and quick to run, but they were also very thirsty. The squires collected some sugar-cane stalks and with great care approached the horses, offering these as a lure. Again and again the horses squealed and spun away before any of the squires could get hold of them, but with patience and persistence they eventually succeeded in capturing eight of them. With these horses and the two captured earlier, they now had ten good horses and five bad ones between them.

Meanwhile, the knights who had charged with Richard had also had a chance to rest and drink. When he called for a new charge, they all stood, but he waved them down and chose from among the knights who had remained behind before. Aimery was not entirely disappointed. Every muscle in his body ached from the horrible dragging he had endured. He had bruises everywhere, and one of his eyes was swollen almost shut and several of his teeth were loose. He presumed these injuries, too, had happened while he was being dragged, since many stones had been flung back at him by his captor's horse.

Much as his body ached, however, he took up a position on the shield wall again and prepared to be a spectator. He no longer believed King Richard and his companions were riding to certain death, but he knew there was no certainty of survival, either.

This time when King Richard charged, however, the Saracens just fell back and parted their ranks for him. The whole troop rode through the Saracen army, and for a heart-stopping moment, Aimery (and the entire Frankish force) thought he had just ridden into a trap and was about to be annihilated. Aimery and half a hundred other men jumped to their feet in alarm, but then the whole troop rode back out of the Saracens the same way they'd ridden in. King Richard turned his horse around again and, evidently ordering his knights to remain where they were, he rode alone toward the Saracen line.

"Holy Virgin Mary!" Aimery gasped. It would take only a single arrow to cut him down now!

But the Saracen line remained immobile, apparently mesmerized.

King Richard was mounted on one of the captured Saracen horses. He looked magnificent as he rode along the length of the Saracen line. He cantered slowly with upraised lance from one end to the other. "Come on!" he shouted, loud enough to be heard even in his own ranks. "Come out and fight!"

While there were few Saracens who understood French, his intentions needed no translation. The Saracen line merely inched away from him whenever he approached. Just by the King's riding back and forth along it, it was being forced backwards. His own troops were as mesmerized by what was happening as the enemy was.

Finally there was a stirring among the enemy. Starting at the back, men started to move. Excited voices wafted through the air, and abruptly the back ranks started to turn and ride away, melting into the distance one after another, until the men in the very front also turned their horses around and picked up an easy canter to try to catch up with the rest.

Richard drew up and sat watching them go, his expression hidden from his own men because he was facing the enemy.

"Is it over?" an archer asked.

"I'm not sure," Aimery admitted.

King Richard was still sitting on his horse and staring to the north. Indeed, he'd shoved his helmet back onto his neck and was shading his eyes with his hand. Aimery followed his gaze. The sun was sinking down the western sky, and although they weren't looking straight into it, it was bright and low enough to make it necessary to squint.

"There's something on the road!" someone exclaimed in excitement.

"There are men and horses approaching from the north!"

"Saracens or Franks?"

"I can't tell yet."

"The Saracens withdrew. They must be Franks. It must be the army of Jerusalem."

At last Aimery could decipher four riders leading the column, but he couldn't make out what was on the banners. He squinted and held his breath as a light sea breeze lifted and then unfurled them with an invisible hand. Gold on white! The crosses of Jerusalem! And beside it: the red cross pattée on a field of gold for Ibelin.

Chapter 22

Jaffa, 1192

ON AUGUST 5 RICHARD THE LIONHEART had seemed invincible—indeed, immortal. Now, less than a fortnight later, he was debilitated by fever, and those closest to him feared for his life. The news of King Richard's fever spread like wildfire through the Frankish camp. He had always been popular with his troops, but after his almost single-handed rescue of Jaffa, he was more a deity than a king. When men heard he was so ill he was delirious and too weak to sit, much less stand, a passive panic spread. The common soldiers began to collect in the streets in front of the citadel where Richard had been carried by his knights, while Masses were read for him to packed churches across the half-ruined city.

The lords collected in the anteroom of his bedchamber, and the stifling heat of August in Jaffa was made more fetid by the stink of medicines, blood drained from the King's veins, clogged sewage in the street below, and the sweat of all of them.

Richard's closest friends were here and his nephew, the new King of Jerusalem. They sat in glum, desultory silence, because there was nothing to say. The fierce Lionheart, who had alone challenged the entire army of Salah ad-Din, was now lying in a bed of sweat-soaked sheets, no longer lucid, and tossing about as if possessed. The doctors knew no cure, so the priests hovered nearby, ready with extreme unction.

Ibelin did not belong to the inner circle, so he had withdrawn to a window niche. From here he could catch a whiff of fresh air off the Mediterranean—when the wind blew. He was joined here by an annoying fly that insisted on crawling along the back of his hand or landing on the back of his neck, despite his repeated and increasingly irritated efforts to chase it away.

His thoughts circled morbidly around what would happen if King Richard died. For the Lionheart's vassals and friends, it would be a catastrophe. Ibelin had heard enough to know that Richard's heir was his treacherous and devious brother John, a man universally seen as unfit to rule. For the French King, on the other hand, King Richard's death would be a godsend. Philip II would at once set to work stealing all the Plantagenet's continental possessions. And Jerusalem? Since the English King had already declared his intent to return home, it arguably made no difference if he departed the Holy Land bound for England or for the grave. Either way, the crusaders would go too. The Kingdom of Jerusalem would be left to its own devices to defend itself as best it could.

At least they were rid of Lusignan—and while Champagne had been disappointingly indecisive during the march south from Acre, when Ibelin had explained what they'd done, he had embraced the plan. In retrospect, Ibelin felt a little guilty for not proposing it to him at the time, and concluded that Champagne—unlike Lusignan—might prove amenable to advice and guidance. He certainly seemed enchanted with Isabella, and that gave Ibelin double leverage.

But the question remained whether the barons and men of Outremer had sufficient resources to hold on to the territories the crusaders had won for them. Tyre seemed secure, and Acre was turning into a bustling city, the harbor choked with ships eager to carry all the goods that could make the Kingdom rich again. Haifa, Caesarea, and Arsur were hesitantly coming back to life—but only insomuch as Syrian, Coptic, and Armenian merchants were willing to cross borders with the goods transshipped and exported through these ports to the Western world. The flow of goods, and so the income, would stop instantly if the Sultan ordered his troops to stop it. Furthermore, the countryside in between these cities was empty. No one wanted to risk settling anywhere but behind high walls, and that meant that the cities were completely dependent on imports of food. It also meant that Salah ad-Din's forces could surround each isolated city and reduce them one after another as soon as King Richard and the crusaders were gone.

The door to the sickroom opened, and all heads turned to see who emerged. The Bishop of Salisbury stood in the doorway and requested in a low but clear voice, "My lord of Champagne, my lord of Ibelin, the King is asking for you."

"He's lucid?" Champagne asked, jumping to his feet and plunging past the Bishop into the sickroom. Ibelin followed him at a more decorous pace, and the Bishop closed the door behind him.

The smells were even worse here than in the anteroom, and the sight of the usually so robust and powerful King lying listlessly and shining with sweat on crumpled sheets was shocking. But his eyes met Ibelin's, and he gestured very faintly with his hand for him to approach.

"My lords." His voice was little more than a raw whisper. "We must treat with Salah ad-Din."

Champagne glanced at Ibelin, and seeing his consent, nodded vigorously.

"I want—you—" his eyes were no longer blue but smoke gray, and they were leveled at Ibelin— "to be my envoy."

"As you wish, my lord," Ibelin answered, surprised by how honored he felt.

"Go to him. Say—we have both suffered enough. We have—exhausted— one another. Tell him—if he grants me—terms—I will go home. But, if not—I will stay—and fight him." Ibelin and Champagne exchanged a glance; the Lionheart couldn't have fought a kitten in his present state.

The King saw and understood their look, but he insisted, "Don't—bury— me—yet."

"Of course not, uncle!" Champagne assured him.

Ibelin confined himself to saying, "I will go. What terms do you want me to offer? The status quo?"

King Richard nodded. "And Sidon—Beirut—the coast—from Ascalon to Antioch. True Cross."

Ibelin nodded again. "We'll start with that, and settle for the status quo."

King Richard managed a ghost of a smile. "You understand me. Yes."

Ramla, August 1192

The arrival of Ibn Barzan in the service of the English King caused a minor sensation in the Sultan's immediate household. Although they had long since learned through spies that the English King and the most respected baron of Jerusalem were reconciled through the marriage of the King's nephew to the baron's stepdaughter, they had not expected Ibn Barzan to enjoy so much trust that he would be the English King's envoy.

Because Ramla had not been rebuilt, the Sultan and his entire army was camped outside the city, on the fertile plain whose produce had once filled the coffers of the Baron of Ramla and Mirabel. The Sultan had a massive tent, divided by silk brocade walls into multiple chambers. He was traveling with three of his concubines, who were guarded by eunuchs in a cloth harem. He had his own chamber for bathing and sleeping, another for praying and a chamber for conducting business, as well as a spacious and particularly ornate chamber for holding councils or audiences. He sent for his brother and eldest son, and they joined him in his office to discuss the unexpected visitor.

Al-Adil welcomed the development, saying it simplified matters. Since Ibn Barzan spoke for the barons of Jerusalem, if he also spoke for Malik Rik, there was no longer any risk of them disagreeing or misunderstanding what had been said. Salah ad-Din's eldest son al-Afdal, on the other hand, was still smoldering over the shame of Jaffa. He had been a witness to the stubborn and insolent refusal of the Sultan's army to continue charging the Frankish position on August 5, and he had seen Malik Rik's unanswered challenge to the whole Saracen line.

Al-Adil found his nephew's assertion that if he had not been "wounded" he would have taken up Malik Rik's challenge somewhat disingenuous. He had, in fact, suffered little more than a facial scratch. This, to be sure, had swollen up the side of his face badly and pulled his mouth temporarily out of shape. It might, if he was unlucky, even leave a permanent scar, but it was hardly life-threatening, and it would not have seriously impeded his ability to fight on horseback. That al-Afdal would have been killed if he had taken on Malik Rik was equally evident to both his father and uncle, so they said nothing and let al-Afdal keep his pride.

Now, however, the teenager's venomous demands that Ibn Barzan be torn limb from limb or cut to pieces were getting on al-Adil's nerves. He glanced to his brother to see if the Sultan was going to silence his foolish whelp or leave it to him to do it. He was relieved when his brother made a dismissive gesture and remarked dryly, "Civilized people do not kill envoys, puppy."

Al-Afdal flushed at the insult and opened his mouth to protest, but his father cut him off with an upturned hand. "Do not make me angry. Go tell Imad ad-Din to escort Ibn Barzan to my audience chamber and to stay with him there while we change." The Sultan and his brother were dressed very simply at the moment, for they had not been expecting guests.

Imad ad-Din had no reason to like Ibn Barzan. On the contrary, he was inwardly indignant at the way he had treated his friend Humphrey de Toron. As a good servant to his Sultan, however, he graciously received the Frankish envoy, ensured that he was comfortable, and ordered chilled water served to him from a silver decanter into a ruby-red glass. Since there was still no sign of the Sultan or his brother, however, Imad ad-Din had no choice but to reluctantly engage the unwelcome guest in small talk.

Sinking onto the abundant pile of cushions to one side of Ibn Barzan (to leave the cushions opposite vacant for the Sultan and his brother), he eyed the unwelcome visitor through a superficial smile. Ibn Barzan was a striking man. God had made him tall, but Imad ad-Din had to admire how straight he sat for a man his age. Equally notable was how slender he was without being fragile. The Sultan had a very noticeable potbelly these days, but not Ibn Barzan. His stomach was flat and firm, his chest and arms muscular. Only his face showed his age and the strain of five years of continuous warfare.

"I am sorry you did not bring my good friend Humphrey de Toron with you, my lord," Imad ad-Din opened.

"My former son-in-law is now on Cyprus with the Lusignan brothers," Ibelin answered readily.

"A very talented young man," Imad ad-Din noted.

"Undoubtedly," Ibelin agreed. "It was his misfortune to be his father's only son. As a younger son, he would have been free to pursue a Church career. I'm sure he would have made an outstanding scholar. As an abbot or bishop, he would have been greatly admired by all."

Imad ad-Din raised his eyebrows in a gesture of disagreement, but said nothing. Instead he asked, "And the English King's nephew: he is more suited to be King, although he has so little sense of honor?"

"In what way does the Count of Champagne lack honor?" Ibelin asked back in evident surprise.

"What honorable man would marry a woman carrying another man's child?" Imad ad-Din asked back, unable to disguise his revulsion for such a filthy relationship.

"Ah," Ibelin nodded, "I understand." Once reminded, Ibelin remembered that Sharia Law expressly prohibited marriage to a pregnant widow. "But this is not dishonorable among Franks," he told the Sultan's secretary. "On the contrary, the Count of Champagne is much admired, indeed revered as *exceptionally* honorable, because he has assumed responsibility for his wife's unborn child—as Joseph did for Jesus."

Imad ad-Din made a face and shook his head in irritation. He was relieved that the arrival of the Sultan, with his brother and son, made an answer to such nonsense unnecessary.

Ibelin got to his feet at the sight of the Sultan and bowed from the waist, while Imad ad-Din bowed his head all the way to the floor. The Sultan seated himself directly opposite Ibelin, flanked by his brother and son, and made sure Ibelin had received refreshments before inquiring about his journey and health. He used the assurances of good health from his guest to segue into inquiring after King Richard's health. "We hear he has been very ill." The Sultan wanted his guest to know how well informed he was. "Has he regained lucidity?"

"Well enough to give me his instructions," Ibelin answered steadily. He had not doubted for a minute that Salah ad-Din knew the state of King Richard's health—probably as well as any of them.

"I hear he craves fruit," the Sultan continued. "If you would allow me, I will send him the very best plums and pears from Damascus as a gift for Malik Rik from me. We just received a caravan with fresh fruit."

Ibelin bowed his head again in thanks. "That is very generous of you, Excellency, and would be most welcome."

"The air of Jaffa is not the best. I suspect he would feel better sooner if he moved to someplace higher."

"The air of Jaffa was left putrid with corpses, but it has improved much over the last week," Ibelin answered with a smile, taking mental note that the Sultan still had his eyes on Jaffa and would attack the moment Richard was gone.

The Sultan's mouth smiled back; his eyes did not. "What is it that Malik Rik has asked you to convey to me?"

"Nothing that you do not already know: that your army is exhausted, your emirs in rebellion, your troops insolent, and your treasury depleted."

As Ibn Barzan spoke, al-Afdal's face flushed, and he could not contain his indignation. Even before Ibelin had fully finished, he burst out, "Those are lies! All lies! We are a thousand times stronger than you! The emirs worship my father—"

"Oh, is that why they refused to obey his orders in front of Jaffa? Is that why Malik Rik could challenge your whole army, and not one man was willing to cross swords with him? I was led to believe your father was very angry about that." Ibelin's eyes cut to the Sultan, who was looking distinctly annoyed.

"Lies!" his son replied hotly. "Any one of us could kill Malik Rik with one hand tied behind his back—"

"Enough," his father silenced him sharply, and answered himself. "Malik Rik's own brother is in revolt against him. His former ally, Malik Phil, is in league with his enemies and preparing to invade his lands. If he survives his current illness—may Allah grant that he does—he must return across the sea, and with him will go all the others who came from the West."

"Indeed," Ibelin agreed. "And I will be glad to see them go." Their eyes locked. Ibelin continued. "In our Holy Book it is written: there is a time for war and a time for peace. A time to sow and a time to reap. It is time for the men of war to return home and for us to sow our fallow fields."

"Let Malik Rik depart with his invaders." The Sultan dismissed them with a wave of his hand, and then looked more intently than ever at Ibelin. "After they have left, if you acknowledge that you have been worshiping a prophet, not a God, and heed the word of Mohammed, may God's blessings be upon him, then I will give you all of Palestine as your *iqta*."

"There are many men who have fought loyally with you for decades, Excellency, who would rightly object to such a generous gift to a new convert." Ibelin glanced significantly at al-Adil.

"Let me and God deal with them, for His joy in saving your soul would far outweigh any perceived injustice visited upon others."

"I am too insignificant to presume to know what will bring joy to the heart of God, but I trust that He will inspire me to do that which pleases Him, and that is to bring peace to His homeland. Will you not listen to King Richard's terms?"

Salah ad-Din held his eyes, and he saw that Ibn Barzan was not in the least tempted by his offer. He nodded curtly.

"King Richard is willing to recognize your control of the highlands, including Jerusalem, in exchange for your recognition of Frankish suzerainty over the coast and coastal plain from Ascalon to Latakia. He proposes an exchange of prisoners, to include all captives taken from the Kingdom of Jerusalem after Hattin and still in slavery. Last but not least, he demands the return of the Cross captured at Hattin that we revere, but which is worthless to you."

Al-Afdal looked flabbergasted, al-Adil bemused, and Salah ad-Din stony. "I will consult with my emirs and other advisors," he told Ibn Barzan dryly. "Is there anything you would like while you are waiting? Food, or a bath, perhaps a woman? I have many very delectable slave girls, some of whom are blond and Christian."

Ibelin concluded that the Sultan was furious with him and refused to react to the provocation. "I'm not in the mood, but if you have any wine from Ibelin I would enjoy that."

The Sultan smiled coldly and flung at him ascerbically, "You'll have to grow it yourself!" Then, ordering Imad ad-Din to see what refreshments he could find, he departed in obvious ill temper.

Jaffa, August 1192

The Sultan flatly refused to return the True Cross, dismissed as preposterous the recognition of Frankish control over any place not securely in Frankish hands (i.e., Beirut and Sidon), and demanded that the Franks withdraw from Ascalon, Gaza, Darum, and Jaffa as well. The only territory he was willing to allow them to retain was the coast from Arsur to Tyre. It was this answer that Ibelin brought back to Jaffa.

Although Ibelin had been told that the English King was much better, he was still in bed. When he was told these terms, he turned his head to the wall, and did not speak for so long that Ibelin began to wonder if he had been dismissed. "Should I leave you, my lord?" he asked softly.

Richard shook his head, but he continued to stare at the wall. Ibelin began to fear that while the fever had broken, so had the Lionheart's vaunted spirit. He did not like this reaction at all.

Champagne stepped closer to the bed. "Salah ad-Din knows you are ill and thinks we are helpless. Maybe we should undertake a quick offensive to demonstrate we are not without claws?"

Richard nodded, but so wearily that Champagne didn't know if he really approved or not. He looked to his father-in-law.

"Maybe a different envoy would be more successful, my liege," Ibelin suggested softly.

King Richard's head rolled back, and he stared at him. "Why do you say that?" His voice was definitely stronger than it had been at their last meeting, and that was encouraging. His eyes were more focused, too.

Ibelin shrugged. "He offered me all of Palestine and I turned it down. That annoyed him."

"I daresay. It would have annoyed me, too," the King of England quipped with a flicker of humor. "Why did you turn it down?"

"The price was my soul."

"Conversion?"

"Yes."

King Richard nodded and tried to sit up, gesturing for his nephew to help him. Champagne jumped forward, grasped him under the arm, and helped him to sit up, as one of his squires hastened over to stack pillows up against the headboard for him. Sitting up, King Richard no longer looked like a man about to die, and there was a spark of more than life in his eyes as well. There was still fire in his soul. "Look, Ibelin—if he respects you *that* much, then you are the best man for the job. Now tell me this: what do you honestly think he might concede?"

"He will never sign a peace treaty, because he has vowed to drive us into the sea. To accept in writing the Christian right to a sovereign presence here—no matter how small—is anathema to him. The most you can hope for is truce."

"Fair enough. I intend to go home and teach Johnny a lesson he won't forget—and Philip, too. But I will come back and finish what I started." The Lionheart's voice was not yet strong enough to carry across a battlefield, but the flame of determination was clearly burning again.

Ibelin smiled. "In that case, my lord, we have common ground. How many years do you need to teach your brother a lesson?"

"Two; but then I'll need time to mobilize resources and build a fleet. Make it three."

"Good," Ibelin agreed.

"Next: the True Cross. What do you think, Ibelin? Can we get it back?" the King asked.

"No," Ibelin admitted.

King Richard was astonished. "Why ever not? It means nothing to them."

"That's exactly why we won't get it back. They've long since melted down the reliquary for its valuable metals and stones, and they've tossed away the wood inside."

Richard was so appalled that he sat bolt upright. "Ibelin! Are you serious? You think it's irretrievably lost?"

"Yes. To them it was just a piece of wood. A worthless piece of wood."

"Even when I was negotiating for its return at Acre? You think they didn't have it then?"

"Very probably not. That may be one reason the Sultan delayed and prevaricated. He might have been trying to find it—or something he could pass off as the sacred relic. He had something that he made Guy de Lusignan swear upon when he let him go—but between then and when you came, he had precious little use for a relic he did not revere."

Richard thought about this and shook his head in disbelief, but he was also a practical man. He moved on. "What about the Sultan's territorial demands?"

"Salah ad-Din cannot in any circumstances leave Ascalon in your hands. It controls the flow of men and treasure from Egypt, upon which he depends to maintain power in Damascus."

King Richard didn't answer at once, but the glitter in his eyes was enough to make Ibelin understand how much he resisted this concession. Ibelin could still picture the King of England stripped to the waist as he helped heave stones up from the beach to rebuild the defenses. When Richard spoke, however, he took Ibelin by surprise with his reasoning. "I need Ascalon to be able to attack Cairo. That's what I intend to do when I return—without the damn French or anyone else to get in my way!"

Ibelin nodded understanding, but he remained certain that Salah ad-Din would not give up Ascalon. Then he had an idea. "Well, if your main concern is using it as a base for a future campaign, would it be good enough if we agreed to *both* leave it vacant for the duration of the truce?"

Richard's eyebrows lifted for a second, and then he nodded. "Yes. As long as they have no garrison in it, I should be able to take it immediately—a first strike before he knows I'm coming, if I time it right." Ibelin had the impression that just thinking about coming back with fresh troops and no nagging allies was revitalizing the sick King.

"But Jaffa's mine and Henri's!" Richard hastened to declare. "Nothing will induce me to give it up!"

"Salah ad-Din knows that," Ibelin answered with a faint smile. "And so does everyone in his army. They have mentally already conceded everything from Acre to Jaffa." He paused as the English King nodded, and then risked broaching the next topic. "My lord, I took the liberty of suggesting a prisoner exchange."

"Of course," King Richard readily agreed. "Total. Both sides return their prisoners, with no additional ransom demands." Ibelin was relieved that he had read the English King's concern for his men correctly. Richard added, "We have a lot more of them than they have of us, anyway, so that shouldn't be a problem, should it?"

Ibelin stiffened. "My lord King," he started, and stopped.

"Yes?"

"That's not strictly true. I mean, we may have captured more Saracen fighting men since your arrival, but they still hold thousands of men taken at Hattin, and more than thirty thousand women and children."

The look the Lionheart gave Ibelin belied all slanders that he was a man most concerned with his own glory; he was stricken. "Christ forgive me, Ibelin! I had completely forgotten that," he murmured sincerely. Then, after a stunned moment, he asked, "What can we do for them? What would we have to give up?"

"Darum," Ibelin answered, noting, "Gaza is untenable without Ascalon anyway."

Richard understood about Gaza, and he turned to his nephew. "It's your kingdom, Henri. Can you defend it without Darum?"

Henri glanced at his father-in-law and announced, "Uncle, my wife, the Queen of Jerusalem, has begged me not to forget the women and children in captivity. She would willingly give up Darum for the prisoners."

Richard was looking hard at his nephew, and after a moment he pointed out, "That wasn't my question."

Ibelin came to his son-in-law's rescue. "The Kingdom is defensible without Darum, my lord King, as long as we have Ibelin to protect Jaffa's flank."

"Hmm." Richard considered Ibelin critically.

"That's why it was built—at a time when the Saracens controlled Ascalon."

"All right; if you two are in agreement on this, I won't stand in your way," King Richard declared.

Ramla, August 1192

Ibelin had the impression that his reception was much warmer this time. Khalid al-Hamar came out to greet him before he even dismounted and graciously escorted him to the Sultan's tent. Furthermore, it was the Sultan's brother, rather than Imad ad-Din, who saw that he was made comfortable and received refreshments while he waited in the luxurious silk chamber. Al-Adil also stayed to chat with him while they waited for the Sultan.

"We hear that Malik Rik is recovering these days," al-Adil opened, in a tone that made it sound like he was delighted by the news.

"Indeed; did your spy also try to take credit for his improving health?" While this remark was a joke, Ibelin wanted al-Adil to know that they were perfectly aware of his spy network.

Al-Adil laughed. "No, no, but he suggested the Sultan's fruits had been decisive."

"A loyal slave to the Sultan would be wise to suggest that," Ibelin suggested, and they both laughed.

"Tell me, how is the stallion I sent to my friend Malik Rik doing?"

"He seems to be recovering from the sores in his mouth. I have been riding him with only a halter, and he behaves so well I may never put a bit in his mouth again."

"Ah, interesting. You think he had something wrong with his mouth?" al-Adil pretended innocence.

"Yes, I'm quite sure," Ibelin assured him.

"I hear very good things about your stud," al-Adil continued jocularly. "Maybe if we conclude a truce, you will allow me to visit?"

"I would be honored, my lord," Ibelin said dutifully. The thought that Sir Bartholomew's grandson Joscelyn was probably the source of al-Adil's information about his stud, however, made him sad.

The Sultan's arrival ended their small talk. Ibelin was relieved to see he had left his son out of this meeting. After the usual pleasantries, they got down to business. Salah ad-Din was clearly pleased with the notion of a three-year truce, adding eight months to the duration for reasons Ibelin did not need to know. The Sultan didn't even blink at the refusal to surrender Jaffa (as Ibelin had predicted), and he frowned at the notion of both sides abandoning Ascalon, but after a moment he agreed, on the condition that the Franks first dismantled the walls.

"They cost the King of England a small fortune," Ibelin protested. "You cannot expect him to just tear them down."

"Either he tears them down or there is no truce," Salah ad-Din shot back firmly, adding with a smile, "but I am prepared to compensate him for his investment. Would ten thousand gold bezants be enough?"

Ibelin's first instinct was to bargain, but then he decided against it. The most important provision of the treaty was yet to come, so he agreed, and Salah ad-Din nodded satisfaction.

"That leaves the prisoner exchange," Ibelin opened. "We are prepared to return all the prisoners we hold—"

"That you have not mercilessly executed," the Sultan reminded him of Acre.

"Treaties must be upheld on both sides," Ibelin replied calmly. "It was in your hands to save them."

The Sultan dismissed this with a wave of his hand and urged, "Go on. You will return all the prisoners you hold in exchange for a Frank apiece?"

"No, for all Christians taken captive at and since Hattin," Ibelin told him firmly, hoping his inner tension did not show.

"Impossible," Salah ad-Din answered dismissively.

"Why?"

"It's been five years. I have no idea where most of them are. They are the property of thousands of my subjects. I cannot just expropriate them."

"You were prepared to return twenty-five hundred for the garrison of Acre."

"Yes, and it was in large part because I had so much trouble finding even that many that I was late meeting the terms of the treaty. There is no way I can find over forty thousand men, women, and children."

It would have been easier to argue with him if Ibelin had not believed him, but he did. He could imagine just how difficult it would be to find captives sold in markets as far away as Mosul and Cairo. But he could not just abandon them, either. The image of the slave column being driven out of Jerusalem still haunted him. "What is Darum worth to you, your Excellency?"

"Darum?" The Sultan looked interested. "You would abandon Darum as well as Gaza and Ascalon?"

"For as many captives as you can find, but on no account less than twenty thousand."

"Twenty thousand Frankish slaves who may be anywhere?" The Sultan still sounded skeptical.

"If you offer to pay for them, people will come forward," Ibelin insisted.

"If I offer to pay enough, you are right, but twenty thousand slaves will cost me at least two hundred thousand dinars, probably more."

"Yes. What would it cost to take Darum from a Templar garrison?"

"Templars?"

"Of course. If they evacuate Gaza, they will be compensated with Darum."

The Sultan glanced at his brother. Al-Adil asked pointedly, "Will you take the women back as well? Would they count towards the twenty thousand?"

"Yes, of course," Ibelin assured him.

Al-Adil shrugged and looked at his brother as he said, "In that case, I don't see why not. We can replace whores easily enough."

Ibelin clamped his teeth to stop from reacting to the calculated insult. He forced himself to wait for the Sultan's reply.

Salah ad-Din shook his head, narrowed his eyes slightly, and looked Ibelin straight in the eye. "No. For twenty thousand captives, Darum is not enough. I will need Ramla and Ibelin as well."

Balian stopped breathing. He just sat there, knowing it was an impossible choice. A choice no man should be forced to make. Ibelin. His birthplace and happy childhood. His heritage and identity. The pomegranate orchards. The vineyards. . . . Or twenty thousand Christian slaves. Sir Bartholomew's daughters, if they were still alive and could be found. The men and women Heraclius had abandoned for the sake of his gold plate. . . .

Ibelin let out his breath slowly. He could prevaricate, pretend he needed to consult with King Richard and the Count of Champagne, but in his heart he knew the decision was his. Champagne and King Richard would accept whatever decision he made about Ibelin and Ramla. But would Zoë and the children? They would have no choice but to accept his decision, but would they hate him for it? Would they ruin the rest of his life with recriminations and reproaches? Zoë might understand. She had spoken of a life in Christ's footsteps as a "monument" to His glory. But what about the children, who were utterly dependent upon him for their future? The thought of John looking at him with resentment was torture, and he squirmed physically.

Salah ad-Din and al-Adil could see that he was struggling with himself, and they waited with bated breath for his answer.

Balian found it difficult to speak, but he could not sit there in silence forever. He forced himself to say it: "You may have Ibelin, Excellency—and Ramla. But," Ibelin's voice gathered strength as he continued, "you must document the return of at least twenty thousand Christian slaves," his voice had turned forceful, almost threatening, "or the treaty will be invalid. God is my witness," and he raised his right hand in a gesture of swearing an oath, "if you break your word in this regard, King Richard will return with a new Western army. He has promised me that, and his word is good."

Salah ad-Din's nostrils flared slightly, and his lips tightened. He did not doubt King Richard's determination to return once he had settled his problems at home—whether the treaty was broken or not. Their war was not yet over. The truce served both sides merely as a means to gain the strength to attack again. They both knew that. It was Ibn Barzan whom the Sultan did not understand. He shook his head. "I do not know if I should laugh or weep for you, Ibn Barzan. As a Believer you could be prince of all Palestine, but for your childish religion with its worship of idols and females, you make yourself a pauper."

Balian smiled sadly, the worst over now. He had spurned temptation and committed himself. "Christ was born and died a pauper," he reminded the wealthy master of Syria and Egypt. "Should I disdain to follow in His footsteps?"

The Sultan could only shake his head in bafflement.

Jaffa, September 2, 1192

The entire Saracen delegation, headed by al-Adil and al-Afdal, was ushered into King Richard's presence. For the occasion he had left his bed and was dressed in a brilliant marigold shirt and yellow hose, over which he wore a red silk surcoat with golden lions embroidered upon it. He wore knee-high, red suede boots, golden spurs, and the crown of England. He was propped up in an armed chair on the dais, surrounded by the highest clergy of the land. In the hall, the barons of Jerusalem and the Grand Masters of the Hospitallers and Templars stood with King Richard's vassals and knights. They were all in armor and the best surcoats they could find after so many months campaigning.

The Saracen delegation looked considerably more magnificent. Peacock feathers and glittering jewels adorned their turbans. The gold and silver on the hilts of their swords and daggers glinted in the sunlight. Their bodies were encased in bright-colored silk brocade woven into elaborate patterns, their boots were tasseled, and gold embroidery traced quotes from the Koran on their sleeves.

In addition to the Sultan's brother and eldest son, all the emirs granted land along the new border were present to swear their agreement with the truce, and Ibelin noted that the ambitious red-haired Khalid al-Hamar was among them;

apparently he had been awarded an *iqta* at last. Altogether, it made a gaggle of almost twenty.

At the sight of al-Adil, King Richard pushed himself to his feet, and the English King and the Kurdish general embraced in a gesture of friendship. Then al-Adil stepped back, removed a copy of the treaty from his tunic, and handed it to King Richard with a bow. King Richard handed it on to the Patriarch with the words, "I have not the strength to read it, but I have agreed to the terms. Here is my hand on it." He held out his hand to al-Adil, who took it with a smile that seemed sincere. "As for the oath," Richard continued, "kings do not swear, but my nephew, the Masters, and the barons will swear to maintain the peace for the designated time."

Al-Adil nodded, because all this had been agreed in advance—just as it had been agreed that when a return Frankish delegation went to Ramla on the following day to swear the oath in front of the Sultan, Salah ad-Din would not personally swear. Instead, the men representing them would do that twice: once here and once in Ramla.

Richard sank back onto his chair, and the Patriarch and the imam accompanying the Saracen delegation alternated reading the terms of the treaty in Latin and Arabic. At the end, the assembled nobles raised their hands and swore to uphold the terms for three years and eight months.

The formalities over, the Franks and Saracens sat down together for a good-natured feast accompanied by jokes, laughter, and apparent goodwill. The mutual respect most of these men had for one another as fighting men was real enough, and the relief that—for the moment—they need not fear death on the morrow was genuine. The Third Crusade was over, and they were glad of it.

For most of the men in the room, their spirits were also buoyed up by the knowledge they would soon be going home. But Ibelin could not share that joy; he had no home to return to.

Chapter 23

Acre, October 1192

KING RICHARD SAILED FOR HOME ON October 9. His wife and sister had already departed in a separate ship, but the King remained to pay his debts and collect as many of his men returning from captivity as possible. The weather was turning unpredictable, however, with the frequent rain showers and sudden squalls that made the Mediterranean treacherous at this time of year. Henri worried that his uncle had left his departure too late, but King Richard was confident that he'd make a quick crossing and be back in Normandy by Christmas, ready to take on his brother and Philip of France with the start of the New Year.

While the crusaders departed by sea, the returning captives began to straggle in through the landward gates. They came in uneven, sporadic groups, herded together by the officials responsible for reporting the numbers of repurchased slaves to the Sultan. Once the Sultan had paid the owners their fixed fee, the former slaves were kept together in local prisons all across the Sultan's territories until the local authorities deemed there were enough to justify an escort to Frankish territory.

Beatrice and Constance had found one another before they left Aleppo, but Beatrice was saddened that Father Francis had died months earlier and would not be granted the grace of a Christian burial. As they had a year earlier, Bart and Amalric also joined them, and this time Constance's younger daughter Anne was tossed in with the other women. She was now thirteen, overly thin, and so timid that she hardly dared look anyone in the eye, even her mother. Her French was fragmenting, too, all but lost under a layer of Arabic, but none of that mattered to Constance now that they were together again.

When, however, they were told they were being transported to Acre, both women resisted vehemently—Beatrice because her youngest son, Joscelyn, was still missing, and Constance because her older daughter Melusinde had not been brought to the collection center, either. No one listened to the protests of a couple of female slaves (or former slaves), however, and both women were unceremoniously tied to the others in the convoy. They had the option of walking or being dragged.

Constance reacted by screaming abuse at the soldiers in charge. Her fit of anguished fury frightened her sister much more than the indifferent Saracen guards. Beatrice put her arm around her sister's shoulder and tried to calm her, while Anne clung to her waist in evident terror. "Connie, calm down. There's nothing we can do about it now. Melusinde may have ended up in a different city and be on her way to Acre just as we are, or she might be there already. If not, once we're safe we can make inquiries." Then, leaning closer to speak directly into her sister's ear, she pleaded, "Please hush; you're upsetting Anne."

The appeal to her maternal duties seemed to penetrate Constance's brain, and she stopped screaming. Putting her arms around her little girl, who was now almost as tall as she was, she laid her cheek on the girl's head, and together they shuffled forward with the rest of the freed—but still bound—slaves.

Since the women and even many of the youths, like Bart, were not used to walking distances, the slave column made very slow progress. They managed little more than ten miles a day, and they often slept in the open, or in barns with livestock. The food was sparse and of low quality, since those responsible had more interest in pocketing a portion of the allotted upkeep funds than in the welfare of their charges. Only the fact that the Sultan wanted twenty thousand humans delivered across the border *alive* induced the men in charge of them to feed them at all.

The Sultan's orders did not provide any other form of protection, however, and the guards felt entitled to the sexual services of these long-since dishonored women and former slaves. They routinely picked out girls to sleep with, some keeping a girl with them as their personal sex partner for the whole journey, others changing partners at whim. Occasionally they fought over one girl or another. Beatrice and Constance were considered far too old and ugly to be of interest anymore, but one of the younger guards took a fancy to Anne. When he beckoned to her, she turned her face into her mother's chest and started trembling so violently that even the guard was shocked.

While the guard stood looking perplexed, Bart, in obvious terror that something terrible would happen to the rest of the family if she did not obey, hissed to Anne that she "shouldn't make a scene" and tried to push her over to the guard. Amalric, in contrast, walked over to the guard belligerently. He was taller than the guard and much more muscular. He didn't stop until he was no more than a foot away, and he looked down on the guard from his superior height. "If you touch my cousin, I'll kill you," Amalric snarled.

"You wouldn't dare!" the guard retorted.

Amalric answered by punching him so hard in the kidney that he crumpled up in pain. Then, before he could cry for assistance, Amalric kicked him in the balls as well. He collapsed on his knees, his face screwed up with pain. Amalric spat on him. Then he turned and herded his family through the astonished crowd of ex-slaves to the far side of the barn.

Beatrice had been terrified that the other guards would take some sort of revenge upon them, but either they had not seen what happened or they didn't care. The young man himself was so ashamed of being bested by a slave that he kept as far away from them as possible after that.

After almost a month, the slave convoy finally reached the border with Frankish territory. They knew they had reached the border because suddenly the land was empty and untended. The fields lay fallow and the pastures were thick with scrub growth. Worse: the abandoned villages were slowly falling to ruin, the doors and shutters unhinged, the kitchen gardens gone to weeds, the livestock pens all broken down.

The sight of this neglect sent shivers down Beatrice's spine, and for the first time since they had learned they were to be set free, she began to wonder about what lay ahead. She began to face not the abstract ideas of "freedom" and "home," but the reality of returning to a rump state impoverished by five years of invasion, destruction, and war. No one had told them the terms of the treaty that had set them free, but no matter how good the overall terms might be, Beatrice recognized that her personal fate, and that of her children, depended on the fate of her father—and that of the Lord of Ibelin. What if both were dead?

She'd caught snatches of conversation between the guards that seemed to suggest " Ibn Barzan" had played a key role in negotiating the release of the captives. Was that Ibelin? If so, he was apparently still a powerful and respected lord. Indeed, the Saracen officials seemed to be a little in awe of him, mentioning him in the same breath as the Sultan, but Beatrice couldn't be 100 per cent sure that " Ibn Barzan" was Balian d'Ibelin.

And even if, or particularly if, Ibelin was such a great and important lord, would he have time to help the former-slave children of a tenant? Beatrice knew her father had been a trusted vassal, a man Ibelin respected, liked, and valued, but her father had been nearing seventy year *before* Hattin. So many men had died in that horrible two-day battle, as many from heat stroke as from the blows of the enemy. Was it reasonable to imagine an old man would have survived? It was far more likely that he had been dead these past five years. And if he were indeed dead, who would remind Ibelin that he'd had two daughters and five grandchildren?

Beatrice concluded it was far more probable that Constance's husband Gautier had survived. He'd been in his prime, and a competent knight. Yet even if it were more probable he had survived, there was no *certainty* of it. Nor did survival mean freedom. The overwhelming majority of the men who survived Hattin had been taken captive. If Gautier had been one of them, who would have paid his ransom? Beatrice did not know whether the truce terms included the release of captive fighting men, since all the slaves in their little convoy were women and youths.

Yet most disturbing of all was the thought that even if Gautier were alive and free, he might not be *willing* to take Constance back. It was all very well for the Church to call marriage indissoluble, but was it reasonable to expect a man to receive back into his house, bed, and affections a woman who had known dozens of other men? The fact that Constance had wanted none of them and they had raped her was immaterial. Beatrice remembered her brother-in-law as a man proud to a fault. A wife who had been deeply humiliated and abused would not suit him.

Constance shared Beatrice's assessment. The closer they got to release, the more frequently Constance whispered in growing distress, "Gautier will never take me back. Never. He'll find some way to discard me."

At least Beatrice didn't have to worry about that; her husband had been buried three years before Hattin. But she did worry about how she, as a widow, was to raise her two sons—or three if they ever found Joscelyn. Even if their land were returned to them, who was to say the tenant farmers would also return—if they lived at all? If they didn't, who would work the land?

It wasn't that she personally shied from work after five years as a slave. On the contrary, she knew she was strong enough to do anything. But one woman would not be enough, and while Amalric was strong and likewise determined to survive, Bart was broken. As the incident with Anne had shown, he was not prepared to stand up for himself or his family. While things might get better once they left Saracen territory and control, Beatrice questioned whether he would ever recover his health, much less make up for the lost years of training.

Knights were not born; they were made—by intensive training at arms and on horseback, training Bart had not received. Nor could she imagine where she would find the money to buy the horses, arms, and armor he would need to begin learning his profession. Beatrice had no illusions: even if they could return to the manor that had been theirs before Hattin, it would look no better (and possibly worse) than the ghost towns they passed through. Amalric and she might be able to patch together a hovel to live in, but it would be years before they could eke out enough of a living to pay for armor or destriers for Bart. And what if they didn't get their manor back?

As for Anne, from what little they had coaxed out of her, she had first had her genitals sheered in half with a crude knife and then been sold as a concubine to a man of middle age and—at least to Anne—repulsive appearance. Because of the genital mutilation, all intercourse was extremely painful, effectively torture. Furthermore, she found it and the other things he had done to her repulsive because of her tender age and her aversion to him. In short, she had been damaged both physically and mentally to the point that she could never be sent to marriage bed. While the peace of a convent would undoubtedly be the best for her, where was Constance to find a dowry? And would a convent take a former sex slave?

They had reached a small river, the banks overgrown with scrub brush and the water running muddy brown. Here the escort stopped, although it was hours before sunset. Someone asked what was going on and was brushed off with the word, "Wait."

Beatrice descended the banks of the river to wash and cool her feet in the flowing waters. The sun was still high and hot, the banks of the river alive with insects, disturbed by the human invasion. Beatrice hitched up her skirts and stepped carefully into the slowly flowing water, unable to see the bottom because the muddy water was opaque. Her foot slipped on the slick stones underneath and she almost fell, but recovered before she landed completely in the water. As she straightened, her eye caught sight of something fluttering in the distance on the far side of the river. It was still far away, and yet something about it ignited inner excitement. It was horsemen, and after five years in Syria, Beatrice's heart raced as she recognized the gleam of sunlight on chain mail and the naked helmets of Frankish knights. A second later she realized that the white banner streaming out behind them bore the splayed red cross of the the Knights Templar. "Templars!" Beatrice cried out and started scrambling up the far bank.

Five minutes later, a patrol of Templar sergeants commanded by a single knight reached the river. The mere sight of the Templars produced a rush among the slaves. None of them could wait to reach the protection of these Christian soldiers, so they scrambled in undignified eagerness across the river, dragging their little bundles of belongings behind them, indifferent to getting wet or muddy.

The Templars tried to tell them to slow down, but no one heeded them. They wanted the Templars between themselves and the Saracens. At last the

Templar knight, a very young man who spoke French with a heavy German accent, ordered the freed captives to stand still so he could check the inventory presented by the Saracen escort commander. Only after the number of slaves had been verified did he countersign one copy of the inventory and tuck the second inside his gambeson.

Finally the Saracen escort remounted and swung their horses around to return eastward. The Templars, meanwhile, assured the former slaves that they had only two more miles to go to a shelter where they would spend the night.

The Templars were emotionless, efficient, and all business as they led the freed slaves. They shook their heads in answer to all questions, indicating they would not answer, and they avoided eye contact. Indeed, they kept their eyes on the road ahead. It was as if they disliked or disdained their charges, Beatrice thought. Did they think they had betrayed Christ? Or was it because they considered them all whores?

After what seemed like a long hour, a sugar mill and refinery came into view. Without irrigation, the cane fields that once surrounded it had died. Cactus, thorns, and gorse had taken root instead. But the mill itself was clearly visible at one end with broken bronze vats heaped around it, and smoke wafted from one of the six chimneys.

"That's pork!" someone cried out. "They're roasting pork!"

With an exuberant cheer some of the younger ex-slaves, including Amalric, started running, but Beatrice didn't have the energy. She also remained wary of what reception they would receive. Would the men here be as cool and disdainful as the Templars? Just then, from the far end of the refinery, a half-dozen figures emerged. They wore the habit of Hospitaller sisters—and to Beatrice's unutterable relief, they were all smiling.

As they poured into the sugar mill, the released captives found themselves in an improvised kitchen, complete with stew brewing over the fire and fresh bread heaped in front of a converted oven. There was even a long sideboard laden with hard cheese, sausage, and apples, while fresh water was available from the well beside the mill. The former slaves, particularly the youths, fell upon the food like a ravenous horde of wolves, while others gathered around the well for a drink of the clean, cool water after the long march.

Beatrice and most of the other women, however, were more attracted to the piles of clothing neatly stacked up on the opposite sideboard. There were heaps of braies for both men and women, shifts, kirtles, and scarves for women, hose and shirts for men, sandals for everyone. One of the Hospitaller sisters came over, still smiling, to explain that these clothes were donations from the citizens of Acre and Tyre. Everyone could pick out one complete outfit for themselves.

Beatrice and Constance could not contain contain themselves. While Constance dived for the sandals and started trying on pair after pair until she found some that felt comfortable, Beatrice grabbed a pair of braies, took the first clean shift and kirtle that came to hand, and most precious of all, a linen scarf. For the first time in five years, she would be able to cover her hideously shaved head like a respectable woman.

As she wound the linen around her head, one of the sisters came to help her, bringing a pin. Only then did Beatrice realize her hands were trembling. "You don't know how good it is to be able to cover my head," she told the sister, embarrassed by her show of emotion.

The Hospitaller sister laid her hand on Beatrice's shoulder reassuringly, "You are not the first returnee to tell us that. Take a second if you want. We can find more."

Beatrice did take a second, not for herself but for Anne. Taking the scarf to her bewildered-looking niece, she offered to show her how to wrap it. Anne looked up at her with wide eyes. "But—but I'm not—not clean—"

"It doesn't matter anymore. Here, I'll show you." When she finished with the scarf, she led Anne back to the pile of clothes and helped her pick out a shift, a pretty kirtle, and a pair of sandals. The kirtle was a bright yellow color, and Anne kept stroking it as if she could not believe it was hers. Amalric, on the other hand, couldn't find any hose big enough for him, and the pair he finally settled on ended two inches above his ankles. He loudly declaimed that he didn't give a damn: the main thing was that they were breeches and not a kaftan. Bart seemed pleased to be wearing hose again, too, but he was increasingly silent.

Meanwhile the sun had set, and the Hospitaller sisters directed the former slaves to a large warehouse that stood at right angles to the factory itself. Here straw pallets lined the wall, each with a blanket. While some of the returnees took advantage of the pallets at once, most were still too excited to sleep just yet. Instead they gathered around the millstone, where the Hospitallers were offering a small ration of wine.

When the sister handed the pottery mug to Anne, she sniffed it and made a face, shaking her head vehemently. Bart, in contrast, gulped down the wine so fast that it went down the wrong way, and he ended up coughing up most of it.

Seeing what had happened, the sister returned to give him a second helping. "Here you go, young man, but not so fast this time," she advised indulgently.

Bart, red-faced, muttered, "Thank you, ma'am."

The sister's eyes took in Beatrice and Amalric, who were obviously with Bart. "Are you a family?" she asked.

"Yes, or what's left of it," Beatrice answered for them. "My name is Beatrice d'Auber, and my father—"

"Is Sir Bartholomew!" the sister answered, her face breaking into a broad smile. "Holy Virgin Mary! Your father has nearly killed himself with worry, prayer, and battlefield heroics! I can't begin to tell you all he has been through! But, wait! You wouldn't be Constance, would you?" she addressed Constance, who nodded vigorously.

"And this is your daughter?" Sister Adela's eyes took in Anne on Constance's arm.

"We're missing my baby Joscelyn and Constance's older girl, Melusinde," Beatrice told her.

"Oh, of course! You don't know. Joscelyn is already in Tyre!"

"What?" Beatrice asked in disbelief.

"It's a long story." Sister Adela diverted further questions until she could think of a way to gently break the news of Joscelyn's conversion and attitude.

"And Melusinde?" Constance asked hopefully.

"Nothing yet," Sister Adela answered deftly, "but the process of returning the slaves is far from over. There's no reason to assume the worst. What we must do instead is to get word to your father! He will be overjoyed to see you, and you need not worry about your future. *Two* queens are anxious to welcome you home." Then, because she could no longer contain her own joy, Adela embraced the remnants of Sir Bartholomew's family one after another, with as much feeling as if they were her own.

Only when she started crying from relief did Beatrice realize just how much she had feared her father would be dead, and how desperately she wanted to see him again.

Acre, Christmas Eve 1192

The Ibelins now lived in a suite of rooms in the royal palace in Acre. The choice was not entirely voluntary, since the owners of the house in Tyre had returned after five years in Pisa and demanded restitution. Balian had opted to leave the horses at his increasingly substantial stud outside Tyre, while accepting Queen Isabella's offer of a suite at the royal palace. Her court was there, and the High Court also met frequently in Acre, since they needed to re-establish coherent government after the chaos of the preceding five years. Yet while

Isabella and Henri de Champagne had been generous, Maria Zoë was acutely aware that her husband was unhappy.

The loss of Ibelin and Ramla still weighed heavily on him. He said he did not regret the choice he had made, but he worried what legacy he would leave his sons. As a result, he and Reginald de Sidon, now her son-in-law, were poring over maps again, making plans for a new assault on Sidon and Beirut. Champagne had promised that if they could re-establish Christian control from Tyre to Tripoli, Balian would be given the lordship of Beirut. Of course, they would have to wait until the end of the truce before making an attempt, and three years was a long time for impatient men.

Maria Zoë watched the two men from the window niche while pretending to read the beautifully illustrated "Song of Alexander" that King Richard had found among Isaac Comnenus' treasure on Cyprus and had given her as a parting gift. Reginald appeared rejuvenated by his marriage to Helvis. More surprising, Maria Zoë thought, Helvis seemed remarkably content for a girl married to a man old enough to be her grandfather. Helvis was proud to be a "married woman," and liked being seen at Reginald's side. It gave her a sense of status and security—not to mention that he doted on her and gave her almost anything she asked for.

Balian, in contrast, looked older than his forty-three years, and despite his restless interest in the assault on Sidon and Beirut, Maria Zoë sensed that his heart was not in it. Much as he longed for a lordship to call his own, he was profoundly tired of fighting. More than once, and often at unexpected moments, he muttered things like: "Too many people have died" or "Blood cannot produce a harvest."

A knock on the door was followed by the appearance of Helvis. She was dressed primly with a starched white wimple encasing her fresh young face, and she announced boldly, "Reggie, I need your help."

Sidon at once straightened and with a smile to Balian announced, "My lady calls," before following Helvis out of the room, leaving Balian brooding over the map.

Maria Zoë put aside her book and stood. John had been begging to start training as a squire, and Maria Zoë had asked Champagne about a position with him. She hadn't yet broached the subject with Balian, however, because he seemed reluctant to be separated from John. Thinking this might be a good moment, she stepped down from the window niche, but got no farther. Another knock on the door made Maria Zoë freeze and Balian spin around, startled. "Yes?"

The man who entered wore a bright turban of silver silk, fastened together with a huge sapphire, but his beard was bright red. Balian recognized him at once. It would be too much to say he smiled, but his expression was welcoming as he exclaimed, "Khalid al-Hamar, I did not expect to see you again so soon."

The newcomer bowed deeply to Ibelin and then glanced at Maria Zoë, still standing on the step down from the window seat. He looked politely in the opposite direction, expecting her to modestly dart out of the room.

Maria Zoë glanced at Balian for guidance, and he shook his head, introducing her instead in Arabic with a provocative flourish, "My lady, Dowager Queen of Jerusalem, Lady of Nablus, Ramla, Mirabel, and Ibelin, Maria Comnena."

Khalid looked at him uncomprehending, before remarking, "You Franks have no honor. A wife is a treasure that should be kept as such—under lock and key—not exposed to the rude gawking of strangers."

"Why? Are you afraid your wives will run away? I have no such fear, Khalid. My lady has cleaved onto me even in my hour of greatest misfortune. As for your gawking, it does no harm."

Khalid shook his head in bemusement, before asking with a provocative smirk, "Are you not ashamed to let another man rape your wife with his eyes?"

"Are you not man enough to look at a woman without lust?" Ibelin countered with raised eyebrows before adding, "If not, then look, but God help you if you insult her in word or deed—for then I will kill you, ambassador or not."

Their eyes locked until Khalid nodded and with a faint smile admitted, "I believe you. But what is the point of keeping women where they do not belong? We have important matters to discuss. This is no time to be distracted by the callings of the flesh!"

"Nor will I be by the presence of my lady, because, Khalid, she is so much more than a creature of the flesh. A woman is like a book of poetry. No matter how exquisite the cover, its value lies in the thoughts and sentiments contained inside. A man who confines himself to looking at the cover, or just feeling the pages, denies himself the greatest riches of all: those that satisfy his mind, heart, and soul. It is because I honor those qualities in my wife, that I will not banish her as if she were nothing but an irrational animal placed on earth by God to satisfy my lust."

"Your false religion misleads you in this as in much less. Women are without the rationality that sets man above beasts, and—unless kept under lock and key to be enjoyed only as appropriate—they distract us from our duty to Allah."

"Indeed, one of us is mistaken, Khalid, but for the present let us agree to disagree on this as we also disagree on the divinity of Christ."

Khalid nodded and, studiously looking away from Maria Zoë, announced: "I bring a message from my master, may God's blessings be upon him, the Sultan Salah ad-Din."

"Then you are doubly welcome," Balian answered with a bow. "Please, make yourself comfortable, and I will send for refreshments."

The entire exchange had been in Arabic, leaving Maria Zoë uncertain what was being said. At this point, however, Balian turned to her and explained, "Emir Khalid al-Hamar has brought a message from Salah ad-Din. I expect it is news of Sir Bartholomew's missing granddaughter."

When the trickle of slaves had tapered off and Constance's daughter Melusinde had still not returned, Ibelin had sent a personal message to Salah ad-Din inquiring after her. He had provided her name, description, and information about the date and place of her capture, as well as when and where she had been separated from her mother. That had been more than a month ago.

"Should I leave you alone?"

"Of course not! I just gave our friend Khalid a lecture on the nature of woman. We agreed to disagree. Besides," Balian added, "when I am the Sultan's guest, I respect his customs; I expect the same courtesy from him and his servants in return. I would be grateful, however, if you could send to the kitchens for suitable refreshments."

When Maria Zoë returned, she found her husband and his guest already in earnest conversation, so she resumed her place on the window seat, picked up the book, and again pretended to read, while surreptitiously watching her husband's face. It was flushed, and she sensed that he was excited about something. His shoulders were straighter than they had been for months, his neck stretched, and his eyes glittering with attention. His guest looked quite pleased with himself as well. It would seem, Maria Zoë concluded, that the girl had been found.

Moments later Georgios arrived with a tray of refreshments, and the mood at the table shifted. The men slid into small talk, Maria Zoë surmised, and she dropped her eyes to the text of her book in case they looked her way. Laughter from her husband and her guest drew her attention once or twice—but then as the guest rose to depart, the intensity returned to her husband's face and he nodded several times in answer to the other's message. Perhaps the guest was saying when and where Melusinde would be returned?

The guest bowed deeply one last time to her husband and then withdrew without even acknowledging Maria Zoë's presence; he was intent on pretending she did not exist. As soon as the door fell closed behind him, Maria Zoë set her book aside and asked eagerly, "They've found Melusinde?"

Balian had been gazing at the closed door, lost in thought. At her words his shoulders sank, and as he turned around he shook his head and admitted dully, "No. They haven't." Taking a deep breath, he continued, "The Sultan swears he made inquiries across all his territories, but no one came forward. She may already be dead. . . . Or perhaps the man who owns her values her more than the price offered by the Sultan for her return, although Khalid claims the Sultan offered double the normal price." Balian paused before asking in a low voice, "How in God's name am I going to tell Constance—on Christmas Eve!—that her daughter is irretrievably lost?"

Maria Zoë grabbed his hand and raised it to her lips. Their eyes met. "*I'll* tell her," she assured him. Then she modified it to "Beatrice and I will tell her," knowing it would be useful to engage the support of the elder and more level-headed of the Auber sisters. But at the moment, she wasn't worried about Constance. What distressed her was to see her husband looking so defeated. Yet something had invigorated him only moments earlier. "But you seemed so pleased," she prodded. "When I returned, you looked as if you had had good news."

Balian started slightly. "Yes, God forgive me, I was pleased. You see, Khalid told me the real reason he was here was to negotiate with Champagne. The Sultan is offering a minor modification of the borders established by the Truce of Ramla."

"Ibelin?" Maria Zoë guessed, her spirits already soaring.

Balian shook his head. "Not quite. What the Sultan offered is the territory that made up the lordship of Caymont. According to Khalid, he made the return conditional on Champagne bestowing it upon me as my fief. Why would Salah ad-Din do such a thing?" He asked baffled.

Maria Zoë shrugged. "That's not so hard to fathom. He'd rather you were content with Caymont than coveting Beirut. Or, should I say, he'd rather see you as Lord of Caymont than Lord of Beirut."

"And you think I have a right to accept Caymont?" Balian pressed her.

Maria Zoë sifted rapidly through her memory for everything she knew about this lordship in her former kingdom. "It was made vacant at Hattin, when Guillaume and his son were both killed."

"Yes. There are no other claimants," Balian confirmed. "Still . . ."

"What is it? Why are you hesitating? You *were* pleased when he told you. I could see it not only in your face but in your bearing."

"Am I that easy to read?"

She smiled softly and reminded him, "Beloved, I've been your wife for fifteen years." She squeezed his hands and looked him in the eye. "What makes you hesitate?"

"I once told the Sultan that if God had wanted me to be a great lord, he would have made me one."

"Ah." Maria Zoë considered that, nodding slowly, before asking, "And you haven't noticed that you *are* a great lord?"

"I have nothing!" Ibelin snapped back, frowning.

"Nothing," Maria Zoë repeated. "Except the attentive ear of the King and Queen, the respect of the High Court, the loyalty of the army, the gratitude—not to say adulation—of the released slaves, the love of the common people. No voice in this kingdom carries more weight than yours. Is that nothing?"

Balian drew a breath and held it. He did not want to seem indifferent or ungrateful for the things she had listed. "The mood of kings and common people is fickle, Zoë; tomorrow I may be hated or just forgotten."

"And God? Do you think His love is fickle, too? Don't you think it possible that God is giving you Caymont because *He* thinks you deserve a material reward?"

"Through the Sultan of Syria? The man who has taken Jerusalem from us?"

"It's a small barony, like Ibelin, but rich," Maria Zoë remarked rather than answering directly.

"Smaller, actually. Six knights, I believe, was all it owed to the Crown."

"It had sugar plantations, oil mills, and vineyards," Maria countered.

"Yes, I think you're right," Balian conceded. "It would be enough to give our sons an inheritance and Margaret a dowry. . . ."

"Yes, it would—without diminishing in any way your stature in this kingdom or detracting from your more important legacy."

He looked at her, uncomprehending.

"You gave up Ibelin for the freedom of thousands. That is the legacy your children will never forget. It is an example they will find hard to live up to."

He answered by pulling her into his arms and kissing her firmly and gratefully. "You are right to remind me I have riches beyond measure—riches that cannot be measured in acres or income—because I have you, Zoë. You are my greatest treasure, an endless wonder, greater than the most splendid poetry on earth."

Maria Zoë hadn't a clue what he was talking about, but it didn't matter. He was standing straighter again, and she could feel energy pulsing through his veins. His face was lit from the inside. She knew she had to foster that newfound flame of hope. "Balian, tonight we will celebrate the birth of Christ," she reminded him. "Rising up from the grave, He brought us all new life. In His name, it is time to stop mourning what we have lost, and to concentrate instead on rebuilding what we still have."

ꟾistorical Afterword

BALIAN D'IBELIN WAS INDEED GIVEN THE lordship of Caymont near Acre, and as stepfather to the Queen he was viewed as the most senior of all the barons in the truncated Kingdom of Jerusalem. The last royal charter still in existence today that he witnessed dates from late 1193, which has led most historians to assume he died about this time. However, the records are not complete, and there could well be other explanations why he did not witness royal charters. The fact is, we do not know the date or place of his death.

Maria Comnena lived until 1217, by which time her great-granddaughter Isabella II (also known as Yolanda) was Queen of Jerusalem.

Guy de Lusignan died in late 1194 and bequeathed Cyprus to his brother Geoffrey, who had already returned to Europe and was not interested in it. The leading Latin noblemen on Cyprus chose Aimery as their new overlord. Within two years Aimery had pacified the island, established a Latin clergy, and submitted the island to the Holy Roman Emperor in exchange for a crown. He was crowned King of Cyprus in September 1197, shortly after the death of his wife Eschiva. His eldest son, Hugh, married Alice, the daughter of Queen Isabella I of Jerusalem by Henri de Champagne. They founded a dynasty that lasted over three hundred years.

Henri de Champagne was never crowned King of Jerusalem, always styling himself only the Count of Champagne. He and Isabella had three daughters together before he was killed in a bizarre accident in November 1197. The barons of Jerusalem chose Aimery de Lusignan as Isabella's fourth husband, and they were married in late 1197 or early 1198. They both lived until 1205. Isabella's only son came from this last marriage. The boy died as an infant, however, and Isabella was succeeded by her daughter by Conrad de Montferrat, known in history as Maria de Montferrat.

John d'Ibelin, Balian's eldest son, was made Constable of Jerusalem in or around 1198 by Aimery de Lusignan, but he exchanged this position for the lordship of Beirut, which had been recaptured from the Saracens in 1197. At King Aimery's death he was named regent of Jerusalem to rule for his immature neice Maria de Montferrat. He held the position for five years until a husband was found for her. He was later to lead a successful baronial revolt against the Holy Roman Emperor, but that is material for another novel.

Philip d'Ibelin, Balian's second son, served as regent of Cyprus during the minority of Henry I (son of Hugh I) of Cyprus. His eldest son rose to be Count of Jaffa and Ascalon and took part in the Seventh Crusade alongside King Louis IX of France. He was also a renowned jurist who composed a major work on the constitution of the Kingdom of Jerusalem.

Helvis, Balian's eldest daughter, married Reginald de Sidon, and their eldest son, Balian, inherited Sidon from his father. After Reginald de Sidon's death Helvis married Guy de Montfort, a brother of Simon de Montfort the Elder, an uncle of the English constitutional reformer, Simon de Montfort the Younger.

Margaret, Balian's younger daughter, married first Hugh of Tiberius, and later Walter of Caesarea.

The Ibelin family was considered "semi-royal" for the next three hundred years, and Ibelins intermarried into the royal houses of Cyprus and Armenia.

For those of you interested in following Balian, Maria Comnena, and their children in the decades following the Third Crusade, I plan two additional novels. The next, *The Last Crusader Kingdom*, will describe the establishment of the Latin Kingdom of Cyprus. A second novel, *Barons against the Emperor*, will describe his son John's struggle to defend the constitutional rights of the High Court against the despotic ambitions of Emperor Friedrich II.

Historical Note

BALIAN D'IBELIN WAS AN IMPORTANT HISTORICAL figure whose name and deeds are depicted in the contemporary chronicles of both Christians and Muslims. Yet while his contributions to the politics of his age are part of the historical record, many of the facts about his personal life went unrecorded. We do not know the dates of either his birth or his death, and sources (or contemporary interpretations of contradictory medieval copies of lost sources) differ on other important facts.

Given these gaps and contradictions, this novel has opted for a lucid story line that is not inconsistent with known facts and in no way violates the historical record, but condenses or alters the exact timing of some events to make the story more coherent and dramatically effective. Below is a summary of the historical facts that form the basis of this novel, noting any deviations made in the novel.

- While it is recorded that Salah ad-Din sent an escort of fifty Mamlukes to accompany Maria Comnena from Jerusalem to safety in Christian territory, it is not recorded where she went. Some sources claim she went to Tripoli or even Antioch, but there is no compelling reason for her to go to either place. She is unlikely to have gone to Constantinople, as her own family had largely been exterminated by the Emperor Andronicus when he seized power, and the new Emperor Isaac II Angelus would have been unlikely to welcome a more prominent member of the imperial family. I have chosen to locate her in Tyre, as this is a convenient device to show what was happening in this city at a critical time in history and is not impossible. She was certainly recorded as present in Tyre a couple of years later.

- Imam Ghazali was a Muslim theologian, jurist and philosopher, and author of *The Revivifaction of Religious Sciences* (*Ihya' Ulum al-Din* or *Ihya'u Ulumiddin*). He lived from 1050 to 1111. The theses on women presented by Imad ad-Din and attributed to Ghazali were derived from the above work by Aisha Mernissi in her excellent analysis of sexual relations in Islam *Beyond the Veil.*

- Imad ad-Din's description of the fate of Christian women after the fall of Jerusalem, described in Chapter 2, is a direct quote from Imad ad-Din al-Isfahani's account of the conquest of Jerusalem and the aftermath.

- At the surrender of Jerusalem, the *Old French Continuation of William of Tyre* (aka the *Lyon Continuation of William of Tyre*) claims Ibelin offered to stand surety for all the Christians who could not pay their ransom and that he was turned down by the Sultan. Some sources report that Salah ad-Din's brother, al-Adil, asked for a thousand slaves as a gift and was given them, followed by Ibelin, who asked for five hundred. According to these sources, the Patriarch was also present and also asked for five hundred slaves, but Imad ad-Din claims the Patriarch left the city with wagons laden full of treasure worth two hundred thousand dinars—in short, enough to pay for twenty thousand men, or much more than was needed to pay for the fifteen thousand mostly women and children going into slavery. I find it incredible that the Patriarch would have had the effrontery to ask Salah ad-Din to "give" him five hundred slaves when he could have purchased the freedom of all. I have therefore left the Patriarch out of this scene altogether.

- The Christians were given forty days to raise their ransoms, which from October 2 would have been November 10. The Christian refugees would have needed ten to twelve days to cover the hundred miles from Jerusalem to Tyre, so Balian would have arrived in Tyre on or about November 20 or 21. However, the *Old French Continuation of William of Tyre* claims that Salah ad-Din's siege of Tyre started on October 31. Ibn al-Athir, on the other hand, stressed that Salah ad-Din spent time in Jerusalem after taking control (i.e. after the Christians had evacuated), setting up madrassas and the like. Furthermore, Salah ad-Din spent time in Acre on his way from Jerusalem to Tyre. In consequence, Ibn al-Athir dates Salah ad-Din's resumption of the siege of Tyre at November 26, which I find more probable.

• Salah ad-Din sent for William Marquis de Montferrat and offered to release him in exchange for the surrender of Tyre. Not only did his son Conrad refuse, but the Arab chronicles claim that he fired a crossbow at his father to underline his point.

• According to the *Old French Continuation of William of Tyre*, Salah ad-Din sent Guy de Lusignan to Nablus after the Frankish surrender of Ascalon (September 1187), and Queen Sibylla was allowed to join him there because Salah ad-Din "did not want her in Jerusalem once he was besieging it." The same chronicle reports, however, that in 1188, Sibylla is in Tripoli, admonishing Salah ad-Din to keep his word to release her husband. German sources report Sibylla trying to "flee from Tyre" by ship and being prevented from leaving by Conrad de Montferrat. It is difficult to reconcile these different accounts, so I have developed a plausible, but not recorded, sequence of events that incorporates all three reports. Sibylla's pregnancy and miscarriage are pure fabrication.

• Reginald de Sidon was given a safe-conduct by Salah ad-Din that was broken when he tried to leave the Sultan's camp and return to his castle of Belfort (sometimes written as Beaufort). He was then tortured within sight of the men holding the castle until he ordered them to surrender. This behavior on Salah ad-Din's part will surely come as a shock to those who hold fast to the romantic view of Salah ad-Din as a "chivalrous" Saracen who was consistently generous and gentle to his enemies—but it is, unfortunately, incontestable historical fact.

• Allegedly "out of remorse," Salah ad-Din gave Sidon back half his lordship as a *iqta*, but within a year, a Frankish force that tried to regain control of Sidon was repulsed. In the early thirteenth century, however, Salah ad-Din's successor al-Adil allegedly granted the remaining half of the lordship to Reginald de Sidon's son, Balian, and it was said that Sidon was the only lordship held from both the Sultan of Damascus and the King of Jerusalem.

- Sometime after Hattin, Reginald de Sidon married Helvis d'Ibelin, Balian's eldest daughter. The couple eventually had several children together, including a son, Balian, who was his father's oldest surviving son and so his heir. Helvis could not have been born before 1178 and was not yet ten at Hattin, while Reginald de Sidon had previously been married to Agnes de Courtenay (as her third husband), so he was probably older than her father. The marriage must be seen as a political alliance between the only barons (besides Tripoli) to escape Hattin, both of whom undoubtedly felt vulnerable in the post-Hattin environment.

- Gerard de Ridefort, Grand Master of the Knights Templar, was released from captivity in exchange for the surrender of Gaza, although this was explicitly against the Templar Rule.

- The story of two Christian slaves falling into each other's arms when one of their masters visited the other is recorded in Arab chronicles as proof of how many Christian slaves were taken. According to these accounts they were sisters who had not seen one another since the fall of Jerusalem.

- The date of Guy de Lusignan's release from Saracen captivity is variously given as May 10 or July, and he is said to have been reunited with Sibylla in either Tortosa or Tripoli on July 4. The former was in the County of Tripoli, so the term "Tripoli" may still relate to Tortosa. To reconcile the accounts, I have opted for a May release date but a long journey, putting him in Tripoli in early July, and a reunion with Sibylla in the city of Tripoli, in order to have them present during the dramatic arrival of the Sicilian fleet that ended Salah ad-Din's siege of Tripoli. There is a moving account in the *Itinerarium Peregrinorum et Gesta Regis Ricardi* (*Itinerarium*) describing the citizens lining the wall and anxiously trying to determine whether the fleet was friendly or hostile. It describes how they cheered on recognizing "Christian symbols," and the answering cheers of the sailors.

- Geoffrey de Lusignan arrived in the Holy Land a year later, but I felt it was useful to introduce him sooner. He is said to have been the major impetus behind Guy's leaving Antioch and setting up the siege of Acre. Showing him convincing Guy to break his oath is consistent with his later role as the most aggressive of the Lusignan brothers.

- Kerak was surrendered in November 1188 and Montreal in May 1189; the date of Humphrey de Toron's release is recorded as May 1189. For literary cohesion, I chose to treat the surrender of both castles and Humphrey's release in a single episode.

- The attempt by Frankish forces from Tyre to retake Sidon is historical fact. Although the names of the Frankish leaders are not recorded, Sidon himself had the most reason to want his lordship back and would have had the greatest local knowledge of the territory, making him the most logical choice for commander. Ibelin, on the other hand, was either already his father-in-law or soon to be so. He therefore likewise had an interest in securing control of Sidon for his daughter. The participation of Toron and Aimery de Lusignan was literary license.

- The siege camp at Acre experienced extreme shortages in the winter of 1190-1191, for which the sources hostile to Montferrat melodramatically blame him. These sources are so biased, however, that I felt it made more sense to consider another possibility—namely, the simple fact that sailing south could be very difficult, especially in winter. An attempt to relieve Tyre from Tripoli, for example, ended in failure because of contrary winds, and Richard the Lionheart almost didn't make it to Jaffa in time for the same reason.

- Conrad de Montferrat was stabbed to death in April 1192 by two assassins. The most likely version of the murder is that Conrad had offended the leader of the Assassins, the "Old Man of the Mountain," by seizing a ship belonging to the sect, murdering the crew, and refusing to pay compensation to the "Old Man." This is why I inserted the incident with the ship into the narrative—to make the later assassination comprehensible.

- Isabella was taken forcibly from Humphrey de Toron's tent at the siege camp of Acre and turned over to an ecclesiastical court that ruled on the validity of her marriage. The clerics, unnamed except for the Archbishop of Pisa and the Archbishop of Canterbury, ruled that Isabella had been too young to consent at the time of her marriage and that she could marry whomever she wanted. Clerical chroniclers writing decades after the fact (and possibly more concerned with preventing claims to Champagne by the descendants of Isabella's third husband, Henri de

Champagne) try to argue that all the judges were corrupted by Montferrat. Given that Isabella's age is indisputable, the vehement fulmina-
tions against Montferrat ring ridiculous. More interesting, according
to the *Lyon Continuation of William of Tyre*, Maria Comnena told her
daughter she would have to renounce Humphrey to gain her father's
inheritance. This is strong evidence that the High Court had chosen
Montferrat as her husband—and was not going to fall for Sibylla's trick
of promising to set aside an unpopular husband only to marry him
again once crowned.

- Even the sources biased against Montferrat agree that a knight challenged Toron to judicial combat and that Toron just stared at the gage.
  The challenger is not named, only referred to as the Butler (in medieval
  times a powerful position usually held by a vassal) of Senlis, so I felt
  free to make it my fictional character, Henri d'Ibelin. All chronicles
  agree that Humphrey was "pretty" "like a girl," "cowardly and effeminate." Although not explicit, the implication is that Toron was homo-
  sexual and that the marriage had not been consummated. For a more
  detailed examination of this controversial incident, see my essay on
  "The Abduction of Isabella."

- King Richard's fleet was scattered by a storm in which three ships
  wrecked on the Cypriot coast, and the vessel carrying Joanna Plantagenet and Richard's betrothed, Berengaria of Navarre, was driven to
  Limassol. Isaac Comnenus plundered the ships, imprisoned the survivors, and threatened the two queens. Richard arrived dramatically
  just as Isaac Comnenus' patience was wearing thin, and he responded
  to Richard's requests for the return of his treasure with insults that
  provoked an assault.

- Richard stormed the beach by Limassol in a dramatic amphibious
  assault without horses. He surprised Isaac Comnenus' army outside
  the city the next dawn. His subsequent conquest of Cyprus was swift,
  largely due to the unpopularity of Isaac Comnenus.

- Guy and Geoffrey de Lusignan sailed for Cyprus to secure King Richard's support for Guy, arriving on May 11. Although Aimery is not
  mentioned, he would almost certainly have been with his brothers. Furthermore, since historically Aimery would later become King of Cyprus

and his role in pacifying and establishing a viable Latin kingdom on Cyprus is the subject of my next book, I wanted to foreshadow these events in this scene.

- Richard is said to have gone out to meet the three ships, coming from the direction of Acre, in a skiff and then to have rushed back to make ready a suitable feast. Richard married Berengaria in Limassol on the next day. Shortly afterwards, Isaac agreed to join the crusade, only to then flee in the night. After that Richard set out to take control of the island, and within fifteen days he had secured the unconditional surrender of Isaac. He set up his own administration and then continued to Acre, arriving there June 8, roughly six weeks after Philip of France.

- Although the Queens of England and Sicily traveled with Richard, they are not mentioned as being in the camp, only being settled in the royal palace after Acre is taken. I think it a reasonable assumption that they would have remained in comparative safety and comfort aboard one of the larger ships.

- The accounts of the massacre of hostages at Acre sometimes imply that women and children were also killed, but the most reliable contemporary sources speak of hostages from the garrison, and these could only have been fighting men. The numbers also vary, but twenty-five hundred is the most reasonable figure given. The description of men awaiting the True Cross and their distress when, after three weeks of excuses from Salah ad-Din, it is not delivered is vividly described in the *Lyon Continuation of William of Tyre*. This document, which is almost certainly based on the firsthand account by someone from Outremer (possibly Ernoul) rather than accounts from crusaders alone, stresses the "great sorrow and tears."

- There is no evidence that Ibelin took part in the Battle of Arsuf, but *poulain* lords and troops did. Including him was a means of describing this critical and famous battle. To exclude it would have detracted from the overall value of the book.

- According to English sources, Balian was seen leaving the Sultan's camp by Stephen de Turnham, but later and in Arab sources Humphrey de Toron is named as one of Richard's negotiators. Aside from the fact that the English may have simply confused Turnham (a familiar name) with Toron (an unfamiliar one), I have chosen, for greater cohesion and to keep the (already large) number of characters down, to make Toron Richard's first envoy throughout.

- The number of times, the locations, and the dates of the diplomatic contacts that took place between Richard and Salah ad-Din on one hand and Montferrat and Salah ad-Din on the other is unclear from the chronicles. There is agreement that there was considerable back-and-forth in late October and early November. I have simplified things in the text for coherence, clarity, and pace.

- The Arab historian Baha ad-Din states explicitly that the suggestion of a marriage between al-Adil and Joanna Plantagenet was al-Adil's idea, and that Salah ad-Din approved the proposal "as a joke" because he knew Richard would refuse. Baha ad-Din claims that Richard rejected it because "the Christians" could not accept the marriage of his sister to a Muslim without the Pope's consent, which would take three months, but he could offer one of his nieces instead! Both sides jocularly continued to refer to this offer from time to time, but neither side appears to have taken it too seriously.

- In April 1192, Richard received news that his brother John was in rebellion, had expelled his chancellor from the Kingdom, and was besieging his supporters. The next day he announced his intention to return home, but was implored by the leaders of the army to first ensure that the Kingdom of Jerusalem had a king. He asked which of the two kings should be recognized, and the army "unanimously" chose Conrad de Montferrat—because Guy had done nothing to win back his kingdom (after losing it in the first place). Richard swallowed this decision and sanctioned it. It is unlikely that the entire "army" would be consulted, nor did the many crusades have any legal right to determine who should be King of Jerusalem. The High Court, on the other hand, did have that constitutional right and I believe it was the High Court, not the entire crusading force, that was consulted and which chose Montferrat.

- King Richard sent Henri de Champagne and two other retainers (Otto de Transinges and William de Cáyeu) to Tyre to bring Montferrat the news; to keep the number of characters down, I only refer to Henri de

Champagne. Although he was not explicitly named, it seems logical that Balian would go with them, representing the *poulains* for two reasons: he was Isabella's stepfather, and he had been largely responsible for her marriage to Montferrat in 1190.

• The assassination of Conrad de Montferrat occurred as described, although allegedly he went to dine without Isabella because she was "late at the baths." I doubt church chroniclers really knew why, and in any case the fight I describe in this novel was a literary device to reflect on their relationship. It was immediately rumored that the assassins had been hired by Salah ad-Din—or Richard. Richard was even charged with the assassination at his trial before the Imperial Diet after his arrest by the Holy Roman Emperor. But he had no motive for murder after acknowledging Conrad as King, and he was in a great hurry to get home. Nor did Salah ad-Din have any clear motive at this point. Other rumors suggested Humphrey de Toron was behind it. That Conrad had in some way offended the Old Man of the Mountain seems the most plausible explanation.

• Some accounts claim that one of the assassins had been in Ibelin's service so that they would have access to Montferrat, which is not completely logical. The assassins' method was to win the trust of their victim, and that was done better within his own household. Ibelin was often nowhere near Montferrat, reducing the opportunity to strike. I have therefore not followed this version of events.

• The French demanded that Isabella surrender Tyre to them, but she refused. The *Itinerarium*, which is shamelessly biased in favor of Richard I, claims she refused on the grounds that her dying husband admonished her to give it to no one but Richard. Since Richard had been Montferrat's bitter opponent up until only a few days earlier, I find that very unlikely. It is far more probable that she was interested in upholding the constitution and independence of her kingdom, which meant deferring to the High Court.

• Accounts claiming that Henri de Champagne was acclaimed and elected by "the common people" of Tyre are nonsense. "The people" had nothing to say about who was elected King of Jerusalem, much less the marriage of a princess or a widow. The High Court of Jerusalem,

on the other hand, both elected kings and selected consorts for their
queens. It was without doubt the High Court of Jerusalem that selected
Henri de Champagne as Isabella's next husband. That her stepfather, as
one of the most influential members of the High Court, would have a
particularly strong voice in such a decision is logical and is supported
by the high standing the Ibelins had ever after.

- The chronicles say that Isabella went to meet Henri de Champagne
  to assure him she was willing to marry him. Allegedly it was this
  meeting that overcame his reluctance to enter a bigamous marriage.
  The accounts stress that he was very pleased with her and later could
  not bear to be separated from her.

- The second attempt to capture Jerusalem took place over King Richard's objections (he preferred an assault on Cairo), and the decision to
  abandon the attempt was made by an elected council made up of five
  French, five local lords, five Templars, and five Hospitallers. Allegedly
  the decision was unanimous, but presumably only after the local lords,
  Templars, and Hospitallers had convinced the reluctant French that
  holding Jerusalem would be impossible even if they could take it.

- The Frankish army withdrew from their positions before Jerusalem on
  July 4, and Richard did not return to Acre until July 26. His wife and
  sister would certainly have heard about the withdrawal long before he
  arrived. The attack on Jaffa started either immediately or two days after
  Richard's arrival at Acre, and he received the news either that same
  night or after nearly a week. I condensed events for dramatic effect.

- The French refused to relieve Jaffa, and the army of Jerusalem with the
  Templars and Hospitallers was stopped on the road near Caesarea. The
  Count of Champagne loaded a ship with as many men as possible and
  sailed to Jaffa. The accounts are so fixated on what happened to King
  Richard, however, that what happened to the army of Jerusalem after
  Champagne left it is not clear. The army did, however, somehow rejoin
  Richard at Jaffa without a fight, so I invented this maneuver along the
  shore and Ibelin's role in devising it.

- The accounts also differ on how long it took Richard to reach Jaffa,
  some saying he arrived in the morning after a night departure, others

that he was becalmed for three days. I've chosen a compromise of a one-day delay.

- The chronicles describe Richard entering by a postern and mounting a spiral stairway into the Templar commandery; presumably he knew about the door from earlier stays in the city.

- The accounts explicitly mention the large number of pigs killed and that the Frankish dead were heaped up with the pigs as an insult. Likewise, the broken wine casks and the slaughter of men in the infirmary are recorded.

- The *Itinerarium* describes the surprise attack on Richard's camp on August 5, saying that some men didn't have time to put on even their braies. It describes Richard riding clear through the Saracen lines, then bringing a horse to the Earl of Leicester, and finally rescuing Ralph de Mauleon from being dragged off as a prisoner. To keep the number of characters down, I substituted Aimery de Lusignan for Ralph de Mauleon, and al-Afdal for his brother al-Zahir.

- Both the *Itinerarium* and the *Lyon Continuation of William of Tyre* claim al-Adil offered Richard a horse (or two) during the battle on August 5. The *Itinerarium* paints it as a chivalrous gesture between brothers-in-arms. The *Lyon Continuation*, which follows the lost *Chronicle of Ernoul* more closely, paints it as a trick. I've opted for the version offered by a contemporary from Outremer, rather than one by an English clerk writing after the legend of Salah ad-Din as "the chivalrous Saracen" had already taken root.

- Baha ad-Din relates that toward the end of the day King Richard rode up and down the entire Saracen line, challenging anyone to fight with him—and no one dared.

- Ibelin was instrumental in negotiating the truce between Richard of England and Salah ad-Din that ended the Third Crusade. Significantly, this agreement, known as the Treaty of Ramla, left Ibelin's own baronies of Ibelin, Ramla, and Mirabel in Saracen hands.

- Although an "exchange of prisoners" was included in the treaty, the return of tens of thousands of captives is not explicitly mentioned in the chronicles. On the other hand, tens of thousands of Christians (some estimates put the number as high as 100,000) had been enslaved after the collapse of the Kingdom of Jerusalem. Most of these were women and children, many the families of surviving fighting men. Others were the husbands, sons and fathers of women who had escaped to Tyre. The human drama was *real* and acute—even if ignored by churchman living half a world away and writing decades after the fact. Furthermore, it is recorded that Ibelin offered to stand surety for the poor unable to pay their ransom after the surrender of Jerusalem; it is unlikely that someone who felt that strong a responsibility for the women and children sent into slavery would forget them easily. The fact that Ibelin negotiated the Treaty of Ramla yet failed to obtain the return of his own baronies, although they lay very close to Jaffa, may be an indication of Frankish weakness, or—as I chose to interpret in this novel—an indication of Ibelin's continued willness to put the fate of innocent women and children ahead of his own material well-being.

- The oath-taking for the Treaty of Ramla was conducted twice, with al-Adil and al-Afdal taking the leading role for the Saracens, and Champagne and Ibelin the principals for the Franks.

- Female genital mutilation (female circumcision) was widely practiced in Muslim society in the Middle Ages and more than 90% of Egyptian women over the age of 15 have been victims of it even today. Islamic scholars recommended female genital mutilation for even adult sexual slaves.

- The lordship of Caymont near Acre was restored to the Kingdom of Jerusalem at a slightly later date in a separate agreement, and allegedly Salah ad-Din designated it was to go to Ibelin. Unlike Sidon, however, he did not grant it directly as an *iqta*, but rather returned it to the Kingdom, and Queen Isabella bestowed it on her stepfather as a fief.

- All dialogue is, of course, fictional, and so is Ernoul's song.

The Abduction of Isabella

In November 1190, Princess Isabella of Jerusalem, then eighteen years old, was forcibly removed from the tent she was sharing with her husband Humphrey de Toron in the Frankish camp besieging the city of Acre. Just days earlier, her elder sister, Queen Sibylla, had died, making Isabella the hereditary queen of the all but nonexistent—yet symbolically important—Kingdom of Jerusalem. A short time after her abduction, she married Conrad, Marquis de Montferrat—making him, through her, the de facto King of Jerusalem. This high-profile abduction and marriage scandalized later Church chroniclers and is often cited to this day as evidence of the perfidy of Conrad de Montferrat and his accomplices. The latter included Isabella's mother, Maria Comnena, and her stepfather, Balian d'Ibelin.

The anonymous author of the *Itinerarium Peregrinorum et Gesta Regis Ricardi* (*Itinerarium*), for example, describes with blistering outrage how Conrad de Montferrat had long schemed to "steal" the throne of Jerusalem, and at last stuck upon the idea of abducting Isabella—a crime the author compares to the abduction of Helen of Sparta by Paris of Troy, "only worse." To achieve his plan, the *Itinerarium* claims, Conrad "surpassed the deceits of Sinon, the eloquence of Ulysses, and the forked tongue of Mithridates." Conrad, according to this English cleric writing after the fact, set about bribing, flattering, and corrupting bishops and barons alike as never before in recorded history. Throughout, the chronicler says, Conrad was aided and abetted by three barons of the Kingdom of Jerusalem (Sidon, Haifa, and Ibelin) who combined (according to our chronicler) "the treachery of Judas, the cruelty of Nero, and the wickedness of Herod, and everything the present age abhors and ancient times condemned." Really? The author certainly brings no evidence of a single act of treachery, cruelty, or wickedness —beyond this one alleged abduction, which (as we shall see) was neither an abduction nor a travesty of justice, much less a case of rape.

Indeed, this chronicler himself admits that Isabella was not removed from Humphrey's tent by Conrad himself, nor was she handed over to him. On the contrary, she was put into the care of clerical "sequesterers," whose role was to assure her safety and prevent a further abduction "while a clerical court debated the case for a divorce." Furthermore, in the very next paragraph, our anonymous slanderer of some of the most courageous and pious lords of Jerusalem, declares that although Isabella at first resisted the idea of divorcing her husband Humphrey, she was soon persuaded to consent to divorce because "a woman's opinion changes very easily" and "a girl is easily taught to do what is morally wrong."

While the *Itinerarium* admits that Isabella's marriage to Humphrey was reviewed by a church court, it hides this fact under the abuse it heaps upon the clerics involved. Another contemporary chronicle, the *Lyon Continuation of William of Tyre*, explains in far more neutral and objective language that the case hinged on the important principle of consent. By the twelfth century, marriage could only be valid in canonical law if both parties (i.e., including Isabella) consented. The issue at hand was whether Isabella had consented to her marriage to Humphrey at the time it was contracted.

The *Lyon Continuation* further notes that Isabella and Humphrey testified before the church tribunal separately. In her testimony, Isabella asserted she had *not* consented to her marriage to Humphrey, while Humphrey claimed she *had*. The *Lyon Continuation* also provides the colorful detail that another witness, who had been present at Isabella and Humphrey's wedding, at once called Humphrey a liar, and challenged him to prove in combat that he spoke the truth. Humphrey, the chronicler says, refused to "take up the gage." At this point the chronicler states that Humphrey was "cowardly and effeminate."

Both accounts (the *Itinerarium* and the *Lyon Continuation*) agree that following the testimony and deliberations, the Church council ruled that Isabella's marriage to Humphrey was invalid. There was only one dissenting voice, that of the Archbishop of Canterbury. However, both chroniclers insist that this decision was reached because Conrad corrupted *all* the other clerics, particularly the Papal Legate, the Archbishop of Pisa. The *Lyon Continuation* claims that the Archbishop of Pisa ruled the marriage invalid and allowed Isabella to marry Conrad only because Conrad promised commercial advantages for Pisa should he win Isabella and become King. The *Itinerarium*, on the other hand, claims Conrad "poured out enormous generosity to corrupt judicial integrity with the enchantment of gold."

There are a lot of problems with the clerical outrage over Isabella's "abduction"—not to mention the dismissal of Isabella's change of heart as due to the inherent moral frailty of females. There are also problems with the slander heaped on the barons and bishops who dared to support Conrad de Montferrat's suit for Isabella.

Let's go back to the basic facts of the case, as laid out by the chroniclers themselves but stripped of moral judgments and slander:

- Isabella was removed from Humphrey de Toron's tent against her will.

- She was not, however, taken by Conrad or raped by him.

- Rather, she was turned over to neutral third parties and sequestered and protected by them.

- Meanwhile, a Church court was convened to rule on the validity of her marriage to Humphrey.

- The case hinged on the important theological principle of consent.

- Humphrey claimed that Isabella had consented to the marriage, but when challenged by a witness to the wedding, he "said nothing" and backed down.

- Isabella testified before the tribunal that she had not consented to her marriage.

- The court ruled that Isabella's marriage to Humphrey had not been valid.

- On November 25, with either the French Bishop of Beauvais or the Papal Legate himself presiding, Isabella married Conrad. Since a clerical court had just ruled that no marriage was valid without the consent of the bride, we can be confident that she consented to this marriage. In fact, as the *Itinerarium* (vituperously) reports, "She was not ashamed to say . . . she went with the Marquis of her own accord."

To understand what really happened in the siege camp at Acre in November 1190, we need to look beyond what the Church chronicles write about the abduction itself.

The story really begins ten years before the alleged abduction in 1180, when Isabella was just eight years old. Until this time, Isabella had lived in the care and custody of her mother, the Greek princess and Dowager Queen of Jerusalem, Maria Commena. In 1180, King Baldwin IV (Isabella's half-brother) arranged the betrothal of Isabella to Humphrey de Toron. Having promised this marriage without the consent of Isabella's mother or stepfather, the King ordered the physical removal of Isabella from her mother and stepfather's care and sent her to live with her future husband, his mother, and his stepfather. The latter was the infamous Reynald de Châtillon, notorious for having seduced the Princess of Antioch, tortured the Archbishop of Antioch, and sacked the Christian island of Cyprus. Isabella was effectively imprisoned in his border fortress at Kerak, and his wife, Stephanie de Milly, explicitly prohibited Isabella from even visiting her mother for three years.

In November 1183, when Isabella was just eleven years old, Reynald and his wife held a marriage feast to celebrate the wedding of Isabella and Humphrey. They invited all the nobles of the Kingdom to witness the feast. Unfortunately, before most of the wedding guests could arrive, Salah ad-Din's army surrounded the castle and laid siege to it. The wedding took place, and a few weeks later the army of Jerusalem relieved the castle, chasing Salah ad-Din's forces away.

Note that at the time the wedding took place, Isabella was not only a prisoner of her in-laws, she was only eleven years old. Canonical law in the twelfth century established the "age of consent" for girls at twelve. Isabella, therefore, could not legally consent to her wedding even if she wanted to. The marriage had been planned by the King, however, and carried out by one of the most powerful barons during a crisis. No one seems to have dared challenge it at the time.

At the death of Baldwin V three years later, Isabella's older sister, Queen Sibylla, was first in line to the throne, but found herself opposed by almost the entire High Court of Jerusalem (the body that was constitutionally required to consent to each new monarch). The opposition sprang not from objections to Sibylla herself, but from the fact that the bishops and barons of the Kingdom almost unanimously detested her husband, Guy de Lusignan. Although she could not gain the consent of the High Court necessary to make her coronation legal, she managed to convince a minority of the secular and ecclesiastical lords to crown her Queen by promising to divorce Guy and choose a new husband. Once anointed, Sibylla promptly betrayed her supporters by declaring that her "new" husband was the same as her old husband: Guy de Lusignan. She then crowned him herself (at least according to some accounts).

This struck many people at the time as duplicitous, to say the least, and the majority of the barons and bishops decided that since she had not had their consent in the first place, she and her husband were usurpers. They agreed to crown her younger sister Isabella (then fourteen years old) instead. The assumption was that since they commanded far larger numbers of troops than did Sibylla's supporters (many of whom now felt duped and were dissatisfied anyway, no doubt), they would be able to quickly depose Sibylla and Guy.

The plan, however, came to nothing because Isabella's husband, Humphrey de Toron, had no stomach for a civil war (or a crown, it seems), and chose to sneak away in the dark of night to do homage to Sibylla and Guy. The baronial revolt collapsed. Almost everyone eventually did homage to Guy, and he promptly led them all to an avoidable defeat at the Battle of Hattin. With the field army annihilated, the complete occupation of the Kingdom by the forces of Salah ad-Din followed—with the important exception of Tyre.

Tyre only avoided the fate of the rest of the Kingdom because of the timely arrival of a certain Italian nobleman, Conrad de Montferrat, who rallied the defenders and defied Salah ad-Din. Montferrat came from a very good and well-connected family. He was first cousin to both the Holy Roman Emperor and King Louis VII of France. Furthermore, his elder brother had been Sibylla of Jerusalem's first husband (before Guy), and his younger brother had been married to the daughter of the Greek Emperor Manuel I. Furthermore, he defended Tyre twice against the vastly superior armies of Salah ad-Din, and by holding Tyre he enabled the Franks to retain a bridgehead by which troops, weapons, and supplies could be funneled back into the Holy Land for a new crusade to retake Jerusalem. While Conrad was performing this heroic function, Guy de Lusignan was an (admittedly unwilling) "guest" of Salah ad-Din, a prisoner of war following his self-engineered defeat at Hattin.

So at the time of the infamous abduction, Guy was an anointed king, but one who derived his right to the throne from his now deceased wife (Sibylla died in early November 1190), and furthermore a king viewed by most of his subjects as a usurper—even before he'd lost the entire Kingdom through his incompetence. It is fair to say that in November 1190 Guy was not popular among the surviving barons, bishops, or commons of the Kingdom of Jerusalem, and they were eager to see the Kingdom pass into the hands of someone they respected and trusted. The death of Sibylla provided the perfect opportunity to crown a new king, because with her death the crown legally passed to her sister Isabella, and according to the constitution of the Kingdom, the husband of the Queen ruled with her as her consort.

The problem faced by the barons and bishops of Jerusalem in 1190, however, was that Isabella was still married to the same man who had betrayed them in 1186: Humphrey de Toron. He was clearly not interested in a crown, and it didn't help matters that he'd been in a Saracen prison for two years. Perhaps more damning still, he was allegedly "more like a woman than a man: he had a gentle manner and a stammer" (according to the *Itinerarium*).

Whatever the reason, we know that the barons and bishops of Jerusalem were not prepared to make the same mistake they had made four years earlier when they had done homage to a man they knew was incompetent (Guy de Lusignan). They absolutely refused to acknowledge Isabella's right to the throne unless she *first* set aside her unsuitable husband and took a man acceptable to them. We know this because the *Lyon Continuation* is based on a lost chronicle written by a certain Ernoul, who was an intimate of the Ibelin family and so of Isabella and her mother, and provides the following insight. Having admitted that Isabella "did not want to [divorce Humphrey], because she loved [him]," the *Lyon Continuation* explains that her mother Maria Comnena persuasively argued that *so long as she (Isabella) was Humphrey's wife*, "she could have neither honor nor her father's kingdom." Moreover, Queen Maria reminded her daughter that "when she had married she was still under age, and for that reason the validity of the marriage could be challenged." At which point, the continuation of Tyre reports, "Isabella consented to her mother's wishes."

In short, Isabella had a change of heart during the Church trial not because "a woman's opinion changes very easily," but because she was a realist—who wanted a crown. Far from being a victim manipulated by others or a fickle, immoral girl, she was an intelligent princess with an understanding of politics.

As for the Church court, it was not "corrupted" by Conrad or anyone else. It simply ruled based on the unalterable fact that Isabella had very publicly wed Humphrey before she had reached the legal age of consent. In short, whether she had voiced consent or not—indeed, whether she loved, adored, and positively desired Humphrey or not—she was not legally *capable* of consenting.

No violent abduction and no travesty of justice took place in Acre in 1190. Rather, a mature young woman recognized what was in her best interests and the interests of her kingdom: to divorce an unpopular and ineffective husband and marry a man respected by the peers of the realm. To do so, she allowed the marriage she had been forced into as an eleven-year-old to be recognized for what it was—a mockery. Isabella's marriage in 1183 as a child prisoner of a notoriously brutal man, not her marriage in 1190 as an eighteen-year-old queen, was the real "abduction" of Isabella.

Glossary

Abaya: a black garment, worn by Islamic women, that completely covers the head and body in a single, flowing, unfitted fashion so that no contours or limbs can be seen. It leaves only the face, but not the neck, visible and is often supplemented with a mask or "veil" that covers the lower half of the face, leaving only a slit for the eyes between the top of the abaya (which covers the forehead) and the mask or veil across the lower half of the face.

Aketon: a padded and quilted garment, usually of linen, worn under or instead of chain mail.

Aventail: a flap of chain mail, attached to the coif, to cover the lower part of the face, secured by a leather thong to the brow band.

Battlement: a low wall built on the roof of a tower or other building in a castle, fortified manor, or church, with alternating higher segments for sheltering behind and lower segments for shooting from.

Buss: a large combination oared and sailing vessel whose design was derived from Norse cargo (not raiding) vessels. Busses had substantial cargo capacity, but were also swift and maneuverable. They could be two- or even three-masted.

Cantle: the raised part of a saddle behind the seat; in this period it was high and strong, made of wood, to help keep a knight in the saddle even after taking a blow from a lance.

Cervelliere: an open-faced helmet that covered the skull like a close-fitting, brimless cap; usually worn over a chain-mail coif.

Chain mail (mail): flexible armor composed of interlinking riveted rings of metal. Each link passes through four others.

Chausses: mail leggings to protect a knight's legs in combat.

Cincenelles: Apparently some kind of fly. According to the *Itinerarium Peregrinorum et Gesta Regis Ricardi* (Book 5, Chapter 44): "At Ibelin flies called cincenelles ravage[d] the faces of the army with their stings, so that they look[ed] like lepers." I have not been able to find a modern word for the insects.

Coif: a chain-mail hood, either separate from or attached to the hauberk.

Conroi: a medieval cavalry formation in which the riders rode stirrup to stirrup in rows that enabled a maximum number of lances to come to bear, but also massed the power of the charge.

Crenels: the indentations or loopholes in the top of a battlement or wall.

Crenelate: the act of adding defensive battlements to a building.

Emir: Saracen rank or title similar to barons in the Frankish armies. Emirs controlled territory or administrative units that generated substantial income and were required to raise troops to serve under the Sultan. Unlike barons in the feudal West, however, their fiefs or *iqtas* were not hereditary, but held only at the pleasure of the Sultan. In theory, the Sultan could dismiss them, but he was also dependent upon them and the troops they could muster, making the relationship much more complex. Emirs had no religious function.

Faranj: Arab term for crusaders and their descendants in Outremer.

Fief: land held on a hereditary basis in return for military service.

Fetlock: the lowest joint in a horse's leg.

Frank: the contemporary term used to describe Latin Christians (crusaders, pilgrims, and their descendants) in the Middle East, regardless of their country of origin. The Arab term "faranj" derived from this.

Destrier: a horse specially bred and trained for mounted combat; a charger or warhorse. These horses had to have the strength to carry a man in full armor at a gallop, but sprinting (for a charge) was more important than endurance, and high spirits and temper were valued. Over time the horses were increasingly trained to take part in battle by kicking and biting, thereby becoming an additional weapon of the knight.

Dromond: a large vessel with two to three lateen sails and two banks of oars. These vessels were built very strongly and were consequently slower, but offered more spacious accommodation than galleys.

Garderobe: a toilet, usually built on the exterior wall of a residence or fortification, that in rural settings emptied directly into the surrounding ditch or moat, or in cities into an external pottery drainage pipe leading down to the city's sewage system.

Hajj: the Muslim pilgrimage to Mecca, one of the five duties of a good Muslim.

Hauberk: a chain-mail shirt, either long- or short-sleeved, that in this period reached to just above the knee.

Iqta: a Seljuk institution similar to a fief in feudal Europe, but not hereditary. It was a gift of land or other sources of revenue from an overlord to a subject that could be retracted at any time at the whim of the overlord.

Imam: a Muslim religious leader and scholar who leads prayers in the mosques.

Jihad: Muslim holy war, usually interpreted as a war against nonbelievers to spread the faith of Islam.

Kettle helm: an open-faced helmet with a broad rim, common among infantry.

Lance: a cavalry weapon approximately fourteen feet long, made of wood and tipped with a steel head.

Madrassa: A Muslim theological seminary.

Malik Rik: Saracen term for King Richard.

Melee: a form of tournament in which two teams of knights face off across a large natural landscape and fight in conditions very similar to real combat, across ditches, hedges, swamps, streams, and so on. These were very popular in the late twelfth century—and very dangerous, often resulting in injuries and even deaths to both men and horses. The modern meaning of any confused, hand-to-hand fight among a large number of people derives from the medieval meaning.

Merlon: the solid part of a battlement or parapet between two openings or "crenels."

Muezzin: The man who calls Muslims to prayer, usually from a minaret, five times a day.

Outremer: A French term meaning "overseas," used to describe the crusader kingdoms (Kingdom of Jerusalem, County of Tripoli, County of Edessa, and Principality of Antioch) established in the Holy Land after the First Crusade.

Pommel: 1) the raised portion in front of the seat of a saddle; 2) the round portion of a sword above the hand grip.

Palfrey: a riding horse bred and trained to be calm, with comfortable gaits, and capable of traveling long distances.

Parapet: A wall with crenelation built on a rampart or outer defensive work.

Quintain: a pivoted gibbet-like structure with a shield suspended from one arm and a bag of sand from the other, used to train men for mounted combat.

Rampart: an earthen embankment surmounted by a parapet, encircling a castle or city as a defense against attack.

Saracen: a collective term meaning "easterner" that referred to any of the ethnically diverse Muslim opponents of the Franks.

Scabbard (also sheath): the protective outer case of an edged weapon, particularly a sword or dagger.

Snecka: a square-sailed warship or galley that was very swift and maneuverable but had only a single bank of oars in addition to the sail, and so a very low freeboard. These evolved from Viking raiding ships. Some, however, appear to have had battering rams, as is described in the attack of Richard I's galleys on an Arab ship off Acre.

Sufi: Members of an Islamic mystical sect; Islamic scholars.

Surcoat: the loose, flowing cloth garment worn over armor; in this period it was slit up the front and back for riding and hung to mid-calf. It could be sleeveless or have short, wide, elbow-length sleeves. It could be of cotton, linen, or silk and was often brightly dyed, woven, or embroidered with the wearer's coat of arms.

Tenant-in-chief: an individual holding land directly from the crown. A baron.

Turcopoles: troops drawn from the Orthodox Christian population of the crusader states. These were not, as was often claimed, Muslim converts, nor were they the children of mixed marriages.

Vassal: an individual holding a fief (land) in exchange for military service.

Also by Helena P. Schrader

A landless knight,
A leper king,
And the struggle for Jerusalem.

A Biographical Novel of Balian d'Ibelin, Book I

Buy Now!

A united enemy,
A divided kingdom,
And the struggle for Jerusalem.

A Biographical Novel of Balian d'Ibelin, Book II

Buy Now!

A crusader in search of faith,
　　A lame lady in search of revenge,
　　　　And a king who would be a saint.

St. Louis' Knight takes you to the Holy Land in the 13th century: a world of crusaders, holy men, and assassins.

Buy Now!

Additional Reading

FOR MORE READING ON THE HISTORICAL Balian d'Ibelin, the crusader states, and the crusades, I recommend the following sources:

Barber, Malcolm, *The Crusader States*, Yale University Press, 2012.

Barber, Richard, *The Knight and Chivalry*, Boydell Press, 1970.

Bartlett, W. B., *Downfall of the Crusader Kingdom*, The History Press Ltd, 2010.

Boas, Adrian J., *Crusader Archaeology: The Material Culture of the Latin East*, Routledge, London, 1999.

Conder, Claude Reignier, *The Latin Kingdom of Jerusalem, 1099 to 1291 AD*, Committee of the Palestine Exploration Fund, 1897.

Edbury, Peter W., *John of Ibelin and the Kingdom of Jerusalem*, The Boydell Press, 1997.

Edbury, Peter W., *The Conquest of Jerusalem and the Third Crusade: Sources in Translation*, Ashgate Publishing Ltd., 1998.

Edbury, Peter W., *The Kingdom of Cyprus and the Crusades, 1191–1374*, Cambridge University Press, 1991.

Edbury, Peter W., and John Gordon Rowe, *William of Tyre: Historian of the Latin East*, Cambridge University Press, 1988.

Edge, David, and John Miles Paddock, *Arms & Armor of the Medieval Knight*, Saturn Books, 1996.

Ehrenkreutz, Andrew S., *Saladin*, State University of New York Press, 1972.

Folda, Jaroslav, *Crusader Art: The Art of the Crusaders in the Holy Land, 1099-1291*, Ashgate Publishing, 2008.

Gabrieli, Francesco, *Arab Historians of the Crusades*, University of California Press, 1969.

Hamilton, Bernard, *The Leper King and His Heirs: Baldwin IV and the Crusader Kingdom of Jerusalem*, Cambridge University Press, 2000.

Hamilton, Bernard, "Women in the Crusader States: The Queens of Jerusalem 1100–90," in *Medieval Women*, David Baker (ed.), Basil Blackwell, 1978.

Hopkins, Andrea, *Knights: The Complete Story of the Age of Chivalry, from Historical Fact to Tales of Romance and Poetry*, Collins and Brown Ltd, 1990.

Jotischky, Andrew, *Crusading and the Crusader States*, Pearson Longman, 2004.

Maalouf, Amin, *The Crusades through Arab Eyes*, Schocken Books, 1984.

Miller, David, *Richard the Lionheart: The Mighty Crusader*, Phoenix, 2013.

Miller, Timothy S., and John W. Nesbitt, *Walking Corpses: Leprosy in Byzantium and the Medieval West*, Cornell University Press, 2014.

Morgan, Margaret Ruth, *The Chronicle of Ernoul and the Continuations of William of Tyre*, Oxford Historical Monographs, Oxford University Press, 1973.

Nicolle, David, *Hattin 1187: Saladin's Greatest Victory*, Osprey Military Campaign Series, 1993.

Pringle, Denys, *Secular Buildings in the Crusader Kingdom of Jerusalem: An Archaeological Gazetteer*, Cambridge University Press, 1997.

Riley-Smith, Jonathan, ed., *The Atlas of the Crusades*, Facts on File, 1991.

Runciman, Sir Steven, *The Families of Outremer: The Feudal Nobility of the Crusader Kingdom of Jerusalem, 1099-1291*, Athlone Press, 1960.

Stark, Rodney, *God's Battalions: The Case for the Crusades*, HarperCollins, 2010.

I also recommend the following websites/blogs:

    http://DefenderofJerusalem.com

    http://defendingcrusaderkingdoms.blogspot.com

    http://Tales-of-Chivalry.com

    http://helenapschrader.com

    http://schradershistoricalfiction.blogspot.com

    http://crusadesandcrusaders.com

    http://realcrusadeshistory.com

CPSIA information can be obtained
at www.ICGtesting.com
Printed in the USA
LVOW08s0128250417

532058LV00001B/77/P